COLORADO CRIMES

COLORADO CRIMES

THREE ROMANCE MYSTERIES

LISA HARRIS

BARBOUR PUBLISHING

ISBN 978-1-60260-497-1

Cover thumbnails:
Design by Kirk DouPonce, DogEared Design
Illustration by Jody Williams

Published by Barbour Publishing, Inc., P.O. Box 719, Uhrichsville, OH 44683, www.barbourbooks.com

Our mission is to publish and distribute inspirational products offering exceptional value and biblical encouragement to the masses.

Printed in the United States of America.

RECIPE FOR MURDER

Dedication:

Many thanks to my fantastic Cozy Mystery Crit Group whose watchful eyes and encouraging words helped me to bring Pricilla's story to life, and to Candy and Laurie Alice for all their awesome input. A special thank you, also, to my wonderful family and their constant cheering me on this writer's journey. And lastly, to my fearless editor, Susan Downs, for believing in me and my story.

Retirement was not what Pricilla Crumb envisioned. If asked, she would compare it to one of her prized cheese soufflés gone flat. Dull and disappointing. Thankfully, her son, Nathan, had been desperate enough to fly her to the upscale hunting lodge he owned, or more than likely she'd be sitting at her card table right now, putting together one of those five-hundred-piece puzzles her next-door neighbor had given her last Christmas. Filling in for Nathan's full-time cook, who had come down with a serious case of the West Nile virus four months ago, had, it seemed, become her escape from the yawning predictability of retirement.

Pricilla sorted through the stack of cookbooks piled beside her on the kitchen's granite countertop. Most of tonight's menu had been set three days ago, but a problem had arisen with the appetizer. Rendezvous, Colorado, might not be the smallest dot on the state map, but it certainly lacked some of the conveniences of Seattle, one of them being oysters, a key ingredient for her grilled oyster dish.

At least the lodge's newly remodeled kitchen left nothing to complain about. The antique-styled cabinets, professional appliances, and aged ceiling beams that added a finishing touch to the spacious room, were a chef's dream. Already, Pricilla hoped that the temporary position would become permanent. Moving back to Colorado and near her son would be worth giving up a few conveniences of the city.

Penelope, her Persian cat, paraded into the room and pressed against her legs.

"Where have you been? Hiding under the bed again?" With the top of her foot, Pricilla rubbed Penelope under the chin. "You'll have to wait awhile, my sweet, unless you have an idea for the perfect starter."

She flipped through another book of appetizers then dog-eared one of the pages. Finally, she'd found something suitable. Salmon-filled tartlets would be an ideal choice start to tonight's dinner.

The timer on the oven buzzed, and Pricilla crossed the hardwood floor to check on her cake. With the weather still surprisingly warm as the calendar moved into October, the baked Alaska flambé would be the perfect ending to the meal. Presentation, as she'd always taught her students, was half the goal with food preparation, and the lighting of the meringue would be the highlight of the evening. She had seen Julia Child present the flaming dessert on television with awed reactions. Pricilla foresaw nothing less for tonight.

Nathan entered the kitchen and kissed her on the forehead, frowning when he saw the stack of cookbooks. "Mom, I thought you promised me you'd keep the menu simple tonight."

She eyed her son's tall, handsome frame before pulling the almond and orange cake from the oven and setting it on a rack. "I haven't prepared anything I wouldn't have fixed for your father for a typical Sunday afternoon meal. Roast pork, herbed oven-roasted potatoes— "

"I admit that you're anything but a typical cook, but"—he glanced at the opened cookbook—"salmon-filled tartlets?"

"They're delicious. You'll love them." She paused, trying to remember if she'd checked the expiration date on the smoked salmon. Surely she had. It was second nature by now.

"I'm sure I will," Nathan continued, "but a simple pot roast with vegetables on the side would have been fine."

She dismissed his concerns with the wave of her hand and checked on the rising dough for her yeast rolls. "The reputation of this lodge is at stake, and I don't plan to have anything to do with tarnishing it. Which reminds me." She turned toward him, her hands placed firmly on her hips. "You must speak to the owner of the grocery store. There are a number of things they don't carry, making it quite inconvenient—"

"Mom, my regular cook never had a problem with getting what she needed." He cocked his head and shot her a smile. "I'm sure that the guests will be happy with whatever you fix. You are Pricilla Crumb, hostess and cook extraordinaire, are you not? Besides, I didn't bring you up here to work you to death. You need to relax a bit."

She couldn't help but smile back. He always knew how to appease her. Without a doubt he had her completely wrapped around his finger. She'd do anything for him, and he knew it.

"I suppose I am a bit keyed up." Pricilla rubbed her hands on her apron. "It's just with all the guests arriving in the next few hours, as well as Max and his daughter Trisha. . ." Pricilla turned back to her bowl of dough, pausing for emphasis. There was no reason to pass up an opportunity to further her plan. "Trisha's such a sweet girl. It's strange that the two of you have never met, despite all the years I've known Max." She glanced at her son.

"It is strange, isn't it?" His expression confirmed he wasn't a bit moved by her ploys of innocence. "Especially considering the fact that you've told me about her at least a half dozen times. And that's just since yesterday." Nathan leaned against the counter. "Let's see. Trisha is a graphic designer with long hair, stunning eyes, and. . .how could I forget? She's single."

Pricilla ignored her son's teasing tone. *Single* was the key word here, because she had a plan. She was certain that sparks would fly once the two of them met. With her matchmaking skills sharpened and detailed plans in place, she was convinced that Trisha Summers was the perfect antidote to her son's lonely heart.

Nathan popped a handful of walnuts into his mouth from a ceramic bowl on the counter. "Why are you so worried about me, despite the fact that I keep assuring you that I'm not lonely? I love running the lodge, meeting new people, and—"

"Running this lodge, no matter how successful, will never bring you true happiness—or give me grandchildren." There. She'd made her point.

"Okay, but what about you, Mom?" He leaned down and caught her gaze, his eyes suddenly dark and serious. "Don't you think it would be far more suitable to find someone for yourself before attempting to try and find a match for your only son?"

Pricilla frowned. That was an entirely different subject. She dropped the ball of dough onto a floured board and started kneading. "I'm not convinced life gives second chances when it comes to true love."

When her husband, Marty, died, she decided to thank the good Lord for loaning him to her for almost forty years. She'd found love once and wasn't certain she'd ever find what she had with him again. Still, while she wouldn't ever admit to anyone that she was lonely, it was hard not to wonder at times what it would be like to share her life with someone other than Penelope.

Max Summers sneaked a hot yeast roll from the bread basket, intent on avoiding Pricilla's watchful gaze. He thought the chances of her catching him, though, were slim. With all the guests here and dinner about to be served, she was running around with the precision of a military general and finishing up last-minute details. He'd rarely seen her more in her element.

"I saw you sneak that roll, Max Summers."

He sat back on the bar stool and shot her his most guilty expression. "You know I never could resist your cooking. And I'm not the only one. I just saw one of your guests steal out of the dining room with a plateful of appetizers."

"Charles Woodruff, I assume?" Pricilla frowned. "He's already complained that dinner was being served too late. Like seven o'clock is an uncivilized hour to eat."

"Do you expect all the guests to be as cantankerous as Mr. Woodruff?"

Despite the warmth of the kitchen, Pricilla's silver hair lay in perfect curls against the nape of her neck, and her face, with just a hint of makeup, still looked fresh. The years might have added a few wrinkles and age spots, but he still found her beautiful.

"It's a small crowd this week. Charles's wife, Claire, seems sweet. The quiet type, I understand, who spends most of her time reading romance novels." Pricilla pulled out another pan of hot rolls from the top oven, the heavenly smell reminding him just how hungry he was. "There are also three college buddies who return each year. Let's see, I think their names are Simon Wheeler, Anthony Mills, and Michael Smythe. Nathan told me that they're businessmen who made it big with their. . .their dot company—"

"Dot-com company." Max stifled a laugh. Pricilla knew nothing about computers. E-mail correspondence would have been the perfect way for them to keep in touch, but she insisted on the old-fashioned method, the post office.

"Anyway," Pricilla continued, "Nathan said they were among the few who managed to survive the fallout in the nineties. Apparently they sold the company a couple years ago for quite a fortune."

He watched her flutter around the kitchen and found himself worrying about her. Even with Misty, the housekeeper, helping, he knew that cooking three meals a day for all the guests and staff of the resort lodge wasn't easy.

He finished the last of his roll. "You're overdoing it, Pricilla."

Pricilla put her fists against her hips and frowned. "Why? Because I'm retired and should be sitting out on my back porch, knitting or, even better, categorizing my dozens of herbal pills and vitamins like my friend Madge?"

"I do remember that Madge's obsession with supplements was a bit extreme, but what's wrong with knitting?" Max smiled. He loved to tease her. "I can't remember my mother ever being without knitting needles in her hands."

Her eyes widened. "I wasn't trying to imply that there's anything wrong with knitting, it's just that—"

"Don't worry." This time Max didn't even try not to laugh. "I can't see you knitting either."

"Thank you. I think." Pricilla frowned and peeked into the bottom oven, letting the savory scent of marinated pork fill the room.

"It smells fantastic." Max knew she loved compliments, and he tried to hand them out freely.

"Let's hope the guests agree."

"Undoubtedly they will."

Pricilla had always been the perfect cook and hostess, and he was quite sure she missed teaching her students at the Willow Hill Private Academy for Girls how to become the same. Times had changed too much, though. Today's generation rarely cooked from scratch anymore, and formal dinners around the family table were becoming a thing of the past. The principal had insisted Pricilla retire and instead hired a girl straight out of university whose idea of a home-cooked meal was frozen lasagna from the supermarket. For Pricilla, leaving behind the academy had been like losing a part of herself.

He, on the other hand, didn't miss working. After giving thirty-five years to his country and the United States Air Force, he loved his newfound freedom. Last week he'd gone fishing four days in a row, just because he wanted to.

"Where's your daughter?" Pricilla brushed some flour off her apron, making sure it didn't get on her red pants suit, then pulled a large glass bowl out of one of the oak cabinets. "I haven't seen her since you arrived, and I'm anxious to introduce her to Nathan."

"I'm already ahead of you." Max watched her expression closely. "Introductions have been made, and the last time I peeked into Nathan's office, they were still talking."

Pricilla's eyes widened. "Really?"

"Really."

He couldn't believe he'd agreed to conspire with her in her most recent scheme to match up his business-oriented daughter with Pricilla's like-minded son. His real reason to come for the week, though, had nothing to do with his daughter's love life. He watched as Pricilla busied herself at the stove. Stirring, tasting. . .adding a bit of salt and pepper. . .then stirring some more.

Violet had been gone almost five years now, and while he still missed her, he had to admit he wouldn't mind sharing his life with someone as fun-loving as Pricilla, even if she was a bit overbearing at times. The problem was, he knew that Pricilla saw him as nothing more than a close friend. Even through their years of correspondence, that fact never changed. Still, he loved the intelligent conversations with her and wondered if perhaps God might grant him one last chance to change their relationship into something more permanent.

Someone screamed.

"What in the world—" Max jumped off the bar stool and ran out of the kitchen, with Pricilla following.

The scream had originated from the second floor of the log-styled building. Max rushed up the staircase and down the hall, stopping at the first open door. Claire Woodruff was bent over her husband, her face paler than a December sky. Charles Woodruff sat slumped sideways in a wingback chair beside the fireplace, his face contorted and pink. A half empty plate of Pricilla's tartlets lay strewn across the stone hearth.

"It's Charles." Claire stood up to face Max, her expression void of any emotion. "I think. . .I think he's dead."

Charles Woodruff was dead, and, for all Pricilla knew, her salmon tartlets had killed him. She'd said as much to Max as she had hurried from the Woodruffs' room after seeing the body. She knew first-hand about food poisoning, though she wasn't sure how long it took for someone to succumb to death after ingesting fatal morsels. Charles couldn't have been dead longer than thirty minutes or so after eating them. She'd set the appetizers on the warmer on the buffet table, never intending that anyone eat them until dinner was announced.

"It wasn't you, Pricilla," Max said while entering the kitchen twenty minutes later.

"You don't know that." She poured extra cleanser on the counter and began scrubbing in vigorous circles. The local detective was upstairs right now doing whatever it was that the authorities did in a situation like this. She shuddered, thinking of what poor Mrs. Woodruff might be going through with her husband dying during their romantic week away in the mountains.

Max closed the distance between them and stood beside her at the counter. "Pricilla, you're upset and not thinking clearly—"

"He died eating my tartlets. The evidence was right there!" She threw the sponge into the sink. "Speaking of evidence, I'm tampering with it—"

Max grabbed her wrists and gently pulled her into a hug "This wasn't your fault. He could have had heart problems."

"Claire said he was in perfect health."

"People in the best of health often die unexpectedly. It could have been any number of things—heart attack, stroke, a ruptured aorta—"

"Stop, Max, please. How would you feel if your prized tartlets were the last thing someone ingested before he died?"

She pulled away from him, desperate for something to keep her busy while she waited for the authorities to interrogate her. Nathan was with the police, and Trisha had volunteered to stay with Claire, leaving her to fend for the other guests. She mulled over her options. She could whip up a batch of cinnamon rolls or perhaps one of her lemon crumb cakes. No. No one would want to sample her cooking after tonight. Max leaned against the edge of the counter and caught her gaze. "I think he was fortunate to have tried some of your wonderful cooking before dying."

Pricilla turned away from him. "Max, you're absolutely impossible. Just last week I read an article about an entire family dying from salmonella poisoning. Something in the stuffed pasta shells—"

"You read too much."

"But this wasn't fiction." She shivered, and it wasn't from the drop in temperature as night descended on the mountains around them. "This really happened. . .like tonight really happened."

"Cases like that are very rare, and I simply can't imagine anything being wrong with your tartlets."

"They'll have to test them." This had her worried.

Max grabbed a glass from the cupboard and headed toward the fridge. "More than likely they will announce that Mr. Woodruff had a heart attack, and there will be no need to even test the contents of your appetizers."

"I've hidden them in the bottom of the deep freeze in a trash bag. I can't have someone else coming down for a late night snack and falling over dead."

That sudden thought bothered her. What if someone else had sampled one of her appetizers and succumbed to Mr. Woodruff's fate? On the other hand—

"Perhaps Mr. Woodruff's death was actually a blessing," she stated.

Max stopped pouring the soda into his glass and looked up at her, a surprised expression written across his face. "A blessing?"

"Of course, it's a dreadful shame for Mr. Woodruff, but what if all the guests had eaten them?" Pricilla stared out the window, where the last of the sunlight was fading beyond the mountains peaks. "One by one we all could have dropped off like flies. It would have been like some nightmare out of *And Then There Were None*—you know, one of Agatha Christie's best mysteries."

"Like I said, you've been reading too many novels, Pricilla." Max set down his glass and grabbed the kettle off the stove. "What you need is a nice, relaxing cup of tea."

Pricilla frowned as Max proceeded to fill the kettle. Her head was pounding, and she was certain her blood pressure had risen a notch or two. She'd have to remember to take her medicine tonight. Leave it to Max, with his orderly, military mind-set, to think that a cup of tea could smooth over the raw reality of death.

Nathan entered the room with Trisha right behind him.

"I've been upstairs with Detective Carter," Nathan said. "He'll want to talk to all of us. Quite routine, of course, since he believes Mr. Woodruff died from natural causes."

"Natural causes?" Pricilla's stomach churned. "How long has Detective Carter been working for the department?"

"I don't know. Six. . .eight months at the most. He's the sheriff's nephew but he seems like he knows what he's doing. Not much ever happens in

Rendezvous to merit a large show of force. The sheriff is back East at a conference of some type, apparently."

Her son's comments were anything but assuring.

Nathan grabbed a handful of peanuts and popped a few in his mouth. "Are you all right, Mom? You're looking a bit pale."

"How can you be so calm about all of this, Nathan?" Pricilla felt the veins in her neck pulsate. Was she the only one taking this event seriously? "There's a dead man in one of your upstairs suites."

"Your mother thinks she poisoned Mr. Woodruff with one of her tartlets." Max took a sip of his drink.

"What?" Nathan and Trisha's simultaneous response only added to the pain of Pricilla's pounding temples.

"That's ridiculous," Nathan said.

"Completely," Max echoed. "I've been trying to convince her otherwise, but your mother's stubborn."

"I know."

Pricilla fumed. They were talking as if she weren't in the room. It was a habit that irritated her.

Nathan caught her gaze. "Does this have anything to do with Dr. Witherspoon?"

"Of course not." Pricilla clutched her stomach. "That was an entirely different situation. Dr. Witherspoon and his wife simply suffered from cramps, vomiting, and nausea. . . . Charles Woodruff is dead."

"Who's Dr. Witherspoon?" Trisha asked Pricilla.

She went back to cleaning the counters. The detective might confiscate her tartlets, but at least the kitchen would be sparkling. "He was a friend of my late husband's. We invited him and his wife over for dinner. Nathan must have been about twelve at the time. Apparently I hadn't noticed that the mayonnaise had expired. We all ended up in the emergency room for hours. It was dreadful."

Trisha covered her mouth with her hand. "Oh my, that is awful."

"Terrible," Max echoed.

Pricilla frowned. Max and Trisha were showing far too much interest in an event she would prefer to forget. "I wish Nathan hadn't brought it up. It was such a humiliating moment."

"Since then, my mother's been fanatical about checking expiration dates and making certain of where everything comes from." Nathan wrapped his arm around his mother's shoulder. "And that's the very reason why I'm certain your tartlets couldn't have been the reason for Charles Woodruff's demise."

Trisha folded her arms across her chest and frowned. "Mrs. Crumb, I can see how it's possible for that situation to make you overreact today, but the truth is, no one knows what has happened, except that Mr. Woodruff is dead.

And I, for one, am certain it wasn't from your tartlets. This is nothing more than an unfortunate event that has us all on edge."

Pricilla wanted to believe Trisha—all of them, in fact—but that didn't take away the overwhelming guilt. She felt like she had when their neighbor had to drive them all to the hospital. She'd let them all down, including Nathan—and now she was afraid she'd let him down again. Not only would her reputation as a hostess and cook be ruined, but the future of Nathan's lodge could be forever tarnished because of her. No one would return to a place where the cook had killed one of the guests.

The kettle began to whistle, and Max pulled it off the burner. "I thought we could all use a cup of tea."

Pricilla busied herself pulling boxes of tea and sugar out of the cupboard. Three boxes of prepackaged cookies sat on the bottom shelf. She cringed at the thought of serving a store-bought dessert, but decided to pull them out anyway.

She turned around and watched as Trisha filled a tray with mugs. The girl was beautiful in her loose-fitting pants suit and open-toed shoes. Her hair lay in soft ringlets around her shoulders. Pricilla was certain she highlighted it, but the honey color accented her skin tone to perfection. And Trisha was also completely efficient. That was one reason Pricilla loved Trisha and knew the young woman would be perfect for her son. Already, she'd managed to help bring calm to the chaos of the evening.

But any thoughts of matchmaking had to be set aside for the time being. Pricilla knew what she must do now. The salmon had smelt funny, she was sure of it, looking back. She must not have looked at the expiration date. And the cream cheese. She couldn't be sure about that ingredient's freshness either. Why hadn't she been more careful? She of all people knew of the dangers of food poisoning. She set the tea and cookies down on the counter and cleared her throat. A hot cup of tea would never fix what had happened today.

"If you will all excuse me, there's something I must do. I'm going find the detective and confess that I poisoned Charles Woodruff."

Max stared at Pricilla, certain he'd heard her wrong. He knew she was stubborn, but this was absurd. He was tempted to drag the rest of the tartlets out of the freezer and eat one just to prove to her that there was nothing wrong with them. Only the remote chance that she was right stopped him.

Pricilla slipped out of the room before anyone could think of something to say. Then Max set his drink down on the counter. "I'm going to try and talk some sense into that woman."

"It won't do any good, I'm afraid," Nathan said. "You know my mother. Once she gets something into her head, it's impossible to reason with her or change her mind."

Max stopped and turned around in the doorway. He noticed the circles under Nathan's eyes. Maybe his playing it cool was an act. Max didn't blame him at all for being upset, though. Having a death occur on one's premises was nerve-racking no matter what the circumstances. Max shifted his feet. "You don't think it's possible that there was something wrong with the tartlets—"

"Of course not." Nathan grabbed another handful of nuts and shook them in the palm of his hand. "I just don't know what else to say to her."

"I think I'll skip the tea for now. I'm going to see if I can do something for Claire." Trisha laid a hand on Max's shoulder. "Dad, why don't you see if you can talk some sense into Mrs. Crumb? What we don't need are rumors circulating about poisoned tartlets, so you need to convince her to keep quiet. And to not worry."

Max let out a deep sigh and nodded. That would be easier said than done.

Pricilla caught Detective Carter outside as he was heading toward his unmarked car. She felt her knees tremble as the gravel drive crunched beneath her shoes. Darkness had fallen, but the front of the lodge was well lit by domed lights.

"Detective, I need to speak to you regarding an urgent matter."

The detective adjusted his glasses. "I'm sorry, Miss—"

"Mrs. Pricilla Crumb."

"Mrs. Crumb, then. I am sorry, but right now I have to make arrangements for a body to be transported, and—"

"What I have to say is regarding the body, er. . .Mr. Woodruff." Using the word *body* seemed uncivilized and disrespectful.

He stood looking at her, notebook in hand and pen in his shirt pocket, clearly uninterested in her or whatever information she might have.

Pricilla held her head high. "I believe that I am the one who murdered Mr. Woodruff."

This got his attention. "Excuse me?"

"The victim, Mr. Woodruff, was in the process of consuming one of my salmon-filled tartlets when he expired."

"Expired?"

"Passed away." Pricilla shook her head. She had no idea it would be so difficult to turn herself in.

"Mrs. . . .Crumb." The bald detective shook his head. "I'm sure that you have the best intentions of helping by confessing to the crime, but I've seen situations like this dozens of times."

She didn't understand. "When the chef killed a guest?"

The man shook his head again. "No, when a man died from a heart attack."

"A heart attack."

"For now, I'm convinced that there was no foul play involved in Mr. Woodruff's death, so please don't give another thought about the. . ."

"Tartlets." The man should be taking notes.

"Tartlets. Yes. I'm certain there is nothing at all for you to worry about."

Confirmation from the law should have cleared her mind, but she couldn't be completely certain until her appetizers were tested. "Do you have a lab where they can be tested?"

He shoved his notebook in his back pants pocket. "We will take every step to find out exactly how Mr. Woodruff died, but as I said, I'm sure you have nothing to worry about in regard to your dinner. Now, if you'll excuse me. I need to head back into town."

What else could she say? More than likely, she thought cynically, the detective was trying to quickly wrap up the case to impress his uncle. She turned back to the lodge, irritated that the man had dismissed her declaration of guilt.

"Pricilla?" Max stopped her at the edge of the sidewalk as the detective peeled out of the driveway. "What did you tell the detective?"

She tried to ignore Max's intense gaze. "Simply that I was concerned my tartlets might have been involved in Mr. Woodruff's demise."

"Pricilla—"

"He told me they believed Mr. Woodruff died of natural causes."

"So are you convinced finally that you had nothing to do with the man's death?"

Pricilla bit her lip. "I need to go see if I can help Claire. She must be so upset."

"You didn't answer my question."

"I've always taken pride in my cooking, and to think that I could have poisoned someone—"

"You still aren't answering my question."

"I want them to test the appetizers. Then I can be certain."

"I suppose that's reasonable, but—"

"No buts, Max. I want—"

The shriek of the smoke alarm interrupted Pricilla.

Max's eyes widened. "Something's on fire."

He sniffed the air and dashed up the porch stairs, taking the steps two at a time.

Pricilla hurried behind Max into the house and toward the persistent blare of the smoke detector. The soles of her shoes clicked against the gray-tiled floor of the entryway as she struggled to keep up with him. The minute she entered the kitchen, she saw the thick gray cloud of smoke that poured out of the oven.

Her roast pork!

Pricilla pressed the palm of her hand against her mouth and tried not to choke on the fumes. How could she have forgotten to turn off the oven?

"Open the back door! I'll get the windows!" Max shouted.

Pricilla's eyes watered as she hurried to open the door and grab a pair of pot holders to fan the fire alarm. So much for her perfect dinner. Her tartlets were hidden in the back of the deep-freeze as possible evidence for Mr. Woodruff's death, the roast pork was a piece of charcoal, and her almond and orange cake for the baked Alaska flambé sat dried out on the countertop. All her grand visions of wowing the guests vanished.

The buzzing alarm finally stopped.

Nathan stepped inside the kitchen doorway and coughed. "What happened? I was out at the barn, telling Oscar about Charles and warning dinner would be late."

Neither Oscar Philips, Nathan's professional guide, nor any of the guests would be eating dinner soon. With a pot holder in each hand, Pricilla pulled out the pan holding the charred remains. "My roast pork. Need I say more?"

"With all that's happened tonight, I'm not at all surprised no one remembered to turn the oven off." Nathan crossed the room and took the heavy dish out of her hands.

"Not only that, the dial is set as high as it can go. I must have turned it up instead of off. Strange—I never do that sort of thing. No wonder it set off the smoke alarm." Pricilla fanned herself with the pot holders as Max took the pan from Nathan then went to throw it into the garbage bin outside. "At least the smoke's clearing. What a complete waste."

"Don't worry about it, Mom."

The roast wasn't all she was worried about.

"What about the guests? Everyone must be starving." She started to rummage through the refrigerator, trying to come up with a spur-of-the-moment meal for ten people. "There are some cold cuts for sandwiches and—"

"I meant it when I said don't worry about it, Mom. Simon Wheeler and his buddies left for town a few minutes ago. I gave them a voucher to the Rendezvous Bar and Grill, so they'll be fine."

"What about Trisha and Max and—"

"Trisha is upstairs with Claire, and I've already told her I'd bring her something to eat after everything settles down. She wanted to stay with Claire until she fell asleep." Nathan wrapped his arm around his mother and pulled her close. "I'll make sandwiches for Trisha and me. I'll make you one as well if you promise to forget about the kitchen and then go get some sleep. It's been a long day for all of us."

Pricilla shook her head. The thought of food made her stomach revolt. "I couldn't eat a bite, but I do need to salvage what I can from tonight's fiasco."

Max returned with the now-empty baking dish and started rinsing it in the sink. "I heard what Nathan said, and he's right, Pricilla. We all need a good night's sleep. Especially you."

"Just a few more minutes." She grabbed a food storage bag out of a drawer and started putting the rolls in it. Reheated, she could serve them for lunch tomorrow with the beef stew she planned to fix. That is if anyone would dare try her cooking.

Misty, the housekeeper, entered the kitchen out of breath. "Sorry I've not been here to help clean up, Mrs. Crumb. Trisha asked me to get some things out of Mrs. Woodruff's car for her. The woman's quite distraught. We heard the smoke alarm go off, but by the time we convinced Claire to hurry outside in case it was a real fire, the alarm had stopped. Is everything all right?"

"I apparently never turned off the oven," Pricilla said, trying to take comfort in the fact that it was only her roast pork and not the lodge that had been demolished. "If you're hungry—"

"Oh no, ma'am." The young woman pressed her hands against her stomach. "I could never eat after seeing Mr. Woodruff hunched over like a rag doll in that chair. I've never seen a dead person in real life before, you know, and his skin was so pale and—"

"We all saw him, as well." Pricilla shuddered at the image, not wanting to be reminded of the details. "It's been a disturbing evening for all of us."

"I feel sorry for his wife," Misty said, "though if you ask me, Mr. Woodruff wasn't the nicest man in the world."

"Why do you say that?" Pricilla asked, busying herself with the last of the cleanup while the men started making the sandwiches.

Misty's gaze dropped, and Pricilla wondered if the housekeeper knew something the rest of them didn't. Nathan had told her Misty had worked for him about eight years, so Pricilla was quite certain that the twenty-something-year-old knew a lot about the guests. Especially guests who returned every year.

Misty pulled on a strand of her long blond hair and began twirling it with her fingers. "Didn't you hear them fighting this afternoon?"

"All couples fight from time to time." While Pricilla would never admit to intentionally listening to their conversation, she was certain that everyone in the lodge had witnessed Mr. and Mrs. Woodruff's raised voices as they went up to their room. She hadn't made out everything they were saying, but the tone of their conversation was evident. Charles had been furious about something. "Conflict and problem solving are a part of being married."

"That might be true, but engaging in an argument with Charles Woodruff has never been difficult." Nathan opened the almost empty jar of mayonnaise and began spreading some on the bread he'd laid out. "Even I had a heated discussion with the man on his arrival. He never was very amiable."

Misty shuddered. "If you don't mind, I'd like to go home now. My heart just won't stop pounding."

"Of course you can," Pricilla assured her. "It's been a rough evening on all of us."

Nathan held up the jar as Misty headed out the back door toward her cabin. "Is there any more?"

"Top shelf in the pantry." There was something else bothering her, and Pricilla wondered if she should say what was on her mind. "You know, Misty does have an interesting point."

"What's that?" Max asked.

"From what I've noticed, Charles wasn't exactly the most well-liked person. What if it wasn't my tartlets that poisoned him, and he didn't have a heart attack—"

"Don't even go there, Mom." Nathan frowned as he grabbed the new jar off the shelf.

"He's right, Pricilla." Max turned around and faced her. "I don't think we have anything to worry about this being anything other than a heart attack."

The men had to be right. She'd never sleep tonight if she let her mind wander in the direction of murder—because that would mean there was a murderer on the loose.

Still, if there was a hint of foul play, she wasn't certain a small town like Rendezvous would have the necessary resources to deal with a situation like this. How long might it take before Detective Carter managed to obtain the results? She wasn't convinced of the man's competence. It wasn't as if they had a team of crime scene investigators on hand like they did on television. They'd have to call for help and there was no telling how long that might take. Pricilla remembered Nathan saying that the last unexplained death that had occurred in this town was ten years ago. The town librarian had been found dead at the bank of Lake Paytah wearing a purple scuba diving suit. To this day the crime hadn't been solved.

Pricilla grabbed some foil from the drawer to begin wrapping up the cake. She might have watched too many reruns of *Murder, She Wrote* and *Father Dowling*, but all the same, she couldn't shake the eerie feeling she had about the whole situation. A dead man wasn't exactly something she had to deal with every day.

"Has anyone called a doctor to come check on Claire?" Pricilla asked, still trying to get the image of Charles Woodruff's body out of her mind.

"I did. Doc Freeman's up the mountain, delivering a baby." Nathan dumped a handful of potato chips beside the sandwich on his plate and then did the same for Trisha's plate. "He said he wouldn't be available until the morning, and he couldn't do much anyway. Said to give Claire an over-the-counter sleeping pill if she wanted it, and to call him tomorrow. I offered her one and she took it, so hopefully she'll get some rest tonight."

She watched Max pull a cold drink out of the refrigerator and pop the tab open, but despite his presence, the situation still left her feeling vulnerable. The sheriff was out of town and had left an inexperienced detective in charge. Now the town's one doctor was unavailable.

"What does one do around here if there's a real crisis?"

Nathan laughed, breaking some of the tension in the room. "We've always done pretty well at avoiding one until tonight."

At least if she was in the middle of a crisis, which was the way she classified this situation, Nathan and Max were the two men she'd want to have by her side. A wave of exhaustion struck her, and she grabbed the edge of the counter to steady herself. Glancing around the kitchen, she decided it was clean enough for now. Any more excitement tonight and they'd be calling Dr. Freeman for her.

"I think I'll take a cup of herbal tea now after all and then go on to bed. I was planning to check on Claire myself, but it seems as if Trisha has everything under control." Pricilla set a mug of lukewarm water in the microwave to reheat it and pressed START. "I remember the night Marty died. The reality of what had happened didn't hit me until the next day. Tomorrow will be difficult."

"You're right," Nathan said. "Claire and Charles didn't have any close family. I've told her she's welcome to stay a few extra days if she needs to."

"What about tomorrow's hunting trip?" Max asked before chomping into his sandwich.

Nathan wiped a crumb off his chin. "The detective said we can go ahead with the hunting trip as planned. I know it will be early, Mom, but—"

The microwave dinged and Pricilla pulled the mug out. "I'll have a hot breakfast on the table by six."

Max watched Pricilla walk out of the kitchen. No matter what the cause of Charles Woodruff's death, the evening had been quite disturbing to all of them. Pricilla's believing it was her fault only compounded the matter. And as unrealistic as it was, thoughts of a real murderer made his skin crawl.

Needing something stronger than a cup of tea, Max poured himself a mug of leftover coffee from the coffee maker to go with his sandwich then offered Nathan some of the hazelnut-flavored brew.

"Guess I need something to wash this food down with. Can't help but wish I was eating some of my mom's roast and hot yeast rolls right now, though."

"I'm with you on that one." Max chuckled.

Nathan rested his hands against the counter. "I'm worried about her."

Max took a sip of the coffee and decided to nuke it in the microwave. "Pricilla's a strong woman. Imaginative, granted, but very strong. She'll be fine."

"I know. It's just that she worked so hard on tonight's dinner, and now to have her think that she murdered someone with her tartlets. . ."

Max tried not to laugh.

While the very idea of Pricilla's tartlets being the cause of Mr. Woodruff's demise was absurd, he knew it made perfect sense to her. Maybe that was one reason he enjoyed being around her so much. He never knew what to expect from her. She had that offbeat, quirky sense of humor that always made him smile. And the older he got, the more important laughter became.

"You know I would never tease her. It's actually much more than that." What could he say? That he had another reason for coming? Could he tell Nathan he'd hoped that he and Pricilla might discover something deeper than friendship?

"You're in love with her, aren't you?"

Max caught Nathan's gaze and swallowed hard, amazed at Nathan's perception.

"*Love* is a pretty strong word." He wanted a change in his relationship with Pricilla, but was he ready to say he loved her? He pulled the sugar bowl out of the cupboard and added two spoonfuls to his coffee before heating both mugs in the microwave. "She makes me smile and feel young. I can talk to her about anything, from politics, to spiritual issues, to the latest reality show."

"You're going to have your hands full."

This time Max laughed out loud. "Trust me. I've known your mother long enough to know both her weaknesses and her strengths. I spent over half my life in the military, learning how to negotiate, talk peace, and delegate responsibilities. I think I'm prepared to handle just about anything."

"Your daughter's a lot like you, you know." Nathan took a sip of his coffee. "I'm impressed with the way she's jumped in and helped to smooth out a difficult situation with my guests."

Max didn't miss the smile that reached all the way to the corners of Nathan's eyes. For once it seemed that Pricilla might have been right on track when she decided to put her matchmaking skills to the test. The spark between Nathan and Trisha seemed to have been lit from the moment they met.

"Trisha's always had her head on straight. I don't know what I'd do without her."

Nathan set his mug down on the counter with a *thud*. "My mother's trying to set me up with her, isn't she?"

"And it's taken you this long to figure that out?"

Nathan shook his head. "So you're in on it?"

"I'll never admit to that."

Now it was Nathan's turn to laugh. "It doesn't matter, I suppose. I really like Trisha. She might not be the outdoor type, but I've already discovered that we have plenty of things in common. Books, science-fiction movies, country music. . ."

"You still sound a bit hesitant."

"Let's just say I've never made time for having a relationship. The lodge is my life, and I love what I do."

"And now?"

Nathan shrugged a shoulder. "I don't know, except I'm glad I'm working at the lodge this week instead of hunting."

"Just promise me that you won't tell your mother, or Trisha, we had this discussion."

"Don't worry," Nathan said. "This time I have as much at stake as you do."

Normally, the scent of frying bacon and a glass of orange juice was enough to get Pricilla going. This morning she'd gone for a cup of coffee, something she normally avoided because of the caffeine, but even her second cup wasn't doing the trick.

"Good morning." Max's smile was far too cheery. "Did you sleep well?"

"Barely a wink." She wouldn't tell him that when she *had* slept, her sleep had been full of troubled dreams.

"You should have taken one of your sleeping pills."

"I would have, but I needed to get up early, and I didn't want to take the chance of being drowsy." She yawned. "Now I'm regretting it."

"What can I do to help?" He tugged on the bottom of his hunter green jacket.

Pricilla glanced at him. She'd always thought Max handsome, with his bright blue eyes and dark brows. His hair had grayed over the years, but he still was as handsome as he'd been when they'd first met, with his broad shoulders and military physique. . . .

She shook her head and tried to control her rambling thoughts. "The sausage needs to be turned. I just need to finish cooking the rest of the pancake batter, and we can eat."

Max grabbed a pair of tongs and begun turning the thick slices of sausage. "Would it help if I stayed behind? I wouldn't mind a bit."

"Yes, you would." She ignored the strong urge to accept his offer. "You'd be holed up with a bunch of women for a week and be miserable."

"I'd get your cooking every night."

Pricilla could feel the heat rising in her cheeks and tried to decipher the look in Max's eyes. "If you bring some game back, I promise to make you a full course meal fit for a king when you return."

"With one of your lemon crumb cakes for dessert?"

"Of course." She busied herself with flipping the pancakes. "I'll watch the sausage, if you wouldn't mind ringing the bell on the front porch and calling everyone in to eat?"

As Pricilla watched Max leave the room, she tried to swallow the disappointment she felt, knowing he wouldn't be here for most of the week. The feeling surprised her. She'd always enjoyed Max's company, but they rarely had the opportunity to spend time with each other. Phone calls and letters had been their way of communicating. Why then would she feel any different this morning? More than likely it was simply because she was sleep deprived. She never functioned well this early in the morning.

A loud *crash* resounded from outside. Then someone yelled.

Max?

It was a sudden déjà vu from the night before. Pricilla's heart shuddered, as she jerked the sausage off the stove and dashed toward the front door. One dead body had been enough to leave her on edge. A second incident might just be enough to push her tumbling over the side.

Pricilla stumbled out the front door and found Max lying face down at the bottom of the stairs on a patch of grass. She ran across the porch, ignoring the achy throb in her left hip that told her to slow down. If anything happened to Max she'd never forgive herself for inviting him here.

Oh Lord, please let him be all right—

Her mind tried to push away the insane image that they had a murderer on the loose, but after a restless night with little sleep, she wasn't thinking clearly. Bizarre dreams of Charles Woodruff sitting in front of the fireplace, eating piles and piles of her tartlets before keeling over didn't help either. No, she had to believe Max and Nathan's strong admonitions that she had nothing to do with Charles's untimely demise. That was difficult to achieve. Surely it wasn't simply a coincidence that first Charles had collapsed and now Max?

She knelt beside him and reached for his wrist to check his pulse. Nothing. She tried his neck, but she still couldn't feel anything. No pulse meant—

Max groaned. He slowly rolled into a sitting position, and Pricilla let out a sigh of relief. He might be injured, but at least he wasn't dead. And there was no sign of blood.

Her heart pounded. "What in the world happened?"

"It's my ankle. I tripped."

She grabbed his arm to help him up, but he stopped her. He may not have lost his life to some crazed lunatic, but he obviously felt he'd lost a measure of his dignity. Ignoring her offer to help, he struggled to stand.

After a minute of trying, he sat back down on the grass and squeezed his eyes shut. "I think I'm going to need your help after all."

Somehow, between the two of them, they managed to get him onto the porch steps where he could sit and elevate his leg.

Once he was settled, Pricilla glanced out across the front grounds. The thick vegetation provided plenty of places where a perpetrator could disappear. The same thing was true along the front of the lodge. Thick shrubs lined the porch. If someone had pushed Max, there were plenty of places to hide, but why? A connection to Charles didn't make sense. The two men didn't even know each other.

Unless the lodge was the connection. Was there someone with a vendetta against Nathan? Perhaps a disgruntled employee who wanted retribution?

She'd have to ask her son.

She sat beside Max and rested his foot in her lap despite his protests. "I need to know if someone pushed you."

"If someone pushed me?" His eyes widened as she worked to untie the laces, and she wasn't sure if it was from the pain or her question.

"This isn't an episode of *Murder, She Wrote*, Pricilla. I tripped."

"All right. But I couldn't help wondering. I just thought with Charles—" Pricilla closed her mouth, feeling quite foolish. Max obviously wasn't connecting the two incidents. Nathan wouldn't either.

She untied the shoe and gently pulled it from his foot.

"Ouch."

"I'm sorry, but your shoe has to come off. Your ankle is already beginning to swell."

"I'm the one who should be sorry." Max shook his head. "I shouldn't have snapped at you. This certainly isn't your fault. I've either broken it, or done a fine job of twisting it. So much for my plans for the week."

She could read the disappointment in his face. "Your hunting trip—"

"I know. Of all the ridiculous things to have happen." Pricilla managed to keep her mouth shut this time and let him rant. "For thirty-five years I trained soldiers, led reconnaissance missions, and tracked down bad guys, with nothing more than a few scratches, and now I've tripped down a stupid staircase and broken something."

She started to take off his thick black sock then stopped. *What did one do with a broken bone?*

Pricilla shuddered at the thought. She'd mastered the art of cooking, but broken bones, blood. . .dead bodies. . .these were things she couldn't handle. She tried to focus on the issue at hand. They should immobilize the ankle, and they needed ice. She knew that. But a doctor would need to look at it.

She put down his foot gently on the step then started up the stairs. "I'll get the keys to the car and some ice from the kitchen. I'm going to take you into town to the clinic."

There were no arguments from Max as Pricilla hurried into the house. The smell of burnt pancakes wafted from the kitchen. Great. Not only had she managed to totally destroy last night's dinner, now she was doing a good job of ruining today's breakfast. Thankfully she'd thought to pull the sausage off the burner, but the last batch of pancakes hadn't fared so well. She turned off the electric skillet then dumped the blackened pancakes down the garbage disposal.

Pricilla let out a sigh. At least this morning the damage was far less, though if she wasn't careful, her entire reputation as a good cook was going to be ruined even if her tartlets weren't the cause of Charles Woodruff's death.

She put the sausage in a warming dish and shoved it into the oven. Where was Misty when she needed her?

As if she'd heard the question, Misty appeared in the back doorway.

"You're late," Pricilla said, before the young woman had a chance to speak.

"I'm sorry, Mrs. Crumb. The children were difficult this morning and—"

"It's all right." She waved her hand. She knew she shouldn't take out her frustration on Misty.

Pricilla grabbed the keys from the kitchen drawer and a bag of frozen peas, all the while giving Misty instructions as to how she wanted breakfast served. By the time she made it back to the porch, Trisha was kneeling beside her father.

The young woman looked up at Pricilla. "I told Dad if he really wanted to stay behind with the women this week, he could have come up with an easier solution."

"You're a bunch of laughs, Trisha," Max said with a frown. "Help me to the car, will you?"

Five minutes later, Pricilla was driving Max into town. Trisha stayed behind to keep an eye on Claire. Max, stretched out in the back sat seat with the bag of frozen peas resting on his ankle, was quiet as Pricilla followed the dirt road that would soon be covered in snow.

While she was relieved that Max's fall seemed to be a completely isolated incident, it didn't change the fact that she could still be responsible for Charles's death. She wondered how long they sent one to prison for involuntary manslaughter.

She also wondered if any of the guests had decided to show up and eat the breakfast Misty was now serving. Already, she could envision poisonous mushrooms in her fluffy omelets and botulism in the homemade sausage.

"You're still blaming yourself, aren't you?"

Pricilla coughed, wondering how Max always seemed to read her mind. "I can't help it. I've got this feeling that something's wrong, and if it wasn't my tartlets. . ." She couldn't let herself think too long on the alternative. "Do you really think Charles died of natural causes?"

"Of course." Was that hesitation in his voice, or was she imagining that as well? "Just because someone dies unexpectedly doesn't mean foul play is involved. And it certainly doesn't mean your tartlets were involved."

"We'll see." She hoped they would have some answers from the toxicology report soon. Waiting was torture.

Max reached up and patted her arm. "Didn't Jesus say not to worry about your life?"

"He said don't worry about tomorrow, but He also said each day has enough trouble of its own. Seems like during these past twenty-four hours we've had enough trouble for at least a month or two."

His deep laughed stopped abruptly as the right tire hit a pothole.

"Sorry. Is the pain bad?"

"Minimal."

She didn't believe him at all, but Max was a soldier, and his type didn't give in to pain.

"You have to admit it's odd." Pricilla hoped that talking would distract him from the pain. "First Charles keels over and dies unexpectedly and then you fall down the stairs."

"It's a coincidence, Pricilla. Nothing more. Let the detective handle things and forget it."

She didn't miss the sharp look he shot her. It was time to drop the subject.

Doc Freeman was back in the clinic and his diagnosis was better than Max expected. But as they left two hours later to head back to the lodge, he was still furious at himself. Even a sprained ankle, the doctor had informed him, could take up to six weeks to fully mend. Possibly longer at his age.

Despite his frustration, he was proud of Pricilla. While they had waited in the cramped lobby, not once had she brought up the subject of Charles's death. Not that he wasn't convinced that her mind was still fully engaged and trying to figure out what had happened, but at least she'd kept any comments to herself. Instead, they passed the time talking about their last vacations, what was happening in their churches, and their children.

He carefully turned his leg to try and relieve some of the pressure. "I appreciate your taking me to the doctor this morning."

"At least it's not broken."

He might be furious at himself for making such a stupid error, but there was a bright side to it all. "There is something good that will come out of this."

"And what would that be?"

"When's the last time we were able to spend an entire week together?"

Her brow wrinkled slightly. "I don't believe we ever have."

Max nodded. "Exactly."

She frowned, but he didn't miss the twinkle in her eyes. "You just want to keep your eye on me, don't you?"

"Perhaps partly, but I am looking forward to some of your cooking."

Hearing her laughter reminded him of why he'd always been drawn to

Pricilla and what a kind-hearted woman she was.

"If I can manage to get through a meal without burning something."

"I'm sure the rest of the week will be different."

Max leaned back in the seat and smiled, thankful that the painkillers the doctor had given him were finally starting to kick in. While Pricilla might be nosy and even meddlesome at times, he also knew that she was also forgiving, loving, and would do anything for anyone. He couldn't help but love her. . . .

Love her?

The thought took him by surprise. Had Nathan been right? He shifted again and looked at her out of the corner of his eye. He fought the urge to reach out and run his fingers down the side of her cheek. In the week ahead of him, he was going to have nothing to do but spend time with Pricilla. She might be full of matchmaking schemes for their children, but he wondered if she ever thought about herself. Maybe she wasn't the only one who needed a matchmaking plan to put into action.

"I do have one question for you," Pricilla said as they turned off the main road and onto the dirt lane that would take them back to the lodge.

He temporarily set aside his thoughts of courting. "What's that?"

"You don't have to go down the stairs on the front porch to ring the bell. How did you end up falling down the stairs?"

Max knew he had to choose his words carefully. He wasn't sure he should tell her. All she needed was more fuel for her imagination. Something that was already close to exploding into an inferno. "There is one other thing that happened this morning that I didn't tell you."

"What are you talking about?"

"It's probably nothing."

"Max. . ."

"I was about to ring the bell, when I noticed something moving along the side of the barn. At first I thought it might be an animal, but as I moved toward the stairs, it was obvious that it wasn't."

"It was a person?"

"Yes, but I'm not sure who." He shrugged. "More than likely it was just Oscar getting things together for the hunting trip."

Pricilla slowed the car as they drove through the main gate. "Seems strange that someone would be lurking around the barn. Even Oscar would use the main entrance."

"It was nothing, Pricilla. I shouldn't have told you." He leaned down to the floorboard to pick up his sack of prescriptions and winced at the movement. The doctor had told him to take the medicine and rest for a couple of days, a plan he fully intended to follow.

Pricilla put her foot on the brake and brought the car to a jolting stop.

"Maybe you should tell the sheriff then."

"What?" Max winced at the pain and braced himself with his hands against the dashboard.

"Look." She sucked in a deep breath.

Max's jaw line tensed. Any plans for romance might very well have to be laid to rest. The lodge was surrounded by sheriff's vehicles.

Pricilla parked the car in front of the lodge, but didn't make any move to get out. A wave of dizziness swept over her. She prayed she wouldn't pass out and make a total fool out of herself, but three vehicles clearly meant that Charles's death had not occurred under ordinary circumstances. Which left two alternatives in her mind. Either Charles had died from food poisoning. . .or there was a murderer involved. Both options left her wanting to jump on the next airplane back to Seattle.

"Aren't you getting out of the car?" Max asked.

"If I have a choice? No." Pricilla dangled the keys in front of her. "There are two options we're looking at here, Max, and I don't like either one. The authorities are here, which means that either my tartlets were involved with Charles's death, or someone murdered him."

He shook his head. "We don't know anything yet."

"Then why are there three, count them, three of the sheriff's cars outside the lodge the morning after one of the guests keels over with no warning?"

Max drummed his fingers on the armrest. "There could be a number of other explanations."

"Give me one." She waited for him to respond. He didn't, making an even stronger argument for her deductions. "You see. You can't think of any other options either."

He shot her a wry smile. "Maybe something happened while we were gone this morning."

She didn't like this explanation any better. "Like what? Guest number two collapses after eating my homemade sausage—"

Max reached out to squeeze her hand. "I told you to stop blaming yourself. Until they find absolute proof that you were involved, you need to stop worrying."

"*Stop worrying!*" She thumped the steering wheel in frustration. "That, my dear, is certainly easier said than done."

Pricilla stepped out of the car then yanked the rented crutches out of the back. Max was not helping. Something had obviously happened, and she had an unsettled feeling in her stomach that said it wasn't good.

Max hobbled beside her down the graveled driveway until they reached the porch, where she managed to help him up the stairs and into the lodge.

"Mom. I'm glad you're back." Nathan's boots thudded against the smooth tiled entryway as he met them inside the lodge. "I'm sorry about the injury, Max. Are you all right?"

Max paused in the doorway. "Thankfully, the doctor says it's just sprained."

Pricilla touched the sleeve of her son's sweater. "Please tell us what's going on here. Considering the size of Rendezvous, it looks as if the cavalry has arrived."

From the troubled expression on Nathan's face, she sensed he was worried. "I guess you could say that. Detective Carter decided to show up with reinforcements."

"I can see that, but why?" Pricilla followed the men down the short hallway toward the living room.

"Apparently there have been some unsettling findings regarding Mr. Woodruff's death, though I can't get anything out of the detective. We're all supposed to meet in the living room."

"Wonderful. He's summoning us like a group of suspects."

"Mrs. Crumb." Detective Carter met them in the hallway. His voice was friendly, but the sentiment was short lived. "We've been awaiting your arrival. I'm sure you're anxious to hear our preliminary findings."

"I'm surprised you have something to report so soon." Pricilla looked the detective in the eye and frowned. The man was obviously out to prove something, though what, she wasn't sure.

"It's my job to bring about justice as quickly as possible."

Pricilla entered the living room behind Max then took a seat between him and Nathan on the soft leather couch. While she'd always enjoyed the open and rustic décor of the room, with its wooden ceiling beams and beautiful pine furniture, today it seemed as cold as the expressions on the guests' faces. Claire's pale appearance emphasized the fact that she would rather be anywhere else. And the men, no doubt, would rather be heading for the mountains and their chance for another trophy.

Simon seemed the most sullen of the three friends. He looked liked he hadn't shaved in several days and the old baseball cap shoved backward on his head managed only to partly cover his unruly mop of dark, curly hair. Anthony perched on the edge of his chair next to Simon, wearing a red T-shirt and flannel shirt that both looked as if they'd been slept in. He eyed the doorway as if he were contemplating a quick getaway. Michael was the only one who apparently hadn't broken away from the formalities of the business world's dress code. Clean shaven, with only a goatee marking his chocolate-colored skin, and decked out in a fleece vest and camouflage pants, he could have posed as a model for any number of hunting magazines.

Pricilla turned her attention to Detective Carter, who stood with his back to the fireplace as he pulled out his little notebook from the back pocket of his pants.

The detective cleared his throat as Oscar and Misty slipped into the room then flipped open his spiraled notepad. "I'm sure you're wondering why I've called you all together this morning. What I had hoped would be a simple case of a heart attack has unfortunately turned into something much more serious."

Pricilla's eyes widened. She didn't like where this was going. Had Charles Woodruff died of food poisoning, or something more sinister?

"Normally an autopsy takes at least twenty-four hours," the detective continued, "but thankfully things fell into place a bit quicker on this case. At first it appeared that there was no real reason to even have an autopsy performed, but during my investigation yesterday, several things stood out that bothered me."

Pricilla saw Claire catch her breath. Yesterday, the detective had assured them that there was no reason to suspect foul play. What had happened between then and now to bring such a turnaround in his position? Certainly Sheriff Tucker wouldn't be handling things this way if he were here. Having them assemble in the living room like a bunch of suspects and Detective Carter carrying on as if he were a Sherlock Holmes wannabe was nothing more than a theatrical stunt.

The detective took a step away from the fireplace and tapped his pen against the notebook. "The first thing that struck me was Mrs. Woodruff's insistence that her husband was in perfect health. To any officer of the law, this raises a question in his mind, when one then expires so unexpectedly. Secondly, there was Mrs. Crumb's assertion that her tartlets had been the cause of his untimely death."

Max reached out and took Pricilla's hand. Despite the comfort it gave her, this time she avoided his gaze. No one had to remind her that, even after living sixty plus years, she still hadn't mastered the art of patience. Oh no. She had to be the one to throw herself in front of the detective, practically begging for him to haul her off to jail for murder. Maybe someday she'd learn to keep her mouth shut, but that wasn't going to help her today.

The detective turned toward her, and she heard the *clank* of his metal handcuffs. "Both instances sent up red flags in my mind. While it will still be some time before the toxicology report is in as well as the official autopsy report from the coroner, the preliminary results are startling."

Pricilla leaned forward in her chair and forced herself not to jump up and grab the detective's notebook from him so she could get to the bottom line.

But the man wasn't finished. "Before I accepted the position of detective to the fine town of Rendezvous and the surrounding areas, I was privileged to participate in a number of forensic classes in Denver. The presence of poisons in a deceased body can be detected in outward signs. For instance, cyanide has a bitter almond odor detectable on the body. Be that as it may, few people are able to detect the smell of hydrogen cyanide. Fortunately, I happen to be one who can."

The detective addressed them as if they were a group of college freshmen who didn't know anything. "Cyanide also turns the blood a bright cherry red. And this precisely is what was discovered in Mr. Woodruff's body. While the findings are preliminary, of course, I have enough to warrant an investigation."

Pricilla had to force herself to take a breath. Cyanide? Surely the detective wasn't accusing her of purposely poisoning Charles?

"Mrs. Crumb"—the detective shortened the gap between them—"you can rest assured that while we will have to test your tartlets, at the present moment, we don't suspect that they had anything to do with Mr. Woodruff's death, though I can't tell you the specifics as to why at the moment."

Pricilla let out an audible sigh of relief.

"But we do, in fact, have reason to believe that Charles Woodruff might have been murdered." He tapped the notebook against the palm of his hand. "I must ask you to stay away from the crime scene."

Max raised his hand. "May I ask a question?"

The detective shoved his notebook back into his pocket. "Before I try to answer any questions, there is one more thing that must be made clear. No one will be allowed to leave the area until further notice. That will be all for now."

A number of audible moans filled the room at the untimely announcement. Several of them gathered around the detective, firing off questions to the balding man, while others slipped out of the room. Claire sat riveted in her seat.

Pricilla slipped into the chair beside her. "I'm sorry about all of this. I know it must be frightening. If there's anything I can do—"

The woman stared at the braided rug at her feet. "The detective told me ahead of time what he was going to announce. I just didn't expect it to be such a shock, hearing it the second time."

Pricilla tugged on the edge of her jacket, searching for words of encouragement. "Do you have family? Anyone close who could come be with you during this difficult time?"

Claire hiccupped and wiped a tear from her cheek with the back of her hand. "Charles and I had plenty of social friends, but no true friends."

"What about funeral arrangements?" Pricilla pulled out a clean tissue from her pocket and handed it to Claire.

The woman nodded her thanks then blew her nose. "Once the state is finished with his body, I'm having it sent to California where I'll bury him. . .and then have a small memorial service that likely no one will attend."

"I'm sure that's not true."

"You didn't know my husband." For the first time, Claire turned and looked at her. "There was a charismatic side of him that people liked, so much so that he was planning to go into politics. But he was so afraid people would find out that he wasn't perfect. We had to have the right house, the right car, the right vacation. Eventually he cut us off from all our friends, family. . . ."

"Do you have a church family?"

Claire let out a low chuckle. "Charles wasn't one for religion, and I pretty much gave up what little faith I had when I met him."

The thought broke Pricilla's heart. She wasn't sure she would have made it after Marty died, if it hadn't been for her relationship with God along with the support of her friends at church, and her family. Unfortunately, she'd met far too many people like Claire. Women, especially, who had left their faith because of a boyfriend or husband. It might take time for Claire to realize how important it was, but there was always hope.

"It's never too late to—"

"It's too late for Charles." Claire stood up and wrapped her sweater around her. "I'm sorry, Mrs. Crumb. I appreciate your kindness, but all of this has been such a shock. I think I will go upstairs and rest. They've moved me to another room, thankfully, and your son is being kind enough to allow me to stay. I just wished things would have turned out different."

"We all do, Mrs. Woodruff."

Pricilla got up slowly from the cushioned chair and felt quite her age at the moment. There was no doubt about another thing as well. Her guest list had just turned into a suspect list—for murder.

"We've got to think of something better than this." Pricilla looked over the list before handing it on to Trisha. "Until our detective finishes his investigation, I can hardly see a man like Simon Wheeler playing a competitive game of croquet."

Trisha threw the notebook down onto Nathan's desk and nodded her head. "You do have a point, but we've got to decide on something."

Nathan raked his fingers through his hair. "That's easy to say, but if I wanted to be an entertainment director, I'd have applied for a position on the *Love Boat*."

Pricilla stifled a laugh, but she had to agree. Hunting, fishing, and camping trips were what had made the lodge a success. Canceling the hunting trip, and the men's chances for another set of antlers for their trophy walls, was like a death sentence. Max, Nathan, Trisha, and Pricilla had worked for an hour to come up with ideas to keep their guests happy until the detective let them go. Carter had insisted that the hunting trip be postponed. The whole procedure was becoming ridiculous, and it was evident that Detective Carter was determined to stay in control.

Pricilla tried to come up with something unique. Hunting. . .guns—that was it!

She sat forward on the edge of her chair. "What do these men like to do?"

Nathan shot her a puzzled look. "They love to hunt."

"Exactly. Which means these men love guns. They love to shoot and compete. So what about setting up some sort of competition for them?"

"Skeet shooting and clay targets." Max threw out.

"And we could bring in some of the locals?" Trisha grabbed the notepad and started jotting down ideas.

Nathan tapped the edge of his desk and smiled. "That's the best idea we've heard so far. As long as the competition is kept a safe distance from the house, we could invite the community and not worry about the crime scene. We could even throw in a few prizes. We need to start calling everyone we know in town—"

The phone rang. Nathan answered it and then frowned.

"No, I can only verify what the police report says. We have no further information for you," he said firmly. "No, the victim's wife isn't making any statements, and neither is the lodge. No. . .no. . .I'm sorry, but this is private property and we'd rather not have any photographers disrupting our other guests' visits. Sorry I can't help you further. Thank you. Good-bye." Nathan was shaking his head as he hung up.

"Great. The *Rendezvous Sentinel* got word of Charles and now they're going to put the story on tomorrow's front page. They don't know yet that it may be murder, but how many reservations will it kill? We've already had two cancellations just today. I'll go out of business if this keeps up."

"The town paper is small potatoes, but it can tip off bigger media," said Trisha. "We can post an announcement on the lodge's Web site. But I think you need to get on the phone and call the sheriff and the editor and the chamber of commerce and the state tourism council and your pastor and your attorney and anyone else you can think of." She took a breath. "We can't just roll over dead."

She stood up and strode toward the picture window that looked out over the snow-dusted mountain.

"You're right. I called and left Sheriff Tucker a message right after the detective made his announcement and called off the hunting trip. I'm waiting to hear back from him."

There was a knock on the door and Pricilla glanced up to see Simon Wheeler in the doorway.

"Mr. Wheeler, can I help you?" Nathan stood and walked to the door.

The frown on the guest's face made it clear that his reason for stopping by Nathan's office was not for a pleasant chat. "I came here to go hunting and paid a lot of money to get what I have always considered to be the best hunting experience around."

"I'm glad you think that way, Mr.—"

"I'm not finished. What has happened here is unacceptable—"

"Mr. Wheeler"—Nathan held up his hand—"you have to understand that while the lodge plans to do all it can to compensate for your week, there are simply things that are out of our control. If you have a problem with the way things stand then you'll need to take your complaints to the detective."

"I've done that, but that man won't change his mind." Simon stepped forward and slapped his hands against the top of the desk. "What do you suppose we do in the meantime? I didn't come here to sit around reading and drinking hot chocolate all day."

"I'm sure you didn't." Nathan held up his notepad. "The four of us have been putting together a program of activities that should keep everyone busy until the detective gives the word that we all can leave."

Mr. Wheeler looked skeptical. "Activities? This isn't a junior high camp."

"Of course not." Trisha stepped forward, giving the man her best smile. "We are thinking more in line of things like a skeet-shooting competition with prizes."

The man rubbed his goatee.

"And plenty of food," Pricilla added.

Trisha nodded. "Give the detective another day or two and in the meantime, I'm sure that Nathan will do all he can to get permission to get the hunting trip back on the calendar."

Pricilla smiled with relief as Simon finally left the room. Trisha was not only beautiful, but an intelligent negotiator as well. The girl was the perfect complement for Nathan. Listening to the young woman's well-spoken argument had brought a ray of hope. And, despite Charles's untimely demise, Cupid's arrow might hit Nathan and Trisha after all.

Detective Carter appeared in the doorway. "Sorry to bother you, Nathan. I'm on my way back to the station and wondered if you wouldn't mind coming with me? I just have a few questions I'd like to ask you."

Any relief Pricilla had felt vanished. "I think it's time you called your lawyer, Nathan."

Nathan stood up and grabbed his coat off the rack. "I don't have anything to hide, Mom. Besides, the sooner we find the truth, the sooner we can get our lives back to normal."

For the first time in twenty-odd years, Pricilla decided to forgo the planned home-cooked spread and decided to serve cold cuts for lunch. While such fare might be common for half the population's noon meal, she'd always insisted on something heartier, and over the years had pledged to avoid serving cold sandwiches to company. In spite of all her good intentions, though, today it couldn't be avoided. She could only hope that the guests wouldn't complain about her lowered standards if she did it just this once.

She stood with the refrigerator door open, debating if roast beef, ham, and turkey would be enough of a selection. Her mother had taught her the importance of making meal time a priority family time. Meals in her house growing up had always been a place where family members came together to share what had happened during the day. Pricilla had, in turn, carried on the same tradition in her own family, and while she couldn't implement such traditions on the guests, it was her responsibility to insure they had the most pleasant dining experience possible. Withdrawing a bag of carrots from the refrigerator to add to her pile of lunch ingredients, she tried to ignore the strong feelings of guilt that began to surface at her compromise.

Guilt—and anger.

She pulled a knife out of the butcher block and started slicing the carrots into thin julienne strips. Taking Max to the doctor might have given her less time to prepare lunch, but the morning's time crunch wasn't what had her upset. What worried her was Nathan. She slammed the knife against the wooden cutting board. Detective Carter had no right to haul her son down to the station. She'd watched enough episodes of *Father Dowling* to know what that implied. A friendly invitation to the sheriff's office meant nothing other than her son was now considered a suspect in a murder investigation. A thought that was absolutely ridiculous.

Pricilla dropped the knife and gnawed on her lower lip. With the detective's decision to involve her son, the stakes had just risen substantially. There was no way she was going to trust the detective's investigative skills, and someone had to save her son's reputation. People were already canceling their reservations after learning about the demise of one of the guests. And an arrest, even if it were false, could ruin Nathan's business.

She started cutting the carrots again. Her mother's dining philosophy had given her an idea. For centuries, good food had been a key ingredient for breaking down barriers and getting people to talk—something she was determined to do with the guests and employees of the lodge. For her plan to work, sandwiches would never suffice. If she hurried, she just might be able to pull it off.

For the first time all morning Pricilla smiled, because while cold cuts and cheese slices wouldn't hit the mark, she knew exactly what would.

Max jerked up in his chair then winced as a blast of pain shot through his ankle. "Pricilla?"

"Sorry. I didn't mean to disturb you." She set a small tray of snacks and sodas at the edge of a puzzle table Nathan had set up beside Max's chair on the front porch of the lodge. "Go back to sleep."

Max closed his eyes, but even with them shut, he could feel Pricilla's penetrating gaze on him.

He opened them again. "Where is everyone?"

"After a bit of persuading by Nathan, Detective Carter allowed Oscar to take the men fishing this morning. They should be back soon for lunch. Claire's sleeping, and Trisha's in her room reading. Nathan's still at the police station."

"I thought it seemed awfully quiet." He held up his hand to block the sun as she stood in front of him with her hands behind her back. "What's wrong?"

"Nothing that can't wait." She sat down and gripped the edges of the padded chair until her knuckles turned white. "It's really not that important."

While he'd never understand why Pricilla couldn't just get to the point, he doubted her blasé response came close to what she actually felt. He also knew her well enough to know that he'd never be able to sleep now. She'd stare at him until he gave her his full attention.

"Of course, it's important." He sat up and helped himself to a cracker and dip. "This is delicious. What is it?"

She loosened her grip on the armrest. "It's homemade liver pâté. I forgot about it with all that's happened. Thought you might be hungry."

Pâté? He frowned. He'd made it a rule to avoid anything that an animal had thought with, tasted with, or. . .well, any other number of other unmentionable things. Still, he wasn't surprised at all that Pricilla could make even liver taste as good as filet mignon.

"I never thought I liked pâté, but this is wonderful." He took another scoop of the dip with his cracker and chuckled. "You know, I'd forgotten, but every year Violet used to bring homemade pâté to the church's Christmas party. She told me it was the one sophisticated recipe in her repertoire, which if you remember, was very limited."

"Was it good?"

He laughed at the memory. "I tried it one time and one time only. Violet had dozens of wonderful qualities, but cooking wasn't one of them. The year before she died, I found her uneaten pâté in the church trashcan. Saundra Huff caught me and made me promise to never tell Violet what she'd done, horrified she might hurt Violet's feelings. Saundra couldn't stand the idea of Violet taking her pâté home when no one had touched it. I never had the heart to tell her."

Pricilla's expression softened. "I'm glad you didn't."

"Me, too, but there's no telling how many years Saundra and the other women had been trying to save Violet's feelings."

"Everyone always loved Violet." She stared at the puzzle he'd started before deciding to take a nap and picked up one of the edges of the Thomas Kinkade picture. "Do you still miss her?"

He popped open the tab of his drink. "I'll always miss her, but I also know that it's time to move on."

He studied Pricilla's profile and caught the seriousness in her expression. He couldn't stand the fact that she was unhappy, and he wanted to be the one to bring a smile to her face. Maybe it was time to tell her how he felt.

"You know, Pricilla, sometimes I think—"

He stopped.

With her focus on the puzzle, it was obvious that her mind was miles away, and besides, this wasn't the time to state his intentions. He couldn't really blame her. Obviously she was quite upset by the fact that Nathan was at this moment being questioned by Detective Carter. If the detective's interest had been in Trisha, or Pricilla for that matter, Max would be ready to engage the man in a duel.

A slight breeze tugged at the collar of his light jacket. He gazed out across the rugged terrain where the aspen trees had already begun to fade and would be bare by the end of the month. The ski resorts were still waiting for powder as the snowfall only reached the highest peaks of the mountains at this point. More than likely the coming snowstorms would more than make up for what was lacking right now. He never failed to be amazed at the wonder of God's beauty. And the stark contrast of man's behavior.

"Pricilla?"

She turned to him, brushing a silver curl away from her face. "I'm sorry. I must have missed the last thing you said."

"Never mind." He smiled. "I thought you hated puzzles."

"Normally I do." She picked up an edge piece and snapped it into place along the outer rim.

"It's Nathan, isn't it?"

She picked up another piece. "I'm worried."

"Me, too, but God convicted me of something this morning."

"What's that?" Looking up at him, she caught his gaze.

"No matter what is going on around us, He's our only true place of refuge. Admittedly, I've tried to rely on my own efforts for most of my life, but the older I get, the more I realize that it doesn't work that way."

Pricilla nodded and leaned back in her chair. "I always loved the verse that says, 'I will take refuge in the shadow of your wings until the disaster has passed.' But what if this disaster doesn't pass?"

"What do you mean?"

"What if they arrest Nathan and—"

"They're not going to arrest him."

"You don't know that." She picked up a cracker and nibbled on it. "What do you think about Detective Carter?"

"What about him?" he asked.

"Do you think he knows what he's doing?"

"Of course he knows what he's doing. Otherwise, he wouldn't have been hired for the job."

"Don't you remember that his uncle's the sheriff?"

"So?" He knew where she was going with her line of questioning, but they couldn't just assume that Detective Carter had been hired simply as a favor to the family. This wasn't the Mafia, whose members stayed in the family business simply because of their last name.

Pricilla shook her head. "Carter could have got the position without being qualified. Max, this is serious. They've just taken Nathan down to the station for questioning. He could be arrested."

"They're not going to arrest him."

She let out a sigh. "Misty told me someone overheard him and Charles having an argument. Someone must have told the detective."

"Just because he argued with the man doesn't mean he killed him."

There was nothing like small towns when it came to letting rumors run loose. And Max knew that rumors could do as much, if not more, damage than the truth. But that didn't mean that questioning Nathan wasn't purely routine.

She leaned forward and caught his gaze. "Of course Nathan didn't kill him. You and I know that, but what about the detective?"

"I'm sure that the man is simply doing his job and looking into every angle—"

"My son's not an angle, and I don't intend for his reputation to be shredded to bits."

He took another sip of his drink. "You really don't like the detective, do you?"

"I've always had this second sense about people."

"Does this include your matchmaking skills?"

Pricilla frowned. "Detective Carter has more conceit than experience. A lethal combination if you ask me."

"Then what do you intend to do?"

"I intend to find out who murdered Charles Woodruff."

Max dropped his drink against the armrest, barely stopping it from tipping over. "You can't be serious." Except he knew she was.

"I'm very serious." Pricilla pulled a small notepad out of her apron pocket and flipped it open. "We need a list of suspects."

"Suspects? You know, you're starting to sound like the detective." She shot him a glaring look. "Sorry, go ahead."

"I've already made out a list of possible suspects that includes both lodge guests and workers. There's a total of ten. To save time, though, I've eliminated the two of us, as well as Nathan and Trisha. In each suspect, we're looking for secrets, a possible link to the crime, and, most importantly, a motive."

"What about opportunity?" He tried not to laugh. He couldn't believe he was going along with her scheme. But on the other hand, what other choice did he really have? "I like that one, because I have an alibi."

"I've already taken you off my list of suspects, but that's not necessarily true."

He frowned. "That I don't have an alibi?"

"If Charles was poisoned, say in his tea, we all had ample time to slip something into his mug."

Max considered her argument. "I suppose that's true—"

"But since I'm certain you for one did not murder Charles Woodruff, I'm not including you in my suspect list."

"Are you sure about that?"

"Max."

"Sorry." No matter how much he enjoyed teasing her, he supposed that now wasn't the time.

Pricilla skirted around the puzzle table and walked to the porch rail. "Suspect one, and the most obvious, of course, is Claire Woodruff, the victim's wife. She has an obvious link to the victim."

"As well as motive. Several heard them fighting."

Pricilla nodded and wrote something in her notebook. "We need to find out, then, what she's hiding. Next suspects: Simon Wheeler, Michael Smythe, and Anthony Mills."

"Three businessmen who had met Charles on a previous hunting trip."

"Great." Pricilla continued scribbling. "We've got our connection."

"Motive?"

"That's what we need to find out. Maybe they interact with Charles somehow in the business world. I'll make a note to follow up on that issue." She scribbled some notes and then tapped the pen against the pad. "Next on the list is Oscar Philips. For starters, I don't like the man."

Max shook his head. "That's not applicable. Miss Marple may have had a certain intuition to solve a crime, as you say you have, but in real life, whether or not you like someone really doesn't count."

Pricilla pressed the notebook against her waist. "I didn't know you read mystery novels."

"I've always loved characters like Hercule Poirot and Sherlock Homes, but, as I just said, in the real world, what one thinks about a suspect really doesn't apply. It's always about the evidence."

She shot him a smile. "I think I've found myself quite a partner."

Max smiled back despite himself. Partners in crime would be more like it. While part of him was trying to figure out how to get her to lose interest in this ridiculous pursuit of justice, Max couldn't help but admire her determination. Her hazel eyes sparkled in the mid-morning sun, and no matter what her schemes might be to serve up justice in this situation, he knew he was hooked.

"So," Pricilla continued, "back to Oscar. He definitely knew Charles from coming to the lodge the past few years."

"You've got your link to the crime."

"And I'm sure he has a secret. Have you ever tried to really talk to him?"

He took another sip of his drink. "Can't say that I have."

"That's because you can't. He's evasive, shifty, suspicious—"

"And you, as I've said more than once, I'm sure, have an overactive imagination."

She cleared her throat as if dismissing his last comment. "Last on the list is Misty Majors. She has the same connection as Oscar, but that's all I have on her so far." Pricilla dropped the notebook and pen onto her chair and folded her arms across her chest. "What do you think?"

"Not bad." Max shifted in the chair and tried to find a more comfortable position for his foot. "You've got your list. Now what? It seems pretty full of holes to me."

"I'm afraid you're right. We're left with more questions than answers." She picked up the notebook and pen, tapped the pen against the pad, and cocked her head. "But I've already got that part figured out. Take in a deep breath."

He filled his lungs with the savory sent of lunch. "I smell food? What is it?"

Pricilla sat back down beside him. "My trump card. Herbed beef stew and a slice of my lemon crumb cake."

"That's your trump card?"

Pricilla smiled and nodded her head. "Think about it. One bite of my stew and the guests will open up, allowing me to fill in the blanks."

He lowered his brow, not convinced in the validity of her experiment. "That's your plan?"

"Do you like my pâté?"

"Excuse me?"

"My pâté. Do you like it?"

"It's delicious." He took another bite for emphasis. "But I already told you that."

She pointed a finger at him. "And that's not all you told me. One bite and you were telling me all about Violet's pâté and the secret of how everyone hated it—"

"Now wait a minute. I don't see how you can compare Violet's pâté with finding out who murdered Charles Woodruff."

"Why not? I need you to help me, Max."

"I don't know." He shook his head. "I'm worried that you're overdoing it for one thing, trying to get involved in an official investigation—"

"I'm fine, I promise."

Despite his best effort to stop Pricilla's harebrained idea, he knew there was no way out of this one.

"Please."

"On two conditions," he said, shaking his finger at her like a stern headmaster. "You run every scheme of yours by me first, and everything you find out, you pass on to the detective."

She frowned, but nodded her head in agreement. He'd keep his promise to help her, but only to try and keep her out of trouble. Something he wasn't sure he'd actually be able to do.

Pricilla breathed in the spicy scent of her stew and smiled. She knew Max thought her idea to interview the guests was ridiculous, but she was convinced her plan was going to work. Lunch would be informal today, served in the smaller dining room that looked out across the mountains. She'd even sent Misty on an errand so the woman wouldn't get in the way of her investigation. Of course, Misty would have to be interviewed at some point as well, but Pricilla had that planned for later. All she needed now for her idea to work was simmering bowls of stew, hot yeast rolls, a listening ear—and her suspects.

Standing in the corner of the room, she took a quick inventory of the table settings to make sure she hadn't forgotten anything. She still needed to put out the glasses and debated between the thick moose mugs or one of Nathan's latest purchases, eight-ounce tumblers with a colored drawing of the same animal on one side. Like every room in the lodge, this one had its own unique décor. From the moose tableware and faux antler utensils, to the antler chandelier hanging above the rustic table and the carved moose on the back of each chair—it was the setting any hunter or fisherman would love. She was counting on the relaxed atmosphere of the room to help ease her guests into a worthwhile conversation that would give her the answers she was looking for.

She turned toward the door as Max hobbled into the room, the rubber tips of his crutches thumping against the wood floor. He tottered for a moment then plopped down on a cowhide chair beside the crackling fireplace.

"Are you all right?" Forgetting the glasses, Pricilla hurried past the edge of the sideboard warmer to where he sat.

"I'm fine."

"But should you be up and around?"

"It's lunchtime." He flashed her a grin. "You know I can't resist your cooking."

"But you're not supposed to be in here. . . ." Pricilla stopped. While she didn't want to appear impolite, she also couldn't have her carefully laid plans infringed upon. The more people in the room, the less of a chance the guests would open up.

She caught his perplexed expression and frowned. "I'm sorry. I didn't mean it like that. It's just that—"

"Don't worry." The corners of his lips curled into a smile. "I just needed to stretch and thought you might want to know that the men are back from their fishing trip. Judging from the strong odor that passed by me a few minutes ago, I'm assuming they'll take a while to clean up."

Glancing at her watch, she decided on the tumblers and moved to place one at each setting. "Did they have a big catch?"

He shrugged and settled back into the chair. "You'll have to ask them, but I got the impression that none of them were very happy. Which means—"

"They'll be less likely to open up."

Frustrated, Pricilla finished putting out the glasses and lifted the lid off the stew to stir the savory mixture. She'd done all she could do. Now it was a matter of praying her plan would unfold to her advantage. She might not uncover any dark secrets in the course of the next couple hours, but any hint as to the motive behind Charles Woodruff's demise would place her one step ahead of the detective. And it was far more likely that the guests would leak information to her before ever coming forward with clues for the detective.

Max tapped one of his crutches against the floor. "You're taking this far too seriously, Pricilla."

She turned to face him. "A man's dead and my son's been taken to the sheriff's office for questioning. I don't think anything I do from this point on is taking it too seriously."

"Come sit down." Max patted the ottoman in front of him.

She hesitated for a moment then placed the lid back on the warmer before crossing the room.

"Can I give you a few tips?" he asked.

She sat down and reached into her pocket. After thirty-plus years in the air force, he must have learned a thing or two about extracting information from the enemy. "Should I get out my notebook?"

"Not now." He reached out and squeezed her hands. "The first step in any investigation is to relax. I want you to take a deep breath then let it out slowly."

Pricilla smiled and nodded her head. She couldn't resist his dimpled grin. Her heart felt like a jackhammer at a Seattle construction site, but she forced herself to close her eyes and take a deep breath. Strange. Not only was her heart pounding, but even with her eyes shut she felt dizzy. She opened her eyes. It had to be nerves. Who wouldn't be upset? Her son was right now being interrogated by the detective?

She couldn't smell the stew anymore. Instead, the scent of Max's cologne filled her senses. She'd never stopped to notice just how blue his eyes were. Blue like the color of the Colorado columbine. His hair had grayed but was still thick with a bit of curl around the ends. The saying that men aged gracefully was certainly correct in Max's case. Now that she thought about it, he'd only grown more handsome in the past few years.

She shook her head. How in the world had her thoughts shifted from her son's dilemma to the color of Max's eyes? Undoubtedly, she was feeling overly emotional today. After finding one dead body, making a false confession to murder, fearing for Max's life—and now her son's future—no wonder she felt as if she'd gone over the edge. Still, if she didn't know better, it would seem that her unbidden thoughts were leaning toward something romantic. But that was absurd. Max had always been. . .well. . .Max. Longtime friend, emotional support, and the one person who could always make Marty and her laugh. It had never mattered that his eyes reminded her of Paul Newman, or that his cologne left her head reeling.

She cleared her throat, and forced herself to refocus on the issue at hand. "What's step two?"

He shifted in the chair and readjusted his foot. "You've already completed step number two."

"I have?" Considering all her sleuthing knowledge came from books and TV shows, his statement pleased her. "And what would step two be?" she asked.

"Completing a factual analysis of the information surrounding the crime. In other words, what you have in your notebook for a start. A suspect list."

"And the next step?"

"Using your suspect list, find a viable motive behind Charles's murder."

Pricilla clenched her jaw. He was right. So she had a list of suspects and their connection to the crime. Unless she could gather more pertinent information from the guests, she'd be no help in ensuring her son didn't take the rap for the murder.

Ten minutes later, Max had left and Simon and Anthony were arriving, freshly showered from their morning fishing trip on Lake Paytah. With a brief explanation that Michael was not feeling well and wanted to skip lunch, they sat down at the end of the round table, and nodded when she set the bowls in front of them. Apparently they were hungry, because neither of them spoke as they dug into the thick stew.

She filled a plate with the hot rolls and set it before them. "How was the lake this morning, gentlemen?"

Simon grunted and took another bite of his stew.

She bustled around the table and handed them each an extra napkin. Apparently Max had been right that they weren't happy over the morning's trip. "Was it that bad?"

"Yep." Anthony's response was just as ambiguous. Pricilla frowned. "Didn't you catch anything?"

"Nope."

Her eyes narrowed at Simon's curt response. She didn't want to hover over them like some bumbling private investigator, but in order to gather the information she needed, she was going to have to find a way to engage them in a discussion. This couldn't be a one-sided conversation, though at the moment she wondered if these men were capable of much more. Still, she had no intentions of giving up just because up to this point they'd only grunted or spoken in monosyllables.

She grabbed the water pitcher off the sideboard and topped off their already full glasses. Whether it was needed or not, she needed an excuse to stay in the room.

"Last time I went fishing with Nathan, we caught our limit of rainbow trout." She began serving another loaf of fresh bread. "Let me tell you, it was one of the tastiest meals I've ever had. Several of those trout were over twelve inches long. We fried them up and ate them with coleslaw and hushpuppies on the side. . . ."

Pricilla stopped talking.

Both men had dropped their spoons into their bowls and were staring at her as if she'd grown horns.

"Not *real* puppies, of course," she hurried on to explain. "My mother was from the South, and she always served those little fried dumplings of cornmeal. Normally you eat them with catfish, but. . ." Biting her lip, she stopped. She'd obviously wandered onto the wrong topic. "Anyway, I hope you like today's menu."

She dusted off her hands on her apron. This was getting absurd. They were going to be finished with their meal before she was able to add even a trace of evidence into her notebook. Trying to look busy, she wondered what she could say to get them to talk. Frankly, if she could do things her way, she'd opt to find a small room with a bald light and use more forceful tactics. Just because such methods were considered extreme, why beat around the bush when the truth might be easily discovered with a bit of creativity?

She piled a second plate with hot bread then placed it on the table in front of the men, contemplating what to say next. While it was true that subtlety had never been her strongest point, she was certain that her cooking would eventually make up for any problems she might encounter in getting the men to talk. Even if she hadn't served fresh fish.

"Sad thing about Mr. Woodruff, isn't it?" she began, trying once again to fuel the dying conversation.

"Yep" was the only response she got. She needed a question that couldn't be answered with a simple yes or no. Or, in their case, no yeps and grunts.

Pretending to brush crumbs off the tablecloth, Pricilla reached out to straighten one of the silverware settings. "Did either of you know him well?"

Anthony wiped his mouth with a napkin. "The three of us went hunting with him once."

At last a complete sentence. She decided to push for more. "What was he like? I didn't really know the man at all except for a brief exchange before his untimely passing."

Simon looked to his friend. "Pretty quiet, wouldn't you say?"

"Yep. He was pretty quiet. Kept to himself."

While she couldn't really call it progress, at least she had them talking. "I understand you both are businessmen. Did you ever meet him in a professional capacity?"

She didn't miss the look that passed between the two men, nor the silent pause that followed her question.

Anthony reached for another piece of bread, his face void of expression. "You obviously haven't heard about the man's reputation. He wasn't exactly the kind of person one chooses to do business with. Always cutthroat and out to win, no matter what."

Unable to take notes, Pricilla told herself to find out more about this hunting trip of theirs. For whatever reason, the men obviously harbored bad feelings toward Mr. Woodruff. Whether or not they'd go into greater detail was another question.

"I understand you own a. . .dot-com company," she continued, hoping she'd phrased it correctly. With technology advancing as rapidly as it did, she found it amazing how anyone could keep up with what was going on. She was probably one of the few remaining holdouts of the modern world who still didn't have her own computer or e-mail account.

"We did," Simon quipped. "Sold it a few years back for a nice profit."

"We're preparing to launch a new online consulting business in the next few months."

Anthony's addition gave her little to go on. "Is that how you first met up with Mr. Woodruff? In business circles, I mean."

The two men didn't have to say anything for Pricilla to realize that she'd pushed them too far.

"Now listen here." Simon shoved his bowl away from the edge of the table then scooted back his chair. "I'll be the first to admit that I didn't like the man, but that doesn't mean that I killed him."

"Same here." Anthony folded his arms across his chest and eyed her warily. "Did the detective set you up to ask us about our relationship with Charles?"

Pricilla wanted to laugh at the question. If only they knew the real motivation behind her line of questioning, they'd more than likely turn her over to the detective.

She waved her hand in the air and tried to shrug aside the comment. "Just curious is all."

The men rose from the table and mumbled their thanks for the lunch as they left the room. The interview was over. Clearing their dirty dishes from the table, Pricilla prepared the table for the next guests, hoping that whoever once said that curiosity killed the cat had been mistaken.

Max slipped into the dining room, amused at the interchange he'd overheard between Pricilla and the men. While he had to admit her plan did have merit, she obviously picked the wrong two men to start off with. He chuckled to himself. One had to give her credit. He'd been involved in literally hundreds of official interviews throughout his career as an officer and not once had anyone had the idea to offer a homemade meal in order to get the conversation to flow. Obviously, the problem had been Pricilla's rusty interviewing tactics and not the food.

Pricilla placed her hand against her chest when she saw him. "How long have you been standing there?"

"Long enough to hear the end of your conversation with the men."

"They didn't even try the cake." Pricilla's expression fell. "It didn't exactly go as smoothly as I'd intended."

Max leaned against the end of the table. "What if I interrogate the next suspect?"

"I thought you were against all of this."

He hobbled his way around the table to one of the chairs and sat down. "I am, but it's starting to rain, and I've worked on the puzzle until I can't see straight with my bifocals anymore. And besides all that, I'm hungry. Who's left on your list?"

"Michael, Claire—"

"Misty." Max smiled as the young woman entered the room. No time like the present to show Pricilla firsthand a thing or two about how to handle a proper interview. "I was just sitting down to eat. Would you care to join me?"

He ignored Pricilla's glare as the young woman set a package down at the end of the table. "I'm flattered for the offer, Mr. Summers, but I'm just here to give Mrs. Crumb the package I picked up in town for her. Besides, it's probably not appropriate for me to be eating with one of the guests."

"She's quite right, Max." Pricilla nodded her head. "And I hadn't really planned—"

"It's not a problem at all." He reached for a piece of bread and spread on some butter. "Who wants to bother with formalities? I hate to eat alone."

With hunting now out of the picture and the detective's directive that they all stay near the lodge, it didn't hurt to have something to occupy his time. Eating at the table with Misty, and whoever else showed up, was bound to break down barriers. Besides, how difficult could an undercover interview with an attractive young woman be?

Pricilla frowned as Misty took a seat across the table from Max. While she couldn't complain about the housekeeper's efficiency, allowing the staff to eat with the guests was not acceptable. What if someone joined them while Misty, their housekeeper, was sitting at the table, eating and laughing like one of the paying guests? Certainly Nathan would hold to the same standards, believing it wasn't the impression a top-rated lodge should ever leave.

She placed two bowls of steaming stew in front of Max and Misty but this time didn't smile at the savory scent wafting through the room.

Max smiled up at her. "This looks delicious, Pricilla. Thank you."

"And thank you, Mr. Summers, for inviting me to join you." Misty put her napkin in her lap, clearly thrilled to have been asked to stay for lunch. "While the food is always wonderful, today's company simply can't be beat."

"Please, why don't you call me Max?"

"And you can call me Misty."

The housekeeper laughed, or rather, she giggled like a schoolgirl on a date. Pricilla's brow puckered. Certainly the young woman wasn't flirting with Max? He was over twice her age.

"I'd hoped for the chance to chat with you at some point during the week," Misty said between spoonfuls.

"Really?" Max sat back in his chair.

"I always find older men so much more interesting than those my own age."

Max winked at Pricilla as she set a plate of hot bread on the table, but the gesture did little to erase her growing irritation.

So this was how he ran his investigations with attractive younger women? Put on the charm like Cary Grant and then sit back and watch it all unfold? The way Misty was opening up under his well-seasoned plan, he would have the case solved by the end of the meal. Clearly she didn't need to be a part of this.

Pricilla cleared her throat. "I need to check on some things in the kitchen. If you need seconds, there is plenty of food on the sideboard."

"Why don't you join us, Mrs. Crumb?" Misty asked.

Why did *Mrs. Crumb* sound so old-fashioned and downright ancient coming from Misty—whose pert smile and bright blue eyes lit up her wrinkle-free face like a ripe peach?

Pricilla forced a smile across her lips. "Thank you, but I want to make sure that things are ready for tonight's meal."

Max waved his hand in the air without looking up. "Then don't worry about us. We'll be fine."

"I'll be in to help you shortly." Misty patted Max's hand, a gesture Pricilla didn't miss. "And I'll be sure and take good care of Max in the meantime."

Pricilla picked up the package and hurried toward the kitchen, wondering why, all of a sudden, there was a lump the size of the Rocky Mountains in her throat. Maybe she would have done better with her own investigation if she'd tried buttering up the men before launching her questions, but one didn't have to be so obvious.

Pricilla pulled a stack of cloth napkins out of the bottom kitchen drawer and began running the taupe material through iron napkin rings she'd found at one of the local shops. Surely she wasn't feeling jealous. She and Max had known each other for years, and she'd never looked at him as anything more than a close friend. Just because Misty was pretty, jovial, and less than half her age—okay, far less than half her age—didn't mean that the girl was interested in Max. She was simply being friendly.

Once again, it had to be the stress. It was true that Max had always been there for her, flying in when her husband died and sending frequent letters as he could truly sympathize with her after losing his own wife. He'd been there to give her spiritual advice when she needed it and sent her small gifts on her birthday and for Christmas. But if it was nothing more than friendship she felt toward him, then why did her heart pound when she pictured Max's dimpled smile? And why did her heart sink when the housekeeper had his full attention?

"Mrs. Crumb?"

Pricilla set down the last napkin and turned around as Trisha walked into the room. "Did you get some rest?"

"Sort of." The young woman plopped down on a bar stool before resting her chin in her hands. "I thought reading would distract me, but I've read the same page at least a dozen times, and I couldn't tell you a thing of what I read. So much for the back cover's claims to grab my attention from page one and not let go until the last sentence."

"I'm sure it's not the book." Pricilla joined her at the counter, mirroring Trisha's glum expression. "I understand completely. This whole situation has left me on edge, and now with Nathan down at the sheriff's office. . ."

Trisha slid off her chunky bracelet and rolled it between her fingers. "I know you're worried about him. It's strange. I've known Nathan for just a matter of days but there's this connection between us. Maybe it's just because you and Dad have always been close."

Or maybe it was something much deeper. Pricilla smiled despite the somber mood of the day. No matter what was going on around them, she still believed firmly that Nathan and Trisha were right for each other. All they needed were a few more nudges in the right direction and human nature would take care of the rest.

"I checked on Claire before coming down," Trisha said.

"How is she?" Pricilla pulled a bag of red and green peppers from the fridge and laid them beside the cutting board, mentally calculating how much she should chop for tonight's antipasto pasta salad.

"I tried to convince her to let me bring her some lunch, but she wasn't interested."

Pricilla frowned. "Surely I can come up with something tempting to whet her appetite. I know it's difficult, but she has to eat. I'll take something up to her in a little bit."

Trisha took a piece of red pepper and popped it into her mouth. "I'm afraid she thinks the detective suspects her."

Pricilla rested her knife against the board. "What do you think?"

"I don't know." Trisha scrunched her lips together. "I suppose being the spouse of a murdered man makes one an automatic suspect. She did tell me she was Charles's beneficiary, and, from what I gathered, has a lot to gain financially from his death."

"And from the way everyone seems to have disliked him, perhaps she didn't have much to lose." Pricilla closed her mouth, wanting to bite back her words. "I'm sorry. I shouldn't have said that."

"Don't worry. I'm sure we've all thought that a time or two. If he was murdered, as the authorities believe, someone obviously didn't like him."

"I suppose you're right."

Pricilla went back to chopping the peppers. She knew little about Charles Woodruff, and speaking ill of the man would gain nothing. Money was always a possible motive, and she needed to add it to her notebook once she was done making her salad.

Trisha leaned back, stretching the muscles in her shoulders. "Do you know where my dad is?"

Pricilla scowled. Here was a subject she'd like to avoid. "He's in the dining room, eating lunch with Misty."

"With Misty?"

"I had the brilliant idea to see if we could find out more about Charles and his relationship with the guests. He chose Misty."

Trisha cocked her head. "If I didn't know better, I'd say you almost sound a bit. . .jealous?"

"Of course not." Pricilla dismissed the idea. "It's just the stress of this whole ordeal has me feeling a bit off. Aren't you planning to eat something?"

"I'm not really hungry. What's for lunch?"

"Stew, hot yeast rolls, and lemon crumb cake."

Trisha mulled over her choices. "Is there any cereal and milk? On any other day, I'd go nuts for a bowl of homemade stew, especially with the takeout I eat everyday, but—"

"Don't worry. I understand." Pricilla waved her hand in front of her. "If you look in the pantry, I'm sure you'll find something you like."

"Thanks." Trisha snatched a spoon from the silverware drawer then headed for the pantry. "I'll grab myself a bowl of cereal then give my book another try."

Pricilla dumped the peppers into the large fluted bowl she'd already filled with pasta, sausage, tomatoes, and cheeses. All she needed to make now was the dressing. Standing in front of the cupboard, she pulled out the balsamic vinegar then rested her hands against the smooth counter as Trisha left the room.

She couldn't stand it any longer. What was Misty telling Max? Despite the ridiculous pangs of jealousy she may or may not be experiencing, the truth was, Misty might hold information that might be valuable in solving the crime—and possibly saving her son. Slamming the cupboard door shut, she hurried back down the hall and planted herself outside the doorway of the dining room. Eavesdropping might not be the most ethical behavior, but as someone somewhere once said, desperate times call for desperate measures.

Max knew he was making progress. He took another bite of the stew and listened to Misty who was obviously familiar with the guests, knew things the rest of them might never find out. While he was never one to sit around and gossip, today his purpose was to extract as much information as he could regarding Charles Woodruff's relationship to the other guests—as resourcefully as possible.

He wiped his chin with his napkin and leaned back in his chair. "You must know a lot about the ins and outs of the lodge as well as the guests, Misty. You've been working here for. . .how many years?"

"I started working here eight years ago last July. It's hard to believe that much time has passed." Misty sighed, fiddling with her spoon. "My husband left me when my girls were still in diapers. They're nine and ten now. Don't know what I would have done if Nathan hadn't hired me. Out of work with only a high school education. Makes life difficult."

He helped himself to another roll then reached for the butter dish. "Seems like you've done well for yourself."

She nodded. "The job came with a cabin that's become home, and who can complain about waking up to a view of the Rocky Mountains every morning?"

Max took a sip of his drink, ready to push the conversation a step further. "You knew Charles Woodruff from years past. What's your take on all of this? Do you really think that one of us could have bumped him off?"

"It is hard to imagine, isn't it?" Misty giggled again. "Did you know the man had false teeth?"

"Really?" His eyes widened, but he mirrored her grin. "Not a motive for murder, I don't suppose."

"Of course not, but I could tell you things—"

"Let's stick to things regarding the case for now." On the surface, Misty didn't seem to be hiding anything. In the long run, he calculated, direct questions would get the most information out of her.

"Okay." Misty leaned forward in her seat as if she were afraid someone else might be listening. "Here's an interesting fact, then. Charles bought out Simon Wheeler and Anthony Mill's failing business a few months ago. Makes you wonder what kind of hard feelings there might have been between them."

Bingo.

Max knew he was onto something, but he kept his expression neutral. "That is interesting. I wonder what circumstances surrounded the buyout?"

"From what I heard, it wasn't a pleasant takeover." Misty fiddled with the edge of her napkin. "Just my opinion, of course, but I could definitely sense animosity between Charles and those men. And I certainly don't think they intended to come here at the same time, either. I overheard there was a conflict with the Woodruffs' original reservation and they had to change it at the last minute."

Max rubbed his chin with the tips of his fingers. Pricilla was going to be pleased with what he was coming up with. It might not be anything, but he'd learned from experience never to ignore information, no matter how minute. Had one of them been planning to knock off Charles, or had it been a spur of the moment decision when they found out he was staying at the lodge? Either way, the men already had a connection to the victim, and now they had a motive.

"Enough about Charles and the other men." Misty swung her long hair behind her shoulder. "If you ask me, they're all nothing more than stuffy businessmen who care more about making money than who they step on. As for me—"

Max tried to interpret the gleam in her eye. "What about you?"

"I'm looking for someone much more stable. Someone older who realizes that there's much more to life than earning a fortune or stomping on other people to get ahead. . . Someone like you."

Max swallowed hard. Surely she wasn't implying that she was interested in him? He was imagining things. Of course he was. He felt something pat his foot, and he froze. Had he just bumped the edge of the table leg, or was it Misty?

"I, um. . ." What could he say? "Can I get you a piece of Pricilla's lemon crumb cake?" He scooted back from the table and then winced, remembering his sprained foot.

Misty laughed as she moved around the table. "I think you'd better let me get it."

He watched out of the corner of his eye while she served up two thick slices of the cake, with its rich, lemony frosting. At least Pricilla was nowhere near. He'd sensed before she left the room that she hadn't been happy with him eating lunch with Misty, though he wasn't sure why. Unless she could be. . .jealous.

The thought was highly unlikely, but he smiled anyway, liking the idea that Pricilla might actually have feelings for him. Misty set a piece of cake in front of him, and he took a big bite of the moist treat. Maybe there was hope for him and Pricilla after all. But he still had to deal with Misty.

He ate his cake in silence, trying to avoid Misty's steady gaze.

"How long do you plan on staying at the lodge?" she asked after a minute had passed. "I understand you've recently retired."

Max coughed, wondering what her questions were leading to. "Yes, I was in the air force."

"Wow." He might as well have told her he was an astronaut or the president of the United States. She looked just as impressed. "I've never been able to resist a man in uniform. There's just something about those starched collars and shiny buttons that leave me completely breathless. Crazy, isn't it? I'd love to see you in your uniform—"

"You know, Misty, it's been wonderful eating lunch with you, but I—" He shoved his plate away from the edge of the table, avoiding her fervent gaze. "Time for my afternoon nap, you know."

He groaned as he rose from the table. Not so much from his throbbing foot, but more in an attempt to emphasis the age difference between them. Surely Misty saw him as practically ancient.

"Let's do it again then, soon." Misty's eyes hadn't lost their gleam. "I'd love to hear all about your military experiences. It sounds so. . .so manly."

Max tried not to choke. Misty's interest had nothing to do with the suspects or the recent murder and everything to do with him. Throwing his napkin on the table, he hobbled out of the room like a coon with his tail on fire.

By the time Pricilla saw Max round the corner, it was too late. He slammed into her, the rubber knob on the bottom of his crutch jamming against the end of her shoe and barely missing her toes.

"Max!" Pricilla pressed her back against the wall, thankful neither of them had fallen. Feeling young at heart would do little to curb the probable injuries of such an accident. Max's fall this morning was proof of that. "What in the world are you doing?"

"I could ask you the same thing." A streak of pain reflected in the corner of his eyes, as he must have bumped his sore ankle, but she also didn't miss the hint of amusement they held. He knew exactly what she had been doing.

"Eavesdropping?" His grin spoke volumes.

"What happened?" Misty bustled around the corner, saving Pricilla from answering his question. "Are you both all right?"

Misty looked straight at her.

"Yes. I was just. . ." Pricilla tugged at the bottom of her red tunic in an attempt to get her composure back. She certainly couldn't confess she'd been eavesdropping on their conversation. At least not to Misty.

"Just a bit of a collision," Max said, coming to her rescue. "Why don't we go sit on the porch for a while, Pricilla? This old man's tired."

Pricilla stifled a laugh. While eavesdropping, she hadn't missed Misty's clear advances or Max's attempts to thwart them. Having to take a nap was a ready excuse she found extremely amusing.

"Are you sure you're all right?" Misty still looked worried.

"We're fine. Really." Pricilla blew out a short breath. If Misty had been the one to discover her spying, she'd never have lived it down. Thankfully, she only had to deal with Max.

Misty shrugged. "If you're sure, I guess I'll head for the kitchen and make sure everything is cleaned up for this evening."

"Good idea, Misty." Even Max appeared relieved that she was leaving.

Any feelings of jealousy Pricilla had once entertained had dissipated and were replaced with amusement. While the idea of Misty coming on to Max seemed ridiculous, it was even more ridiculous to think that Max might go along with it. Hadn't Pricilla known him long enough to know that his integrity was far too great for him to falsely encourage someone—even during an "investigation"?

Pricilla followed Max outside into the afternoon sunlight and breathed in the sharp scent of the surrounding pine trees. How she could have ever managed to be jealous of Misty, she couldn't imagine.

Max laid his crutches against the wall and slid awkwardly into his favorite chair. "How much of our conversation did you overhear?"

Pricilla raised her voice a notch in an attempt to imitate Misty's higher pitched tone. "I've never been able to resist a man in uniform. I'd love to see yours—"

"Please." He rubbed his temples with his fingers and shook his head. "I don't remember the last time I've felt so embarrassed."

"Why? You should feel honored. She's young and beautiful, and in reality a very sweet girl."

He held up his hand in defense. "A sweet girl who needs to find someone her own age."

Pricilla felt the wheels in her mind begin to spin at the comment. Things were turning out well between Trisha and Nathan so far; what if—

"Don't even go there, Pricilla."

"Go where?" She tried to shoot him an innocent look, but he obviously didn't buy it.

"A love match for Misty." He pointed his finger at her and shook his head. "You've forgotten how well I know you. You see a damsel in distress and immediately send out the call for Prince Charming."

"That's not true—"

"Isn't it?"

She avoided his gaze this time. He did know her far too well. Penelope jumped up into her lap and began purring, giving Pricilla something to focus on other than Max's intense gaze.

Max cleared his throat. "I came up with a motive for you."

Pricilla couldn't help but grin. He obviously didn't want to discuss Misty anymore, and she was glad. Neither did she. Still, she couldn't help but be relieved that Max cared less about Misty's advances, though why it even mattered to her in the first place she wasn't quite sure. There was nothing wrong with Max finding love again. Quite the contrary. Wasn't it true that most couples who had satisfying marriages more often than not went on to marry again after one of them died? On the other hand, marriage at her age seemed far too complicated for some reason. She shook her head. Max was right. It was time to change the subject.

"I overheard something about Simon and Anthony's business?"

He let out a low chuckle at her confession. "Interesting, isn't it? I'm still trying to connect the dots. The three of them sold their online business for a huge profit, and then Simon and Anthony turned around and lost everything to Charles. But how?"

"There are never any guarantees in the business world. One day a millionaire, the next day bankrupt." Pricilla leaned against the thick cushions of the chair and stared down the empty road that lead to the lodge. She glanced at her watch. It was almost two o'clock and Nathan still wasn't home. Her worry was escalating into full-fledged anxiety.

Max tapped his fingers against the arm of the chair. "I thought I'd do a bit of research online from Nathan's computer once he returns. Maybe I'll find out something."

Trying to push aside her worry for her son, she pulled out her notebook, wondering now if she should have signed up for the computer class that had been offered to their Golden Oldies group at church last spring. Up to this point, she'd never thought that a machine could actually be an ally. In her opinion, computers ended up making people work harder rather than ease the burden of labor. She'd always seen the contraption as one of man's unidentifiable enemies—too complicated, too time consuming, and too antisocial.

She flipped the notebook open and jotted down a reminder to talk to Claire about the takeover. Computers might be out of her league, but she could deal with pen and paper. "I can't help you with any online research, but I will speak to Claire about her husband's business. She should know something."

Whether or not Claire would tell her was another issue.

"I have to be honest, Pricilla. After today's experience, I'm even more convinced that we really should leave this to Detective Carter." Max fiddled with the zipper on his jacket. "No matter how valid your motivation to get involved, this isn't our business. It's simply too dangerous. It's not a military investigation or even a civilian issue. This is a murder investigation that needs to be handled correctly by the authorities."

Pricilla frowned, disagreeing with his assessment. It *was* their business. Or at least hers. She'd never been one to let an injustice go, and she wouldn't start now. True, murder was out of her league, but with a little creativity. . .

"Maybe we need to try a different approach," she offered.

"Like what? You were subtle, I was blunt, and neither approach got us very far."

She didn't like the way the conversation was headed. She knew Max had never been of the opinion that what she was doing was appropriate, but up until now he'd at least gone along with her ideas—harebrained as they might be at times.

"I don't know." She felt uneasy under his intense gaze. "I'm not content to sit around and wait for the detective to arrest someone. Especially if that someone is innocent."

"You're worrying again. I still say we step back completely, and let the authorities handle things."

Pricilla frowned. He might be right, but that didn't lessen her resolve to do what she could to find out the truth. It wasn't as if she thought Nathan would actually be in trouble with the law. No one in his right mind would ever seriously entertain the thought that Nathan could have done such a vile act, and certainly not if they really knew him. Maybe that was part of her fear. The detective was new to the department and didn't know Nathan. The facts said someone overheard her son arguing with the victim shortly before the murder took place. That's what the detective would focus on.

Nathan's pickup truck spun into the circular drive. After parking the vehicle at an odd angle in front of the lodge, he slid out from the driver's side, worry lines clearly marking his forehead.

His boots clattered up the front steps. "I'll be in my office if anyone needs me."

Pricilla jumped as the screen door slammed shut behind him. "I take it things didn't go well."

Max squeezed her hand. "They didn't arrest him. He probably just needs to cool off."

"Slight comfort when you know that the detective could still show up any minute and arrest him."

"I've told you before, and I firmly believe it. They're not going to arrest your son."

Pricilla glanced at the house. "I'm going inside to talk to him."

"He looked like he wanted to be left alone."

She headed for the front door. "He's my son. I don't have to leave him alone."

Pricilla knocked on the doorframe of Nathan's office before entering. He sat in his chair with his eyes closed, as if he were trying to compose himself.

"Do you want me to come back later?" Despite her last words to Max, she did respect her son's privacy. But that didn't lessen her desire to fix everything for him.

He opened his eyes and rested his hands on the desktop. "Come in and shut the door."

She closed the door behind her then sat across from him in a pine chair that matched the rest of the office's rustic decor. "What happened?"

Her son tapped his hands against the desk and breathed in deeply. "Before I get to our friend Detective Carter, I just got off the phone with a TV news producer from clear across the state. I told him the same thing I told our little newspaper and, luckily, no one knows yet that Charles was murdered. But it's only a matter of time."

"I'm sorry, Nathan. I'm sure it will all work out. God's in control, despite what it looks like to us," said Pricilla. "Now, what about your talk with Carter?"

"In his typically brusque manner, he asked an assortment of questions, like my relationship with Charles and the lodge's financial situation." He paused. "I'm trying to see things from the authorities' point of view, but it's hard."

"What do you mean?"

Nathan shook his head. "I see now why you don't like Detective Carter."

She cringed inside at the comment. While his statement was true, she really had tried to keep the opinion to herself. "Were my feelings that obvious?"

"Aren't they always?"

Pricilla had to laugh. She'd never been accused of being ambiguous. "Tell me about your argument with Charles."

His face hardened into a scowl. "I'll be the first to admit that it was a bit heated, but Charles was an arrogant man who never accepted anything less than what he wanted."

"And he didn't get it this time?"

"It was out of the question. He wanted a different guide. No explanations, just a different guide or this would be his last year supporting my lodge."

Pricilla mulled over the new information. "A strange request."

"Especially considering the fact that Oscar is my best guide and has gone with Charles in the past with no problems that I'm aware of. You'd have to know Charles, though, to fully understand."

"What do you mean?" Pricilla refrained from pulling out her notebook again. She didn't know how this latest tidbit of information fit into the larger scope of things, but she was determined to find out.

Nathan picked up a pen and tapped the end against a blank pad of paper. "To put it nicely, he was high maintenance. He's been coming for the past five or six years, and every year it's the same thing. He complained at the drop of a hat, always insisted on special meal requests, and frankly, never had anything nice to say to anyone."

"Why didn't you just refuse him a room, then? Say you were booked or make up some sort of excuse."

"Believe me, I considered that seriously, but normally the man brought several people with him, and I couldn't afford to turn down that kind of business. Often those he invited came back the next year on their own. So whatever I thought about the man personally, he was good for business."

Not anymore.

Pricilla let out a deep sigh and tried to make heads or tails out of the information. She might hate jigsaws, but this was a puzzle she was determined to solve. All she needed was a bit of patience and the pieces would eventually come together.

Nathan cleared his throat and flipped on his computer. "This year his wife booked, and I couldn't say no. Even though it was just the two of them. Some sort of marital retreat, she told me."

"Surely an argument with Charles couldn't be considered grounds as a motive for murder. I mean, you'd think they'd have to come up with something a bit more solid."

Nathan rubbed the back of his neck with his hand while the monitor warmed up. "While I think I convinced the detective that I had nothing to do with Charles's death, I can't be sure. The man seems to think he's an updated version of Columbo."

Pricilla chuckled at the image. "So he actually thinks you're capable of murder?"

He shrugged. "Who knows what the man is thinking, but to his credit, he's thorough. I have a feeling he's trying to please his uncle, or at least live up to the older man's solid reputation."

"And going about it all the wrong way." She pulled out her notebook, unable to stop herself anymore. She scribbled yet another question regarding the conflict between Oscar and Charles. Unfortunately, her questions were beginning to far outweigh any answers she might have come up with.

"What's that?"

"This?" She tapped the thin pad on her leg and smiled at him. "Just keeping my own notes of what's going on. I refuse to have your name marred because the detective was in too much of a hurry to solve the case. What about Claire, for instance? Surely she'd have a stronger motive than you and warrants a ride downtown. I've heard there was a life insurance policy involved—"

"Mom, please don't tell me you've become a Jessica Fletcher wannabe?"

She avoided his sharp gaze. "Okay, I won't."

"Have you?"

A knock on the door stopped her from answering his question.

"Come in."

Pricilla hated the fatigue in her son's voice, but didn't miss the way his eyes lit up when Trisha stepped into the room.

"Sorry to interrupt—"

"No, please come in, Trisha." Nathan stood and offered her a chair next to Pricilla.

Trisha tugged on the gauzy sleeve of her vintage-looking blouse and sat down. "I saw your truck parked outside and wanted to know how things went."

He took a seat and straightened out his arms in front of him. "No handcuffs yet."

Trisha smiled. "I guess that's a good sign."

Pricilla didn't miss the strong currents that had vibrated across the room at Trisha's entrance. They might not see it yet, but she was certain that it wasn't going to take much more pushing on her end for this relationship to blossom into something serious. "Nathan, I have an idea."

He raised his brows in a silent question.

"Take Trisha fishing for the rest of the afternoon." She shoved the notebook back into her pocket, her mind having shifted to a much more pleasant pursuit. "You might not catch anything, but at least you'll be away from the lodge for a while. You need a break and things are quiet here."

He rubbed his chin. "I don't know—"

Trisha sat forward, looking uncomfortable. "Please don't feel pressured on my account—"

"Trust me, the idea is appealing." Nathan's smile lit up his eyes. "And it's even more appealing if you'd agree to come with me. It's just that—"

"That what?" Pricilla felt determined not to let a murder investigation hinder any chances of the two of them getting together.

He stared at the computer screen. "Besides needing to catch up on this month's accounting, I guess I'm just worried about not being here if something else happens—"

"Nothing else will happen," Pricilla interrupted. "Max and I will be here with Misty. What could go wrong?"

"What could go wrong?" Nathan eyed her curiously. "What hasn't gone wrong?"

Pricilla pressed her lips together. Perhaps it wasn't the most logical question to ask, considering all that had happened in the past forty-eight hours, but still. . .

Nathan stood and leaned against the desk with his palms. "Are you up to it, Trisha? Despite the fact that everything seems to be falling down around us with no end in sight, my mom's right. I really could use a break."

"Do I dare admit I've never been fishing in my life?" She shot him a sheepish grin.

"You've never been fishing?"

"I thought I'd hinted earlier that I'm not exactly the outdoor type. I'm willing to attempt a go of it, though."

"A positive attitude and one of my fishing rods are all you'll need." Nathan walked around the desk toward Trisha. "And you're sure you don't mind, Mom?"

"Not at all."

"You can call me on my cell phone if you need anything."

Pricilla smiled as the two stepped out of the office. Murder or not, there was no reason to put aside her matchmaking plans. And besides, she had plans herself. With tonight's dinner ready for the grill, she had just enough time to go upstairs and have a heart-to-heart chat with Charles's widow.

10

Pricilla set the hot bowl of stew on the wicker tray then paused for a moment to make sure she hadn't forgotten anything. Despite her earlier failure in using comfort food to extract information during her interrogation, she still believed her idea had merit. And if nothing else, it was her Christian duty. Claire Woodruff had been through a horrifying ordeal. Bringing her a meal was the least Pricilla could do. "Pricilla?"

She turned sharply, paying for it with a piercing pain that shot through her hip. "You scared me, Max."

He folded his arms across his chest and leaned against the counter. "Hmm . . .jumpy and a bit on edge. Seems suspicious to me."

She frowned at the comment. "I thought I'd been eliminated from the suspect list."

"Then let's look again at the facts." Max hobbled toward her, a wide grin across his face. "You now hold a tray filled with an assortment of mouthwatering treats. Because of the fancy tea cloth, we'll deduce that it is for a woman. Now, I just spoke to Trisha who was on her way to go fishing with Nathan, a fact that I plan to return to in just a minute, by the way. Misty's already eaten, as we both know. So. . .that leaves Claire, number one suspect on the detective's list—and most likely in your book as well."

Pricilla cleared her throat. "She's a woman who needs a friend. And a good home-cooked meal to keep up her strength won't hurt either."

She held up her head in mock challenge. It wasn't a lie. Not even a stretch of the truth if one thought about it. The woman had just lost her husband.

"All of that might be true, but"—he pointed to the pocket of her tunic, which held her notebook—"you can't tell me that you didn't plan to ask a few pointed questions while you're up there."

"Only if the opportunity arises. She might need someone to talk to." *Or someone to confess to,* though she wouldn't dare say that aloud.

Deciding to add a piece of her cake to the tray, she took down a saucer from the cupboard and cut a thick slice of the dessert. She did have a list of questions she wanted to ask the woman, and while she very well might not get the chance, she planned to at least try. She believed Claire held the key to much of the investigation, and unless she had been totally oblivious to her husband's work, she had to know something about Charles's relationship with

Anthony and the other men.

Max picked up the knife she left on the platter and cut himself a thin piece of cake. "I'm not going to convince you to stop your investigation, am I?"

"Nope." She set the saucer on the tray. She didn't want to argue with him, but she couldn't deny her convictions either. It was time to change the subject. "I thought you were taking a nap."

"I'm still going to. There's one other thing I want to talk to you about first. Nathan and Trisha."

Pricilla frowned. Surely he hadn't changed his mind about their matchmaking scheme.

"I don't know if you had a hand in things," he began before she had a chance to defend herself, "but my daughter's going fishing."

She couldn't read his expression. "And that's a. . .good thing?" She might as well hope for the best in a situation like this.

"Yes, it is." Now, Max's smile reached his eyes. "You know Trisha. She loves the opera, museums, and designer clothes. To get a man to convince her to wear jeans and an old shirt and go fishing. . .well, the girl's smitten, if you ask me."

Pricilla laughed and picked up the tray. At least one of her plans was headed in the right direction. Maybe she could go into the matchmaking business if her stint as an amateur detective didn't pay off.

"So you're not opposed to my matchmaking attempts?"

"I definitely think you should stick with those skills rather than your detective work. In the long run, you're liable to get into a lot less trouble. Murder is permanent."

Pricilla shuddered. He was right. Murder was a serious offense, especially considering the likelihood that someone currently staying under this roof had executed the deadly plan.

Max said good luck as she left the kitchen, and five minutes later Pricilla knocked gently on the door of the Elk Room, where Nathan had moved Claire after her husband's passing. She entered when she heard a soft "come in."

Claire lay on top of the elk-print duvet, dressed in a plush terry-cloth robe and pink slippers.

"I thought you might be hungry." Pricilla set the tray on the pine nightstand beside the bed, careful not to knock over Claire's pill bottles, and sent up a short prayer for wisdom. She was definitely going to need it.

Claire rubbed her swollen eyes then closed the book on her lap and set it aside. "I don't know if I can eat—"

"You have to. I know it's difficult, but you won't be able to do anything if you don't keep up your strength." Pricilla folded her hands together, hoping she could find a way to convince the woman not only to eat something, but to open up to her, as well. "Do you mind if I stay for a few minutes? It might help to have someone to talk to."

Claire shrugged. "Let me go get a tissue from the bathroom."

"Would you like me to get it for you?"

"No. I can do it."

As Claire left the room, Pricilla glanced at the steamy book cover on the bed. While she hadn't read the romance novel, she was quite certain Claire's tears stemmed from her current situation and not her choice of reading material.

Scooting a chair a few inches away from the wall, she took a seat and adjusted her bifocals. What would Lilian Jackson Braun's fictional detective Qwilleran have done in a situation like this? No doubt he would turn to his crime-sniffing cats Koko and Yum Yum to find the answers. Unfortunately, her own feline friend, Penelope, had never portrayed such high levels of intelligence. Penelope preferred sleeping under a bed or other tight quarters. Still, pet P.I. or not, a good detective could find things that other people would miss.

She slowly took in the details of the room, trying to imprint the image in her mind. A seasoned investigator would notice the pair of women's shoes laying by the fireplace, covered with smudges of mud on the heels, the generic bottles of vitamins, the makeup and jewelry sitting on the dresser, and Charles's open suitcase on the floor.

Concentrating, she pressed her lips together. Among Claire's possessions, there had to be some clue of who hated Charles enough to kill him. No murderer could perform his deadly deed without leaving behind evidence.

"Sorry." Claire walked back into the bedroom with a fistful of tissues and wearing a dark shade of red lipstick that made her pretty face look even paler. "Nothing prepares you for something like this, does it?"

"No." Pricilla thought back to her own experience of losing her husband unexpectedly. "How are you doing today?"

"I don't know." Claire stopped at the picture window that looked out over the mountains toward the north. "I don't know what I'm going to do now. Our marriage wasn't perfect, but it was what I knew. I haven't been on my own since. . .well, I've never been on my own."

"I know how you feel. I lost my husband almost three years ago. We married right out of college."

Frowning, Claire walked to the bed and plopped down on it before picking up a piece of bread and nibbling on the corner. "How did he die?"

"Marty was out playing golf and collapsed on the green with a heart attack."

"So he died doing something he loved."

Pricilla nodded. "After he retired, he golfed at least once a week. It was strange. I almost always joined him except that one Saturday."

Claire's expression softened. "So you weren't there when he died."

Pricilla closed her eyes as the vivid memories returned. "By the time I got to the hospital it was too late."

"I'm sorry." Claire crossed her legs. "And now? Does it get any better?"

"The pain will ease, though I don't know if it ever goes away completely. We'd just celebrated our forty-third anniversary. You can't be married to someone for that long without it taking time to get used to being alone again."

Pricilla stopped. She hadn't come to talk about her own loss. If Claire was going to heal, she needed to find a way to release the uncomfortable flood of emotions she had to be experiencing. "Tell me about Charles."

A shadow crossed Claire's face. "We'd been married almost twenty years. Doesn't seem long compared to the number of years you spent with your husband, but we did have a good marriage. He was always bringing me flowers and presents."

Claire's claim surprised Pricilla. Not that she had any reason to doubt the woman, but even she had heard Charles and Claire's vicious argument the day they checked in. Not a sign of a marriage gone bad perhaps, but from her own observations, she couldn't help but wonder if Claire was hiding something.

Or perhaps Pricilla was being too critical. Marriages today were difficult to sustain and no one escaped without an occasional rift. The fact that Claire and Charles had stayed together twenty years and beaten the statistics that would have had them divorced years ago had to be evidence that they were doing something right.

Claire dug her fingers into the fabric of the comforter. "Most people didn't know Charles the way I did. They saw him as a ruthless businessman. No one understood how great the pressure was on him. He had a lot to live up to. His father's expectations, for one, in running the family business, and he always had his hand in a number of other projects."

"I understood he had some business contacts with the other men staying at the lodge this week. Anthony Mills and Simon Wheeler?" Pricilla decided to take the opportunities as they came.

"Really? I wouldn't know. For the most part I stayed out of all his business dealings, though I think it had something to do with a lawsuit he'd recently filed regarding a takeover." Claire shrugged. "We entertained his clients from time to time, but he preferred to meet them at the office or an expensive restaurant. He told me that all his hard work kept him feeling young. In reality, it kept him running, but he loved it. He even planned to go into politics. Said I would make the perfect governor's wife."

Pricilla filed away the new information as Claire spoke about her husband. Perhaps the shock of his death hadn't yet completely worn off. It was after the funeral was over and after everyone had gone home that Pricilla had found handling Marty's death the most difficult. At times, the business of widowhood had completely overwhelmed her. So many details that had to be taken care of. So many daily reminders of what she'd lost.

Pricilla leaned forward, not wanting their conversation to end yet. "And what did you think about the idea of becoming a governor's wife?"

Claire seemed to consider the question. "I was always right there on Charles's arm when he needed me. He always told me that he would take me places with him, and not just physical destinations like Europe and the Caribbean which we frequently traveled through, as well. He was determined to make it socially."

"Where did you come from?"

Claire's laugh seemed to be laced with a hint of bitterness. "A wealthy section of Chicago. Left when I was sixteen. Thought I could make a go of it in Hollywood as an actress. Apparently I didn't have that certain charisma it takes for one to make it past the first round of auditions. I modeled a bit but never landed anything big. That was probably why I always had a hard time believing that Charles would pick me from the dozens of other girls who would have married him in a second. Of course, my parents believed he wanted to marry me for my money, but I knew that wasn't true."

Once again, Pricilla wished she could pull out her notebook and jot down a few comments. Not that her memory was unreliable, but writing had always helped her to solidify things in her mind. Thankfully, while she couldn't run an investigation in the open like Detective Carter could, she was still getting an interesting picture of Claire and her relationship with Charles.

"What was it that drew you to him?" Pricilla asked.

"The first time we met it was his eyes. I'd just left an audition. It hadn't gone well, and I needed to take a walk and compose myself. I ran into Charles—literally—on the corner of West Sunset Boulevard and Whitley Avenue. We stood on the curb for twenty minutes or so, just talking. Didn't take us long to find out that we were both from Chicago and had a lot in common.

"He invited me to lunch, and while it wasn't something I normally did with a complete stranger, I couldn't help but say yes. And the whole time I couldn't keep my eyes off of him. He was tall and handsome, with eyes the color of sapphires. Strong and intense."

Either Claire really had loved her husband and had nothing to do with his murder, or she was putting on a good front. Or maybe she was just lost in the past. A past that was perhaps full of happier memories than the present. That was something Pricilla was determined to find out. For somewhere along the line, Charles had changed from a dashing Casanova to a hard-nosed businessman. Hadn't Claire changed as well?

As Claire talked about their first few years of marriage and their struggle to have children, Pricilla forced herself to simply listen to Claire talk without any interruptions. She knew it was necessary to get the most out of their chat. Even if she didn't discover any leads for the case, at least she'd now have an insight into the Woodruffs' life.

After a few minutes, Claire took a deep breath, pausing from her monologue. "It's hard to believe he's dead. I have the money to do anything I want, but the things I once thought were so important don't seem to matter anymore."

Pricilla nodded. All the money in the world couldn't take away the pain of losing a spouse. She knew that. But there was something else niggling at Pricilla's mind as well. What the woman needed now was something that could only be found in a relationship with Christ. "You said you'd given up your faith when you met Charles. Does that mean you don't believe in God?"

"I did once." Claire shrugged and avoided Pricilla's gaze.

"And now?"

"I can't even tell you when I stopped believing. I stopped feeling God's presence, and He certainly hasn't been there for me lately."

Pricilla didn't miss the bitterness that once again edged Claire's voice, but she knew firsthand that there was only one way to find peace and assurance in such a terrible loss.

Please help me to show her You, Lord.

Pricilla worked to choose her words carefully. "I've lived a lot of years, and I'm still learning how to rely on Christ as my Savior. There's a verse in the Bible that talks about taking refuge in the shadow of God's wing until the disaster has passed. I'm convinced a relationship with Christ is the only way to truly find peace in the midst of pain. Our own strength is never enough."

Claire held up her hand. "But don't you see? This is never going to end. Charles is dead, and I have to pick up the pieces. If God were really in control, He would have stopped all of this from ever happening."

"Why?" Pricilla shook her head. "Just because things go wrong in our life isn't proof that God's goodness is any less. Unfortunately the bad choices people make are what lead to sin's consequences. Not God's choices."

Claire's eyes darkened, and Pricilla knew she had pushed the conversation too far for the moment. Claire moved to stand up and knocked over a bottle of vitamins, jumping up as the small tablets scattered across the carpet.

Pricilla stood up as well. "Let me help you pick them up."

The woman glanced up at her, and Pricilla tried to decipher the look of fear in her expression. "No, please. I just need to be alone. I'm sorry. . . ."

Claire knelt down on the carpet and began picking up the small pills.

Not knowing what else to do, Pricilla left the room, wondering exactly what it was she'd just seen in the woman's eyes.

Pricilla found Max sitting on the porch, dozing with a book in his hand and Penelope purring on his lap. At least his choice of reading material was better than Claire's, though she herself preferred a good cozy mystery over Max's science fiction books any day. She did wonder, however, if perhaps after this week's events, her reading choices would change to something a little less. . .deadly.

He opened his eyes as she sat down beside him.

"How did it go?" he asked, stifling a yawn.

She pulled out her notebook, not sure what she should write down first. "I learned more about Claire and Charles. According to her, they had a great marriage and were climbing the social ladder straight into politics."

"Interesting." Max rubbed Penelope behind her ears. Both of them still looked half asleep. "Is Claire still at the top of your suspect list after your interview?"

She paused at his question, unsure of the answer. On one hand, it was easy to sympathize with the woman and disregard any suspicions that she might have been involved in her husband's demise. She appeared to have cared about Charles, and did seem to be mourning over her loss. On the other hand, Claire had both motive and opportunity and could easily be covering up any animosity she'd held against her husband.

"I think it's still possible she's hiding something, but someone—or rather two someones—have just moved up on my list."

"Who's that?"

"Anthony and Simon." Pricilla tapped her pen against her paper, certain she was onto something. "Apparently, not only was there a takeover but, according to Claire, a lawsuit as well."

Max's brow rose. "This continues to get more and more interesting."

"You mentioned doing an Internet search on the computer." She dropped the pen and paper onto her lap, praying that they were finally making a step in the right direction. "Could you find specific information on this lawsuit Charles evidently brought against the two men?"

"If the files are public record, it should be fairly easy to find, I suppose." Max rubbed his chin and nodded. "Their motivation for murder is certainly growing. If they made a fortune off a dot-com business and later lost their investments to Charles, they'd have plenty of reason to hate the man."

She knew he was right, but she also couldn't forget her conversation with Claire. "There is something else bothering me, though it doesn't have to do with our suspect list per se."

"What's that?"

Pricilla started doodling a flower on the corner of the open notebook. "Claire asked me why God didn't stop Charles from dying. In other words, if God was in control, why did He let something like this happen?"

"Ah! The age-old question of man. How could a good God let bad things happen?" Max patted his propped up foot and smiled. "And your answer?"

"I told her that things going wrong in our lives weren't proof that God's goodness is any less. Man's bad choices are what lead to sin's consequences."

He nodded. "Good answer."

Pricilla wasn't so sure. "If it was such a great answer then why did she practically kick me out of the room after that?"

"You must have touched a nerve."

She considered his words. Besides physical clues of a crime, there had to be emotional clues as well. Changes in behavior. Uncharacteristic reactions. Had Claire's reaction been one of guilt to a crime, or was it simply that she regretted the fact she'd turned her back on God?

The problem was Pricilla had nothing to compare with what she saw in Claire's behavior today. If she didn't know how the woman normally acted, how could she make an accurate judgment on how she'd conducted herself today? Pricilla had spent little time with either of the Woodruffs before Charles's death. All she had were comments from Nathan and the others who had seen little good in the man.

There was truth in the saying that there is always more than one side to every story. What if Charles had simply been misunderstood? She let out a deep sigh. That didn't change the fact that someone had hated him enough to murder him.

Pricilla added some squiggly lines to her drawing. "No matter what the truth, I can't help but feel sorry for Claire. She seems so lost. They never were able to have children, so she really is alone."

"It's sad to see someone as attractive as she is drawn to the wrong things for fulfillment. Charles had money, but that didn't bring them happiness in the end."

"True, but there's another thing that bothers me about our conversation. She portrayed Charles like a charming Romeo, which is not at all the way everyone else saw him." She set the pens in her lap and caught Max's gaze. "Granted, I didn't really know the man, but it's obvious Nathan didn't like him, not to mention Simon and his friends. And then there was the rift between him and Oscar."

"Now that's interesting."

"And also a bit odd when you start noticing that practically everyone here had a bone to pick with the man."

"Except his wife."

"Exactly. Which is one reason I can't help but think that she's hiding something."

"Like what?"

Pricilla shook her head, wishing she had the answers. "I don't know yet, but the woman portrayed Charles as too perfect. You know how much I loved Marty, but I'd also be the first to admit that he wasn't perfect. And the same is true for any other couple, I'd think. From everyone that I've talked to, Charles simply wasn't a likable man. He couldn't have been that different in his marriage."

Max folded his hands in his lap. "I see what you're saying, but I still think you're grabbing at straws, Pricilla."

She frowned. Maybe she was. In any case, she didn't seem to be making progress toward the truth, which made her all the more determined to go a step further. "I'm going to go interview Oscar now."

"Pricilla—"

She stood up and made sure to add a measure of determination to her voice. "You can come with me if you'd like, but I plan on talking with him."

Hobbling down the path toward the barn, Max listened to Pricilla vocalize her theories regarding the case while he made sure one of his crutches didn't hit a hole and land him flat on his back again. The last thing he needed right now was another fall. Someone had to watch out for Pricilla, and at the moment, he wanted that someone to be him.

While he normally preferred the warmer winters of New Mexico, he had to admit today was beautiful. The harsh Colorado cold he'd wanted to avoid hadn't yet hit this part of the state, allowing him to enjoy the last of the golden foliage that surrounded them.

"At least something's going right." Pricilla stopped beside a group of white-barked aspen trees and waited for him to catch up with her.

"What's that?" he asked, wondering if he'd missed something she'd said.

"Our children. How do you think Trisha is faring?"

He smiled at the image of his daughter standing on the edge of the lake, reeling in a plump catch. "In the capable hands of your son? I'm sure she's having the time of her life. They seem perfect for each other."

Max glanced at Pricilla out of the corner of his eye. The brisk mountain air had brought out the color in her lined complexion, giving her cheeks a rosy glow—and causing his heart to palpitate. What he really had wanted to say was that the two of them might be perfect together, but after so many years of friendship, he was finding it difficult to figure out a way to change things between them. He didn't want to do anything to ruin their friendship. Maybe they could find a way to start slowly.

Like dating?

The unexpected thought made him want to chuckle. Dating in college had been one thing, but how did one start over forty years later in the courting game? Dinner and a movie seemed too cliché. Sports like rollerblading and bicycling were out of the question, especially with his injured foot. Playing board games around the fireplace might be nice, but would Pricilla think an evening of Scrabble and PBS too dull?

With the Rocky Mountains surrounding them, he followed the winding dirt path beside her, wondering how life had suddenly become so complicated. The whole dating idea seemed ridiculous, which made him wonder if he wasn't looking at the situation in the wrong light. Who said that courtship had to be formal, especially among two friends who had known each other half their lifetimes?

There was another issue that would have to be addressed, as well. While his heart might feel as if he were twenty-five again, the reality was that he was living in a sixty-five-year-old body, and both he and Pricilla were set in their ways. While he didn't like the idea of a long-distance relationship, in order for something to develop between them they would both have to make changes. Moving to Colorado had never been a part of his game plan, and he was certain that Pricilla would have the same reservations about moving to New Mexico and away from her son.

Maybe finding love a second time around wasn't going to be as easy as he'd hoped.

Shoving aside his jumbled feelings for the moment, he stopped beside her a few yards away from the entrance of the barn, sure that the two-story structure was the dream of any rancher. Surrounded by pine and aspen trees, the building's solid timber walls fit perfectly into the mountain scenery.

He glanced at Pricilla, surprised she didn't have her notebook and pen out, though he supposed this was a covert operation. "So what's our plan this time? I noticed that you're not carrying a picnic basket full of your cooking."

Her serious expression didn't waver. "I did consider the idea, but thought that might be going a bit overboard."

Max stopped himself from laughing out loud. Since when did Pricilla worry about going overboard? "So any alternative plans?"

"I guess we'll play it by ear. My plans haven't worked so far. I'm hoping to shake my first impressions of the man that weren't good. Maybe that will change if I talk to him for a while."

Somehow Max had his doubts that Oscar would pour on the charm at their arrival. Once Max's eyes adjusted to the dimness of the barn after the bright sunlight, he found his assumptions to be correct. It didn't take words to know that Oscar wasn't happy about the delay in the hunting trip. His sour expression said it all. He stood along one wall of the barn, his broad frame bent over a hunting rifle. Except for the tattoo on his left arm, the guide reminded Max of one of his old military buddies. Rock solid and built like a mountain man.

"Afternoon, Oscar." Pricilla's chipper voice rang out as they walked past the man's pickup and crossed the cement floor of the barn.

The guide glanced at them briefly before shoving a bronze cleaning brush into the bore of the rifle. "Afternoon."

Max studied the number of high-quality hunting rifles lining the wall and smiled. While he would have preferred not to be a part of Pricilla's wild goose chase to find the murderer, at least he'd found an item of common ground. It looked as if Pricilla wouldn't need any of her lemon crumb cake to get Oscar to talk after all. While her endeavors to coax her suspects to confess were original, he was quite certain that she was out of her league with Oscar. She might know how to whip up an irresistible four-course meal, but he knew his weapons.

He stopped beside Oscar and nodded his approval. "A Winchester M70. Nice firearm. Basic but very accurate. One of the best bolt-action rifles, three-position safety—"

"You sound pretty familiar with your weapons." Oscar took the rifle out of the gun vise and handed it to Max.

Max ran his fingers along the silky walnut stock. He didn't have to pretend to be interested in firearms. "After thirty plus years in the military, I learned a thing or two."

"This one's the Featherweight model and has the standard recoil pad." Oscar folded his arms across his chest. "I use it mainly for beginning hunters, though personally I've always liked its feel and accuracy."

"Max is being far too modest when he says he knows a thing or two." Pricilla took a step back, her smile forced. He'd forgotten she'd always been skittish around guns. "Max was a small-arms expert in the air force."

"That's impressive." Oscar took the rifle back and took aim at an undisclosed target on the other side of the barn. He pulled on the trigger. "Bang."

Pricilla put her hand over her heart.

"Don't worry." Oscar chuckled as he laid the rifle back in the vise. "I'm in the middle of cleaning it. It's not loaded."

As amusing as Oscar's simulation had been, Max couldn't blame her reaction. With the rifle in the guide's hands, Max certainly didn't want to be the one to discover Oscar was the murderer. He'd prefer Oscar to be friend rather than foe any day.

Oscar leaned against the workbench, his brow raised in question. "So did the two of you need something?"

Apparently, Show and Tell was over. Max looked to Pricilla to answer the guide's question.

"Nothing in particular," she said. "I think we're all feeling cooped up after the hunting trip was canceled."

Oscar sprayed cleaning solvent on the brush he'd used a few minutes ago. "Believe me, that's not all I'm feeling. Can't believe that bald-headed detective had the gall to cancel."

"Still, it's a tragedy about Charles Woodruff, don't you think?" Pricilla wet her lips. "You must have known him fairly well after spending a number of hunting seasons with him."

"Not by choice. It was my job." Oscar's frown deepened, and Max wondered if Pricilla's line of question was too direct. Subtlety took skill.

"I could have done without him on those trips. Never thought he treated folks well, especially Mrs. Woodruff."

"Strange." Pricilla cocked her head. "Claire told me that she and her husband had a good relationship."

"Things are rarely the way they appear. You should know that." Oscar set down the spray can and looked Pricilla in the eye. "You're not out to catch the murderer, now are you, Mrs. Crumb?"

Pricilla held his gaze without flinching. "I believe that's Detective Carter's job."

Max noted the heated glances that passed between Oscar and Pricilla and decided it was time to cut the interview short. "My foot's throbbing, and I need to go and rest my leg, Pricilla. If you're ready to walk back to the house, I think I've had enough exercise for the day."

"I. . .of course." She glanced at him, looking distracted. "Thanks for the demonstration, Oscar. If you'll excuse us—"

Pricilla followed Max back toward the house, feeling as if the questioning had all been in vain. The only new thing she'd learned was the fact that Oscar believed Charles hadn't treated Claire the way he should have. That discovery, though, didn't surprise her at all.

She tried to organize her thoughts as she and Max made their way up the dirt path and across the gravel driveway. There was another thing that was bothering her. "I suppose if Oscar was the murderer he'd have used the gun he was cleaning rather than poison."

Max shrugged. "It does seem that a bullet in the back of the head would be more his style. Besides, poison's normally connected to women's crimes more so than to men's."

Which led them back to Claire. Or simply in circles. She wasn't sure which.

Pricilla stomped up the porch steps, trying to get the mud off her shoes. "The only common denominator I can find is that no one seemed fond of Charles. But that's not a reason to kill a man."

"We're obviously missing something. Let's examine it more closely." Max sat down in his chair and propped up his foot. "Why do people take the life of someone else?"

She plopped down beside him and mulled over the question. "There could be any number of reasons. Jealousy, murder, blackmail, infidelity, lust. . .the list could go on and on."

"Exactly." He rested his elbows against the arms of the chair. "Anything, in fact, that's in line with the sinful nature."

The thought sent a shiver up her spine. She'd told Claire that humanity's bad choices were what led to sin's consequences. This was true both in the physical sense, as with Charles's death, and in the spiritual sense. Hadn't Paul spoken in Galatians on how the acts of the sinful nature led to death? Murder sounded vile and contemptible, but she'd always been struck by the sins Paul listed.

"What are you thinking?" Max broke into her thoughts.

"I'm thinking how thankful I am for Christ's sacrifice and His forgiveness. It's what the murderer needs. . .what Claire is searching for." She gazed out toward the jagged mountains. "When Paul lists the acts of the sinful nature, he adds things like discord, jealousy, and selfish ambition—things we've all had to deal with—alongside sexual immorality and debauchery. Simply put, we've all sinned. If it wasn't for Christ's death, we'd all be held accountable."

"It's a stark reminder of just how much He loved us, isn't it?"

A shriek of laughter pulled Pricilla away from her somber thoughts. Trisha and Nathan staggered up the drive like a couple of teenagers. Pricilla adjusted her bifocals. If she didn't know better, she'd have thought they were both plastered.

Nathan had his arm around Trisha, whose oversized sweatshirt and jeans were drenched.

Pricilla scooted Penelope off her lap and scurried to the railing. "What in the world happened?"

"Would you believe I fell in the lake?" Trisha's giggle filled the air as she shoved a strand of wet hair from her forehead. "Nathan had to pull me out."

Apparently, Trisha had been Nathan's only catch for the day, but from the look on his face he hadn't minded at all.

Pricilla's motherly instincts took over. "You need to get upstairs, Trisha, and into some warm clothes before you catch your death from pneumonia."

"I know." Trisha laughed. "Thanks, Nathan, for a wonderful time." She laughed again and slopped up the porch steps.

The young woman's cheeks were flushed as Pricilla hurried beside her up the stairs, leaving Pricilla to wonder if the reaction was from the cold or from Trisha's obvious growing feelings toward Nathan.

12

Pricilla followed Trisha into the Santa Fe room with a stack of towels she'd grabbed out of the upstairs hall closet.

"My friends back home are never going to believe I went fishing, let alone that I fell into the lake." Trisha shivered as she crossed the threshold, but it didn't stop her laughter from ringing out. "Fishing has never been on my to-do list, but I have to say, I had so much fun with Nathan today."

Pricilla couldn't help but echo Trisha's laugh. "Right now, the only thing on your to-do list is to get into some dry clothes."

The drapes that framed the large picture window were open, letting in the last of the afternoon light and some warmth. The sun had begun its descent toward the crest of the mountain range. Once it dropped behind the jagged skyline the temperature would begin to drop as well. Obviously, though, any thoughts of an approaching cold front, or the fact that she was drenched from head to toe, were far from the young woman's mind. One didn't need a degree in psychology to see that the chances of Nathan and Trisha's relationship becoming a lasting one were rising.

And Pricilla couldn't be happier.

She handed Trisha the towels and scurried her into the bathroom. "Would you like me to light the fire before I go?"

Trisha nodded. "That would be wonderful. If you don't mind waiting, I'll be out in just a minute."

Pricilla smiled at the young woman's unbridled enthusiasm, remembering the day she first met Marty. She'd gone home that night and told her roommate she'd just met the man she was going to marry. Love at first sight might seem unbelievable to some people, but she knew it was possible. It might be a while before Trisha and Nathan knew how deep their feelings for each other were, but the beginning seeds of a relationship were already there.

Stopping in front of the stone fireplace, she pulled the box of matches off the mantle. She'd chosen this room for Trisha. Instead of the hunting theme that most of the rooms had, this suite had a Spanish décor with an iron headboard for the bed and matching vanity. The red and green plaids, solids, and floral fabrics of the quilt were picked up in the curtains and throw pillows, giving the room a cozy feel.

Trisha was more than likely used to more modern furnishings, and certainly more modern conveniences than the lodge offered, but despite the fact she was a city girl, the glow in her cheeks was proof that a bit of sunshine, fishing. . .and romance. . .were the perfect prescription for any overworked corporate employee's life.

Pricilla struck a match and moved the yellow flame beneath the pile of kindling in the fireplace. The fire flickered for a few moments, almost dying out, then began to lick the fuel, spreading its fingers around the logs.

A few minutes later, Trisha stepped out of the bathroom, dressed in wool slacks and a long-sleeved top.

"That was quick." Pricilla threw the used match into the fire. "Do you feel better?"

"Definitely warmer. Thank you." Trisha rubbed the ends of her hair with one of the towels. "I need to finish getting ready, but I was wondering. . .would you mind talking for a few minutes?"

"Of course not."

Trisha hung up the towel on the back of the bathroom door then grabbed a black sweater off the vanity chair and slid the sweater on. "My mom and I were always close. I miss having a motherly figure in my life. Especially when it comes to issues of the heart."

Like falling in love?

Trisha grabbed her makeup bag off her bed, stubbing her toe as she rounded the corner. "Akk. . ."

Even a bumped foot couldn't erase the glow on Trisha's face. She sat down at the mirror and unzipped the bag before reapplying her makeup, the smile never leaving her lips. "I suppose it could be a bit awkward for me to talk to you about Nathan. I mean, he is your son. I just feel comfortable around you."

"I don't mind at all." Pricilla leaned forward in the chair she'd chosen for the talk. "So, what do you think about Nathan?"

The question was too forward, but Pricilla couldn't help it. She wanted to know the answer.

Trisha's brow furrowed as she set down her brush, and Pricilla wondered if she had indeed overstepped her boundaries.

"I'm sorry. If my question was too personal—"

"No." Trisha held up her hand. "It's just that I feel guilty, like I should be in mourning instead of out fishing. I mean, the past couple days have been so weird. With Mr. Woodruff's death and all. Honestly, the whole situation's been more than a little bit frightening."

"I certainly agree with you on that point."

Trisha turned toward Pricilla. "But I can't deny the attraction I feel toward Nathan. He's different from anyone else I've ever met."

Pricilla opened her mouth to make a comment then forced herself to shut it. If she wanted Trisha to open up in front of her, she was going to have to give her the opportunity.

"The thing is," Trisha continued as she applied her mascara, "I've had plenty of dates, but this is the first time that I've ever considered giving someone a chance—which surprises me. I've always thought I was too set in my ways and too strong willed for a relationship to really work. Marriage and family have always been out there in the future, but up until now I've never met anyone who makes my heart thud or makes me laugh."

"And now?"

The smile was back on Trisha's face. "I don't know how to describe it, but Nathan brings out something inside me I've never felt before."

"I'm so happy for you. For both of you." Pricilla reached and gave Trisha a hug. She understood the need to share her life with someone. It was interesting how similar their situations seemed. At least on the surface. She'd thought from time to time how nice it would be to remarry. To let someone into her life who would eat supper with her, share the household responsibilities, and help fill the lonely nights. She missed the companionship of marriage. Wouldn't someone like Max do exactly that?

The question caught her off guard, and suddenly the room began to feel warm. While she'd entertained the thought of remarriage, there was another side to the coin. She enjoyed the freedom to make her own decisions and wasn't sure if she were ready to give that up. And besides, it wasn't as if Max had feelings for her beyond friendship.

Pricilla told Trisha she'd see her at dinner then closed the door to the room behind her. Trisha had mentioned Mr. Woodruff's death, reminding her again that his demise had set her on edge and had her doing things she wouldn't normally do. Not only did they all want to know who had killed the man, she couldn't shake the underlying fear that someone else might be next on the murderer's list. And then there had been her ridiculous feelings of jealousy toward Misty of all people. Something totally out of character for her.

No. Nathan and Trisha had a chance to find true love with each other, but she and Max were a totally different story. They were too good of friends and too set in their ways to think about a relationship.

With her temples throbbing like a jackhammer, Pricilla poured herself a glass of water from the kitchen tap and swallowed two aspirin. Talking with Trisha had been pleasant, but dinner had been a strained ordeal. At least everyone's appetite seemed fine as there had been little of the marinated barbeque meat or salads left, but there hadn't been much conversation during the meal, as everyone seemed to be lost in his or her own thoughts.

She needed to get her mind off the particulars of the case, but was finding it impossible to do so. Her visits with both Claire and Oscar had forced her to realize that there was more involved in the case than she, for now anyway, had been able to work out. Nothing added up. Her fingers drummed against the notebook in her pocket as she tried to force the pieces of the puzzle to fit into something that made sense.

Drawing in a deep breath, she made a mental list for tomorrow's breakfast. The sausage casserole was in the refrigerator along with the fruit salad Misty had made before dinner. There would be little to do tomorrow. . .except prepare meals and try to fill in the missing holes in her investigation. Why was it, though, that nothing she had done so far had brought her any closer to the truth?

She turned off the kitchen light and headed for the living room, her mind trying to wrap itself around the problem. All of the guests, who were also prime suspects according to Detective Carter, were gathered in the spacious room, trying to whittle away the last hours of the evening and add some sense of normalcy to the tense circumstances. Only Claire had decided to go straight to her room after dinner.

Snow had begun to fall outside. Even standing beside the roaring fire did little to take the chill out of the air. Everyone was ready for the murderer to be caught—and the sooner the better.

The grandfather clock in the corner chimed eight. While bits of laughter floated across the room from time to time, it was obvious that everyone was on edge. Despite the detective's order, he could only hold them at the lodge for so long. No one liked the idea that they were confined with a killer on the loose—maybe even among them right now.

Simon and his friends were engaged in a friendly round of poker at the far end of the room. Max and Trisha sat across the room playing a game of Risk. Pricilla had forgotten how much he liked board games and wondered when the last time was that she'd played. She normally spent her afternoons and evenings in the garden, reading, or on one of her latest hobbies. Tonight, even Max's Thomas Kincade puzzle sounded tempting. Anything to break the tension.

"You look cold. I thought you might like some hot chocolate."

Pricilla looked up at Nathan who stood in front of her with two steaming mugs in his hands. "It does sound good, actually. Thank you."

"She's beautiful, isn't she?"

Pricilla followed his gaze, stopping at Trisha. "Definitely your best choice yet. Why aren't you over there playing with them?"

"I just got here myself. Had a bunch of paperwork to finish up before tomorrow. What do you think about her?"

She took a sip of her drink. "She's smart, pretty, a hard worker.... I think you need to hold on to her."

"I think so, too."

Pricilla smiled at her son's comment. She'd expected to have to come up with a lot more scheming with her matchmaking plans, but it was turning out that she didn't have to do anything. Sometimes, love took on a life of its own.

Nathan held the mug between his hands, his gaze focused on the other side of the room. "I know it's not possible, but I don't want her to leave after this week."

"Have you guys talked about a possible future together?"

"It's all happened so quick. I don't want to come across too strong. At least I still have a few days left before she and her father leave."

Pricilla frowned at the thought. Of course, Max would be leaving, too. The idea shouldn't surprise her, but it did. She'd enjoyed their time together these past few days, and while she knew now that her supposed feelings of jealousy were nothing more than the results of stress, one thing was clear. His going back to New Mexico was going to leave an empty space right in the middle of her heart.

Max rolled the dice then smiled in triumph as he won against two of Trisha's armies in the Ukraine. "Could it be that your old man just might have the lead in the game for once?"

"The game is far from over, and I'm about to conquer South America." Trisha laughed then leaned forward and caught his gaze. "Honestly, I'm surprised you're making any headway through all of this."

His brows rose in question. "Why would you say that?"

"You've spent the past fifteen minutes continuously glancing at Pricilla."

He leaned back and folded his arms across his chest. "I could say the same for you."

Her attempts to convey an innocent expression didn't fool him at all.

"What do you mean?"

"What do I mean?" He nodded his head toward the fireplace where Pricilla and Nathan stood talking and drinking hot chocolate. "You're only losing because you can't keep your eyes off Nathan."

"That's not true—"

"Isn't it?"

Trisha frowned, but he didn't miss the sparkle in her eyes. "And I thought a nice dueling game of Risk would be a great father-daughter activity tonight, considering everything that's happened."

His smile widened. "It is. I'm enjoying every minute of it."

She handed him one of the dice then rolled her two across the board, wincing at the snake eyes that looked up at her. "Face it, Dad. You'd rather be with Pricilla—"

"And you'd rather be with Nathan."

Max laughed. Falling in love was a complicated thing. He'd never expect both him and Trisha to have their hearts taken at the same time.

He rolled again, beating her last army on Australia. "What do you like about him?"

She groaned and tossed him the dice, her face flushed with a rosy blush. "He's so different from the guys I meet. They're focused on getting ahead in their careers. If they find time for a family, good, but it's not a priority. Nathan's business is important to him, but he also likes to fish and hunt, and he's already showed me that there's more to life than work, something I tend to be a bit obsessed with." She shook her head. "It all seems so fast. . .so out of control even. I mean, I've only known him a few days, yet part of me feels like I've known him forever."

Max rested his elbows on the table. "It's funny. I've known Pricilla forever, and I'm just now realizing that I want more from our relationship."

"Do you believe in love at first sight?"

He had to consider the question. "I don't know that I've ever thought about it. I first met your mother when she was fourteen years old. One day, I turned around and she'd become a woman. That was the moment I knew I loved her. I was home on leave, and some friends and I were invited to her eighteenth birthday party. She was the one distraction that had me considering going AWOL."

"I'm not surprised at all. Mom was a wonderful woman." Trisha shoved a piece of hair behind her ear. "I never believed in love at first sight. . .until now."

"Then what are you doing?"

"What do you mean?"

Max slapped his hands against the table. "Stay here."

With a new resolve, Max rose from the table and hobbled across the room to where Pricilla and Nathan stood.

"How's the game going?" Nathan asked.

Max caught the longing in the young man's eyes. It was clear he'd rather be sitting at the table with Trisha. "Thought you might want to take my place."

Nathan grinned. "Are you sure? I thought this was a father-daughter evening."

"Who are we kidding? You'd rather be with Trisha, and I'd love to keep Pricilla company." He leaned forward. "By the way, I'm winning, but she's good."

Nathan laughed. "I think I can handle myself. I—"

Misty burst into the room. Pricilla jumped beside Max, dropping her mug. The ceramic slammed against the stone hearth.

"I'm sorry." Misty held her hand against her chest. "But it's Claire. She's missing."

Pricilla's hot chocolate seeped across the stone hearth and onto the carpet, but Pricilla couldn't move. She had suspected Claire had something to hide and now she was certain.

Nathan stepped forward. "I want you to take a deep breath, Misty, and calm down."

Everyone's gaze was riveted on the young housekeeper as she took a few deep breaths and tried to relax before she continued talking. "Claire asked me to bring her a cup of tea at eight o'clock, so I made some for her, headed for her room, and knocked on her door. She didn't answer. I thought she might be asleep, but I was worried about the woman. I mean she just lost her husband, and I know how awful it feels to have someone walk out on you, though it wasn't as if Charles did it on purpose, I suppose. I mean—"

Nathan laid his hand on her shoulder. "Why don't you stick to what happened to Claire for now?"

"I'm sorry. You're right. It's just that—never mind." She flipped back a section of her blond hair. "Anyway, I opened Claire's door and saw that she wasn't in her room. I looked in the bathroom and even on the outside balcony, but she wasn't there. That wasn't the most bizarre thing, though. I've been cleaning her room everyday, so I know what should be there. And, well, her purse and most of her clothes are now gone."

Pricilla's eyes widened. She glanced around the room at each of the guests—or *suspects*, as she was sure Detective Carter had officially labeled them all. It was like a scene from one of Agatha Christie's mystery novels. They were all gathered in the parlor, and there was a murderer on the loose. It could be any one of them. And now Claire was missing. And in Pricilla's mind, if she'd run away from the lodge, it could mean only one of two things. Either Claire was the murderer, or she had something to hide.

Pricilla worked to swallow the lump that had risen in her throat. Maybe there was a third possibility? Could the murderer have struck again? She shook her head. Nathan was right. They all needed to calm down. Jumping to conclusions would do nothing but ensure a panic.

She tugged on Nathan's sleeve and pulled him aside. The room was filled with the murmur of voices. As much as Pricilla didn't like Detective Carter and his patronizing methods, even she knew when to draw the line. "We need to call the sheriff."

"Just a minute." He held up his hand and addressed the group. "Before we overreact to the situation, we need to do our own quick search of the lodge. Claire could have gone for a walk, gone out to see the horses in the barn, or any number of things."

Trisha glanced out the window. "Her car's still here. That may mean she hasn't left the property."

Nathan nodded. "See what I mean? More than likely she just stepped out of her room. No use calling the detective unless we have a real crisis to report. Now. Let's all split up to look for her, and meet back here in fifteen minutes."

Misty knelt and began to pick up the shards of broken ceramic. "I'll clean up the mess, Mrs. Crumb. Feel free to go look for Mrs. Woodruff with the others."

Pricilla nodded her thanks and headed for the kitchen. Max hobbled along beside her down the long, narrow hallway. Misty had probably had enough stress for one night, and she couldn't blame the young woman. Pricilla slowed her steps. She'd never noticed how eerie the lodge felt at night. The iron sconces left shadows dancing on the walls. A dog barked in the distance, but beside that there was little noise but the sound of her footsteps and the uneven thump of Max's crutches on the hardwood floor.

"I never knew how exciting life could be with you," Max said, breaking the silence between them. "I'd planned to ask you to join me for a game of Scrabble until this most recent incident occurred."

She laughed. "This is becoming to be too much excitement, if you ask me."

"I agree. I'm too old for games of cloak-and-dagger."

"Except there are no spies involved in this game. Only dead bodies and a lodge full of suspects."

The kitchen light was on, and Oscar was filling a plate with leftovers. He balanced the food and soda in his hands then shut the refrigerator door with his foot. "Hope you don't mind, Mrs. Crumb. One of the horses is a bit colicky tonight, and I've been tied up in the barn until now."

"Of course I don't mind." Pricilla paused at the bar. "Have you seen Mrs. Woodruff? She seems to be missing."

"No." Oscar's brow narrowed. "I haven't seen her at all today, in fact. Is something wrong?"

Max laid his crutches against the counter. "We don't know yet. We're trying to find her."

Oscar pulled out a roll of plastic wrap and covered his plate. "I just came from the barn. Unless I missed her in the dark. . ."

Pricilla shook her head. "I don't suppose there would have been any reason for her to go to the barn, but just in case, would you mind walking there with me once you get your food together? Max can't be on crutches in the dark, and I'd prefer not to go alone."

Oscar shrugged. "I'm ready now."

"Pricilla, I think you should—"

"I'll be fine." She glanced at Max, whose expression told her clearly that he wasn't happy with her plan. "Like Nathan said, she's probably gone for a walk or some other harmless activity. Don't worry."

She grabbed a flashlight from the junk drawer by the stove and stepped out the back door with Oscar before Max could stop her. While she'd far rather be sitting in front of the fireplace, playing a game of Scrabble with Max, she was determined to get to the bottom of things. This new twist in the case had her mind scrambling once again to put the pieces together. What she had, though, wasn't enough to finish the outer edges of even the simplest puzzle.

Pricilla's breath blew out in white puffs in front of her. "It's been a strange week, hasn't it?"

"Yep," Oscar mumbled.

"I've never been involved in a murder investigation."

Oscar grunted, and Pricilla felt a sense of déjà vu. Apparently, like Simon and his buddies, conversations weren't Oscar's forte. How was one supposed to do a thorough investigation when constantly greeted with grunts and one-syllable answers?

She shone the flashlight down the moonlit path, making sure she walked slow enough to avoid the ruts, while at the same time trying to keep up with Oscar's long steps.

Moonlight caught Oscar's rigid jaw line, and she shivered. Taking a deep breath, she reminded herself that the chances of Oscar having anything to do with the murder were slim. He had no known motive except that he, like everyone else, had disliked the dead man. The reason for Charles's dislike of Oscar was still unclear in her mind, but she wasn't convinced it had anything to do with the murder.

She looked up at the aspen trees that swayed in the wind along the path like a group of dancers. The snow had stopped falling, leaving a dusting of white powder that glistened beneath the glow of the moon's light. They were almost halfway to the barn. She decided to make another stab at a conversation.

"Have you always lived in Colorado?"

"Kansas originally."

"Any family?"

The darkness masked his expression this time. "My parents died in a car crash when I was seventeen. My sister still lives in Kansas."

"Is she married?"

"Five years, to a computer geek from Cincinnati."

"And what about you?" She steered the conversation back to him. "Why'd you move to Colorado?"

He let out a breath that clouded the cold air as they neared the barn. "My friends used to spend their breaks skiing in the mountains, but my family could never afford it. Went camping a few times and discovered I liked the outdoors. I may never be able to afford a condo in Breckenridge, but at least I'm here more than one or two weeks out of the year."

She tried to sense bitterness in his words for growing up poor, but if it was there, it didn't show. Besides, the man had a point. Two weeks out of the year wasn't nearly long enough to enjoy the beauty of this area.

The barn was dark except for a lit light bulb at the entrance. Oscar flipped on another light, illuminating the rack of guns on the far wall.

"Mrs. Woodruff?" Pricilla's voice echoed in the large structure. She breathed in the fresh scent of the hay. "Mrs. Woodruff, are you here?"

There was no answer except for the low snort of a horse in one of the stalls.

"I don't think she's here." Oscar set his plate of food down on a long wooden counter.

Pricilla turned to face him. "Did you know her well?"

"Mrs. Woodruff?" He shrugged a shoulder. "Why would I have known her?"

"She stayed at the lodge a number of times. You must have run into her once or twice."

Oscar rubbed his goatee and shook his head. "Of course I saw her around. I just don't normally have a lot of contact with those who don't go hunting, and Mrs. Woodruff never did."

Pricilla paused, wondering if once again she was pushing too hard. Max had warned her that her snooping into the case was going to get her into trouble. With a wall full of hunting rifles and a possible murderer standing in front of her, she hoped this wasn't the time Max proved himself right. She was too far from the house for anyone to hear her scream if he was.

Oscar popped open the tab of his cola.

Pricilla jumped then chided herself for her uneasiness.

He blew on the fizz before taking a sip. "I'll let you know if I see Mrs. Woodruff, but until then I have dinner to eat and a horse to tend to—"

"Of course." Pricilla took a step backward. "Thanks for letting me walk with you. I'm sure they've already found her by now anyway."

She walked slowly back to the lodge, hoping someone had actually found Claire. While Pricilla wanted the woman to be innocent, Claire did have both motive and opportunity.

Something howled in the distance, sending goose bumps down Pricilla's spine. She pulled her sweater around her, wishing she'd grabbed her heavy coat before coming out here. Max had been right. Once again she'd acted before thinking and would risk the chance of getting sick if she didn't get warm soon.

Her beam caught movement up ahead, and she froze. Another howl broke through the stillness of the night, but this time it was closer. Something was out there. A wolf? A dog? She had her mind set on staying clear of a murderer, not a wild animal that might cross her path.

"Pricilla, it's me."

"Max?" She raised the flashlight and shined the light in his eyes.

"Put that thing down." He reached out and shoved the beam of light back down to the ground.

With her heart racing, she took a deep breath. "What in the world are you doing out here? You don't even have a flashlight."

"It's a full moon and I have two perfectly good weapons." He held up one of the crutches.

She pressed her hand against her chest. "You about gave me a heart attack."

"What about me?" The combination of the sound of his voice and the light of her flashlight were enough to tell her that he wasn't smiling. "You go tearing off in the dark with a possible murderer without thinking twice about it."

"I—"

"I'm not finished yet. You seem to have forgotten that there's a murderer on the loose. Otherwise you wouldn't have done something as foolish as go out in the dark with one of the suspects. Besides, you really didn't think I was going to let you go off by yourself, did you?"

"What could you have done? You have a sprained foot—" Pricilla bit back the comment. He was right. She hadn't thought. If Oscar had wanted to harm her, there wouldn't have been anything she could have done. Wit and mental power might be handy in a game of Scrabble or Risk, but she would have been no match physically to a thirty-something-year-old male with a rack of rifles on the wall. Who was she fooling?

She shook her head. "Of course, you're right, Max. I'm sorry."

"You should be." The lines around his eyes softened. "You had me worried that something awful was going to happen to you."

"Have they found Claire yet?"

"I don't know. I've been wobbling toward the barn the whole time you were gone."

She couldn't help but chuckle at his comment. "I'm sorry, but it does make a humorous picture. Your running after me in the dark on your crutches. . . I am sorry."

"Just stop taking so many gambles with your life." Did she sense a hint of amusement in his voice? "As much as I am opposed to getting involved with this entire mess, there is something else I found out tonight."

Pricilla stopped. "What is it?"

"I found a few moments to do a bit of digging around on the Internet and came across an interesting interview."

"Yes—?"

Max started back up the path, this time in the light of her flashlight. "After the dot-com business was sold, Michael Smythe took his share of the money and pursued a lifetime dream to become an independent producer of video games. His first game was an immediate success."

She kicked a rock out of the path with the toe of her shoe. "No connection to Charles, though, right?"

"Not yet, but in digging deeper, I discovered that while Michael didn't partner with the two men, he did invest heavily in their endeavor."

The lights of the lodge lit the path and Pricilla turned off her flashlight. "So when Simon and Anthony lost all their money, Michael took a big hit as well."

"A huge loss, apparently."

"Which keeps all three of them on the list of suspects."

Max nodded. "Especially considering the fact that the takeover was not pretty."

At the lodge, Nathan paced across the porch, talking to someone on his cell phone, his fist balled at his side. Trisha leaned against the rail. There was no one else on the porch.

"Have you found her?" Pricilla rushed up the stairs, ignoring the throb in her hip.

Trisha turned and shook her head. "Not unless you found her in the barn."

Nathan flipped the phone shut and joined the three of them.

"Did you call the detective?" Max asked.

"No, the detective called me." Worry lines were etched into his forehead. "He had a follow-up question to our conversation earlier today. I didn't tell him about Claire."

Trisha rested her hand on Nathan's arm. "I think you need to call him back and tell him what's happened."

Nathan's frown deepened. "As much as I don't want to, I suppose I should."

Trisha was right, of course. They would have to call the detective. But that didn't mean she would have to stay up and see him. Surely he wouldn't have the gall to get her out of bed.

"Since there's nothing else I can do, I think I'm going to head up to bed.

We can talk more about what you found out tomorrow."

Max smiled at her. Maybe he'd forgiven her.

He headed into the house behind her. "Chicken."

Or maybe not.

She turned to face him. "Okay. I admit it, Max. I'm avoiding an encounter with the detective."

"Sleep well." He winked at her and headed toward the kitchen. "I'll see you in the morning."

"Good night."

At the end of the upstairs hallway, Pricilla paused at her room. Was it only a few short days ago that she'd looked forward to a quiet week with Max and Trisha? Life had gotten complicated, and quickly. She preferred murder and mysteries to be savored within the pages of a good book—not experienced in real life. Who was she to think she could solve a real life whodunit? Pulling her key from her pocket, she slid it into the lock. Miss Marple had an uncanny intuition. Father Brown had a deepened spiritual insight. She, on the other hand, had—

Pricilla froze. The door wasn't locked. She tried to relax. Undoubtedly she'd simply forgotten to lock it.

Slowly, she pushed the door open. Claire was sitting on her bed.

"I have to tell someone the truth." The woman's stoic expression never wavered as she spoke. "I'm the one who murdered Charles."

14

Pricilla leaned against the doorframe for support. The day had obviously been too tiring for her. Here she was, a sixty-four-year-old woman with bifocals and a girdle, standing in the doorway of her room, listening to a murder confession.

Things like this didn't happen to people like her. They happened to priests, and ministers, and undercover FBI agents.

She took a tentative step forward. Maybe it was time to add a hearing aid to the list. "What did you say?"

"I said I killed Charles."

Pricilla shook her head to try and clear it. "You're confessing to his murder?"

In actuality, Pricilla wasn't so much surprised at the fact that it had actually been Claire who did it but that the woman was confessing to her that she had done it.

Claire raked her fingers through her hair and nodded. "Whoever said that confession was good for the soul was right. I've felt like I was going to be eaten alive by the guilt. I finally couldn't take it anymore."

Pricilla studied Claire's face. Her eyes were red and swollen from crying, but a sense of relief was obvious in her expression as well. Stress did weird things to people. Having one's husband murdered would certainly top her list.

Claire dug into the comforter with her fists. In her jeans and forest green sweater, and painted nails, she looked like a typical hotel guest. Nothing about her stood out. In fact, she looked a bit vulnerable. Certainly not capable of murder. . . Or was she?

Pricilla took a step toward the bed. "Are you sure you're not just overwrought? You've been through a traumatic experience."

"There's nothing wrong with me." She hiccupped. "Well, nothing besides the fact that I will live out the rest of my life in prison."

A shadow crossed Claire's face, and Pricilla wondered if she'd actually thought through the consequences of her actions or if her only goal had been to confess. Something definitely wasn't right. "Have you been drinking?"

Claire shook her head. "I hiccup when I'm nervous."

Pricilla chewed on her bottom lip. Out of all the scenarios she had played through her mind in solving the case, this certainly hadn't been one of them. A clandestine meeting at night in her own room seemed more like something from a B-rated movie than from her own life.

Pricilla sat down on the bed beside her. "Tell me what happened?"

Claire hiccupped again then clinched her hands against her stomach. "I've made so many bad choices, I don't know where to begin."

Max would be furious to know that she was sitting beside a confessed murderer, but at the moment she didn't feel any fear. Only a deep sorrow and pity for the woman. Besides, Claire was obviously in a daze.

"Try starting from the beginning," Pricilla suggested. "It always helps."

Claire took a laborious breath. "I planned it weeks ago after I found out he was cheating on me. I used a slow acting poison from a private source. You wouldn't believe how easy it is to get your hands on something like that. Cost me a fortune, all right, but took little effort. Charles thought the pills were vitamins. Something to help boost his immune system. He worked so many hours and was always tired. He'd take anything I suggested that might give him that extra boost. He never complained when I reminded him every morning to take them. Never suspected a thing."

"Why are you telling me this now? Why confess?"

Claire shrugged. "Besides the fact that I couldn't hold the truth inside a second more, I'm pretty sure the authorities would find out eventually. Once the toxicology report comes in, they'll search my things and find a trail that leads to me. It would be funny if it wasn't so tragic. I couldn't wait for Charles to die. But now that he's gone, I actually regret killing him."

Pricilla tried to picture the woman in a jail cell. Overcrowded conditions. Prison garb. Greasy food. The images were far from pleasant, and Claire certainly wasn't the kind of person one imagined visiting in cellblock D. Sculpted eyebrows, manicured nails, and a bit of plastic surgery and liposuction thrown in along the way... Not exactly the poster girl for your local prison population.

Pricilla fought to understand. "Lots of husbands cheat on their wives but that doesn't give their wives the license to kill them. Did he abuse you?"

"Not physically, but there are plenty of other kinds of abuse." She kept her voice calm with barely any inflection. "I never thought it would have driven me to murder either, but my marriage was a farce, far from the perfect situation I tried to show everyone."

Claire got up and walked to the window. Pulling open the heavy drapes, she let the moonlight spill across the bedspread with a forest scene pattern. "Six months ago, I found out that my husband was having an affair with his secretary, and I confronted him."

Pricilla didn't know what to say. She'd informally counseled dozens of people over the years. Young mothers who needed an older woman to talk to.

Someone who wouldn't judge, could give advice freely, and most importantly, someone who would just listen. The advice part came easily. She'd worked hard to make sure that she listened as well.

But this was different. She'd heard women pour out their hearts over husbands who'd left them with small children, or who had deserted them after their children had left home. Women who'd lost everything they had because of their husband's indiscretions. But murder was completely out of her league.

"I'm sorry," she said, simply.

Claire ran her fingers down the thick drapes. "I know that I was as much to blame for our problems as he was. It's ironic, really. This trip was supposed to be a chance for us to make things right in our relationship. On the surface, anyway. I knew nothing would ever change between us.

"There were money problems, as well. He would never have divorced me. I have my own money from my father's estate. Divorce would have completely ruined him financially, something he would never have handled. He was content to pretend that all was well with us, another one of his lies."

Pricilla leaned back and rested her hands on the bed. "So what happens now?"

Claire's gaze dropped, and she scuffed the toe of her leather boots against the carpet. Maybe the reality of what she'd done in confessing was starting to sink in. "I suppose the detective will need to be called."

"He should be on his way actually. Misty told us you'd disappeared, and we've all been out looking for you."

"So, I've become a fugitive." Claire laughed, a short hollow laugh. "Can I ask you something?"

"Of course."

Claire came and sat back down on the bed beside Pricilla. "Did you mean it when you said that God was good, and that He was in control?"

"Yes."

"Do you think He could ever make something out of the mess I've made of my life?"

Pricilla closed her eyes and quickly prayed for wisdom. Then she said, "One thing I've been struck with lately is that we've all sinned. Your consequences might be greater right now, but God speaks just as loudly against those who envy and gossip. Something I'm sure we're all guilty of. To God, sin is sin, but He promises us that for those who trust Him and serve Him, He will forgive us our sins and purify us."

"I find that hard to believe. I took a life. . . ." Claire wiped away a tear and sniffled.

"There are tissues in the bathroom," Pricilla suggested.

"Thanks," Claire said vaguely. She walked into the bathroom, shutting the door behind her. Pricilla had a few moments to catch her breath. The window was too small for Claire to crawl through, so she didn't have to worry about the woman escaping.

Claire's confession had Pricilla's mind spinning. How could someone kill her husband? Divorce was extreme enough, but murder was so. . .so final. She pulled off her sweater and threw it on the bed. If Nathan had managed to get a hold of the detective, he could be here any minute. And she was sure that the detective would find pleasure in arresting Claire. He'd have his murderer and the case would be solved. And a case closed would please his uncle. All her harebrained ideas had done nothing to solve the case.

Someone knocked on the door.

She crossed the room to open it.

"Detective Carter!"

"Mrs. Crumb—" The bathroom door opened behind her, and the detective's eyes widened. "And Mrs. Woodruff?"

Pricilla cleared her throat. "I found her."

"I can see that." He pulled off his glasses and waved them at her. "And do you know what the penalty is for harboring a suspect in a murder investigation?"

Did he just accuse her of a crime? "Harboring a suspect? Detective Carter, that's ridiculous. I wasn't harboring anyone. I found Claire in my room. Surely you don't think that I would ever do such a. . .such an illegal thing."

"Don't I?" He slid his glasses back on and caught her gaze.

"It's not her fault." Claire grabbed her purse and squeezed it against her chest as she walked toward the detective. "I was in her room when she came in. Mrs. Crumb didn't have any choice but to listen to me confess—"

"Confess to what?" Claire had the detective's full attention.

The woman held her head up high. "I'm the one who poisoned my husband."

The detective folded his hands across his chest and stood looking at both women for a moment. "Now isn't this an interesting turn of events. Are you willing to come down to the station and make a complete confession?"

"Yes." Claire's voice wavered.

The detective pulled a pair of handcuffs out of his back pocket.

Pricilla stepped between Claire and Detective Carter. "Do you have to handcuff her?"

"As much as I'd like to humor you, Mrs. Crumb, my only goal is to see that justice is served, and in doing that it is my duty to uphold the letter of the law." The detective glanced at Claire as if evaluating his decision. "But I suppose I could make an exception this time."

Pricilla nodded in surprise. It was the first glimpse of humanity she'd seen in the man.

Claire preceded the detective out of the room, a glazed expression across her face. Pricilla looked at the clock. Nine. Just an hour ago she'd been about to play an innocent board game. Now all Pricilla knew how to do was pray.

Three hours later, Pricilla glanced at the digital clock. Again. She couldn't sleep. She threw off the comforter. Maybe she was just hot. The logs in the fireplace no longer burned with their orangish glow, but the room was stuffy. Rolling over, she pushed off the thick comforter and let out a deep breath. She needed to relax, but all she could see was Claire's face as she confessed that she'd murdered her husband.

She turned over the other way, but it was no use. If she took a sleeping pill this late at night, she'd never get up in the morning. A cup of tea was the second best thing.

Flipping on the light beside her bed, she sat up and yawned then wrapped her robe firmly around her. She found her slippers under the bed and padded downstairs to the kitchen. Apparently, she wasn't the only one who couldn't sleep. Trisha sat on one of the bar stools with a mug in one hand and a book in the other.

Pricilla stopped in the doorway. "Can't sleep either?"

Trisha set down the book and shook her head. "Every time I close my eyes, I see the look on Claire's face as the detective carted her off to jail. The whole thing is too weird. I don't understand why she would confess like that. There's got to be something else going on."

"I know what you mean, but what?" Pricilla grabbed a cup and filled it with water before putting it in the microwave. "I have some over-the-counter sleeping pills, if you want to try one."

Trisha lifted up her mug. "I'm trying hot milk, but it's not working."

"Never worked for me either."

With the water heating, Pricilla flipped through the tea canister and debated over what kind she wanted. Avoiding caffeine was a no-brainer. Too much of the stimulant and she wouldn't be able to sleep, even with a pill.

One blend claimed it would relax her so she would be able to sleep like a baby. It had been years since she'd slept like a baby, but it was worth a try.

"I had a friend who had some interesting remedies for falling asleep." Pricilla leaned against the counter and waited for the water to heat up. "Marjorie was convinced that sleeping with her head facing north guaranteed a good night's sleep. Something to do with the magnetic field of the planet or something."

Trisha took another sip of her milk and grimaced. "My mom always told me to lie in bed and wiggle my toes. It was supposed to relax me."

The microwave beeped and after taking out the mug, Pricilla dropped her tea bag into the hot water. "Maybe I should try both suggestions."

"I suppose it couldn't hurt, though I don't know if Nathan would appreciate my rearranging the furniture to ensure I was lying in the right direction." Trisha got up and dumped the rest of her milk down the drain. "So, you have some magic pills, do you?"

Pricilla chuckled. "When you get to be my age, you can't be without them."

Pulling her plastic pillbox out of the cupboard, she set it down on the counter and noted Trisha's raised brow. "Don't tell me that your father doesn't have one of these stashed away. It's all part of the joys of growing old."

Pricilla ran her finger across the plastic container. From painkillers to blood pressure medicine, herbal vitamins to sleeping pills, she'd managed to organize her daily doses down to a science.

"Now for sleeping pills. These are prescription, so Detective Carter would come after me if I gave them to anyone. These two contain an antihistamine, so you might feel sluggish come morning." Pricilla popped open one of the compartments. "And this one"—she popped open another—"is a dietary supplement that is supposed to help regulate your sleep-wake cycle. You can take your pick."

Trisha tapped one of the pills with the tip of her finger. "Wow. I have a choice? I had no idea there was a selection."

"Believe me, this is only the beginning of what's available." She nudged Trisha with her shoulder. "Personally, I avoid them whenever possible, but my doctor agreed it's all right every now and then, so I like to be prepared. And frankly, I'd say involvement in a murder investigation is a valid reason."

"At least the case is pretty much closed now." Trisha poured a glass of water and took a sip. "How in the world do you keep these straight?"

"Get to be my age and you won't have a problem. Unless, of course, you suffer with memory loss." She caught the worried expression on Trisha's face. "It's really not that bad. I've got an herbal pill for that as well."

Trisha guffawed. "I needed to laugh. Life's become too serious lately."

Pricilla handed her one of the pills. "This is a mild one. Take it and go on up to bed. You can sleep in tomorrow as late as you want."

Trisha grabbed the pill, but Pricilla didn't miss the blush that crept up the young woman's face. "Well, the detective finally said we are all free to come and go as we like. With the men leaving on their hunting trip tomorrow, Nathan's planning to take off a couple of hours so that he can take me out to breakfast in town."

Pricilla beamed inwardly. "I'll make sure you wake up. You'll be missing my peaches and cream French toast, but I have the feeling that neither of you will mind a bit."

"Somehow I have a feeling that you're right." Trisha swallowed the pill with a glass of water then kissed Pricilla on the cheek. "Thank you for everything."

"You're welcome." She'd always wanted a daughter. A daughter-in-law would be just fine. "Sleep tight."

Pricilla took a sip of her tea and watched as Trisha floated out of the kitchen. She needed to finish her drink and try to sleep as well. She'd never make it through tomorrow if she didn't get some rest.

She wondered how Claire was doing right now. At some point, the shock of what had happened was going to wear off. That's when things would get really tough. That's when she would really need a relationship with Christ to get her through. Without it, Pricilla honestly didn't know how people coped with tragedies. She'd keep praying for Claire and maybe even visit her. There was nothing else she could do at this point.

Pricilla started down the hall toward the stairs. Something niggled at the back of her mind, but she couldn't put a finger on it. Ever since she'd talked to Claire that time in the woman's bedroom, she had felt that something was off. A small detail that didn't add up. Feeling the stiffness in her joints, she took the stairs slowly. Max would tell her that she was overtired and being paranoid, and he was probably right. She was also certain that he was thrilled she was out of the detective business for good. And so was she. . .for the most part. There had been something exciting about planning, trying to phrase the right questions, and putting together the pieces of the puzzle.

But all of that was over now.

Pricilla yawned and tried for the third time to read the recipe out of the cookbook for peaches and cream French toast. Three hours of sleep wasn't enough to keep a snail moving at half speed, and it certainly wasn't enough to keep her eyelids open. Her vision doubled as she tried adjusting her bifocals. Maybe she should serve something simpler this morning—like cold cereal and bananas.

But of course she wouldn't.

Instead she poured herself a cup of coffee—thick and black—and tried to wake up. It wasn't as if she needed as much sleep as she did when she was younger, or that she'd never suffered from sleepless nights before, but there was a minimum amount required to function. She obviously hadn't reached that point.

She flipped the pages of the recipe book and settled on cherry-cinnamon muffins. Fifteen minutes prep time she could handle. Add a few simple side items like yogurt and bacon, and her guests would be happy. There might even be time for a midmorning nap, something she seldom indulged in.

Pricilla paused before pulling out the ingredients for the muffins. Her spiral detective notebook sat beside the recipe book, an empty page staring up at her. She flipped through the slips of paper and frowned. So much for her lists of suspects, motivations, and interviews. All they had got her was knee deep into a number of embarrassing situations and not one step closer in solving the case.

But life was back to normal now. She no longer had to worry anymore about interrogations, clues. . .or Detective Carter for that matter.

"Good morning." Max's voice rang entirely too chipper from the kitchen doorway.

She turned to face him. "Why the super-sized grin this morning?"

He bridged the gap between them, his crutches thudding against the floor. "Nothing like a good night's sleep after a murder's been solved."

Pricilla groaned. "I take it you weren't up half the night then."

"And you were?"

She pointed to the box of tea on the counter and shook her head. "Let's just say, don't believe the one that claims you'll sleep like a baby after drinking it. Of course, I'm sure they would include murder as an exemption in their ads."

Max folded his arms across his chest and chuckled. "Of all people, I thought you would have slept good last night, knowing the case is solved."

"One would think." She tried to open the jar of sour cherries then handed it to Max.

"It couldn't have ended better to me." He strained, balancing on his good foot, then popped open the jar. "With life back to normal, I can spend the rest of the week with you without your little notebook coming between us."

Pricilla ran her hand down her cheek, suddenly wishing she'd spent more time trying to erase the crow's feet and age spots. "Glad you slept well."

"And why didn't you? You should be relieved."

"I am." Pricilla pulled a glass bowl out of the bottom cupboard then went in search of the measuring cups. "But I don't understand how Claire could have killed her husband. She told me he was unfaithful to her. If you ask me, he should be the one locked up for his indiscretions. Instead, she's going to pay for her decision the rest of her life."

"But isn't that what it comes down to? It was her decision." Max popped one of the sour cherries into his mouth. "Besides, I'm sure there's more to the story than either of us will ever know."

"I suppose, but don't you wonder how God could have allowed the woman to suffer so much pain that she in turn took someone's life?"

Max knitted his brow and appeared to mull over his answer. "I would assume there's got to be a lot of baggage that goes behind a decision like Claire's. You can't blame God for her bad choice."

"Of course, you're right." She measured the flour and dumped it into the bowl. "It's still sad though. Her life will never be the same again, no matter what happens."

"I was wondering. . ." Max cleared his throat and dropped his gaze for a moment. "I was wondering if you felt like going into town today? I thought I could take you out to lunch. Might be a nice break for you, considering everything that's happened here the past couple of days."

Pricilla smiled. If Misty served lunch, she should be able to enjoy a quiet break with Max. She'd planned a special celebration dinner tonight, but if she left a list of things for Misty to get done, she should have plenty of time to have everything ready by seven.

She watched as Max fidgeted in front of her. Funny how the mention of them going to lunch had him squirming like a seventeen-year-old asking her out to the prom. She shook her head. It must be her imagination. The lack of sleep could do funny things to a person. Besides, it wasn't as if this were a date or anything. They would go to the Rendezvous Bar and Grill, or one of the small town's other restaurants and enjoy the establishment's specials for the day that would be enhanced by engaging conversation.

She felt her heart skip a beat. "Lunch would be perfect."

Twenty minutes later, with the muffins in the oven and Misty setting up the dining room for breakfast, Pricilla headed upstairs. She expected that there would be quite a few smiling faces this morning, but the nagging feeling that something wasn't right continued to pester her. She wanted to know how Claire could have been driven to murder her husband.

Pricilla stopped in front of the Elk Room and hesitated. The detective had already made a search last night and removed all the evidence. What could a bit of snooping on her behalf matter at this point? It wasn't as if she expected to find any more clues. Even she knew that the case would soon be officially closed by the coroner and sheriff's department. There was nothing left for her to discover. But that didn't stop her from wanting to take one last look.

"Mom?"

Pricilla pulled her hand back from the door knob like it was a hot ember. She shoved her hands behind her back. "Nathan, you scared me."

"What are you doing?" He cocked his head, seemingly amused at the fact that he'd caught her red-handed. "In case you forgot, the case is closed."

"I know. I was just. . ." She took a step away from the door, swallowed any feelings of guilt, and decided to change the subject. "Where are you off to this morning? You're looking quite handsome."

He tugged on the collar of his muted green sweater and grinned. "I'm taking Trisha out for breakfast. I'm assuming you approve?"

She smiled and the tension of the moment began to fade. "You know I do, and a date is definitely a step in the right direction."

"As long as it's the first of many."

Pricilla smiled to herself. It was obvious Nathan was smitten. So much, in fact, that the mere thought of Trisha had him losing his concentration and forgetting the fact that he'd caught his mother about to go into Claire's room to investigate a closed case.

She reached up and brushed off a piece of lint from his shoulder. "I hope it will be the first of many as well."

"Did you see the *Rendezvous Sentinel* this morning? They just announced Charles's death and put a stock photo of the lodge on the front page. They'll be calling today, though, now that Claire has been arrested. I plan to be away from the phone, giving my attention to more important things. Like Trisha." He smiled. "I just wish we had more time before she had to leave."

"A long-distance relationship is always an option for a while." Pricilla tried to ignore the reminder that Max would be leaving in four days, as well.

"I've never believed in a long-distance relationship, but I've decided to talk to her about that this morning. Time's running out and nothing will happen if I don't take a chance."

Life was full of taking chances. Was that what Claire had done? Took a chance that killing her husband would bring her something better in life? That something certainly wasn't prison. Questions continued to nag Pricilla. What had Claire hoped for in killing him? Revenge? Freedom?

He reached down and kissed her on the cheek. "I'm meeting Trisha downstairs in a few minutes, so I'd better get going."

Pricilla rested her hand on his arm. "Can I ask you a question first?"

"Of course." He leaned against the wall. "What is it?"

"Why do you think she did it? Claire, I mean. Why do you think she killed her husband?"

He shrugged a shoulder. "Does it really matter? I mean, she's admitted to the crime and the authorities have arrested her. She had motive and opportunity. As to exactly why. . .I suppose we'll never know."

She shook her head. She wanted answers. "I don't understand what would motivate a person to commit such a dreadful act. On the surface, Claire had everything. Money, success, beauty. . .but obviously none of that was enough. She wanted more and, for whatever reason, believed that with Charles out of the way, she'd find it."

Nathan scratched his chin. "Think about it. Are success and riches ever enough? Most people spend their whole lives searching for something they can never keep. They don't seem to realize that we enter into the world with nothing and we all leave this world with nothing."

" 'Store up for yourselves treasures in heaven.' " She quoted the verse from the book of Matthew and wrinkled her brow. "Is that the answer then? Claire was too caught up in getting ahead in life that she failed to look at the consequences?"

"And failed to realize that the stakes are bigger than making it financially, or climbing to the top of the social ladder." Nathan drew in a deep breath. "I think you need to let it go."

She nodded. "I know."

She glanced at the closed door. He was right, of course, but that didn't change the fact that it still beckoned her to open it. There would be no answers inside Claire's room as to why she'd done what she'd done, but the pull to investigate was there all the same.

She cleared her throat and decided to ask one last question. "There's one other thing that's been bothering me. A small detail of the case that was never resolved. If Simon Wheeler and Anthony Mills lost their business, how did they manage to pay for this expensive week?"

Nathan's brow rose at the question. "If I remember correctly, the entire week's bill was paid by the third party in their group, Michael Smythe."

Once again, questions began to surface as to the connection between Charles

Woodruff and the three businessmen, but with Claire's confession, there obviously wasn't a link between the three men and Charles's death.

"Anything else?"

"No, just enjoy yourself."

"You don't have to worry about that. I'll see you later."

Pricilla watched Nathan slip down the stairs and out of view. The hallway was empty now, giving her the opportunity to do one final thing with the investigation before she could put it behind her. Pulling the master key from her pocket, she slipped it into the lock and turned the knob.

Inside, she went to the window and drew back the curtains, letting a flood of morning sunshine filter into the room. Misty hadn't come to clean yet, but the detective had emptied the room of all of Claire's possessions. It was a bleak reminder that Claire would not be coming back.

This time, there were no details of the room to consider. No pairs of shoes, or makeup, or jewelry. Columbo would find that one last scrap of evidence that would explain why Claire had made that fateful decision. The one thing that had been nagging at his mind that would pull all the pieces of the puzzle together and explain the case.

But there wasn't anything to find. Claire had confessed and, depending on a judge's pronouncement, she'd likely spend the next few decades behind bars. Taking one last look around the room, Pricilla sighed and opened the door. Max and Nathan, as usual, were right. It was time to give up her role of detective.

Penelope whisked passed her legs and into the room.

"Not now, Penelope." Pricilla spun around. "You're going to get me into trouble if I get caught snooping in here."

The cat slipped under the bed. Pricilla eyed the open door. Someone was coming up the steps. She shut the door then turned back to find the cat. Of all days for Penelope to pull one of her stunts. But she couldn't leave her here.

She bent down beside the bed, one leg at a time. Her hip protested, but she ignored the ache. "Penelope. Come here, kitty, kitty."

The cat lay contentedly beyond her grasp.

And that wasn't all that lay under that bed. She was going to have to remind Misty to do a better job at cleaning under the beds. Besides a number of dust bunnies, there was an ink pen, two earrings, and several pills.

Pricilla grabbed the pills and sat up, hitting her head on the edge of the nightstand.

"Ouch!"

The pain faded quickly as she stared at the two small pills. There had been a bottle of vitamins sitting on the nightstand the day she first tried questioning Claire. The event replayed clearly in her mind. The woman had knocked them over, spilling the contents across the thick carpet. Something had bothered Pricilla then, but she hadn't been able to put a finger on it. Holding the capsules in the palm of her hand, she pulled herself up onto the bed then adjusted her bifocals.

Pricilla might not be licensed to run the local pharmacy, but between her collection of herbal and prescription pills and those of her friends, she was quite certain of two things. One, these were the pills Claire had spilled, and two, these pills were not vitamins. She studied the markings closely. She'd bet her bottle of elderberry capsules that these were natural herbs used as a diuretic, the same ones, in fact, her good friend Marge took. Claire had implied that these were the pills that had killed Charles. And that she'd paid a fortune for the slow-acting poison. Pricilla was grasping at straws, and she knew it, but something wasn't adding up. The case was closed, and she might still be looking for a way to save Claire, but the question still remained. Penelope stole out from under the bed and rubbed against Pricilla's legs. Could Claire have inadvertently been giving her husband something quite harmless instead of the poison she thought she was giving him?

If that was true, then someone else had murdered Charles Woodruff.

Max took a bite of the muffin and kept his gaze on the *Rendezvous Sentinel*'s sports page in front of him. His mind, though, was elsewhere. He'd waited far too long to state his intentions to Pricilla and no matter what today brought, this was going to be the day he told her how he felt. No more excuses. No more looking for ways a relationship at their age couldn't work. And no more getting sidetracked by another one of her wild goose chases. Charles Woodruff's death had been solved, he had a lunch date with Pricilla, and while the Rendezvous Bar and Grill might not be the most romantic setting he could think of, once he told her how he felt he hoped it wouldn't matter.

"Max?"

He smiled. Pricilla stood in the doorway, wearing a tiger print, loose-fitting pants suit. Most women would have avoided the boldest outfit on the rack, but it looked perfect on her.

While he felt sorry for Claire Woodruff, he was admittedly glad she was in jail. Today, he'd have Pricilla all to himself, and he would have time to go forward with his own matchmaking plans. If they were as successful as the schemes they had hatched for Trisha and Nathan, there might even be something permanent in store for him and Pricilla in the near future.

"You're looking a tad more chipper." He patted the seat next to him. "Did you get some breakfast?"

"I can't think about food right now." Pricilla waved away the offer with her hand. "Claire might be innocent."

"Oh no." Max held the newspaper back up in front of his face, wishing he could momentarily disappear.

Claire had been sent to the slammer. . .locked in the poky. . .thrown in the penitentiary. . .case closed. So that meant Pricilla had *not* just said that Claire Woodruff was innocent, because it wasn't true. It couldn't be.

Pricilla slid into the chair next to him at the breakfast table and jabbed at the black-and-white newsprint. "Didn't you hear me?"

"I heard someone say that Claire was innocent, which can't be true," he said behind the cover of the paper. "So I'll have to say no."

Pricilla poked harder at the paper, her finger ripping a hole through tomorrow's weather forecast.

"Pricilla." He lowered the paper slowly then folded it into quarters, reminding himself that this was the woman he loved, and that her quirkiness just made her all the more endearing. Didn't it?

"I'm serious, Max. I think Claire might be innocent." She dropped two small pills on the white tablecloth and beamed in triumph.

He didn't get it. "Don't tell me this is your proof."

"Just hear me out."

He knew he didn't have a choice. So much for his grand plans of declaring his undying love to her without any distractions or interruptions. By the time he managed to tell her how he felt, he would be locked away in a retirement home.

He rested his elbows on the table. "Go ahead."

Pricilla leaned forward, her face looking as solemn as his commanding officers who sent him off to the Vietnam War. Not a good sign. She was dead serious.

"First of all," Pricilla began, "I admit that I might simply feel sorry for the woman and want to absolve Claire from her husband's death, but that doesn't change the fact that something doesn't add up."

"What doesn't add up?" He forced himself to look interested as he asked the question. He didn't want to go through this again. "The woman confessed to her husband's murder. Period. Case closed."

She held up a finger in her defense. "And how many people have confessed to crimes they either didn't commit or, as in Claire's case, thought they committed but really didn't?"

"You're kidding me, right? Why would she do that?" The room started slowly spinning in circles, as if the earth had finally fallen off its axis. "You're telling me that you think she only *believes* she committed the murder, but in reality she didn't?"

For the first time, Pricilla smiled. "So you do understand?"

His eyes narrowed. "Not at all."

She laid her hand on his arm, and he tried to ignore the effect she had on him. How could this woman make his heart race like he was nineteen again, while at the same time drive him insane with her off-the-wall ideas?

"Just listen to the facts, Max. Claire said she found a seller who sold her a slow-acting poison that cost a lot of money. What if this seller took advantage of Claire, and instead of giving her the poison, substituted it for a harmless drug so he'd make more money off of her?" She held up the pills in her hands. "Like these pills."

She still wasn't making any sense. "Where did you get these?"

"The day I went up to talk to Claire about the murder, she knocked over a bottle of vitamins. Something bothered me about the experience at the time, but I couldn't put my finger on it. Today, under her bed, I found two of the same pills from the bottle she knocked over—except that these aren't vitamins. That's what had been niggling at the back of my mind. If I'm not mistaken, these are the same pills that my friend Marge takes. Diuretics. A relatively harmless pill, for most people. Certainly not anything that would poison someone over a matter of weeks and then kill him."

He struggled to put the pieces together. "And how do you know that those are the pills she gave him, thinking they were poison?"

"I don't for sure, but she said she put the pills in a vitamin bottle because she knew he'd take them without complaining, and I only saw one vitamin bottle. And when she knocked it over, she acted jumpy, like she didn't want me to discover that there weren't really vitamins inside the bottle. Of course, she thought they were poison, even more reason for me not to see them."

Max rubbed his temples. He was worried because he was beginning to understand what she was saying. How was it that Pricilla could manage to make her theory sound so logical? Surely there was little merit to the idea, but what if she was right? Was the real murderer getting off scot-free? The thought sent a shiver down his spine. He had wanted to put this entire ordeal behind him, but Pricilla, as usual, had other ideas.

He didn't want to let himself agree with her logic. Not this time. "I still think you need to leave things alone. If we have to, we can go and talk to the detective. Tell him what you found and let him handle it."

She crossed her legs and leaned against the back of the chair. "I have a plan first."

A plan? Max tapped his fingers against the table. Of course she had a plan.

"My theory is easy enough to prove. I want to go into town and have the pills analyzed at the pharmacy. Then I want to talk to Claire in jail."

Thirty minutes later, Pricilla stood in line at the local pharmacy with the two pills in a plastic bag. Max stood beside her, his face grim. She couldn't blame him. He wasn't the only one frustrated that the case wasn't closed. Frustrated that there might be one missing piece that could completely change the outcome of the investigation. The only thing that made her smile was the fact that all her hard work as an undercover detective might actually pay off.

Not that she wanted to ever be involved in a murder investigation again. Not at all. She'd come to that conclusion at four o'clock this morning when she was lying in bed, wide awake. Frankly, her experiences in investigating Charles Woodruff's murder had left her believing that crime solving really should be left to the authorities—except perhaps Detective Carter—and that her ability to find this possible significant piece of the case was nothing more than a coincidence.

An elderly gentleman took his prescription from the pharmacist, leaving her free to speak to the middle-aged woman.

"I have a rather odd question, I'm afraid." Pricilla set the bag of pills down on the counter. "I need to know exactly what these are."

The woman chuckled and tucked a strand of her short hair behind her ear. "You'd be surprised how often people ask me that very question. Pills get dumped in their purse or onto the carpet—"

Pricilla cleared her throat. "Well, I'm certainly glad I'm not the only one who's ever asked."

"These are diuretics." The pharmacist held up the pills in her hand. "They're used for removing water from the body by—"

"Thank you. I do know what a diuretic is, I was just afraid it might be something a bit more—" Max thumped her foot with the end of his crutch, and she switched the direction of the conversation. "Anyway, thank you. I know how important it is to keep one's prescription medicines straight."

"It's very important. Please don't hesitate to ask if you have questions like this again."

Max followed her out to the car. "You've got to learn when it's time to ask a question and when it's time to be quiet."

She ignored his reprimand. "We got our answer, didn't we? These pills couldn't have killed Charles Woodruff, and if Claire confirms that this was what she gave her husband, then there's another murderer on the loose."

After a quick stop at the instant photo booth tourists used on Main Street, Pricilla pulled into the driveway of the sheriff's office. Max hobbled behind her toward the glass doors that led to the small detention facility on the west side of the building.

"I don't get it, Pricilla." She could hear him huffing as he struggled up the sidewalk. "Secret photos and one of your cakes?"

She caught his odd expression, surprised he'd held off his questions this long. "Both are a part of my plan."

Max stopped along the cement walk. "They're not going to let you give food to an inmate, and—"

* * *

"Don't worry." Pricilla kept on walking. "The cake's not for Claire."

"I don't think they allow you to bribe the officials, either," Max mumbled, but she was already through the glass doors.

He let out a sharp breath then hurried to catch up with her. If she wasn't careful, he'd end up visiting her behind bars. He could see the headlines now: Woman Arrested for Attempting to Bribe Local Authorities with Slice of Succulent Cake. . . .

By the time he got inside, she was standing in front of a row of lockers.

"Can you believe this?"

"What?"

"We can't take anything inside if we want to see one of the inmates." She jiggled the key on the locker. "Do you have a quarter? I used the last of mine at the photo booth."

"A quarter." Max fished some change out of his pocket then handed her the coin.

He should have stayed home. At least then he could be lounging on the front porch of the lodge with a good book and a plate of Pricilla's cookies, instead of chasing empty clues.

She dumped her coat and her purse into the metal box then headed toward the reception desk with the cake.

He decided not to even ask.

"Detective Carter." Patricia greeted the man matter-of-factly.

"Ah, Mrs. Crumb. I wasn't expecting to see you today."

"We're here to visit Claire Woodruff," Pricilla announced to the balding detective.

The officer scratched the back of his head. "First of all, the only thing that you're allowed to bring in here are your keys and identification. There are lockers on the other side of the glass doors where you can store your things."

"I understand, but first let me ask you if it's possible to see Claire."

The man shoved his glasses up the bridge of his nose. "You have to have an appointment before you're allowed to visit with one of our inmates."

"I don't have an appointment. Would you—"

"Appointments need to be made twenty-four hours in advance."

"Wait a minute." Pricilla shook her head. "Mrs. Woodruff was only arrested last night, so there was no way that I could have made an appointment twenty-four hours ago."

"Well, then, only family can see her, and I know for certain that you are *not* family." The detective picked up his pen. "I can make an appointment for you for next Wednesday."

"Next Wednesday?"

"And don't bring anything into this lobby with you next time, or you won't be allowed to visit."

"It's just a cake." She held it out to him, as if the scent of the citrus would change his mind. "One of my lemon crumb cakes."

"That's nice, but it's still not allowed. No snacks, packages, drugs, or contraband for our inmates."

Her lips curved into a frown. "I wouldn't consider my cake contraband, and besides, it's not for one of your inmates."

"Pricilla, I think we should leave now," Max prompted, but she stood her ground.

"Is the sheriff back in town?" she asked.

Max cocked his head. *What was this? Plan B?*

The detective glanced toward one of the back offices. "He's on duty right now."

"I'd like to see him, please."

Max wondered if he should turn around and walk right out the door and wait for her in the car. Doing things the proper way would be too simple when Pricilla was involved. But, he had to admit, not nearly as interesting.

A minute later, a stocky officer with graying hair strode across the lobby. "Mrs. Crumb! It's such a pleasure to see you."

Max couldn't help but smile to himself. Of course. Pricilla had an inside contact. Why had he ever questioned the fact that she had a plan?

"Sheriff Tucker. How was your trip back East?" Pricilla grasped the man's hands.

"Great, but it's always good to be home. I arrived back in town last night."

"And your wife and that precious granddaughter of yours? How are they?"

The sheriff pulled his wallet out of his back pocket and flipped it open to a picture of a sleeping infant. "They're both fine, thank you. It's hard to believe, but little Hailey will be four weeks old next Sunday."

Pricilla glanced at the department store photo and grinned. "She's grown so much and is positively adorable. Sheriff, I want you to meet my dear friend, Max Summers. He's up visiting from New Mexico."

"It's nice to meet you, Mr. Summers."

Max reached out to shake his hand. "Nice to meet you, too."

"I know Sheriff Tucker from church," Pricilla said. "Some of the ladies organized a few meals to help out when his daughter was in the hospital, delivering Hailey."

"A couple meals?" The sheriff shoved his wallet back into his pocket and laughed. "This woman could feed an army with the food she brought my kids. Allowed me to sample a few of the dishes. Juicy ribs, roast with gravy and mashed potatoes. . ."

The descriptions were enough to make Max's stomach growl. "No one would argue that Pricilla is an excellent cook."

A blush crept up Pricilla's face as she picked up the cake off the counter.

"The detective here implied that I shouldn't have brought a cake, but after promising you I'd make you and your wife one, I hadn't thought that there would be a problem for me to bring it to you at the station."

"Of course it's not a problem." The sheriff took the dessert and smiled. "Can I sneak a piece before I clock out tonight?"

"I'll leave that for you and your conscience to settle. I know how much your wife loves lemon cake." Pricilla laughed. "Now, Sheriff, there is one other thing—"

Max leaned against the counter, eager to see what would happen next. Pricilla was obviously born with an extra measure of charm, because considering the pleased expression on the sheriff's face, he looked as if he would grant her anything she asked for. Detective Carter, on the other hand, wasn't looking quite as compliant.

"We're here to see Claire Woodruff," Pricilla began. "She had been a guest at my son's lodge and doesn't know a soul in the area. We'd really like to see her if it wouldn't be too much trouble."

"Well, there are rules, you know, that even one of your lemon crumb cakes can't get around." The sheriff laughed again, and his belly shook. "You'll have to wait until visiting hours start, but I don't see a problem in waiving the twenty-four hour rule in this case. Do you, Carter?"

"I. . .of course not."

Pricilla clasped her hands together. "I certainly appreciate it, Sheriff. I've just been so worried about the woman."

"We will have to see a photo ID and run a background check. Regulations, you know, even for people we're acquainted with. But my nephew here will take care of that, and then you can see her in about forty-five minutes if she's in agreement."

Pricilla noted Carter's grimace, but forty-five minutes later, he ushered her and Max into a pale green room lined with chairs. The detective told them where to sit, and it was another five minutes before he led Claire into the room.

The detective stood at the door. "Visitation will be over in exactly thirty minutes."

Claire walked toward them slowly, looking surprised. Her face was pale and there were bags under her eyes. "How nice of you to come by. I—"

"Are you all right?" Pricilla frowned, wishing she could have bit back the words the moment they'd surfaced. Of course the woman wasn't all right. She'd been arrested for killing her husband and now faced a lifetime behind bars. "I'm sorry. I shouldn't have asked such an insensitive question."

Claire sat down on the edge of the seat and rubbed her hands against the legs of her orange prison garb. "I've just gone from socialite to jail inmate. You can't go much lower than that."

Max leaned forward. "What about your bond?"

"My case is supposed to go before a judge today and my lawyer's getting my money together. Some of Charles's assets have been frozen, but thankfully it shouldn't be a problem. I'd sell my right arm to get out of here if I had to."

Pricilla squeezed her hand. "Maybe it won't be that difficult."

Claire's brow narrowed. "What do you mean?"

Max nudged Pricilla with his elbow and she nodded slightly. He was right. She was going to have to be careful about what she said. For all she knew, this was going to turn into nothing more than another dead end.

Pricilla pulled from her pocket the photo she'd taken of the two pills, and showed it to Claire. The clarity wasn't perfect, but it was good enough for what she needed. "I found these pills under your bed at the lodge. I need to know if these are the same pills you used to poison your husband."

Claire covered her hand with her mouth and nodded her head. "I don't want to think about it."

"Claire, I know you're upset, but I need you to listen to me very carefully. I don't know where you got these pills, but they are simply a mild diuretic."

"No." She wrung her hands together. "The man I bought them from told me they were a slow-acting poison. He couldn't guarantee how long it would take for them to work, but he assured me they would."

Pricilla looked to Max. There was one more thing she had to ask.

"I have one more question for you. Is it possible that whoever sold you the pills was simply trying to extract money from you?" She patted her pocket. "These pills couldn't have poisoned Charles."

Pricilla studied the woman's face. Instead of relief, though, she saw fear in Claire's eyes. A lab test would prove for certain what the pills were, but her previous theory now moved to the forefront. If Claire didn't kill her husband, then who did?

17

Max slid into the booth across from Pricilla and tapped his fingers against the brown Formica table. Just when the murder of Charles Woodruff had come to a nice and neat conclusion, Pricilla had managed to find a way to blow the case wide open with two tiny diuretic pills.

He picked up the plastic menu and studied the lunch items. Ham, roast beef, meatloaf. . . His stomach growled. There might be a murderer on the loose, but he still had his appetite. The Rendezvous Bar and Grill had been overly crowded, so he'd suggested they stop for lunch at Tiffany's. The small café, located just off Main Street, was quiet, and he hoped for a chance to talk to Pricilla about something besides Charles Woodruff's death—namely, the fact that he had waited far too long to declare his intentions toward her.

But there was another issue that had to be resolved before he could bring any plans of romance into the conversation.

He looked up at her and caught her gaze. "You know we have to talk to the detective about what you found out from Claire."

She pulled off her coat and laid it on the seat beside her. "Yes, but I thought we should discuss the new development first."

He had no desire to discuss the details of the case. While he could see that Pricilla actually might be on to something with her diuretic pills, that didn't change the fact that this was the detective's investigation. Not theirs. And Max was finished playing her bumbling sidekick.

She pulled out her compact and dabbed powder on her nose. "I want to be able to give the detective something more. If nothing else, a well thought out theory so he won't simply dismiss what I have to say as the ramblings of some crazy old woman looking to be the next Jessica Fletcher."

"No one thinks you're a crazy old woman."

She grinned, and his heart thudded offbeat in a peculiar rhythm that might have had him worried under other circumstances. He didn't know why, exactly, but there was no doubt that Pricilla had stolen his heart. With all her quirks and eccentricities, she'd managed to not only step in and fill the lonely ache inside him, but give him a reason to smile again. He'd never believed that growing older meant growing old, and she was the perfect antidote to life this side of middle age.

Pricilla hugged the menu to her chest. "If Claire really is innocent, I need to come up with a solid hypothesis on who committed the crime. While I never liked Oscar, he doesn't seem to have a strong motive for murder. What do you think?"

He glanced again at the daily special and decided on meatloaf and mashed potatoes before answering her question. "There were definite underlying hostilities between the two men, but no matter who actually killed Charles, you can't forget that Claire's far from innocent."

She frowned. "I suppose you are right, though I admit that I'd hoped that in the end Claire would be absolved of all wrongdoing."

"Intent can be just as deadly as the actual crime."

Pricilla sighed and signaled for the waitress. "Are you thirsty, Max? I think I need a strong cup of coffee before I can even think about eating lunch."

He nodded and two minutes later, he was sipping black coffee and mentally strategizing his next move. A move that had nothing to do with Pricilla's continuing investigation. He'd rehearsed the conversation a thousand times in his mind.

Pricilla—he'd look deep into her eyes as he spoke—*we've known each other a long time, and despite the fact that we always lived miles apart, our families still managed to go through many of life's ups and downs together. From raising teenagers, to empty nests, to the loss of our spouses, to retirement. . . I don't know how you will feel about this, but I'd like to see our relationship move beyond friendship. I'm sixty-five years old, but you make me feel as if I'm thirty-five again. And while I never thought that I would feel this way again, if you're willing to take a chance*—

"On the other hand, the real murderer could be Simon or Anthony." Pricilla leaned forward and rested her elbows on the table, jerking him from his thoughts as she spoke. "They had a strong motive as well as opportunity."

"They were always near the top of my suspect list." Max stopped then frowned. She had done it again. Pulled him off track from his task at hand. How could one woo a lady's heart when she had murder on her mind? "Pricilla."

"I do have a theory—"

"Pricilla." He took a deep breath. "I don't want to talk about Claire right now. I don't want to talk about Charles Woodruff, or anyone who might have killed him. Not Oscar, or Anthony, or Simon—"

"All right." She knitted her brow together and shot him a confused expression. "What do you want to talk about?"

"Us." Max cringed the moment he spoke. He'd planned to be subtle at first, but instead he'd blurted it out.

"Us?"

He cleared his throat and fiddled with his half-empty mug. "I didn't mean it to come out so. . .so stern, but yes. Us. The truth is, I care about you as a woman, and a friend, but I've come to realize that I care about you in a far deeper way, as well. I know we're past the age most people think about falling in love, but that's just it. I love being with you. And I've fallen in love with you. In spite of the craziness of this week, I've been happy because I'm with you."

Her eyes widened, but he'd gotten this far and there was no turning back now. "I'm sure this comes as a bit of a surprise, and I'm not asking for you to say anything you're not ready to, but if you've ever considered the idea of something developing between us, even for a moment, then. . .well, just think about it."

Pricilla was certain her heart was going to explode. Had he just declared his intentions toward her? For a moment she didn't think she was going to be able to take another breath.

Max Summers loved her.

He loved her?

She gulped in a deep breath of air and took in the woodsy scent of his cologne. Shaking her head, she tried to pull her thoughts together. She'd never thought about Max romantically. Or had she? It was true that she'd been affected by the same bright blue eyes that stared at her right now. And if she was honest with herself, her pulse had fluttered a time or two, and her heart had pounded at least once at his dimpled grin. Then there had been the embarrassing scene with Misty when she'd believed that the young woman had her sights set on Max—

Pricilla had convinced herself that there weren't feelings of interest on her part, but because they were in the middle of a murder investigation, everything had been knocked off kilter. Could her reactions be proof that she felt something deeper as well?

Max's face turned a pale shade of gray. "I didn't mean to be so abrupt, but I've waited long enough to tell you how I feel."

And she'd waited too long to respond. "You just. . .you just caught me off guard."

"Have you ever thought about something developing between us beyond the friendship we share?"

"I don't know. I—"

The waitress chose that moment to come take their order. Pricilla would have preferred for her and Max to leave so they could find a place to talk without any interruptions. His declaration had her mind spinning in opposite directions, but instead she settled on a toasted cheese sandwich and a side salad, hoping she'd still be able to eat when the food arrived.

Once the waitress had left, he grasped her hands and caught her gaze.

"I don't want to lose our friendship, Pricilla, but I'm not getting any younger. I want to take a chance to find happiness again. . .with you."

Her heart fluttered. If she were honest with herself, there was no one she enjoyed being around more. Max made her feel cherished and appreciated. Who said you have to be twenty to fall in love?

Love?

The word surprised her, but for the first time Pricilla realized that the comfortable relationship she had developed with Max throughout the years had turned into that very thing.

She was in love with Max. And he was in love with her.

The thought brought a smile to her lips. What that meant to their future, she had no idea, but for the moment, it didn't matter. "Do you remember when you caught me eavesdropping on you and Misty?"

He laughed. "It was a scene I'll likely never forget."

"I was jealous of Misty."

"What?"

Confessions of guilt weren't normally her forte, but for some reason it was important for him to know. "Misty is pretty, outgoing, half my age. . .and she was coming on to you."

"No, she wasn't."

Pricilla cocked her head and raised the pitch of her voice. "I'm looking for someone much more stable. Someone older who realizes—"

"All right." He shook his head and grinned. "Enough—"

"Someone like you, Max."

"I said enough." There was a twinkle in his eye. "So, I haven't taken you totally by surprise?"

"No, I am totally surprised, yet looking back, I think I've felt the same way for quite some time and never knew it."

He squeezed her hands, and she wondered what was in store for the two of them. Life had become comfortable, even predictable—barring the recent murder, of course—and the thought of something new on the horizon sent a shiver of excitement down her spine.

The waitress placed their orders in front of them. Pricilla stared at her plate. There was one thing she still had to ask him.

"What happens now?" She picked up her fork and pushed a piece of tomato around. "You're leaving in a couple of days, and I don't think either of us is ready to make a huge move at this point."

Max shrugged. "All I know is that the very questions you're probably asking yourself right now are the same questions that have kept me from telling you how I feel. And trust me, I've thought of all the reasons why a relationship between us won't work. We're too old, too set in our ways, live too many miles apart. . . Yet I'm convinced we can figure out a way to make this work."

"I know you're right."

He said a prayer for the food then dug into his meatloaf. "So, what is your theory?"

There was a look of contentment on his face, but she was still reeling over his statement and was having a hard time getting her mind focused back on lunch, let alone the Woodruff case. "My theory?"

"You said you had a theory."

Trying to settle her mind, she put the cloth napkin in her lap. What was her theory?

She chuckled. "It's not fair to take me completely off guard with thoughts of love and romance then ask me my theories on the murder investigation."

"Then how about we spend the rest of lunch without any mention of Claire, or the case?"

"Agreed."

Max reached out and squeezed Pricilla's hand. No matter what happened with the rest of the investigation, she knew one thing was certain. Life would never be the same again.

For the second time that day, Pricilla pulled the car into the gravel parking lot in front of the sheriff's office. A storm gathered in the distance, but for now, warm rays of sunshine still filtered through the darkening clouds above them, helping to lessen the sharp chill of the afternoon breeze. She turned off the car and glanced at Max.

He still carried himself as a commanding officer. Pressed shirt and slacks, military haircut, broad shoulders and upright posture that gave him an air of authority. . . Falling in love again had not been on her agenda. It was hard to imagine that so much had changed between them in such a short time.

She raised her head toward the glass doors of the building. Her interest in the Woodruff case had waned somewhat since Max's confession. Not that she wasn't still intent on finding out the truth, but her feelings toward Max had taken a sudden precedence, and she was having a hard time formulating exactly what she wanted to tell the sheriff. Formulating *any* of her thoughts for that matter.

Max opened his door and reached for the crutches. "Are you coming?"

"I think so." She pushed back an errant curl from the side of her face. "I'm still a little dazed from our conversation at lunch."

Part of her told her his confession of love had been nothing more than a figment of her imagination—but his nervous smile told her otherwise.

"I suppose it is a bit awkward." He pulled his door shut, stopping the sound of the howling wind. "That was one thing that made me hesitate to say anything to you sooner." His eyes darkened. "I've been worried that in telling you how I feel, I'd ruin our friendship—"

"No. It's not that at all." She tapped her hands against the steering wheel. Knowing what to say had rarely been a problem, but sitting beside him, discussing their relationship, left her feeling like a tongue-tied teenager. "You've awakened feelings I didn't know I had, and now I'm trying to untangle them all. Does that make any sense?"

Max chuckled. "Complete sense. But all we have to do is take things a day at a time and see what happens."

She nodded and opened her door, realizing that it was time now to see what would happen when she told the detective about the two little pills that might change the entire direction of the case. Something she was dreading to have to do, because she had a feeling that the detective wasn't going to be keen on her findings now that he thought the case had been wrapped up nicely like an early birthday present.

As Pricilla hurried into the building, letting Max hold the door for her, she felt the heat rise in her cheeks over his chivalrous action. Which was ridiculous. Max was a gentleman and always held the door for ladies. It was the realization that he was doing it for her as a part of a courting ritual that had her feeling tingly from head to toe.

Inside the sterile reception, she was disappointed to see Detective Carter standing behind the reception desk with no sign of the sheriff. On her way up the sidewalk, she'd decided that if at all possible she'd bypass the detective with her information, even though he'd been technically in charge of the case.

"Good afternoon again, Detective." She set her purse down. "Is the sheriff still in?"

"Nope. He'll be out the rest of the day." The detective picked up a folder then leaned against the desk with a sigh. "Is there something else you need, Mrs. Crumb? Visiting hours are over until Saturday."

"I'm not here to see Claire, but I suppose if the sheriff is gone, then I will need to speak to you." She swallowed her disappointment. "It's regarding the Woodruff case."

"Of course." His stern expression made it perfectly clear that he wasn't pleased with the interruption. "Mrs. Crumb, if you've forgotten, the initial investigation will more than likely be officially closed by the end of the day. Then Mrs. Woodruff will be arraigned and her preliminary hearing date set."

Pricilla gnawed on the edge of her lip. "I don't know how to say this, other to come straight out and tell you. I don't believe Mrs. Woodruff killed her husband."

"Mrs. Crumb"—the detective folded his arms across his chest and shook his head—"I realize that you have been playing the part of an investigator during this case, and that's fine for fiction and the movies, but this is real life. And in real life, it's the law that handles cases like Mrs. Woodruff's. Not a novice detective like yourself."

Pricilla felt her blood pressure rise as she fought to control her growing temper. "Detective Carter, I resent your implications that I—"

Max leaned over and nudged her gently. His reminders were becoming far too frequent, though even she admitted to the fact that she needed someone to keep her in line when it came to the balding detective.

She decided to start again. "Will you just let me explain?"

He glanced at his watch. "You have exactly one minute."

Pricilla frowned, but her determination didn't waiver. She set the bag of pills on the counter, and told him step-by-step what she'd discovered both at the lodge and from Claire this morning.

"So, if these were the pills Claire was using to poison her husband, and they're nothing more than water pills, the conclusion is quite obvious. Claire Woodruff might have intended to dispose of Charles, but what she gave him was harmless."

The detective stared at her, his arms still crossed until she finished. "And that's it?"

"That's what?"

"Did you consider that fact that Mrs. Woodruff is used to living life among the upper class? She probably has a large home, expensive cars, and all the similar trappings of money. But murder is a serious crime, and she's intelligent enough to try and find a way out." He leaned forward, resting his hands against the desk. "Confession might relieve the soul, but when the reality of what she's done begins to sink in, I'm not surprised at all at her attempts to get you on her side with this. . .this concocted plan to set a guilty woman free."

"Excuse me?" Pricilla's eyes widened. "She didn't come to me with a concocted plan to get out of jail. The woman was genuinely surprised when I told her what I'd discovered."

The detective took a step back, obviously debating whether or not he should consider her story.

She, on the other hand, wasn't finished stating her case. "If I'm correct, then by your doing nothing, the real murderer could very well be running free tonight. I also know your uncle well enough to recognize that he will be quite impressed when he finds out that you followed through on a lead and ended up cracking the case and finding the real offender."

He shook his head. "What if you're wrong?"

She held his gaze. "What if I'm right?"

She'd hit a nerve with the detective, she could tell. He took the pills and dropped them into an envelope. "We have the rest of the contents from their room at the lodge, so it will only be a matter of time before we find any discrepancies, if there are indeed any to be found."

"Perhaps. But then again, perhaps not."

Max cleared his throat. "I think it's time we headed back to the lodge."

"I was just thinking the same thing." Pricilla nodded her head. "Good day, Detective Carter."

Pricilla waited until they were outside and out of earshot from the detective before she spoke again. "I can't imagine where that man got his manners. Certainly not from his uncle. At least we still have our list of possible suspects. Now it's up to us to set a trap for the murderer."

Max slid into the front seat of the car, trying to decipher Pricilla's last comment.

He'd hoped that by going to the sheriff's office and informing the detective of what they'd found out, she'd give up any ideas of pursuing a possible second murderer. He'd also hoped, if nothing else, that his confession over lunch would be a strong enough distraction to convince her to leave things alone. Now, he wasn't sure it was.

He glanced at her out of the corner of his eye as she drove down the main street of town. Past the *Rendezvous Sentinel*'s offices. Past the Starlight Theater, Allie's Antiques, and the Baker's Dozen, a bakery that threw in an extra item for every dozen you bought. Tourists loved the quaint, old-fashioned look of the town that boasted numerous bed and breakfasts and three nearby ski resorts. Up until now, the town of Rendezvous had also boasted of the fact that violent crime was virtually nonexistent. The thought that there was a murderer on the loose, who was staying at the lodge, no less, did little to ease his worry. All the more reason that the sheriff's office should handle things and not Pricilla, his self-appointed private investigator and novice detective.

She pulled onto the dirt road that headed out of town and toward the lodge. "You're awfully quiet."

"I've been thinking."

"So have I."

He frowned. "You're not seriously considering setting a trap to catch a murderer, Pricilla. Are you?"

"I still have a few details to work out, and I'm going to have to convince Nathan to call in a favor for me, but yes. I have a plan."

He forced himself to ask the question. "What is your plan?"

A smile tugged at the corners of her mouth. "Think about all the great literary detectives and how they pinned down the suspect. They all had a plan. A moment of truth when they forced a confession out of the suspect then pulled on the noose until the suspect had nowhere to run."

"And how do you expect to do this?"

"I had already planned dinner tonight to be a celebration. Everyone will be gathered together in the dining room, and just at the point when their appetites are satisfied, I'll stand and address the group."

Max winced as the bumpy road jostled the car and, in turn, his injured foot. Unfortunately, his foot wasn't his biggest concern at the moment. "So, you're planning the clichéd dinner party where the detective corners the murderer with his wit and intellectual brilliance."

"I wouldn't say it's a cliché."

"And I wouldn't say you're Sherlock Holmes."

His comment put a sour look on her face, but he didn't care. He wanted their relationship to have a happy ending—and it wasn't going to if she started accusing people of murder.

Pricilla pulled into the driveway of the lodge, knowing Max wasn't impressed with her idea. Maybe she was pushing things too far. She'd been lucky. . .or rather blessed. . .that nothing had happened to her during her informal interrogation of the suspects. But what could happen over beef burgundy and roasted vegetables, in a room full of people?

She parked the car and turned off the engine. "Are you mad at me?"

"For some reason, I've always had a hard time staying mad at you." As he gave her a lopsided grin, she felt a surge of relief shoot through her. "But that doesn't mean I'm ready for you to play the role of Sherlock Holmes."

"And why not, Dr. Watson? I've always thought we made a good team. And I promise not to do anything foolish."

His brows rose in question. "Is that something you can promise?"

"You have to admit that I've had at least one or two good ideas regarding the case so far."

He drew in a deep breath and let it out slowly. "You get Nathan's permission, and I'll back you up."

She smiled and got out of the car. There was something else to make her smile, as well. Nathan and Trisha sat on the porch together, enjoying the afternoon. She might not be certain what would happen between her and Max as far as their future, but she wouldn't be disappointed at all if wedding bells sounded in the future for their children, something that ranked far higher than solving the Woodruff case.

She sat down in a cushioned chair beside Max on the porch and addressed their children. "Hope you're enjoying the last of this weather. Looks like a storm will hit later this evening."

Trisha shivered and pulled her sweater around her shoulders. "The temperature has already begun to drop in the past thirty minutes, but I love watching the storms come in."

Nathan crossed his ankles and leaned back. "Where have the two of you been?"

Ignoring the twinkle in her son's eye, Pricilla glanced at Max. She'd tell Nathan later about what had happened in her own love life, but for now, they needed to deal with a much more serious matter.

"We've been at the sheriff's office," Pricilla began. "There have been some new developments in the case since last night, and there's a good chance that Claire didn't murder her husband."

"What?" Surprise marked Trisha's expression.

Briefly, Pricilla summarized the latest findings in the case.

When she was finished, Nathan shook his head. "You've got to be kidding. What does the detective say about all of this?"

Pricilla laughed. "He's skeptical, but I think he sees the merit in what I showed him."

Nathan slapped his hands against his thighs. "Just when I think the trouble's behind us, another threat pops up."

Pricilla smiled. She had hoped that the possible threat to the lodge would be motivation enough to get her son to agree to her idea. That last thing any of them wanted was for the lodge's reputation to be tarnished further. Solving the crime was the only way to guarantee that things would actually get back to normal.

"There's something else." She worked to keep her expression composed. "I need your help."

Nathan held up his hand. "Mom, I thought I told you to stay out of it. Let the detective do his job."

"All I'm planning is a simple dinner party. Everyone else will think it's a celebration of the Woodruff case being closed. If we can catch the real murderer off guard, we might be able to find out the truth."

"Sounds a bit old-fashioned, if you ask me. I mean, with DNA analysis and forensic science, I'm not sure I see the value in simply trying to catch the murderer off guard." Her son turned to Max. "Don't tell me you're going along with this?"

"I don't think you're going to talk her out of it."

Worried lines crossed Nathan's brow. "So you agree that bringing a group of suspects together, like the last chapter of a mystery novel, including a possible murderer, is a good idea? That with a few, well-planned-out words we can actually catch the person who killed Charles Woodruff?"

Pricilla fidgeted in her chair. Nathan was weakening. She could see it in his eyes.

"You know your mother." Max glanced in her direction and winked. "She tends to be quite persuasive."

"Yes, I do." Pricilla puckered her brow. They were doing it again. Talking as if she weren't there.

"And knowing you, Mother, the idea will probably work."

She leaned forward. "So you'll help?"

"I don't suppose we have anything to lose? Tell me what you need me to do."

Pricilla set the last silver spoon on the table then stood back to admire the effect. Tonight, she'd decided against the normal stoneware place settings and their rustic forest scenes and decided instead to use the formal white dishes with the gold rim. She ran her hand across the smooth mauve tablecloth and smiled. With the table set and a buffet ready, the truth of who really killed Charles Woodruff was about to be discovered.

Rain tapped against the windows as the temperature outdoors continued to drop. Shivering, she added two logs to the fire and watched as the yellow flames came back to life. The atmosphere was perfect. She dimmed the overhead lights, and the crystal glasses caught the golden reflection of the fireplace. A flash of lightning lit up the floor-to-ceiling windows. Seconds later, thunder rumbled in the distance.

She checked her watch. It was fifteen minutes before seven. She had included Oscar and Misty on the guest list, and while the invitation might seem a bit unorthodox with the case closed and a mood of celebration in the air, she was convinced that no one would mind. The ease of the buffet would make the dinner elegant, yet simple enough to ensure that everyone had a good time.

Lighting the three ivory candles that made up the centerpiece, she then blew out the match, inhaling the woodsy scent of the smoke. Everything was ready.

Max entered the room early, giving her the extra boost of confidence she needed for the rest of the evening. He looked stunning in a gray suit jacket and paisley tie, the perfect attire for a formal dinner party. Perfect enough for her heart to thud and her knees to quiver at the site of him and his gorgeous blue eyes.

But as they both knew, she had something far different than a social—or romantic—occasion in mind tonight. A rush of adrenalin surged through her. She felt like Jessica Fletcher on the brink of solving one of her cases. And if her theory was right, Pricilla would prove to Detective Carter that while she might be a novice, her intuition was rarely off track.

Granted, she didn't have the authority of a badge to back her up, but she'd followed the clues of the case and interviewed the suspects until she'd discovered a loose end in the detective's theory. Who said that this gray-haired retiree needed to stick to card games and knitting needles to fill her time? She was about to prove them all wrong.

Max popped a crouton from the sideboard into his mouth. "Are you ready for this?"

"I think so." She nodded and drew in a slow, calming breath. "Do you think I'm doing the right thing?"

He leaned into his crutches. "You're staking a lot on your convictions, but that's one of the things I admire about you the most. Your determination to stand up for justice, no matter what the cost."

Pricilla laughed. "You're making me seem far more noble than I feel. But you're right about one thing. While Claire might be guilty of intending to murder her husband, I honestly don't believe that she was the one who killed Charles. I just don't know if I can prove it."

"We will see, but hopefully, in the next hour or so, you'll be able to do just that."

Pricilla checked her watch and another wave of adrenalin shot through her. She tried to relax, but found it impossible. Ten more minutes. Then she'd either be able to prove her theory that Claire was innocent—or end up making a complete fool out of herself.

"Pricilla?"

She glanced up and realized she had missed something Max had said. "I'm sorry. I'm nervous."

"You don't have to go through with this—"

"No, I feel like I have to."

She rechecked the dishes on the sideboard to make sure she hadn't forgotten something from tonight's menu. It was simply the way she was. She couldn't stand for anything to be left undone. Solving Charles Woodruff's death was no different. Not finding out the truth at this point would be failure.

Convinced that everything was in order, she turned to Max. "Do you have any last minute theories?"

"Actually, I do." Max hobbled over to the fireplace and laid his crutches down before sitting on the stone hearth. "I spent a good hour online before coming down here, looking deeper into Simon and Anthony's failed business that Charles took over."

He had her full attention now. "And?"

"While I'm sure the detective has looked into the connection, I did find something very interesting. Simon's family owns a large orchard in western Colorado. They grow peaches, cherries, and have even started growing grapes in the past five years."

She lowered her brow, not yet following his theory. "So what's the connection?"

"Peach pits contain cyanide, and the leaves of certain cherry trees can also be highly poisonous—"

"And Detective Carter is certain that the final lab test will prove that Charles died of cyanide poisoning." Everything started to click together. Maybe she hadn't been that far off after all.

Max shrugged a shoulder. "Of course, I've also thought of the possibility that it's nothing more than a coincidence. From what I read online, it would take a lot of peach pits to kill a person."

"But if someone knew what they were doing—"

"True, but even the diuretic pills could be nothing more than a red herring. I still think that the most logical conclusion is that Claire is the guilty party."

Pricilla crossed the Oriental rug and stood in front of him. "Then let's pray that truth prevails tonight. I'm ready to put this behind me."

"I'm ready as well." He reached out and took her hands. "Mainly, because there are a lot of other things I'd rather be discussing with you than Charles Woodruff."

Pricilla felt a blush cross her cheeks. "For instance?"

"Like what the future holds for you and me."

Her pulse quickened. He was right. There were still a lot of things they needed to talk about. While preparing dinner, she had mulled over the obstacles standing between them and still hadn't come to any firm conclusions as to what might work. The barriers that had made him hesitate to talk to her about his feelings in the first place hadn't disappeared because she'd admitted she shared his feelings. There were genuine concerns that would have to be dealt with, because a long-distance relationship was never the best solution.

But she wasn't sure how to change that. He'd mentioned things like being old and stubborn as well as the distance between them. Max hated the cold Colorado winters, and she didn't fancy the New Mexico summers. Then there was the lodge and the job she hoped would become permanent. Nathan needed her, and she needed something to keep her busy. Whatever she and Max decided in the end, it would take a whole lot of compromise from both of them.

He rubbed the back of her hand with his thumb. "You're not having second thoughts are you? About us, I mean."

"No." She smiled, certain that any compromises on her part would be worth it. "But you are right about the fact that there are a few complications we will have to look at."

"In the meantime, I think we both need to subscribe to a cheap phone plan."

"And take out stock in the U.S. Post Office." Pricilla laughed. "Have you thought about extending your trip?"

His smile dissolved into a frown. "If I hadn't promised to coordinate one of our local children's Christmas-toy drives this year, I'd consider it, but don't worry. I'm planning to return here soon."

"I'm counting on it."

Pricilla pulled her hands away from Max as Nathan entered the room with Trisha. It was time to push any ideas of romance aside and remember that there was a far more serious matter to deal with at the moment.

One by one the guests entered the dining room. The murmur of conversation and sporadic laughter filtered throughout the room as they began to fill their plates. Pricilla smiled in anticipation. They had no idea that she had set a trap for Charles Woodruff's real murderer, and if everything went according to plan, there would be a second arrest made tonight—and the Woodruff case would *finally* be closed.

She served herself from the buffet then sat beside Max at the table. Eating slowly, she enjoyed the beef, the roasted vegetables, and rice pilaf—but her mind was elsewhere as she studied the guests. Anthony roared with amusement as he threw out the punch line of some hunting joke. His buddies, Simon and Michael, joined in the laughter. None of them looked as if they'd recently been involved in a deed as grim as murder. Instead, they were probably thinking about how relieved they were to be leaving in the morning for their long-awaited hunting trip.

Oscar, looking as if he felt out of place, chuckled at something Anthony said the far end of the table. Undoubtedly, he would prefer to be out tracking game rather than dressing in a button-down shirt and slacks to attend a formal dinner. Nathan and Trisha were deep in their own conversation and looked as if they'd forgotten that the rest of them were in the room. Even Misty seemed to be enjoying herself as she filled her plate with another helping of food.

At seven forty-five, the guests began to push back their plates, contented expressions on their faces. Satisfied that the timing was perfect, Pricilla tapped her glass and moved to stand behind her chair. Clearing her throat, she attempted to address the group formally, as Hercule Poirot might have done when wrapping up one of his own famous cases.

"Before dessert is served, I'd like to make an announcement." She gripped the curved back of the chair to steady her hands and ignored the annoyed expression Simon gave Anthony. "As we all know, the detective's original theory regarding the death of Charles Woodruff was a simple matter of marital indiscretions gone wrong, but several things that have occurred lately made me question that conclusion and realize that there were indeed several other factors involved."

Pricilla noted the puzzled looks that crossed the faces of her guests and beamed, gaining confidence as she continued to speak. "As we all know, Charles Woodruff was poisoned, but it seems that the case isn't as tied up as everyone once thought. In fact. . ." Pricilla paused for a moment for effect. "It is my belief that the real murderer is right here in this room."

Someone coughed.

Several squirmed in their chairs.

Pricilla kept smiling. It was the reaction she'd hoped for.

"There were plenty of motives among you," she continued, "but the question is, who of the guests, or workers, would stoop low enough for murder? Simon Wheeler and Anthony Mills hated Charles and the fact that he'd taken over their failing business, leaving them bankrupt and giving them both motive and opportunity for the crime. And while Michael hadn't been involved in the actual business dealings, he had invested heavily in the project."

Simon's face turned pale. Anthony gripped his napkin between his fingers like a vise. Michael shoved his chair back from the table. "You can't be serious, Mrs. Crumb. You're accusing us of murder?"

"Not yet. There is also the fact that Charles demanded he be given a new guide this year. For whatever reason, he couldn't stand Oscar." Pricilla watched the guide's jaw tense as her words began to sink in. "It was obvious that the rift between the two men ran deep. Deep enough for one to murder the other, perhaps? And I can't forget the fact that Misty knows far more about the guests than anyone might imagine. I've heard a few of her stories myself. Could something she overheard have led her to murder?"

Apparently, the shock of what she was suggesting had rendered them all speechless, including the real murderer who, up to this point, had thought that he, or she, was getting off scot-free. Now was the moment when she'd bring her rehearsed monologue to a close. With a few well-chosen words, she needed to give the impression that she knew without a doubt who had performed the dreadful deed.

She cleared her throat again and continued. "On the day following Claire's arrest, I discovered a vital clue that made me believe that while Claire might have *intended* to kill her husband, she wasn't the one who administered the final dose that took his life. That, of course, left us with the startling fact that someone other than the victim's wife, someone seated at this very table, was responsible for Charles's untimely demise. And with the evidence piling up, the identity of the antagonist began to take form."

No one moved. The room was silent except for the rain splattering against the widows and the occasional crackle of the fire in the stone hearth. Pricilla turned to each of the guests, one by one, until her gaze finally rested on Max who gave her a subtle smile of encouragement.

A clap of thunder shook the room.

A chair squeaked at the other end of the table. Misty shoved back her seat and let it crash to the floor. "Charles Woodruff paid me to be quiet over the fact that his wife was having an affair." She stumbled toward the door. "But I didn't have anything to do with his murder. I promise. I could never murder anyone."

Someone's fork clanked against the edge of a plate, but no one else spoke. No one else confessed. No one else moved.

Pricilla sat down, numb over the fact that her plan hadn't worked. This wasn't what she had envisioned. If Misty was telling the truth and Claire had been the one unfaithful to her husband, then she had the perfect motive to get Charles out of the picture. An uneasy feeling grew in her stomach. What if the detective had been right all along? What if Claire had somehow set up Pricilla, and, in turn, she had played into her hands?

But the woman couldn't have done that.

Or could she?

Others began to rise from the table.

The vein on Simon's neck pulsed as he stopped in front of her. "Your lunchtime interrogation was one thing, but to accuse one of us point blank of murder? This time you went too far."

Michael nodded. "Don't expect us to be back next year. Your little charade, the clichéd dinner party straight out of the pages of some dusty mystery novel, did you really think it would work?"

Anthony and Oscar said nothing as they walked past. But they didn't have to. Pricilla knew what they were thinking. She had gone too far this time. Those two tiny diuretic pills had ended up causing her a mountain of trouble and, worse, the loss of business for Nathan's lodge.

Max, Nathan, and Trisha stayed to help her pick up what remained of her dignity. Max squeezed Pricilla's shoulder, but even his touch did little to relieve her frustration.

She leaned her elbows against the table and shook her head. "I don't think I've ever been so embarrassed in my life. My grand finale, the clichéd dinner party, as everyone called it, was a total disaster."

"I did try to warn you, Mrs. Crumb." The detective stepped into the room, his ever-present notebook in hand. "There's no doubt in my mind Claire Woodruff killed her husband, and now it looks as if I have even further proof that the lab results will confirm."

Pricilla cringed. The balding officer had been right all along. Nathan had convinced Detective Carter to stand in the wings for the dramatic conclusion, and the confession from the murderer. So much for the theatrics of well-known TV detectives like Dr. Mark Sloan who never had a problem finding out the identity of the murderer.

"What about the person she was having an affair with?" Pricilla knew she was grasping at motives, but if there was any chance to save her self-respect, she'd take it. "We had four capable suspects sitting in this room who might have been involved, and Misty must know—"

"Be assured that while I'm quite certain that Misty's statement will only strengthen the district attorney's case against Mrs. Woodruff, I will follow up on the housekeeper's admission. But, Mrs. Crumb"—the detective shoved his notebook into his back pocket and caught her gaze—"I, as an officer of the law, must advise you to stop making any more attempts to play detective."

Nathan nodded. "He's right, Mom. You've done everything you could. Even I have to agree that it's time you let the sheriff wrap things up."

"I know." Pricilla stood up wishing she could disappear into the polished floorboards. "I think it's time for me to go to bed. All of you were right from the very beginning. I have no business playing the part of a detective. I'm a sixty-four-year-old retiree who needs to find a real hobby."

"Pricilla, you did your best—"

"Don't worry about me. I'm fine." She waved her hand at Max's attempt to comfort her and headed for the hallway.

"Mrs. Crumb?"

Pricilla stopped as Misty entered the room. The young housekeeper's face was wet with tears.

"I owe you all an apology." Misty glanced at the detective then back to Pricilla. "I didn't mean to cause such a scene, it was just. . .it was just that I was taken by surprise at your remarks, Mrs. Crumb."

"It doesn't matter now." Pricilla shrugged. "The detective will want to talk to you, I know, but I'm the one who should apologize for treating my son's guests as suspects when there was no solid evidence that anyone was guilty. Claire's affair is simply more proof that she's guilty."

"You might be right, but at least let me clear my conscience." Misty took a deep breath and wiped the tears off her cheeks. "What I did was wrong, and it's been bothering me for months. I blackmailed Charles over the fact that his wife was having an affair with Oscar—"

"With Oscar?" Pricilla froze at the name.

Maybe her theory wasn't so far off after all. Claire planned to poison her husband so she could be with Oscar, but if Oscar got impatient. . .

"You were right in what you said about me and my knowing things about the guests." Misty wrung her hands together as she continued, her words breaking into Pricilla's thoughts. "My job lets me find out a lot of things that I'm sure the guests don't want me to know about. Like Claire's affair for one. I never intended to blackmail Mr. Woodruff, but neither did I turn down his generous offer to keep quiet. He told me that her indiscretions might ruin his chances of gaining a political office, something he refused to let happen." She turned to Nathan. "And it isn't at all that I don't appreciate my salary, Mr. Crumb, but I have to think about my children's future, and—"

"We understand, Miss—" The detective cocked his head and waited for an answer.

"Majors. Misty Majors."

"Miss Majors. In the light of your confession, I'm afraid I'm going to have to insist that you come down to the station with me now so I can take a complete statement—"

"Wait a minute." Pricilla's mind was still reeling with Misty's news, but she wondered if she'd done enough damage for one night, or did she dare press the subject further?

"What is it, Mrs. Crumb?" The detective was not smiling.

A truck peeled out of the driveway, and Pricilla caught a glimpse of the dark pickup in the outside lights. The pieces of the puzzle were falling into place. Why hadn't she figured it out before? Shoving her shoulders back, she held her chin high. She had one last attempt to save her reputation.

She turned to the detective. "If Misty's telling the truth, then I believe that the real murderer, Oscar Philips, is making his escape."

Carter ran to the window and shoved back the curtains. Tires spun on the gravel outside the lodge then the pickup raced down the long driveway toward town. Pricilla stared out the darkened window from behind the detective, wondering if Oscar's reaction would prove to be yet another odd twist in the case, or something totally unrelated. She'd never liked Oscar, but that wasn't proof that he'd committed murder. Running from the scene of an investigation, unofficial or not, shined a whole new light on things. Either Oscar had something to hide—like murder—or he had a lot of explaining to do for taking off in such a huff.

The detective addressed Pricilla. "I'm not convinced you're right, Mrs. Crumb, but I'm also not going to take any chances. I'm putting an APB out on Mr. Philips and going after him myself."

Without another word, the detective strode toward the front door and let himself out.

"I'm in shock." Pricilla crossed the room and stared out the window as the detective turned on his lights and sped away from the lodge. "Oscar was never at the top of my list of suspects, though I suppose now he should have been. I'm just having a hard time picturing Claire and Oscar together. What a mess."

Nathan leaned against the back of one of the chairs. "A very tangled mess."

"Now I feel doubly guilty that I didn't speak up sooner. . .and because of my children, guilty that I did."

A look of fear shot across Misty's face. She sucked in a deep breath and started to hyperventilate. Trisha crossed to the fireplace where Misty stood and put an arm around the woman.

Pricilla fingered the jacquard striped drapery, not feeling quite as sympathetic. "Knowing what you just told us would have tied Claire to Oscar, which would have given him a stronger motive from the beginning."

"And would have explained why Charles was so opposed to Oscar leading the hunt," Nathan added.

"I'm sorry I didn't speak up. I know you're right." Misty leaned back against the stone hearth and sobbed. "The detective's going to arrest me, isn't he? What about my children—"

"I don't know if he'll arrest you." Pricilla laced her fingers behind her back. A part of her did feel sorry for the woman, but withholding evidence had its own consequences. "Since the man you were blackmailing is dead, I don't see why anyone would press charges. And besides, from what you said, it seemed more like he was paying you off rather than you truly blackmailing him."

"I never meant to get involved." Misty wiped her face with her sleeve and headed toward the table. "I'm going to clean up. If the detective returns, you can tell him I'll be in my cabin."

"It looks as if I owe you an apology, Mom," Nathan said as Misty started clearing the table. "Time will tell for certain if you were right, but if I was a betting man, I'd stake my lodge on the fact that Oscar is guilty."

"I agree, but we'll have to wait to find out for sure. While the dinner party didn't bring about the confession I'd hoped for, maybe this is the next best thing." Pricilla shook her head. "In the meantime, I'll make some more coffee. I know I won't be able to get to sleep for a long time."

"I'll help." Trisha followed Pricilla into the kitchen while the men moved into the living room to talk. "I thought the case was closed with Claire's arrest, and now Oscar is mixed up in the whole thing? I just don't get it."

Pricilla pulled a fresh bag of cinnamon hazelnut coffee from the cupboard. "I don't have all the answers at this point, only that Claire definitely wasn't the only one involved. Tonight proved that."

"How about a more pleasant topic for now?" Trisha began filling a wicker tray with coffee mugs. "Tell me what's going on between you and Dad. I can't get over the way he looks at you."

Pricilla felt the heat in her cheeks. Had it really been that obvious? No matter, she knew she deserved the nosy question. She'd certainly asked her fair share of interfering questions in her time, most recently with her attempts to play matchmaker between Trisha and Nathan.

"Is that the motive behind your offer to help?" Pricilla stifled a laugh as she filled the coffee carafe with fresh water. "A chance to find out about me and Max?"

"Not fair." Trisha laughed as she pulled out a stack of saucers and added it to the tray. "But I do admit I've been dying to ask you."

This time Pricilla didn't try to stop the laughter from bubbling out. Not only was laughter a huge relief after the stress of the evening, but she wasn't sure she could suppress her feelings regarding Max any longer.

Pricilla poured the grounds into the filter. "Romance is definitely a more pleasant subject than murder."

"Definitely." Trisha shivered and started setting mugs on a tray. "You don't mind my asking, do you?"

"No. The way I keep secrets, or shall I say the way I don't keep secrets, you were bound to find out sooner rather than later."

"So—" Trisha stopped and faced her.

Pricilla paused. Up until this point, she'd spent the past six hours pondering Max's lunchtime declaration and its consequences. Saying it aloud would make it seem real. Like there was no turning back. Like her life had just changed forever.

Pricilla cleared her throat. "Your father took me out to lunch today, and he brought up the possibility of our relationship growing into something. . . something other than friendship."

"I knew it!" Trisha leaned against the counter and beamed. "And your feelings?"

"I realized that what I felt for him had already begun to change to something beyond friendship, but I hadn't let myself see it."

"And what about the fact that he lives over two hundred miles away?"

Pricilla frowned at the reminder. She wanted to spend the next few days reveling in the fact that Max loved her, not worrying about tomorrow. The Bible was right when it taught that each day had enough trouble of its own. The last few days had certainly had their share.

"I could ask you the same question," Pricilla began. "What about you and Nathan?"

Trisha busied herself with filling the tray with mugs, sugar, and cream.

Pricilla wondered if she'd overstepped her place. "I'm sorry—"

"No." A smile tugged at Trisha's lips. "It's just that I never expected to fall in. . .well, to fall for anyone. Not this quickly anyway."

Pricilla smiled. She'd known from the moment she'd met Marty that he was the one for her, so love at first sight didn't surprise her at all. In her own situation, it might have taken longer with Max for her to discover her true feelings, but she also knew that true love was worth waiting for.

"Sometimes," Pricilla began, "God's timing surprises us, but if we're in His will, it's always right."

Trisha nodded. "That's exactly how I feel. Like this is God's timing and it's right."

"I just wish all of us lived closer together. I'm not sure I'm up to a long-distance relationship."

Trisha let the pile of teaspoons clank together. "I know that things have moved fast—maybe too fast—between Nathan and me, but I'm thinking about moving to Rendezvous. It would give us a chance to see if things might really work out between us."

Now Pricilla was the one beaming. "I think that's fantastic."

"Really?"

Pricilla squeezed Trisha's hand. "You don't have to seek my approval.

You've already got it."

"Thank you." Trisha folded her arms across her chest and faced Pricilla. "I've been building up my online clients for the past year and had planned to quit my day job in the next few months. I could find a small place in town. Neither of us wants to deal with a long-distance relationship. If nothing else, a move like this would give me the push I need to take my graphic design skills to the next level."

Pricilla watched Trisha's animated expression light up her face, and a twinge of reservation swept over her. Trisha was ready to change her entire life for a possible relationship with Nathan. Pricilla wasn't sure she herself was so flexible. How long would it take for her and Max to figure things out between them? How long did it take to adjust to the idea of falling in love the second time around?

The phone on the kitchen wall rang, and Pricilla's heart thudded. All of that was going to have to wait for now because at the moment, there was a far more pressing question at hand. One she hoped to have an answer to tonight. Was Oscar Philips the man guilty of poisoning Charles Woodruff?

While the detective's admission didn't come easily, at eleven o'clock the next morning, he admitted to Pricilla that her theory had been correct. Nathan, busy updating the lodge's Web site and getting a statement ready for the reporters' calls that he knew would be coming, insisted she be the one to announce the authorities' findings to the guests.

Max handed her a mug of black coffee as the guests, along with Misty, filed into the living room. "So you get to play the role of Columbo after all. The brilliant detective whose final monologue lets everyone know, for certain this time, whodunit."

"Except this time the murderer won't be here." She chuckled, warming her hands on the mug with a sigh of relief. No one could be happier than she was that this ordeal was over.

Last night's rain had turned into snow sometime during the night, covering the ground with the white powder that had, in turn, melted this morning, leaving a slushy mess and temperatures that hovered just above freezing. But even the bad weather couldn't dampen her spirits. Oscar was in jail, and the case against him was as solid as the thick wooden beams above her.

"I don't think the detective is quite as thrilled with my sharing the public details of the case as the sheriff is."

Max squeezed her hand. "You deserve it."

She took a sip of the hot drink and watched as Misty slipped into a padded rocker. The normally extroverted housekeeper appeared subdued after spending the morning talking with Detective Carter. She'd obviously learned a thing or two about the merits of minding one's business in her line of work.

Simon, Anthony, and Michael, on the other hand, were full of smiles as they marched into the room and took a seat along the leather couch. While this year's holiday might not have ranked high on their list of top vacations, Nathan's offer to give them a complementary week at the lodge with their spouses, including a four-day hunting trip into the mountains, had obviously soothed their spirits.

Pricilla set her cup down and smoothed the front of her slacks. She made her way to the center of the room, where Detective Carter had addressed them a mere three days ago. It was hard to believe how much had changed in such a short span of time. A man was dead, and the lives of two others destroyed. And in a complete opposite turn of events, she was looking at a future with Max. The thought made her smile and gave her the extra boost of confidence she needed.

The low murmurs in the room silenced as she clasped her hands in front of her. "First of all, I want to apologize to all of you for last night's dinner. I may have seemed a bit overconfident. I'm sorry for contriving the scene. However, it may not have turned out exactly as I intended but in the end, instead of a confession to murder, Oscar was stopped last night a few miles outside of Rendezvous and taken into the sheriff's office for questioning. As the detective explained to me, it didn't take long for the pieces of the puzzle to finally come together and, while there are certainly a few loose ends that will be tied up in the next few days, the sheriff suggested that an update for those involved would be well received."

The fire crackled behind her as she took a step forward onto the multicolored braided rug. "Apparently, when Oscar discovered that Misty knew about his affair with Claire—not to mention the fact that his deed had been announced to the entire group—he panicked, knowing it wouldn't be long until he was tied to the murder of Charles. Though Oscar wasn't at the top of my suspect list, looking back, there were plenty of clues along the way. He mentioned his poor family, and I caught hints of bitterness in his expression as the wealthy dined and vacationed yearly in the lodge. He, in turn, spent his days cleaning the barns and looking after those who never gave him a second glance. The rich wife of one of the guests turned out to be the perfect target.

"Claire only told part of the truth when she mentioned her husband's indiscretions and left out some important details regarding her own. More than likely, Oscar had tried to convince Claire to leave her husband for him in order to gain control of her fortune. When that didn't work, he convinced her to do something more drastic—murder. He must have had an incredible hold on her, but Charles also hadn't been the greatest husband, so Claire was vulnerable. Her attempts to murder her husband, though, didn't work. Instead of poisoning him slowly, the pills she bought turned out to be nothing more than a mild diuretic. With Charles still alive, Oscar got impatient and, blinded by greed, decided to take things into his own hands. He believed that not only would the two of them get away with the deed, but that he'd be set up financially for life."

Pricilla paused in her monologue. "There were other clues. Questions as to why Charles fought with Nathan over the guide. When Charles found out that Oscar would be leading the hunting party, he wanted nothing to do with the man. And knowing his wife was having an affair with the guide was a compelling reason."

She glanced at Misty who was staring at the floor. "Misty's involvement was accidental. When, during last year's hunting trip, Charles found out from Misty that his wife was having an affair with Oscar, he was willing to pay whatever it would take to keep the affair a secret. A divorce would ruin him financially since he'd married Claire for her money, and as a man wanting to go into politics, the affair wouldn't ride well either. There were other things that raised questions throughout the investigation—like the fact that Claire's shoes had been covered with mud from the barn, pointing to the fact that she'd been there to see Oscar.

"The most convincing evidence found so far among Oscar's things was the poison that, in the preliminary testing, matches a substance in the tea Charles drank with my tartlets—a high dose of cyanide extracted from cherry tree leaves. According to the sheriff's investigation, Claire decided to break things off with Oscar after Charles's death because she couldn't stand the guilt in thinking she had killed her husband. Oscar had even been the one to turn up the oven that set off the fire alarm in a desperate attempt to distract everyone so he could talk to Claire.

"And lastly, there are other details of the case, undoubtedly, that won't be released until the trial, but any questions you might have can be addressed to the detective, whom I'd like to thank for following up on my theory despite the fact that he wasn't convinced I was anywhere near the truth."

Pricilla sat down exhausted but relieved that the murder of Charles Woodruff had finally been solved. What Claire did was wrong, and she would still have to deal with the consequences of her actions, but Pricilla promised herself that she would continue to pray that one day Claire would understand the truth that God is good, and that He could forgive her. Perhaps with some help, one day she'd be able to make something of her life again. And the same, she hoped, would be true for Misty as well.

Max ignored everyone else in the room and joined Pricilla on the cushioned love seat, appropriate, she thought, for what she was feeling at the moment.

"I'm proud of you." He ran his thumb down her cheek and smiled. "And now, what do you say we forget about Jessica Fletcher and Columbo and Sherlock Holmes and Dr. Watson and concentrate on us?"

She nodded as he leaned in and kissed her gently on the lips. The newness of his touch left her heart reeling, convincing her that a second chance on love was something worth pursuing.

"I'd like to make a toast—to my mother," Nathan announced to the group, raising his cup of coffee in the air. "For sticking to your convictions, following the evidence, and for being the best novice detective I've ever met."

"Here, here."

"Well done."

She felt the heat rising in her cheeks, something that had been happening far too often lately, and decided that there was only one thing left to say. "Anyone ready for a thick slice of my lemon crumb cake?"

Pricilla Crumb's Recipe for Lemon Crumb Cake

Cake:
3 cups flour
3 teaspoons baking powder
¼ teaspoon salt
1 ½ cups butter, softened
3 large eggs + 1 egg white
1 ½ cups sour cream
1 ½ teaspoons lemon zest

Crumb Mixture Filling:
1 cup flour
½ cup brown sugar, packed
½ teaspoon cinnamon
¼ teaspoon nutmeg
⅓ cup butter, softened

Heat oven to 375°. Coat a 13 x 9-inch baking pan with nonstick cooking spray. Set aside. To prepare the cake, combine flour, baking powder, salt, and butter. Beat on low speed for 30 seconds. Continue beating, adding one large egg at a time, then egg white, sour cream, and lemon zest. Beat another two minutes on medium high.

In a separate bowl, prepare crumb mixture filling by whisking together flour, brown sugar, cinnamon, and nutmeg. Stir in butter until mixture is moistened and starts to stick together.

Pour half of batter into prepared baking pan. Sprinkle crumb mixture filling evenly across the top then cover with remaining cake batter, careful not to mix the filling into the batter. Bake for 30-35 minutes, or until done. Cool completely on a wire rack.

Frosting:
8 ounces cream cheese, softened
¾ cup unsalted butter, softened
2 cups powdered sugar, sifted before measuring
¼ cup heavy cream
⅓ cup lemon curd

With an electric mixer, blend together: cream cheese, butter, sugar, cream, and lemon curd. When cake is completely cooled, frost and enjoy!

BAKER'S FATAL DOZEN

Dedication:

A big thanks to Susan, Lynette, Rhonda, and Darlene. I'd be lost without your honest critiques. And to my mom. Thanks for always being there for me.

Pricilla Crumb snatched a pile of envelopes from the mailbox and shivered in the chilly May breeze. A letter from Max Summers rested on top. She sighed in frustration. She'd come to the conclusion that a long-distance relationship was no different than the *Titanic* on that fateful night it struck an iceberg. Both were poised for inevitable disaster. That, in her mind, described her relationship with Max Summers. Seven months ago they decided to try to move beyond their thirty-year friendship and give love a chance. After being married to her first husband for over four decades before he died, Pricilla had come to believe that life didn't give second chances when it came to true love. Max had changed all of that—for a while anyway.

Making her way up the front steps of her son's two-story hunting lodge, she shoved the stack of correspondence under her arm then ripped open the red envelope that had Max's return address on the front. Yanking out the birthday card, she eyed the picture of a cake and a plump baby staring back at her.

Pricilla sat down on one of the padded wicker rocking chairs on the porch and read the card. "To another sixty-five years of feeling young at heart."

While the sentiment was appreciated, turning sixty-five had never felt quite so. . .well, so old. She could tolerate the blood pressure pills and the occasional Metamucil. It was the glance in the mirror this morning that had reminded her that while she might still feel young at heart, her body had decided to grow old without her. Not that she wanted to return to the age of high heels and miniskirts. Not at all. But an occasional day without having to wear bifocals would be nice or, at the very least, being able to remember where she put them.

And it wasn't as if she didn't appreciate the card either, because she did. The same as she looked forward to her biweekly phone calls with Max. The problem was that their relationship had hit a slump of predictability. They'd both decided that at some point, if they wanted their relationship to continue, they'd have to figure out a way to shorten the miles between them. But that meant one, or both, of them would have to move. And neither of them, it seemed, was ready to make the transition.

Max, who wasn't fond of the cold Colorado winters, dreaded the idea of giving up the warmer climate of New Mexico. Pricilla's temporary job of cooking for her son's lodge had saved her from the mundane routine of retirement and was currently in a state of semi-permanence, something she was quite happy about. Cooking had been her passion since she won the first annual Rocky Mountain Amateur Chef Competition thirty-five years ago, before she'd moved to Seattle and started teaching at the Willow Hill Private Academy for Girls.

She flipped the card back open and read the last sentence again. *Try to stay out of trouble until I see you again! Love, Max.*

Pricilla chuckled, realizing exactly what he was implying, but he had no need to worry as she had no plans to get involved in another whodunit. Frankly, her experience in helping to solve Charles Woodruff's murder left her believing that crime solving really should be left to the authorities (with the exception of Detective Raymond Carter), and that her ability to solve the case was nothing more than a coincidence.

Penelope, her Persian cat, jumped up on her lap and yawned, as her son Nathan clambered up the porch steps in his work boots.

"Good morning, Nathan."

"Good morning, Mom." He plopped down beside her then rested his boots on another chair.

Even at seven in the morning, she knew he'd been up for hours, making sure things at the lodge were ready for another day. With three newly hired trail guides, Rendezvous Hunting Lodge and Resort offered everything from horseback riding to fishing to hiking, and had become one of the premiere places to vacation in the mountains of Colorado.

Nathan took in a deep breath then lay back against the padded headrest. "Don't tell me you're making cinnamon rolls for breakfast."

"Complete with cream cheese frosting." She knew he couldn't resist her breakfast specialty. "It was a request from one of your guests."

Pricilla glanced at her watch. They still needed another ten minutes to bake, but already the sweet scent of the baking rolls wafted out the front door, and her stomach rumbled.

"Maybe I need to put in a few more special requests." Nathan was six feet two and, since childhood, had never seemed to get his fill of food. "I don't remember the last time you made some of those gooey rolls for me."

"You'd better watch what you're saying."She handed him the mail, keeping Max's card for herself. "If I'm not spoiling you, Trisha is."

"I am a lucky man, then." Nathan glanced at the card she held. "A card from Max?"

"Yes."

"How is he?"

She tapped the envelope against the palm of her hand. "He's doing well. I'll tell him you asked next time he calls."

"Tell him he missed the birthday party I threw for you last night—"

"Nathan, that's not exactly fair."

Her son tended to be overly protective of her, something that amused her greatly, considering she remembered the exact complaint coming from his mouth as an independent teenager. Besides, Max had planned to fly up for her birthday until two old buddies invited him to go on a fishing trip to Lake Pleasant. She'd insisted he join them, and after hesitating, he promised to fly up to Rendezvous in a couple weeks to see her.

Nathan's frown made it clear how he felt. He never could keep his feelings to himself. "I just don't think that phone calls are good enough. I've never believed in long-distance relationships."

"People do it all the time."

He started flipping through the mail, his frown still in place. "Why don't the two of you make the move? Trisha was hesitant about moving to Colorado, but she loves living here now."

No matter where she and Max were in their relationship, Pricilla was certain she'd been right on track when she decided to put her matchmaking skills to the test between Nathan and Trisha, who also happened to be Max's only daughter. Sparks between them had ignited the moment they met, and she was convinced that Trisha was the perfect antidote to her son's once lonely heart. The girl was not only beautiful with her highlighted hair that accented her skin tone to perfection, she was also smart, efficient, and—

"Why doesn't Max make the move?"

Now Pricilla was the one to frown. "Moving when you're thirty is one thing. Once you get to be our age, moving from the couch to the bedroom can become an ordeal."

"And that's coming from the woman who's making my lodge a success with her gourmet three-course meals and to-die-for cinnamon rolls?" Nathan laughed. "What is it you're worried about this morning, Mom? Your birthday? You might have just turned sixty-five, but you're hardly ready for the geriatrics' ward."

"I never said I was. But every May twelfth I turn another year older. While it's not exactly something new for me, I do have to deal with the fact that my body's aging faster than my mind."

She patted the back of her hair, as if it were a case in point, and made a mental note to make an appointment at Iris's Beauty Salon for tomorrow afternoon. It was time for another perm, and maybe she'd do something different this time. She could have it colored black or maybe burgundy. . . .

It was time to get the focus of the conversation away from her and Max. "So when are you going to ask Trisha to marry you?"

"When the time is right." He leaned forward as if he were afraid Trisha would hear him despite the fact that she was a dozen miles away in her condo in the mountainous town of Rendezvous. "I bought the ring."

"That's a good first step." At least one person in their family was making progress in a relationship. "Now you have to ask her."

"I'm just waiting for the perfect moment."

Pricilla stopped rocking. Maybe that was the problem with her and Max. Maybe they were waiting for the perfect moment for everything to fall together. Something told her, though, that the perfect moment would never come unless they made it happen.

After her first husband, Marty, died, she'd eventually found the strength to be grateful that the good Lord had lent him to her for over forty years. Still, while she'd never admitted even to Max that she was lonely, it was hard not to wonder at times what it would be like to share her life with him on a day-to-day basis.

Three hours later Pricilla headed into the small town of Rendezvous. With breakfast over and Misty, who'd moved up from housekeeper to Pricilla's full-time kitchen assistant, finishing the cleanup, Pricilla had time to pick up a few things in town for tonight's dinner. She'd already prepared ten sack lunches for those going on a day hike with one of the guides, so no one should need her until dinnertime.

While she sometimes missed the bustle of Seattle and its conveniences, she'd grown up in the Colorado Mountains and loved being back. She'd also gotten to know the owner of the local grocery store, who now went out of his way to order for her whatever she needed. Her menu choices had never been ordinary. Her favorite pastime was experimenting with everything from hors d'oeuvres like stuffed eggs and salmon-filled tartlets (which had almost gotten her arrested once), to spectacular desserts like caramel custard with flaming peaches or her famed lemon crumb cake.

Today, though, she had only one stop to make. The Baker's Dozen carried the best pastries and fresh bread from here to Denver, and while she couldn't say she particularly liked the proprietor, Reggie Pierce, and his overbearing ways, his cream fillings, in particular, were divine. And buying his fresh baguettes and sourdough loaves certainly saved her time in the kitchen.

Pricilla parked the car in front of the shop and breathed in the fresh mountain air as she stepped out of her car. Normally, with spring officially here, Rendezvous' population, which hovered just under three thousand, would drop slightly until the snows came again, but today, despite the fact that ski season was over, the streets still bustled with a few remaining tourists.

The bell on the door jingled as she went inside the bakery and caught the aroma of fresh yeast bread. A large glass case displayed every pastry imaginable. The Baker's Dozen had become quite popular with not only the town and its tourists, but across the nation through its new Internet and mail order service. While Pricilla might know nothing about computers or how to use the Internet, Reggie's wife, her good friend Annabelle, had told her that Reggie predicted that their online business would soon surpass local sales in the shop.

Pricilla stood at the counter, wondering why there was no one in the room to help her. Normally, Reggie enjoyed running the front room himself, but today the only noise was the whirl of the ceiling fans above her. She tapped her fingers on the glass case and studied today's selection. While she preferred making her own desserts, the Italian shortbread cookies looked scrumptious. If nothing else, she would order half a dozen for herself. Of course if she ordered a dozen, Reggie would throw in one more for free. . . .

Pricilla frowned, wishing the counter had a bell she could ring for faster service. While most of tonight's dinner was already in the final stages of preparation, that didn't mean she had time to dawdle in town.

"Reggie? Hello?"

She glanced back at the door and noted that the CLOSED sign that hung on the glass was facing her. The shop should be open. She slipped behind the counter and through a small back room until she was standing outside on a tiled patio.

"Reggie—?"

That's when she saw him.

Pricilla couldn't breathe. Her stomach clenched. Reggie Pierce lay on the tiled patio with a large vase smashed to pieces around his head, his face colorless with no signs of movement. Reggie Pierce was—at least in Pricilla's mind—dead.

2

Pricilla took a step back from the body. There was no doubt about it. Reggie Pierce was dead.

She squeezed her eyes shut. It was happening again. A mere seven months ago she'd seen Charles Woodruff's lifeless body slumped in a wing-back chair beside one of the fireplaces at the lodge. Charles Woodruff's death had been enough to leave her on edge, and now a second dead body. . . Maybe if she concentrated hard enough she would be able to wake up and all of this would be nothing more than a bad dream. She counted to five then opened her eyes again.

Reggie still lay in the same spot.

She struggled to take a deep breath and wondered where the nearest phone was. Sheriff Tucker would have to be informed immediately. Pricilla leaned down and picked up a jagged piece from the broken terra cotta pot before looking up at the overhead balcony that led from the Pierce residence. Could one of the pots have simply fallen off the edge of the balcony, or had this been a deliberate act of murder?

Heels clicked on the tile behind Pricilla, and she turned around to see who was there.

"Reggie?" Annabelle Pierce, Reggie's wife, stopped halfway across the patio, her hands covering her mouth.

O Lord, please give me the right words.

"I'm so sorry, Annabelle. I'm afraid Reggie is. . .he's dead." Pricilla closed the distance between them, wishing there were a way to undo what had happened. But there wasn't, and right now all she knew to do was keep a line of prayer open and continue to ask God for wisdom.

Annabelle leaned over the lifeless body of her husband, her chest heaving with emotion. "What happened?"

Pricilla shook her head. "I don't know exactly, but it seems that a pot fell from the balcony. We need to call—"

"911." Annabelle fumbled, trying to open her crocheted handbag, then dropped it, scattering the contents across the stone flooring. She fell to her knees. "If we hurry, maybe they can do something—"

"It's too late." Pricilla bent over Annabelle's slender form and tried to steady the sobbing woman.

Instead of being comforted, Annabelle feverishly started grabbing tubes of lipstick, tissues, and an assortment of other items and began shoving them back into her purse.

Pricilla picked up the cell phone that had slidden behind a potted plant and punched in 911. Annabelle certainly wasn't in the right frame of mind to make the call. When the phone failed to ring, she checked the face of the phone.

The battery was dead.

"Where are all the employees?" Pricilla asked. While she needed a phone, the last thing they needed was a bunch of people stumbling onto the outdoor patio and making a mess of the scene in case Reggie's death had been a crime.

"In the staff room." Annabelle's breaths came in ragged spurts. "Reggie had called a meeting, but when he didn't show up. . ."

"You came to look for him?"

Annabelle nodded her head.

"Mrs. Pierce, I. . ."A young man who looked to be in his late twenties stopped short at the edge of the patio. "What in the world. . . ?"

Pricilla stepped forward. "Mr. . . ."

"Robinson. Darren Robinson." The man pushed his thick glasses up the bridge of his nose. "I'm one of Mr. Pierce's employees."

"Darren, I'm Pricilla Crumb. As you can see, Mr. Pierce has. . .well. . .been involved in an unfortunate accident."

"The sheriff?" Darren walked toward the body. "Has he been called?"

"The battery's dead," Pricilla said, holding up Annabelle's phone. "And please, don't touch anything. The authorities will need to investigate the scene."

"Of course." Darren slipped a cell phone out of his pocket and turned to face her. "I'll make the call."

Annabelle stood and grabbed Pricilla's forearm. "Ezri and Stewart just returned from the university. They can't see their father like this. . . ."

"I just left them in the staff room," Darren said.

Pricilla nodded, knowing it was up to her to keep everyone calm until the authorities arrived. "Darren, would you please bring Ezri and Stewart into the front bakery where we will wait for the sheriff? You also might lock that side door and let the other employees know what has happened."

"Certainly," he said with the phone to his ear.

With the rest of the employees taken care of for now, Pricilla led Annabelle into the shop, where she obediently sat on one of the wooden benches that lined the front windows. Pricilla flipped the sign in the window to CLOSED then took a seat beside the distraught woman. Everywhere she looked there were pastries, fresh baguettes, and donuts. The once-pleasing aroma of sweets that filled the room now made her stomach churn.

Her mind raced with the implications of what had just transpired. "Who was supposed to be minding the store?"

"I don't know." Annabelle stared at the busy pattern of the tiled floor. "Monday staff meetings were common. Reggie normally assigned someone to stay out front while we met. I never heard anything. How could I have missed it?"

"So you didn't hear a crash?"

Annabelle shook her head. "I don't know what I'm going to do now. And Ezri and Stewart. I'd looked forward to your meeting them, but now. . ."

Pricilla reached out and squeezed Annabelle's hand, wishing she were better at finding words of comfort. Annabelle had become a regular visitor at the lodge, coming to have tea at least once a week with Pricilla. But despite their newfound friendship, there were just certain things that one could never prepare for, and this was certainly one of them.

Pricilla wished she had her notebook. While she was no expert on the intricacies of solving a case, she had been successful in catching Charles Woodruff's murderer and in the process had learned a thing or two. There was no doubt that because of their friendship, Annabelle would tell her things that she would never mention to the sheriff

Ezri and Stewart entered from the front of the shop. Introductions were brief. As they sat on either side of their mother and waited silently for the sheriff, Pricilla tried to remember what Annabelle had told her about her children.

Stewart was twenty years old and, according to his mother, lazy. He looked so much like his father with his dark hair and eyes that Pricilla couldn't help but wonder if he took after his father in other ways as well—like a bad temper and an overt fondness for material things. But the outward similarities stopped with his physical features. Reggie, always dressed neat and proper, would never have worn cutoffs and an old sweatshirt like the ones Stewart sported today.

Pricilla turned to study Ezri. She favored her mother as far as looks went. Tall and slender with short, kinky blond hair and blue eyes, she'd just finished her junior year at Columbia University, studying marketing. While Pricilla certainly didn't want to put either of Reggie's children on the suspect list, she also knew from their mother that neither of them had a good relationship with their father. And, if she remembered correctly, Stewart was studying forensic science. Was it possible he knew enough about criminal behavior from classes and online research to be dangerous?

Pricilla shook her head. Just because she'd once found herself involved in trying to solve a murder didn't mean that was the case again this time. Annabelle's children were the victims here, not suspects.

Five minutes later, and much to Pricilla's displeasure, Detective Carter arrived with the coroner. Sheriff Tucker, it seemed, was working another case and was currently unavailable. Pricilla had hoped that the chief himself would be free to investigate instead of sending his nephew, who, from the look on his face, felt the same way about seeing her. The two of them had clashed during Mr. Woodruff's case, where the detective thought Pricilla had no business being involved. That might have been true, but it wasn't as if she'd chosen to have another murder take place practically at her feet.

The glass door to the bakery clicked shut behind the detective. "Ahh, Mrs. Crumb, we meet again."

"So it seems, Detective."

He turned to Annabelle and her children. "Mrs. Pierce, while I know this is a difficult situation for you, I will need to get a signed statement from each of you. If you would go upstairs to your apartment while I make an initial examination of the scene and the coroner begins his investigation, I'll join you shortly." The detective addressed Pricilla again. "I will need a statement from you as well, Mrs. Crumb. Why don't you show us the body, then perhaps you could serve some tea to help calm everyone's nerves. You are proficient in the kitchen, are you not?"

"An award-winning chef, actually," Pricilla murmured under her breath as she led the detective and the coroner out back.

Detective Carter surveyed the scene, shining a flashlight across the smooth stones. "A light shone on the ground at various angles, even outside in broad daylight, creates new shadows that, in turn, could expose evidence."

"Really." Pricilla wasn't impressed.

Leave it to Detective Carter to show off his knowledge of crime scene procedure. She normally didn't carry such a strong dislike toward people, but there was something about the detective that never failed to rub her the wrong way.

He let the beam of light follow the outer path of the broken vase. "What surprises me the most is how we meet again in such unpleasant circumstances, Mrs. Crumb."

"It's certainly not by my choosing."

The bald detective flicked off the flashlight then pulled out a spiral notebook from his back pocket and flipped it open. "Before I start my investigation, I need to know if you're planning to take the credit for Reggie's demise or if I should look elsewhere."

"Excuse me?"

His deep-throated laugh grated on her nerves. "It was a joke, Mrs. Crumb. Relax. Though I must say, even to a seasoned investigator, the fact that you're here once again at the scene of a murder does leave one to wonder if it's simply a coincidence. . .or something else."

Pricilla frowned at the statement. Just because she'd once believed she'd poisoned someone with her salmon tartlets and had foolishly admitted doing so to the detective didn't mean he had to bring it up. "I'm here because I'm the one who found Reggie's body."

Carter folded his arms across his chest. "Now this is getting more and more interesting by the minute. Did you know that statistically that means you are the one most likely to have killed him?"

Pricilla couldn't believe the man's ridiculous accusation. "No, I didn't know that, but I'm not a statistic."

"True, but I must caution you about one thing before I begin my investigation. I have to insist that just because you facilitated one or two aspects of Mr. Woodruff's case doesn't mean I need your help again."

"And I have no plans of offering it."

Maybe she wasn't a seasoned detective, but to speak to her as if she'd hindered his previous investigation instead of helped it wasn't right. If her memory served her correctly, which she knew it did, she was the reason Charles Woodruff's real murderer was behind bars.

"Detective, I need you to come take a look at something." The coroner knelt beside the body, his gaze focused on the deceased man.

"Why don't you go on up and wait with Mrs. Pierce," Carter said. "I won't be long."

Thankful to get away, Pricilla took the winding staircase that led from the back of the store up to Annabelle's spacious home. The upstairs apartment had changed little from the last time Pricilla had been here. On one of her previous visits, Annabelle had given her a complete tour of the four-bedroom residence with its formal décor.

There was one thing that was notably different, Pricilla observed as she stepped into the living room and noted the familiar leather couches, oriental rugs, and polished brass fixtures. Reggie, who'd had a bit of an obsessive-compulsive disorder, had always insisted that everything stay in its proper place. This morning, though, there was a sense of disorganization to the room. It wasn't something that the detective would pick up on, since he'd more than likely never been here before. To Pricilla, on the other hand, the subtle differences were obvious.

A stack of mail lay scattered on the floor beside the antique desk, throw pillows were out of place, and the couch didn't line up along the lines of the wood flooring. Something had happened in this room.

Annabelle stood alone beside the sliding glass windows that led to the balcony. "I told Ezri and Stewart to wait in their rooms for now. I need your help, Pricilla. Everyone in town knows how you saved Claire from going to prison for life and helped to find Mr. Woodruff's real murderer and—"

"I can't get involved in another official investigation." Pricilla leaned against the back of the couch and gnawed on her lip. Not only did she have no business getting mixed up in another case, she'd never hear the end of it from the detective, her son, or Max.

"You don't understand. I'm afraid. . .I think I know what happened."

Pricilla's brow rose in question. "The police haven't even determined whether or not it was an accident—"

"It couldn't have been an accident. I'd never keep pots on the edge of the balcony." Annabelle wrung her hands together. "I'm only going to tell you this because you're my friend and I trust you. I'm afraid the police are going to find out that Stewart might have been involved. They had a horrible fight this morning, and then. . .and then Reggie told him he was cutting him out of his will."

Pricilla had tried to reach Max for the past three days, but a fishing trip with two of his buddies had cut him off from all forms of communication. So much for modern conveniences. She cradled the cordless phone against her ear and paced the lodge's recently renovated kitchen, waiting for Max to answer. He was due to return this morning, so with a bit of luck she'd be able to reach him before she had to leave for Reggie Pierce's funeral.

On the fourth ring, he finally picked up. "Hello?"

She clicked her black heels against the hardwood floor. "Max, it's Pricilla."

"Well, this is a nice surprise."

Pricilla couldn't help but smile at the sound of his voice. Her heart thudded, but this time it wasn't the menacing jolt of the *Titanic* bumping against an iceberg. No matter how difficult their long-distance relationship might be, Max still made her feel young and alive again. Maybe there was hope for them after all.

"How was your trip?" she asked.

"We just pulled in about twenty minutes ago. The weather was perfect and the fishing even better."

She heard the smile in his voice as she stopped in front of the counter to drum her nails against the hard surface, wishing she had something more pleasant to tell him in return. "I need to talk to you—"

"What's wrong?"

"It's not me. I'm fine, it's just that. . ."

Pricilla closed her eyes and wondered if this was really a good idea. The last thing she needed was for Max to worry about her—something she knew he would do once he found out what had happened to Reggie. Max had been far from happy with her involvement in the Woodruff case, but what else could she have done? Not only had her reputation as a chef been at stake, the future of her son's lodge had hung in the balance as well. If she hadn't stepped in, Charles Woodruff's death might very well still be labeled unsolved, like the case of the town librarian who'd been found dead eleven years ago on the bank of Lake Paytah, wearing a purple scuba diving suit.

"Do you remember Annabelle Pierce?" Pricilla began pacing the large kitchen again. "She and her husband own the bakery in town."

"I remember her. What was her husband's name. . .Reagan?"

"Reggie."

"Wasn't he a bit—"

"Obnoxious? Yes, he was."

Reggie's temper had put him at odds with most of the town at one time or another. He'd even been kicked out of a town hall meeting for arguing with the mayor over the newly proposed town dump. If it weren't for his melt-in-your-mouth baked goods, no doubt most of the town would have been in favor of ousting the man into the next county—or state for that matter.

Pricilla swallowed hard. It was time to get to the point. "I found Reggie dead outside his shop this morning."

Max's silence spoke volumes. She'd known he wouldn't be happy that she'd stumbled upon another investigation, but it wasn't as if she'd intended to walk into the Baker's Dozen and find a dead body.

Pricilla filled a glass of water from the kitchen faucet and took a sip. "Annabelle asked me to help find out the truth behind her husband's death. She needs me to—"

Max groaned. "Annabelle needs you to be her friend. The police will solve the case." He paused. "I'm sorry. I don't mean to sound harsh, it's just that I worry about you."

"But don't you see? I'm in a position to help her. People will tell me things they'd never tell the police."

"That doesn't matter. Getting involved with the detective's job is only asking for trouble." Max was silent again for a moment. "Have you talked to Nathan and Trisha about this?"

"We had dinner together last night and the subject did come up."

"And. . ."

Pricilla hesitated. "They were cautious but understood my need to help Annabelle."

"Pricilla. . ."

She set her glass down with a *thud.* "All right, maybe *understood* isn't the right word, but they're not going to try and stop me."

"You know I can't stop you either, but I've tried to tell you this before. You're not Jessica Fletcher, and this isn't another episode of *Murder, She Wrote* where the story is wrapped up neatly at the end of the hour. If Reggie's death was a crime, then there's a murderer involved, and in playing amateur sleuth, you could end up putting your life in jeopardy."

An hour later Pricilla stood beside Nathan and Trisha and tugged at the bottom of her bodice, wishing her one black dress wasn't so uncomfortable. Reggie Pierce's funeral had been attended by less than a dozen people, and there were now even fewer people at the graveside service. Of those who had managed to make their way down the gravel road to attend the short service, most looked as if they'd rather be anywhere but standing together on a patch of green grass, remembering Reggie's far-from-perfect life.

While it was not yet noon, the sun was warm enough to bring trickles of perspiration to Pricilla's brow and make her wish for a moment that she, like the majority of the town, had decided to stay home. Apparently, no matter how good Reggie Pierce's pastries and sourdough loaves tasted, the man simply wasn't liked by the people of Rendezvous.

Stewart stood beside his mother, dressed in black jeans and a T-shirt. The scowl on his face made Pricilla wonder just how deep the conflict between the father and son had run. Had Reggie's pledge to cut him out of his will been simply words spoken in the heat of the moment, or had he planned to follow through with his threat?

Ezri's face looked pale and void of emotion as she held on to her mother's arm. What secrets had she held regarding her feelings toward her father?

And then there was Annabelle. While the spouse of a victim was often the first person to suspect in a murder investigation, Pricilla had dismissed that idea before ever allowing it to take root. Sixty-five years had given her more than purple trails of varicose veins in her legs and crow's-feet at her temples. It had given her an inherent insight into other people's character. And Annabelle was not a murderer.

With the monotone voice of the minister rambling on in the background, Pricilla replayed Max's last words to her on the telephone.

"If Reggie's death was a crime. . ."

Certainly being involved in Charles Woodruff's murder investigation had changed her perspective on life. She didn't want to automatically see a villain behind every bush, but even Annabelle was convinced that her husband's death hadn't been a simple accident. If that were the case, weren't the chances high that whoever had done the ruthless deed was right here among them?

Pricilla couldn't help but study the small number of guests surrounding the gravesite. She'd made no promises to Max. Surely observing the guests couldn't get her into trouble.

Several of the workers from the bakery stood toward the back of the group, including Darren. His help on the day of Reggie's demise had been welcomed, but she wondered why a seemingly intelligent man his age was stuck working in the back of a bakery. Several of the other workers had immigrated from Mexico. Were they grateful to Reggie for their weekly paychecks, or did they hold a different sentiment entirely?

Nathan nudged her with his elbow. "Mom, the service is over."

Yanked out of her thoughts, Pricilla looked around at the guests who were already beginning to leave and sighed. If she didn't stay focused, her sleuthing was going to get her into trouble. "I'd like to speak to Annabelle before we leave."

Nathan nodded. "Trisha and I will meet you at the car."

Pricilla waited until Annabelle had finished speaking to the minister. "Do you want to talk?"

Annabelle nodded then slid her hand into the crook of Pricilla's arm. They strolled back toward the funeral home in silence for the first several minutes. Aspen trees shimmered in the wind beside the perfectly manicured lawn, while the sweet scent of lilacs filled the air. On any other day, the scene would have been perfect. Today it did little to lift the heavy atmosphere that hovered around them.

It was Annabelle who broke the silence. "Detective Carter stopped by to see me this morning. Because of some other evidence that came up, the coroner opened a murder investigation into Reggie's death."

"Oh my." While the words didn't truly come as a surprise, to hear her friend speak them aloud still chilled Pricilla's heart. "I'm so sorry. I know this has to be a frightening experience."

"Without a doubt, but it's more than that. His death has made me face my own life. Everyone knows that our time here on earth is limited, but that's easy to ignore until something like this happens."

"When someone close to you dies, it's natural to examine your life." Pricilla skirted around a mud puddle left from the previous night's rain. "I remember feeling that way when Marty passed away."

But Pricilla hadn't had to deal with the added strain of a murder investigation.

Annabelle stopped and turned toward Pricilla. "You don't have to worry about where you're going when your time comes. Your faith is strong. I once gave my life to Christ, but lately. . .I just can't see God forgiving me for the way I've been living my life the past twenty-odd years."

"It's never too late."

"It's too late for Reggie." Annabelle started walking again along the path edged with blue and white columbine in full bloom. "When I first married him he was so different. I fell in love with him because he was ambitious, and yet he cared for those around him. I never expected success to consume him the way it did. His entire life started to revolve around making money. I'd hoped that moving here to a slower pace of life would help settle him, but nothing changed."

The silence hung between them until Annabelle spoke again. "I feel as if my entire body's being crushed. Like some python's squeezing the life out of me."

Normally, what to say had never been an issue for Pricilla, but at the moment, she had to struggle for the right words. "You don't have to do this on your own, Annabelle. The Bible describes us all as weak vessels. Jars of clay. It's His power that allows us to be crushed from life's circumstances without being destroyed."

"I just don't know. It's so hard. I think Ezri's seeing someone, Stewart's not doing well in school, and neither will talk to me."

Pricilla squeezed her friend's hand. "Promise me you'll think about what I said?"

Annabelle nodded, slowing as they neared the entrance of the funeral home. "There was one other thing I needed to say to you. It was wrong of me to ask you to help. I was upset and not thinking straight. To even think that Stewart might have had something to do with Reggie's death. . . The thought is simply inconceivable. I shouldn't have said anything."

"Please don't worry about it. I understand."

Annabelle stopped outside the front door of the funeral home. "I suppose I should go back in and at least thank the staff."

"I'll plan to call you tomorrow and see how you're doing. And if you need anything. . ." Pricilla hugged her then headed toward the car where Nathan and Trisha waited for her.

Someone shouting at the back of the parking lot caught her attention. Two people stood beside a black sports car, arguing. Pricilla was about to ignore them when she realized one of them was Ezri.

Wondering why the young woman wasn't inside with her mother and afraid there might be a problem, Pricilla walked past the next row of cars to see what was going on.

The dark-haired man with Ezri banged his fist on the hood then jumped into the car. With a grind of tires against the gravel, he headed out of the parking lot.

Pricilla hurried across the uneven surface, trying not to choke on the car's exhaust fumes. "Ezri, are you all right?"

Ezri stood motionless for a moment, her eyes rimmed with tears. Finally, she brushed the back of her hand across her face and drew in a deep breath. "I'm fine. It was nothing, just. . ."

"Who was that man?"

"No one, just a friend." She reached out and gripped Pricilla's arm. "Please, Mrs. Crumb. You can't tell my mother about any of this. . .promise me, please."

"Will you at least tell me why you're so upset? All I want to do is help—"

"I'm sorry. I can't." Ezri turned and ran toward the funeral home, her heels crunching across the gravel.

Pricilla stared after her, wondering what exactly it was that she'd just seen, and why Ezri seemed so afraid.

Max tried to ignore the fact that the hired taxicab driver was hitting every bump in the dirt road leading up to the lodge and instead focused on the surrounding mountainous area. While he loved New Mexico, he had to admit that Colorado offered its own unique setting with its snowcapped mountains, pale aspen trees, and lazy rivers. Of course for him there was an even stronger draw.

Pricilla.

He'd never expected to fall in love with his good friend's wife, but it had been four years since Marty passed away, and he knew there was no turning back now. He closed his eyes for a moment and pictured her pervasive smile and boisterous laugh. Silver hair lying in perfect curls against the nape of her neck. Wide hazel eyes that took in far more than most realized. He let out a slow sigh. While the years had added wrinkles and age spots, he still found her beautiful and completely enchanting.

There was only one problem. Their relationship, which he'd boldly taken from a lifelong friendship to a budding romance over lunch at Tiffany's seven months ago, had begun to wither.

Max rested his hand against his suitcase and fiddled with the airline tag. The two hundred or so miles of topography between them had proven to be more of a hindrance than he'd ever imagined it could be. Declarations of love rarely accounted for such practical matters, but moving forward had proved difficult for two retirees set in their ways. And he certainly wasn't getting any younger.

Frowning, he shifted his weight and tried to get comfortable in the worn leather seats. The truth was they both had their reasons. For starters, he hated the Colorado winters, and she wasn't fond of New Mexico's hot summers. Trivial, he supposed, in the light of love and companionship, but nevertheless the barriers did exist.

No matter what obstacles had come between them, though, Max felt his heart race as the lofty structure of the Rendezvous Hunting Lodge and Resort finally came into view, and along with it, a dynamic showing of God's masterpiece. Nestled into a grove of aspen trees, the popular tourist destination was framed with the stunning backdrop of the Colorado Rockies. For a hunter, the lodge was paradise.

The taxi pulled to a stop in front of the lodge. Max alighted from the four-door vehicle, wondering for the first time if he'd made a mistake by not informing Pricilla of his unscheduled arrival. Trisha, his daughter, had assured him that he was welcome to stay in her spare bedroom though it wasn't set up for guests. He, in turn, had assured her that all he needed was a bed and a shower. Thirty-five years in the military had taught him that he needed far less to get by on than most people could even begin to imagine.

With the driver paid and his bags unloaded on the wide, wooden porch, Max stepped onto the gray-tiled floor of the entryway. He rang the bell at the front desk before walking into the living room. From the heavy wooden ceiling beams to the rustic pine furniture to the unique cozy rugs, every room added to the ambiance of the mountain setting. The woody fragrance from the fireplace filled his senses. With Pricilla beside him, perhaps the long, cold winters wouldn't seem quite so chilly.

"Can I help you?"

Max spun around and smiled at the familiar voice. Today Pricilla wore a striking red and black pantsuit, and while her taste in clothes ran as bold as her personality, she always looked beautiful to him.

"Max?"

"Pricilla." How he'd let two hundred miles come between them, he had no idea. If he was half as smart as he'd like to think he was, he ought to pop the question right now and forget about all the obstacles that stood between them. "You haven't aged a day since I saw you last."

Pricilla stopped at the edge of the hardwood floor, and the corners of her lips formed a smile. "Either I'm dreaming, or I'm experiencing a sudden onset of Alzheimer's and forgot you were coming."

He'd always loved her sense of humor. "Neither. I wanted to surprise you."

He bridged the gap between them, ignoring the slight awkwardness of the moment, and ran his finger down her cheek before kissing her gently on the lips. "I missed you."

Pricilla pressed the back of her hair with the tips of her fingers. "You know, you really should have called so I could have had a room ready for you, and—"

"You look beautiful." He set his bags down on the floor and took her hand. The delight in her expression was obvious. "I'm staying with Trisha because I didn't want to take advantage of your son. The rooms are for revenue, not for pining suitors."

"You always did know how to win a girl's heart, didn't you?" Her laugh reminded him of just how happy she made him when they were together. "Are you hungry?"

"Starved."

"Good." She laughed again. "Come into the kitchen. We just finished lunch, but I think there's enough left over for you."

He followed her down the short hall, where the smells of her tantalizing cooking filled the air. The cup of coffee and small package of peanuts the airline had offered hadn't been near enough. "What's on the menu?"

She glanced back at him before stepping into the large, open kitchen that had been remodeled last year. "Chicken with a Cajun cream sauce, angel hair pasta, and a new recipe I tried out for peach cobbler."

"Peach cobbler?" Max's stomach grumbled. "I knew I wouldn't be disappointed."

"So the truth comes out." She stopped and rested her hand against the granite counter. Her voice was stern, but there was a twinkle in her eye. "Did you really miss me or are you only here for my fine cuisine, Mr. Summers?"

He shook his head. "There's no competition there. I'd choose an evening with you and a loaf of stale bread over a five-star meal without you any day."

She beamed. "Good answer. Now wash your hands, and I'll dish you up some lunch."

She'd always amazed him. Cooking three meals a day for the guests and staff couldn't be an easy job, yet she always prepared something out of the ordinary. Pricilla cooked the way she approached life, with zeal and enthusiasm. Those traits were only two of many that had drawn him to her.

Misty Majors, Pricilla's full-time assistant, entered the kitchen with a stack of dirty dishes from the dining room. "Why, Mr. Summers. What a surprise. It's good to see you, sir."

Max hesitantly returned a smile to the young woman whom he'd once interviewed as a suspect in a murder case. Apparently age was irrelevant to her, because despite his experience in dealing with hundreds of such interviews, Misty's blatant interest in him had had him running out of the room like a coon with his tail on fire. "It's good to see you, Misty."

"It's been a long time."

His gaze returned to Pricilla. "Too long." It was true. Twice in seven months wasn't enough. He'd flown up to see her at Christmastime, and in return Pricilla had visited at the end of February, when they'd celebrated a belated Valentine's Day and for some unknown reason she'd managed to avoid the subject of a permanent commitment. Now he realized what a fool he'd been, taking the chance of losing her. He should have stated his feelings outright. If he planned on making things permanent between them, something was going to have to change.

Misty left the room as Max reached for a towel to dry his hands. "So how is Annabelle? I was sorry to hear about the loss of her husband."

"Annabelle?" Pricilla put her hands against her hips. This time she wasn't smiling. "I should have known."

"Known what?"

"That you had an ulterior motive."

"An ulterior. . .I'm sorry." Max paused. Pricilla had a way of knocking down his sense of diplomacy, but while there was nothing wrong with his concern, perhaps he had jumped into the subject too soon. "I'm just extremely curious about the fact that barely seven months after Charles Woodruff's death, you manage to stumble over another dead body."

"It's purely coincidence."

"Don't get me wrong, you're not on my suspect list." He shot her a smile. "I know you better than to think you did it. But there's a murderer on the loose, and with one solved case under your belt and dreams of being Jessica Fletcher in the back of your mind—"

"That's not true."

"Isn't it?" He didn't want to widen the point of contention between them, but he couldn't help but worry about her and her seemingly fearless attempts at playing the role of amateur detective. "I know that once you have something set in your mind it's nearly impossible to change it. I just want you to promise to let Carter handle this one."

"Like he handled the last one?" Her eyes widened. "The man's incompetent and you talk about my being the amateur—"

"I'm sorry." Max held up his hand. It was time to switch gears. "Let's not fight. I have a present for you."

"Bribery?" Gifts always brought a smile to Pricilla's face and today was no exception. "I have to admit I like the way your mind works."

"Let me eat, and then I'll show you."

After Max finished his second helping of her peach cobbler, Pricilla watched as he pulled a large, rectangular bag from his carry-on and set it on the dining room table. Her change in attitude had nothing to do with the gift. She'd never been able to resist Max's charm.

Her eyes narrowed as he unzipped the case. "What is it?"

"A laptop." He set it on the table, obviously proud.

She leaned in closer and squinted at the shiny silver machine. "A computer?"

Max nodded. "Sit down beside me."

"I don't need a computer."

"You just don't know you need it. We can communicate and send e-mails to each other. Once you get the hang of it, you'll love it."

Reluctantly, she took the chair beside him. Even though she'd thought once or twice how a computer could have helped her to solve Charles Woodruff's murder sooner, she still didn't see how such an apparatus could ever be of real benefit. She'd said it before, and nothing had changed. Computers simply ended up making people work harder rather than taking away some of the burden of labor. They were too complicated, too time consuming, and too antisocial. And besides, who wanted to be stuck in front of a screen all day?

She watched as Max pushed a button and the machine whirled to life. She supposed that she should at least try to seem interested. After all, he did travel all the way from New Mexico to see her. Something told her, though, that as innocent as Max appeared, he had a hidden agenda behind the surprise visit and the computer that tied back to the death of Charles Woodruff.

And now Reggie Pierce.

She tried to feign interest. "So you and I can send e-mails to each other?"

"E-mails, pictures, and that's just the beginning of what you can do. . . ."

Pricilla stared at the photo of a purple iris that filled the screen as she tuned out Max's voice. There was nothing wrong with her way of sending a letter. Flowery stationery, her favorite ink pen, and an hour in the garden were all she needed. She even loved the trip to the post office where she could choose what kind of stamp she wanted while catching up on all the latest news in town. No computer could do all of that for her.

Max leaned forward and his shoulder brushed against hers as he rambled on about out-boxes, in-boxes, and signature lines. She loved having him near her. There was something about him that made her feel young and alive again. She never thought anyone would have ever taken the place of Marty, and in a real sense, no one ever could. But Max was different. Max was. . .Max. But while he was nothing like Marty, losing one husband made her extremely cautious about losing her heart again.

"Pricilla?"

Her gaze broke away from the screen that now was a mess of cold, sterile typing. "Sorry."

He sat back and caught her gaze. "Have you heard a word I've said?"

She offered him a weak smile. "I know that we can send e-mails, and you mentioned something about in-boxes and the Internet—"

"You'll catch on quickly. I promise." He was far too excited. "Now, look at this."

Thirty minutes later Pricilla rubbed her neck and tried to get rid of the crick that had started at the base of her skull and was now working its way down her spine. She'd tried her best to pay attention to Max's crash course she'd secretly nicknamed the World Wild Web 101, but she was afraid that the learning curve was too great. What was the old saying? You can't teach an old dog new tricks? Replace dogs and tricks with a sixty-five-year-old grandma-wannabe and a state-of-the-art laptop, and you'd about have it right.

She stole a glance at Max and caught sight of his blue eyes. She'd always said they reminded her of the columbine in the spring. And they were smiling. Computers. . .Reggie Pierce's death. . .their uncertain relationship. . .nothing seemed to matter at the moment except for the fact that Max Summers was sitting beside her and he loved her. Even at sixty-five, he still had the same broad, strong shoulders and a military physique from frequent workouts. Seeing him was enough to make up for his wanting her to learn how to use a computer and send e-mails. Truth was she'd missed him.

". . .this is where you can organize messages. Save those you want to keep, or throw away those you don't need any longer."

Pricilla's gaze flicked back to the screen, and she forced herself to concentrate. After Charles Woodruff's death, Max had used her son's computer to research three of the suspects. What if she could do the same thing for the suspects in Reggie Pierce's case?

She stared at the emblems on the bottom of the screen. "Can I get on the Internet?"

"Good question." He smiled. No matter what the mirror told her every morning, she knew Max saw beyond her wrinkles and age spots. "All you have to do is click on this icon like this. Nathan's wireless system makes it easy. You can log on from anywhere in the lodge."

"Log on. . .icons. . .wireless—"

"You'll get the hang of it quickly." He squeezed her hand. "I promise."

Someone in high heels walked across the hardwood floor. Pricilla turned to see Annabelle in the doorway, her eyes puffy from lack of sleep.

Pricilla sat up straight. "Annabelle? I didn't hear you come in."

The woman clutched the doorframe and took a step back. "I'm sorry. You have company. I'll come back later—"

"No. It's fine." Pricilla stood and crossed the room

Annabelle grasped Pricilla's hands. "I. . .I need to talk."

With Max settled on the front porch with a crossword puzzle and a third helping of peach cobbler, Pricilla quickly fixed a pot of tea then joined Annabelle in the living room. It was the least she could do for the woman who had just lost her husband.

Annabelle stirred her drink then poured another spoonful of sugar in the cup before taking a sip. "I hardly know where to start. It's been almost a week, and I still keep thinking that I'm going to wake up and this will all be nothing but a bad dream."

"You've got to grieve and give it time." Pricilla put her used tea bag on an empty plate, wishing she could take away the woman's pain. "Healing will come eventually."

Annabelle gazed out the window. "We fought before he died, and the last words I said to him were horrible. I. . .I threatened to leave him."

Pricilla wasn't surprised at all. "Frankly, Reggie wasn't the easiest man to get along with. I certainly don't think you should blame yourself. I'm sure you had a good reason."

"But I loved him. I never would have left him."

Pricilla stared at the floral pattern on the delicate cup and saucer and bit her tongue. Subtlety wasn't exactly one of her strong suits, and speaking ill of Annabelle's dead husband, no matter how true, was wrong. Honestly. She knew better than that. "I'm sorry—"

"No, it's all right. I'm not blind to the fact that no one in town liked him."

"Reggie was simply a man who was. . ." Pricilla quickly searched for the right word, determined not to make the same mistake again. But what could she say that was both truthful and yet not condemning? Reggie had been demanding, difficult, and overbearing, and those three words barely began to describe the man.

Annabelle leaned back in her chair and ran her fingers through her short, curly hair. "I feel so guilty."

"Guilty?" The detective might be looking at motives for foul play, but Pricilla would never believe Annabelle had been involved in her husband's death. "Why?"

"I just wish things had been different." Annabelle wrung her hands. "I feel guilty that I didn't spend more time working on my marriage, or more time being a better wife. . .or more time being the spiritual example I should have been."

Even though Reggie had never entered a church building and had always seemed proud of the fact, Annabelle had never given up hope that her husband would one day understand why she believed as she did. But Pricilla was certain that her friend's faith had suffered because of it.

"I can't imagine that God. . ." Annabelle shook her head. "Why should God forgive me if Reggie couldn't?"

"Forgive you for what exactly?"

Before she could answer, the cell phone in Annabelle's purse rang. She pulled it out of the black bag. "Excuse me, if it's one of my children. . ."

Pricilla nodded as Annabelle mumbled a hello. While she didn't believe that Ezri or Stewart had enjoyed a healthy relationship with their father, the situation was still tragic.

Annabelle's face paled.

"What is it?" Pricilla set down her tea and leaned forward.

Annabelle clicked the phone shut. "It was Detective Carter. I think I've just become his number-one suspect."

Max flipped through the pages of his favorite hunting magazine while he waited for Pricilla, who sat beside him on the couch, to get off the phone. Normally, he would enjoy the full-page advertisement on the latest hunting gear, or the feature story on Alaska's big game, but this evening he found it hard to concentrate no matter how interesting the subject. He'd been right about Pricilla. Her success in solving the murder of Charles Woodruff was influencing the situation with Annabelle. Pricilla might say she had no intentions of getting involved, but he knew her better than that. Instead of dishing up a second helping of peach cobbler, he was afraid she was about to dish up a second helping of trouble.

He flicked on the small table lamp beside the leather couch he sat on and forced himself to read what he was sure would prove to be an informative article packed full of proven scouting tips. Within seconds the page became a blur. Pricilla's voice lowered beside him, then there was a long pause. He held his breath until she began talking again, but he couldn't make sense of the conversation.

Shoving the magazine into the rack beside him, he folded his arms across his chest and heaved a deep sigh. It wasn't as if he didn't trust Pricilla's instincts, because they were typically on target. Nor did he believe she was incapable of solving a crime—including Reggie Pierce's. But murder was. . .well. . .murder, and he didn't want her involved.

The cozy living room, with its high ceiling and glossy wooden floors, reverberated with the sounds of a few lingering guests playing a lively game of cards, but he finally had to admit defeat and tuned out the murmurs of conversation interspersed with laughter to once again listen to Pricilla. The concern in her voice was what had him worried. She would never sit back and allow the detective—and a bumbling one at that in her opinion—do his job when she believed that justice wasn't being served. Her brief experience as an amateur detective last year had transformed her into a sixty-five-year-old investigator—enterprising, fearless, and out to save the world.

He lifted his head as the phone clicked shut.

Pricilla laid the phone on the end table and slid closer to him. "That was Annabelle."

"I figured as much." He was determined not to overreact, or nag, or any other number of things he longed to do. "Did she talk to the detective?"

"Yes, and it doesn't look good. I'm afraid her fear of being Detective Carter's number-one suspect isn't far from the truth." She shook her head, allowing a fringe of silver curls to bounce around the nape of her neck. "She's innocent, Max."

He wasn't convinced. "People have secrets, things that you might never even begin to guess—"

"I can't imagine Annabelle having a secret so shocking that she would murder her husband because of it." She caught his gaze and frowned. "We've become close friends during the past few months, and while she'd always hinted at unhappiness in her marriage, murder is a whole other thing."

"Perhaps."

With a cozy fire in the hearth to ward off the final chill of spring and soft music playing in the background, the last thing he wanted to do was argue. Or talk about Annabelle Pierce. His chief objective originally might have been to ensure Pricilla stayed out of trouble, but the truth was, he'd shown up on her doorstep for a much more significant reason. He had every intention of reviving their stagnant relationship. He'd missed her, and with marriage in the back of his mind, he knew it was time to begin courting again. First things first, though. "What did the detective say?"

Pricilla lowered her gaze and began picking at a chipped nail. "They found a new will Reggie presumably had typed up. It was unsigned and dated the day before he died. He cut both Annabelle and the children out of his will."

"Presumably." Max sucked in his breath. If Reggie had indeed written the will, it was definitely a motive for murder. "Had he threatened Annabelle with this information, or even told her about it?"

From the look on her face, Pricilla obviously realized how damaging the evidence was. "Yes, but she didn't believe he would actually go through with it. Reggie was a hard man to get along with. He always looked for leverage to get what he wanted. It's strange. Somehow, in spite of his cantankerous character, she still loved him."

Even Max couldn't help but feel sorry for the woman. "How's she doing?"

"Annabelle's a strong woman. It will take time, but I think she'll pull through."

Max drummed his fingers against the leather armrest. Maybe Pricilla was right. She was a good judge of character and was rarely wrong when it came to her gut instincts about people. But if Annabelle hadn't killed off her husband in a fit of rage, then who had?

Pricilla rested her hand against his arm. "I thought I would stop by the bakery tomorrow. To support the business, of course."

He definitely smelled an ulterior motive in this vein of the conversation. "Just for support?"

"If I happen to find out a clue relevant to the case, it would be wrong to dismiss it." She flashed him a pleading look that was going to get him in the end. "Annabelle can't afford to close down the bakery, and the sheriff told her that as long as the police have access to whatever they need, she'll be allowed to keep it running."

"So you'll just purchase a few dozen pastries and perhaps some of their baguettes?" He didn't buy her reasoning, but resisting her was impossible.

"Annabelle's a good friend, and I have to support her. Besides that, they have the most divine Italian shortbread cookies. You'd love them."

"After three helpings of your peach cobbler, I hardly think I need to indulge on shortbread." He patted his stomach and laughed. "I suppose a trip to the bakery wouldn't hurt anything, though I'm quite certain you're hoping to find more than just a sampling of pastries."

Pricilla eyed the assortment of pastries beneath the glass case and felt her mouth water. She'd definitely discovered one of her weaknesses. She could hardly resist driving by the quaint bakery without stopping in for a taste of a fresh fruit tart or perhaps a chocolate truffle, and today was no exception. The shopping list in her pocket crinkled between her fingers. Five long baguettes would never be enough. Of course, she could simply go to the grocery store to buy all the baguettes she needed, as well as get the ingredients to make tonight's dessert herself. She was quite adept at making her own delicious cakes and pastries, but then she might miss a chance to gather information on Reggie's death, which, besides supporting Annabelle's business, was the real reason she was here.

She turned to Max, who was drooling over a tray of almond cream pastries. "Would you like one?"

"One?" His gaze shifted to the cream horns. "How in the world would I ever choose just one? The selection is incredible."

"You can't. I've sampled all of them, and trust me, you can't go wrong with any of them." She laughed and hoped the indulgence didn't show too much on her waistline. "Reggie learned how to make pastries from a chef in Paris. Of course, now that Reggie's dead. . ."

Now that Reggie was dead what?

Annabelle relied on the income of the bakery to support her family. With two kids in college, finances had to be tight no matter how well the business was thriving. And then there was the added complication of the mail-order side of the company. Annabelle had always been highly involved in the business, and they had a full-time baker capable of keeping up with the demand, but if she were arrested for the murder of her husband that would change everything.

A cherry tart caught Pricilla's eye, but she forced herself to focus. Pastries and cream-filled cakes were not why she was here. She was here to help Annabelle find out who murdered her husband, and if that meant talking to employees, making phone calls, or even doing a bit of undercover sleuthing, she would do it.

She clicked her fingers against the glass and wondered why no one was working in the front. Everything in the store looked normal. The glass and chrome had been polished, the floor swept, and even the hand-painted OPEN sign hung in place out front. All as if nothing had changed. For a moment she expected Reggie to walk through the swinging wooden doors from the back with his gruff exterior and long apron covered in flour and smears of chocolate.

But of course he didn't.

A knot twisted inside Pricilla's stomach as she tried to block out the imprint of the last time she'd seen Reggie. Cold stone flooring. . .the shattered vase. . .his motionless body. . . At least she hadn't come alone this time. Max had agreed to accompany her to the bakery, mumbling some excuse about needing to get out of the house and into the fresh air, but his words didn't fool her. He was here to keep an eye on her. In fact, it wouldn't surprise her at all if her son had put him up to the idea. Honestly, how much trouble did they really think she could get into at a bakery—unless it had to do with consuming too many calories?

She stole a peek at Max's reflection in the glass and felt her heart trip. Part of her hoped she was wrong and that he had really come to Colorado to see her and not just to ensure she didn't try her hand at being Jessica Fletcher once again. He looked quite handsome in khaki pants and a checkered, button-down shirt. She couldn't help it. When Max was with her, fears about the future began to melt away along with all her excuses as to why a permanent relationship with him couldn't work.

Ezri stepped into the storefront from the back room, forcing Pricilla once again to concentrate on the issue at hand. The young woman's neon orange outfit did little to perk up the somber expression on her face.

She ran her hand through her cropped hair. "Mrs. Crumb, I'm so sorry I kept you waiting. I was filling an order in the back. We're a bit understaffed today."

"I know this is a hard time for you, but it's good to see you." Pricilla set her purse on the counter and gave her a reassuring smile. "I thought perhaps you might be closing early for the day?"

The young woman shook her head. "Mother insists we need to keep the store open."

Pricilla tugged Max toward the counter. "I'd like to introduce you to Max Summers. He's a good friend of mine."

"It's nice to meet you." Ezri cocked her head and stared at him. "You're Mr. Summers? Trisha's father?"

"Yes. Do you know her?"

For the first time, Ezri's face lit up. "She's such a sweet person. She comes in from time to time and always orders one Napoleon and one lemon tart."

Max smiled. "I'd forgotten those are her favorites. She's always had a sweet tooth."

"She's told me what a great dad she has. It's nice to meet you in person." Ezri's gaze clouded over.

Max took a step forward. "I'm so sorry about what happened to your father, Ezri."

"Unfortunately, my father and I were never close. Business always came first for him." She held up her hand as if to dismiss in one sweep all the pent-up pain and rejection she felt. "Anyway, it's really good to meet you."

"It's nice to meet you, too."

Pricilla pulled out her wallet. "We thought we'd stir up a bit of business for you. I need five baguettes and two dozen of your individual meringue-almond cakes."

"Mmm, these are one of my favorites." Ezri pulled out a white box and began filling it with a layer of the round cakes. "I'm sure your guests will enjoy them."

"Speak for yourself." Max now had his sights on a row of walnut puffs. "Who says I'm going to let Pricilla share them with our guests?"

If it was true that the way to a man's heart was through his stomach, Pricilla had certainly knocked on the right door. "I'm convinced I've inhaled at least a thousand calories just by standing here."

Ezri laughed, but the sound rang hollow. Pricilla couldn't help but remember the incident in the parking lot the day of the funeral. Ezri's expression had bothered her that day, and if her assumptions were correct, the girl was still worried about something.

"What is it, Ezri? You look. . .scared."

Ezri glanced toward the back room before reaching for another meringue-almond cake with a pair of tongs. "It's nothing. Really."

"I might not know you well, but I do know your mother, and I'm concerned for all of you."

Ezri set the box on the counter and stared at the speckled Formica top. "I don't know if I should say anything, Mrs. Crumb."

Pricilla ignored Max's disapproving look and continued. "I know your mother and that she could never be involved, but we need to find some sort of evidence to the contrary. If you know something—anything that might help—you can tell me."

Ezri leaned forward, sending Pricilla a strong whiff of the girl's perfume. "Part of the problem is Detective Carter. I know it's his job, but the detective is constantly snooping around and asking questions."

"What kind of questions?"

"For one, he's been grilling all the employees, which I can understand, but it's just the way he goes about it." She tugged at the bottom of her shirt. "He gives me the creeps."

Pricilla shot Max a look of triumph. She obviously wasn't the only one who found the detective's tactics both irritating and unprofessional. "And. . ."

"Well, Darren Robinson is a college student my dad hired for the summer. He's really good at computers and has been updating the bakery's Web sites and doing other things that will boost the mail-order business." Ezri shivered despite the warmth in the storefront. "He's a nice enough guy, who keeps to himself, but. . ."

Pricilla pressed against the counter to ensure she didn't miss anything. "Do you think he had something to do with your father's death?"

"Not Darren, but what worries me is what he told the detective. He said he saw Stewart on the balcony moments before my dad died. He was standing behind the pot and looking down on the patio." Tears welled up in Ezri's eyes. "I just don't think Mom could handle the fact that Stewart may have been involved."

Pricilla didn't like what she was hearing, but at the same time, she was quite certain that dropping a heavy pot from a balcony would never be Stewart's modus operandi. The boy was studying forensic science. Certainly if he'd wanted to kill his father, he would have come up with something a bit more scientific, wouldn't he? Still, such reasoning wasn't enough to dismiss the young man as a suspect.

"Do you think your brother is capable of murder?"

Ezri shrugged a shoulder. "I won't lie. Stewart is a lot like my dad was when it comes to living the good life. He wants to live it up without any of the responsibility and doesn't want to hear you say it won't work."

"Maybe I could talk to him."

Max finally spoke up again. "I'm sure the detective has done that, Pricilla."

"He did." Ezri grabbed five of the wrapped baguettes, placed them on the counter, and began ringing up the sale. "But Stewart isn't talking much to anyone right now, and I doubt you'd be any different."

Pricilla knew Max wouldn't approve of her next question, but she asked it anyway. "Do you know where your brother is right now?"

Ezri shrugged. "I know where he's supposed to be. In the back, filling orders from our Web site. Instead, he's probably down at the pool hall."

Stewart wasn't at the pool hall as Ezri had predicted. Pricilla swallowed her disappointment and followed Max past a vintage photo shop, a travel agent, and a gift shop as they walked toward the car.

"It's just as well," he told her. "I hardly think that the pool hall is an appropriate place for either of us."

She swallowed her frustration. "This is Rendezvous, Max. Not Las Vegas."

"True, but—"

"Wait a minute." Pricilla stopped just past the corner drugstore where the street opened up to the town park. "There he is."

Stewart sat on one of the wrought iron benches, his hands stuffed inside his jacket pockets, simply staring across the empty playground. Dark, unruly hair that needed a good haircut. A red T-shirt and shorts that looked as if they'd been slept in for the past week. Pricilla tossed the baguettes onto the backseat of the car and tried to come up with an opening line that would get him to talk. She couldn't imagine the three of them having many shared interests, but there had to be at least one common denominator.

Annabelle's plea for help replayed in her mind. Until the truth behind Reggie's death was revealed, Annabelle wouldn't be able to go on with her life. It was enough to propel Priscilla down the cobblestone walk toward the young man. With a new wave of determination and a box of meringue-almond cakes, Pricilla hurried toward Stewart.

"Pricilla, wait." Max sped to catch up with her.

"I know what you're going to say." She turned to face him with the box of cakes against her chest. "And you have every right."

Max closed his mouth.

He obviously thought she agreed with his hesitation to grill Stewart, but she wasn't ready to completely concede. "All I want to do is ask him a couple questions."

"A couple questions?"

"If nothing else, he's Annabelle's son and it would be rude not to express my condolences."

Pricilla knew he didn't buy her reasoning, but it was the best she could come up with at the moment. And besides that, it really was true. She hadn't had the chance to talk with Stewart at the funeral and tell him how sorry she was for his loss.

"Please, Max."

"Just be careful. If he is the murderer..."

"He's Annabelle's son."

"Which doesn't make him innocent, and you know it."

She approached the young man from the side. "Stewart?"

There was no reaction.

Max pointed to the pair of earphones.

Pricilla slid into the space beside Stewart. According to Nathan, the park had been constructed five years ago. The surrounding mountains, with a dusting of snow along the top, made the spot a perfect photo op. But Pricilla had her doubts that Stewart noticed any of it. And since talking wasn't getting his attention, she hoped the fresh pastries would. She opened the lid of the box of still warm cakes and waited a few seconds for the warm scent of almonds to fill the air.

Stewart turned then pulled the earphones out. "Mrs. Crumb...and Mr...."

Max stood in front of them, looking almost as uncomfortable as Stewart did. "Summers. Max Summers."

Stewart nodded.

Pricilla waited a few more seconds. "Would you like a cake? They're fresh from the oven."

He shrugged.

She'd obviously taken him off guard, which might be a good thing. Pricilla decided to seize the opportunity. She handed him one of the cakes. "I'd be ten pounds lighter if it weren't for your father's bakery."

Pricilla frowned as he shoved a bite into his mouth. That wasn't at all what she'd intended to say. Ezri had said he didn't talk much, and now he had an excuse. The last thing the boy wanted, she was sure, was yet another reminder of his father's death.

She cleared her throat. She might as well get the condolence part over with so she could find some less shaky ground between them. "What I really wanted to say was that I haven't had a chance to tell you how sorry I am about your father's death. I know this is a very difficult time for you."

Stewart shrugged again before taking another bite. This was going to be harder than she thought. If she, of all people, couldn't start a conversation, she wasn't sure who could.

"So you think I killed my father?" His words were somewhat garbled with a mouthful of meringue. But not so garbled that she couldn't understand.

"I certainly didn't say that."

"You didn't have to." He brushed the crumbs from the edges of his mouth and stood. "I know what people are thinking in this small town. I'm the prodigal son who didn't want to come home. Everyone knows about the fight I had with my dad the morning he died."

"I did hear that there had been some problems—"

"Did my mom also tell you that he was planning to cut me out of the will?"

"Well. . ."

Stewart's laugh rang hollow. "So I have the perfect motive."

"Stewart."

"And don't forget opportunity. Darren can place me at the scene of the crime moments before the actual murder."

She hadn't expected the boy to practically confess to a crime before she'd even asked her questions. "None of that means you killed your father."

"Doesn't it? The detective is pretty convinced. I've seen the look on his face. Even my mother has doubts of my innocence."

"Your mother loves you."

Stewart didn't reply.

"Do you want to tell me about the fight you had with your dad?" Pricilla prodded.

To her surprise, Stewart sat back down beside her. She offered him another almond cake, and he took it. The features on his face softened. He was nothing more than a confused adolescent with some growing up to do. The murder of his father, no matter where their relationship stood, had to have put a kink in the process.

Max moved to the other side of the bench and sat without saying a word.

"My father and I never got along. He was always busy with work. Too busy to attend little league games and track meets."

Pricilla bit the edge of her lip to refrain from making a comment. There was no doubt that the boy needed to talk. If she interrupted at this point she'd probably lose her advantage.

"In New York he had his restaurant," Stewart continued. "It was like his first-born son. It got all his attention. When they decided to move here, my mom promised me things would be different. I believed her at first. The only thing was, school holidays are also peak times for the store. So when I was home from college, I worked."

Stewart fiddled with the white cord of his headphones. "The morning he was murdered, my father told me that I was nothing more than a lazy bum who didn't deserve a dime of his hard-earned money. I told him I didn't want any of it, slammed the door, and walked out of the house. Some of his last words to me were that he was cutting me out of his will. I wasn't surprised. He loved to dictate my life but never took the time to really know what I wanted." He slapped his hands against his thighs. "At least everybody's happy now. The town has the perfect scapegoat, saving its touristy image, and the detective can put another star on his badge for another solved murder."

"If the detective had any real evidence that you'd killed your father, he'd have already arrested you," Pricilla insisted. "I've worked with the man before, and while it's true he can be quite blunt, I think it's mainly because he's motivated to do his job and keep this community safe." Pricilla couldn't believe she was defending the detective, but if digging out a few morsels of truth helped reassure Stewart, it was worth it. "I don't think he'd ever do anything to hurt you on purpose."

"Tell that to yourself next time you're hauled down to the sheriff's office in front of your friends for a couple hours of questioning. I'll bet you'll think plenty different."

She had no intention of getting hauled down to the sheriff's office for any reason, but she did understand his point.

Stewart shook his head and frowned. The hard lines that had creased his forehead earlier returned. The moment of confession was over.

Pricilla closed the lid of the bakery box and considered Stewart's words. She wasn't convinced yet of his guilt but still needed to ask one more question. And since he seemed to be playing things straight, so would she. "Did you kill your father, Stewart?"

Stewart shoved his hands back into his pockets and rose to leave. "Since you seem so keen on playing the role of detective, why don't you figure that out yourself?"

Pricilla breathed in the aroma of the fresh bakery items that sat behind her in the car and kept her eyes on the winding road that led back to the lodge.

Max had taken exactly thirty seconds once they were back in the car to dive into the box of pastries to ensure they were suitable for the guests. Or so he claimed. "So what are you thinking?" she asked.

He took another bite. "How glad I am that you didn't give all these pastries to Stewart. It's got to be one of the most divine pastries I've ever tasted. Besides yours, of course—"

"I wasn't talking about almond cream and apricot fillings." Pricilla couldn't help but laugh. "And there's a glob of something at the corner of your mouth."

Max quickly wiped it away before finishing the last bite.

She slowed down to turn the corner on to the road that led to the lodge.

"I was referring to our talk with Ezri, Darren's claim of seeing Stewart at the crime scene moments before Reggie's untimely death, our unexpected talk with Stewart. . .all of it."

"What am I thinking?" He closed the lid of the box, keeping his promise to only sample one, and set it on the backseat next to the other groceries they'd picked up. "The exact same thing as when you thought you'd murdered Charles Woodruff with one of your salmon-filled tartlets. I think you need to let the detective handle things."

"What if he arrests the wrong person?"

"You worry too much."

Only with good reason. "Would you trust the detective if it were your neck on the line?"

The pregnant pause that followed gave ample clue as to what he was about to say. Max cleared his throat. "Let's just say I'm glad I'm not in the position to find out."

Pricilla rolled down her window a couple inches. While there was a place for air conditioners, there was nothing like breathing in the fresh mountain air in springtime. "You must have an opinion about Stewart. You saw the boy. If you ask me, he's simply hurting over his father's death, which is a different emotion altogether from guilt. I don't think Stewart Pierce killed his father."

"While you might be right, he does have both motive and means. And there was a lot of anger in that boy that even you can't deny."

"True, but a lot of people get angry without unleashing their anger in the form of a crime."

"Sometimes all it takes is one pivotal moment to prove what's really inside a person. For the good and for the bad."

"That's a bit negative, don't you think?"

"God created man to be complex and to make his own decisions." Max reached back and opened the lid of the pastry box. "That's what makes us unique."

"What am I going to feed my guests tonight?"

"Stewart had two."

"I needed something to keep the boy talking." She shot him a grin. "What if I promise to make cinnamon rolls for you in the morning?"

He smiled and flipped the lid shut. There was no doubt that the way to Max's heart was through his stomach. And she supposed he had a point about the complexity of man, but she preferred to look at the situation in a less philosophical manner.

The lodge came into view. Nathan and Trisha stood on the porch and waved.

"At least we have something to celebrate in the midst of all this. Now all we need is for Nathan to finally pop the question."

Which made her feel a bit guilty about being happy over her son's relationship with Trisha when Annabelle was still in mourning. But not enough to completely douse the joy she felt over possible upcoming nuptials between the two. She'd seen the changes in Nathan. Trisha's move to Rendezvous so they could give their relationship a go was the best thing that had happened in as long as she could remember.

Pricilla pulled into the drive and parked the car then adjusted her bifocals. Trisha had a tissue in her hand. "Max, she looks as if she's been crying."

With her arms filled with baguettes, Pricilla got out of the car and hurried up the front steps. Max followed close behind with the pastries and the rest of the groceries. All she needed was another disaster to strike. Dealing with the aftereffects of Reggie's death gave her enough to fret over. Trisha blew her nose and leaned against the railing. The young woman's normally stunning eyes were red and puffy. If something was wrong with her. . .or if Nathan had broken up with her. . .well, her son would never hear the end of it. She adored Trisha, and it was high time her son got married and produced a grandchild.

Nathan took the pile of baguettes and motioned toward the front door. "Would the two of you mind coming inside? Trisha and I will put the groceries away then meet you in the living room. We have something to tell you."

Pricilla sat on the edge of the couch beside Max and braced herself for the bad news. While she didn't want to jump to conclusions, the clues all led to the same place. Trisha had been crying, and now the couple had something to tell her and Max. She could think of only one scenario that included Trisha crying and both Nathan and Trisha insisting on talking to the two of them together.

Nathan and Trisha were breaking up.

The very idea sent a band of shivers up her spine and turned her stomach sour. How could Nathan even consider such a thing? He'd finally found the perfect woman—thanks to his mother, she might add—but now, for some lame reason, he was ready to throw it all away?

The first time she'd met Trish, she knew that the young woman was ideal for her son. Not only was she smart, extremely attractive, and a Christian, she was single. That singleness, though, hadn't taken long to change once Pricilla had put her matchmaking skills into play. Trisha Summers was simply everything Pricilla had imagined in a daughter-in-law. And she had no intention of losing the girl.

She dug her nails into the arm of the couch. "I think Nathan and Trisha are breaking up."

"Breaking up?" The statement obviously caught Max off guard. "I can't imagine that. I don't ever remember seeing Trisha happier than she is now."

"I know she's been happy with Nathan, but something's wrong." Pricilla fiddled with the fringe on a throw pillow and wished she had something productive to do with her hands. She'd never been good at simply sitting. And waiting was even worse. "Didn't you notice she's been crying?"

Max continued thumbing through a hunting magazine. "She told me last night she thought she was coming down with a cold. I gave her some of my vitamin C tablets, and she went to bed early."

Pricilla still wasn't convinced that a lack of vitamins was Trisha's only problem. "What if my son has come down with a case of cold feet and has called things off between them?"

"It certainly wouldn't be the first time a couple broke up, but I think you're worrying over nothing." Max set down the magazine and gave her his full attention. "And speaking of doubts, I've been thinking a lot about you and me lately. I know this isn't the time for me to bring this up, but it seems to me that a case of cold feet might apply in our relationship as well."

Pricilla grimaced at the sting of his words, but only because she knew they were true. While neither of them had made the offer to move and change their relationship from a long-distance one to one where they actually lived in the same county, she had been the one who pulled back every time the subject of something permanent was broached.

It wasn't as if she didn't love Max or that she didn't enjoy his company. Far from it. Even now, his presence brought her a sense of security and stability. But what if that wasn't enough?

She knew that when he left to go back to New Mexico in a few days, the same fears would surface. Once, she'd thought it would just be a matter of time before she could shove her doubts aside. Doubts that she could truly find love the second time around. Doubts that at sixty-five she would be able to—or simply willing to—make the necessary adjustments. Doubts that she would be able to get over a second broken heart if something were to happen to Max.

More and more she wasn't so sure.

Even so, being afraid of losing Max like she'd lost Marty seemed a lame excuse. She'd never give up the forty-three years she'd had with her first husband in order to have saved her heart when he died. So why was making things permanent with Max any different? He was the best thing in her life right now, and she knew she'd be a fool to give him up.

"Max, I just don't—"

Trisha and Nathan entered the room then sat across from her and Max, leaving Max's comment hanging. For now, anyway. She knew it would only be a matter of time before the issue came up again.

Trisha blew her nose as tears formed in the corners of her eyes. Whatever the future held between her and Max, Pricilla couldn't stand the thought of her son breaking Trisha's heart.

Pricilla furrowed her brow. "How could you, Nathan?"

Her son shot her a blank look. "How could I what?"

"Look at her. She's crying."

"Crying? No." Trisha gave her a faint smile then blew her nose again. "Allergies. I'm absolutely miserable."

"Allergies?" Pricilla felt a wave of relief wash over her. "Why, that's wonderful."

"Wonderful?" Nathan wrapped his arm about Trisha and pulled her close.

"I didn't mean wonderful as in I'm-glad-you're-not-feeling-well. Not at all. I simply meant. . ."

Pricilla huffed out a deep sigh. Why did she always manage to get herself into such embarrassing messes? Jumping to conclusions. . .overlooking crucial pieces of evidence. . .and most importantly, allowing her fears to take over. Some detective she was. The entire thing was really Reggie Pierce's fault. If he hadn't gone and gotten himself murdered, she wouldn't be trying to turn every situation into an investigation. She glanced at Max, who, instead of coming to her rescue, seemed just as ready for an explanation.

Pricilla offered them all a weak smile. "Trisha looked as if she was crying, so first thing of course I imagined was that the two of you had broken things off."

"Quite the opposite, Mom."

Nathan held out Trisha's left hand. Pricilla's eyes widened. How in the world had she missed such a stunning ring? The diamond had to be at least half a carat.

"Trisha and I are engaged."

"Engaged?" Max broke into a grin. "Congratulations!"

Pricilla flew across the thick area rug to gather her son and future daughter-in-law into her arms. She might actually get the chance to hold her grandbabies before they sent her away to an old age home after all.

Max watched Pricilla out of the corner of his eye while she rambled on to Trisha about wedding dresses and colors. He was definitely going to have his work cut out for him in the coming weeks.

He caught snippets of the conversation between giggles and laughter. *Wedding planners. . .antique lace. . .no reason to wait too long. . .*

No reason to wait too long.

He might not know a thing about invitation etiquette and caterers, but that one phrase stuck with him. He'd sensed Pricilla's hesitation in their own relationship, and even though he realized they still had a number of obstacles standing between them, he truly wanted things to work out. When she'd flown down to see him in February, he'd considered proposing, but somehow she'd always managed to steer the subject away from anything permanent. To him, it was clear. For whatever reason, Pricilla wasn't ready to take the next step. And while he knew he loved her, he also knew that he wasn't content to wait indefinitely for her to decide what she wanted.

Even though she'd slept restlessly the night before, Pricilla still rose before the sun managed to make an appearance above the horizon. By nine o'clock she'd fed all the guests a hearty breakfast of scrambled eggs, biscuits and gravy, bacon, hash browns, and blueberry muffins, chatted with Trisha about a local florist when she dropped Max off at the lodge, and set up a tour of the bakery for half past ten with Annabelle. If she was to discover any new insights into Reggie's case—especially certain noteworthy details the pushy detective might overlook—meeting Annabelle's employees was essential.

Max wandered into the kitchen with a crossword puzzle in one hand and an empty coffee mug in the other. How could his eyes, ones that reminded her of Frank Sinatra, and his cologne, which always left her head reeling, leave her breathless one minute and ready to run away the next? She couldn't forget his comment from yesterday, and even after tossing and turning all night she still wasn't ready to respond to it. Even so, her stomach flipped as Max, wearing his worn loafers, shot her a grin before moving silently across the kitchen to refill his coffee mug from the coffeepot.

Watching him out of the corner of her eye, she stirred the stew she'd made for today's lunch and wished she had a clear response for him. She'd written down a dozen excuses in her journal last night, but that's all that they had been, excuses. Funny. She'd never before been accused of having cold feet—especially considering she normally jumped into things rather than stopping to examine the consequences—but for some reason love had tangled up her emotions and brought about the most unexpected reaction: a case of cold feet as difficult to unravel as the case of their local dead baker.

Turning down the stove a notch, she waited until Max was finished doctoring his drink before speaking. "I feel as if I owe you an apology for yesterday."

"An apology?" He took a sip then wrapped his hands around the hot mug. Even with spring in the air, the morning still had a slight chill. "What for?"

"For being the one with cold feet in this relationship. For not knowing where we're going, or even where I want things to go."

His gaze never left her face. "You don't owe me an apology. I shouldn't have broached the subject like that."

She wiped her hands on her apron before covering the bowl of coleslaw with plastic wrap and putting it in the refrigerator. "You were right. I have been hesitant to let our relationship go ahead, and I'm not even sure why. When you're here, I feel young again, and when you're away, I miss you, but it's hard to stay truly connected only through phone calls and letters."

She eyed the laptop on the dining room table. He had promised more lessons today, but she was quite certain that even daily e-mails would never take the place of face-to-face contact. In order for things to work between them, something was going to have to change. But she wasn't sure she was willing to pack up her life and move to New Mexico. Even for Max.

"Part of the problem, I'm sure, is that living so far apart simply isn't conducive to a growing relationship." Max leaned against the granite counter. "And I admit that I've been just as stubborn at the thought of moving here."

"It's completely understandable considering the fact that you've lived in New Mexico your entire life. You're a leader in the church and in the community—"

"The very same reasons I can't ask you to leave here. And besides that, I haven't seen you so happy since before Marty died."

Max's statement simply confirmed what she'd been feeling. She was happy here and had seen the thought of moving to New Mexico as a choice between doing something she loved, and finding love.

He bridged the gap between them and took her hand. "Like it or not, we're no longer two naïve teenagers ready to step out together and face the world. We've already faced many of the ups and downs of life head-on, which tends to give us a completely different outlook. And there's something else I think we're both forgetting. I realized yesterday that we've been going about this relationship all wrong."

"What do you mean?"

He squeezed her hand. "We need to pray about our relationship, Pricilla. It's something I admit that I haven't done nearly as much as I should have. I don't know. Maybe you're not the only one with cold feet."

Pricilla pressed her lips together. It was one thing for her to have cold feet, but for him to have them as well. . . She sighed. Of course he was right. How had she managed to spend time trying to convince Annabelle to keep praying and to give her loss to Christ, yet had rarely taken time to bathe her own relationship with Max in prayer?

It was time she laid it all before her heavenly Father. "It's interesting how you can give advice on how to give it all to God, but when it comes to putting that advice into practice yourself, it often gets lost in the bustle of life."

"Like with Annabelle?"

Pricilla nodded. "I've been trying to encourage her to not give up and to let God be her source of strength, but she feels guilty over Reggie's death."

"Guilty?"

"Guilty that she didn't work harder to make things work between them." Pricilla paused, startled at the correlation to her own life. Was she going to feel guilty one day for letting a second chance for love pass her by because she was afraid, or perhaps unwilling to take a chance?

Max shoved his now cold coffee into the microwave. "What did Paul say in 2 Corinthians? 'We are hard pressed on every side, but not crushed'?"

Pricilla nodded. She knew the verse well. "And 'struck down, but not destroyed.'"

Walking through difficulties was never easy. She watched Max grab the last blueberry muffin from the serving plate then take a bite while he waited for his coffee to finish heating up. Part of her longed for more intimate moments like this. Moments when she could bask in the familiarity of the two of them together. Conversations in the kitchen. . .over breakfast. . .perhaps under a starlit sky. Surely this was something she could get used to again.

The microwave beeped and Max took the mug back out. "I overheard you talking with Annabelle this morning. How is she?"

"About the same. Still trying to find her footing in all of this. I told her I'd stop by this morning. She's going to give me a tour of the bakery."

"Along with a chance to cross-examine the employees?" Max's eyebrows rose while she tried to ignore the unasked questions.

"You wouldn't mind if I happened to stop and chat with some of the employees, would you?"

"And if I did, would that make any difference?"

She caught the teasing in his voice despite his serious expression. "I—"

"I'm sorry." He winked at her. "Admittedly, that was an unfair question. I'll come along if I can play Watson on this quest."

She smiled, relieved that he had agreed to come with her, even if it was only to keep an eye on her. "Of course you can, Doctor."

Pricilla dropped the lid onto the pot to let the stew simmer. It was amazing how a brand-new day—and talking with Max—made it easier to put things in a different perspective. She'd been foolish to worry over Trisha and Nathan's relationship, and perhaps she was foolish to worry about her own relationship with Max as well. Obviously, the stress over finding Reggie's body and the subsequent concern for Annabelle were taking their toll. As grateful as she was to Max for humoring her on her quest to see what she could find out at the bakery, she knew that his unspoken concerns to stay out of it had validity. What right did she have to overstep Detective Carter's authority in the case, no matter what her personal feelings were regarding the man? The very fact that she'd solved one investigation didn't mean she'd have the same success with Reggie's case.

But Annabelle had asked for her help, and for Pricilla, that was all the motivation she needed.

Max followed Pricilla and Annabelle through the back room of the bakery, surprised at how interesting the tour had been. Of course, part of his interest might be due to the variety of samples they'd been offered. Top of the list so far was the strawberry cream cheese tart that would force him to double his normal daily workout, but it had been a sacrifice well worth it.

Annabelle signaled them both to follow her to where a man was pulling a long pan of tart shells from the oven. "I know you wanted to meet our staff. I'll have to hire at least two more full-time workers in the next few weeks, but for now I want you to meet José, who's our incredible chef, as I'm sure you both can testify to. Reggie might have taught him everything he knows, but the man is also extremely talented. I'm not sure what I would do without him."

As soon as the chef had set down the tray, Pricilla stretched out her hand to greet him. "It's nice to meet you, José. We're regular customers of the bakery."

The man nodded but avoided Pricilla's gaze, something that didn't stop her from continuing. "How long have you lived in Rendezvous?"

"Six years."

"You must have known Mr. Pierce well, then."

"He was a fair boss who taught me well." No sign of bitterness was reflected in the man's eyes as he spoke.

Annabelle nodded across the room at a second man who could have been José's twin with his short stature, dark hair, and narrow eyes. "His brother Naldo works primarily in filling orders for our online business, where, as you already know, we ship our products all over the country."

Naldo nodded but didn't move from where he stood assembling packages of bakery items to be mailed. Neither man appeared inclined to talk, let alone succumb to an unscheduled cross-examination by an amateur detective.

A timer went off and José jumped. "I'm sorry, but if you'll excuse me. . ."

"Of course." Annabelle turned as another man entered the warm back room of the bakery. "And this is Darren Robinson, computer geek extraordinaire—his words, not mine—but I must agree, as he's quadrupled our business with our new Web site and other ideas, like using the bakery here as a test market for our products."

The phone rang in the corner of the room that had been partitioned off into a small office. Annabelle took a step toward the metal desk that was piled with folders. "I'm expecting a phone call from my estate attorney and need to answer that. Darren, if you wouldn't mind filling our guests in on some of the details of the mail-order side of the business, I'd appreciate it."

With a nod from Darren, Annabelle's heels clicked across the tile flooring as she hurried to pick up the phone.

Darren clasped his hands together and gave them a lopsided grin. "Is there anything in particular you'd like to know, Mrs. Crumb?"

Max looked at Pricilla, knowing exactly what questions she'd like to ask. Without a badge, though, her line of questioning was limited. A blessing, from his point of view.

Pricilla flashed Darren a smile. "It sounds as if you're quite the computer expert."

A slight blush crept up the young man's cheeks. "I've been teased a time or two that I'd rather hang out with my Intel Xeon than—"

"Your what?" Pricilla shook her head.

"My computer."

"Oh—"

"And why not? The information and possibilities are endless. Give me a little bit of time, and I can tell you where you went to college, which credit cards you own, and where you took your last vacation."

This time Pricilla stood speechless, and Max forced himself not to chuckle out loud. "Didn't I tell you a computer would be useful?"

Pricilla cleared her throat. "Can you really do all those things?"

"Well, at the very least, I can probably find out where you went to college and if you have a blog or a MySpace account online—"

"A blog?" Pricilla was definitely out of her territory this time. "Never mind. But I do have a question for you."

Darren shoved his hands into his jeans pockets and shrugged. "Shoot."

"Do you give lessons?"

"Lessons?" The young man reached up to push his thick glasses up the bridge of his nose.

"Computer lessons. I have a new one, but unfortunately I'm quite illiterate when it comes to electronic things." Her gaze shifted briefly to Max. "I know nothing about blogs or any of that, but I am particularly interested in learning how to use the Internet."

Max recognized exactly where her line of questioning was heading, and he wasn't sure he liked it. Still, what better way to find out everything she could about Reggie and the other suspects? "I didn't know you were so interested, Pricilla."

She shot him a knowing look. "It is the wave of the future."

Ten minutes later they were heading out the bakery's driveway with a computer lesson lined up for the following week.

Pricilla turned on her blinker and waited for a family of tourists to pass in front of them before merging onto Main Street. "Did you notice anything about José?"

"Besides the fact that he makes some of the best tarts I've ever tasted?"

She frowned, obviously not in the mood for jokes. "Yes, besides that fact."

"Then no."

"He seemed very nervous, and his gaze kept shifting."

"He's a chef who makes a mean strawberry tart."

Pricilla sucked in her breath. "There he is again!"

She slammed on the brakes, and Max's hands hit the dashboard with a *thud.*

"Ouch! What are you talking about?"

"In the rearview mirror. It's the stranger who fought with Ezri the day of the funeral." She pulled the car against the curb, this time slowing to a stop. "He came out of the alley beside the bakery. I think it's time to add another suspect to my list."

Almost a week later, Pricilla finished frosting the last section of the cake then licked what was left of the lemon icing off the spatula. The sweet taste seemed a sharp contrast to her sour mood. Five days had passed since her unsuccessful visit to the bakery, where she'd learned nothing more than the fact that José and Naldo were nervous types (suspicious behavior perhaps, but not a valid reason to suspect them for murder), and that Darren was a computer wiz, which certainly wasn't a crime either. Even adding a seventh possible suspect had rendered no further evidence toward the truth. So, in regard to her investigation, she'd accomplished nothing.

Conversely, over the weekend the detective had taken in Annabelle for another round of questioning with the claims that forensics had uncovered further proof that foul play had been involved in Reggie's death. While no arrests had yet been made, or any details revealed, Annabelle had called Pricilla yesterday morning, certain that at any moment the detective would arrive at her doorstep with a warrant in his hands.

Something still didn't seem right in Pricilla's mind, and after their talk, she was even more convinced that Annabelle was innocent. But she hadn't been able to put her finger on the missing piece. Mulling over the list of suspects had done nothing more than leave her eyes blurred with fatigue and her brain refusing to cooperate.

As had the suspects themselves. Attempts to talk to Stewart on Friday at the bakery had left her with nothing more than an impression of an immature boy who needed a sense of direction in his life—but no signs of a murderer. Ezri was hiding something, Pricilla was certain, but she had a feeling it had nothing to do with her father's death and everything to do with her seventh suspect. That brought her back around to the bakery's two nervous employees and Darren the computer wiz. At least she still had her computer lesson with Darren in two days, but she was beginning to wonder if that, too, would lead to yet another dead end. With the progress she was making, she was liable to have more luck figuring out how to maneuver through the intricacies of the World Wide Web than making a breakthrough in the mystery surrounding Reggie's death. Stumbling across Charles Woodruff's murderer last October had obviously had nothing to do with her brilliant investigative skills, but instead had simply been a matter of luck.

Pricilla covered the cake before crossing out the last item on her to-do list for the lodge and glanced at the clock that hung on the wall. No matter what her frustrations over the case, she knew that Reggie's death and Annabelle's potential conviction weren't the real source of her restlessness. In less than thirty minutes, she would drive Max to the airport to catch his flight back to New Mexico. Instead of the sense of relief she thought she'd have, the very idea of his leaving left her feeling emptier than she'd ever imagined.

After his suggestion that she had cold feet, she'd decided that she needed time to not only pray about their relationship but time to step back and think about it—with Max on the other side of the state line. But in spite of her decision, the past week had been one of those nostalgic times she knew she would file in the recesses of her memory and pull out on a rainy day to savor.

He'd taken her out for dinner twice, to church on Sunday, and for a long drive into the mountains where they'd gone sightseeing like a couple of tourists. Even so, between wedding plans for Nathan and Trisha and late night Scrabble games, he'd avoided any further discussion of their future. The only thing that had been resolved between them had been their decision to pray about the situation until they saw each other again. And while prayer was definitely a step in the right direction, it had yet to clarify for her which direction her heart wanted their relationship to go.

Ignoring thoughts of cold feet versus lifelong commitment, Pricilla pulled a small notebook and pencil from the pocket of her sweater, for once thankful that she had something to think about besides Max. She'd compiled a list of suspects with as many details as she could, such as their links to the crime, motive, and opportunity. Filling in opportunity had been easy. All seven of her suspects had opportunity, except for perhaps Ezri's mystery man. Motives, on the other hand, had been harder to decipher. Even with her outspoken methods and candid questions, she'd discovered nothing that led to intent.

Max stepped into the kitchen, set his suitcase on the floor, and laid his carry-on bag on the table, interrupting her train of thought. "Are you about ready to go?"

Pricilla flipped the notebook shut and shoved it in her pocket before turning around to face him. Blue eyes. . .broad shoulders. . .and that smile. Since when had the option of doing something she loved and choosing love ever been an issue in the first place? Especially with Max involved. Somehow love was never that simple.

She cleared her throat. "Yes, I was just. . .just making sure everything was ready for lunch."

"And the notebook?"

A wave of awkwardness rolled through the warmth of the kitchen. The sweet scent of lemons mingled with the chowder simmering on the stove, yet did nothing to whet her appetite.

Max had told her that he'd come to the same conclusion regarding Annabelle's innocence, but that left him worried that the real murderer was still lurking about. He wasn't happy with Pricilla's quest to find the truth, especially since he was leaving. "You promised me you would let the detective handle the case."

"I promised not to do anything foolish that would land me in jail—"

"Or in the morgue. There's a killer on the loose. . .remember." Max held up his hand and sighed. "I'm sorry. I'm not going to be here much longer, so let's promise that there will be no more talk of Reggie, or sleuthing, or suspects—"

"Or Detective Carter."

"Definitely not him." He returned her smile, making her heart ache all the more.

There was no doubt about it. She was going to have to make a decision. And soon.

An hour later Max stood at the airport window and watched Pricilla drive away, afraid he'd just made the biggest mistake of his life. He tapped the edge of his ticket against the palm of his hand, eyed the check-in counter, and weighed his options. One, he could fly home as planned and continue trying to make their relationship work through phone calls, letters, and now e-mail. But even the latest technology wasn't able to bridge a gap of two hundred miles and bring them together for a weekly game of Scrabble or a romantic dinner out. And even that wouldn't have been enough.

His other option was to stay in Rendezvous, rent a place in town, and propose. Selling his house had been on his mind for months, but he'd always stopped before taking the plunge and actually calling a Realtor. The more he thought about it, though, the house was far too big, too quiet. . .and Pricilla wasn't there.

There was another thing to consider as well. He'd been praying about his relationship with Pricilla for the past few days, and somehow he knew that if he walked away now, he'd lose her forever. How he'd allowed stubbornness and his own reservations to get him this far, he wasn't sure, but there was no way to get around the truth. He was lonely, and he loved her.

Not that he was looking simply for companionship. Not at all. Despite Pricilla's somewhat quirky ways at times and the fact that she seemed to have a nose for trouble, he still wanted her in his life—for the rest of his life. She made him smile like no one else could. She was funny, smart, and made his heart thud like he was seventeen again. He'd never win her heart completely if he didn't take a chance.

And this time his staying would have nothing to do with Reggie Pierce's death, or whether or not Annabelle was truly innocent. While it was true he worried about Pricilla's often unconventional attempts to play the role of amateur detective á la Jessica Fletcher, he couldn't change who she was. . .nor did he want to. It was part of what he loved about her. Her innate desire to find out the truth no matter how difficult the process.

The automatic doors opened beside him, allowing the scent of freshly mown grass to fill the air. He took in a deep breath and smiled in resolve. Just because they weren't in what society called the prime of their lives was no reason they couldn't find a bit of happiness together. Since living hundreds of miles apart wasn't working, it was time he stepped up and made the move. What difference did it really make anyway, whether he was in New Mexico or Colorado? Only one option would give him what he really wanted.

Grabbing his suitcase in one hand and his carry-on in the other, he stepped to the curb and flagged down a taxi.

Pricilla bent down and snipped off another daffodil to add to the bunch she already had in her hand. A fresh bouquet of flowers, even with her limited choices at this time of year, would go a long way to boost her spirits. She fingered the yellow bloom. With Max gone, she'd finally get a chance to be able to sort through her feelings. She needed the space to decide if she really was suffering from a case of cold feet. . .or if she was ready to take the plunge into something more permanent.

Like matrimony.

The word brought an assortment of feelings to the surface that only forty-three years married to the same man could bring. Like any couple, her and Marty's life together had been full of joy and disappointment, hard work and fun, struggles and contentment. Then life had intervened and taken Marty from her. His dying, while a part of life, had never been an easy phase for her. A time to be born and a time to die. A time to grieve and a time to dance. A time to love. . .

And for her a second chance for love?

Glancing up, she saw no signs, in the cloudless blue sky, of the plane that was taking Max back to New Mexico. All she could see were the Rocky Mountains that loomed between them. Perhaps the truth was that the distance between them had kept her from having to make a decision. But the time for decision was coming.

She walked slowly along the front of the lodge then stopped and clipped a few cuts of ferns for the bouquet. Beside her small herb garden, the grounds would soon be sprinkled with a covering of spring flowers. Bleeding hearts, sweet William, tiger lilies, and peonies. . . If her heavenly Creator cared about each colorful bloom, He certainly cared about her own personal dilemma. Glad that no one was around to hear her audible mumblings, she cut a sprig of rosemary for supper and began praying.

"The truth is, Lord, I am finally happy for the first time since Marty died. Nathan needs me here, and honestly, it's good to feel needed." She crumbled the blades of rosemary between her fingers and took in a deep breath of the fragrant herb.

Despite the hectic pace, she loved the chance to cook, create menus, and make the guests happy. Retirement, in her mind, had been as eventful as one of her prized cheese soufflés gone flat. Dull, dreary, and monotonous. No matter how strong her feelings were for Max, she needed a purpose for her life.

"What do you think, Lord? Maybe I'm just afraid I'll move to New Mexico only to have everything fall apart, leaving me with nothing."

It was better this way. Wasn't it?

A horn honked as a car pulled into the circular drive. Pricilla stood up and immediately regretted the abrupt move. "Who in the world. . . ?"

Rubbing the small of her back with her free hand, she squinted into the afternoon sun and tried to determine who was in the taxi. No new guests were scheduled to arrive until tomorrow, and rarely did anyone show up without a reservation, as the lodge stayed full most of the year.

The car stopped in front of the porch, and someone stepped out of the back seat. With his back toward her, the man set his suitcase and carry-on bag on the ground then turned to pay the driver.

Max? It couldn't be. He was twenty thousand feet up in the air. . . .

"Pricilla."

Leaving his bags beside the porch, Max walked toward her with a lopsided grin on his face. "I had this crazy idea about staying here in Colorado. Renting an apartment, taking you out to dinner once a week, maybe working part-time for your son as a handyman. I don't know. But what I do know is that it would beat long-distance phone calls and e-mails." He paused to take a breath. "What do you think?"

"I. . ." She pulled the flowers to her chest and felt her heart pounding against the crushed blooms. "I don't know what to say."

He stopped right in front of her. "Say that you want me to stay. That you wouldn't mind putting up with an old, retired, and rather predictable gentleman, who loves fishing, peach cobbler, and you, though certainly not in that order—"

She reached out and placed her finger against his lips, smiling at his nervous chatter. "I want you to stay."

"Really?" He grasped her hand. "Something told me that if I left today I'd lose you forever. I'm just not willing to do that."

"I don't want to lose you either." Pricilla shook her head, certain she was dreaming. He was really willing to give it all up for her? "What about your house, your hunting buddies. . .your life in New Mexico? You'd give it all up? For me?"

"Yes, because I'd like to give it. . .to give us. . .a try."

Pricilla's lips curled into a smile. She let the bouquet of flowers tumble to the ground and wrapped her arms around his neck. Only God knew what the future held, but for the first time in a long while everything seemed all right again in the world.

Max looked across the table in the Rendezvous Bar and Grill, noted Pricilla's flushed cheeks, and knew he'd made the right decision. While she studied the dessert menu posted at the end of the table, he knew her mind wasn't on which piece of pie she might order but on their relationship. Not that Pricilla was ready to say yes to his proposal if he asked her today. He knew that. But he'd finally be able to court her properly. And what did he really have to lose? He could always fly back and go hunting with his buddies once or twice a year. And he'd be with Pricilla the rest of the time.

She sneezed and picked up her sweater off the bench beside her. Her notebook fell out on the table along with a packet of tissues.

Max reached across the table and picked up the spiral pad.

A grimace crossed her face as she grabbed it back. "You're not going to get after me for playing the role of Miss Marple again, are you?"

"No, because I know that if I do you'll have me running back to New Mexico faster than a wild bronco." He winked at her. He'd already decided that he was going to quit worrying about her investigative tendencies, even if that meant taking on the role of Dr. Watson to her Sherlock Holmes.

"Good. Then I suppose I could keep you around."

Her laughter and smile made his pulse race. "Where are you in your questioning?"

Pricilla flipped open the notebook then set it in front of him. "I've gone through each of the suspects one by one, including, of course, the bakery's three full-time workers. Also on the list are Ezri and Stewart, and as much as I believe she's innocent, I couldn't completely eliminate Annabelle. I've also added Ezri's mystery man since he seems to always show up at interesting times and is somehow connected to her."

"What about outsiders?"

"While I realize that it's possible that someone outside this list was responsible for Reggie's demise, no one reported seeing anyone else on the premises that morning." For the first time since his return, she frowned. "Without the added benefit of the forensic science information the detective has, I've decided to keep my list to these seven. But as you can see, motivations are quite limited."

Max couldn't help but chuckle inside. He might have taught her a thing or two about the art of interrogation from his own experiences in the military, but it was obvious she was struggling this time around. On television the suspects often seem ready to confess at the end of the show, but in real life, he found that was rarely the case. That was certainly true right now.

The waitress brought two orders of French dip and salads, set them on the table in front of them, and promised to return with refills on their water. After asking the blessing for the meal, Max chomped into his sandwich, hungrier than he'd realized. Watching Pricilla eat, he realized how much he enjoyed moments like this. Moments together he'd like to get used to.

She reached out and grabbed Max's hand. She jutted her chin toward the counter. "It's him again."

Max leaned forward. "Who?"

"Ezri's mystery man. He's paying for an order of takeout." Pricilla scooted to the edge of the booth and squinted through the top of her bifocals. "He's not getting away from me this time."

Pricilla reached for her sweater, but Max stopped her by tightening his grip on her hand. "It's one thing to take a tour of the bakery and meet Annabelle's workers. But you don't know anything about this man. What if he's the murderer and you start asking him a bunch of pointed questions? What if. . ."

Max stopped and rubbed his temple with the fingertips of his free hand. He'd practically accused a complete stranger of being involved in Reggie's death. For all he knew, the man could be a minister or a doctor. The whole situation was getting completely out of hand. Besides that, the young man was half his age and obviously worked out. No match for either of them if accusations began to fly and things got ugly. Dealing with this man would take a gun and a badge behind any finger pointing.

"I just want to talk to him." Pricilla pulled her hand away. "Annabelle is desperate for answers. If she goes to jail, what about her children and her business?"

He took in a deep breath and reminded himself of all the reasons why he'd decided to give up his life in New Mexico to spend it with Pricilla. "That's what I love about you. You've always cared about people enough to get involved in their lives. But this is different. Tell the sheriff about your suspicions and let him talk to the guy this time."

She shook her head. "All I'm going to do is ask him a few questions."

"Like what?" Max turned around to get a second glance at the man. "He's huge, and I don't think he's one to chat about a murder investigation over a cup of tea—especially if you're naming him as a suspect."

Pricilla's jaw tensed as she watched the front counter. The man was still waiting for his order. "All I plan to do is mention that I saw him with Ezri, and how I wondered if he was a friend of hers."

Leaning forward, Max lowered his voice. "And then what? Do you really think he's going to open up and tell you, a complete stranger, that he murdered Reggie? Or perhaps how he planned the man's demise with Ezri's help?"

"Max!"

"I'm sorry, but—"

"What about Sherlock Holmes and Dr. Watson?" Pricilla grabbed her notebook off the table. "I thought we were a team."

"We are, but—"

"He's just got his order. I've got to catch him before he gets away."

Before Max could mutter another word, she'd slid out of the booth and was gone. He eyed his sandwich and salad and felt his stomach growl. So much for lunch. With a resigned sigh, he headed for the front of the restaurant where Pricilla was leaving in pursuit of Ezri's mystery man, who carried a bag of takeout under his arm. Even Pricilla's suspect was going to get to eat lunch.

"Sir."

Max paused in the doorway at the cashier's sharp voice.

"Sir, you haven't paid."

Max turned around. Of all the ridiculous things. But he couldn't argue. The teenager, sporting a silver nose ring and eying him accusingly, was right. Pricilla was going to get him into serious trouble one day. He could see the headlines now: MAN ARRESTED FOR FAILING TO PAY FOR LUNCH. He took a deep breath and dug his wallet out of his pocket. Twenty dollars would more than cover the bill and leave a hefty tip to a waitress who had yet to refill their water. He set the money on the counter.

She chomped on a piece of gum and glared at him. "I need to see your bill with that."

"I don't have a bill."

"Then you'll have to wait until the waitress rings one up for you."

This conversation was going nowhere quickly. "I'm in a hurry, can't you—"

"I need the bill."

Max scanned the crowded restaurant for the waitress, but there was no sign of the redhead. "You can still see what I ordered on my table, because I didn't have a chance to finish it. Two orders of French dip sandwiches and salads. Water to drink. Nothing on your menu is over nine bucks."

The girl was still frowning.

Max slapped another five on the counter. "Will this cover any inconvenience?"

She fingered the additional bill. "Well, I suppose this would cover whatever was on the bill—"

"Thank you." Max hurried out the door and glanced up and down Main Street for Pricilla's bright pink sweater.

She was nowhere to be seen.

Pricilla slipped around the corner of Main and Aspen and pressed her hand against her chest. Max had been wrong. Ezri's mystery man's physique wasn't proving to be a physical threat to her life, but his fast pace might. The man was only half a block ahead of her, but so far he hadn't heard her attempts to get his attention. More than likely he was listening to one of those new-fangled headsets with music loud enough to leave him deaf before he was thirty.

Trying to control her labored breathing, she walked past the local pet shop and wished she'd worn her walking shoes. If he went much farther, she'd have to admit defeat. He had to be stopping soon, though. The only thing left on this street was the snowmobile shop on the corner. Beyond that, the paved road turned into a dirt path that led up into the mountains.

A large neon sign stood in front of the one-story building that rented snowmobiles and ATVs to tourists. Pricilla's eyes widened as the man struck off across the parking lot where a couple dozen all-terrain vehicles were parked.

"Surely he's not planning to ride one of those..."

The man jumped on one of the ATVs.

Pricilla shook her head and scurried toward him, but he was too far away. She'd never reach him in time. "No, no, no..."

Quickly she weighed her options. There wasn't a salesperson in sight to help her. Not that they would want to rent to a gray-haired granny sporting heels and a pleated skirt. He gunned the engine. Pricilla waved her arms to get his attention, but he was busy getting his helmet on.

She eyed one of the models. The key was in the ignition. Once, about fifteen years ago, she and Marty had rented a couple of ATVs and ridden for several hours through the desert. Maneuvering an ATV might not be like driving a car, but how hard could it be? The man was pulling out of the parking lot. She couldn't simply take it, of course. And besides, she wasn't even sure she could remember how to start the thing.

"You've done this before, and it can't be that difficult." Pricilla hiked her leg over the seat and tried turning the key.

Nothing.

She had to hurry. She could still see the flame-colored vehicle as the man headed down the dirt trail, but it wouldn't be long until he disappeared from view behind the trees. She tried turning the key again and this time the engine roared to life. There was a helmet on the handlebars, and she shoved it on her head before buckling the strap.

No doubt this was one of those situations where Max would demand she stop and consider carefully what she was about to do. But a picture of Annabelle flashed through her mind. She'd mentioned her fears that Ezri was seeing someone and had been very secretive about the relationship. Pricilla had seen firsthand how one bad egg could ruin a girl for life. Maybe there was no connection to Reggie's death, but she'd never forgive herself if she didn't at least try.

The vehicle jerked forward, almost knocking her off. She was going to get herself killed before ever leaving the parking lot. Inching forward, she pushed harder on the accelerator, allowing it to sputter ahead. One hand on the gas, the other on the brake, it was simple. All she had to do was follow Ezri's mystery man and find out where he was staying. With an extra spurt of gas to the engine, she flew forward toward the dirt road.

Max stood on the edge of the sidewalk, wondering how Pricilla could have simply vanished. Her car was still parked in front of the Rendezvous Bar and Grill, which meant she couldn't have gone far, but a glance down both sides of the street revealed nothing more than a couple small groups of tourists enjoying a day of shopping. Which way had she gone?

Frustrated, he headed north on Main, glancing into store windows in hopes of catching a glimpse of her pink sweater behind a display of old-fashioned trunks or maybe a rack of postcards. Three blocks later, he paused again at the corner boasting the only stoplight in town. Considering the town of Rendezvous had only one main street, there weren't a lot of places where one could simply disappear. Straight ahead led to the park. To the right was the road to Nathan's lodge, and the road to the left went past an ATV rental place as it began its ascent into the mountains. He simply had no idea which way to go.

Knowing Pricilla's inclination to get into trouble didn't help calm his anxiety either. He scratched behind his ear and decided to backtrack along the other side of the street. There had to be a logical explanation somewhere. If Pricilla's mystery man was connected to Ezri, it made sense that Pricilla had followed him back to the bakery. If nothing else, it was worth a try.

Crossing the street, he admitted to himself that his decision to return to Rendezvous was not turning out the way he'd expected. In less than an hour, he'd assumed his role of Dr. Watson despite his better judgment, paid for a supposed celebratory meal he hadn't had a chance to enjoy, and lost Pricilla. How could the woman be such a magnet for trouble?

As Max approached the bakery, a flash of color caught his eye at the end of the alley that ran alongside the store. He adjusted his bifocals. It was definitely not Pricilla, but someone was rummaging through a bag beside a Dumpster. He took a couple steps into the alley. It was Naldo—or José. He couldn't tell for sure which brother, but there was one thing he could tell. The man wasn't taking out the trash. Max watched as the other man pulled out a dark green sack from the large Dumpster and began sifting through its contents. Every few seconds he glanced back at the bakery, then continued his search.

Max searched for a legitimate explanation. Not that going through trash was unheard of. He knew about the sport of Dumpster diving from a nephew of his who claimed he'd given up shopping retail because of his regular dives. But except for a few stale donuts and bagels, Max couldn't imagine what one of the Baker's Dozen employees would be doing sorting through trash. And considering that the bakery was the site of a recent murder, he couldn't help but wonder if there was a connection.

He strolled past the alley, trying to look inconspicuous by appearing to be interested in the latest spring collection of women's wear displayed in a store window. He counted to thirty, then spun around to return for a second look down the alley. The man was gone. Max didn't stop to consider the consequences. He slipped down the alley and found the grocery sack the man had been going through. It was nothing more than a bunch of discarded mail, mainly junk mail, the kind that had a habit of collecting faster than the layer of dust in his living room.

He picked up one of the envelopes from the sack, flipped it over, and read the address. Darren Robinson. He picked up another envelope from a credit card company. Again, the letter had been forwarded to the bakery and addressed to Darren Robinson.

A door squeaked open behind him. Max shoved a piece of the mail into his back pocket, threw the rest of the evidence into the Dumpster, and spun around.

Annabelle stood in the doorway, dressed in a blue jogging suit. "Why, Mr. Summers. What a surprise. It's good to see you again."

"I'm afraid I've. . ." He stammered, irritated that he'd let his curiosity get the best of him. And he'd gotten onto Pricilla for being impulsive.

"Did you need something?" The smile on the woman's lips didn't mask the dark shadows under her eyes.

"I'm looking for Pricilla, actually. Have you seen her?"

"Not today." If the women found it odd that she'd caught him behind her shop, going through the Dumpster, she didn't show it.

"I'm sure she's fine, she. . ." He didn't know how to explain the fact that he'd managed to lose Pricilla while eating lunch in town.

"You know, your timing is perfect, if you have a few minutes."

"My timing?"

"Ezri's out, Stewart's working up front, and Naldo just finished baking a new batch of samples. We need someone to taste them."

Max took in a deep breath of chocolate, caramel, and every other sinfully delicious pastry the bakery made and wondered how he could refuse. "But Pricilla. . ."

"I can have Stewart send her back if she shows up." She waved him inside. "Do you like macaroons?"

He followed her to a table set up on the far side of the room. "If you're talking about one of those divine coconut cookies Pricilla likes to make for her guests."

"That's exactly what I'm talking about, but these are homemade coconut almond macaroons filled with bittersweet chocolate cream and just a hint of orange marmalade inside."

Max's mouth began to water.

"Don't forget the bittersweet chocolate and roasted coconut on the outside."

He smiled. "And you want me to be a taste tester."

"Are you game?"

He glanced at the door. "I really should try and find Pricilla. . ."

"It will take five minutes, and I'm sure she's fine. Mr. Cadwell is having a shoe sale. Fifty percent off. She told me she planned to stop by and probably just forgot to tell you."

Max hesitated. Annabelle was right. Letting his imagination get away from him was only going to up his blood pressure. He worried too much. Just because Reggie Pierce had met a tragic ending didn't mean there was a murderer around every corner. Besides that, he knew how much Pricilla loved to talk. He eyed the tray of desserts and cleared his throat. Pricilla was fine.

"I don't ever remember turning down a chance to sample desserts of any kind. Especially when the words *chocolate*, *coconut*, and *orange marmalade* are all in the same sentence."

"And that's not all," Annabelle rushed on. "We're trying out a new triple chocolate cheesecake, and raspberry bars—raspberry preserves inside a buttery, almond crumb crust."

Max rested a hand on his stomach, knowing exactly what Pricilla would say if she were here. But surely calories didn't matter for the moment. Naldo and José were busy at work. He could always use the opportunity to see if what had just happened outside at the Dumpster had any relevance to the case.

"You're going to love these." Annabelle sat down at a small table and motioned for Max to join her. "Naldo wants to add a few more choices to our selection and prepared these to see what I think."

"I saw Naldo, or maybe his brother, outside a couple of minutes ago."

"Naldo stepped out for a bit of air, I believe. Are you ready?"

He eyed a tray filled with samples of dessert and smiled. A few minutes longer wouldn't hurt. Annabelle picked up a bite-sized macaroon and Max followed suit. The creamy chocolate blending in with the coconut and marmalade swirled on his taste buds.

"Now this is fantastic."

"I agree, but there's more."

Max took a second bite of the macaroon for good measure, certain that moving to Rendezvous was going to prove to be hazardous to his health. Between the bakery and Pricilla's cooking he wasn't sure how he was going to avoid gaining weight.

He took a sip of water from the glass Annabelle offered then eyed the next selection. Cheesecake was one of his favorites. A buzzer went off across the kitchen and Max glanced up. Naldo and José, along with a couple helpers, were hard at work baking. Now was as good a time as any to voice his recent concerns.

"I know it's none of my business," he began, "but Naldo was sifting through the trash in your Dumpster."

Annabelle looked up. "That's odd."

"I thought so as well, though normally I suppose I wouldn't feel compelled to say anything. It's just that with the death of your husband. . ." He caught her flickering gaze. "I'm sorry."

"It's okay. I appreciate your concern." She picked up a bite-sized piece of cheesecake. "While I can't imagine why he would go through the Dumpster, I also don't see how it could have any connection to my husband's death."

"Normally I would agree. What struck me, though, was that he was looking through Darren Robinson's mail."

"That's even stranger." She wiped the corners of her mouth with a napkin. "But I still can't see a connection to my husband's death. Can you?"

"No. . . Not at the moment anyway."

Max pulled out the envelope from his back pocket. It had been forwarded, in care of the bakery. "Does Darren have all his mail forwarded here?"

"Yes. He said it would be easier for him since he was only going to be here temporarily and doesn't have a permanent address."

Max set the letter on the table and reached for a raspberry bar. "Where is he living right now?"

"He moved in with a couple friends on the edge of town. I don't think it's anything worth bragging about, but the rent is cheap and the neighborhood is decent."

He took a bite of the crunchy raspberry bar and smiled. At least this wasn't a competition. He'd never be able to choose his favorite of the three.

Annabelle took a sip of her water. "I could simply ask Naldo what he was doing."

"I'm not sure that's a good idea. I think it best to leave all lines of questioning to the police—"

"Naldo."

His concern fell on deaf ears. So much for trying not to get involved. How was he ever going to convince Pricilla about the dangers of investigating once she knew what he'd been up to?

Naldo stopped at the table with a broad smile across his face. He wiped his hands against his white apron that was covered with flour and smears of chocolate. "Mrs. Pierce? Do you like them?"

"You've outdone yourself again, Naldo. As always."

"Mr. . . ."

Max nodded. "Mr. Summers. Max Summers."

"Do you like them, Mr. Summers?"

"They're fantastic."

Naldo moved to leave, but Annabelle stopped him. "There is one other small thing, Naldo. I'm sure it's nothing, but with the recent death of my husband, you must understand that I'm. . .concerned about what happens around here."

Naldo's brow lowered. "Of course, Mrs. Pierce."

Annabelle picked up the envelope from the table and handed it to Naldo. "Mr. Summers, as a friend, is looking into the death of my husband and saw you going through the trash. Looking specifically, it seems, in Darren Robinson's mail. I wondered if you could tell me why."

"I. . ." Naldo glanced away briefly. "I received a letter from home this week and can't find it. I thought perhaps it had gotten thrown away with the trash. I have no reason to look through Darren's mail."

Max was certain the man was lying.

"You know that Mr. Pierce always treated my brother and me well," Naldo continued. "I never would have done anything to hurt him. . .or you and his children."

"I know that, Naldo. Thank you for your explanation. You and your brother have always been hard workers and you know I appreciate that. I was certain you had a plausible explanation."

"Thank you, ma'am." Naldo bowed his head then returned to the kitchen.

"You don't believe him, do you?" A shadow crossed Annabelle's face as she picked up another raspberry bar and took a bite.

"I believe he respects you and your late husband, though I'm not convinced about his excuse. But you were right. It's probably nothing." Max looked at his watch. "I really should go and find Pricilla."

"Of course." Annabelle stood. "Thank you for your help with the pastries . . .and for your concern for me and my family."

Max said good-bye then hurried out the back alley to the street. Just like he'd done with Pricilla's disappearance, he refused to make a mountain out of a molehill, but one thing seemed obvious. Naldo was hiding something.

Every joint of Pricilla's body ached from the continual jolt of the uneven terrain as she rode the ATV up the bumpy mountain road. She already regretted her impulsive decision and knew she should stop. The only problem was that she wasn't sure if she could stop. And of course, at some point she'd return the quad. She'd simply have to explain that she'd been after a suspect in a murder investigation, and if she lost the man she might miss an important lead. She'd worry then whether or not they believed her.

Another bump on the road shook the ATV. Not only were the trees lining the trail getting denser, but the dirt road was getting steeper, and she wasn't sure anymore that the owners of the ATV she'd "borrowed" were going to look at her acquisition that way. Why couldn't she have simply admitted defeat and waited for a more opportune time to track down the man?

Except who was to say that she'd ever get another chance. Keeping her speed constant, she somehow managed to keep the other vehicle in sight. The driver had made no sign that he noticed anyone was behind him, which was fine with her. She'd much rather keep her presence undisclosed than have him think someone was stalking him.

A large bump in the road bounced her ATV into the air. Slamming down on the seat, she realized the truth in the saying that you're only as young as you feel, because at the moment, she was feeling quite old. Her body, with all the normal aches and pains of a sixty-five-year-old, wasn't meant to fly down a dirt road—in a skirt, no less—on an off-road vehicle.

She gripped the handles and attempted to avoid a second bump, but that only managed to pull her off course. The ATV veered off the path and she lost control. A tree loomed ahead of her. Pulling to the right with every ounce of strength she had left, she missed the tree by inches. . .and ran into a juniper shrub. Entangled by the bush, the engine sputtered then stopped.

With her entire body numb from the vibration of the vehicle, Pricilla didn't move for a full thirty seconds. Finally, she pulled the helmet off her head and assessed the damages. Her skirt had caught on something and was torn. A bruise was forming on her left calf, and her arms felt like limp spaghetti. At least she'd live.

Pricilla drew in a sharp breath and tried to ignore the stab of pain in her lungs, brought on by the cool mountain air. A lark called out in the distance. Blue spruce, evergreens, and aspen trees crowded around her. A crisp, spring wind blew across her face, but all she felt was a deep ache in every muscle and joint. Climbing slowly off the bike, she stood up straight. She'd be sore tomorrow—and the day after that, no doubt. What she really wanted right now was a hot bath with a handful of Epsom salts thrown in. Instead, she had two options, and they both, unfortunately, involved exercise. Walk back to town, or continue on to the nearest cabin. She adjusted her bifocals and looked ahead. There was a cabin not five hundred yards from her. . .with the flame-colored ATV parked outside.

Leaving the quad bike to be dealt with later, Pricilla made her way toward the cabin, stopping only once she'd reached the bottom of the porch stairs. The one-story house sat surrounded by a grove of aspen trees, and a trail of smoke rose from the chimney. But there was no trace of the man. Max was going to be furious at her impulsiveness, but she'd come this far. She might as well go the rest of the way.

With a dose of determination, she marched up the steps and knocked on the door. Someone pulled back a lace curtain and peered out the front window. A moment later the door opened.

"Mrs. Crumb?"

"Ezri?" Pricilla wasn't sure who was the most surprised.

Ezri tugged on the bottom of her tan leather jacket and cocked her head. "Mrs. Crumb? I—"

"Who is it, sweetheart?" Ezri's mystery man stepped in behind her and peered over her head.

Pricilla cleared her throat. "This is rather awkward, and I am sorry for barging in on you like this, Ezri, as it's really none of my business, but. . .you know, I haven't met your friend."

"This is Kent Walters." Ezri glanced behind her. "My. . .my husband."

"Your husband? Oh." Pricilla's eyes widened as she tried to process Ezri's statement. "I had no idea you were married."

"Neither did anyone else until now." Kent, who towered over Ezri by several inches, came forward and shook Pricilla's hand. "It's nice to meet you, Mrs. Crumb."

Ezri ignored her husband's questioning stare. "Mrs. Crumb, you must be cold. Please come in."

Pricilla shivered in response. "I'm fine, really, though it is a bit chilly now that the sun has started going down."

"You can sit by the fire and warm up." Ezri pulled a stack of books off a worn wingback chair and patted the back of the seat. "Would you like some hot chocolate? I've even got some of those miniature marshmallows."

"That would be nice. Thank you." Pricilla went to stand in front of the hearth, not sure if the chills she felt were from the weather or the strange situation she'd just stepped into.

The fire crackled, and she breathed in the fresh scent of pine. Pricilla fingered the notebook inside her skirt pocket and mentally added two questions to her list. Was there any connection in all of this to Reggie's death? Or had she simply uncovered a whole other mystery? Somehow, she knew she needed to find out the answers to both, because whether or not Ezri had been involved with her father's death, Pricilla had obviously stumbled onto something significant.

Ezri hesitated for a moment in the doorway to the kitchen as if she wasn't quite sure whether or not Pricilla should be left alone with Kent. "I'll be right back with the hot chocolate."

Pricilla's adrenaline raced as she glanced around the room. The small living area was sparsely furnished, but red fringed throw pillows, paired with a multicolored afghan on the couch and a handful of pictures, added just enough warmth to make the room homey. While she was shocked to hear that Ezri was married—a fact she was quite certain her mother had no inkling of—at least a cup of hot chocolate might give her time to figure out exactly what was going on.

Pricilla's gaze stopped at a wedding photo of Ezri and Kent. Unlike the trendy jacket, T-shirt, and low-cut jeans Ezri wore today, the white dress was simple and elegant.

She picked up the silver frame off the mantel to study the picture closer. "Ezri made a beautiful bride."

Kent cleared his throat. "Yes, she did."

He turned to her, allowing Pricilla to get a close look at him for the first time. Standing at least six foot two, he was muscular with bright blue eyes, and quite handsome. His expression softened as he gazed at the photo of his wife. While Max had to be correct in his assessment that the man worked out, there was nothing sinister about him. Just from the look in his eyes, it was obvious that he loved Ezri.

Pricilla ran her finger down the edge of the frame. "It's too bad her mother wasn't able to help plan the wedding."

"I guess you've figured out by now that we married in a very untraditional manner." He picked up a piece of candy out of a bowl from the hearth and unwrapped it. "I tried to talk her out of eloping, but Ezri insisted we keep it a secret."

Pricilla set the photo back down and took a seat in the wingback chair. "Why the secrecy?"

"You'll have to ask Ezri that question." He popped the chocolate into his mouth. "I'm not even sure why she told you who I was. She's the one who insisted that we keep our relationship a secret. Something hard to do as a newlywed, let me tell you."

Pricilla caught his slight blush. "How long have you been married?"

"Almost two months." He shoved the wrapper into his jeans pocket and reached for a second piece of candy. "I've seen you around town, haven't I?"

"Perhaps." Pricilla nodded, wondering how much she should admit to regarding her afternoon escapade. "I. . .I have to confess that I followed you here today."

She braced for his response, hoping she wouldn't be the only one coming clean.

"You followed me here?"

"I borrowed one of the ATVs from town." Pricilla cringed, realizing how lame her excuse was going to sound. The way things were headed, she'd be the one ending up in a jail cell.

"Really? I'm working at the shop for the summer. They let me use one of their ATVs to get around. Renting a car became too expensive." He shook his head. "I don't understand, though. Why were you following me?"

Ezri returned with two large mugs of hot chocolate and handed one to Pricilla. "Kent, please. Mrs. Crumb is a close friend of my mother's. I'm sure she has a perfectly good reason. Don't you, Mrs. Crumb?"

"Ezri, can I talk to you in the kitchen for a minute?" He turned to Pricilla, his expression guarded. "You don't mind, do you, Mrs. Crumb?"

"Kent—"

"I don't mind at all." Pricilla touched the young woman's sleeve. "Really, Ezri, it's fine. And by the time you get back, I might actually have warmed up enough to chat for a few minutes."

Pricilla took a sip of the chocolate and let the hot liquid warm her insides as the couple left the room. Not that Ezri would want to chat with her. Pricilla had somehow managed to show up unannounced on their doorstep and gain a confession before she'd even posed her first question. She bet the detective couldn't have done that well if he'd tried. But that still left her with the fact that Ezri was feeling vulnerable, and answering a slew of questions might not go over well.

Two minutes later the back door slammed shut as Ezri returned to the living room again. "You'll have to forgive Kent. He knows how badly I've been hurt in the past with my father, and he's always been very protective of me. He wasn't sure how to react with your showing up unexpectedly and then my blurting out that we're married."

"He seems like a nice man." Pricilla prayed for wisdom as she spoke. Outside appearances often meant nothing. A secret marriage could easily be the tip of the iceberg for a multitude of other skeletons. And she couldn't forget Reggie's murder.

"Kent is wonderful." Ezri sat on the edge of the brick hearth with a dreamy look of one in love. "He spoils me like I'm a princess."

For a moment, Pricilla saw the familiar reflection of her own self all those years ago. She, too, had been young, in love, and ready to conquer the world with her hero. Losing Marty had been like losing half of her soul. And it had taught her that happily ever after doesn't last forever.

Starting a relationship with Max had been completely unexpected. He'd waltzed into her life like a handsome knight on horseback and reminded her of the delights of falling in love for the first time. Having cold feet hadn't stopped her heart from beating fast in his presence or her cheeks from blushing at his compliments. Somehow, Max had managed to start erasing any doubts she harbored over finding love the second time.

But she wasn't here for Max.

Pushing thoughts of her own romantic saga aside, Pricilla pressed on with the matter at hand. "Tell me about Kent."

Ezri stretched out her legs and crossed her ankles. "I met him two years ago in an English lit class. For me, it was love at first sight. He was so handsome and dreamy, like Jane Austen's Mr. Darcy and Lord Byron wrapped up into one."

Pricilla laughed at the comparison. "As I recall from my own literature classes, Lord Byron was somewhat of a scandalous hero, was he not?"

Ezri leaned forward and winked. "Eloping is rather scandalous, don't you think?"

"True." If thoughts of scandal hadn't stopped Ezri from going ahead with the elopement, Pricilla couldn't help but wonder what else the young woman might dare to try. Murder, perhaps? "Kent seemed surprised that you told me the truth about your marriage. And, I have to admit, so was I."

Ezri shrugged. "Even I'm astounded over the confession. I don't know. I saw you standing there with Kent behind me, and it just slipped out. Truth is, I'm tired of keeping secrets and sneaking around. It's been awful not telling my mother."

Pricilla shook her head. She had yet to understand the couple's reasoning for keeping the relationship a secret. "If it's been so awful, then why haven't you told her?"

Ezri took a sip of her drink then held the steamy cup under her chin. "It's complicated."

"Love often is, but I'd think your mother would be thrilled to know that you've found someone who loves you so much."

"I know." Ezri's relaxed pose was fading. "I used to have dreams of a beautiful church wedding, with me in a long satin dress with a train that went on forever. Funny how life sometimes gets in the way."

"What exactly got in the way?"

"You mean who." Ezri fiddled with the gold chain of her necklace. "It was my father. While everyone knew he could be temperamental, I'm sure my mother kept certain things even from you. He was extremely controlling. For example, in order to pay for our schooling, we had to return home every summer and work at the bakery where he paid us minimum wage and made us miserable. Marriage was another issue with him. Not that he was against my getting married one day, I suppose, but not until I had a diploma in my hand. If he knew I'd married Kent, he'd have cut me off financially, and then I wouldn't have been able to afford to stay in school."

Pricilla didn't like where the conversation was heading. "So this is all about money?"

Ezri frowned. "You make me sound like a fortune hunter."

"But why not just wait?"

Ezri took a sip of her hot chocolate and spilled a drop on her shirt. She pulled a tissue out of her pocket and dabbed at the stain. "Kent wouldn't have waited for me forever."

"If he truly loves you—"

"Please, Mrs. Crumb." Ezri set her mug on the hearth and walked across the worn carpet. "I know enough to realize that no guy is going to wait around for a girl whose father dominates her life and refuses to let her marry."

Pricilla understood the girl's dilemma but still wasn't convinced that Kent had been worth the deception. "What about the fight you had with Kent after your father's funeral? I hate to say it, but from what I saw, he seemed as domineering as your father."

"Kent is nothing like my father." Ezri stopped in front of the fireplace and faced Pricilla. "He's kind, gentle, compassionate. . . ." She shook her head and threw the tissue into the fire. Within seconds it had disintegrated. "He believed we should tell my mother that we're married, but I felt like she'd had enough shocking news lately."

"Your mother's stronger than you think, Ezri."

"Maybe, but losing a husband then finding out her daughter had eloped all in the same week didn't seem right." Ezri shrugged. "I guess I'm still waiting for the right moment."

"So Kent is living here while you wait to tell your mom?"

"This place belongs to his grandfather." Ezri ran her fingers across the stone hearth. "I love it up here on the mountain. And best of all, it gives us a place to be together when I'm not working at the bakery."

As a mother, Pricilla knew that if Ezri were her child, she'd want to know the truth. "You need to tell your mom."

"I know. But now she's dealing with my father's death, and the detective—"

"Keeping secrets only causes trouble in the end."

"Like murder?" Ezri sat back down. "Kent's one of your suspects, isn't he?"

"I'm not a detective."

"Mom told me that you were looking into things for her and trying to find out the truth. I guess Kent might have looked a bit suspicious if you didn't know who he was. Of course, I suppose I'm on the list as well, aren't I?"

Pricilla pressed her hand against her pocket and felt the notebook. "I admit to being curious. That's the reason I followed him here. I was worried about you."

Pricilla set her empty mug on the hearth and realized she was still just as worried about Ezri. With her father out of the picture, she could bring her marriage out into the open. Was freedom from her father motive enough for murder?

Ezri glanced outside where Kent was chopping wood. "So what now?"

"I'd say that's up to you."

When the neon sign of the snowmobile shop came into view, Pricilla felt her breath catch. She'd hardly noticed the bumps and ruts she'd traveled over for the past few minutes. All she'd been able to think about was Ezri's foolish elopement and her own foolish, impulsive act. While she'd tried to convince Ezri that it was time to face the truth and confess to her mother, she knew she had her own confession to make. Hopefully the owners of the four-wheeler would be sympathetic and not press charges.

Kent had offered to follow her back down to the shop and explain the situation to his boss, but Pricilla had graciously declined his offer, insisting that she was going to have to own up to her actions.

Pulling into the parking lot, she maneuvered past a row of discounted bikes. Max had probably called the sheriff by now and put out a missing persons report on her. What was he going to say when he found out where she'd really been? She pressed on the brake and managed to stop without running into anything.

"There she is, Detective." A balding man came storming out of the shop with none other than Detective Carter on his tail. "I'd say the description I gave you fit perfectly. Late sixties, gray hair. . ."

Late sixties? Pricilla let out a sharp huff. That boy needed a new pair of glasses. Ignoring the commotion as the two men shuffled across the parking lot to where she had parked, she attempted to climb off the bike. Her legs went limp, and this time it wasn't from the jostling of the quad. Somehow she knew that whatever excuse she gave for her impulsive behavior, it wasn't going to work with the detective.

Gripping the handles, she braced herself for the encounter. "Detective Carter. I hadn't expected to run into you today."

"So you didn't plan to steal this quad bike?"

"I didn't steal it, I just. . ." Just what? For the first time in her life her curiosity and impulsiveness were about to give her a federal record. "I take full responsibility for my actions."

The detective shook his head. "Pricilla Crumb, I'm afraid I'm going to have to place you under arrest for the unauthorized possession of this all-terrain vehicle."

11

Pricilla clenched the arms of the metal chair in Detective Carter's small office and tried not to panic. Max had warned her that her attempts to play detective would only get her into trouble. And his predictions had just come true. The detective might not have forced her to wear handcuffs on the short ride to the sheriff's office, but she knew he was on his way to start the fingerprinting process followed by half a dozen mug shots. She glanced down at her black skirt and wondered what she'd look like in bright orange. Mouthwatering gourmet meals and walks in the mountains would be replaced by an hour of fresh air a day and manual labor.

Surely this wasn't happening.

Needing to focus on something besides her current state as an apprehended felon, she glanced around the office. Two glass walls overlooked the lobby of the station that was quiet at the moment. Obviously, no one else had decided to go chasing after a murder suspect in a pilfered off-road vehicle. The second pair of walls was lined with plaques and diplomas. It seemed the detective was creating a name for himself in the area of law enforcement.

Or at least trying to. Considering his brusque manners and gruff behavior, she still wasn't convinced of his competence.

Standing to examine the plaques more carefully, she dismissed the thought and wondered why Detective Carter always managed to rub her the wrong way. He was just a man doing his best to get ahead in this world. And besides that, it couldn't be easy trying to live up to a reputation like his uncle's. Sheriff Tucker had spent seventeen years as a top-ranking officer in the New York police department before taking on a quieter position as sheriff in the mountainous town of Rendezvous.

A photo of a woman and child sat on Carter's desk. Funny. She'd never thought of the detective as a family man. Because he'd always come across as cold, she'd always assumed he was single. Maybe those were qualities he left behind at the office.

Pricilla turned around as the glass door clicked open. "Detective, I was just looking at your photo. Is this your family?"

Carter set a folder on his desk. "My wife and daughter."

"Your wife is gorgeous, and so is your little girl. How old is she?"

"Sammy will be three next month."

Pricilla pointed to the displayed awards, hoping to avoid the inevitable booking procedure. "Quite impressive. Degrees in criminal justice and law couldn't have been easy."

The detective sat down at his desk with a shrug. "After a couple more years of experience under my belt, I'm planning on joining the FBI."

"That's a noble goal."

"One I've had since I was thirteen years old." He picked up a pencil and tapped it against his desk. "Mrs. Crumb, enough of my life. I have some news you're going to be happy about."

She perched on the edge of her chair, wondering why his expression didn't match his words. "I could use some good news right now."

"The owners of the shop dropped the charges against you."

"Really?" A ripple of relief surged through her. "Why?"

"Kent managed to explain to them the reasoning behind the escapade. One that I have to admit I'm not quite clear on myself at this point. Chasing suspects and stealing vehicles are bound to get you in trouble."

She ignored the implications as she rose from her chair. "So I'm free to go?"

"Not quite yet." The man had yet to smile. "Have a seat, please."

"All right." She drew out her words, feeling as if she wasn't going to like where this conversation was headed.

The detective steepled his hands in front of him. "Mrs. Crumb, let's be honest for a few minutes. I know you don't like me."

A *whoosh* of air escaped her lungs. This was what he wanted to talk about? The constant clashing of their personalities? "Of course I don't dislike you, I just—"

"I said let's be honest, Mrs. Crumb." He held up his hand to stop her. "You dislike my straightforward methods to find justice. And most importantly, you dislike the fact that I'm about to arrest your friend for murder."

The mention of Annabelle soured her stomach. "Like you, all I want is for justice to be done, but Annabelle is innocent."

Carter shook his head. "That's not what the evidence says, but regardless of the facts of the case, let me try and put things a different way. I admire your deep passion to help people, but—"

"Really?" She ignored the *but*, finding it hard to believe that he admired anything about her, considering the mess she'd just gotten herself into.

"Yes, I do. But it's time that you and I came to an understanding. I'm the detective here, sworn to uphold the law. You, on the other hand, cook at a local lodge."

"I'm the chef—"

"Fine, so you're a chef at a local lodge. I thought I made myself clear during Charles Woodruff's murder investigation. You have no business following suspects, interrogating—"

"I never interrogated anyone." Her fleeting attempts to defend herself were likely to get her into more trouble, but there was no one else in the room to speak on her behalf. Perhaps she should have agreed to the offer for a lawyer after all. "Detective Carter, all I did was ask a few simple questions—"

"Please, Mrs. Crumb." He scratched the top of his bald head. "This isn't television where you snoop around until the murderer confesses his—or her—deadly deed. There's no prewritten script here. A man's been murdered and there's a killer on the loose. Neither is it a tea party or a Saturday morning with the knitting club."

Pricilla frowned. Just because she was old enough to be his grandmother didn't mean he had to stick her in the corner with a pair of knitting needles.

The detective leaned forward and caught her gaze. "What's it going to take to get you to leave things up to me?"

"Are you wanting to strike a deal?"

"No, I'm *wanting* you to stay out of my investigation."

Pricilla folded her arms across her chest. "Did you know that Kent and Ezri are married?"

Detective Carter shook his head. "I'm not following."

"It's just a simple question. Did you know that Kent Walters and Ezri Pierce are married?"

"No." He flipped his pencil against the desk. "Did you know that Stewart dropped out of school two months ago?"

Pricilla lowered her head. "No."

"What is your point then, Mrs. Crumb?" The detective leaned forward. "As you can see, you're not the only one capable of gathering pertinent information."

"I still believe that people will tell me things they would never tell you. And no matter what the evidence shows at this point, I'm acquainted with Annabelle well enough to know that she never would have killed her husband. There's a piece of the puzzle that is still missing."

"I'm afraid you're quite naive, Mrs. Crumb. Refreshing, perhaps, to see in a person, but in the real world, it just doesn't work. How well do we really know anyone? I could quote case after case where the nice man next door was eventually arrested for some ghastly crime no one thought he could have committed."

"That's quite a cynical view of life, don't you think?"

"No, it's realistic. And the other thing to consider is that you don't hold a badge."

She knew he was right, but she couldn't forget the broken expression on

Annabelle's face. There had to be something she could do. "So, what if I promise not to actively seek out new information regarding the investigation?"

Carter's forehead wrinkled into half a dozen narrow folds. "What does that mean?"

"It means that I won't chase after possible suspects on borrowed quad bikes—"

"*Stolen* quad bikes."

Pricilla tried not to choke on her next word. "Agreed."

"Here's the deal. If you happen to come across information regarding the death of Reggie Pierce, you may ask a few subtle questions, but you also will promise to pass on any information you receive directly to me."

Pricilla smiled. "So, I'm your. . .assistant."

"Absolutely not." Carter's expression morphed into one of disbelief. "But I can't forbid you from keeping your eyes and ears open. You'll pass on any information, and you'll avoid situations that get you arrested. Next time things might not go so easy for you on this end of the law."

"So, if I'm not your assistant, how about your stool pigeon?"

"My what?"

"Your mole." She couldn't help but beam as the detective squirmed in his seat. "You know. Your informant. Isn't that police lingo?"

A vein protruded in the detective's thick neck. "Mrs. Crumb, you are not working for me. You are not my informant or my mole. Do I make myself clear?"

"Perfectly."

"Good. Now you can go."

Pricilla leaned forward. "One last question. Do you happen to know where Max is? I thought he might have been worried and called here to find out where I was."

The detective jutted his chin toward the glass wall. Max was talking to the receptionist at the front desk. Her confidence vanished, leaving her feeling like a schoolgirl being picked up from the principal's office for unruly behavior.

Pricilla stood to thank the detective. In her quest for justice, she'd made a crucial mistake in disregarding the consequences. And Max was sure to be upset at her impulsiveness. It was time to see just what her actions were going to cost her.

Max barely had a chance to ask the receptionist about Pricilla's whereabouts before she emerged from the detective's office. After wandering around town another thirty minutes, asking shopkeepers if they'd seen her, he'd decided that his only alternative was to go to the sheriff.

He stepped toward her, still uncertain as to what he should say. The scolding he'd wanted to give her seemed inappropriate. Especially in light of his recent impulsive act.

"I'm a bit confused," he began. "The receptionist mentioned something about a quad bike."

It didn't make sense. This was Pricilla they were talking about.

Her gaze dropped to the floor. "If you want to know the truth, I borrowed . . .stole. . .an ATV from the shop down the road in order to follow my suspect."

Max shook his head. Surely he'd heard her wrong. "You did what?"

"It all made perfect sense at the time. The man was getting away and I was afraid I'd lose him."

"On an ATV?" She started toward the door and he hurried to catch up. Suddenly his escapade outside the bakery seemed tame. "You're sixty-five years old, Pricilla—"

"A fact that I don't need to be reminded of." She reached up and rubbed her shoulder with one hand. "I'm going to be sore for the next month."

"But on an ATV?" He still didn't believe her.

She stopped in front of the door and caught his gaze. "The man happened to be Kent Walters. Ezri's husband."

"Wait a minute? Ezri's husband?"

She held up the keys to her car and dangled them in front of his face. "Would you mind driving home? I'll tell you all about it on the way."

"Of course not." He closed his mouth. While she might not have been entirely scrupulous in her behavior, from the looks of things, Pricilla had just discovered another twist in the case. Unlike himself, who'd dug up nothing more than a pile of unwanted junk mail.

She managed a half smile. "Thanks."

He held the door open for her then followed her out into the sunshine as she continued to ramble. She always rambled when she was nervous. Deciding not to try to get a word in, he simply listened as they walked the two blocks to where the car was parked.

Once he'd started the motor and pulled away, Pricilla's recap of what had happened only managed to raise his blood pressure a notch and solidify the thought that this time Pricilla had allowed her curiosity to get the best of her. And she seemed to have forgotten as well that, while her cat Penelope might have the fabled nine lives, as a woman of sixty-five she did not.

"I'm sorry about this whole mess." She let out a heavy sigh. "You were right. You're always right."

Perhaps she'd learned something from this experience after all.

"Right about what?" he prodded.

"You warned me that getting involved in this case would only get me into trouble."

"Pricilla—"

"But stealing a quad bike to chase down a suspect. . ." She shook her head. "This time I obviously went way too far."

He didn't say anything, still unsure as to how he should respond.

"So. . ." Pricilla blew out a sharp breath and kept her gaze straight ahead.

"So what?"

She clasped her hands in her lap. "I thought you might have something scathing to say to reprimand me."

Following the curve of the road bordered by a row of pine trees, Max glanced at her out of the corner of his eye. He'd felt a bit guilty over ratting on Naldo for digging through the trash, though he had no plans at the moment of telling Pricilla what he'd been doing for the past hour. While he didn't believe the man's explanation, he was also pretty certain the incident didn't have anything to do with Reggie's murder. Pricilla, on the other hand, had been stalking suspects, stealing property, and interrogating innocent people—assuming Kent was innocent. The crazy thing about all of this was he knew that Pricilla would never hurt anyone intentionally. Not that motive always justified the actions, but in her case it couldn't help but push the scales slightly in her favor. He had to give her credit for that.

"Max?"

He needed to say something, but he still wasn't sure if he should laugh out loud or give her a good old-fashioned spanking. "I don't want you to think that just because I decided to take the next step and see where our relationship might be heading that I have some sort of control over you, but that doesn't change the fact that you've let your obsession with the case send you spiraling in the wrong direction."

"And. . ."

"And I'm worried that next time the outcome won't be in your favor."

Pricilla's fingernails gnawed on the door handle. "Don't get me wrong. I take full responsibility for my own actions, but that doesn't change the reality that something's not right with the case. Detective Carter is planning on arresting Annabelle."

While he couldn't ignore the fervor in her voice, that didn't justify the fact that if she didn't stay out of the detective's way, at some point she was going to find herself in serious trouble. And it scared him. "What if it's her son or Ezri who killed Reggie? Then what?"

Pricilla pursed her lips. "I'll accept the truth when it's finally revealed, but the man's got an agenda."

"Who?"

"The detective."

"And why do you think he has an agenda?"

"He wants to join the FBI."

Max frowned. "And that gives him an agenda?"

"Yes. . .no. . .I don't know, Max."

He pulled the car into the driveway of the lodge and parked beside a beat-up, two-door vehicle. "Promise me, agenda or not, that you'll stay out of this. Please."

Her lips smacked together. "I almost forgot."

"Forgot what?"

"That car must belong to Darren Robinson. I'd completely forgotten he promised me computer lessons today."

Max groaned inwardly. Here they went again. He knew that despite what had happened earlier today, Pricilla's agenda for computer lessons had little to do with learning to surf the Internet, and everything to do with assessing one of her suspects. And it was hardly a surprise that the appointment had slipped her mind between her unethical pursuit of Kent up the mountain and her subsequent visit to the detective's office.

"You promised to stay out of trouble, Pricilla," he warned.

She opened her door and scooted toward the edge. "Which is something I have every intention of doing. I'm only going to keep my eyes and ears open in case I stumble across any information relevant to the case. And even you have to admit that Darren Robinson is certainly relevant to the case."

Pricilla scooted her chair a couple of inches closer to the laptop so she could read the fuzzy screen that had just popped up. Darren might be charming and intelligent, but she wasn't going to let herself forget that he was a suspect in Reggie Pierce's murder.

She glanced at the young man sitting beside her at the kitchen table. His pressed khaki pants and button-down shirt looked sharp, and his manners were just as meticulous. Opportunity was the only thing she had on the young man, though. Reggie had given him a decent job, and he'd proved his worth in the business. Killing Reggie didn't make sense. But even if she didn't find any information to pass on to the detective regarding the case, she could always learn a thing or two about computers in the process.

"Mrs. Crumb?" The young man pushed his thick glasses up the bridge of his nose.

Whacking her leg on the edge of the table, Pricilla winced then forced herself away from her contemplations on the case and reminded herself why she was here.

"I'm sorry, Darren." She scrambled for a proper response. All she needed was for the young man to guess her real interest behind her request for a computer lesson. "Like I told you, the World Wide Web, and all aspects of computers for that matter, might as well be a language from an entirely different planet. My mind tends to. . .wander a tad."

"You're making it too complicated." His encouraging smile reached the corners of his hazel eyes, and she relaxed a bit. "A few simple guidelines and you can find out anything you want."

Pricilla determined to focus on the matter at hand, because there were a number of things she wanted to research once she learned to navigate the inner workings of modern technology. The detective's comment on Stewart dropping out of school for one, and Reggie's business background for another.

She drew in a deep breath. "How about showing me how to get to the bakery's Web site for starters?"

With a few clicks from Darren, a picture of the Baker's Dozen filled the screen. Pricilla studied the familiar storefront with its view of the Rocky Mountains in the background. The company logo crossed the top and a row of photos of bakery products edged the left side of the screen.

Darren leaned back. "You try it yourself now."

With Darren's encouragement and occasional instructions, Pricilla maneuvered through Italian pastries, specialty cakes, and mouthwatering chocolates, gaining confidence with every screen she opened. Maybe there was something to this computer craze after all. Shopping from the comfort of her own home would have its benefits, though perhaps not for her waistline or her pocketbook.

But she was interested in more than cream puffs and puff pastry. The more she knew about Reggie and his employees, the closer she would be to the answer behind the baker's fatal encounter.

An hour later Pricilla was still convinced Darren made it look far easier than it really was, but at least she could accomplish some of the basics. Being left alone to maneuver her way through the information would be a test she hoped she could pass, but either way, she was impressed with what she'd managed to learn.

She folded her hands in her lap, certain her brain would shut down if she had to think anymore today. "You're quite a wiz at this computer stuff."

"I spend more time in front of a screen than around people."

Pricilla decided to take the opening to find out more about the young man. "What about your family?"

"I don't see them much between school and work."

He pressed his hands against the table and sat up straight. His ease in communicating seemed to diminish as they switched to a personal subject. But Pricilla wanted to know more.

"Are you close to them?"

Darren scooted his chair back. "I'm an only child and my parents. . .well, let's just say they were never around much. Especially my father. Besides, I spent most of my life off at boarding school."

Darren's friendly smile melted into a deep frown that consumed his face and left a shadow across his eyes. She'd obviously hit upon a subject that he'd prefer to avoid.

Pricilla bit her lip and wondered how she always managed to hit a raw nerve. "I'm sorry. I didn't mean to bring up an unpleasant subject."

"No, it's fine. My father died a few years ago, then my mom remarried and now lives in Alaska. I'm pretty much on my own now." Darren's shrug was unconvincing. "None of us were ever particularly close. Like I said, my father was busy with work, and my mom. . ."

Darren clamped his mouth shut as if he'd said too much.

Pricilla decided she'd pressed the subject enough for now. "I'm sorry I brought up the subject, but I do appreciate all your help today."

She slid her chair back and stood to stretch her tight muscles while

Darren gathered his cell phone and keys off the table without another word. She wasn't sure if she'd stumbled on something significant or simply a young man's loneliness.

She didn't want to read things into what he'd said, but his reaction did show that everyone has a secret, or at the least things they don't want to talk about. Darren Robinson might not be on the top of her suspect list, but until the killer confessed, she refused to eliminate any of them.

Max set his crossword puzzle on the arm of the porch chair and ran his fingers across the back of Penelope, Pricilla's Persian cat, who lay curled up contentedly in his lap. He had to chuckle to himself. The more he thought about it, the more he found humor in the entire four-wheeler escapade.

He squinted through the bright afternoon sunlight at the stunning backdrop of aspen and pine trees that surrounded the lodge. Truth be told, he'd have loved to see her scooting up the mountain behind the wheel of the ATV. Pricilla in a helmet with the wind blowing against the folds of her skirt as she sped across the rough terrain was a picture even he was finding hard to imagine. He couldn't help but chuckle out loud, but humorous antics aside, part of him wondered if she'd ever stop playing the role of detective and decide to settle down with him.

Not that he had ever expected her to get involved in yet another murder. And surely the odds of it ever happening again were slim to none. It wasn't as if she were Jessica Fletcher, whose scriptwriters ensured she encountered at least one dead body every episode. No, Pricilla was more like a twist on Hyacinth Bucket, PBS's unconventional busybody who'd somehow managed to trade in her guest list for a list of suspects.

Max scratched Penelope behind the ears and listened to the cat purr. If he was honest with himself, his plans to move to Colorado had been a spur-of-the-moment decision. No different, really, than Pricilla's impulsive act to chase after a murder victim in an off-road vehicle. Love, mystery, and old age all seemed to be factors in both of their madcap decisions.

He glanced up as Pricilla strolled across the porch with a plate of brownies in one hand and a tall glass of milk in the other. The brownies were no doubt a peace offering, and one he would accept with no qualms. No matter what she did, he couldn't deny the fact that he loved Pricilla and couldn't stay annoyed at her for too long. Pricilla was. . .well. . .Pricilla, and the enthusiastic way she faced life was part of what he loved about her. It just happened to be the part that most often got her in trouble.

She set the dessert and glass of milk on a small side table beside his padded chair and shot him a smile. "Are you still mad at me?"

He took the largest brownie off the plate and cocked his head. "For some strange reason, you're hard to stay mad at."

She slid into the chair beside him and reached out to squeeze his free hand. "I know I've been a bit obsessed with the case and trying to prove that Annabelle is innocent, but I never should have let things get out of hand like they did today."

"You're a good friend, Pricilla." He laced her fingers between his as he took a nibble of the rich chocolate. "No one could ever deny that fact."

She didn't look convinced. "Being a good friend doesn't excuse the fact that I foolishly embarked on a reckless escapade that could have had serious consequences. Both physical and legal."

"That's true, but no one will ever doubt that your motives are pure."

"Pure motives don't justify illegal actions." Pricilla grabbed one of the brownies and took a big bite.

Max stifled a laugh at the intensity in her voice, knowing that no matter what he said, it was going to take more than his encouragement and a chocolate brownie to ease Pricilla's guilt in this situation. "That might be true, but even a court of law takes into consideration the reasoning behind an act when pronouncing judgment."

"So you're trying to tell me that the motives behind my actions excuse or even justify what I did?"

"I'm trying to tell you to stop being so hard on yourself. We all make mistakes."

"I agree with that." She wiped a crumb off the front of her dress. "It's interesting. At Reggie's funeral I remember talking to Annabelle about how we are all weak vessels. Paul describes us as jars of clay. My point was that although we can be crushed from life's circumstances, we are not destroyed. At that point, though, I was thinking about how Annabelle's entire life had changed in one moment, but it applies to all of us."

"And makes you realize not only how worthless man really is, but how Christ changed all of that through His death on the cross." He reached for his milk and took a sip. "It always amazes me that it's through the trials and tribulations we face that God's glory is the most apparent."

"How do I make Annabelle understand that?"

"By believing it first yourself."

"Ouch." She winced at his answer. "Touché."

"I'm sorry—"

"No, you're right. It's a lesson I have to take to heart before I can ever make someone else understand."

Somehow, he had no doubts that she would take it to heart. "By the way, how did the computer lesson go? I've been wondering where you were. Darren left close to an hour ago."

"I decided to put what I learned into practice and 'surf the Web,' as they say, for a while."

He glanced at her out of the corner of his eye as he took a bite of his brownie and frowned. She'd forced too much enthusiasm into that last sentence. Something was afoot.

"Pricilla?"

"Yes?"

Her response came far too quickly. The brownies were more than a peace offering. They were smoothing out the edges for what was to come.

He set his glass down and caught her gaze. "You found out something, didn't you?"

"I know I promised to stay out of the investigation, but even the detective said if I happened to hear something or—"

"Purposefully stumble across something on the Web?" Had she learned nothing from her recent madcap adventure?

"All I wanted to do was try out some of the things Darren taught me. I thought I would Google a few names—"

"Google a few names?"

"You might not find all of this quite so humorous when you find out what I discovered."

Max drew in a deep breath. "Humorous" wasn't at all what he would call the situation. "I'm listening."

"Reggie Pierce used to own an upscale restaurant in New York." Pricilla leaned forward and looked at him intently. "Annabelle mentioned it a few times, but from what I read, even her descriptions didn't do it justice. I'd always assumed that the pressure of running such an upscale venture became too much, and Reggie wanted a slower pace. Now I'm not so sure."

He had to admit his own growing sense of curiosity, though he'd never admit it to Pricilla. "Why's that?"

Her eyes widened. "Seven years ago Reggie's business partner died under mysterious circumstances. And the overall consensus is that he was murdered."

Pricilla stepped out of the warm sunshine and into the air-conditioned climate of the bakery. Breathing deeply, she let the savory scents of yeast bread and sweet chocolate fill her lungs. Ezri stood behind the counter, filling an order for a mother with two small children in tow. While Ezri's taste in clothes ran along the lines of eccentric with her vintage fringe vest and embroidered black jeans, today there was something different about her. Her smile was broader, and there was a lilt to her voice.

"Mrs. Crumb. It's so good to see you." Ezri waved a pair of metal tongs in Pricilla's direction. "I'll be with you in just a moment."

"No hurry." Pricilla crossed the checkered tiled floor, stopping in front of the glass-covered pastries. "It will give me time to decide what I need this morning."

Breakfast had been hours ago. A blueberry muffin would hold her over until lunchtime and certainly wouldn't do too much damage to her waistline. On the other hand, the éclairs looked extra good today.

Two minutes later the bell at the front door jingled as the mother bustled her children outside, their angelic faces covered with chocolate from their pastries.

Pricilla eyed the fresh loaves of bread that would go perfectly with tonight's dinner of beef medallions and roasted vegetables and made her decision. She tapped on the glass. "I'll take five loaves of the sourdough and one of your strawberry cheesecakes. I thought an extra dessert during coffee would be nice for the guests."

"A perfect choice, Mrs. Crumb." Ezri grabbed a sack from the counter that had the Baker's Dozen's logo printed across the top.

Pricilla studied the row of pastries for a second time and couldn't resist. Blueberry muffins were good, but the éclairs looked irresistible. It was too bad Annabelle owned a bakery and not a health food store. "And you can throw in two of your cream-filled éclairs for me as well."

Pricilla didn't miss the sparkle in Ezri's eyes as she slid the first mouthwatering éclair into a small white box, but she was quite certain that the young woman's beaming smile had nothing to do with éclairs.

Still, before she went any further with her questions, she had a confession to make. "I never was able to apologize to you for what happened yesterday—"

"Trust me, Mrs. Crumb. You don't owe me an apology." Ezri set the box down and leaned against the display counter. The grin never left her face as she held out her hand, showing off the diamond wedding ring that encircled her finger.

"Why, Ezri, it's stunning." Pricilla studied the young woman's pear-shaped diamond and felt a wave of relief flood through her. Maybe something good had come out of yesterday's fiasco. "So you told your mother?"

Ezri pressed her hand against her heart. "I've never been so relieved about anything in my entire life. There are no secrets about Kent and our marriage anymore. And it's all due to you."

"I don't know that I deserve any of the credit." Pricilla ran her fingers across the empty space on her own left hand. For months after Marty's death she'd continued to wear the ring he'd given her decades before. The day she finally laid it to rest in the back of her jewelry box had brought with it a flurry of emotions, and while she still missed the ring on her finger, now she could only think of Max and wonder if she was ready to accept such a commitment from him.

Ezri rested her hands against the counter. "Trust me, Mrs. Crumb. If it wasn't for your showing up yesterday and knocking some sense into me, I'd still be trying to live a double life."

Shoving aside her own relationship questions, Pricilla tried to focus on the matter at hand. "What does your mother think about Kent?"

Ezri slid a loaf of bread into a sack. "Besides the adjustment to knowing that her little girl is married, I think she's happy. She seems to like Kent and knows that he makes me happy. I never should have kept it a secret, but at least things seem to have worked out finally."

"I'm really happy for you, Ezri. You've been through a lot lately and the last thing you need is the stress of keeping more secrets."

Ezri nodded toward the back of the bakery. "My mother's upstairs, and I know she'd love to see you. I can finish getting your order boxed up and have it waiting for you."

Pricilla nodded, but her stomach recoiled at the reason she needed to see Annabelle. Things had worked out for Ezri and Kent, but what was going to happen if the detective dragged Annabelle off to jail and managed to slap her with a murder conviction? Ezri might have Kent to give her a sense of stability, but the two of them should be enjoying life as newlyweds, not having to deal with the reality of Annabelle's possible prison sentence.

And what about Stewart? At twenty years old, he still had a lot of growing up to do. With the little she knew about the young man, it seemed obvious that losing a second parent could be permanently detrimental.

Pricilla trembled at the thought. She had to find out the truth. "I had planned to go see your mother, but I wondered if I could ask you something first."

"Of course."

Pricilla paused for a moment as Detective Carter's harsh words of warning repeated themselves in her mind. No. All she was doing was taking advantage of the opportunity, something he had grudgingly given her permission to do. Certainly there was nothing wrong with that.

Pricilla cleared her throat. "I know this is none of my business, but I can't help but be worried about your brother. I understand he dropped out of school?"

Ezri's smile vanished. "He didn't kill our father—"

"I know." Pricilla held up her hand. "I'd never accuse him of murder, Ezri. That wasn't my intention. But I am concerned."

Ezri slipped another loaf of bread into the sack. "I have to admit I'm worried, too. I'm not positive, but I'm pretty sure he's run up a lot of debt. Please don't tell my mother. If anyone should be cured of keeping secrets, it's me, but I don't know what to do, and until I have proof. . ."

Pricilla shook her head. "Your mother needs to know, Ezri. The detective is aware that your brother dropped out of school, and if there's debt involved, he probably already knows. It's always better to simply come clean."

Ezri stared at the rows of baked goods in front of her, her face now void of the joy it had held only moments before. "I heard them fighting a few weeks back because dad wouldn't give him any extra money. Stewart liked to live well, but frankly, he's lazy."

"Laziness isn't a motive for murder, but I am concerned how the detective will look at things. He's determined to wrap up this case, and the last thing I want is your mother or your brother—"

"We both know my mother didn't have anything to do with my father's death." Ezri's voice rose a notch. "And neither did my brother, Mrs. Crumb. I'm certain of it. Stewart might be lazy and even a bit irresponsible, but he's not a murderer."

Pricilla covered the young woman's hand with her own and squeezed gently, wishing she could give her more assurances. "I'm going to do everything I can to help, Ezri. I promise."

A moment later Pricilla took the narrow flight of steps to the upstairs apartment. There was no getting around the facts. If Stewart had known that his father had been in the process of cutting him out of his will, then he had the perfect motivation for murder.

Pricilla found Annabelle sitting at an antique desk with a pen in her hand, staring at a blank card. The grieving woman didn't even move as one of the wooden floor boards in the living room creaked beneath Pricilla's weight.

Pricilla paused at the edge of the oriental rug. There had been no attempts made to tidy the normally organized room. Papers were scattered across the floor. Three empty pizza boxes lay discarded on the dining room table. Even the sink was full of dirty dishes.

"Annabelle?"

Annabelle continued staring at the card. "I need to send thank-you notes to people. Reggie didn't have a lot of friends, but there were flowers and cards. His aunt who's almost ninety even sent five hundred dollars for the kids' education."

Pricilla raised her eyebrows. "That was generous."

"It was very nice of her, wasn't it? Except five hundred dollars won't even pay for one class." She shook her head and looked up for the first time. "I'm sorry—"

Pricilla bridged the gap between them and rested her hand on Annabelle's shoulder. Her friend's normal stylish attire had been discarded for old jeans and a T-shirt, matching the disheveled room. "You don't ever have to be sorry for grieving. It's a natural part of the process."

"I know, but I had been feeling better. I've been thinking about what we talked about. How I need to let God forgive me and allow Him to give me strength." She pointed to a Bible that lay open to the book of Philippians. "I read this morning how Paul says that Christ will take our weak mortal bodies and change them into glorious bodies like His own."

"It's a beautiful passage, isn't it?"

"Yes, but then it keeps hitting me again. Reggie's dead, and all the detective's evidence is pointing at me, which means I'll probably end up being arrested." She caught Pricilla's gaze. "You believe that I'm innocent, don't you, Pricilla?"

"That's why I'm here."

Annabelle reached out to squeeze Pricilla's hand and let a smile cross her lips for the first time. "I don't know what I'd do without you."

"What I want you to do right now is go sit on the couch, and I'll make you some tea."

"I'd like that." Annabelle dropped the pen, which slid off the desk and onto the floor, but she didn't bother to pick it up. "I need to tell you something first, though. It's about Ezri."

"She showed me her ring." Pricilla bustled into the kitchen that opened into the living room, and filled the teapot with water from the tap. "Are you doing okay after finding out about her marriage?"

Annabelle labored across the room before stopping to lean against the back of the couch. "In not knowing what's going to happen to me, I'm relieved she has someone who will take care of her."

"We're going to find out the truth, Annabelle."

Annabelle sighed audibly. "Sometimes I'm not sure that discovering the truth is the best thing."

Pricilla looked up from the granite counter where she was assembling the milk and sugar and paused to look at her friend. Women in the church had organized a few meals after the funeral, but Annabelle was too high-strung this morning and probably hadn't eaten anything decent for days despite the offered help. "Can I make you some toast or an omelet?"

Annabelle shook her head. "Tea is fine, thank you."

Pricilla pulled out a pair of mugs from the cupboard and decided she wouldn't leave until the dishes were done and she'd helped to catch up on some of the housekeeping. "What did you want to talk to me about?"

Annabelle pressed her hands against her heart. "It seems that the detective is digging into everything I've ever said or done until he finds that final piece of evidence that will put me away for life."

"He is persistent, but in all honesty, I think he only wants to find the truth." Pricilla located the box of tea bags, surprised she'd just defended the detective. Perhaps seeing the photo of his wife and daughter had added a bit of humanity to the balding lawman.

Annabelle shoved back a strand of her bleached hair that was beginning to show streaks of gray.

"You need to relax, Annabelle."

"I know, but I have to show you something." She pulled something out of the back of the desk drawer then perched on the edge of the bar stool facing the kitchen.

She slapped a photo on the bar and pushed it toward Pricilla. "This is Riley Folk. Ezri's biological father."

Pricilla dropped the saucer she was holding against the counter. She moved to catch it, but instead the small plate cracked in two against the hard surface. "I'm sorry."

"Forget about it."

Pricilla held up the broken pieces. "I just. . .I had no idea you were married before—"

"I wasn't. I learned the hard way that secrets cause nothing but trouble in the end. Reggie found out the day before he died."

"I. . .I don't know what to say."

Pricilla turned away to dump the broken pieces of the saucer into the trash can. Max had tried to tell her that everyone has secrets, but she'd refused to believe that Annabelle had any secrets—or at least any secrets worth murdering for. But hidden beneath the polished exterior of their marriage had been at least one skeleton.

Annabelle fingered the photo. "I've always been ashamed of what happened. Reggie never knew until he found this picture."

Pricilla studied the picture of the man. "Who was Riley?"

"No one, really." Annabelle shrugged. "A man who happened to fill my loneliness while Reggie worked late hours. I finally broke it off, but when Ezri was born there was no doubt in my mind who the father was. Blond hair, blue eyes. . .Reggie never suspected a thing."

The teakettle whistled, and Pricilla was thankful for the distraction. She knew Annabelle had regrets in her past, but she'd never expected something like this. She was always amazed at people who balked at the morality of the Bible without considering the heaviness of sin's consequences—like the ones Annabelle had been living with and would continue to live with for the rest of her life.

Pushing all doubts of Annabelle's innocence aside, Pricilla poured the hot water into the teacups and slid one across the bar to Annabelle. "I have to say, I'm not sure I understand why you wanted to tell me. Does this have something to do with Reggie's death?"

Annabelle grasped her cup with two hands. "I don't know if it has anything to do with it or not, but something else is bothering me. You know how Reggie was impulsive about keeping everything in perfect order. He even kept his sock drawer color-coordinated." She waved her arm toward the messy living area. "As you can see, his tidiness never completely rubbed off on me, but I always tried to keep things clean. Anyway, lately he started blaming me for various things that were out of place. I'd noticed it, too, but it wasn't me. Every once in a while I'd find things moved around the house. Little things that I never would have noticed except for Reggie's idiosyncrasies to have everything in its exact spot. It was how he found the photo, trying to figure out what else was out of place."

Pricilla worked to fit the pieces together, but inevitably something was missing. "I'm not sure how all of this fits together, but since we're talking about secrets, I do have a question for you."

Annabelle took a sip of her tea. "Ask me anything. I'm tired of secrets and am determined not to keep any more."

Pricilla decided to be completely forthright. "All right then. I'm curious about Reggie's previous business partner, William Roberts. I'm only bringing up the subject because anything I can find out about, the detective is sure to find out about as well, if he hasn't already."

"I'm not sure that there's a whole lot to tell. Reggie and William owned a successful restaurant in New York. Reggie's plan was always to make it big, then eventually retire to the mountains in Colorado and start a bakery, which is exactly what he ended up doing. The restaurant did very well until William's death. Reggie was good at investing in a number of diverse markets with his profits. Stocks, bonds, art, even jewelry. He was ruthless in business and always did whatever it took to get ahead."

"How did William die? The article I read wasn't conclusive."

Annabelle shrugged. "That's because we never really knew what happened. The police finally decided that his death was a suicide, but I'm not sure. He didn't seem like the kind of man who would kill himself. It was a strange time. The restaurant began to suffer with the bad publicity, so Reggie decided to pull out while things were still ahead and moved us all here."

"Sounds like that might have been the best thing, considering the circumstances."

"I've always felt a bit guilty, though." Annabelle rested her tea on the counter. "We didn't even attend William's funeral. Our entire family came down with a case of the flu. It was horrible. William's wife and her son left immediately after the funeral and headed for her parents' home on Nantucket Island. Not that the two of us were close, but I never saw her again."

"I think we've talked enough about the past for today." Pricilla noted the dark circles under Annabelle's eyes, even more noticeable against her pallid skin color. "There is only one thing you can do right now, Annabelle."

"What is that?"

"You need to continue searching to rediscover God's love. He's the only one who will never let you down. And the one place where you will be able to find the strength to make it through this difficult time."

An hour later, with the kitchen cleaned and the living room tidied, Pricilla made her way back down the staircase from Annabelle's apartment toward her car, still trying to ignore nigglings of doubt in the back of her mind. The last thing she wanted to believe was that Annabelle could have been involved in something as horrid as murder. But she also knew that life with Reggie could be unbearable. There was one looming reality she couldn't shake. He'd discovered a shocking secret and had threatened to leave her out of his will.

And now Annabelle was free.

Pricilla hammered the blade of the knife into the carrot like a machete flying through the overgrowth of a dense jungle. She needed to have dinner ready for the lodge's guests in thirty minutes, but all she could think about was Annabelle and her confession.

Max stood beside her at the counter, roped into chopping tomatoes and yellow peppers for the salad because Misty had needed to take her youngest daughter to the doctor. Thankfully, everything else for the three-course meal was ready.

Pricilla picked up another carrot and started chopping again despite twinges of arthritis that told her to slow down and continue at a reasonable pace.

Max reached out and covered Pricilla's hand before sliding the butcher knife away from her. "You're hacking at these carrots like they're a troop of enemy soldiers coming at you. You're going to cut one of your fingers off."

Pricilla held up her hands in defeat. "I'm sorry. My mind is a million miles away right now."

"Or more precisely in the town of Rendezvous at a quaint little bakery?"

Pricilla frowned. "I wish I could tell you everything Annabelle shared with me—"

"What you and Annabelle discussed needs to stay between you and Annabelle, but that doesn't change the fact that I am concerned. You're too caught up in this case for your own good."

"I'm fine, Max. Really. Right now all we need to be worried about is Annabelle." Pricilla dumped the carrots into the salad bowl then rested her hands against the counter. "She's the one facing time in prison if new evidence doesn't show up."

Max added the tomatoes he'd chopped to the bowl. "I know Annabelle is a good friend of yours, and that you're determined to find out the truth, but I think you need to prepare yourself for the reality that she might have been involved. She, above anyone else, seems to have the perfect motive."

Pricilla squeezed her eyes shut, hating the fact that Max was right. Already, she'd discovered enough secrets in that family to sink the *Titanic*, and if truth be told, any one of them could have been a part of it.

" 'He reveals deep and hidden things; he knows what lies in darkness, and light dwells with him.'" She blew out a labored breath, mulling over the words from Daniel for the second time since her morning devotional. "Why does it seem that the older I get, the more questions I have for God? Not that I doubt His authority and sovereignty, but I do question man's consistent weakness."

Max went back to work on chopping a pepper. "It's a tough question that only God truly understands. He might have created man in His image, but He also gave us choices. That's what makes us human."

"Humans who, more often than not, seem to choose the wrong direction that in turn causes a domino effect of consequences." Pricilla picked up her notebook from the counter and flipped it open. "Speaking of consequences, I've added at least one new motive. Stewart dropped out of school and his father refused to give him the money he wanted. Add to that, Ezri is pretty certain he's run up debt that he can't pay off."

Pricilla didn't feel comfortable mentioning Annabelle's indiscretions at this point, though she knew that if the facts continued to implicate her friend, the detective would need to know the truth. For now, though, she'd continue praying that her instincts were right, and that Annabelle's moments of carelessness years earlier hadn't led her to make an even bigger mistake with Reggie.

Max snatched the notebook out of her hands. "I thought the incident with that ATV had cured you of your involvement, Pricilla."

"It cured me of doing something foolish without thinking through the consequences. Even the detective is open to my input as long as I pass any information on to him."

"Input that you might happen to stumble across, not information you seek out."

Pricilla ignored the warning. "I need to talk to Stewart."

"And you really believe that Detective Carter won't put you behind bars for meddling in his case?"

"Don't be ridiculous. Nothing like that will happen again." She held up her hand. "No more four-wheelers. Scout's honor."

Max's laugh surprised her. He grabbed her hands before pulling them against his chest. "How can it be that the very thing I love the most about you, your care and compassion for others, happens to also be the one thing that gets you into the most trouble?"

"At least you're able to see the good side of my somewhat suspect character traits." Looking into his blue eyes, all the doubts she'd harbored regarding their relationship began to slip. Max was the one person who continued to believe in her no matter what.

"And where do you think we might find Stewart?" she asked him.

"Ezri said he spends most of his time hanging out at the pool hall."

"You'll come with me?"

Max shot her a grin. "Someone needs to keep you out of trouble. And besides that, the sooner this case is solved, the sooner we can start making progress on our relationship."

Max stepped into the darkened pool hall behind Pricilla and wondered if he'd been too quick to offer her help on her mission to question Stewart. Not that the atmosphere was as bad as he'd imagined. The setting seemed to be more of a hangout for young people than a smoky bar for brawling hoodlums, but he still felt out of his element. Loud music played in the background. Some boys' band with repetitive lyrics he couldn't understand. Even the pungent smells from the kitchen were geared toward the younger crowed with its heart-attack-inducing greasy choices, which he avoided—like French fries and fried burgers.

He hated feeling his age.

"There he is."

Max glanced in the direction Pricilla pointed. Stewart leaned against the wall with a pool cue in one hand and a bottle of water in the other. At least the young man didn't appear to be drinking alcohol.

Max squinted across the room at Stewart. After their last interview with him, Max wasn't sure he wanted to go another round. He turned back to Pricilla. "What are you going to do? Offer to play a round of pool with him?"

"Of course not." Pricilla flashed him an annoyed look. "That would be ridiculous. And besides, do you actually think he would agree to play with me? I've never touched one of these poles in my life."

"It's a pool cue."

"Whatever." The look of determination in Pricilla's eyes had yet to waver. "That's why you're going to offer."

"I'm going to what?" Max choked on the words.

"It's a perfect plan. We need a way to get him to relax and trust us."

"I haven't played pool for years—"

Pricilla frowned and rested her hands on her hips. "I've seen that trophy you won."

"From 1967!"

"You'll do fine."

Pricilla was already halfway across the tiled floor by the time Max recovered his bearings. A little friendly competition during his early military days couldn't begin to have any impact on what might happen today if he attempted to play a game of pool. Besides, with Pricilla instigating one question after another to the poor chap, it hardly seemed like a way to get the young man to relax and open up.

"Max." Pricilla waved at him from the other side of the room.

Max made his way past cracked vinyl chairs and small, round tables and wondered if he would set off an alarm escaping through the emergency exit to his left. Why did his intentions to be the gallant hero in helping Pricilla with her oddball quests always seem to land him in a boiling pot of trouble? He had no doubt that that was exactly where this innocent escapade was headed.

As promised, Pricilla greeted the young man then suggested a friendly game of pool between the two men.

Stewart slouched against the wall. "I was waiting for friends, but they're late."

Max seized his one way out. "We don't have to play—"

"Max." Pricilla's gaze bore through him, more pointed than the end of a pool cue.

Max rephrased his sentence. "You don't mind?"

Stewart tossed the empty plastic water bottle into the trash and shrugged. "Beats doing nothing."

The young man positioned the balls on the table and racked them up. Max grabbed a pool cue and chalked the end, wondering if he could come up with a last minute reprieve. A quick glance at Pricilla reminded him of her determination. Her mind was made up, and leaving now would only result in having to defend himself later. Something he'd prefer not to do.

With her notebook peeking out from her jacket pocket, all she needed was Columbo's trench coat and she'd fit the part of detective to a T. And like Columbo, she didn't seem to have any intention of waiting to toss out the first question. "Your mother told me that you were studying forensic science. Is that right? It sounds like such a fascinating subject to me."

Stewart shrugged as he lined up his pool cue for the opening shot. "Some of the classes have been interesting. Beats working in a bakery all summer long."

"What classes will you be taking next semester?"

Stewart's staid expression never changed. "Not sure if I'm going back."

Max took his turn at the table and somehow managed to drop a solid ball into a corner pocket.

Stewart stood up straight for the first time and nodded his head. "Not bad for an old man."

Max lined up for another shot and decided to take the young man's words as a compliment. "Thanks."

He frowned as another ball hit the side of the table and bounced away from the pocket he'd been aiming at. Pricilla wasn't going to hear the end of this. He was sacrificing his pride for the sake of her investigation. She'd better come up with some answers. Fast.

In the meantime, though, it might not hurt to do some of the talking himself. It was going to take more than chitchat to break the ice between them. "It took me awhile to find out what I wanted to do with my life. After two semesters of classes at a community college down in New Mexico, I dropped out of school against my father's wishes."

He avoided Pricilla's gaze. Perhaps his line of questioning wasn't going in the direction she'd planned, but if she intended to drop any bombshell questions regarding Reggie's death, she was going to need all the warming up possible.

Stewart grabbed some chalk from a ledge along the wall. "What did you end up doing?"

"I joined the military."

"Whoa. That would be way too much discipline for me."

Max studied his next shot, wishing he'd done better in geometry. Mathematics and angles had never been his forte. "I'm certainly not saying that the military is for everyone, but I do believe that it's perfectly normal to take time to discover what you want to do for the rest of your life. For me, though, the military became exactly that. I eventually learned to negotiate, plan strategic campaigns for the military attacks, and even interrogate prisoners."

"Really?" Admiration dawned in the young man's eyes. Maybe they were making progress after all.

Max pulled back his pool cue and clipped his intended ball too far to the right. "It might not have taught me all the skills I need for a game of pool. . ."

Stewart laughed as he approached the table for his turn.

". . .but it did teach me discipline along with essential life skills that I would have been able to use whether I'd served only one term or made serving my country a lifetime career."

Max winked at Pricilla, whose smile of thanks sent a shiver of emotions running through him. Perched atop the vinyl bar stool, she looked prettier than any of the twenty-something girls who sat laughing too loudly at one of the back tables. Pricilla's silver hair lay in perfect curls against the nape of her neck, and her face, with just a hint of makeup, still looked fresh. The years might have added a few wrinkles, but they had brought with them an extra dose of grace and charm, and he still found her beautiful.

Maybe being over the hill wasn't so bad after all.

Stewart paused at the corner of the table. "I've always wanted to run my own business."

"You're in the perfect position then." Pricilla's voice competed against the background music. "The Baker's Dozen has potential for growth, and you've got the opportunity to learn how it works from the ground up."

Stewart didn't look convinced. "Working the cash register and filling boxes with donuts isn't exactly running a business."

"My experience with negotiations and interrogations didn't happen overnight. It never does. I first had to survive boot camp then work my way up the ladder." Max sank a clean shot. "It's the same with anything. You've got to prove yourself and pay your dues. In the end, though, it's worth it."

"I suppose you've got a point."

"Have you ever thought about helping your mother run the bakery someday?" Pricilla's question was met with serious contemplation from Stewart.

"I don't want anything to do with the bakery."

"Why not?"

"Why should I? I've already told you how my father cared more about his work than he ever did about his family." Stewart's pool cue scraped against the green felt as he scratched the shot. "I don't owe him anything."

Pricilla slid off the stool and moved to stand beside the pool table. "Who do you think killed him?"

The bottom of Stewart's pool cue hit the ground. Pricilla had asked one question too many, taking her friendly chat to the despised level of an interrogation.

"That old detective sent you back to get more information out of me, didn't he?"

"Trust me, Stewart." Max tried not to laugh at the image. "Detective Carter would quit before he ever gave Pricilla a badge and sent her out on an investigation. Pricilla's concerned for your family. That's all."

Pricilla cleared her throat. "And considering how the last time we talked you practically confessed to murdering your father—"

"I didn't confess to anything."

"True, but you were the one willing to give us both a motive and an opportunity."

"If you're digging for evidence, I'll give you more." Stewart dropped a striped ball into a hole, then lined up for another shot. "Two months ago I dropped out of school. Never told my dad. I knew he'd cut me off entirely if he ever found out that I was spending his money without earning a single hour of college credit.

"That was the problem with him. As long as we did what he wanted, he never bothered us. He chose the classes on forensic science for me with some sort of unreasonable expectations that I'd become a doctor or a top FBI agent. He never asked me what I wanted to do with my life." The veins in Stewart's neck began to bulge as he sank another ball into a corner pocket. "And if he knew the truth. . ."

Pricilla took a step closer to the table. "What is the truth, Stewart?"

"The truth? Is that what you want to know? How about the fact that I've run up more debt than the bakery brings in in a year? I tried to tell him that I was in trouble the week before he died. But do you think he cared, or would even listen to me?"

"Your father loved you, Stewart."

"Really? Funny. I never saw it, yet still I thought maybe, just maybe, he'd treat me like his son one day. Not that I expected him to welcome me with open arms and a big party, but I thought he'd at least hear me out." Stewart grasped his pool cue with both hands and split it in two across his leg. "Right before he died, he threatened to cut me out of his will. Something he obviously would have followed through with if someone hadn't killed him."

"Stewart." Max took a step closer. "This isn't going to help."

The owner of the establishment stepped out from behind the counter. "Young man, I'd suggest you stop right now, or I'm going to call the sheriff."

Stewart threw a cue ball toward the owner, barely missing Pricilla in the process. Instead it shattered a glass case behind the counter. "You wanted more evidence, didn't you? What are you thinking right now? Reckless son murders his father in order to get his hands on his inheritance. It fits, doesn't it?"

"Stewart." Max grabbed the broken stick out of the young man's hand, then looked up as Detective Carter stepped into the room. With the broken cue stick in his hands and Pricilla's recent exploits, he was quite certain this wasn't going to look good to the detective.

"I can't believe this." The balding officer stomped across the floor. "I was walking by and happened to hear a bit of ruckus. I want all three of you to come with me down to the station. Now!"

"But I—"

"Yes, you, too, Mrs. Crumb. I would have thought that our talk yesterday would have made more of an impact on you. Stealing a four-wheeler and now a barroom brawl."

"Detective Carter." Pricilla's face had turned an ashen shade of gray. "I will not have my name marred with untrue facts."

Max grimaced at her attempts to clear her good name. So much for her promises that nothing like this would ever happen again. Innocent or not, Pricilla was being hauled down to the sheriff's office for disturbing the peace. And he was going with her.

Pricilla sat with her hands in her lap in Detective Carter's now familiar office. The two glass walls seemed to close in on her. The detective stood, leaning against his desk with an unmistakable scowl written across his face. Max sat hunched down in his chair beside her as if he wished he could disappear into the floor boards. That was something she'd like to do at the moment as well.

Carter pulled the small notebook and pen from his shirt pocket. "Before I go and talk to Stewart, I wanted to see the two of you alone."

"This is all an innocent misunderstanding, Detective. . ."

Pricilla paused, afraid that anything she said would only make things worse. She might not have participated in Stewart's bout of temper, but in reality she had instigated it with her pointed questions. The young man had been on the edge of exploding, and she'd managed to add fuel to the flame.

"It goes beyond an innocent misunderstanding, Mrs. Crumb, when we're looking at over three hundred dollars in damages. I want to know what happened." The detective folded his arms across his chest. "Surely you weren't back on the sleuthing trail, now, were you?"

Pricilla swallowed hard. "I was worried about Stewart. As a friend."

"Worried?" The detective didn't seem pleased with her answer. "And why were you worried?"

Pricilla glanced at Max, who had yet to say a word. He avoided her gaze. "I suppose it will all come out in the end, so there's no use in keeping any secrets."

"No, there isn't." Detective Carter shoved his glasses up the bridge of his nose, then poised his pen to write. "Keeping secrets would mean that not only did you go beyond our agreement to cross-examine Stewart—"

"We weren't cross-examining Stewart—"

". . .it would also mean that you didn't pass along vital information to me regarding my ongoing investigation." He ignored her input and tapped on the notebook. "There's a name for that, you know. Withholding evidence."

"I get the point." Pricilla squirmed in her chair. "First of all, Stewart dropped out of school two months ago."

The detective didn't look impressed. "I am aware of that fact, Mrs. Crumb. I told you that the last time you were here."

"I know."

She fiddled with her purse strap, wishing there was a way out of spilling the information she had. Max had warned her that her probing would get her into trouble, and as always, he'd been right. Only now she'd dragged him into the situation as an accomplice.

She stared at the lined patterns on the tiled floor. "There is more."

"Good, because at the moment that's the only thing keeping you out of a jail cell."

"Detective Carter." Max spoke up for the first time, exasperation filling his voice. "Both you and I know that you have nothing on either Pricilla or me that would merit holding us in a jail cell. I'd appreciate it if you'd avoid using theatrics in this interview."

"Fine." The detective shrugged. "Please continue, Mrs. Crumb. Out of respect for justice in this situation, since we've now had to rule out jail time."

While she might dislike the detective's methods, she couldn't help but smile at Max's attempt to save her honor. Carter's sullen expression emphasized the fact that he wasn't happy with either one of them at the moment, but perhaps all wasn't lost. And one thing was for certain. She was done probing for evidence in this case. No more Holmes and Watson. No more interviews, questions, or digging for the truth, since all she ever seemed to manage was soiling her own reputation.

"Mrs. Crumb."

"I'm sorry." She worked to focus on the issue at hand. "Apparently Stewart has been involved in some sort of gambling and has racked up quite a large debt."

"How much?"

"I don't know exactly, though I'd venture to guess that the figures are substantial. Five or six figures perhaps?"

The detective whistled under his breath. "That is substantial. What else?"

While Pricilla didn't like where the conversation was going, she knew she had no choice but to come clean on what she'd learned. "Stewart came to his father about a week before Reggie was killed and asked for money."

"Hmmm. . ." Carter rubbed his chin. "Now this is getting interesting. You might have just won a free get-out-of-jail card."

Max cleared his throat.

"Sorry." The detective scribbled some more notes. "What else do you have?"

"Nothing really, except for the fact that Reggie and Stewart did have a big fight, and Stewart threatened to take him out of his will."

"That's certainly not nothing. We know that Reggie planned to follow through with cutting the entire family out of his will. That leaves us with a bottom line that Stewart now has motive and opportunity."

Pricilla felt her stomach lurch. "I never meant to imply that the boy killed his father—"

"You didn't have to. The evidence always speaks loud and clear on its own."

Pricilla felt forced to backpedal away from the hole she'd just dug for herself. And Stewart. "Certainly he has a temper and needs to grow up, but my gut tells me that he's innocent."

"Like Annabelle?"

"Yes, like Annabelle. . ."

Pricilla closed her mouth. Gut feelings weren't going to get her anywhere in this office. How could she explain, using evidence, that she believed something—or someone else—had to be involved? Even she couldn't come to that conclusion with the evidence she'd gathered. The truth was, she simply didn't want Annabelle to suffer any more than she already had. Stewart's conviction would hurt Annabelle more than if she herself was sent to prison. There was no way around the facts, though. Stewart had both motive and opportunity, whether she liked it or not.

Pricilla uncrossed her legs and slid forward in her chair, ready to leave. "Can we go now?"

"After my required lecture. You know I'm not happy with either of you." His thick glasses had slipped down the bridge of his nose, giving him the air of a disgruntled professor. He shoved them back into place with his forefinger.

She was getting tired of defending herself. "We had nothing to do with the broken pool cue or the broken glass—"

The detective held up his hand. "Nevertheless, I was forced to arrest you yesterday, and now you've been involved, innocent or not, with a brawl at the pool hall. Hardly behavior for one of the leading figures of our community."

Pricilla frowned, certain that the detective's comment was meant in jest.

But the detective didn't look amused. "I suppose a thank-you is in order, though. With the evidence I've already collected on Stewart, I now have enough to go to the DA."

"What about Annabelle?"

"Let's just say that I'm not completely eliminating any family members at this point." The detective shoved his notebook and pen back into his front pocket. "And Mrs. Crumb?"

"Yes?"

"In the meantime, please try and stay out of trouble."

"I want you to know that I'm finished." Pricilla braced herself against the car door as Max took the curve in the road that led toward the lodge a few miles an hour too fast.

"Finished with what?"

Rows of pine trees streaked by as gravel crunched beneath the tires. "I'm finished with my role of amateur sleuth. No more Miss Marple, Jessica Fletcher, or Sherlock Holmes."

Max shot her a wry look. "Does that mean I can't be your Dr. Watson anymore?"

"Stop teasing. I saw the way you looked at me in the sheriff's office."

"I was honestly madder at his tactics than yours. Neither of us could have predicted Stewart's explosion."

Pricilla gripped the door handle. "Can you slow down just a little bit, please?"

"I'm sorry." He let up on the gas. "My mind isn't exactly on the road at the moment."

"Neither is mine. I've presumably managed to get Annabelle's son arrested for murder."

Max reached out and squeezed her hand. "If he does end up getting arrested, you had nothing to do with it. The truth would have come out one way or another. And Stewart's the one who will have to pay the consequences."

"I suppose." She glanced down at Max's solid hand that enclosed hers. He always made her feel so safe and protected. "What I do know is that I'm finished with the whole sleuthing thing. I'm now simply Pricilla Crumb, chef at the Rendezvous Hunting Lodge and Resort."

"And girlfriend to Max Summers?"

She caught the gleam in his eye and felt a rush of adrenaline fill her heart. "Girlfriend sounds a bit. . .juvenile, don't you think?"

"Juvenile or not, with sleuthing out of the way, there might actually be time to give our relationship a go." He raised her hand to his lips and kissed her fingertips. "What do you think?"

That Max Summers was more romantic than Clark Gable and Cary Grant rolled into one sweet package?

She let out the breath she'd been holding. "I think that can be arranged."

"Good."

Outside they were surrounded by dozens of shimmering aspen trees, a colorful display of spring flowers, and the mighty Rocky Mountains, but all she could see at the moment was Max's handsome profile. He'd swept in unexpectedly and brought things into her life she'd forgotten were missing. Widowhood had left her longing for someone to hold her hand when she was lonely, someone to laugh with and cry with. Max was filling up the lonely spots.

Annabelle's lost expression flashed through the recesses of her mind. Her friend might not have had an ideal marriage with Reggie, but they'd still managed to stick together for all those years. Pricilla understood the pain of losing a husband. That's why the thought of loving then losing Max had her running scared at times. But even her sometimes irrational fears couldn't compare with what Annabelle was going through.

"I'm still worried about Annabelle. My gut tells me that Stewart wouldn't murder anyone. I just wish there was a way to prove it—"

"Pricilla—"

"Don't worry. I meant what I said about staying out of the investigation, but I still can't help but worry about Annabelle's family."

Max pulled into the driveway of the lodge and parked the car in an empty space. "All Annabelle needs at this point is a friend, and nothing more."

"I know. You're right."

He squeezed her hand one last time before opening his car door and letting in a gush of warm spring air. "Of course I'm right."

Chuckling, Pricilla made her way up to the porch where Nathan and Trisha sat in the afternoon sun, drinking lemonade and snacking on a plate of her double fudge brownies.

Pricilla noticed the bleak expressions that crossed the couple's faces and paused at the top of the stairs. "Surely my brownies aren't that bad."

"Of course not. They're the only appealing thing I see at the moment." Trisha folded her arms across her chest and shot Pricilla an exasperated look. "Nathan and I have just officially had our first fight."

"I'm shocked it took you this long." Max stopped behind Pricilla and laughed. "And if you're wondering if it will be your last, I can assure you that it won't."

Pricilla picked up Penelope from her padded perch on one of the chairs and sat down with the cat across from the couple. "Do I dare ask you what you fought about, or would that be sticking my nose into yet another subject that isn't my business?"

"It's not a secret at all." Nathan held up the hunters' calendar that normally hung above his desk in his office. "We're trying to set a date."

"For the wedding?" Pricilla didn't understand the problem.

Trisha shrugged. "Sounds petty, I know, but nailing down a date that will work for both of us is proving to be a tad difficult."

"A tad?" Nathan dropped the calendar onto an empty chair. "How about impossible?"

"Don't start it all again." Max grabbed a brownie from the plate then sat down, seemingly amused with the situation. "Why don't you simply hire one of those wedding planners who will make all the major decisions for you? If you can't set a date, how in the world will you choose colors, flowers, dresses, and all the other stuff that women insist on when it comes to planning a wedding?"

Pricilla frowned. "Are you trying to pick a fight with me now?"

Max winked at her. "Nothing of the sort. I was simply trying to help."

"That's not helping, Dad." Trisha waved her hands in the air. "And please don't even go there. This is my wedding, and I refuse to have the details handled by a stranger."

"It's *our* wedding," Nathan cut in.

"Of course it's our wedding, but—"

"Elope with the girl, Nathan." Max crossed his ankles, looking completely relaxed. "It's the only way to survive your upcoming nuptials."

"They wouldn't dare." Pricilla had held her tongue long enough. "They'd forever have the wrath of a mother who's been dreaming of her only son's wedding for over thirty years."

"Mother—"

"What? Is it asking too much to be a part of the wedding of my son and the woman he loves?" Pricilla grabbed a brownie, pulled a walnut off the top, then hesitated before sticking it into her mouth. "What's the problem with deciding on a date anyway? I would think that out of 365 days in a year you could agree on at least one date."

Trisha flicked her fingers against the calendar. "Hunting season."

"Hunting season is not the problem—"

"Of course it is, Nathan." Trisha rolled her eyes. "I have to plan my wedding around hunting season. And I've always wanted a fall wedding."

"Women are stubborn, Nathan." Max still looked as if he were enjoying the conflict. "You're going to have to get used to it."

"You're not helping, Dad."

Pricilla felt her blood pressure rising. She'd deal with Max later. Right now there was a wedding to rescue. "Trish is right, but what you should be thinking about is that the actual wedding is only one day out of your life together. I think you're both forgetting that what really counts is the marriage. Not the wedding. If you can't learn to give and take now, it's going to be rough."

Nathan raked his fingers through his hair. "I love Trisha, you all know that, but I've been a bachelor for so long—"

"And that makes you some sort of hero who deserves special treatment?" Pricilla frowned. The entire conversation was getting ridiculous. "Trisha left her home and moved to Colorado so the two of you could make a go of this relationship. Give and take is what will make your marriage work."

Pricilla stopped. Weren't Nathan's excuses the same excuses she'd been throwing out regarding her relationship with Max? She was too old to make another big change in her life. Too stuck in her ways to make the necessary adjustments that would give their relationship a chance. Max had made the first move in agreeing to stay in Rendezvous, and instead of being grateful she continued to push him away with her excuses.

Trisha clasped her hands in her lap. "Your mother's right, you know."

Nathan dropped the calendar to the floor. "That I'm being the stubborn one."

"I didn't say—"

"I know. I'm sorry." He reached out and wrapped his hands around Trisha's. "My mom is right. A relationship is all about give and take, but we've somehow gotten so caught up in this wedding planning stuff that we've forgotten what's really important."

"And what is that?"

"You and I living the rest of our lives together." Nathan leaned forward and kissed Trisha slowly on the lips. "I'm sorry."

A glow flickered once again in Trisha's eyes as she looked at him. "Me, too."

Nathan stood then pulled Trisha to her feet. "How about we go for a walk and figure out a compromise. The weather's perfect. . .you're perfect. . ."

She let out a soft giggle. "I think we can do that."

Taking Trisha's hand, Nathan led her toward the stairs. "We'll be back in a little bit."

Pricilla watched them walk across the lawn that was edged with yellow primroses and sweet violets, their arms around each other. "They make a sweet couple, don't they? There's something so romantic about being young and in love."

Max quirked an eyebrow. "Versus being old and in love."

"I didn't mean that at all." She caught his smile and tried to understand the countless emotions that filled her heart, knowing Max loved her. Joy mixed with fear and contentment. Perhaps she was making it all too complicated. "There's nothing like falling in love for the first time and promising the rest of your life to another person. I'd given up on ever having grandkids until now."

"You know we've got our own quandary to work out."

"I know, and I think I've figured out at least part of what's been bothering me." Pricilla swallowed hard. How was it that solving dilemmas between Trisha and Nathan seemed so simple compared to her own life?

"Okay. What have you figured out?"

"Your moving here does change everything."

"In a bad way?"

"Of course not. In a different way." Pricilla stared out across the green grass as the silhouette of Nathan and Trisha disappeared into a grove of pine trees. "Listening to the two of them made me think. When you were in New Mexico, I didn't have to think seriously about where our relationship was going because of the distance between us. But now. . ."

"I'm here and you have to decide."

"Exactly." Pricilla nodded. At least he seemed to understand. "And it's not as if I don't want things to move forward between us, but this is scary for me, Max. I loved one man for forty-three years. Falling in love again is wonderful, beautiful, and exciting, but also very unexpected. And even a bit scary."

"I guess it boils down to one question, then." His gaze caught hers. "Do you want me to stay, Pricilla?"

Pricilla stepped into the fourth townhouse she and Max had looked at in the past two hours. All of their charming features, as the Realtor called them, were beginning to blur together. One bedroom versus two bedrooms. Wood fireplaces versus gas. An extra half bath versus an extra full bath. . . She glanced at the tacky gold curtains hanging above a large picture window. None of that really mattered. What really mattered was that Max was staying.

That *was* what mattered most. Wasn't it?

She studied him as he circled the living room, looking like a serious renter. Max, with his gorgeous blue eyes and handsome physique, was staying because of her. That very idea kept repeating in her mind over and over and made her heart pound with anticipation. It was what she wanted, of course, because with him living close by they would have a chance to see if their relationship really had a chance.

No.

Not *if* their relationship had a chance. It would allow what they already had to blossom and grow into marriage. Which was what they both wanted. Max would rent a small place for six months or so, and in the meantime they would spend time together like any other dating couple until he proposed.

Except if that were true, then why did she have to keep telling herself that this was what she wanted?

She ran her fingers across a dusty windowsill in the small living room and decided to focus on the matter at hand. House shopping. The view of the Rocky Mountains from the front window was stunning. A bit of spring cleaning and new curtains could easily transform the neglected dwelling into the perfect bachelor pad. If they married. . .once they married. . .there would be further logistics to work out, but those things didn't have to be decided at this point. All she needed to focus on now was that Max had decided to give up his life in New Mexico for her. And that he loved her.

Pricilla stayed in the background as Max chatted with the Realtor, Marilee Baxter, a middle-aged woman who sported tweezed eyebrows, fake fingernails, and a wad of gum that seemed the essence of unprofessionalism. At least she had the decency to wear an outfit that covered up her lush curves, unlike some women prone to display all their assets in low-cut, tightly fitting attire.

"What is this for?" Max stared at one of the living room walls that had an indented arched space.

"It's called an art nook." Marilee moved in beside him, her hands waving along with her enthused explanation. "It's a charming place to feature a lovely antique vase, or—"

"I don't own any vases." Max frowned.

"If you don't have any vases, perhaps you could hang a small framed picture." Marilee brought her hand to her mouth and shuddered. "Of course, now any mention of a vase reminds me of Reggie Pierce. You have heard the horrible news about poor old Reggie, Rendezvous' famed baker, haven't you?"

"Yes, I—"

Marilee didn't even pause for Max's reply. "Everyone in town's talking about how someone knocked him off with a heavy vase. Have you ever imagined such an awful way to die?" The woman finally paused to take a breath and snap her gum. "Haven't had this much excitement since Naomi Tucker, the town librarian, was found dead eleven years ago on the bank of Lake Paytah, wearing a purple scuba diving suit."

"I'm not sure that *excitement* is the right word." Max glanced in Pricilla's direction. "Pricilla actually was—"

Pricilla shook her head and moved to stand beside him. The last thing she needed was the entire town talking about how she had been the one to discover Reggie's body. Thanks to the detective, no doubt, her name had stayed out of the paper, a fact she would be eternally grateful for. Not only did the omission keep the lodge out of any connection to a second murder, she also had no desire to have her name aligned once again with such an awful event. Apparently Detective Carter was good for something after all.

One slipped word to Marilee, though, and Pricilla was quite certain that her involvement in yet a second murder investigation would become as legendary as the deceased town librarian.

"What about Pricilla?" Marilee spoke as if Pricilla were in the room and she was looking for the latest town gossip to spread through the fertile grapevine.

Pricilla decided to speak up for the first time. "Max was only saying that because I'm friends with Reggie's wife, Annabelle, and the news came as quite a shock to all of us."

Max flashed Pricilla an apologetic look. He'd have to get used to the small-town mentality where gossip spread faster than a wildfire and never came out the same story at the other end.

"Such a sad account." Marilee folded her arms across her chest. "I ate at Reggie's restaurant in New York years ago while in town for a conference."

"Really?" Pricilla couldn't help but ask the probing question. She might have promised to stop her investigation, but the fact that Reggie's partner from that very New York restaurant had mysteriously died before the place shut down wasn't a piece of information that she could simply forget. And while she couldn't see how it had any relevance to Reggie's death, she was curious about the place. "What was the restaurant like?"

Max glanced at his watch. "Perhaps we should continue the tour of this place. It is getting late—"

"I was quite impressed, actually." Marilee leaned against the stone fireplace, seemingly absorbed with the new topic. "It catered to a wealthier crowd and the food was sensational. You're a chef, aren't you, Mrs. Crumb?"

"Yes."

"You would have loved this place. It was tucked away at the end of a quiet street, but that didn't stop the crowds from coming. When I ate there, we waited an hour and a half for a table for four, and let me tell you, it was worth every minute. They had a chef straight from some fancy chef school in Paris who could turn out the most divine escargot, baked shallots, and the pasta… well, it was an experience I'll never forget."

To the woman's advantage, she had just set upon Pricilla's favorite topic. "You're making me hungry, and it's not even dinnertime yet."

"Just the savory smells alone, at this restaurant, would have packed on the calories." Marilee's smile faded. "There was something strange about their move here, though."

Pricilla took a step forward. "What was that?"

"Perhaps we could look at the kitchen—"

"I've always believed that Reggie must have had a stash of cash somewhere," Marilee continued, ignoring Max's comment. "The restaurant had a priceless collection of antiques displayed that was quite stunning. Things like rare porcelain pieces, turquoise corded vases, and a number of valuable prints. I've always had quite an eye for expensive antiques, so naturally, when the family moved here and I became their Realtor, I expected them to buy one of the more upscale accommodations Rendezvous has to offer. We have some spectacular pieces of property available, you know."

"Naturally."

Max might not be smiling along with his sarcastic comment, but Pricilla couldn't help but urge the woman to continue. "And why didn't they? Buy something more exclusive, I mean?"

"Frankly, I'm not sure. Their decision to move in above the bakery surprised me. Granted, not only is it convenient, but the accommodations are quite large and well built. But still. One would assume that they would have had the money to move into something a bit more luxurious." Marilee leaned forward and lowered her voice. "On the other hand, I have heard rumors that the reason they moved here was because the restaurant went belly-up. It's hard for me to imagine how, except for some sort of problem in the management, but nevertheless, it would be a shame to have had to sell all those beautiful pieces."

"Ladies, if you don't mind." Max stepped in between them. "While the subject of a dead man's antiques and hidden stash of money is fascinating, at the moment I'm more interested in finding a place that will hold *my* antiques. A cracked leather sofa, a worn plaid recliner, and half a dozen cheap, secondhand prints."

Marilee's eyes widened for a brief second before she gained back her composure. Undoubtedly, hearing the word *antique* anywhere near the words *cracked leather*, *worn plaid*, and *cheap* was turning her stomach sour.

Pricilla tried not to laugh as Marilee cleared her throat and addressed Max. "My apologies, Mr. Summers. You're completely correct in your statement that we need to get back to the business at hand. I don't know what got into me. Shall we hurry on to the kitchen then? You're going to absolutely love the charming bay window in the breakfast nook."

"I'm sure I will." Max brushed against Pricilla as Marilee sped toward the kitchen and stopped. "I thought Miss Marple had vanished from the picture."

"She has." Pricilla frowned. "Only she seems to have left behind her friend, Miss Curiosity, who simply can't be held accountable for asking a few innocent questions."

"Innocent?" He squeezed her arm and placed an unexpected kiss on her cheek. "You know you're incurable, Mrs. Crumb."

By the fifth house, Max was beginning to question his decision to leave New Mexico and rent a house. Not that he had changed his mind about being closer to Pricilla, but he did wish that there was another way. His place back home had a large storage shed for his tools and various woodworking hobbies. None of these houses had an area for him to tinker around on his latest project.

And there was another thing that was bothering him. Pricilla. Not that she'd said anything specifically, but he was quite certain that she still had doubts regarding their relationship.

Marilee's phone rang with some fast-paced rap song that sounded as loud and flamboyant as the woman herself. "If you will both excuse me for a moment."

With a nod of her head, she disappeared off onto the back porch that overlooked the mountains. The one *charming* asset of the place Max actually agreed with her on.

Pricilla stared out the window, her arms crossed and her lips puckered into a frown.

Max moved to stand beside her. "Another beautiful view."

"True."

A one-word response from her could only mean one thing. "What's wrong, Pricilla?"

She spun toward him and forced a smile. "Nothing. I just. . .I suppose I'm just worried a bit that you really want to go through with this move. I mean, it is a rather big change."

"Do you want me to move closer?" While he was uncertain where their conversation was leading, he was afraid he wasn't going to like the final destination.

"Of course I want you nearby. I just don't want you to ever feel. . . obligated."

The tone of her voice was far from convincing. "Are you really sure you want me to stay, Pricilla?"

He brushed his fingers across her forearm. He hated to ask her a second time, but he couldn't ignore the flicker of doubt in her eyes that had seemed to grow with each house they'd stepped inside. He knew that his move to Colorado had been a rather impulsive one, and he had made it a priority to pray that they make the right decision, but something still wasn't right.

He stepped back to lean against the kitchen counter. "I need to know where you want our relationship to go."

Pricilla's eyes widened. "You know I want you to stay."

"Actually, I'm not convinced. And while I don't want to say good-bye. . ."

She turned back to the window, her silence speaking more than words ever could. "I know you've wanted me to be more decisive regarding our relationship, and I honestly don't know why I feel so confused."

"Does it have anything to do with Marty?"

"I loved Marty for over half my life, but this is more than losing him." Her fingers fumbled with the blue curtains hanging in the window. "Honestly, I don't think my reservations have anything to do with Marty, except for on one level, I suppose. Losing him hurt so much. . .I just don't want to go through it all again."

Max resisted reaching out and pulling her toward him. The last thing he wanted to do was completely push her away. "I understand what it's like to lose someone you love, but I'm sixty-five years old. I'm not getting any younger."

Max closed his eyes for a moment and prayed for the right words. He never had been good at discussing his feelings, but this moment, of all moments, he was going to have to make a gallant try.

Pricilla swung around to face him. "I don't know if I'm ready, Max."

"I—"

Marilee waltzed back into the kitchen and shoved her phone into her black bag. "So, where were we?"

"I'm sorry, but..." Max ignored the woman's bright expression and turned to Pricilla, who avoided his gaze. His heart sank like a downed missile. "I'm sorry, Marilee, but there's been a slight change of plans."

Pricilla didn't remember the last time she'd felt so completely guilt-ridden. Most likely not since she believed herself to have poisoned Mr. Woodruff with one of her salmon-filled tartlets. At least in that case she'd been absolved of the horrific deed, but in this instance, with Max's broken heart exposed beside her, there was no one to blame but herself.

She squeezed on the handle of the car door until her knuckles turned white. How could she have been such a fool and pushed Max away because of her own irrational fears? Staring out the window of the car, she watched the trees fly by as Max drove her back to the lodge. Life was full of loving and losing. Sixty-five years on this earth had been enough to teach her that. Even the Bible talked about times of laughter and tears, so why, as an individual who, more often than not, tended to jump into things without always fully analyzing the consequences, was she unable to give love a fair shot at happiness?

To give her and Max a fair shot at happiness.

She turned to catch a glimpse of him out of the corner of her eye. He gazed straight ahead, his expression harsher than normal. She knew she'd hurt him tremendously, but no matter how bad she felt, she couldn't find a way to erase the flood of doubts that continued to assault her.

He eased up on the accelerator before turning onto the road that led to the lodge. As soon as he dropped her off, he'd undoubtedly be on the next plane to New Mexico—miles away from the senseless woman who'd just managed to throw her heart away and stomp on his in the process.

She cleared her throat. "I'm sorry."

"You have nothing to be sorry about."

"I have everything to be sorry about. How can I, Ms. Spontaneity, suddenly freeze when it comes to matters of the heart?"

"It happens to the best of us." Max's tone was even, but the hurt in his voice was clear.

"So this has happened to you before?"

"Well...no." He continued to avoid her gaze. "I've only loved two women in my life."

Her and Violet. The guilt Pricilla felt deepened another notch. Violet had been his high school sweetheart before becoming his wife for forty or so years. Did the fact that she *did* love him count for anything at this point?

"I do love you, Max. I just need more time—"

"For what?" Gravel spun beneath the tires as Max took the left curve too sharply. "I've waited for months, and like it or not, I'm not going to be around forever. I was looking forward to sharing my twilight years with you while there was still something left to enjoy. One of these days, I'm going to start forgetting more than just where I laid my glasses or what I had for breakfast yesterday. I'm going to—"

"You're not that old."

"At the moment I'm not feeling that young, either."

Pricilla jumped as her cell phone went off in her purse. The interruption was only going to serve as a delay to the inevitable falling out that was coming between them, and the whole idea made her sick. Digging through the bag, she tried to squeeze out the tears that rimmed her eyes. She'd never meant for things to end this way between them.

"Hello?"

"Mrs. Crumb?" A tentative male voice responded on the other end.

"Yes. Who is this?"

"This is. . .Naldo. I work at the Baker's Dozen in Rendezvous." There was a slight pause on the line. "I'm not sure if you remember meeting me—"

"Of course I remember. Can I help you somehow?"

"I need to speak with you in person."

Pricilla mentally sorted through her calendar for the next couple of days. "I suppose I could drop by the bakery tomorrow—"

"I need to speak with you today, if at all possible."

She furrowed her brow, uncertain of the rationale behind the urgency in his voice. "Well, I suppose I could come today. What did you have in mind?"

"Not the bakery. There's a small Mexican restaurant twenty miles outside of Rendezvous in the town of Mountain Springs. Can you meet me there in half an hour?"

"Half an hour?" Pricilla glanced at her watch. "I don't know. I—"

"Please, Mrs. Crumb. It has to do with Mr. Pierce's death."

Pricilla sucked in a short breath. Max was not going to like this. She'd promised to give up her sleuthing. To forget about Sherlock Holmes and Jessica Fletcher. . .

"Mrs. Crumb, I think I know who killed him."

Pricilla snapped the cell phone shut and dropped it into her purse. If Naldo was telling the truth, then the odds of discovering who had killed Reggie had just risen a notch or two. The logical thing might be to call Carter and tell him what had happened, but she knew she needed to talk to Naldo first.

The problem was explaining it to Max.

"Who was that?" Max gripped the wheel.

"Naldo." Pricilla worked to keep her voice even. "He works for Annabelle at the Baker's Dozen. You met him the day we toured—"

"I remember." Max appeared not to catch the lighthearted mood she attempted to display. "Why would he call you?"

"He. . . Max, would you mind stopping the car for a moment?"

"Stop the car? Why?"

"Please?"

Frowning, Max dropped his speed and edged closer to the side of the road. "What's going on?"

Pricilla held up her hands. "Before I say anything else, please understand that I honestly had every intention of stepping out of the role of detective and leaving the case completely in Carter's hands. No more subtle interviews with suspects. No more notebooks full of motives. No more—"

"I get it, Pricilla." Max was not smiling.

"Just remember, when you start getting mad, that this wasn't my idea."

"What wasn't your idea?" A vein in his neck began to pulse. "What did Naldo want, Pricilla?"

"He thinks he knows who killed Reggie."

Max slammed on the brakes and came to a complete stop. "Pricilla!"

"Stop saying Pricilla like you're calling me to the principal's office to be expelled, or—"

"That's exactly what I'm trying to sound like." He shifted the car into PARK and took his hands off the steering wheel. "This is insane. You need to call Detective Carter right now and tell him about this meeting."

He grabbed for her purse, but she clutched it against her chest. "I don't think that's a good idea."

"Pricilla—"

"Max." She mimicked his patronizing tone.

"I'm sorry, but how in the world could calling the police *not* be a good idea?"

"If he wanted the police involved, don't you think Naldo would have called them up himself? He wants to talk to me. He's scared."

"Of what?"

"I don't know, but I could hear it in his voice."

"Face it, Pricilla. Your instincts about people haven't always been on target."

Now he was beginning to tread on thin ice. "I was right about Ezri having a secret, and Stewart—"

"Fine. Perhaps at times you at least hit the dartboard. . ."Max pounded his hands against the steering wheel. "But there's no way I'm taking you to meet this guy."

"Then I'll go on my own."

She jutted out her chin, annoyed at his negative response. She deserved a bit of credit. It wasn't as if she wanted to apprehend the murderer herself. All she wanted to do was see what Naldo wanted. Besides, how dangerous could it be to meet him at a public place?

Max shifted in his seat and faced her. "Can I ask you a question? Why is it that you're so decisive on this matter, yet falling in love and committing to a person is impossible for you?"

She tried to ignore the sting of his question but couldn't shake off its implications. "It's not impossible, and that wasn't a fair question."

"I'm sorry. You're right. That was a low blow."

"Yes, it was."

He stared at her for a moment as if he didn't know how to respond. "It's just that all the things I love about you are the very same things that get you into trouble and end up keeping us apart. I never know what you want."

"You don't know what I want?" Pricilla blinked back tears of frustration. "I want to erase every fear I have that is standing between you and me and a relationship. I want to let myself forget about the hurt and pain I felt when Marty died, and the knot in my gut that warns me not to go through it again with you. But for whatever reason, that hasn't happened yet. And until it does, it wouldn't be fair to either of us for me to commit to something I'm not completely sure about."

"I guess falling in love is complicated whether you're sixteen or sixty." For the first time, his expression softened, and he smiled at her.

"I guess you're right."

Max shifted the car into DRIVE and glanced into the rearview mirror before swinging a sharp U-turn in the gravel road. "If we're going to get there in time, we'd better get going."

Max followed Pricilla up the flower-lined sidewalk toward the entrance of the restaurant and wondered how he'd managed to once again give in to her. Granted, part of him was interested in what Annabelle's employee had to say, but common sense required them to go to the detective with the lead. Following up on this information themselves was apt to get them into all sorts of trouble. Though surely things couldn't get much worse than Pricilla's recent arrest and their both being hauled down to the sheriff's office.

That is, unless Naldo was the murderer and they were stepping into a trap.

Ignoring the ridiculous thought, Max opened the glass door of the restaurant and released the savory scents of spices and fresh chips into the afternoon air. His stomach growled, reminding him that lunch had been a long time ago. He loved Mexican food—or at least he had twenty years ago. Today spicy foods tended to leave him regretting the indulgence. Perhaps just one order of mild salsa or guacamole with a basket of tortilla chips wouldn't affect him that much.

Pricilla stopped just inside the doorway and turned to him. "Are you sure you're okay with this?"

He glanced inside the quiet restaurant where only a half dozen or so clients were left after the presumed lunch rush. Upbeat salsa music played in the background, far too peppy for his current mood. "It's a little too late to back out now, I suppose."

She shot him a half smile, and his heart lurched. This wasn't fair. Thirty minutes ago she'd managed to break his heart, yet here he stood beside her, hot on the trail of one of her suspects who'd promised them vital information. The way things had gone so far, they were more likely to be classified as criminals along with the likes of Bonnie and Clyde than end up as heroes by solving the case. What did it matter anyway? As soon as they were done here, he planned to drop Pricilla back off at the lodge and catch the next flight to New Mexico.

He turned away from her and took in the dining room that had been decorated in the southwestern flair common to most Mexican restaurants. He just wished her silver curls and hazel eyes hadn't left such a lasting imprint on his mind. He'd have to deal with his heart later. Right now it was up to him to make sure Pricilla didn't get herself into any trouble. Or manage to drag him into it with her.

Pricilla tugged at his sleeve. "I don't want you mad at me for agreeing to come out here. You know I never planned this."

Max couldn't help but laugh at her plea of innocence. "As much as I hate to admit it, it does seem to me that intrigue has a way of finding you whether you want it or not."

"And speaking of intrigue." Pricilla pointed toward the other side of the room. "There he is. And he's alone."

Max nodded as a waitress dressed in a decorative, flared skirt and bright orange blouse approached them with a broad smile.

"Table for two?"

Pricilla shook her head. "Thank you, but we're meeting someone on the other side of the room."

Without another word, she scurried past the waitress and barely missed knocking into a six-foot-tall cactus displaying half a dozen sombreros.

Following her across the room, Max slid into the cracked leather seat beside her and greeted Naldo, who looked as if he'd rather be anywhere else but here at the moment. Perhaps Max wasn't the only one feeling as if this interview might be a mistake.

Naldo swirled his glass of ice water, letting the frozen liquid clink against the edges. "I'm glad you both showed up, but I. . .I'm not sure this was a good idea."

"What is it, Naldo?"

A bead of sweat covered his temple and dripped down the side of Naldo's face. He sopped it up with his napkin before looking up again. "I called you because I owe Mr. Pierce. And like I told you, Mr. Summers, he and his wife have always been good to me."

Pricilla glanced up at Max, but he avoided her gaze. With all that had happened lately, the last thing he wanted to confess to was that he'd tried to do his own investigating.

"Someone's going to get into trouble." Naldo glanced at the exit then leaned forward. "And I have no intentions of being connected to a murder I didn't commit."

Pricilla shivered at the man's words. The word *murder* was enough to make her wish she'd taken Max's advice and forgotten about the whole investigation.

She decided to proceed cautiously. "You said you knew who was responsible for Reggie's death."

"I don't know for sure, but I do know that something odd is going on around that house, and I don't like it." The waiter placed a basket of chips and salsa on the table and Naldo looked relieved over the distraction. He dunked a crisp chip into the salsa. "Mr. Pierce might not have been the nicest man in the world with his temper and all, but he did give me and my brother a chance."

Pricilla eyed the salsa with interest but was quite certain it would be too hot for her taste. More than likely, she was already going to be up half the night, tossing and turning over her fumbled relationship with Max. There was no use adding heartburn to the mix.

"What makes you think something's going on at the Pierce home?"

Naldo took another chip. "First, you need to know that the only reason I'm telling you this is because you both seem like nice people. And when you dropped by the bakery, Mr. Summers, and tried to find out why I was rummaging through the trash. . .well. . .I realized later that I should have told you the truth then."

"You were interviewing suspects?" Pricilla stared at Max.

"It was nothing." Max grabbed a chip and stuffed it in his mouth.

"Nothing?" she pressed.

"Mrs. Crumb?"

Pricilla wavered before turning back to Naldo. She and Max could talk later.

"All I'm going to do is pass on what I know about Mr. Pierce's death. What you do with this information is your business, but don't expect me to go to the police and repeat any of this."

"Okay." Pricilla took a chip from the basket, ready for him to get to the point.

"But first of all, I want to make a deal."

"A deal?" What she needed was information that would be worthwhile to her. . .and to Carter. "I'm not sure what you mean. Could you explain?"

Naldo's gaze shifted to the table. "My brother and I are in the country illegally, and. . .well, with the detective snooping around in his investigation of Mr. Pierce's death, we're getting a bit nervous. I have a family to support back in Mexico. I need this job."

"I'm sorry, but I don't know anything about immigration laws or. . ." Pricilla shook her head and looked to Max.

"Neither Pricilla nor I can make any promises, Naldo." Max spoke up for the first time. "You have to understand that."

"But you can try. Can't you?"

"Why don't we start by you telling us what you know. Then we can go from there."

Naldo scooted back in his chair, and for a moment she was afraid he wasn't going to trust them enough to continue. "I guess I could do that—"

"Are you all ready to order?"

The waitress took the most inopportune time to interrupt. From the way Naldo sat squirming in his chair, Pricilla was certain it wouldn't take much for the man to bolt.

"Why don't you order yourself something to eat if you're hungry," Max told him. "I'll pick up the bill."

Pricilla felt a wave of gratefulness wash over her at Max's offer. Dr. Watson, it seemed, had returned.

"I don't know." Naldo stared at the menu.

Pricilla felt her blood pressure rise a notch. While she did appreciate Max's offer and felt certain that a serving of good food would help put Naldo at ease, waiting on the dark-haired man to tell them what he knew left her with the same feeling she'd had the summer Nathan talked her into bungee jumping off the edge of a bridge.

Thirty long seconds later, Naldo set the menu back on the table. "I'll take a plate of enchiladas rancheras with a side of guacamole."

"Pricilla?" Max seemed anything but anxious.

"Thanks, but I'm really not hungry." Food was the last thing she wanted when a bomb was about to explode in her lap. "But I will take a lemonade, please."

The young woman scribbled something on her pad before turning to Max. "And you, sir?"

"Make that two sides of guacamole, and a bowl of your tortilla soup would be great." Max folded his hands in front of him as the waitress left with their order. "The food smells wonderful here."

"It's the best in the area. My brother and I come here whenever we can."

Pricilla was not in the mood for casual, beat-around-the-bush conversation. "I believe Naldo was getting ready to tell us what he knew regarding the death of Reggie."

"Okay." Naldo rolled his napkin between his fingers. "Three times now I've seen Darren Robinson sneak into the Pierces' upstairs home."

"So that's why you were going through his trash?" Max asked.

"His trash?" Pricilla caught the flicker of guilt in Max's gaze.

Max waved his hand. "It was nothing."

"Thought I might be able to find something. . ." Naldo began.

"We can talk about the trash later. What I want to know is, why would Darren sneak into the Pierces' home?" Pricilla's eyebrows rose.

Naldo dunked another chip in the salsa before taking a bite. "I've been asking myself the same question. Last night I decided to follow him."

Pricilla leaned forward, not wanting to miss a single word. "And. . ."

"He had a key to the front door. Walked in like he owned the place."

"Where were Annabelle and Stewart?"

Max pressed his hands against the tabletop. "If you'd stop interrupting, he'll have a chance to tell us."

"Sorry." Pricilla stifled a grin. While he might never admit it, Max was as anxious as she was to get the truth out of Naldo.

"It was about two-thirty, so they were presumably in bed. I stood near the doorway, careful to stay in the shadows, and I saw Darren pull some papers out of the bottom shelf of the living room bookshelf. The only light in the room was from the full moon, but it was enough to tell me that he was happy. I think he found whatever it was he was after."

Pricilla leaned forward. "Which was. . . ?"

Naldo shrugged. "I never found out, because at that moment someone flipped on a light in the kitchen. It was a miracle neither of us was caught. I am, though, convinced about one thing. Darren found whatever it was he was looking for in the bookcase and would have taken it if someone hadn't scared him away. He managed to sneak out the door while I hid and slipped out a few minutes later. He's been looking for something, and I'm positive he'll be back."

Back at the lodge an hour later, Pricilla sat at the kitchen table and mulled over what Naldo had told them then pondered what Marilee had mentioned regarding her firsthand view of Reggie's New York restaurant. Was there a connection between the stash of money and Reggie's recent death? But how was Darren involved in all of this?

Somehow, on the way home, she'd convinced Max to stay another day, though he refused to discuss the case with her. Or the fact that he'd done a bit of his own investigating without telling her. Not that she had anything at this point either, but if she could find out if Reggie had something worth being killed for. . .

With Max dozing on the front porch of the lodge, Pricilla fired up the laptop. With what Darren taught her about the Internet, it was possible that she could find a connection between the young man and Reggie's past. If not, she had no proof that what Naldo had told her was even true.

All they really had at this point was Naldo's word. There was no proof yet that Darren really was after anything, or that Naldo hadn't made up the entire story. It was hardly enough information to take to the detective, something Pricilla was secretly glad for. She needed time to figure things out, and going to the sheriff would only mean that things were once again out of her hands. For the moment, she'd been given another opportunity to find out the truth. And if she could find a connection between Darren and Reggie she'd be one step ahead.

She began scanning page after page of newspaper clippings on the famed New York restaurant owned by Reggie and his partner, William Roberts. Every review promised that the restaurant would be around for years to come.

But something had gone wrong.

She flipped to the next screen then stopped. A photo on the previous page had looked familiar. Pricilla clicked the back arrow and stared at the photo of William Roberts. . .and his son. It was a snapshot that had been displayed at William's funeral. Her heart thudded inside her chest. He wore glasses now and his hair was longer, but there was no doubt about it. She'd finally found her connection. Darren Robinson's real name was Darren Roberts. And he was the son of Reggie's dead business partner.

For a full thirty seconds, Pricilla couldn't move. She stared at the slightly blurred photo and decided she had to be imagining things. Why in the world would Darren have changed his name then applied for a job with his father's old business partner? None of it made sense, especially the fact that Annabelle had never mentioned who Darren was.

Unless Annabelle didn't know.

Pricilla searched her memory for what she'd learned up to this point about Reggie's former business partner, William Roberts. He had a son who would have been about Darren's age. Darren had told her that he had attended boarding school and had rarely seen his father. Was it possible, too, that Reggie and Annabelle hadn't known the boy? Annabelle had mentioned the fact that she hadn't seen William's wife since before William's funeral. . . . Which meant that Darren could have shown up without them knowing who he was.

She gnawed on the end of her thumbnail. Up to this point, she'd failed to come up with a single motive for Reggie's death under Darren's name in her notebook. Now, in a matter of two hours, his motivation had just shot him to the top of her list.

Pulling out her notebook, she glanced through her scribbled handwriting, trying to tie everything together. Annabelle had once told her that Reggie had always insisted on investing diversely. What if the two business partners had invested in something together besides the antiques the Realtor had mentioned? Something that only the two of them knew about.

Something worth killing for.

She tapped her pen against the table and hoped she was looking in the right direction. Things that could be hidden in a house might range from rare coins to government bonds to jewels. And any of those things could have given Reggie motivation for killing his partner. But the scenario obviously didn't end there. Darren must have found out about his father's investments with Reggie. Investments that Reggie somehow had managed to keep for himself at his partner's death. Pricilla shivered at the two chilling speculations she was left with. Darren took a job at the bakery with the intention of not only finding revenge in killing Reggie, but in getting his hands on a fortune as well.

The problem now was proving her theory.

"What are you working on?"

Pricilla jumped and smacked her leg against the underside of the table. "Ouch."

"Sorry." Max slid into the chair beside her. "I didn't mean to startle you."

Blue eyes stared back at her, but instead of the warmth they normally held, she couldn't miss the reservation in his gaze. She rubbed the top of her knee to ease the throb that was going to leave a nasty bruise. "I'm fine, really."

For a moment, a deafening silence hung between them.

"Can I get you something to drink?" Pricilla jumped up from the table and, once at the counter, began digging through the tray of tea bags. "I know I'd like some tea right now, though I suppose I'd better stick to one without caffeine. You know how too much caffeine makes me jittery and—"

"You're rambling, Pricilla."

"I'm sorry." She'd never felt uncomfortable around Max. . .until now. What if, because of her insane accomplishment of turning him down, she'd ruined their friendship? That was something she couldn't deal with at the moment. She grabbed two of the tea bags then shoved the box back in its rightful place on the counter. "Did you have a nice nap?"

Max tapped his fingers against the table, apparently as uncomfortable as she was. "It was just a short catnap, but I do feel energized."

She grabbed the kettle and began filling it with water. "Why do you suppose they call short naps catnaps? I mean, a short nap for Penelope could be an hour or two—"

"Pricilla, I came in here to tell you something."

She pulled two mugs out of the cupboard then turned to catch his somber expression. Whatever it was, this wasn't going to be good. "What's wrong?"

"I booked a ticket for New Mexico a few minutes ago with the airline. I'm leaving in the morning."

Pricilla felt the air rush out of her lungs. While the news might be expected, it didn't take away the reality that Max's leaving was going to break her heart. No, that was ridiculous. She'd been the one to drive him away. How had their relationship managed to take more twists and turns than a good cozy mystery novel? "You don't have to go—"

His jawline tightened. "I do, and you know it."

"If I had more time—"

"Stop feeling guilty, Pricilla. I know we can't always control how we feel, and this just happens to be a case when one party's feelings are stronger than the other's. It's not your fault."

His words sounded more like they were coming from a defense lawyer standing in front of a judge rather than the jilted party of a relationship gone sour. But despite their softness, the words did nothing to ease the sting of guilt that was welling up around the edges of her heart like an allergic reaction. All of this was her fault. There was no way around it. Surely there was some sort of in-between relationship they could muster to keep.

She poured the hot water over the tea bags then carried the two mugs to the table. "What happens now, then? You leave and I never see you again?"

"Not hardly, considering our children are soon to be married. Besides, it's not as if we have to avoid each other. We'll always be friends, Pricilla." He reached out as if to touch her hand, out of habit perhaps, but then drew it back quickly. "Nothing can change that."

Except she already had changed everything between them. As unintentional and unplanned as her actions had been, she knew she'd have to live with the consequences of losing the second man—and probably the last man—who'd really loved her. Unconditionally with no reservations.

She'd been a fool to let him go.

Max stared at the computer screen and wondered if he'd wake up one day and realize what a fool he'd been for not fighting longer and harder for Pricilla. Except he had tried to stay and fight. She'd made it clear that she didn't want their relationship to go past the boundaries of friendship, and he had to accept that.

But what if they lost their friendship as well?

He took a sip of his tea and winced as the hot drink scalded his tongue. He hated the awkwardness that had wedged a gap between them deeper than all the miles between here and New Mexico ever could have. The laptop's screen saver, a serene rippling brook, splashed across the monitor. Another reminder that all his efforts had been in vain. So much for his brilliant idea to bring them closer together through modern technology. So much for his idea to start courting at sixty-five.

He needed to change the subject. "Who was that in the picture?"

Pricilla set down a mug of tea in front of him and perched on the edge of the chair beside him, ready to run, he supposed, if he said anything out of place. "Did the boy remind you of anyone you know?"

Max turned the screen toward him slightly and moved the mouse to turn off the screen saver. "Not that I can think of."

"Look again."

This time he lowered his bifocals. "I suppose. . .he does look a bit like Darren Robin—"

"Exactly."

Max shrugged, not getting her point. "And there's significance to this?"

"Considering that it's a picture taken with him and his father, William

Roberts, yes. I'd say there's quite a bit of significance involved."

Max mentally rolled his eyes while frowning. So she was off on another red herring chase. When would she learn to trust the detective enough to leave all matters of a murder investigation to him? Perhaps their unexpected breakup had been for the best. It was obvious that she wasn't relinquishing her role as Jessica Fletcher despite the detective's constant verbal warnings and, even more appalling, her recent arrest.

He turned back to his tea and stared down at the dark liquid. "I don't see how it can be the Darren we know. Robinson and Roberts—"

"Darren could have changed his name."

He looked up, catching her gaze. "That doesn't make him a killer."

"Not that information alone, but who did Naldo see snooping around the Pierces' home? Darren Robinson." Pricilla dumped another spoonful of sugar into her tea as her voice rose a notch. "Darren knows something about what his father and Reggie invested in, and I believe he's after it."

He bit the inside of his lip. He hated the fact that she was beginning to make sense. "Pricilla—"

"Think about it, Max. Even you can't deny the fact that I've stumbled upon—"

"Stumbled upon?" His eyes widened at her innocent plea. He might be able to admit that her line of reasoning had possible merit, but he had to draw the line somewhere. She'd found a minuscule crack in the door and had shoved it wide open.

"I didn't call Naldo. He called me, and then—"

"And then you managed to keep that information from Detective Carter while you continued sleuthing on your own."

Max shoved his tea aside and shook his head. Whether or not she had "stumbled" upon the information really wasn't the issue here. He should have driven her directly to the sheriff's office instead of agreeing to the meeting with Naldo. Things were quickly spiraling out of control, and the fact remained that this was a murder investigation—something they both seemed to keep forgetting—not a mystery dinner party with eight guests, a box of clues, and a phony victim.

A man was dead, and there was a murderer on the loose.

"Max?"

He avoided her pleading expression, along with those eyes that always managed to pierce straight through his heart, and held up his hands in defeat. "All right. I'll admit that this is all information worth considering, but you've got to tell the detective what you've discovered."

"I will, but I want to try something first."

That wasn't a good sign. "Pricilla—"

"What's going on, you two?"

Max glanced up at the sound of Nathan's baritone voice as he and Trish entered the kitchen, hand in hand. At least they'd managed to salvage their relationship, unlike his own failed attempts with Pricilla.

"You have perfect timing." Pricilla jumped up from the table and grabbed two more mugs out of the cupboard. "I need to talk to all three of you about something. Sit down, and I'll pour you both a cup of tea."

"What it is, Mom?"

Max caught the questioning look Trisha shot at Nathan as they sat down at the table. Pricilla had a plan, and he was quite certain that her plot was going to not only involve the three of them, but would undoubtedly transform them from respectable citizens into fugitives running from the wrath of Detective Carter. He wasn't sure he was ready this time. Even thirty-five years in the military hadn't prepared him for one of Pricilla's attempts to bring justice back into the world on her terms.

Pricilla set the two mugs in front of their children then slid into her chair while Max waited for the bomb to drop. "I know I promised that I was finished with the investigation of Reggie's death, and I was, scout's honor. But something. . .well, to put it bluntly, I think I know how to catch the killer."

Pricilla waited for a response, but no one said a thing. Instead, blank looks registered on their faces. Max looked as if he preferred to hide beneath the table rather than listen to her latest half-baked, concocted plan, as he was sure to think of it.

Obviously the blunt approach had not been a good choice.

"Max can back me up here." She cleared her throat. She had to make at least one valiant effort before they locked her away on some funny farm. "We think we know who killed him, which means—"

"*We* think we know?"

Pricilla decided to ignore the sting of Max's words. Perhaps switching to the plural to encompass him in her exploits hadn't been the wisest move, but this was going to take every bit of convincing she could muster. Giving herself the greatest advantage was simply good strategy on her part.

Pricilla took another sip of her tea, then, as succinctly and concisely as she could, she recapped the events of the last three hours, starting with the meeting with Naldo and ending with her discovery of Darren's true identity on the Internet. By the time she was finished, their blank looks had been replaced with a hint of interest. Perhaps only a small dose, but she was certain it was there nevertheless.

She leaned forward in her chair. "What do you think?"

"That you need to contact the detective immediately." There was no hesitation in Nathan's voice, a fact Pricilla chose to ignore as she continued.

"So you think my theory has merit?"

"Does that really matter in this instance?" There was no budging her son's stance.

It seemed as if in his eyes, her pursuit of justice should have ended the moment it started. Never mind the fact that Annabelle was likely to go on trial for the murder of her husband, which in turn would affect her children and Kent. . . She felt a knot grow in her stomach. Not that she wanted to believe Darren had a role in Reggie's demise. She had found the young man polite and respectable, hardly the typical stereotype for a murderer. But then was there ever really such a thing? Murderers all had their own character traits, and besides that, facts couldn't be altered like a size twelve pair of pants.

Pricilla took a deep breath and decided to stand by her convictions. "I think it does matter, Nathan."

"As much as I don't want to admit it, I think your theory does have merit." Trisha held her tea mug between both hands and avoided Nathan's sharp look. "But that doesn't change the fact that Nathan is right. The detective needs to be updated on all of this, because frankly this isn't your business. I mean, this is a murder investigation, and just because you once happened to shake down a murderer in a similar situation doesn't mean you need to try it again. You got lucky once. That's not liable to happen a second time."

"Maybe not, but I need you all to hear me out." There was no way she was giving up now. They might not understand her motivation, but fear would not be the thing that stopped her. "Annabelle's future is at stake here, and I promised her that I would do everything I could—"

"Your promise doesn't include risking your life, Mom."

Pricilla wished she could find a way to make her son understand. "My plan is foolproof and safe."

"How can a plan to catch a murderer ever be foolproof and safe?" Trish's brow lowered. The young woman was crossing over to the skeptics' side.

"Look at the facts with me for just a moment." Pricilla was ready to throw out everything she had left. "Naldo saw Darren looking for something in Annabelle's home. We know that whatever he's after, the young man's determined, and after last night's interruption, I have no doubt that he'll be back. More than likely tonight, which means we don't have a lot of time to play around with. Tomorrow he could be gone, along with Reggie's fortune."

"This is all speculation, Mom. So you catch him for breaking and entering." Nathan smacked his hands against the table and shrugged. "You still haven't caught him for murder. Besides that, the kid's smart. If he smells something fishy, he'll be out of there in a heartbeat."

"And how can you be so sure that Annabelle doesn't know about whatever he's looking for?" Max spoke up for the first time. "Maybe she's already liquefied the assets and there's nothing left to find. He could be on a wild goose chase as well."

"Naldo was convinced Darren found what he was looking for. He wasn't able to take it with him last night, which means he'll be back."

"So how do we catch him?"

"Trish." Nathan nudged her with his elbow.

"I'm glad you asked." Pricilla smiled, feeling the rush of impending victory in the air. "We're going to set a trap."

Max sat down in the metal office chair across from Detective Carter's desk, feeling better than he had all day. The three of them hadn't been able to talk Pricilla out of her crazy plan to catch Darren red-handed, but now she sat beside him ready to face the detective, who, he was quite certain, would put a stop to this crazy proposed plot of hers. Watching the detective's lips pucker into a scowl as he slid into his chair convinced Max further that it was inconceivable the detective would allow Pricilla to go ahead with her plan to set up Darren no matter how many times she said it was foolproof.

Catching a murderer was never foolproof, and if he couldn't persuade her of that fact, at least Carter could lay down the law or even threaten arrest, if necessary, to curb her insane plot.

"So, Mrs. Crumb, I understand you have some information for me?" The detective shoved his glasses up the bridge of his nose then steepled his hands in front of him.

Smug with a touch of arrogance. . . For the first time since Max had met the detective he was beginning to like the man, if only because he was the one man who could literally put a stop to Pricilla's plans.

Pricilla perched on the edge of her chair, her bulky purse in her lap. "I did discover something quite interesting today, Detective, though I do hope I'm not wasting your time, bringing you information you already have."

The detective pulled a notebook and pen from his shirt pocket. "As long as you haven't run off with a stolen ATV or been involved in another barroom brawl, I suppose I can give you a few moments of my time."

Pricilla squirmed in her chair. Max smiled. Perfect! In five minutes she'd have shared her information along with her crazy plan, and Carter would respond by having them both thrown out of his office.

As expected, Pricilla started with the phone call from Naldo. The detective's eyes widened through parts of the monologue as his pen took rapid notes, but other than a few grunts, he said nothing. Max listened to Pricilla's description of Darren that made him sound more like a member of the Italian mafia rather than a college-age computer geek. That, though, was fine. The further offtrack she got, the quicker the detective would put an end to this.

Three minutes later Pricilla leaned forward for her closing argument. "So as you can see, the evidence all points to Darren, Detective. He got a job at the bakery not only to get his hands on Reggie's fortune, but to avenge his father's death."

Carter tapped his pen against the blotter on his desk. "Is that everything, Mrs. Crumb?"

"Isn't that enough?"

The detective stared at his handwritten notes then flipped a couple pages as he murmured something incoherent under his breath. "I have to admit that even though this information is coming from an amateur sleuth right out of the pages of an Agatha Christie novel, I think you might have something here."

"You do?" Max spoke up before he could stop himself.

Surely Detective Carter wasn't going along with Pricilla's line of reasoning? Granted, her ideas might warrant a second look at Darren's past involvement with the Pierce family and any connection he might have today, but the detective actually sounded. . .impressed.

Pricilla shot Max a victorious glance then cleared her throat. "Detective, I know you don't like the fact that I've interfered with your investigation a time or two in the past, but I have come up with a solid plan."

"A plan?"

"To trap Darren, of course." She held up her hand. "Before you stop me, please hear me out."

"Okay." Carter leaned back in his chair and folded his arms across his chest. "What do you propose to do?"

What did she propose to do?

Admitting that the information she'd come up with was helpful was one thing, but surely Carter wasn't open to listening to her harebrained scheme. Just because she'd been the one to put an end to their relationship didn't mean he wouldn't continue to be concerned over her wellbeing. He didn't want her involved.

". . .time is running out, and there's not a doubt in my mind, Detective, that Darren will be back tonight for what he left behind at the Pierce residence."

Detective Carter nodded his head. "I like it."

He liked it.

Liked what? Max frowned at the smile that passed between Pricilla and the detective. In his attempts to figure out the detective's motivations, he'd missed the crux of their conversation. And something else was bothering him as well. Since when did Pricilla and Detective Carter smile when in the same room together?

Max squirmed in his chair, shedding his confidence faster than a New Mexico rattlesnake could shed its skin. Had Carter really done the unthinkable and agreed to Pricilla's far-fetched plan? Max had only agreed to come with Pricilla because he knew the detective would put her in her place. And now the man was going along with her idea?

Impossible.

"I'll write a ransom note."

Max jerked his head up at the detective's statement. A ransom note hadn't been a part of Pricilla's plan. "You're going to do what, Detective?"

"Why not?" The lawman shoved his pen and notebook into his pocket and stood.

"It'll work." Pricilla's smile had yet to lessen.

Max shook his head. "I'm sorry, but I'm lost. I thought this entire plot was about arresting Darren."

"It is." Carter braced his hands against the top of the desk. "Haven't you been listening to a thing we've been talking about?"

"I. . ." How had he become the bad guy in this scenario? "Apparently I missed something."

"It's quite simple, really." Pricilla clutched her purse against her chest and stood up. "Looks as if you have a ransom note to write, Detective Carter."

Max frowned in defeat. None of this really mattered to him anyway. Pricilla could go through with her plan and there would be nothing he could do to stop her. He was leaving in the morning for New Mexico.

Two hours later Pricilla stood in the center of Annabelle's living room and faced a windowless wall, trying to ignore the sting of Max's hasty good-bye in the sheriff's parking lot. Not only had she managed to fumble their relationship, she'd apparently shot a hole in their friendship and sunk it as well.

Instead of sulking, though, she forced herself to refocus on the three six-foot-tall cherry bookshelves that stood side by side, encasing half a dozen shelves each. Reggie and Annabelle's collection of books was extensive, from classics like Twain and Dickens to bestselling authors King and Sparks to numerous nonfiction topics and business-related research material. If her theory was correct—and Naldo had been telling the truth—a fortune lay five feet away from her, hidden somewhere inside a secret compartment in the wooden frame.

"Pricilla?"

Pricilla spun around to face Annabelle, whose face had turned as pale as chalk since Pricilla's arrival thirty minutes ago. "I know you're nervous about all of this, but don't worry. It's going to work out fine."

Annabelle wrung her hands together in front of her. "What if it doesn't work?"

"We won't know unless we try, will we?" Pricilla moved across the oriental rug and squeezed her friend's hand. "It's all going to be over soon."

"I know." Annabelle blew her nose with a tissue from her pocket. "I sent Darren on an errand into Mountain Springs. He won't be back for at least another hour."

"Perfect. That will give us the time we need to make the exchange." Pricilla took a deep breath. No matter how knotted her nerves felt at the moment over the situation she'd gotten herself into, she was going to have to be the calm one. "Do you want to help with the search, or would you rather wait in my car?"

"Definitely wait in the car." Annabelle reached for her overnight bag and slung it over her shoulder. "Whatever Darren is after is the reason Reggie is dead, and part of me doesn't even want to know what it is. I still don't know how Reggie could have done this to me."

Pricilla pulled her friend into a hug. "I'm sorry, sweetie. I really am."

Tears welled up in Annabelle's eyes as she took a step back. "I thought I knew Reggie, but I didn't. I didn't know him at all."

"You go on downstairs while I wait for the detective." Pricilla worked to keep her voice even. "We shouldn't be too long."

Annabelle grabbed a black sweater off the back of the couch and headed for the front door. "I do appreciate your letting us stay at the lodge tonight. You've done so much for me. Too much."

"Nonsense. Once Darren finds out that Reggie's fortune has been switched for a ransom note, he's going to be furious. You don't want to be around to see those fireworks explode."

"Mrs. Crumb." Carter appeared in the doorway.

"Detective Carter. Good. You're back."

He shoved his hands into his front pockets and leaned against the doorframe. "Are you ready to go treasure hunting?"

Pricilla shot him a piercing stare. "Someone might hear you."

"Don't worry." The detective held up his hand. "With the investigation still open, no one will question my presence here. It's a small town, but even the news in Rendezvous can't get around that fast, so relax."

"Relax? Right." Annabelle slipped out the door, leaving Pricilla alone with the detective.

"Well, Mrs. Crumb." Carter rubbed his hands together like a kid ready for Christmas. She'd never seen him so. . .so enthusiastic about anything. "It all comes down to this. You find me a million-dollar stash, and I'll take your evidence to the DA. If we find nothing. . .well. . .then you're out of the game."

That sounded more like the detective she knew, and she couldn't help but wonder if he was more excited about finding Reggie's cache or proving her theory wrong. "Nothing like a bit of pressure."

"Now." Carter rested his hands on his hips. "Where exactly did Naldo say Darren had been when he stumbled across something?"

Pricilla walked across the room, stopping in front of the bookshelf. "Right about here."

"Then let's start looking."

Pricilla kicked the baseboard with the toe of her shoe, trying to feel for a slight give in the wood. Anything that might lead them to the alleged fortune Reggie had managed to squirrel away. "So why did you agree to my plan, anyway?"

She moved an inch to the left and jabbed at the board again.

Nothing.

Carter studied the bookshelf beside her. "Now that's a question I've asked myself at least a dozen times in the past two hours."

"Your confidence in me is overwhelming, Detective." Pricilla winced as she eased down on her hands and knees onto the wooden flooring. The last time she'd been in this position had been out of necessity when she spilled a bottle of Madge's expensive herbal supplements across her friend's linoleum kitchen floor. Still, she supposed that the chance of a vast fortune that would set Annabelle and her family up for life was reason enough to succumb to the aches and pains of growing old.

"Anything?" Carter crouched down beside her and ran his fingers across the next piece of baseboard.

"Not yet."

He blew out a deep breath then knocked against the wood. "You're sure Naldo was talking about these bookshelves—"

"Yes. He mentioned the bottom shelf."

"What if he meant floorboards, or—"

"Then why don't you bring him in for questioning?" Pricilla frowned. Just when she thought they'd managed to raise their relationship to the level of tolerance, he had to go and start being difficult again.

"I don't want to bring him in for questioning because we are trying to keep this treasure-hunting business under wraps, remember?" Carter stood and whacked the baseboard with the heel of his shoe. "If Naldo gets wind that the stakes might include a fortune, we'll have this house crawling with treasure hunters before I can count from *uno* to *diez*."

"Fine. Then keep looking."

Pricilla frowned. If they didn't find something soon, her entire theory would be shredded and thrown out with tomorrow's trash. If Naldo had been lying—

"Ouch!"

"Mrs. Crumb. What is it?"

"I just pinched my finger on something." Pricilla shook her finger, hoping to ease the stinging pain. "Wait a minute."

Without another thought to her injured finger, she began pulling the books off the bottom shelf. Two dozen encyclopedias might just be hiding more than an armload of interesting facts. With all the books tossed on the floor, she worked to lift up the bottom shelf.

"Look at this. You didn't have to take out all these books." Carter pulled a pocketknife from his pocket and pried at the bottom baseboard. A six-inch section popped off with a snap.

Pricilla picked up the piece of wood. "What is it?"

Carter motioned toward the small opening. "I suppose you deserve the honors."

Pricilla reached in her hand and pulled out a small black pouch. Diamonds scattered across the wood surface.

Carter started counting. "There's. . ."

"Thirteen."

He sat back on an encyclopedia before shoving it aside. "How appropriate."

"They're beautiful." Pricilla dropped one of the diamonds into the palm of her hand. "How much do you think these are worth?"

"I don't know." Carter held up one of the jewels toward the light. "They'll have to be appraised, of course, but I've heard of high-quality ones that ran for nearly half a million."

"Each?" Pricilla barely got the word out.

"Each."

Pricilla let out a low whistle. "So now we know what Darren was after."

"And what he was willing to kill for."

The next day, Pricilla filled the Styrofoam cup with steaming coffee then glanced around the newly opened convenience store at the edge of town. At nine o'clock the early morning traffic had dissipated, leaving the place quiet except for an old John Denver song that played over the sound system. While she would have preferred something more upbeat to counter her mood, the convenience store owner's choice in music was hardly at the top of her list of priorities. The detective had insisted that the setup here would be perfect in case something went wrong. Something she was praying wouldn't happen.

In the thirty minutes she had been here, she'd roamed the five aisles, counted the number of brands of cough drops, chips, and snack products, and rearranged a stack of crackers that had slid off the shelf. Perhaps her plan hadn't been so brilliant after all. It was a quarter past nine and there was no sign of Darren. He'd probably smelled a trap and run.

What had she been thinking? What had the detective been thinking when he set up this crazy scenario?

She wandered past the selection of drinks in the cooler section that ran along the back wall. Either the cashier was starting to get suspicious that she was stalking the place, or the young man was in on the operation with the detective. Carter had told her not to worry. Right. She'd give Darren another ten minutes before declaring defeat and trying to come up with plan B.

"Mrs. Crumb?" One of the cooler doors shut behind her. She turned around to face Darren. "What are you doing here?"

The boyish gleam she'd once recognized in his eyes had been replaced by a look of irritation. She opened her mouth to say something, but no words came out. She tried clearing her throat. High school students froze during the opening night of their senior play. The stakes here were much higher than a leading role in a three-act performance.

"I know you were expecting Annabelle, but. . ." Pricilla worked to keep her emotions suppressed despite the knot of fear welling up inside her chest. She could do this. "But I'm here instead."

"Great." He popped the tab of his drink and took a swig. "A nosy old woman trying to play the role of Nancy Drew."

"Ouch. You know you were much more pleasant in your role of respectable college student." Pricilla forced herself to look him in the eye and hold her ground. "So, I guess we both know why you're here?"

He shrugged, and she couldn't help but wonder if he really felt as calm as he looked. The whole ensemble—T-shirt, Windbreaker, jogging shorts, and white tennis shoes—gave him the generic look of any other morning jogger. "Is this some nutty idea of Mrs. Pierce's to pay me to be quiet?"

"Because half of the diamonds were your father's?"

His face paled. "How did you—"

"What if I told you there were no diamonds hidden beneath the bookshelf?"

"What?"

Pricilla watched his reaction. "You didn't get a chance to find out, did you, so you're not sure what was in there?"

"Stop trying to play with my mind. I can't imagine Annabelle going to all this trouble for a handful of Monopoly money." He held up the ransom note they'd left. "This is proof enough that I was on the right track, and Annabelle was wise to believe I won't stop until I find it. It was supposed to be so simple."

"Simple, that is, until Reggie realized who you were? The son of his dead business partner."

"No." Darren shoved his hands into the front pockets of his navy blue

Windbreaker. "So what now? You don't really expect me to leave without my father's fortune. I know it's mine. I found out about the existence of the diamonds from some notes of his I found last night. Unless you're in on this with the detective—"

Pricilla searched for the plausible response she'd memorized. "I would say that's highly unlikely, considering the detective has already arrested me once and had me hauled into the sheriff's office a second time because of this entire mess. The man doesn't exactly hold me in the highest regard."

He leaned against one of the cooler doors and combed his fingers through his hair. "This entire situation is ridiculous, you know. I suppose I led Mrs. Pierce to the diamonds last night when she caught me, though I didn't think she saw me. I should never have left without finding them."

"I am, or shall I say Annabelle is, prepared to make a deal with you. You want the diamonds. She wants you out of her life."

Darren smacked his fist against the door. "You know, I would have been halfway to Brazil with the diamonds by now if it hadn't been for a slight interruption in my plan. All I want is what is rightfully mine."

"Even if that means stooping to murder?"

"Reggie deserved to die. He killed my father." Darren grabbed Pricilla's arm. "You know, I'm tired of this. It's time we did this on my terms."

"And what are your terms, Darren?"

"Considering you've just become my hostage, that's none of your business."

Pricilla felt a sharp jab of pain shoot down her arm as Darren pulled her toward the front door of the store. Over a pot of tea the night before, she'd tried to plan what to do if Darren became aggressive, but Carter had assured her the police would be waiting in the wings to jump in at the first sign of trouble.

Well, she was sensing trouble.

Darren's grasp tightened. "You'd better not scream."

One look around the store revealed an empty spot at the counter. Where was that cashier? So much for Carter's assurances of coming to her rescue. Trying to pull away from Darren's grip, she knocked into a display of potato chips. The cans tumbled off the shelf and onto the floor. She lost her footing for an instant as she tripped over one of them, but his hold on her arm never loosened.

She had no one to blame but herself. They'd been looking for more than a simple burglary conviction. She'd wanted a murder confession that would clear Annabelle's name and had believed that raising the stakes would increase the chances Darren would confess. It had taken her an hour and three pieces of her peanut butter pie to convince Carter that out of all the people Darren knew, she was the one he would talk to.

That cockamamie assessment of hers had proven correct. Darren had confessed to her and straight into the hidden microphone of the detective's state-of-the-art recording technology that had picked up every syllable of the man's confession. Its technological advances better not fall short when it came to the ability to rescue hostages and announce their distress.

As Darren's grip tightened, Max's face appeared unexpectedly in the recesses of her mind. In facing the wrath of a murderer, she suddenly realized what a complete fool she'd been to send Max away. All her excuses to guard her heart no longer seemed important. She loved him. And now she might not get the chance to tell him again.

Pricilla tried to suck in some air. The room was starting to spin. She could make out the door ahead of her but still couldn't tell where the cashier was. She was out of breath and her arm was going to have a nasty bruise from Darren's tight hold. Something caught the corner of her eye as Darren pulled her around the last corner before they got to the automatic front door. Betting on her last chance, she grabbed a can of air freshener with her free hand and managed to pop the lid off with her thumb. Praying that her aim would be better than her common sense, she squeezed.

The effect was immediate. A howl rang out. The air smelled of fresh peaches and cinnamon before the room spun out of control. She felt a burst of pain at the back of her skull. Someone shouted.

Then everything went dark.

"Mom?"

Pricilla opened her eyes then shut them against the glare of the sun. Her head pounded beneath the mental fog that enveloped her. "Nathan?"

"How do you feel?"

She forced her eyes open. Plastic seats, metal grill barrier, and the smell of peaches. . . This couldn't be happening. She was sitting in the parking lot of the convenience store in the back of a patrol car.

"Mom?"

"You asked how I feel? Like I have a hangover." She rubbed her temples with her fingertips and struggled to sit up then melted back into the seat. "Not that I've ever had one, but. . .what's going on?"

"You're in the back of Detective Carter's patrol car."

"I can see that, but why?"

Nathan scratched his head and rested against the open doorframe beside her. "You fainted."

"Fainted? I. . .I most certainly did not." Pricilla's eyes widened in horror. "That's impossible."

"As impossible as a person claiming they don't snore because they've never heard themselves. Trust me, you were out cold."

"I don't understand." The throbbing in her temples intensified. "What about Darren?"

Nathan nodded toward the front of the store where Darren leaned against the brick wall with a scowl on his face. "According to the detective, he's waiting for permission to leave so he can go down to the station to file a complaint against the department."

"What?" Pricilla shook her head and tried to clear the ringing noise. Obviously, movement was not a good idea. "I don't understand."

"I'm not sure I understand all of this either, considering I wasn't let in on the final details of this latest escapade of yours." Nathan squatted on the ground beside the car and took her hands. "We just dropped off Max at the airport, and he told me you were through with all of this, which was what I had gathered from yesterday's version of your plan. Then I got a call from Detective Carter a few minutes ago."

"The plan changed." Pricilla winced. So Max was gone, a fact that hurt worse than the growing headache. At least he hadn't seen her in all her humiliation. "We were going to trap Darren and get a confession."

"Well, that's the other interesting thing. The setup you were involved in didn't work. Instead of picking up your conversation with Darren, all that was recorded was John Denver playing in the background. The cashier, an undercover detective, sensed a problem and slapped the handcuffs on Darren, who now claims he was simply leading you outside for some fresh air because you were feeling faint."

She shook her head. This was too much information, too fast. And none of it what she wanted to hear. "And then I passed out?"

"Or hit your head. No one is completely sure what happened."

This was unbelievable. Aches from arthritis and occasional bouts with memory loss, yes, but fainting? "I've never fainted before in my life. Never."

Nathan laid a hand on her shoulder and squeezed gently. "You've been under a lot of pressure lately, Mom, between your job at the lodge, Reggie's murder, and your relationship with Max. I don't think that something like this should be totally unexpected."

"Fainting is what delicate women do in Victorian novels."

"No one would ever call you delicate, Mom."

"But my entire plan was for nothing."

Trisha arrived with a candy bar and a bottle of juice. "An ambulance is on its way, but I thought this might help if you have low blood sugar."

"I don't have low blood sugar—an ambulance?" Pricilla's fingers grasped the edge of the seat. She was not going anywhere in an ambulance.

"Take it. Please." Trisha held out the food. "The detective insisted on getting your head checked out just in case."

Pricilla frowned, ignoring the offer. "I doubt he was worried about a concussion when he said that."

"Mom, take the juice and candy bar."

She didn't feel like arguing, so she took the imposed gifts.

Trisha stood beside Nathan and wrapped her arm around his waist. "Did you hit your head?"

"I think so." Pricilla felt for sore spots with her hand then winced. "Of course, every muscle in my body is aching right now, so I'm not sure what happened."

A phone went off and Trish reached for her back pocket. "Hang on."

"Darren claims you slipped and hit your head on one of the shelves, Mom."

"Nonsense." The throbbing began to intensify. Maybe she had hit her head. She tried to remember exactly what happened. "We were talking, and somewhere in the midst of my questions he confessed to killing Reggie. That had been the plan, but then he must have panicked. He said he was taking me as his hostage."

Nathan frowned, and Pricilla looked away.

"I suppose fainting was a good move on your part, but Darren is still claiming to be the hero in this situation."

Pricilla jutted her chin up at Nathan's last words. "What did you say? The hero?"

"That's what the detective told me."

"This is ridiculous. Someone had to have seen something. What about the video surveillance in the store? All gas stations have security measures like that."

"You're finally awake, Mrs. Crumb?" Nathan moved aside as the detective stepped up to the car and knocked on the top of the roof with his knuckles. "How are you feeling?"

"Better until you had to make that awful noise."

"Sorry."

"I don't know what's going on, Detective, or what Darren told you, but he grabbed me." Pricilla pressed her hand against the door handle and pushed herself up out of the car as she addressed the detective. "He took me hostage—"

"Whoa, slow down, Mom." Nathan reached down to stop her ascent, but she stopped him with the flick of her hand.

"I'm fine."

"You still have to be checked out by a doctor—"

"He's right, Mrs. Crumb, but we've also run into a kink here. I assumed, like you've just said, that Darren tried to grab you, but he says otherwise. We've just been looking at the tape, and unfortunately it isn't clear if Darren grabbed you or if you tripped and Darren was helping you. Low blood sugar perhaps—"

"I don't have low blood sugar." She threw the candy bar and drink into the patrol car. "I'm perfectly healthy."

"I thought I was, too, but somehow I managed to let you talk me into this ridiculous setup." The detective turned to Nathan. "My wife keeps nagging at me to show a little sympathy and listen to others, so I thought, why not? Some of Mrs. Crumb's instincts have in the past proven to be valid, so why not go out on a limb and figure out a way to catch this guy once and for all. Look where Solomon's wisdom got me this time."

"Thanks for the vote of confidence." Pricilla leaned against the car. "But that doesn't change the fact that I still don't understand what happened."

Carter shoved his glasses up the bridge of his nose. "Not only did we not get any sort of confession from Darren—"

"Nathan told me. That wasn't my fault—"

"He also said that he's planning to sue the department." Carter held out his hand. "I'd like my microphone back, please. At least I won't get written up for losing department property along with all my other blunders today."

"It doesn't work." Pricilla worked to unfasten the microphone from inside her blouse pocket.

"Did you have to remind me?"

"Sorry." The hook snagged then finally came loose. "He did confess, you know."

"So you say, but at the moment I can't do anything about it. I'd say that sums up the situation quite nicely."

She held up the faulty device, then with a flare of dramatics dropped it into his open hand. "What about the spray can? Doesn't that prove I was trying to defend myself?"

"You managed to miss Darren and instead hit Detective Markham, who was working the counter. He's in the bathroom, flushing out his eyes. Who's to say who you were aiming at?"

"A bout of insanity, I suppose you'd like to think?"

"A defense lawyer *would* claim something like that."

She ignored his comment. "Does Annabelle get the diamonds?"

"I'm sure that will involve piles of legal hassles. With no physical evidence that he was planning to steal the diamonds, it's going to take a top prosecutor to stop him from claiming a share, which in reality might actually be his."

"I'll testify."

"Don't even go there for now. You're officially off the case. Besides, what we have now is his word against yours. It's a mess. A complete mess." The detective dropped the microphone into his pocket and frowned. "The ambulance just pulled in, finally. I want you completely checked out. I don't need two complaints against the department in one day. I'm never going to hear the end of this as it is."

Trisha rushed to the car, her hands behind her back and a serious expression on her face. "Pricilla, I. . .that was Dad on the phone. He called from the airport to see if he forgot his shaving kit at my house. He said he didn't know about the plan, and—"

"You told him?"

Trisha nodded slowly. "He's meeting us at the hospital."

Pricilla's heart lurched. She'd managed to completely botch her chance at catching Reggie's murderer, but maybe there was a chance to save her relationship with the man she loved.

Max punched the elevator button and frowned at the closed doors. How long did it take for a box the size of a refrigerator carton to drop one story, open its doors, and suck him in? He hated elevators. He hated hospitals even more. Hated the smells, and the green walls, and the constant beeps and whirring sounds of machines. It brought back too many memories of doctor's appointments, hospital stays. . .and Violet.

Violet.

Sometimes it seemed as if she'd been gone forever. Other days it seemed like only yesterday. He'd buried those feelings so deep, he hadn't allowed himself to remember the pain anymore. Pricilla had, though, and he'd ended up losing her because she still felt the heartache of losing someone she loved.

He punched the button again. "I blew it, Lord."

Not that he would have given up forty years of marriage because the ending hurt. Never. But he should have been more patient with Pricilla. Instead of leaving, he should have recognized her fear and waited for her. Things might have turned out differently.

Where are the stairs?

He took a step back and stared down the hallway.

"Dad?"

"Trish."

His daughter strode toward him and smiled. "What are you doing?"

"They told me they put Pricilla in a room upstairs."

"I'll take you to her." She motioned with her hand. "She's down the hallway in the emergency room."

"They told me—"

"Someone told you wrong, Dad. And by the way, she's going to be fine. You can stop worrying." She wrapped her hand around his arm and started walking. "Being here brings back memories of Mom, doesn't it?"

"Your mom hated the hospital, but she never showed it. Always had a smile for the nurses and a good joke for the doctors. I could never be that way. I'd moan and complain until they kicked me out on my backside."

Trish's laugh faded as he passed a bulletin board. Pleas for blood donors. . . cancer support groups. . .information on Alzheimer's. . .

There was too much pain in the world.

Max squeezed his daughter's arm. "Have you ever thought about why?"

"Why what?"

"Why there is so much pain in this world." Their footsteps echoed down the empty hallway. "I lost your mother. Pricilla lost Marty. Annabelle losing

Reggie has brought nothing but heartache to her family, and even to Pricilla, who managed to get herself involved in the entire mess."

"That's Pricilla, Dad. Saying she cares is never enough. She has to jump in and fix everything."

"That's what I love about her. Loved."

She nudged him with her elbow. "You were right the first time, Dad. You love her and she loves you. Why don't you just swallow your pride and give Pricilla the time she needs. She let you go because you weren't ready to wait for her."

"Time I should have been willing to give her."

Max frowned, frustrated at his own stubbornness. He hadn't been willing to wait for the best thing he had going for him in his life. And it had taken almost losing Pricilla to realize she was worth waiting for. For as long as it took. They might not have forty years ahead of them, but he'd take whatever he could get. Because it would be spent with Pricilla. Now he just had to pray that God would give them another chance.

Trish laced her fingers through his and squeezed. "You used to tell me that when God created the world, though, everything He made was good. Sin is what separated us from God. Never God Himself. From the very beginning He's been trying to draw men back to Him. Jesus was the ultimate sacrifice to bring us back to Him."

"Did I ever tell you what a wise daughter I have? I think I just needed to be reminded of what was true." Max stopped at the door to the emergency room and turned to Trisha. "And because I suppose at times it's easier to blame the Creator instead of man's decisions."

"Pain is a part of life, but don't ever let it stop you from living." Trisha reached up and planted a kiss on his cheek. "Now, get in there and talk to her."

Max took a deep breath and crossed the emergency room floor until he got to room 3. He tapped on the door and heard her say "Come in."

Something in his heart trembled when he saw her. Oh yes. He loved her. Still. "Hi."

Pricilla reached up and tried to fix her disheveled hair.

He sat down beside her on the narrow bed. "Don't worry about it. You'll always look beautiful to me. Though I didn't realize that your plan to save Annabelle involved your taking down a murderer and almost getting yourself killed."

"Killed? Obviously reports of my death have been highly exaggerated." She fiddled with the edge of the bed sheet. "The whole plan was a disaster. If you think the detective didn't like me before. . .well, let's just say I'm sure if it were up to him he'd have me thrown back into one of his jail cells."

He decided to ignore her last comment. Even Carter couldn't do that.

"What did the doctor say?"

She touched the side of her head with her hand. "A mild concussion. Nothing to worry about."

From the moment he'd entered the room, he'd tried to gauge her reaction to his presence, and so far he didn't think he was doing very well. She'd yet to smile at him or give any clue that she even wanted him in the room. Perhaps she was simply still frazzled from her experience at the convenience store.

Don't let pain stop you from living.

Trish had been right. He was ready to live again. And Pricilla had brought life back to him. She might kick him out and tell him she never wanted to see him again, but she was going to hear him out.

"Max, I've been a complete fool—"

"Pricilla, I need to say something to you—"

They spoke at the same time.

She held up her hand and shook her head. "Me first. Please. Something happened to me inside that convenience store. When I found out that Darren was the man who had killed Reggie, I knew he wouldn't think twice about murdering me as well. But what scared me the most was the fact that I'd lose you. I should have never let you walk away, Max." She reached out and grasped his hand. "I love you."

Max trembled at her touch. She really loved him? "So I haven't lost you?"

She shook her head and squeezed his hand. "What were you going to say?"

"I. . .I was ready to board the plane this morning and walk out of your life." He caught her gaze. "When Trish told me what had happened, I knew I'd made the biggest mistake of my life. I shouldn't have left. I gave up too soon on us, and I'm not ready to throw away the chance we have for love. Neither of us knows what the future holds. I could die from a heart attack tomorrow, but being together today would make it worth it. Or we could both live another thirty years until we're half senile, and have lost all our teeth, or at least can't remember where we've put them—"

"Oh, Max."

Pricilla's smile made his pulse race.

"Let's promise not to worry about what might happen tomorrow." He reached up to wipe away the tear that slid across her cheek then kissed her gently on the lips. "Pricilla, I want you to be my wife. Will you marry me?"

21

Two days later Pricilla glanced at Max like a smitten schoolgirl while Misty worked her way around the table, serving individual dessert plates of passion fruit tarts. The room was filled with the sweet scent of the buttery crust with its fruit filling and piped meringue on top, but all Pricilla's senses could take in at the moment was Max. Blue eyes stared back at her, leaving her feeling tipsy despite the fact that not a drop of alcohol had been served during tonight's feast.

"The dinner is spectacular, but even more so is the hostess." Max reached for her hand then brought it to his lips like the romantic hero straight out of a black-and-white movie.

Pricilla felt a blush creep up her cheeks as she took a bite of the dessert and savored the tropical taste of the passion fruit. As she'd planned, the atmosphere was perfect. A centerpiece of fresh-cut flowers from the garden and an arrangement of lit candles offered a warm glow to the room, adding yellow radiance to the dimmed lighting. A fire crackled in the fireplace, more for ambiance than for the need of warmth on the drizzly spring night. Even the mahogany table had been set for eight with the lodge's finest gold-rimmed white china, crystal glasses, and sterling silverware.

The setting was perfect. Everything was perfect. Pricilla Crumb was sixty-five years old and hosting her own engagement party. . .to Max. Life didn't get much better than this.

Trish and Nathan had joined them for the celebration along with Annabelle, her children, and new son-in-law. The only downside of the evening was the fact that Darren hadn't been arrested in connection to Reggie's death, and they still didn't know what the outcome would be regarding the investigation. The detective had promised, though, that he would do everything he could to put a close to the case as soon as possible. At least the spotlight had been taken off Annabelle for the moment.

Pricilla's instincts might not have been far off, but the whole experience with her jaunt as a detective—amateurish as it might have been—had taught her a number of important lessons. She had learned the importance of waiting on God instead of jumping into things on her own. It was time to allow God to curb her impulsivities and let Him be the Lord of her life. Additionally, the conflict at the convenience store had taught her that life was short and unpredictable. One never knew what was around the next corner. . .a corner she now knew she wanted to take with Max.

Stewart, who sat across from her, set his fork on his plate and cleared his throat. "Mrs. Crumb, I. . .well. . .I just wanted to apologize. My behavior over the past few weeks has been anything but appropriate. Through my father's death, I was forced to see what happens when revenge and anger take hold of a person. It made me realize that I want to be on the right side of the law. I'm going back to school in the fall and am going to finish my degree in forensic science. Who knows, maybe one day Detective Carter will hire me."

"That's wonderful, Stewart." Pricilla turned to the young man's mother. "Annabelle, you must be so proud of his resolution."

"Very proud." The spark that had been missing for weeks was finally back in Annabelle's eyes.

"You're not the only one with plans to go back to school, little brother." Ezri's broad smile lit up the room. "Kent and I are going to finish our last year of school then return to Rendezvous to help Mom run the business. Kent will have a degree in business, and we want to not only expand the mail-order side of the bakery, but add an ice cream parlor."

"We can certainly use another booming business in this town." Nathan nodded his approval.

"Your mother was the one who brought us all together." Ezri smoothed the wide collar of her shirt and held up her glass of cider. "Thank you, Mrs. Crumb."

Pricilla's eyes moistened with tears. "You're welcome, Ezri."

"Since we're all confessing. . ." Annabelle cleared her throat. "I know a lot can happen in the next year or two, but just the thought of having my kids living nearby brings me a peace. And best of all, I've rededicated my life to Christ. It's time I went forward and became the example and leader I need to be to my children."

The doorbell rang, interrupting the rounds of well wishes for the Pierce family. "Who could that be?"

A moment later Misty announced Detective Carter.

Pricilla pushed her chair back and stood. "Why, Detective Carter. We weren't expecting you."

Carter took off his raincoat and handed it to Misty. "What's the occasion? I seem to have crashed a party."

Pricilla felt a blush creep up her cheeks. "It's an engagement party. . .for Max and me."

Carter ran his hand across his balding head and smiled. "It looks as if congratulations are in order."

"We've just finished dinner, but if you'd like some dessert—"

"No, please, sit down. What I have to say won't take long." He rested his hand against the end chair where Nathan was sitting. "In fact, this setting couldn't be more perfect. I've always wanted to hold a dinner party during which I reveal the real murderer among the assembled list of suspects."

Several let out audible gasps at the detective's announcement. Color drained from Annabelle's face. Pricilla's stomach knotted into a ball. She wasn't going to allow him to ruin this party no matter what the news.

"Detective Carter, please. We are celebrating tonight."

"I suppose then that you don't want to hear that I made an arrest today and am in the process of closing the case."

"You're what?" Pricilla sat back down in her chair.

"You heard me right. I'm closing the case." The detective took off his glasses and cleaned them with the bottom of his shirt. "You might not believe this, but while our setup at the convenience store might not have worked, I managed to get a full confession out of Darren."

Pricilla's brow narrowed in impatience, but she realized that the detective was enjoying his theatrics.

The detective put his glasses back on. "I've spent the past forty-eight hours gathering evidence, and from what I have so far, Darren had always been convinced that Reggie killed his father. A fact, I suppose, that we might never be able to prove. Needless to say, Darren believed it. His plan was to take revenge on his father's death and get his hands on the diamonds. He spent the last month methodically searching the house for the diamonds."

Annabelle shook her head. "Explaining why things were always out of place. And why I thought I'd lost one of my house keys."

"Add to that, he figured that your family would have plenty of motivation to kill Reggie if he played you all against each other. He was the one who typed up the phony *unsigned* will to throw me off the trail."

Annabelle fingered her glass and stared at the clear liquid. "So while my husband didn't live the life of a saint, at least he didn't turn on his family in his last moments."

"You can be assured of that, Mrs. Pierce."

Pricilla had had enough of the detective's theatrics. "I still don't understand how you got him to confess. Last I heard he was planning to sue the department."

Carter smiled. "Let's say that microphone ended up working after all."

Pricilla leaned forward. "You actually taped his confession?"

"Not exactly. He saw you give me back the microphone with your typical dramatic flair, and he thought he'd been busted. I was able to play on that belief and while he thought he was striking a deal with me for a lesser sentence, yesterday he managed to turn himself over for a certain conviction."

Max laughed. "That's unbelievable."

Annabelle rested her arm on her daughter's shoulder. "So does that mean that my family and I are innocent now in the law's eyes?"

"Yes, it does." Carter tapped his fingers against the chair then took a step backward. "I have to run, but I thought you would all enjoy hearing the news."

Nathan held up his glass as the detective grabbed his coat and left the room. "I'd like to propose a toast. To closure for Annabelle and her family, and to the future of Max and Pricilla."

"Here, here!"

Trish winked at her father. "Have you two set a date for the wedding?"

Pricilla looked at Max and offered a wry grin. "Not yet."

"We have." Nathan squeezed Trisha's hand. "October 17."

Pricilla sighed. "I'd say we have some work ahead of us, Max. Wedding dates, decorations—"

"That settles it, sweetheart." Max reached out and took Pricilla's hand. "We're eloping—"

"And deprive me of seeing my mother marry?" Nathan's brow rose. "I think I remember a certain person balking at the idea of her only son eloping."

"It looks as if setting a date is inevitable." Max groaned but didn't lose the twinkle in his eye as he turned to Pricilla. "Something I'm not complaining about one bit."

Pricilla beamed at Max's smile and the lighthearted banter that filled the room, thanking God for once again bringing a second chance at happiness into her life.

CHEF'S DEADLY DISH

The fact that she'd already seen the wedding dress didn't stop Pricilla Crumb's jaw from dropping. She searched for a word of encouragement to give her future daughter-in-law, but none surfaced at the sight of the satin gown hanging like a shapeless gunnysack on Trisha Summers's slender frame.

Lord, this is one of those days when an extra miracle would be greatly appreciated.

Pricilla paced the carpeted floor of suite twenty-three in the Silvermist Lodge and shook her head. With the wedding only three weeks away, the express package had arrived not only late but two sizes too big. Yards of satin swallowed Trisha in their creamy swirls, while the puffy sleeves jutted to the side like oversized football pads.

Trisha blinked back the tears and sniffled as she looked down at Riley Michaels, who'd been called in to help salvage the gown. "It's hopeless, isn't it?"

"Fiddlesticks," Riley spoke through a mouthful of pins. "Nothing's hopeless."

Pricilla moved to hand Trisha another tissue. "If anyone can save your dress, Riley can. She comes highly recommended."

"Thank you, Mrs. Crumb. And she's right, Trisha. You don't need to worry one bit." Riley's brow puckered as she knelt to examine the lace hem, her stoic expression far less encouraging than her words. "Give me a few days, and we'll have this dress looking as if it were made for you."

"Didn't I tell you everything would be all right, Trisha?" Pricilla worked to add some enthusiasm to her words, but she'd never understand the compulsion to buy things off the Internet. And a wedding dress of all things. Even if it was exactly what Trisha had been looking for, the oversized gown simply proved Pricilla's theory that shopping via the World Wide Web was a modern pitfall to be avoided. "I was told you won't find a better seamstress than Riley anywhere around, and from what I've seen so far, I can see why."

"I'm sure you're right." Trisha blew her nose. "But if I didn't know better, I'd say this wedding was jinxed."

"What else has gone wrong?" Riley pulled a pin from her mouth and eased it into the fabric.

Fresh tears brimmed in Trisha's eyes. "For starters, our invitations were printed *Nathan and Janet*, instead of *Nathan and Trisha*."

Half a dozen pins spewed to the floor as Riley burst out laughing. She clasped her hand against her mouth and began picking up the scattered pins. "I'm sorry. They fixed the problem, didn't they?"

"They replaced the invitations, but not the days of stress I had to endure as a result." Trisha wrinkled her reddened nose. "All I have to say is a week's honeymoon in the Bahamas with Nathan can't come soon enough. I'm beginning to dread my own wedding."

"He did get the engagement ring right," Riley said. "It's absolutely stunning."

Trisha smiled for the first time. "It is gorgeous, isn't it? Nathan had it specially made with a stone he got in South Africa when he was there on a hunting trip a few years ago."

"That is so romantic."

While she certainly didn't believe in jinxes, Pricilla had to admit Trisha had a point. With the wedding ceremony around the corner, it seemed that the planning of the blessed event had taken a nosedive and gone completely off course. She'd suggested hiring a wedding coordinator, but Trisha insisted she wanted the experience of planning the event herself. As much as she loved the girl, Pricilla wished she could find a way to knock some sense into her.

"Have you ever thought about eloping?" Riley shoved a lock of her short red hair behind her ear, barely missing a beat as she continued marking the alterations with another pin.

The question produced a pair of raised brows from Trisha, but Pricilla thought the woman had a legitimate point. She glanced down at the simple diamond engagement ring on her own finger and wondered about her upcoming nuptials. The word *elope* had entered into a number of conversations with her fiancé, Max, in hushed tones. Despite the scandalous feel the idea rendered, if the truth be told, it was sounding more and more like a good idea. She didn't need a fancy dress, dozens of guests, and piles of rich food as an essential backdrop for her to proclaim her love to Max. A wedding ring on her finger and a marriage certificate from the court would be enough for her.

Pricilla pulled a complimentary issue of *Food Style* magazine off the coffee table as Trisha jumped into a monologue about why she was insisting on a genuine old-fashioned wedding. But a peek at the magazine only managed to exchange one stressful encounter for another. The glossy photograph of filet mignon and browned-to-perfection potatoes served as a reminder that a substitute chef now stood in Pricilla's kitchen at the Rendezvous Hunting Lodge and Resort. While she looked forward to her role as emcee for the renowned Rocky Mountain Chef Competition, even her son Nathan's repeated assurances that all would be fine under the strict eye of her weekend replacement had done little to erase her apprehensions.

"Have you and Max set a date yet?"

Pricilla's chin tipped up when she realized that Riley was addressing her. "Max and I? Not yet." She glanced back at Trisha. "I believe I have enough to worry about at the moment. I am the mother of the groom, you know."

And her son had always come first.

Riley cocked her head. "I've always believed that there's no use putting off a good thing."

Pricilla flipped the page. At sixty-five, she hadn't expected Prince Charming to come waltzing into her life, but Max Summers, friend of nearly four decades, had indeed swept in and stolen her heart in the process. While she planned to say "I do" before their children considered sending them to a retirement center, two weddings were simply too much to plan at the same time. Especially with all the complications encountered with this one.

Riley stuck in another pin. "How much time do I have?"

Pricilla eyed the digital glow of the hotel clock. "They're serving dinner in twenty-five minutes."

"I'll have to come back at least two more times for fittings. Maybe three."

"That's fine." Trisha nodded at her reflection in the full-length mirror that hung on the wall. "Though, with this weekend's menu, I might not have to have the dress altered quite as much. If it's anything like lunch, I'm bound to gain a few pounds."

"You and me both." Pricilla tossed the magazine back on the table and fished her lipstick from her makeup bag. "But with food prepared by top chefs trying to impress the judges for a $250,000 cash prize, it will be worth indulging."

Riley let out a low whistle. "I could use the $250,000, though I'd never make it past boiling water in a food competition."

"And what would you do with all that cash, Riley?"

"I want to start my own line of wedding and bridesmaid dresses."

"With your talent, I wouldn't be surprised at all if you did just that one day." Pricilla flipped on the light by the desk. It flickered, then finally stayed on. She put on a layer of the lipstick and then dabbed some powder across her forehead, wondering why she even tried to cover up the decades of wrinkles. "Weren't your parents in the restaurant business, Riley?"

"They used to own a seafood restaurant called The Krab Kettle on the Oregon coast, but they sold the place five years ago," Riley said with a sigh. "Both my parents died not too long after that."

"I'm so sorry." Pricilla caught the young woman's grim expression and felt sorry she'd brought up the subject. Maude Lock, one of Pricilla's good friends, had recommended Riley and, in the course of their conversation, had mentioned that the woman's family had once owned a restaurant. She'd failed to mention that the couple was no longer living.

"I heard that the infamous Norton Richards is filling in for one of the contest judges," Riley said, changing the subject. "Is that true?"

"Yes, do you know him?" Pricilla asked.

"By reputation only."

Norton Richards had a legendary reputation. The former food critic was said to be liked by few, hated by many.

But Pricilla preferred to dismiss the gossip. "I'm hoping this weekend proves that the man isn't nearly as vicious as his reputed character."

Riley frowned. "You're far too kind, Pricilla."

"Did he ever review your parents' restaurant?" Trisha asked.

"Theirs, along with dozens of others across the country."

Pricilla snapped her powder compact shut. One thing was certain. From what she'd heard, any event including Richards was bound to be memorable.

Max Summers savored a creamy spoonful of crab bisque soup. Pricilla might have had to twist his arm to get him to attend the three-day competition, but if the main course was even half as good as tonight's appetizer, he'd have to change his tune. He glanced over at her, with her bright hazel eyes and soft, silver curls. His gaze shifted to her soup bowl. Strange. She hadn't touched her food, nor was she smiling.

He set down his spoon. "What's wrong?"

The orange glow of the elaborate candle centerpiece set up in the lodge's Great Room emphasized her solemn expression. "I'm beginning to wonder if your coming with me this weekend was a mistake, Max."

"A mistake?" He reached for a pat of butter and spread it in the middle of a hot bread roll. And she'd been the one complaining how little time they spent together. Things might change after the wedding, but in the meantime he was living in New Mexico doing his best to sell his house, while she continued working at her son's lodge in Colorado. "Why do you say that?"

Pricilla's hand stopped his spoon halfway to his mouth. "Cream-filled bisque and real butter isn't exactly on your diet."

His eyes widened as he breathed in the rich scent of the soup and felt his mouth water. He wasn't giving this up without a fight. "I'm not on a diet."

"Not technically, but have you already forgotten the doctor's report from your last checkup?" She shook her head. "This meal is nothing but high cholesterol, high fat, and high calories."

Max chuckled before downing another bite. "Must be why it tastes so good."

"Max. I'm serious."

"So am I." While he loved Pricilla despite her sometimes unconventional ways, there were certain things he had no intention of changing. It was time to throw it back into her court. "Have you already forgotten that you were the one who wanted us all to come this weekend to relax and enjoy ourselves?"

Which was exactly what he was doing.

His daughter, Trisha, who sat across from them, held out a basket of rolls to Pricilla. Max smiled—the perfect diversion. Even Pricilla couldn't ignore perfectly baked bread. "He's right you know, Mom. All of us need to relax."

Max helped himself to a second roll and added it to his plate. He was relaxing. How could he not? The atmosphere was ideal. The company perfect. And the food, well, you couldn't get much better than this.

It was undeniably the ideal location for this year's cooking contest extravaganza. A low murmur of voices, sprinkled with occasional bits of laughter, filled the lodge's Great Room where the judges, staff, and invited guests—all except the actual contestants—had gathered at the two long, formally dressed tables. Fading rays of sunlight shimmered behind the large windows overlooking the Rocky Mountains. Tomorrow the place would be buzzing with cameras and reporters, but tonight, with a fire crackling in the stone fireplace, the large room had an intimate feel.

A woman with black pants and a silver sequined blouse made her way up to the podium in the front of the room. She couldn't be over thirty-five, but her face barely moved as she glanced over the crowd with her frozen smile. Botox, no doubt, had trapped her expression as it did for thousands of others who refused to believe one could grow old gracefully. But he knew it was possible. Just a glance at Pricilla reminded him of that.

"Good evening, ladies and gentlemen." The Botox woman placed a hand on each side of the podium and leaned forward. "My name is Michelle Vanderbilt, and I'm here to represent *Food Style* magazine as we host a nationwide search for the next master chef."

A twenty-something-year-old, with mousy brown hair and a timid expression to match, snapped photos from the other side of the dining table.

"On behalf of our illustrious magazine, I want to welcome all of you to the stunning Silvermist Lodge, set in the middle of the beautiful Rocky Mountains," Miss Vanderbilt continued. "I hope you all are enjoying your dinner so far. Tonight's menu was planned and created by our six finalists as an informal kickoff before the official opening in the morning. And if tonight is any indication of what's ahead, we can all be assured that none of us will go home hungry."

Max wiped the sides of his mouth with the cloth napkin from his lap, then joined the rest of the audience in their enthusiastic applause. He'd been right. This weekend was bound to be filled with an incredible menu and nothing—not even his lovely fiancée—could stop him from enjoying it to the fullest.

"As you all know, tomorrow begins *Food Style* magazine's celebrated Rocky Mountain Chef Competition. And as one of the premiere cooking contests in the country, this year's prize is not only $250,000, but a one-year scholarship to the prestigious Parisian culinary school, Bon Appétit."

The guests applauded at the announcement.

"We have a few things to discuss before the official opening in the morning. All six of the contestants have checked in, and let me remind you that interaction between contestants and judges is strictly forbidden. Before the main course is served, I'd like to make a few brief introductions and then leave you to enjoy the rest of your meal. I'll begin by introducing our honorary emcee for the event, Pricilla Crumb. Mrs. Crumb taught home economics for thirty-two years at the esteemed Willow Hill Private Academy for Girls in Seattle and currently works as the chef at the famous Hunting Lodge and Resort in Rendezvous, Colorado."

Max nudged Pricilla with his elbow, and she held up her hand and waved as the guests clapped.

"Continuing with our judges, I'd like to welcome Manny Parker from Denver who owns Manny's Grill; Violet Peterson, owner of Le Petit Gourmand, which is also located in Denver; Lyle Simpson, *Food Style* magazine's own food critic; and celebrity chef J. J. Rhymes."

Max joined with the applause while popping a piece of bread into his mouth.

"I'd also like to extend a personal welcome to Norton Richards, renowned food critic, who has graciously agreed to take over for our fifth judge, who was unable to attend due to a last-minute family crisis."

Silence filled the room. A few scattered claps followed.

Miss Vanderbilt cleared her throat. "Lastly, I'd like to remind the judges of the informational meeting we'll be having at eight thirty tonight."

Max leaned in toward Pricilla. "What's the deal with Norton Richards?"

"Where do I begin?" she whispered. "He used to be a food critic who is said to have ruined a few good careers along the way with little regret on his side."

"That bad?"

"Let's just say you never wanted to be caught on the downside of one of his reviews. I'm not sure how true all the rumors are, but supposedly he could shut down a restaurant quicker than it takes to order a dish of crème brûlé."

Max let out a low whistle. "Ouch."

Miss Vanderbilt scanned the audience with her emotionless expression. "Enjoy the rest of your dinner."

The waiters brought out the main course next. Max's mouth watered at the sight of spicy prawns and a juicy steak. Even the vegetables looked to be cooked to perfection. He sampled a prawn and smiled. This was one of the things he looked forward to as Pricilla's husband. She could turn a bad apple into a delectable dish. He took another bite and thought of his still fairly slim waistline. Perhaps she was right. If he wasn't careful, he'd end up looking like his old fishing pal, Bud. Still, for now he planned to enjoy himself.

Dishes clattered at the other end of the table. A chair skidded across the floor. Max looked up.

"I don't have to listen to this! I don't have to listen to any of you!" Norton Richards's voice rose above the chatter in the room. "I came as a favor to Miss Vanderbilt, who knew my presence would boost the ratings of this sorry contest." He threw his napkin onto the table. "But there's no way I'll stand for being treated this way."

Beside Max, Pricilla sucked in a lungful of air. Mr. Richards's chair crashed to the floor as he spun away from the table.

"Mr. Richards, please. . ."

Miss Vanderbilt's words were ignored as Norton Richards stomped from the room.

Pricilla pulled back the heavy curtain of her window. The glowing red clock beside her bed read five after twelve, but she was too keyed up to sleep. Norton's sudden exit from the dining room had startled everyone, bringing an abrupt end to the friendly camaraderie of the evening. Apparently someone didn't like his presence here. She hadn't been able to see who the man had argued with at the dinner table, or hear what had set him off, but that didn't stop her from wondering what could have been said to have provoked such a dramatic outburst.

She tried to focus on the beauty of the quiet night. The last days of summer had already faded into autumn, bringing with it cooler nights at the higher elevations. Moonlight spilled against the circles of the half dozen hot-water pools that lay on the outskirts of the lodge. Swaying aspen trees and shadowy white light lent an eerie feel to the night.

A man shouted.

Pricilla strained to make out two shadows that appeared on the path near the pools. Without her bifocals she was forced to squint. She fumbled for her glasses, slid them on, and then turned back to the window. Two figures struggled in the moonlight, but she couldn't make out the details. Dark clothing. . .a flash of metal. . .glasses on the larger figure. . .

She shuddered.

The lifeless body of Reggie Pierce filled her mind, but she shoved it away. Reggie, and Charles Woodruff for that matter, were completely different situations. Stumbling across murdered victims twice in her life was bad enough. Three times. . .no. Someone crying out in the night didn't mean a murder was taking place.

A second cry shattered the quiet of the night.

Pricilla pulled her robe tighter around her waist and rushed toward the hallway. If she took the side door that led outside, she could get there in a hurry. Her room wasn't far from the pools. Slowing halfway down the stairs, she fought to catch her breath and wondered why she hadn't taken the elevator. Two solved murders might have gained her a measure of respect at the Rendezvous sheriff's office, but it had done little to stop the effects of age. Her left hip groaned and her lungs begged for air. She wasn't prepared to take on a murderer.

Nor would she have to, because there was no murderer—just someone who needed help. She huffed down the stairs, the bunion on her left foot throbbing, and then stopped when she saw a shadowy image through the window at the end of the hall. Her heart caught in her throat. This was no lover's quarrel. She had to do something. She glanced down the empty corridor.

The red fire alarm caught her eye.

No. She couldn't. Or could she? Surely this qualified as an emergency. Without another thought, she pulled the handle. The alarm blasted, and water began to shower from the ceiling.

The sprinkler system?

Cascades of water ran down her face. There was no time to consider the consequences of what she'd just done. Instead, she scurried out the door and down the stone path. Lights from the rooms flickered on one by one, illuminating the garden as the siren continued to scream.

Pricilla froze at the edge of the top hot-water pool. She was too late. Clarissa Fields, one of the contestants, stood over Norton Richards's body, her hands covered in blood.

Please tell me it's not true that you just stumbled across another dead body."

Pricilla's shoulders tensed at the sound of Max's baritone voice. He brushed up beside her, his sleeve wet against her bare arm. A drop of water fell from his nose. Obviously she had more to explain to him than simply how she'd managed to set off both the fire alarm and the sprinkler system. She hesitated with her response, knowing he wasn't going to like her answer. Norton Richards, she'd been told, was very much dead.

"You're soaked."

"And you're avoiding the issue." His hand brushed against her forearm. "Pricilla? What happened? The sprinkler system goes off, the police arrive to investigate an apparent murder, and now I find you out here in the middle of a crime scene?"

"This is unbelievable." A man in a bathrobe and slippers stood beside the yellow crime scene tape and addressed Pricilla. "I used to work installing sprinkler systems. Do you realize that you have more of a chance of getting hit by an asteroid than setting one off by pulling the fire alarm?"

How could news of her misdemeanor travel so quickly? Weren't there more serious matters to deal with? Like murder?

"It was an emergency. I thought—"

"Odds are something like ten million to one." The man shook his head.

"Pricilla has always been one to beat the odds." Max steered her away from the growing crowd. "Forget him. What happened?"

"Norton Richards was murdered. I found him lying at the edge of one of the hot-spring pools." Even in the shadows of the aspen trees surrounding them, she could feel his piercing gaze. She stared at the flashing lights of a police car stopped two dozen feet away at the edge of the parking lot. "Someone else must have heard the screams and called the police—they got here just after I did."

Max ran his fingers through his damp hair and sat down on a weathered bench just outside the partitioned-off crime scene. "Have you already forgotten the last time you stumbled across a dead body?"

She pushed away the lifeless image of Reggie Pierce. "I'd like to forget."

He folded his arms across his chest and caught her gaze. "Let me recap.

You were arrested, knocked out, taken hostage—"

"Okay, okay." She held up her hand. "So things got a bit out of hand—"

"A *bit* out of hand? They're already out of hand this time in my opinion."

She sat down beside him. "Everything turned out fine before."

"Does that really matter?" Max let out a loud "humph." "Along with a murder, there is always a murderer. If this one is loose and thinks you can identify him. . ."

Pricilla felt her stomach clench. "The sheriff believes they already have the suspect in custody."

"Who?"

This was the problem. "When I arrived, Clarissa Fields, one of the contestants, was standing over the body, her hands covered with blood. But I know she didn't do it."

"She didn't?"

"No."

He grasped her hand. "And how do you know that?"

"I knew Clarissa when I taught back in Seattle. She was one of my best students. I knew her family from church. I'm convinced that she's no more a murderer than your. . .than your own mother."

"Wait a minute." Max shook his head. "I'm not accusing anyone, but you're telling me that a man was found dead with someone standing over him, and she was covered in blood? What more evidence do you need?"

She shrugged, wishing she had a more concrete answer. "All I know is that Clarissa didn't do it."

Max fiddled with her diamond engagement ring. "The police will take her down to the station and question her. If she's innocent, they'll find that out on their own. They don't need your help."

"So you'd let an innocent girl get locked up for life on murder charges for a crime she didn't commit?"

"That won't happen." His mouth tightened. "Trust the system this time, Pricilla. I don't want you getting involved."

She frowned. "It's not as if I did any of this on purpose. I was standing at the window of my room and heard someone shouting, so I came outside to see if I could help."

An officer approached them in his regulation forest green button-down uniform shirt, with a shoulder patch that said DEPUTY across the top. "Mrs. Crumb?"

Pricilla's stomach began to churn, and she was quite certain this problem wouldn't be remedied with a handful of antacid tablets. There had to be a law about pulling the fire alarm, or setting off the sprinkler system for that matter. No doubt the man was kind enough to spare her the embarrassment of arresting her in front of her friends.

"I take full responsibility for my actions, Deputy. Pulling the alarm was a foolish and impulsive act. If you want to arrest me. . ." She held out her hands in defeat.

"I haven't had a chance to talk to the manager, but considering the circumstances, I'd imagine that he'd prefer a few wet carpets to a murderer loose on the premises."

"But I'm certain there still is a murderer loose. Clarissa didn't kill Norton Richards."

"Pricilla."

She ignored Max's pointed plea. "She couldn't have."

"So you are acquainted with Clarissa Fields?" The eager look on the deputy's face implied he was ready to wrap up another case.

She frowned. It was time this cowboy slowed down.

"I've known her for years, in fact. I'm an old friend of her family."

"Then the sheriff will want to speak to you briefly, if you don't mind waiting in the lobby for a few minutes."

"Of course not."

He nodded his head and started to walk away.

"Wait a minute." Pricilla hurried toward him, ignoring the throbbing in her hip from hustling down the stairwell. "Are you arresting Clarissa?"

"She's being taken to the sheriff's office for questioning."

"But I know she didn't do it."

The deputy stopped, hands planted firmly against his hips. "Do you have evidence that implicates another person?"

She pressed her lips together. "No."

"Evidence speaks louder than feelings, Mrs. Crumb."

"What about a murder weapon?"

"We are still investigating this murder."

"All I know is that Clarissa isn't capable of murder."

"Ma'am, when you've worked for the department as long as I have, you discover that everyone has a secret. And those secrets lead to all kinds of violence." He tipped his wide-brimmed hat. "The sheriff will meet you in the lobby in five minutes."

Pricilla glanced across the yellow tape line where Clarissa stood with the sheriff. One of the white outdoor lights from the garden revealed long, reddish-brown hair pulled back from her face in a neat ponytail. Her white T-shirt was smudged with blood on the front. The girl looked up at Pricilla. Her complexion had paled to a chalky white. Fear shone in her eyes.

"Mrs. Crumb?" She took a step forward, but the officer stopped her.

Pricilla approached the tape. "May I talk to her?"

"Pricilla." Max grasped her elbow.

"No one can speak to her now," the officer said. "We're taking her down to the station for questioning."

"I didn't stab Mr. Richards, Mrs. Crumb. Please. Promise you'll help me."

"You know I'll do whatever I can."

As the officer led Clarissa to the car, Pricilla melted onto the bench beside Max. "I know I sound crazy, but she didn't do it."

"And you shouldn't get involved." Max stiffened beside her. "And you shouldn't have promised that you'd help her."

But she had, because the authorities were making a mistake. They were missing some clue from the scenario that would be revealed in the light of day. The ambulance pulled out of its parking space, followed by the squad car containing Clarissa. One thing wouldn't change. The medical examiner had arrived, taking with him from the scene Norton Richards in a body bag. There was no denying the fact that someone had taken his life, nor the fact that Clarissa's hands had been covered with the man's blood. Still. . .

Pricilla scanned the growing crowd of spectators that gathered just outside the yellow tape. Clarissa was no murderer. She knew it. Her instincts for people rarely proved her wrong, and she was certain tonight wouldn't be an exception.

Max had insisted on joining Pricilla and the sheriff for the interview. The manager of the hotel had opened up his office to them so they could talk in private and had even brought in a pot of tea. While Max was normally a coffee drinker, the mug of tea gave him something to do besides worry about Pricilla.

When this was over, he planned to sit down with Pricilla and insist she stay out of the case. He had no intention of being an overbearing husband, but when murder was involved, he felt he had the right to put his foot down. Just because things had turned out okay in the past didn't mean they would this time.

Pricilla sat beside him with a cup of steaming tea in her hands, looking more relaxed than he'd expected. Her hair was a bit damp, but her eyes were alert. Truthfully, it was this trait of always wanting to help others that had made him fall in love with her. If only that same attribute didn't always manage to land her in so much hot water.

The sheriff, looking agitated, cleared his throat and pressed the palms of his hands against his tan trousers. "I'm sorry to have to question you so late, but I find it best to talk to witnesses while the scene is fresh in their minds."

"I understand." Pricilla set her tea down on the small end table beside her and crossed her legs.

"How well did you know Clarissa?"

"I've known her since she was about five. Her parents moved to Seattle, where I lived at the time. From Baltimore, I believe."

"What can you tell me about her family?"

Pricilla paused to consider the question. "Let's see. Her parents divorced before they moved to Seattle, so I knew her mom and stepfather. She was an only child, and both sets of grandparents have passed away since I first met them. I also remember that she used to spend summers with her aunt, her mother's sister, back East when she was younger."

Max listened to each question, all thoroughly routine and professional. He'd spent half his life in the military learning how to negotiate, talk peace, and delegate responsibilities, but seeing Pricilla involved once again in a murder investigation left him with knots in his stomach.

If anything happened to her. . .

"Do you have any idea if she might have known Mr. Richards?" The sheriff's tea lay untouched beside him.

"I wouldn't know."

"When's the last time you saw her?"

Pricilla glanced at Max. Was that a sign of guilt in her expression?

She looked away. "About four years ago, right before she left Seattle to work in California."

Aha. How well could she know a person she hadn't seen for that long?

The sheriff cleared his throat and squirmed in his chair. "That's quite awhile, you know. People can change."

"Not Clarissa. She was always a hard worker and very conscientious." Pricilla leaned forward. "Listen. I know you see me as just another civilian witness. An old lady who doesn't know what she's talking about, but I have experience—"

"Pricilla." Max felt his jaw tense. Surely she wasn't planning to bring up Reggie Pierce.

"Please, Max." She rested her hand on his arm. "I want to see the truth, as much as I want to see Clarissa released. You see, I've worked on a couple cases as an unofficial consultant for the sheriff's office back in Rendezvous."

Max shook his head. So much for insisting she not get involved.

The sheriff's brow rose. "You were an unofficial consultant?"

"Just think about it. You want the truth, and I'm in the perfect position to help you find it. I'm one of the only people involved in the contest who can freely speak to the judges, the staff, and the contestants."

He rubbed his chin. "I don't know."

"I'd let you know right away if I found out anything pertaining to the case."

"Please know that I do understand your concern, Mrs. Crumb. And while I appreciate your offer, and I'm sure that you have Clarissa's best interests in mind, I have to go back to the simple fact that a civilian working on a case isn't acceptable."

The sheriff cleared his throat and then stood to shake their hands.

Max smiled. Good. The interview was over, and the sheriff had made his position clear.

Max felt Pricilla stiffen beside him as the man left the room. "He's right, you know."

Loud voices from the lobby interrupted any response Pricilla might have tried to throw back at him. Michelle Vanderbilt, still dressed in her sequined top and black pants, stood at the front counter talking to the manager. Water from the woman's hair dripped on the floor while black makeup smeared beneath her eyes like a raccoon, making Max suddenly grateful he wasn't the one having to deal with the overbearing woman.

When Michelle saw the sheriff emerge from the office, she skittered across the wood floor in her high heels, dragging her assistant with her. "I need to know exactly what's going on. I'm in charge of coordinating this nationally-televised competition, and if the sprinkler system going off wasn't bad enough, news of a murder connected to the competition will leak out and ruin our ratings."

"Or draw viewers to you like flies to manure on a hot summer day," Max commented under his breath.

Pricilla nudged him with her elbow. "Max."

"Have you seen the way she treats her assistant?" he murmured.

"Sarah?"

"I saw her yelling at the poor girl earlier. She doesn't seem to hesitate saying what's on her mind. No matter what it is."

"The woman's under a lot of pressure to make sure everything flows smoothly the next three days. You can hardly blame her for being on top of things."

The sheriff stopped in front of the woman. "I'm sorry, Miss. . ."

"Miss Vanderbilt. Michelle Vanderbilt." She reached out her hand to shake the lawman's. "I represent *Food Style* magazine, one of the country's leading publications, as we host a nationwide search for the next master chef in the Rocky Mountain Chef Competition. Surely you've heard of it?"

Max stifled a laugh. The woman sounded like an infomercial.

"I have just voiced my concerns to the manager," she continued, barely taking a breath. "We chose this lodge, and the town of Silvermist, in an effort to bring a small-town, cozy atmosphere to our competition, but since my arrival, I've been greeted with nothing but hassles. Not only was I put into a regular room instead of the suite I requested because, for some mysterious reason, there wasn't an available upgrade, but room service is slow, and now the sprinkler system has gone off in part of the building because, I'm told, of faulty wiring. Just look at my hair. There's not even a decent hairstylist within fifty miles who can fix this."

"A man was murdered, Miss Vanderbilt—"

"Which is exactly why I'm speaking to you. I will not allow your lack of diligence and an inability to prevent murder, of all things, to mar the magazine's reputation, or my reputation for that matter."

Max leaned toward Pricilla. "This is probably the first murder this town's seen in years, and she's spouting off like we're in a war zone."

"I assure you, ma'am, that we will do all we can to ensure your show continues without interruption." The sheriff turned to the lodge manager. "But with that said, I'm afraid I'm going to have to ask everyone to stay on the hotel premises or speak to me before they leave. And I'll need a list of all the guests and staff. Tomorrow we'll start doing interviews."

"Interviews?" Michelle gripped the edge of her beaded handbag. "Why?"

Max couldn't help but smile as he spoke loud enough for the woman to hear him. "Because we've all just become suspects in a murder investigation."

Pricilla entered the dining room at half past seven the next morning, wishing she'd remained in bed under the warmth of the thick comforter. The last thing she felt like doing was pasting on a smile for a television audience. Already, the large room was filled with reporters, bright lights, and cameras.

Cameras that put ten pounds on a person.

She glanced at the buffet table and sucked in her stomach, hoping the tan color of her new pantsuit didn't add any inches. Bowls of fresh fruit lay beside piles of sausage, biscuits and gravy, and scrambled eggs. No. She'd definitely skip breakfast this morning. Besides the calories, the smell of food that filled the room made her stomach churn. Stumbling over murder victims late at night tended to do that.

Stifling a yawn, she poured herself a cup of black coffee from a carafe, hoping the caffeine would kick in quickly. She'd slept little last night, although looking around, it seemed she wasn't the only one who'd been unable to sleep after all the commotion. The room was already half full, but no one seemed to be moving at full speed.

Michelle Vanderbilt stood in the far corner of the room wearing a lime green skirt and matching jacket. Hands waving, she argued with the sheriff about something. She must have been right about the lack of hairdressers in the area because her blond, highlighted hair didn't look near as chic as it had yesterday.

Of course after last night's episode with the renegade sprinkler system, even Pricilla wished she could sneak away for one of her weekly visits to Iris's Beauty Salon for a touch-up. Thankfully, Trisha had managed to tame her silver curls so they looked acceptable for her upcoming stint in front of the camera. Or so she hoped.

"Good morning." Max stepped up beside her with a plate piled high with every no-no from the doctor's list. He jutted his chin toward the sparring couple. "I see the tyrant's at it again."

Obviously, any lack of sleep had done little to curb his appetite or sense of humor, but for once she wasn't in the mood to nag at him over either. There were too many other things to worry about. "Sleep well?"

He led the way to an empty table toward the back of the room. "Off and on. I'm thankful the sprinklers didn't go off in the rooms, because I'm planning a nap between interviews with the sheriff. Though I suppose someone's in a lot of trouble for not doing their job properly. Apparently, the wiring's a mess."

Pricilla slid into the seat beside him, tired of the constant reminders of the incident even if it wasn't completely her fault. Even the deputy's assurances that no charges would be pressed over her reckless act weren't enough to erase the guilt she felt over her impulsiveness. After last spring's experience with a stolen ATV, she thought she'd learned the dangers of being impulsive.

Apparently I still have a long way to go, Lord.

Her stomach growled, and she snagged a blueberry muffin from Max's plate. Another impulsive act, perhaps, but fainting in front of the camera from not eating would surely be worse than looking a few pounds heavier.

The commotion up front increased.

Max quirked his left brow. "That woman doesn't give up, does she?"

"I don't know." Pricilla didn't try to curb the sarcasm in her voice. "It could have something to do with the fact that someone told her we're all murder suspects."

"And I thought she was upset because someone turned on the hall sprinklers last night and ruined her hair."

"Max."

"Sorry, but you have to admit that the woman's difficult."

"She is a bit overbearing."

"And rude and heartless."

Tossing aside all resolutions to not overindulge over the course of the weekend, Pricilla dabbed a fat pat of real butter in the center of the muffin. A little comfort food couldn't hurt. "Personally, I'd like to cancel the entire show. I'm about ready to open the dessert competition, and I have no idea how to proceed with one man dead and Clarissa not only disqualified as a contestant but now in jail for murder."

She was worried about Clarissa. The girl lying in some dingy jail cell overnight was a frightening image she couldn't shake.

"You'll do great." He squeezed her hand. "Just forget everything that happened last night. The sheriff's department is perfectly able to handle the case and find out the truth. All you have to do is go up there and look gorgeous."

"Funny."

She bit into her muffin and started praying that God would give her a nonimpulsive plan to prove Clarissa's innocence.

"Ladies and gentlemen, I'd like to welcome you to the Fifteenth Annual Rocky Mountain Chef Competition." Pricilla smiled at the audience while trying to ignore the red RECORD light that meant every word she spoke—and every pound and wrinkle on her body—would soon be transmitted and played in thousands of homes across the country. "I'm Pricilla Crumb, and our first competition of the day will be the dessert category."

The applause from the large crowd of spectators who had booked spaces in the audience for the weekend rang across the room. Behind her, the five contestants stood ready at their stations, outfitted in the required chef coats, black pants, aprons, and signature chef hats.

"For those of you who are watching for the first time, I'll explain the rules as we go along. For this morning's competition, all the components of the dessert must be made on-site. Each individual has four hours to make five unique desserts. During this time, judges will be assessing the contestants for their efficiency in using ingredients as well as the cleanliness of their working conditions. With monetary prizes totaling $250,000, the competition goes beyond a simple sampling of the delicacies and includes presentation, artistry, and kitchen management."

She caught Max's gaze, thankful he was in the audience. It didn't matter what had happened last night. She could do this. Adjusting her bifocals, she continued to read the prompter. The audience chuckled on cue at her first joke. So far so good. All she had to do was get through the next forty-five seconds, smile graciously after her closing remarks, and make a graceful exit.

"Lastly, I want to recognize our wonderful sponsor, *Food Style* magazine, and Michelle Vanderbilt, who have worked to make this competition the renowned event it has become." Pricilla smiled graciously on cue. "Let the competition begin."

The red light on the camera went off. She let out a sigh of relief. Turning around, she stepped away from the podium, careful not to stumble on one of the dozens of cords lying across the floor. Graceful and self-assured, she pushed her shoulders back. Max was right. All she needed to do was focus on her responsibilities for the next three days.

The sheriff signaled to someone from the wings. Pricilla moved off the stage as Miss Vanderbilt whispered something to the lawman, and he took his place in front of the audience.

The sheriff cleared his throat and tapped on the microphone. "Before the competition officially starts this morning, I feel it necessary to make several reminders. We are continuing with our interviews this morning."

Miss Vanderbilt's red lips pressed into a frown as the sheriff continued speaking. She obviously wasn't happy with the fact that the sheriff had now taken over her show, even if it was temporary. She jerked around and rushed off the stage area.

"Miss Vanderbilt—" Pricilla tried to warn her, but it was too late.

Miss Vanderbilt's heel caught on one of the cords. A camera flashed. Pricilla blinked. The younger woman's lean frame spilled across the floor.

So much for graceful exits.

Pricilla rested the ice pack against Michelle's wrist. The hotel kitchen wasn't the best place to treat an injury, but it was out of the way of the competition and had plenty of ice.

"Ouch!"

"Sorry." Pricilla moved back and let Michelle hold the pack in place. "It's going to be sore for a while."

Michelle wiped her hand across her cheek. Was the woman actually crying?

"Everything's going to be okay, you know."

"No, it's not." Michelle sniffled and then ran her fingers through her hair. "I'm going to lose my job over this entire fiasco. As if there wasn't already enough stress just trying to enforce the rules on the contestants, now I'm having to deal with a murder."

"Which rules?"

"I caught Freddie Longfellow talking with Lyle Simpson, one of the judges, who then quickly assured me that their conversation hadn't gone any further than discussing an exchange of their suitcases that had been swapped by the bellboy."

"I suppose that's understandable."

"Maybe, but not only is the reputation of the magazine and the competition on the line, but mine as well." She brushed an invisible speck from her skirt. "Though it's not as if I plan to work for *Food Style* magazine forever."

"Really?"

"The magazine, this entire competition. . ." She waved her injured hand toward the Great Room and then winced. "They're simply rungs on the ladder to get me where I want to be."

"Which is?"

"A news anchor of a major network." Michelle cocked her head, looking surprised, as if Pricilla should somehow know. "You really think I've worked all these years for. . .for this?"

"Honestly, I wouldn't know. Seems as if you've already achieved a lot in your life to me."

When Michelle didn't respond, Pricilla glanced across the busy kitchen area where staff members were doing prep work for the lunch crowd. Where was Michelle's assistant? Maybe Sarah would be able to calm her boss's fears.

While Pricilla didn't think the wrist was broken, she'd asked the assistant to arrange for transportation to the doctor.

With no sign of Sarah, she poured a glass of water from the tap and handed Michelle two aspirin from her purse.

The woman downed the medicine and then smacked the glass against the counter. "And you know that all this is Norton Richards's fault, that two-faced weasel."

Now here was an interesting position. Placing all the blame on the murder victim.

Pricilla raised her eyebrows. "How could it be his fault? He's the one lying dead in the morgue."

Michelle dipped her chin. "You obviously didn't know Norton. I knew he'd go to his grave dragging others with him, and it looks like I was right."

Pricilla couldn't help but jump through the door Michelle had just left wide open. What could a few well-posed, investigative questions hurt? She'd proceed cautiously.

"So, were you and Mr. Richards friends?"

"Friends?" Michelle leaned her head back against the wall. "Norton didn't have friends. He had enemies."

"But you knew him?"

Her laugh came out more like a "humph." "Everyone who was anyone in the food industry knew the man. Newspapers and magazines wanted his columns; chefs wanted his respect and five-star reviews. Even nightly news ratings went up with a story about him, so reporters were always digging up something new. He took a few people to the top with him, but most he simply dragged through the gutter then dumped in the sewer when he was finished. The very same thing he's doing with my career even now."

Ouch. So the woman didn't like him. Considering the man's reputation to tick off everyone he came in contact with, that in itself wasn't a motive for murder. But if she had a personal vendetta against him, that might put things in a bit of a different light.

"What motive could he possibly have for wanting to ruin your career?"

"Haven't you been listening?" She blew out an exasperated sigh. "The man didn't need motives, permission, or even a valid reason for that matter. He thrived on making other people's lives miserable."

So much for wanting to believe the man's sordid reputation was simply a rumor, but sometimes the truth did hurt. How many of those taken down by a harsh review from Norton Richards deserved exactly what they got? Surely a man couldn't build a career as one of the country's foremost food critics without telling the truth, as ruthless as his approach might be. One didn't have to like the man to respect his talent. If that was indeed what it was called.

Pricilla searched for her next question. "Where did you first meet him?"

Michelle's laugh competed with the banging of pots and pans and butter sizzling on the stove. With the mouthwatering smells filling the room, missing breakfast might have been a mistake.

"I met Norton at a funeral, believe it or not. One of the editors of the magazine died last year, and he actually showed up to pay his regards."

"Who do you think killed him?"

She shot Pricilla a piercing gaze. "You think I killed him, don't you?"

"No. No, of course not. I was just wondering. There seems to be plenty of people with motives when it comes to Norton. . . ."

Pricilla looked up and immediately closed her mouth. The sheriff stood in front of her, arms folded across his chest. "Mrs. Crumb, could I have a word with you? In private?"

"Of course. I was just. . ." Her heart thudded in her chest. Just what? Interrogating a suspect after she'd specifically been told to stay away from the case? That answer would go over well. "I was helping Miss Vanderbilt. She fell and sprained her wrist."

"I am sorry, Miss Vanderbilt. I understand that the hotel is arranging transport to take you to the doctor?"

"Yes, thank you."

"Good. Then Mrs. Crumb. If you don't mind coming with me."

She minded, all right, but what choice did she have? It wasn't as if she'd done anything wrong, or even illegal. This was a free country, and no one could stop her from asking a few simple, albeit personal, questions that might or might not have any relevance to the case.

She followed the officer down the hall toward the lobby in silence, working to keep up with his long stride. Already the staff was using large vacuums to dry the carpet, making any conversation impossible to hear over the noise. It was just as well. She wasn't sure she wanted to hear what the man had to say or find out how she'd managed to get pushed to the top of his interrogation list.

Today's interview room had been set up in one of the small conference rooms. It was as cold and sterile as a jail cell.

She decided to start the conversation. "When can I see Clarissa?"

"Maybe tomorrow. I'll let you know. She's just been charged with the murder."

Pricilla plunged forward, hoping she wasn't saying something she would later regret. "Clarissa's not guilty."

"Now about Michelle," the sheriff began, ignoring her outburst.

"I was just making conversation with her."

"By asking her if she knew who killed Richards?" He held up his hand. "It's okay."

"What's okay?"

"I took the liberty of calling Detective Raymond Carter last night. I've known the man for a decade, and. . .well. . .while I'm still not too keen about the idea of working with a civilian, there are certain circumstances that have made me reconsider your offer. And as you've just shown me, you're in the perfect position to talk to people without the intimidation of a badge."

"Oh." Pricilla sat back in her chair. Twelve hours ago her involvement wasn't even an option, and now she was being given free rein to investigate? Something wasn't right. "Why the change of heart? You were fairly adamant yesterday that I should stay out of your way. No exceptions allowed."

"Well, for starters. . ." He coughed and tapped his fingers against the gray, speckled conference table. "My reelection is coming up, and I won't have my opponent speaking out against me and the crime rate. You understand, don't you?"

"Of course."

She did understand. For the most part, anyway. But there was something he wasn't telling her. A recently surfaced clue? A piece of evidence pointing to someone else? Or maybe he was telling the truth, and he just wanted her to help him solve the case so he didn't lose his reelection.

The tapping on the table continued. "Carter told me how successful you'd been in working with his department."

Pricilla bit her lip. A compliment from Detective Carter wasn't something to dismiss lightly, but Max was not going to like this.

"What exactly are you saying, Sheriff?"

"To put it bluntly, Mrs. Crumb, I need an inside source. And you're my only candidate."

"Absolutely not, Pricilla." Max held up his hand in protest as if this action would intensify the impact of his words.

Pricilla frowned from behind the round table where they sat near the front of the room, watching the morning competition progress. After two hours, the plated dessert contest was at the halfway mark. The fragrances of chocolate, cinnamon, and vanilla filled the air, but at the moment, her attention was far from the dessert-laden countertops and thick sauces that bubbled on the stovetops.

"Max—"

"Please." He leaned forward and lowered his voice. "No matter what the sheriff told you, tracking down a killer—again—is out of the question."

Pricilla tried to gather her poise as she absorbed Max's too-loud protests. With the attention focused on the competition, no one in the audience seemed to notice his outburst, but that didn't stop Pricilla from cringing. While it was true that the last thing she had expected this morning was Sheriff Lewis's invitation to help solve the case—albeit in an unofficial capacity—she also hadn't expected Max's objections to be quite this strong.

Not that she didn't appreciate his concern over her becoming involved in another murder. It was true that her past experiences in solving crimes had been quite eventful, but in the end the price she'd paid had been worth it. Justice had been served and the real murderers locked up. And like Reggie Pierce's case, she couldn't get around the fact that with Clarissa involved, this case had an added personal element.

"Max, I really do understand your trepidation." The last thing she felt like was arguing, but on the other hand there was a young woman's future at stake. "But you can't honestly expect me to walk away from Clarissa's plight without doing anything."

"Of course not, but—"

"And the sheriff has personally asked for my input in the case."

He folded his arms across his chest. "In an unofficial capacity only."

"Completely unofficial," she conceded. "But even you have to admit that I'm in the perfect position to talk to the judges, the contestants, and the staff who might be involved."

"Which is exactly why I don't want you involved." He leaned forward.

"I have. . .concerns."

"Concerns?" Her frown deepened.

Frankly, she had concerns as well. If Clarissa was innocent, there was a murderer on the loose, and she didn't want an encounter with someone who obviously didn't think twice about ending another person's life. But concerns aside, she had promised Clarissa that she would do whatever she could. And she meant to keep her word.

Pricilla searched for a diplomatic approach to make her point. "Clarissa's life is at stake, Max, and besides, I promise not to get myself into any trouble."

"That's impossible." Max shook his head and frowned. "Pricilla, we've barely been here twenty-four hours, and you've already set off the sprinkler system and landed yourself smack-dab in the middle of a murder investigation. If that's not trouble, then I don't know what is. And if I remember correctly, I heard that very same promise before with Reggie's and Charles Woodruff's investigations—"

"Those situations were different," she insisted.

"How?"

She paused, trying to come up with a legitimate response. "I wasn't asked to help by law enforcement for one thing."

The truth was, she would prefer not to relive the dreadful moments leading up to the discovery of those murders. Instead, she turned her attention to the large viewing screen that had zoomed in on one of the contestants, Maggie Underwood, who was pulling a 9-inch springform pan filled with a chocolate cake from the oven. Pricilla's heart skipped a beat as the young woman fumbled with the hot pan, finally placing the dessert on the counter.

Pricilla let out a sigh of relief. Obviously she wasn't the only one affected by last night's tragedy. Still, despite the somewhat subdued atmosphere, the audience did seem to be enjoying watching the chefs as they whipped, stirred, and concentrated on the tiniest of details to catch the judges' attention.

She couldn't say the same for her and Max. She'd planned to enjoy her weekend, not endure a lengthy inquisition.

"And there is something else that bothers me," Max continued.

Pricilla turned back to him, praying the morning wouldn't end in a fight. "What is that?"

"If you ask me, it seems quite clear that this is an open-and-shut case. How can you argue with the evidence, especially when you were the one first on the scene? Face it, Pricilla. Clarissa was found standing over Norton's body after midnight and covered in blood. What other reason would she have had to be outside at that time of the night before the biggest competition of her life begins?"

Even Pricilla had to admit he had a point, but that didn't lessen the resolve she felt that Clarissa must have had a legitimate reason to have been there. She just wasn't sure what it was. "There has to be a perfectly logical explanation. If I had been the one to stumble across Norton's body in the dark, I would have tried to verify whether he was alive or not and in the process might have gotten his blood all over me."

"You're grasping for straws. Face it, Pricilla." Max shook his head. "You haven't seen Clarissa and her family for several years. Who's to say that Clarissa hasn't changed? People do change, and not always for the better."

She frowned. "You're sounding quite pessimistic."

"No, realistic. And you know it's only because I care." Max took her hand. He might be strongly opinionated, but all it took was one touch to remind her of why she said yes to his proposal of marriage. He made her feel young again—no matter what her bunion was telling her at the moment. "I'm just concerned about your safety, nothing more."

She matched his smile. There was already enough tension in the room—they didn't need to add a misunderstanding between themselves to the mix. "I know."

The screen switched to a close-up of a layered cheesecake, and despite the seriousness of their conversation, Max's expression confirmed he was already anticipating the sample-sized portions that would be handed out to the audience.

But she wasn't done yet. "All I plan to do is ask a few discreet questions."

"Discreet questions?" Max chuckled. "The problem is I remember your previous attempts at interviewing suspects. A barroom brawl and subsequent arrest is far from discreet."

"Would it help if I said I've learned my lesson?"

"No."

"Max. . ."

He let out a deep sigh. "Then humor me, Pricilla. Anything outside the lines of questioning gets run by the sheriff first. He's the one responsible for following up on any and all leads."

"I promise."

He didn't look convinced. "I can't help it. I didn't like it the first time you went head-to-head with a murderer, and I don't like it any better today. If you would only—"

A muffled cry interrupted Max. Pricilla's gaze snapped back toward the screen. Someone in the audience gasped. The smell of burnt sugar filled the room.

The cameras zoomed in on Maggie, who was in the process of grabbing a pan from the stove and dumping its contents into the sink. The audience silenced as the scorched liquid slid from the pot and down the drain.

So much for the raspberry sauce.

Pricilla couldn't help but feel sorry for the girl. A move like that most likely ruined any chances of winning. Pricilla adjusted her bifocals. Maggie turned the tap on and thrust her hand beneath the water. Even without the aid of the cameras, it was obvious the young woman had burned her hand. Pricilla rushed toward her to help, wondering what else could go wrong this weekend.

"It was going to be a chocolate mousse cake," Maggie said between sobs.

Pricilla had led her away from the intense stares of the audience and into the hotel kitchen where she'd doctored Michelle just a couple of short hours ago. One murder and two contestants out in less than twenty-four hours. She didn't like the odds of this game so far.

Maggie wiped her nose with her uninjured hand and sucked in a breath. "I'd even made these cute little chocolate sticks. . .and spun sugar spirals. . .but the raspberry sauce. . ." With her hand still beneath the cool running water, the crying started again.

Pricilla couldn't help but sympathize. In a normal competition, with the stakes as high as they were, the stress levels were tremendous for the contestants. Add a murderer on the loose, and who wouldn't be edgy?

"I don't even know how it happened," Maggie sniffed.

"How what happened?" Pricilla pulled the girl's hand away from the tap water to examine the burn. No blisters were present, and the redness was already almost gone.

"I've made this recipe dozens of times at my uncle's restaurant," Maggie continued. "Everybody loves it. . .and I've never burned it."

"You're just nervous, sweetie. The competition's stressful, and then there's the murder on top of all of that. . . ."

Fresh tears brewed in Maggie's eyes. Pricilla obviously shouldn't have brought up the murder. She glanced at her watch. "Listen, there's still almost an hour and a half left in the competition."

Whether that was enough time, Pricilla wasn't sure, but it was at least worth a try. She patted the small wound with a cloth and handed Maggie a couple of pain relievers. "You can still try."

"I don't know, Mrs. Crumb." Maggie fiddled with the edge of her chef's hat.

"If you ask me, you've come too far to simply give up now."

Maggie sniffled again and nodded her head. "I suppose you're right." She jumped off the barstool and headed back to her station.

The sheriff entered the room as Pricilla was leaving. "It seems like every time I run into you, Mrs. Crumb, you're playing the role of medic."

"Something I'm certainly not, though perhaps we need to open a nurse's station beside your investigation room with all that's happened in the past twenty-four hours."

As they entered the Great Room, Pricilla watched Maggie step into her kitchen, take a deep breath, and start back to work. The audience cheered her return. Pricilla hoped it would be enough to keep her in the competition.

The sheriff folded his arms across his chest and sighed. "I'm on my way to the lobby to meet with the manager. Do you have a few minutes to walk with me?"

"Of course." Pricilla couldn't help but notice the difference between Sheriff Lewis and the small town of Rendezvous' Deputy Carter, who had been anything but happy at her involvement in the two murder cases back home. Obviously the deputy's tune had changed. So much, in fact, that he'd even recommended her to the sheriff, something that still surprised her.

"I can't help but think that there is something very odd about this whole scenario," the sheriff began as they started down the hallway.

"You mean with Maggie?" Pricilla asked, not certain where the man was headed.

"How could a professional cook simply forget about her sauce?"

She pressed her lips together. Maybe Maggie had been hinting at something more than just burned sauce. "Maggie did seem genuinely perplexed as to how her sauce could have burned. What if this didn't occur because she was nervous and simply forgot? She's made the dessert dozens of times and knows what she's doing."

He rubbed his chin with his fingers, obviously trying to connect the dots, something Pricilla had yet to do. "So you're saying she implied someone had been tampering with her equipment."

"Not in so many words. . .but now that I think about it, that was the impression I got."

"Is it possible?"

"I suppose. There are rules set up to keep people out of the kitchens, but if someone has enough motivation, they could find a way around them."

"So someone could have tampered with her equipment. That's a pretty serious accusation."

"Except that leads to the question of motive," Pricilla said. "It doesn't make any sense, at least not in connection with Norton. It only makes sense in light of the competition."

"Maybe Maggie was distracted and burned the sauce because she has a guilty conscience," the sheriff offered.

Pricilla shrugged. Truth be told, she'd burned a few things in the course of her career as a chef. "Even professionals aren't perfect."

"Maybe, but all she needed was a moment of rage, and before she knows it, a man is dead. It's worth looking into anyway." He stopped at the edge of the lobby where complimentary beverages were being offered to the guests. "Coffee?"

Pricilla shook her head and waited while the lawman helped himself to a Styrofoam cup of the strong brew with two sugars and a cream.

"What do you know about Maggie?" He took a sip of his drink and waited for her response.

"Besides her bio in the program? Not a whole lot." Pricilla tried to remember what she'd read about the young woman. "She's twenty-eight, single, and the youngest of the group next to Clarissa. She's worked as a sous chef for the past four years in her uncle's restaurant, Sassy's."

"I've heard of it. That's a pretty classy joint."

"From what I've seen so far, she knows what she's doing and is good at it. Before today's incident, I would have placed her near the top of the contenders. A mistake like that, though, could mean that the competition is pretty much over for her."

"What else?"

Pricilla shrugged. "She seemed nervous on camera today, and while this isn't her first competition, the stress level for all the contestants is high. Not to mention that someone was murdered last night."

"So you think her reaction today is nothing more than nerves?"

Pricilla shrugged, wishing she could give him more. "I don't know."

"What about a connection to Richards?" the sheriff continued.

"None that I know of, though I'm quite certain Norton would have done a review of her uncle's restaurant at one time or another." Pricilla paused. "Still, considering all the bad reviews the man wrote, it's a miracle he lasted this long."

"So you think we're looking at revenge."

"Maybe. What I do know is that you're looking in the wrong place with Clarissa."

"Something you've mentioned at least once or twice already." The man looked away, lost it seemed, in his own evaluation of the case. "The DA wants to wrap this one up quickly."

"As do you."

"So you'll keep your eyes and ears open?" the sheriff asked.

"You know I will." Pricilla paused, wanting to turn the tables before their interview was over. "But there is one other thing I'd like to know."

"What's that?"

"Did Clarissa give you a reason for her being out last night?"

The sheriff glanced around the lobby, which was empty except for a desk clerk and a couple waiting by the front door. "You have to understand, Mrs. Crumb, that anything I tell you must be kept between us in the strictest of confidences."

"Certainly."

"Clarissa's lawyer has talked to her."

"What about her parents?"

"Her mother and stepfather are off on a cruise somewhere in the Caribbean, and we've been unable to reach them as of yet."

"And as for her guilt?"

"She denies any involvement in the murder. Claims she couldn't sleep and decided to go for a walk. While she was coming up the path, she heard two people arguing and went around the pools to avoid them, believing that it had to be some lovers' quarrel. She heard someone yell, then saw someone running."

"And the blood?" Pricilla asked.

"She'd recently taken a CPR class. She claims she was trying to save his life."

"And you believe her." Pricilla phrased her question like a statement.

The sheriff's gaze darted to the right. "Yes. I do. And that's why I need your help. The DA doesn't agree with me. They've gone ahead and charged her."

The hotel manager emerged from a doorway behind the front desk. "Sheriff. . .Mrs. Crumb. . .I'm sorry to interrupt."

The sheriff's eye twitched. "It's fine. I was planning to come talk to you."

Pricilla started to leave.

"Before you leave, Mrs. Crumb, I want to thank you," the manager said.

"Thank me?"

"The electrical inspector's in a ruckus over the sprinkler situation. The man who worked on it is probably going to lose his license. Thankfully, you brought the problem to our attention."

Pricilla swallowed a twinge of guilt. "That wasn't exactly my plan."

The man tugged on his jacket. "I understand, but in a real emergency, the situation could have ended up being far more serious."

"You're welcome. I think. Now if you will both excuse me."

The sheriff's gaze shot to the doorway and then back to her. "Of course, Mrs. Crumb. We can continue our conversation at a later time."

Pricilla returned to the Great Room and forced herself to concentrate on the rest of the dessert segment, certain there was something the lanky lawman wasn't telling her. She'd had the same feeling just a few hours earlier in the conference room after her interview with him but still wasn't sure why. Maggie managed to make a comeback with her chocolate mousse cake, but even that triumph wasn't enough to beat out Freddie Longfellow. As soon as the session was over, Pricilla made a point to snag Freddie in order to congratulate him on his win. . .and to take the opportunity to ask a few questions.

Her smile broadened as she approached him. She had a job to do, and there was no better time than the present. "Congratulations on winning the first round, Mr. Longfellow."

"It's Freddie, please, and thank you." He brushed a tuft of blond hair out of his eyes and smiled at her, apparently trying to transmit some of the charm to her that he'd used earlier. His flamboyant personality had captured the judges' attention as well as the audience's. "I've worked long and hard to win this competition."

"It's far from over."

"True, but this is my third time to compete, and this time I plan to win. I'll be in school in Paris this time next year."

"You sound pretty confident."

He straightened his linen jacket. "I have been told that my distinctive combinations of flavors can't be beat, and I'm counting on it."

Enough to knock off one of the judges? She wasn't ready to dismiss that question yet.

Pricilla decided to pull out the only card she had, not sure where it would lead her. "That doesn't by any chance have to do with your tête-à-tête with Lyle Simpson does it?"

Freddie cleared his throat. "Not that it really is any of your business, Mrs. Crumb, but before rumors start flying as to the validity of my integrity, like I assured Miss Vanderbilt, the bellboy switched my bags with Mr. Simpson's when I checked in. As the competition hadn't even started, I didn't see any harm in knocking on the man's door and retrieving my luggage. And if, for whatever reason, you don't believe my story, the bellboy will back me up."

A nice, pat story, for sure.

But he did have a point. "I'm sorry to have implied otherwise, Mr. . . . Freddie."

Perhaps it was time to steer the conversation clear of accusations before she turned the man off entirely. "To be honest, this year has had a bit of a rough opening with the death of one of the judges, hasn't it? I suppose it has all of us rattled."

"I don't know. From what I've heard, the death of Norton Richards isn't too great a loss."

Pricilla grimaced at the man's blasé comment. "I've always believed that any loss of human life is great."

"True, of course, but the man did have a knack for stirring up trouble." Freddie eyed a tall blond across the room. "Or so I've been told."

Pricilla frowned. "So you didn't know Norton?"

Freddie turned his attention back to Pricilla. For the moment, anyway. "Never saw the man before last night."

Pricilla frowned. Freddie was cocky. Too cocky. And from the look on his face, their conversation was over. "It was nice to chat with you, Mrs. Crumb, but I have a phone call to make before the next competition starts."

Pricilla glanced at her watch. There was an hour and a half until the next competition began, which gave her just enough time to go upstairs to her room, brush her teeth, and perhaps slip in a ten-minute energy nap before she met Max for lunch.

Freddie headed for the blond, while Pricilla took the elevator to her floor.

When she stepped out a few moments later, someone grabbed her arm.

"Pricilla?" Trisha stood in front of her, her face pale.

Pricilla pressed her hand against her chest, with the fear that another murder had taken place. "What's happened?"

"Quick. Into the room."

Pricilla followed her down the carpeted hall, slipping in behind her.

"What in the world are you doing, sneaking about the hotel like this after a. . ."

"A murder?" Trisha paced the floor.

"Exactly. You startled me half to death."

"I'm sorry. I had no intention of scaring you, and I suppose this will seem insignificant in the light of everything that's going on, but. . ." Trisha paused. "You know my engagement ring."

"Of course. Nathan's talked about it enough for me to have its every detail memorized. A pear-shaped diamond he handpicked in South Africa. Custom setting and gold band. . .not another one like it in the world."

"Which is precisely the problem." Trisha held up her left hand as tears welled in her eyes. "It's missing."

Pricilla grasped Trisha's bare hand in horror. Another glitch in the wedding plans wasn't going to go over well at this point, and a lost engagement ring more than fit the definition of catastrophe.

Trisha frowned. "Nathan even reminded me last week to get the ring resized. I'd planned to do it as soon as we got back home, but he was right. I should never have waited."

And he was not going to be happy with the news. The custom-made engagement ring had been designed exclusively for Trisha and couldn't be purchased online or at the mall. Not to mention the sentimental value that was worth even more than the ring itself.

Pricilla perched on the edge of the queen-sized bed and ran her fingers across the thick down comforter. The ring had to be somewhere around the hotel, but where? "When did you last see it?"

"That's the problem. I'm not sure." Trisha rubbed her fingers around the bare spot, the furrows in her brow deepening. "I noticed it was gone yesterday afternoon, but I kept praying I'd find it. I. . .I'm not sure I can tell Nathan."

Pricilla frowned. They'd have to deal with Nathan at some point, but for now Trish was going to have to narrow it down closer than sometime yesterday.

Trisha sat down across from her on the dressing table stool and clasped her hands together. "Riley commented about it yesterday during my fitting. After that, I'm not sure."

"Okay, we know you had it on then," Pricilla began.

The steps to deducing where she'd seen the ring last were no different than deducing who had murdered Norton Richards. Except at least with a murder investigation, the number of suspects could normally be narrowed down to a small handful. Finding the ring could be more like finding a needle in a haystack. But as with any good investigation, they just needed to start at the beginning. "We need to make a timeline."

"All I did yesterday was my fitting with Riley, coffee with Nathan in the restaurant, and then we went for a walk around the lake before dinner in the Great Room." Trisha rose and started pacing the tan carpet again.

A walk around the lake definitely posed a problem by widening the search perimeter. If the ring had fallen off somewhere on the trail, the haystack had just turned into a football field, and it would be nearly impossible to find. From the look on Trisha's face, the same reasoning had gone through her mind as well.

Trisha stopped at the open window that overlooked Silvermist Lake in the distance. Her face paled. "Wait a minute."

"What is it?" Pricilla joined her at the window. While she'd always enjoyed the view of the aspen trees, evergreens, and the lofty Rocky Mountains from her bedroom window at Nathan's lodge, Silvermist Lodge boasted the additional stunning scene of the lake in the forefront of the distant mountains.

Trisha pointed to the placid waters. "We walked around the jogging trail that circles the lake. It's just under three miles. We stopped for a breather, and Nathan tossed a few rocks across the surface. It was so beautiful and clear. . ." She paused, gnawing on her bottom lip.

Pricilla didn't like where this was going. "And. . ."

"Nathan challenged me to skip a stone as many times as he could."

"Then I suppose that's the most logical place to start looking."

Trisha shook her head. "Finding it out there will be impossible."

"Maybe." Pricilla glanced at her watch. "I've got a little less than an hour and a half before I have to be back at the competition."

"We'll never find it—"

"Don't give up yet. I've got an idea."

Forty-five minutes later, Pricilla and Trisha stood at the edge of Silvermist Lake with a metal detector Pricilla had managed to secure from the lodge. Stepping over logs, brush, and wildflowers, they'd scoured the edge of the rocky lake where the engaged couple had taken a break from their walk. So far, they'd turned up five bottle caps and a penny, but there was no sign of the ring.

The frequency of the beeps increased. Pricilla reached down and dug up another coin. This time it was a nickel.

Trisha, who had said little after her initial confession, now stood along the shore of the lake with her arms folded tightly across her chest. "Where in the world did you get the idea to use a metal detector?"

Pricilla walked slowly as she swept the coil back and forth above the ground. "My husband, Marty, was a treasure hunter. Never found any great treasure besides a few coins, an old locket, and some other jewelry, but he still kept up with it throughout the years. If nothing else, it was great exercise for the two of us. We spent a good part of our holidays scouring beaches, parks, and farms across the country. He loved it."

"And you?"

"I loved being with Marty." She smiled at memories of walking along the sandy coastline with the tide tugging at her feet or tramping through the woodlands, all the time with Marty beside her. It had become something they both enjoyed doing together.

Pricilla held up her right hand to show Trisha the gold band encircling her fourth finger. "I found this Celtic ring on the East Coast one summer."

"I've noticed it before. It's beautiful."

Pricilla went back to sweeping the ground, but while the idea of using a metal detector might be novel, she was quickly beginning to regret the idea. She glanced at the water lapping against the shore beside her. No woman her age should don rubber boots and wade out into cold lake water. But that's exactly what she was about to do.

She let the detector hover above the surface of the water, careful as she took her first tentative step.

"Are you sure about this?" Trisha asked.

Pricilla nodded. "This detector is waterproof, so while we're here, we might as well search the water near the shore. It can't be that deep."

"Just be careful." Trisha continued her search along the shore, staying parallel to Pricilla. "What else did you find in your treasure hunts?"

"A rare coin worth about two hundred and fifty dollars and a handful of Civil War bullets. That was pretty much the extent of my findings. Marty found a few more things."

"I'm sure you miss Marty a lot."

"I do. But now that your father's in my life. . ." Pricilla couldn't help but smile. "God made room in my heart to find love again. Something I never thought would happen."

Pricilla inched her way along the shoreline and then moved another foot out.

"Stay near the edge, Pricilla. There's no telling when the bottom drops off, and if you fall in, you'll catch pneumonia. It's got to be freezing now that summer's over."

Pricilla's chuckle rose above the *whir* of the detector. "I seem to remember someone else falling into a lake in an attempt to impress a certain young man."

Trisha and Nathan's first, unofficial date had been to go fishing, something Trisha had never attempted before.

"I've never been an outdoor girl, but Nathan's somehow managed to add fishing and hiking to my list of leisure activities." Trisha stopped at the edge of a thick log that jutted into the water a dozen feet. "But I wasn't trying to impress Nathan. I was just determined to catch as many fish as he did. I guess it didn't work."

Pricilla caught her gaze.

Trisha laughed. "Okay. I was trying to impress him. He had me hooked that very first day. Forget about the fish."

The frequency of the beeps sped up. Pricilla had found something.

She reached into the shallow water and dug in the sand with a stick. A minute later, she pulled up another bottle cap. "At this rate, we'll have the world's largest collection."

"And no ring." The hopelessness in Trisha's expression was back.

"We'll find it." Despite her encouragement, Pricilla knew the words rang hollow.

"It's impossible, and you know it." Tears welled in Trisha's eyes. "I'm just going to have to find a way to break the news to Nathan."

Pricilla kept on, determined to find the ring despite the odds.

Trisha glanced at her watch. "You've got to get back to the lodge. I can't tell you how much I appreciate what you've done, but I'm just going to have to face the truth. The ring is gone."

"Give me five more minutes."

Max peeked into the Silvermist Café, looking for Pricilla in case she'd decided to grab something to eat. She'd told him this morning that she was planning to lie down for a few minutes before lunch, so when she didn't show up, he assumed she'd decided to take a longer nap. As long as she was back in time for the next stage of the competition, some rest would do her good.

He scanned the cozy restaurant with its antique furniture, timber ceiling beams, and picture windows overlooking the lake, turning to leave when he saw no sign of Pricilla. He wasn't worried about her. Not yet anyway. A chalkboard in the doorway announced the specials of the day in colorful chalk: FILET MIGNON WITH GARLIC SHRIMP, and HOMEMADE COCONUT PIE.

Homemade coconut pie. He glanced behind him into the lobby. Still no sign of Pricilla who would, no doubt, quickly point out that he had just sampled half a dozen desserts prepared by master chefs. Still, one slice of pie wouldn't hurt. . . .

His focus snapped back to the restaurant while at the same time he tried to muster his floundering remains of willpower.

A pretty blond hostess approached him, ponytail swinging behind her, menus in hand. "Table for one?"

Max hesitated. If Pricilla ever found out he'd sneaked in for a piece of pie, she'd have him running five miles with Trisha every morning.

Unless. . .

His smile broadened. One of the contestants, Christopher Jeffries, sat alone at a corner table. Early thirties, clean-cut and soft-spoken. . .Max had been impressed with the young man's performance throughout the morning competition. He'd fared well, coming in a close second behind Freddie Longfellow with his mini fruit Pavlovas and chocolate cream puffs, desserts Max had found irresistible.

He decided to take a chance. "I'll be joining Mr. Jeffries."

Thanking the hostess, he made his way to the back of the room. The quicker the case was solved, the sooner Pricilla would be able to put it behind her, and he, in turn, could stop worrying about her. Surely a bit of investigating couldn't hurt. One never knew what a few carefully chosen questions might uncover.

He stopped at the young man's table.

"Are you up for a bit of company?" Max asked. "I'd love to ask you a few questions about the competition, if it's not a bother."

Christopher folded up the newspaper he was reading and pointed to the extra chair. "I don't mind a bit. In fact, I should be preparing for the next round, but I needed a distraction from the contest. Are you a reporter?"

"Not at all. I'm Max Summers. My fiancée, Pricilla Crumb, who's working as the emcee, talked me into coming up for the weekend."

"Christopher Jeffries, though I suppose you already know that." He chuckled. "Are you enjoying the competition so far?"

"The food is out of this world, though for you contestants, the competition must be stressful."

"Incredibly." Christopher dropped the paper onto the table. "I knew it would be. This is the second time I've entered, though I didn't make it to this level last year."

Max nodded at the piece of coconut pie Christopher was in the process of eating. Apparently Max wasn't the only who couldn't turn down the dessert.

"Is it good?"

"Fantastic." The young man took another bite. "You'd think I'd be sick of sweets after this morning, but I walked by and couldn't resist."

The waitress stopped at the table with a glass of ice water. Ignoring the nagging comments he could hear from Pricilla in the back of his mind, Max ordered a slice of the pie for himself.

"Did you know the judge who was murdered?" he asked, jumping into the conversation headfirst once the waitress had left. "Norton Richards?"

Christopher laughed. "And I was expecting the normal questions, like, how long have you been cooking, or what made you choose a career as a chef?"

Max fidgeted in his chair. So much for being subtle. He was losing his touch. "I. . .I suppose the murder is in the forefront of everyone's mind. It definitely is in mine."

"No doubt." Christopher took another bite of pie. "Norton was a friend of my father's actually, if you could call him that. Perhaps an acquaintance is a better word. I never spent any time with the man, but from what I heard, he didn't have any real friends."

Max settled into his chair and started to relax. "So how did your father know him?"

"He's the editor for a small newspaper back in Montana, the same town where Norton was originally from. I used to work at the paper in the summers while I was in college. We ran Norton's weekly columns. That was before he was syndicated across the country."

It was interesting how everyone seemed to have a connection to the dead man. "So did you ever have any run-ins with him?"

"No, but my father did." Christopher took a final bite and then pushed his plate aside. "The small town of Junction, where my dad runs the paper, has a well-known restaurant that draws in the summer tourists. It's run by two brothers who started the place at the end of World War II. They're famous for their buffalo steaks and baked beans.

"Readers began complaining about the harshness of Norton's reviews. He might have been from Junction, but that didn't make people any less forgiving when he began bashing Sal and Winston and their cuisine."

"So what happened?"

"My father threatened to discontinue his column if he didn't write more favorable reviews."

"And did he?"

Christopher signaled the waitress for a refill on his coffee before answering. By now, most of the customers had cleared out, leaving the room quiet except for the hum of the overhead fans. "Apparently Norton didn't allow anyone to dictate what he wrote. He never sent in another review."

"Was it detrimental to the paper?"

"Not a bit, which infuriated Norton. Or so I was told."

The connection was interesting, but certainly not enough to pin a murder on. And Christopher Jeffries seemed far from the type of person to lose his temper in a heated moment. Of course, who was Max to say whether or not there was a murderer lurking within?

The waitress slid a piece of pie across the table in front of Max and then filled Christopher's coffee mug.

Max cleared his throat and opted for another angle once she'd left. "So do you think Clarissa's guilty?"

"I have to say," Christopher said as he added two packets of sugar to his drink, "that I was surprised when the sheriff arrested her. While I'd just met her, she struck me as the sweet girl next door. Can't really see her blowing up and killing someone, but then I'm no psychologist." Christopher leaned forward. "Now Michelle is more what I'd call a viable suspect."

Max's brow rose. "Why is that?"

"She doesn't remember me, I'm sure, but I met her once. She interviewed for a position at my father's paper."

Their world just kept getting smaller and smaller. "I'm having a hard time picturing Michelle stuck in some small town in Montana."

"This was before she hit the big time with the magazine. She was building her résumé and figured a smalltown paper needed an ace reporter to track down stories that would bring in more readers."

"Did she get the job?"

Christopher nodded. "But she only stayed for six weeks before quitting to work for some high-profile job in New York. Made a whole lot more dough, I'm sure."

"When was that?"

"If I remember correctly, it was right before Norton moved away from Junction."

"So Michelle and Norton knew each other?"

"Oh yeah. They knew each other all right." Christopher drummed his fingers against the table, his expression implying they'd been far more than friends. "But she ended up leaving for New York, which I'm assuming ended any relationship they had. Michelle wasn't afraid to do whatever it took to get where she wanted to go."

Including murder? Max took another bite of the pie that suddenly didn't taste quite as good as the first. That was the answer he was going to have to find out.

Pricilla took another step forward, careful not to drift too far from the shore. While the water was less than two feet deep from where she stood, the ground quickly sloped the farther one got from the shore. The last thing she needed to do was lose her footing and fall in.

The beeping increased again. She poked at the spot with her stick, careful not to stir up too much dirt. Probably nothing more than another bottle cap.

Trisha stepped out onto the log hanging over the water. "Be careful."

"I could say the same for you, Trisha, balancing like that. I'd prefer not to have to rescue you."

"I might have a tendency to clumsiness, but I have no intention of joining you in the water, especially without floaters."

Sure enough, it was another bottle cap.

It was time to give up. Jamming the stick into the sandy bottom, Pricilla paused. The stick had found something else. One last attempt wouldn't hurt, even though she was certain it was too big to be a ring. "I found something, but it's probably just a rock. One thing I learned with Marty is that most finds never live up to the anticipation of the moment."

Hands on her knees, Trisha leaned forward as far as she could on the log. "What is it?"

"I don't know."

"Pricilla?"

Her gaze jerked up as the log snapped in two, plunging Trisha into the water below.

Strong waves slapped against Pricilla's legs, knocking her off balance. The metal detector slid from her hands. She lunged for something to hold on to but couldn't reach the branches extending from the broken log. The next second, her feet flew out from under her.

The rocky floor of the lake rushed up to greet her, slamming into her backside, as her rubber boots filled with water. She braced herself with her arms, barely keeping her head out of the water, and managed to stand back up at the same time Trisha came to the surface, gasping for air.

Pricilla reached for Trisha's arm, afraid they would both go down again. Miraculously, they didn't.

Pricilla gulped a deep breath of relief. "Are you okay?"

Trisha pushed a strand of wet hair off her face, then spewed water from her mouth. "Besides startling me to death, nothing seems to be hurt except for my pride. But what about you? I'm so sorry. I looked down, thought I saw something flash in the sunlight, and before I knew it the log had snapped beneath me."

Relieved they were both okay, Pricilla couldn't help but snicker at Trisha's shocked expression and the fact that they must both look like a couple of wet rats. While the water only came up to midthigh, both of them were completely drenched from head to toe. Of course, being thirty years older than Trisha meant that Pricilla would be the one to pay more with bumps and bruises. At least nothing seemed broken.

"I am sorry." Trisha pressed her lips together. "You're sure nothing is strained or broken?"

Pricilla shivered and started sloshing toward the edge of the lake in her waterlogged boots that felt more like lead weights. "If anything is broken, I can't feel it yet."

"Nathan's never going to believe I did this again." With her hands placed firmly on her hips, Trisha blew out a huff. "I seem to have a knack for ruining the great outdoor adventure. Here I am marrying the owner of a hunting lodge, and I can't get near a lake without falling in."

Pricilla chuckled as she grabbed the metal detector and headed toward a large rock near the shore so she could dump the water out of her boots. "Stepping out onto a rotten log over a lake does seem to be a way to substantiate the law of gravity."

"And Murphy's Law," Trisha threw out, wringing out the bottom of her drenched shirt.

Pricilla looked down at her own disheveled outfit. Murphy's Law certainly seemed to be working for her today. How in the world was she going to make herself presentable for the next competition after tromping through the outdoors for over an hour before falling in a lake? She could already hear Max's "I told you so," but this time she could honestly tell him that their excursion had nothing to do with the murder investigation. Surely that would soften his predictable rebuttal that she had a knack for finding trouble.

The metal detector started beeping. Pricilla kicked her toe against yet another bottle cap that lay on the ground and flipped off the machine. This detector had gotten her into enough trouble today.

Still, she couldn't help but wonder what Trisha had seen before tumbling into the water.

"What do you think it was?" she asked as she dumped the water out of her boots.

Trisha shrugged. "I don't know. Something flashed along the bottom of the lake, but I'll probably never be able to find it again."

"Where?" Pricilla shoved her boots back on, ready to rescan the area with the detector if need be.

Trisha reached to snap a stick off the fallen log and poked the stick into the water where she stood. "I don't think there's anything here." She turned back toward the shore and then stopped. "Wait a minute."

Pricilla stood. "What is it?"

"I don't know, but it's big. No wonder I saw it earlier." Trisha nudged a rock away with her shoe and reached down to pull the object out of the water.

Pricilla blinked.

Trisha held a nine-inch chef's knife in her hand. Pricilla's heart began to pulsate. The murder weapon? Norton had been stabbed. And this knife wasn't rusty. She tried to dismiss the obvious conclusions. There had to be a hundred reasons why there was a knife in the water.

But a coincidence? She didn't think so.

Pricilla took in a quick breath. "You don't think that has something to do with the murder—"

"Don't even go there." Trisha shook her head and started for the shore, still holding on to the knife. "I refuse to get involved in another murder investigation. All I plan to do is find a place to dispose of this knife so no one gets hurt."

"But it's completely possible." Pricilla eyed the chef's knife. Black handle, polished edge, laminated steel. . .she'd seen the same type of knife in several of the contestants' kitchens. "If this is the murder weapon, there's no way that Clarissa could have murdered Norton. She wouldn't have had time to dispose of the evidence."

"You're jumping to conclusions."

"Stop and think about it." Shivering, Pricilla followed Trisha onto the rocky beach, thankful no one was in sight. She really didn't want to explain to anyone why the two of them were dripping wet with mucky lake water. "If I caught her red-handed, as the authorities believe, then why was there no evidence of a weapon anywhere around?"

"I don't know. I still say you're jumping to conclusions. For all we know, this knife has been here for months." Trisha combed her fingers through her wet hair. "And not only that, we're pretty far from where the murder was committed."

Pricilla eyed the knife. Trisha was right, of course. Just because they had found a knife the day after a murder was committed didn't mean the two were connected.

On the other hand, she couldn't just dismiss the possibility that the knife was the murder weapon. That evidence alone could save Clarissa. There was only one thing to do.

Pricilla quickened her steps. "We've got to go find the sheriff."

Max stood on the wooden deck of the lodge overlooking the lake. Tables lined the area with umbrellas to shade them from the afternoon sun, and there was still no sign of Pricilla. He was starting to get worried. He'd called her room twice and even went upstairs and knocked on her door, but no one had answered.

Nathan joined him at the railing. "Did you find my mom?"

Max gnawed at the toothpick between his teeth. "No. And I can't imagine where she is."

"I can't find Trisha either." Nathan leaned against the railing beside him. "It's like they've vanished from the lodge."

Max glanced at his watch and frowned. "And Pricilla is supposed to introduce the next competition in a few minutes."

"Both our cars are still out front, so they couldn't have gone too far. Maybe they went for a walk."

"That is a possibility."

Max drummed his fingers against the rail and stared out across Silvermist Lake. Surrounded by evergreens and aspens, this area was one of the most beautiful places he'd ever visited in the Rocky Mountains, but for the moment, he couldn't relax enough to enjoy the scenery. While it was possible that Trisha and Pricilla had gone for a walk and lost track of time, his gut told him there was more to it. And wherever they were, it had to do with Norton Richards's death and the personal invitation the sheriff had recently extended to Pricilla to help out in the case.

He reached into his pocket for an antacid and sent up a prayer for the safety of the two women. Finding himself smack-dab in the middle of a murder investigation—with Pricilla involved—tended to raise his acid level faster than a bowl of red-hot chili.

While he popped two of the chalky pills into his mouth, snippets of the conversation he'd had with Pricilla over breakfast replayed in his mind. He couldn't understand why the sheriff, of all people, had asked Pricilla to get involved. The woman had enough determination to find out the truth without encouragement from the law. Deputy Carter might have been impersonal and even rude at times, but at least he was smart enough not to invite Pricilla to become an informant.

Still, whether he was right or not, nothing excused the fact that neither Pricilla nor Trisha had told anyone where they were going. What if something had gone wrong? Pricilla had tried to dismiss his concerns that she was a magnet for trouble, a theory proved by the last two cases she'd gotten involved in. The last thing he wanted to deal with at the moment was another arrest, or kidnapping. . .or something even worse.

Max turned to Nathan. "I have this sick feeling that both your mother's and my daughter's disappearance have something to do with Norton Richards's murder."

Nathan's eyes widened. "Surely you're not serious."

"I'd prefer not to go that direction, but you know your mom. And I know how determined she is at the moment to ensure Clarissa isn't charged with his murder."

Nathan leaned against the railing. "So you think she's off chasing down a batch of clues?"

Max nodded. "That's exactly what I'm thinking. Pricilla's involvement in two murder investigations has given her just enough confidence to think she knows what she's doing, and enough to get her into trouble."

He knew he should give her more credit. Pricilla was intelligent, compassionate, and most of the time, level-headed, but with his heart on the line, he was bound and determined to make sure nothing happened to her.

Max glanced up at Nathan. "There's another reason why I'm worried."

"What's that?"

"Did your mother tell you about her conversation with the sheriff?"

"No. . ."

"For some crazy reason, he's asked her to be his inside source to the investigation. You know, to keep her eyes and ears open for anything she might pick up from either the contestants or the judges."

"His informant?"

"Yep, and while he might be right about the fact that she's in the perfect position, I'm still tempted to go and have a talk with the man."

"Why haven't you?"

"Because you know as well as I do what your mother's reaction would be. Not only would it infuriate her, I'm afraid she'd lose trust in me. She's a grown woman, and for me to go behind her back and discuss the matter. . ."

Nathan shoved his hands into his pockets. "I, for one, think it's a good idea."

"Except she wasn't exactly pleased with my reaction to the request, and I'm afraid if I stepped in and tried to stop her, she'd end up being all the more determined to get involved. Though now I wish I would have. Especially if she's in trouble."

Max squinted against the bright sun as he scanned the area. A man fished alone in a boat in the middle of the lake. Another couple stood at the water's edge, their arms around each other like they were the only people around for miles. Two others trudged along the shoreline. One carried a metal detector. Now there was an idea for a safe hobby for him and Pricilla to get involved in. One that might keep her busy enough to stay out of trouble.

"Who's that?"

Max's attention snapped back to the present at Nathan's question. "Where?"

Nathan was pointing at the pair in the distance with the metal detector. One of them wore rubber boots. That definitely took Pricilla out of the running and Trisha as well. He couldn't see either woman going out in such unsightly apparel.

"I think it's them," Nathan said.

"I don't think so." He adjusted his bifocals. "The last time I saw Pricilla, she was wearing a red short-sleeved sweater."

Nathan shook his head. "I'm positive it's them. Let's go."

Max hurried behind Nathan down the narrow staircase that led to the lake. Anger started to brew. He thought Pricilla had more sense than to take off without telling anyone where she was going, and that went for his daughter as well. Especially after a murder had taken place. How was he supposed to take care of her if he couldn't even keep track of her?

The two women stopped dead in their tracks when they saw the men approaching. Nathan had been right. And both women were soaking wet. Max wasn't sure if he should stay furious or burst out laughing at their appearance.

Then he saw the knife in Trisha's hand. All the worry he'd felt earlier swept back over him. He opened his mouth, but Nathan was the first to find his voice.

"What in the world happened, Trisha?"

Max's daughter avoided both their gazes.

Now it was Max's turn to press the interrogation. "Pricilla?"

"Before you go off losing a bunch of steam, hold on." Pricilla set the metal detector against the ground and jutted her chin toward Trisha. "We were out looking. . .for something. . .and. . ."

The women exchanged guilty glances.

"Looking for what?" Max demanded.

Pricilla drew in a sharp breath. "For the moment that doesn't matter. The bottom line is I think we found the murder weapon."

Pricilla caught the worry in the men's expressions. And the anger. Max had warned her earlier that morning not to dash off and get herself in trouble, and from where she stood, soaking wet and claiming to have found the murder weapon. . .well, it definitely looked like trouble.

She curled her fingers tighter around the metal detector. "I really can explain."

"I'm the one who needs to explain." Trisha took a step forward.

"Trisha—" Pricilla started.

"It's okay." Trisha held up her hand. "Your mother did this for me, Nathan. For us."

Nathan shook his head. "I don't understand."

"I lost my engagement ring—"

"You *what*?"

"I know." Tears welled in her eyes. "I've been sick over it. I think I might have lost it yesterday while we were throwing rocks. It was a bit loose and. . ."

Nathan frowned. "Thus the metal detector."

"So this wasn't a quest to solve the murder?" Max asked.

"Not at all, and granted, we aren't certain this is the murder weapon."

"Seems too much of a coincidence to me," Max threw in.

Nathan folded his arms across his chest and shook his head. "So you went off looking for your ring. How in the world could you have fallen in. . .again?"

"I told you I wasn't the outdoor type."

He cocked his head, as if waiting for a more reasonable explanation. "Yes, you did."

"I'm better with computers and running board meetings."

"I know."

Trisha stepped forward to put her arms around his neck. "And you still want to marry me?"

"Well, you do look kind of cute when you're wet."

"Nathan. I am sorry about the ring."

Nathan chuckled as he pulled her into his arms and kissed her firmly on the lips.

"What I want to know is if you are both all right," Max said.

"Yes, we're fine," Pricilla assured him.

"As long as you're okay." Nathan kissed Trisha again. "That's all that really matters."

Pricilla cleared her throat and turned to Max. "So am I off the hook, too?"

"Not so fast." He bridged the gap between them and took her hand. "Something tells me that this won't be the last time you stick your nose into this investigation."

"I told you, I couldn't make any promises."

"Even with a possible murder weapon in your possession—"

"A murder weapon that could clear Clarissa. It's the one hole in their case against her."

"Which would mean there's been a murderer on the loose while you've been tromping through the great outdoors alone." Max's brow furrowed.

"You scared me, Pricilla. I'm not ready to lose you."

She shook her head. "You're not going to."

He leaned down and kissed her, reminding her that love can shoot tingles to your toes whether you're sixteen or sixty-five.

He pulled back and ran his thumb down her cheek, making her wish she didn't look like such a mess. Perhaps there was truth in the old adage that true love was blind. Even dripping wet and wearing rubber boots, the spark still simmered.

"I suppose we need to go find the sheriff now," he said.

"Surely even you can't ignore possible evidence."

Nathan and Trisha trudged up the slope ahead of them, arm in arm. Nathan's cell phone rang, and he reached to answer it.

Max took Pricilla's hand, and they followed the younger couple back toward the lodge. Not only was she going to have to find the sheriff, she was going to have to ask Michelle to take her place for the next segment, something she was quite certain Michelle wouldn't mind. Being in front of the camera seemed to be her thing.

Nathan stopped and snapped his phone shut. "Your ring isn't the only thing lost."

"What are you talking about?" Trisha said.

"Our travel agent called to confirm the details on the added excursion I requested."

"And. . ."

"Apparently, the hotel has lost our honeymoon reservation."

There was something to this Murphy's Law. Pricilla had never believed in bad luck, but she couldn't deny the fact that any plans of a relaxing weekend had been waylaid.

I know You're in control, Lord, but things sure do seem to be spiraling out of control.

She trudged toward the lodge behind the others in the cumbersome rubber boots, feeling every aching muscle in her body. A bruise had formed on her right wrist where she'd hit it against a rock, and her head throbbed. While being young at heart might keep her spirit alive, she now had even more reason for steering clear of rigorous outdoor excursions.

Max slowed down to match her pace while Nathan and Trisha hurried ahead, lost in conversation. A misplaced hotel reservation might justifiably seem insignificant compared to a murder, but Pricilla also knew that didn't take away the irritation of the situation. Another fly in the ointment was not what the couple needed at this point.

She stopped at the tackle shop to return the borrowed boots and metal detector, quickly donning her own sturdy shoes again.

"Are you sure you're okay?" Max reached for her hand as they started walking again.

"A bruise or two, but I'm fine." A glance his direction left her heart beating in that familiar pitter-patter rhythm that only a bout of true love could evoke.

He looked as handsome today as he had the first time she'd met him, with his broad shoulders and military physique. Friends for decades, she'd never expected anything more, but somehow they'd found it. And now he was even more handsome. His hair had turned gray, giving him a look of maturity, and he still had a trim figure despite his constant craving for sweets.

A wave of guilt washed over her as they continued toward the lodge. She'd looked forward to this weekend as time together for the two of them. Living hundreds of miles apart wasn't easy, and until the wedding, or until Max's house sold, they had no choice but to endure a long-distance relationship.

Maybe it was time to stop focusing on excuses and simply set the wedding date.

But all thoughts of romance fled as Pricilla stopped at the bottom of the stairs leading up to the lodge's restaurant. Michelle perched at the stop of the stairs, clipboard in hand, her displeasure evident.

Pricilla turned to Max. "Michelle's waiting for me, and you know she isn't going to take my late or untidy appearance well."

"Knowing you, you'll find a way to placate her."

Pricilla had exactly fifteen seconds to figure something out. She took the stairs slowly, forcing a smile as she stepped onto the deck.

Michelle wasn't smiling. "Mrs. Crumb. Where in the world have you been?"

Pricilla scrambled to think of something to say that wouldn't completely erase the tiny bit of dignity she had left. A good reputation had always been important to her, and if she wasn't careful, the professionalism and integrity she worked to portray would be lost in an instant.

She combed her fingers through her disheveled hair. "I was involved in a bit of an accident, Michelle. Trisha and I. . .we. . ."

"I can see you've been involved in some sort of recreation." Michelle's lips puckered. "The next round of the competition begins in ten minutes. I'm already down a judge and a contestant and have a second contestant thinking about dropping out because of this morning's fiasco. Now on top of all that, it seems that my emcee has decided to go swimming. This isn't good for publicity, Mrs. Crumb. For the continuity of the show and for the sponsors who wanted the face of. . .of Julia Child, I need you in front of the camera in. . ." She glanced at her watch. ". . .eight and a half minutes."

"I'm very well aware of that." Pricilla clenched her fists beside her. She was also aware of the fact that she'd never be presentable in twice that amount of time.

Trisha held the knife out of sight behind her back. "This is all my fault, really—"

"It's okay, Trisha," Pricilla said. "Go on upstairs and change. I'll be there shortly."

As Nathan and Trisha skirted away with the evidence, Pricilla wondered if it was even possible to soothe Michelle's ruffled feathers. The woman had tunnel vision when it came to her work. Far be it for even a murder investigation to get in the way of her project.

Pricilla decided on another angle. "While I realize that I've put you in an extremely awkward position, don't you think the sponsors would welcome seeing a bit of the woman who has worked so hard to make this contest the success that it is?"

Max cleared his throat beside her. Pricilla avoided looking at him. There were times when one simply had to pull out all the diplomatic cards available.

"You've done an outstanding job," Pricilla rushed on, "and you deserve some time in the spotlight. This afternoon's opening segment would give you just that. I can't see anyone complaining about that."

"Well, I. . ." Michelle pushed back her highlighted bangs with her fingers. "I suppose no one would mind."

Bingo. Appealing to the woman's vanity had been the right card to play.

Pricilla smiled. "And I promise I'll be ready to go on in time for the next segment."

Michelle checked the schedule she carried. "I'll expect you in front of the camera at two thirty." The frown was back, but Pricilla knew she'd won. The younger woman turned on her high heels. "Don't be late a second time."

With Michelle placated for the moment, Pricilla relaxed. She'd have just enough time to change her clothes, do something to her hair, and grab a quick lunch before resuming her role. Missing one spot was bad enough. Missing the next assigned slot would be unacceptable.

"I'm not sure I trust her."

"What do you mean?" Pricilla walked beside Max across the thick area carpet through the lobby toward the elevator, thankful the lobby was empty for the moment, except for the receptionist who was talking on the phone.

"You told me that when you spoke to Michelle, she admitted to knowing Norton, but that they weren't friends."

Intrigued, Pricilla stopped at the elevator and punched the button. "She seemed quite emphatic on the point, even stating that the man had no friends, only enemies and that he, even beyond the grave, was trying to ruin her career."

"It seems she was quite passionate on the matter." Max folded his arms across his chest. "Why?"

"I don't know if *passionate* is the word, though someone obviously was passionate enough to kill the man."

"Well, I happened to have a chat with Christopher Jeffries while you were out treasure hunting."

"And. . ."

"He emphatically implied that Michelle and Norton were far more than friends at one time."

"Really?" The elevator doors opened, and Pricilla stepped in before Max. "And how would he know something like that?"

Pricilla's interest peaked as Max filled her in on the details of his conversation with Christopher.

"Michelle definitely told me quite the opposite. That they couldn't stand each other." They stepped out of the elevator and walked toward Pricilla's room.

"What is the old saying—opposites attract? They still could have had a romantic encounter."

"Still, it sounds to me as if one of them is lying."

"Maybe, but on the surface I see no reason why Christopher would lie. If you ask me, Michelle has more to hide than her wrinkles."

"Max." She stood at her door, passkey in hand, wondering if there was merit to Max's discovery or if it was nothing more than a thread of gossip.

"We can talk about it later. You change and I'll go save us a table in the restaurant." He leaned down and brushed her lips with his before he walked away, leaving her more to think about than simply a potential murder weapon.

While the women changed into dry clothes and Nathan battled with the travel agent over their lost reservations, Max called the sheriff, who promised to be at the hotel within the next thirty minutes. With the knife now in a plastic baggie procured from the kitchen, he'd gone back downstairs to reserve a table for five from the perky waitress who asked if he was back for seconds on the pie. He wondered for a moment if he could get by with another slice but then decided against it.

The sheriff arrived five minutes after the women, giving them just enough time to order salads and iced teas. Nathan was still pacing on the deck outside the restaurant, on hold with the travel agent who had booked their honeymoon package.

Max slid the evidence across the table to the sheriff.

The lawman's eyes widened. "Where did you find this?"

Pricilla explained the exact location where they'd found the knife.

The sheriff held the bag up in front of him. "There is, of course, no way to know whether or not this is connected to the case at this point, but if it is indeed the murder weapon, it could punch a hole in the DA's case."

"Exactly," Pricilla said, taking a sip of her water. "Which in turn could exonerate Clarissa."

"Potentially." The sheriff slipped the knife into his briefcase. "Anything else?"

Max paused, wondering if he should mention his conversation with Christopher, but decided against it. At this point the truth was still rather fuzzy.

Pricilla leaned forward, her voice lowered. "So what do we do next?"

Max frowned, pointing at her. "This part of *we* has already been in enough trouble this week, wouldn't you say, Pricilla?"

"Max."

The sheriff shrugged. "I realize your concern, but Pricilla has already been a help to the case."

"So you're convinced Clarissa is innocent?" Pricilla asked.

"Yes," he admitted. He stood up and grabbed his bag. "I appreciate your help, but if you will all excuse me, I'll be in touch."

The lawman slipped out of the restaurant as the waitress served their food.

"I'm surprised you didn't order a slice of the coconut pie," Pricilla said as she reached for the pepper.

He felt his cheeks redden and decided to confess. "I had one earlier when I joined Christopher. Though it was in order to further conversation, of course, and not appear to make it an interrogation session."

"Good try." She took a sip of her water.

Wanting to avoid an argument, he jumped into another subject. "So tell me what you all know about Norton Richards."

"I used to follow his column religiously," Trisha admitted. "You've read it before, haven't you?"

Max cleared his throat. "I can't say that I have, actually."

"He was eccentric," Pricilla began. "He had a temper, and of course, a ruthless pen. His reviews were full of wit, but as you know by now, were also very tough."

"Which gave him a love-hate relationship with the world."

"Exactly," Pricilla continued. "Most restaurants hated him, at least those who didn't receive a good review, but the public loved him, and he became a sort of icon. Good reviews, of course, were coveted, because they brought in business. Bad reviews could crush a business with his trademarked phrase 'the deadly dish' that was given to menu items he didn't like."

"Hmm, 'the deadly dish.'" Max set his fork down and frowned. "Seemed to have been a bit of a prophecy."

He felt a shudder run down his spine. No one had expected the killer review of a deadly dish to turn into murder, but unless they were mistaken, that was exactly what had happened.

With Pricilla back to work as the hostess of the contest, Max decided it best to stay away from the samples of gourmet food. As hard as it was to admit, Pricilla did have a point. Fishing and walking down the long hallways of the hotel only went so far to counteract the desserts and high-calorie foods he'd been indulging in this weekend. Besides, he could always make up for anything he missed at supper.

A sense of déjà vu washed over him as he made his way to the small business center adjacent to the hotel's lobby. While he had no illusions of discovering the murderer simply from an online search, anything he could add to the investigation of Norton and his deadly dish was a step closer to getting Pricilla off the case. And his motivation was strong. He'd told her that her involvement with the investigation was sure to lead to trouble, and in less than twenty-four hours, his words had proven true.

It was time to put an end to all of this.

He glanced at his watch. With an hour and a half left in this afternoon's hors d'oeuvre competition, he had just enough time to do a bit of research online. At least Pricilla was safe for now. Surely nothing could happen to her while she stood in front of a television camera.

Armed with a small notebook containing a potential list of suspects, he slid in front of a computer. Besides a twenty-something-year-old wearing headphones while playing an online game, the small room was empty. He grabbed the mouse and clicked on the Internet icon. He'd run background checks from time to time in the military, and while he didn't have nearly the resources he once had, something was better than nothing.

First on his list was one of the judges, Lyle Simpson, owner of an upscale Italian restaurant outside Denver. It didn't take long to find the first round of startling news. Two months ago, Simpson put his restaurant up for sale. He printed out a copy of the article and clicked on another link. Further digging revealed that the former five-star venue was facing bankruptcy. While the notable television personality might be a draw for the competition, apparently the popular chef's business had run amok. He couldn't help but wonder what Michelle would think, knowing that one of her esteemed judges was about to go under financially.

There were other possibilities, of course, that could play into the equation.

Gambling, debt, drinking—if Pricilla were here, she would add a tainted review by Norton to the list. Max jotted down a couple more facts, still unconvinced that a restaurant could go under simply because of one of Norton's so-called deadly reviews. Couldn't it just be nothing more than bad management of a once-superior venue? Or maybe it was simply that Lyle was a better chef than businessman.

He maneuvered his way through the contestants, stopping to print out bios that might be applicable, until he came to Michelle Vanderbilt. Max googled the woman's name and scrolled through the links. Because of her possible romantic connection to Norton, Max would have bet his savings account—if he'd been a gambling man—on her involvement in Norton's murder. Two of the articles revealed career triumphs for the woman while implying the fallout of others in the process. Perhaps Norton wasn't the only person who was eager to take down whoever he could on his way up.

He clicked on a third article. Two years ago Michelle was arrested for attacking a colleague. The charges were later dropped because it was a situation of "she said, she said." Nevertheless, it all seemed to be here. A relationship with the victim, history of violence, possible motive because of rocky history with victim. . .

Someone dumped a large wicker bag on the floor and then slid into the chair beside him. Max looked over at Michelle's assistant, Sarah Reynolds. She wore little makeup beyond lip gloss and perhaps some powder. Black slacks, white sweater, hair pulled back in a ponytail. . .

She smiled at him as she clicked on her own Internet icon. "You're Pricilla Crumb's fiancé, aren't you?"

Max returned her smile and nodded.

"I think it's so romantic for an old. . ." She cleared her throat, shoving a piece of gum into her mouth. "For a couple more advanced in years to find love."

"Advanced in years?" His eyes widened at her choice of words. He'd yet to get to the age where he was ready to be rolled into an old folks' home with his teeth in a cup beside him.

In Michelle's presence, Sarah was hardly noticeable. He'd never heard her say more than "yes, ma'am" or "no, ma'am." While her looks might not be on par with a cover model, he had to give her some credit. She must have a lot of discipline to put up with her demanding boss.

Max closed out the page and grabbed his papers from the printer. He didn't want Sarah to know that he was researching her boss. Still, he might as well take advantage of the opportunity. Anyone working for the magazine would have come in contact with Norton at some point.

"So you're the photographer for this weekend's activities," he threw out.

"Technically, no. I'm actually more of a girl Friday. You know. The ever-faithful and efficient assistant who's taken for granted." The girl's glossy lips widened as she laughed. "Of course, you would know what a girl Friday means. My mom always said I'm too old for my age."

Max raised his brows. *Ouch.* Another reminder of his age.

"I mean the age thing in all due respect, of course." A dreamy look crossed her face as she chomped on her gum. "I should have been born fifty years earlier, when they had real actors like Cary Grant and Clark Gable. The movie *His Girl Friday* has always been one of my favorites. You know, with Cary Grant and Rosalind Russell. Movie stars don't come like him anymore, do they? Though perhaps the movie became like a self-fulfilling prophecy with me becoming a girl Friday. Still, I like a man who's mature and a bit older, like you."

A bit older? Max swallowed hard. He had to be more than thirty years the girl's senior. Avoiding her pensive gaze, he wondered how she could breathe while talking so much. Apparently he hadn't learned his lesson last time about the pitfalls of trying to interview younger—much younger—women. In the first murder investigation Pricilla had dragged him into, he'd offered to interview one of the suspects and then had to leave the room, running like a coon with his tail on fire from the young woman's blatant pursuit.

No. He brushed the ridiculous thought aside. He was simply on edge and reading things into the situation.

"Of course I remember Cary Grant," he started. "Not that I knew him personally, as he was born several decades before I was. . ." Here he went again. It was definitely time to change the subject. Sarah seemed hungry for attention, a definite advantage when extracting information from a source. "So what's your take on the murder?"

"If the rumors are true, that the authorities think Clarissa might be innocent . . ." She leaned forward and lowered her voice. "The top of my list is Violet Peterson."

Max raised his brow. He'd yet to google this judge and restaurant owner. "What do you know about her?"

"A bit of inside info from my job." She looked around the room. Besides the guy playing videos and wearing headphones, the room was still empty.

"It's a recipe for disaster if you ask me." She blew a bubble and then sucked it back in. "Michelle would fire me if she saw me chewing gum."

"What's a recipe for disaster?" he asked, urging her to continue.

"Violet owns this swanky French restaurant. You know the kind you wouldn't dare go into without a suit and tie and that I couldn't afford to go into on the salary the magazine pays me. Anyway, Norton wrote a scandalous review last year that claimed her Coquille St. Jacques and stuffed mushrooms tasted worse than an overcooked microwave dinner. It was so lethal, in fact, that Violet's lawyers served Norton legal papers claiming malice and defamation."

"Did anything come of it?"

"Not yet."

Max tapped his fingers against the desk. "Maybe it's just me, but I have a hard time believing that Norton had that much influence over people. Shutting down restaurants, owners filing for bankruptcy. . .if that were true, then half the restaurants in the country would be out of business simply because Norton didn't like their special of the day or thought there was too much salt in the soufflé."

Sarah crossed her legs, still chomping on her gum. "Look at Elvis and the Beatles, for example."

"Please don't tell me that you're comparing Norton Richards to those music legends."

"Of course not. They had real talent, but that doesn't change the fact that our society will take almost anyone and make them into an icon if they fit the need for the moment."

"So Norton appealed to people's need for what? Finding the best hamburger in town?"

She shook her head. "You definitely didn't know Norton."

"What do you mean?"

"Despite the man's gruff exterior, he really did know what he was talking about. Yes, his words could cut worse than a butcher knife, but for a top-rated review, he expected a lot and thrived on honesty no matter how brutal it might be. His reviews gave some restaurants the well-deserved publicity they needed to boost their clientele, as well."

"So you knew him?"

"You could say that." Sarah's laugh came out more like a snort.

"Meaning. . ."

"Norton Richards didn't have time for people like me. I'm too low on the ladder to be a threat and not high enough to help his career."

"You shouldn't be so hard on yourself."

"Oh, I've never minded flying under the radar. It's allowed me to get information I wouldn't otherwise be able to." She blew another bubble and let it pop. "I'm not naive enough to think I'll make it big in this industry. Fashion, food, and starting the latest craze require finesse. To get anywhere you need to either have that certain charisma or the ability to climb over people on your way to the top."

Like Michelle and Norton?

"So how did you get to know Norton?"

"I worked for him for five years before I was hired by *Food Style* magazine."

"You worked for him?" Max hadn't expected this.

"Norton doesn't do much speaking anymore. . .well, before he died he didn't. . .but besides his restaurant reviews, he used to do speaking engagements, talk shows, radio slots, and the like."

"So you were his assistant."

"Yeah." Sarah punched in an Internet address, pausing until her e-mail service popped up. "But I didn't get a degree in journalism to spend the rest of my life making appointments for other people and making sure their electric bills get paid. That's why I'm getting out."

Max quirked his left eyebrow. "Getting out?"

"I probably shouldn't tell you this, but I've written a book." She turned back to him and leaned forward. "It's a biography of sorts. Unauthorized and currently in the middle of a bidding war with two big New York publishing houses."

Murder aside, the young woman had his curiosity piqued.

She popped her gum. "It's the truth behind a certain icon of the food industry."

Now she really had his attention. "And who would that be?"

Sarah smiled. "Norton Richards."

Max crossed the lobby following the afternoon's competition, still unsure whether he should add Sarah Reynolds to the list of suspects or take her off. She didn't seem to hold animosity toward the man, but dead, Norton would have no rights of privacy, giving Sarah the freedom to write what she wanted. The advance from a bidding war could bring in a hefty amount. What if Norton had tried to stop the unauthorized book from being published? But surely if she'd killed Norton she wouldn't have wanted the information about the book to leak out. On the other hand, such information was bound to come out eventually, and maybe she thought it better to make it public before the police did.

He stopped at the Silvermist Café, wanting to make sure he'd remembered everything. With no competition during the dinner hour, he'd planned a romantic meal for Pricilla on the back deck overlooking the lake. Arriving early, he was assured that his request for a private table and flowers had been filled.

Pricilla entered the dining room five minutes behind him, wearing a deep purple jacket with black slacks. He caught her smile. Time had only managed to make her more beautiful to him. Any regrets of leaving his home in New Mexico to be with her had long since vanished.

Watching her walk across the room toward him, he was reminded that it was time to set a wedding date. He wasn't willing to wait indefinitely for all the details of selling houses and moving to be worked out. At his age, every day was a gift. A gift he intended to share with her. Norton's death had reminded him just how fleeting life really was.

He shoved any thoughts of the investigation aside. Everything he'd learned this afternoon had only managed to muddy the waters. For now he'd keep the latest details of the case to himself and focus on Pricilla, knowing she'd have her own theories to share with him anyway.

"You look beautiful." He took her hands and kissed her briefly on the lips.

Her smile widened. "After your dinner invitation, I decided I should change out of the rubber boots and look for something a bit more appealing."

"Whatever you did worked." He wrapped his arm around her waist, anticipating a quiet hour together. "There's something we need to talk about."

"Is everything all right?"

"Everything is fine," he said, leading her to the table the servers had set for them near the edge of the deck. Late afternoon rays of sunlight scattered across the lake, leaving a glowing hue above the mountains.

"So what did you do during this afternoon's competition?"

He pulled back her chair, wondering how much he should tell her. "A little research. . ."

"Research?"

He'd said the wrong thing, but he wasn't going to let her steer him that direction. Not yet, anyway. He took his seat across from her. "Nothing life-shattering. I'll tell you later about that. First things first. I haven't had enough of you to myself, and for now, I only want to focus on us."

The waitress set down two bowls in front of them. He'd ordered everything ahead of time, from the starter course to the butterflied shrimp and savory rice for the main course, to the dessert.

Pricilla frowned when she saw the creamed asparagus soup.

"It's their special of the day, with top reviews from the customers I interviewed."

She laughed, but from her expression, she wasn't buying into his reasoning.

"You're right." She held up her hand. "I'm not saying a word. This evening's about us, and speaking of us, then, I think it's time we set a date."

"For the wedding?"

"If we don't, the planning stage could go on forever. And I'm not nearly as young as I used to be."

He couldn't help but smile. His thoughts exactly. She was smiling again, too. Perhaps wedding talk would be enough of a distraction for him to get away with the high-cholesterol cheesecake he'd ordered for dessert.

Pricilla took the last bite of her cheesecake and pushed the plate aside. She'd regret finishing the slice later, especially after the huge meal Max had ordered for them, but for now, she was enjoying every minute of the evening. In the past hour, they'd settled on a date for the wedding, discussed where they would live afterward, and how much they were anticipating their children's wedding.

And not even a mention of the murder, for which she was grateful. All she had to do now was check to ensure that a December wedding didn't conflict with her friends' holiday social calendars or her work commitments at the lodge. In a few short months, she'd be Mrs. Max Summers.

She squeezed her eyes shut, picturing the quiet ceremony inside Nathan's lodge with a few select friends and family. Poinsettias for decoration, a violin quartet playing in the background. . .simple, yet elegant.

"Pricilla?"

Her eyes popped open. "Sorry. I was daydreaming about the wedding."

"We don't have to wait that long."

She felt her cheeks redden at his smile. "There's so much to do, and December is only three months away," she began.

He took a sip of his coffee. "I thought we were going to keep things small and intimate."

The word *elope* crossed her mind again. Maybe he was right. Why wait until December? All they had to do was make sure Nathan and Trisha were able to tie the knot. Then they'd be free to tie their own nuptials.

"Let's finalize the details of our wedding after Trisha and Nathan's." She still wanted to deal with the question that had been nagging at her. "You told me you did some research this afternoon."

The murder investigation might have been an off-topic subject for the last hour, but if Max had stumbled across anything important, she needed to know.

"I'll give you five minutes if you promise to go on a walk with me after supper with no mention of the case. I finally have you to myself, and the sky is clear, the stars bright—"

"Okay." Pricilla laughed as he signaled the waitress for coffee refills. There was something about being in love that made her giddy. "You don't have to convince me."

"Well, I'm not sure how much the sheriff knows, or how much he needs to know, but to put it briefly, I had an interesting conversation with Sarah."

"Michelle's assistant?"

The waitress came by with a pot of coffee and filled their cups before they continued their conversation. "Apparently she used to work for Norton."

"Really?" Max had her attention now. She hadn't expected this twist.

"But that's not all. She's just finished an unauthorized manuscript of Norton's life."

Pricilla's head began to spin as he went on to give her the details of their conversation. "Talk about fuel for the fire."

"One that's growing out of control by the minute." Max grabbed a thin stack of folded papers from his jacket pocket. "I don't know if these will help, but I did a bit of my own research today and printed out some bios of most of the main suspects."

"This is great." She set down the sugar spoon for her coffee and began thumbing through the papers. "So all we need to find out now is which suspect was willing to take the matter into his own hands by killing Norton. What about—"

"Wait a minute." Max grasped her hands, shooting a tingling sensation through her that went all the way to her toes. "I believe your five minutes are up."

The question still haunted Pricilla when she awoke the next morning. While the list of viable suspects grew by the hour, only one person had struck the fatal blow that killed Norton. So if Clarissa wasn't the perpetrator, then who was?

She rolled over in the queen-sized bed and shoved off the covers, wishing she could go back to sleep instead of facing another day in front of the cameras. She didn't have to look into the mirror to know that, with the stress of the last two days, her crow's-feet had multiplied, and the circles beneath her eyes darkened. In a world that thrived on youth and beauty, whose idea had it been to stick her in front of the camera?

And what had she been thinking when she said yes?

Pricilla shoved on her slippers and yawned. At least she'd have a chance to speak to Clarissa today. The poor girl's parents—if they even knew yet about the incarceration—must be frantic with worry. It hadn't been so long ago when Pricilla had feared that Deputy Carter was going to drag Nathan into custody during the investigation into Charles Woodruff's murder.

Trisha peeked up from the other side of her bed. "Did I wake you?"

"Trisha?" Pricilla slipped her glasses on and took a second look. "What on earth are you doing on the floor?"

Trisha disappeared behind the thick rose-colored comforter again. "I'm looking for my ring."

"I thought you lost it near the lake."

"I think I did, but I'm not ready to give up." She rounded the foot of the bed on her hands and knees, stopping in front of the dresser. "And I'm still not completely dismissing the possibility that it's in this room."

Pricilla glanced down at the carpet below her. She loved her future daughter-in-law, but there was no way she was going to attempt a search under her bed. Days of flexibility and litheness had ended more than a decade ago when she gave up yoga, and the last place she wanted to find herself was stuck in some precarious position on the floor.

Instead, she slid her robe on and rotated her neck to work out the kinks of sleeping on a too-soft bed. "Did you sleep all right?"

"Besides dreaming that the lake had turned into some huge monster with long fangs?" Trisha peered up at Pricilla beneath a row of bangs. "I still can't believe I lost the ring."

"There's still a chance it might show up."

"Maybe." Trisha dragged a chair across the floor and crawled into the empty spot behind it. "I'm afraid that even if I did drop it in here, more than likely the maid vacuumed it up."

Pricilla sensed the desperation in her voice and searched for a word of encouragement. "I doubt most maids take the time to clean all those hard-to-get spots. You know how most workers are these days."

Trisha was still inching her fingers along the floorboards of the far wall when Pricilla entered the bathroom to brush her teeth and wash her face. At some point, Trisha was going to have to face the fact that the ring was likely lost for good. That is, if the young woman's instincts were right and it had sunk to the bottom of the lake.

After brushing her teeth, Pricilla squeezed a dab of cleanser onto her hands, ran them under the water, and began her morning ritual of attempting to erase the years—a feat that so far had never been accomplished. "So what did you and Nathan do for supper last night?"

"We ended up eating with J. J. Rhymes, one of the judges, and I have to tell you, that man's a born comedian."

"Really?" Pricilla turned off the water and stepped back into the room. While J.J. was on her list of suspects to interview, she'd not yet found the opportunity to talk to the rotund restaurant owner. "What is he like?"

"For starters, he's the only person I've met so far who doesn't seem to have a bone to pick with Norton." Trisha shoved back the heavy drapes and searched along the floorboard beneath the window. "Quite the opposite, actually. Apparently they knew each other from college."

"Really?" Pricilla dabbed her face with one of the plush white towels all hotels seemed to own, wondering if the relationship between Norton and Rhymes could have any relevance to the case. "So they were friends?"

Trisha made her way toward the adjacent wall. "It didn't sound as if they celebrated Christmas or birthdays together, but J.J. claims that his business quadrupled after a five-star review from Norton this past year. Business, apparently, has never been so good."

Certainly didn't sound like a motive for murder, but if Pricilla had learned anything at all during the past two investigations she'd been involved in, it was that most people have hidden agendas. What one saw on the outside was often meant to hide the truth hovering beneath the surface, and at this point, she wasn't yet ready to dismiss anyone except Clarissa as a suspect.

Trisha stood, hands on her hips, eyeing the corner of the room like a surveyor. "He also claimed that a bad review from Norton was most always justly deserved."

"Now that's a first." Pricilla set the towel down and reached for her jar of face cream. "Everyone I've talked to insisted that the man's reviews were unfair. . .or worse. Of course, these were people who found themselves recipients of Norton's 'deadly dish' reviews. The man had to garner fans when he gave out good reviews."

"J.J. received a five-star, the highest award from Norton, so it's no wonder he's not complaining."

Pricilla added an extra layer of cream under her eyes. J.J.'s take on Norton, while not incriminating, was definitely interesting. "Did he happen to give his opinion on the murder?"

"We briefly touched on the subject. He seemed glad that Clarissa was behind bars. When I told him that the authorities had some questions as to her guilt, he reiterated that he thought the government spent far too much time trying to determine people's guilt when the evidence was clear, and in this case at least, he didn't see the need to search any further."

Words from a guilty conscious? Perhaps relief that a scapegoat now sat behind bars? Pricilla frowned. No. That was definitely stretching the situation. Still, his support for the victim did stand out in a murky sea of dislike for Norton. At this point in the investigation, anyone claiming the man was anything but a low-down weasel made an investigator stand up and take note. Time would tell whether or not there was merit to Trisha's observation.

The closet door flew open with a *thud*. Pricilla peeked out of the bathroom with a bottle of liquid base in one hand and a sponge in the other. Trisha had thrown open the closet doors and was now frantically searching the pockets of each article of clothing that was hung up.

"Trisha. . ."

"It's got to be here somewhere. I've searched under the beds, behind the dresser, along the floorboards. . ."

Pricilla set down her makeup and moved to put her hands on Trisha's shoulders. "You'll never find it this way."

Trisha sat down on the bed and combed her fingers through her hair. "I've lost it, haven't I? And I'm not talking just about the ring."

Pricilla sat down beside her. "Everything you're feeling is perfectly normal, but I have to tell you one thing."

Trisha drew her legs up toward her chest and stared at Pricilla with red-rimmed eyes. "What's that?"

"In the end none of this really matters. None of the wedding mishaps. Not even the lost ring."

Trisha's eyes widened. "But this is my wedding. The day I've dreamed of since I was seven."

"Which is exactly my point." Pricilla rushed on to clarify. "Yes, the wedding dress, honeymoon, and ring are important, but what really matters is that you and Nathan work to make yours a marriage that lasts forever. Everyone wants a spectacular wedding. Very few, it seems, want a marriage that works the way God planned."

Trisha wiped her face with the backs of her hands and laughed. "I suppose I have been a bit preoccupied with wedding details lately. I've probably been driving Nathan crazy."

"Nathan loves you."

"I know."

A woman's loud voice rose in volume from outside her room. Michelle? Sarah? She couldn't be sure. "Have you looked inside the dresser?"

"Yes."

"Under the nightstands?"

"Yes—"

A sharp knock rapped at the door, interrupting their conversation.

Pricilla tightened her robe around her waist and hurried to answer it. "Now who could that be?"

Riley stood in the doorway all smiles, looking far too perky for seven in the morning.

"Riley, I—"

"I know I should have called," she interrupted, her smile never failing. "Is Trisha here?"

"Yes." Pricilla stepped aside, and the young woman swept into the room like a tornado.

"I found it."

"You found it?" Trisha shook her head. "Found what?"

Riley dug into her front pocket and held up a ring. Trisha's ring. Pricilla's jaw fell open. Trisha stood beside her speechless as Riley pressed the missing ring into the palm of her hand.

"I don't understand."

"I got up early this morning to work on your dress and found it caught in the hem. It must have gotten wedged on the fabric and fallen off while I was altering it."

"I just can't believe it. . .thank you."

Riley laughed, her red hair bouncing over her eyes. "When I found it amidst the piles of fabric, I knew you must have been frantic, so I rushed right over here."

Trisha slid the ring on her finger and then gave Riley an energetic hug. "I can't thank you enough. And to think of all the trouble I've gotten myself into trying to find it."

"Trouble?"

Pricilla laughed. "You don't want to know."

Trisha held up her hand and stared at the diamond. "I really don't know how to thank you, Riley."

"It's not a problem. I know you must be so relieved."

Pricilla pulled a pressed suit jacket from the closet and turned to the girls. "Why don't the two of you join Max and me for breakfast downstairs?"

Riley shook her head. "Normally I'd jump at the chance, but I've got a wedding dress to finish."

"And I've got to find Nathan and tell him the news."

Pricilla pressed the outfit against her before glancing at her watch. "I'm supposed to meet him in fifteen minutes, which doesn't give me near enough time to put myself together."

Twenty minutes later Pricilla left the room, noting that Trisha couldn't keep her eyes off her ring. At least she had one good reason to smile again despite the seemingly sabotaged wedding.

Not wanting to be later than she already was, Pricilla hurried down the hall outside her room. Halfway down the narrow corridor, someone bounded out of one of the rooms behind her. She turned and cocked her head in order to see the face beneath the pile of clothes the person carried. "Sarah?"

"Mrs. Crumb. Good morning." Sarah moved a jacket aside and shot her a sheepish smile. The young woman was loaded down with clothes, books, and other paraphernalia presumably necessary for today's competition. "Michelle just called me up with a list of things she needs downstairs, including two complete changes of clothes."

"What in the world happened?"

"For starters, someone dumped a glass of grape juice down the front of her suit, and she has a meeting with the hotel manager in five minutes."

A notebook slipped from Sarah's hands, landing at Pricilla's feet. "Why don't you let me help?"

"I would appreciate it." Sarah handed Pricilla the pile of clothes and reached down to pick up the notebook. "I knew it was going to be one of those days when Charlie called before seven."

"Who's Charlie?"

Sarah repositioned the stack of books before heading down the hall again toward the elevator. "Michelle's fiancé. She tends to get a bit animated when she talks to him, especially when he doesn't do what she wants."

"So that's the ruckus I heard while I was getting dressed."

Sarah nodded. "Charlie was supposed to be here for the contest, but now he says he won't make it because he's got some gig his band has to play at."

Pricilla hurried to keep up with the younger woman. "Your job gives you the inside scoop into all kinds of things, doesn't it?"

"Yes, but too often it's information I could do without." Sarah shifted the camera strap higher up on her shoulder.

Pricilla decided to skip any follow-up on that comment. "Why the extra outfit for Michelle?"

"Just in case she needs to change quickly again. She's always been paranoid about looking just right."

"A girl Friday, I believe Max called you."

"Photographer, secretary, gopher. . .and that's just for starters." Sarah laughed, but her smile quickly faded. "I bet Mr. Summers told you about my book, too, didn't he?"

Pricilla pressed her lips together, wondering how much she wanted to admit to knowing. Surely it couldn't hurt, and if anything, she might be able to drag out more information from the girl. "Yes, he did."

"I probably shouldn't have told anyone. I realized that my confession made me look a bit. . .guilty?"

"In what way?" Pricilla asked.

Sarah stopped at the elevator and punched the DOWN button. "It won't take people long to presume that with Norton's death, I stand to make a substantial amount of money on my book, which gives me motivation. You know how death always skyrockets sales. But the truth is, writing someone's secrets isn't the same as killing someone."

Pricilla agreed with the girl's logic, but she also knew that Sarah was right about people's presumptions. If word about the book leaked out, it would definitely look suspicious. "While that might be true, I think you need to consider telling the sheriff. He'll take it better hearing it from you than hearing it elsewhere as a rumor."

"I suppose you're right. If it wasn't for the sheriff's orders to stick around, I'd be gone. Michelle made me so angry yesterday, I threatened to quit. Somehow she made me promise to stay. For now, anyway."

"Max said you are planning to quit as soon as the book deal goes through?"

"And not a moment later."

The elevator doors finally slid open. Pricilla stepped into the empty elevator behind Sarah.

"Thanks so much for helping. I couldn't have done it without you."

The elevator door slid shut. While that probably wasn't true, Pricilla decided to take advantage of the girl's gratitude. Hopefully Sarah wouldn't regret her candid conversation. "I've heard rumors that Michelle had once been romantically involved with Norton."

"Very briefly, but yes. It's a fact I've been debating whether or not to tell the authorities. As much as Michelle drives me crazy, I'd never want to see her get into trouble. They had this love-hate relationship, though honestly,

I think the bottom line was that Michelle wanted to stay on his good side. The exclusive interviews and restaurant critiques he did for the magazine always boosted readership and made Michelle look good."

"Did something go sour between them?"

"A couple months ago, rumors began circulating that the popular column Michelle had been trying to get was going to be given to Norton. Michelle's always wanted her own syndicated column, and this one had the potential to reach millions."

Pricilla whistled as the elevator shuddered to a stop. Michelle's motivation to get rid of Norton had just doubled.

"And there is one other thing."

Pricilla pushed the Close Door button before the elevator doors could open. "What's that?"

"I really don't want Michelle to get into trouble, but. . ." Sarah hesitated. "The night Norton died, he'd called Michelle's room, and after five minutes or so of fighting, Michelle left the room in a huff. I only know this because I was in her room going over the next day's schedule with her."

"Did she leave to go and see Norton?" Pricilla asked.

"That I don't know. But I do know that she left around ten and didn't return until just after midnight."

"Sounds pretty suspicious to me."

"Maybe, but the truth is, as much as the woman drives me crazy, I can't see her murdering anyone."

"Given the right circumstances, one never knows."

Pricilla was still mulling over her latest bit of information when the sheriff flagged her down in the lobby.

"I see I'm not the only one up and about early." The sheriff hurried across the room. "Any news for me?"

"A few tidbits that might interest you."

"As in. . ."

"Michelle had a fight with Norton the night of the murder."

The sheriff rubbed his chin. "She should have told me. That's quite an oversight on her part."

"Yes, she should have."

He glanced at his watch. "Are you still planning to visit Clarissa today?"

"I have a two-hour lunch break starting at noon. Max was planning to drive me into town then."

"Good." He nodded his head and tugged on the edge of his jacket. "I'm meeting with Miss Vanderbilt now—and I'll be sure and ask her about the fight she had with Norton—then I'm heading back to the station with some information."

"Wait, Sheriff." Pricilla wasn't letting him go yet. "What kind of information?"

The sheriff glanced around the lobby. Besides the front desk clerk, the room was empty. Still, he leaned forward and lowered his voice. "We just finished inventorying Clarissa's kitchen."

Pricilla's brow furrowed. From the look on the sheriff's face, it was clear that whatever they'd found, it wasn't good.

"There was one thing missing, but please don't repeat it, as this kind of evidence will end up being crucial to the case."

Pricilla's frown deepened. He was hedging around his answers. It was time to be more direct. "What was missing?"

"A nine-inch knife, identical to the one you found in the lake."

10

Pricilla tapped her hands against the table and waited beside Max for Clarissa to enter the visiting room. She didn't want to worry about the sheriff's announcement concerning the missing knife because, the truth was, anyone could have lifted it from Clarissa's kitchen. But that did little to stop her apprehension. At least the young woman's parents had finally been contacted and were on their way to Colorado. Until they arrived, Pricilla hoped to be a familiar face that could ease some of Clarissa's fears.

One of the deputies opened the door to the small, square room that held nothing more besides tables and chairs for meetings between the prisoners and their families and friends. Clarissa hesitated briefly in the doorway and then entered.

"Mrs. Crumb. I can't thank you enough for coming." She crossed the room and collapsed into the chair across from them.

Her face was pale and her features strained. Whatever the outcome of the case, this experience would change her forever.

"I'm sorry you've had to go through this." Pricilla reached out and squeezed Clarissa's hands. "How are you?"

"Numb. . .worried. . .terrified." The young woman wiped away a tear.

Pricilla nodded to Max. "You remember meeting Max Summers the opening night of the contest."

"Yes, of course, though it seems like a hundred years ago." Clarissa toyed with the end of her ponytail. "It's nice to see you again, Mr. Summers."

"Please call me Max. It's good to see you again as well, though I'm sorry it's not under better circumstances. Pricilla told me about you. All good things."

Clarissa's gaze dropped to the table. "I bet she never imagined having to add my arrest to her repertoire of stories."

Pricilla caught the bitterness in her voice. "Clarissa—"

"I didn't do it, Mrs. Crumb." Clarissa pulled away her hand and tensed her jaw. "I didn't kill Mr. Richards."

"I know, sweetie. That's why we're here."

Her eyes widened. "So you really believe me?"

"I've known you since you were five. I realize that people change and that it's been awhile since I've seen you, but yes, I believe you. You have too much of a heart for people to hurt anyone."

Clarissa's frown deepened. "Try convincing the sheriff of that."

"He wants to help you. It's his job to ensure that the truth is known. And I honestly believe he's doing everything in his power to do just that."

She knotted her fingers together. "But you'll help me, too?"

Max chuckled. "She's already on the case. Pricilla has spent the past forty-eight hours trying to find anything that might lead to who killed Norton."

"Really?" Clarissa's lips curled into a half smile, but even that couldn't erase her hollow expression.

"Really. You're in good hands."

Pricilla felt her cheeks redden as she glanced at Max, knowing it took a lot for him to admit she was involved when he preferred her anywhere else but knee-deep in the middle of a murder mystery.

Clarissa's eyes brightened slightly. "So what have you found out so far?"

Pricilla didn't want to see the light in the young woman's eyes dim again, but everything she had at the moment was inconclusive. She had to start somewhere. "What I've learned is that half of the people involved in the contest had a grudge against Norton. The hardest part isn't going to be finding someone with a motive. It's going to be finding the right motive."

"I can believe that." Clarissa groaned. "I heard a number of the contestants griping when they heard Norton was going to be one of the judges."

"Something that doesn't surprise me at all." Pricilla pulled out her notebook, ready to get to work. "First off, I understand you have a lawyer, right?"

Clarissa nodded. "He's an old family friend who flew in from Seattle yesterday."

"Good. Now you know I want to help in any way I can, but I need you to tell me everything. And I need it to be the truth."

"Okay." Clarissa nodded.

Pricilla tapped her pen against her notebook. "Had you met Norton before this weekend?"

"No. Well, not in person, that is."

Pricilla glanced at Max who looked as intrigued with the conversation as she was. "What do you mean?"

Clarissa rubbed her fingers together. "About two years ago, Norton wrote a review for the restaurant I was working at."

"You were working the night he ate there?"

"Yes. I was a sous chef, working for Jake Filbert at the time."

"I've heard of him."

"He's a wonderful chef, and Norton's review was unwarranted."

"I've heard that while his reviews could be brutal, they were also honest."

"There was nothing honest about this review. Norton complained unendingly about the bland appetizers, tasteless main course, and heavy dessert. Not a word he said was true."

Pricilla pressed her lips together. "Do you think your loyalty to the restaurant could have made your reaction a bit biased?"

Clarissa shook her head. "I believe Norton had a personal vendetta against Jake."

"Why?"

"Jake and Norton went to school together twenty-odd years ago, and they both had dreams to make it big in the industry as chefs. The year they graduated, Jake was admitted into one of Europe's most prestigious cooking schools. Norton wasn't accepted. According to some, he never got over the blow. In the end, Norton found greater success, but grudges can run deep."

"Do you have any proof that Norton meant the review as revenge?" Pricilla asked while scribbling a few notes. There was no use interviewing people if she forgot all the details tomorrow.

"Unfortunately, no. The only thing I could do was write a letter to the editor of the newspaper, but all my efforts ended up backfiring in the end."

"What do you mean?"

"Jake decided that my letter added to the bad publicity and used it as an excuse to fire me."

"Despite his problems with Norton?"

"I tried to ask Jake, but he refused to talk about it. At that point, anything I said would be nothing more than a pile of accusations that I can't substantiate."

"So what happened after you got fired?"

"I found another position eventually, but the damage had been done, especially with my name mentioned in Norton's write-up. I was lucky to have a chance to even participate in the contest, but now, after being arrested for murder. . .well. . .I probably won't be able to find work flipping hamburgers. So much for the chance of winning a scholarship and starting afresh."

Pricilla set down her notebook. Why was it that there were always more questions than answers? "So you saw this contest as a chance to escape from the past and move ahead?"

"Exactly."

"How much does the sheriff know about all of this?"

"He knows about my letter to the editor and my being fired. It seems as if the entire legal system is trying to use the incident as a motive for murder." Clarissa winced. "Which I suppose I can't blame them for. I know it looks bad, but on the other hand this was two years ago. If I'd wanted to knock the guy off, wouldn't I have done it a long time ago?"

"Maybe, but in the end, all it really proves is that you had a bone to pick with Norton like all the rest of them. It doesn't mean you killed him." Pricilla glanced at her notes. She needed more. "What about the other contestants?

Do you know of other motives any of them might have?"

Clarissa's laugh rang hollow. "No one was thrilled to have Norton on the panel of judges, but that doesn't mean they killed him. Myself included."

Max shook his head. "Well, someone killed him."

"And that someone is on the loose." Clarissa shuddered. "I've got to get out of here, but they won't let me go until they get enough evidence to arrest someone else."

"Half the people at that contest have a motive," Pricilla said.

Max leaned back and shook his head. "How in the world could one man have made so many enemies?"

"Greed. . .selfishness. . .pride. . .you name it. Though you have to give the guy some credit. He was the top in his field, and most people took his reviews seriously." Clarissa clasped her hands in front of her. "The question is, what do we do now?"

Pricilla wished she had a more concrete strategy. For now, all she could do was continue keeping her eyes and ears open. "I'll keep interviewing the other contestants and trying to find out as much information as I can. At some point, someone will slip. In fact, we've already found a few discrepancies in several stories. Now it's a matter of sorting through them and finding out which are actually relevant to the case. In the meantime, I'd say that the biggest hole in the case against you is the problem of the missing murder weapon. Trisha and I found a knife in the lake that more than likely is the murder weapon."

"In the lake?" Clarissa's eyes widened.

"It's a long story." Pricilla's gaze shifted to Max, but he was staring straight ahead, making her wonder if he was avoiding her gaze because he was still unhappy about her jaunt in the lake or if he was simply trying not to laugh over the way she'd emerged looking more like a drowned rat than Sherlock Holmes. She cleared her throat. "The bottom line is that you couldn't have been two places at once."

"You're talking about the knife they discovered missing from my kitchen?"

Pricilla nodded. "Just because it was from your kitchen doesn't prove you took it. We all know that while access to the kitchens was supposed to be restricted, it wouldn't have been difficult. And for one of the other contestants, it would have been a snap."

"You keep talking about the contestants. Have you thought about one of the judges, someone from the audience, or even the hotel staff for that matter?"

"At this point I'd say it could be anyone."

Clarissa lowered her chin and stared at the table. "But in the end, I was the one standing over Mr. Richards's body. That's the kind of evidence no one can ignore."

"Maybe, but if that knife proves to be the murder weapon, they will have to release you. How could the murderer be found standing over the victim and the weapon be half a mile away at the same time? The entire scenario is impossible."

"Maybe."

Pricilla felt as if she were grasping for straws and didn't like it. "There are no *maybes* about it. And we'll prove it."

"I do appreciate your help, Mrs. Crumb." Clarissa stood to leave. "If there is anything. . .anything at all that I can do, please tell me."

"You just keep praying that this will all be over soon."

"I hope so."

"Mark my words."

The deputy entered the room. Their time with Clarissa might be over, but Pricilla was far from finished with her investigation.

Once outside, she slid into the front seat beside Max and leaned back, the fatigue of the past few days washing over her like a bad dream.

Max started the engine and eased out of the parking lot into the light traffic that filtered down Main Street. "So what do you think? Do you still believe she's innocent?"

"Without a doubt, though our talk with her did manage to raise more questions than it answered. First of all, I want to know more about Jake Filbert, Clarissa's old boss. Sounds to me as if the man had a reason to have a vendetta against Norton."

"Seems pretty straightforward to me. Norton wrote a bad review because he was jealous of Jake, Clarissa wrote a letter, and Jake fired her for writing it—probably she didn't clear it with him first. Seems nothing more to me than another red herring and not an actual clue into Norton's death."

"I suppose you have a point."

"I personally think we should stick to those who are actually here at the contest."

Pricilla smiled despite the heavy fatigue she felt. He'd said "we." She liked the sound of that. She glanced at Max's profile and wondered how she'd ever thought that she was too old to fall in love again. While love might have a few extra complications the second time around, it was still worth it.

Max braked at the stoplight and tapped his fingers against the steering wheel. "Do you mind if we run by the pharmacy on the way back to the lodge?"

"Of course not." Pricilla noted the sign in the next block flashing LINDA'S DRUGSTORE and felt a ping of worry strike. "Are you all right?"

Max muttered something under his breath as he pulled through the intersection.

"What did you say?"

"Antacids." He gripped the steering wheel and avoided her gaze. "I need some more antacids."

"Antacids?" Pricilla started to shoot him an I-told-you-so glare but stopped. While the man had insisted on indulging in every rich, creamy, and fattening item on the menu the past two days, he'd also managed to make it clear at the sheriff's office that he was on her side. Perhaps he deserved a bit of leeway after all.

She nodded. "Of course we can stop. We have time."

Max pulled into the parking lot and parked. Pricilla hurried with him into the store, wondering how many other people staying for the contest had dropped into the same store for a bottle of antacids because of all the rich foods. The small store had four or five neatly arranged aisles boasting everything from first aid products, over-the-counter medicines, and a variety of health aids. Pricilla stopped and pulled Max behind a large cardboard model promoting a new line of low-carb, ready-to-drink shakes and supplements. On any other day, she might be tempted to add a box or two to the basket she'd grabbed on the way in, but in light of what she'd just seen in aisle three, calorie counting was the last thing on her mind.

Max pulled his arm away from her grip. "What is it?"

"Up ahead." She jutted her chin toward the next aisle.

"Why are we hiding? It's just Michelle—"

"Shh." She peeked around the cardboard model's bulky bicep before grabbing Max's arm again and pulling him next to her. "She's not alone."

Michelle stood beside a row of cold medicines, talking in hushed tones to a man. Late thirties, graying goatee, five-foot-seven at the most. It was the way Michelle stood that made Pricilla assume that this conversation was more than just an encounter with a friend at the store. She tried to make out what they were saying but couldn't follow the garbled whispers.

"Maybe it's a boyfriend," Max said.

Pricilla shook her head. "Sarah told me this morning that Michelle has a fiancé, but he's not supposed to be in town. We've got to get closer so we can hear what they are saying."

"Pricilla—"

She ignored his warning and slid past the bronze hunk until she was partly masked behind a shelf of diet pills. She paused to listen. Still too far away.

"Pricilla."

She swung her elbow around sharply to jab him to be quiet. Too sharply. She gasped. A display of diet drinks tumbled from the shelf, smacking the floor loudly before scattering in every direction.

Michelle's chin jerked up. One can rolled across the shiny surface and stopped at Pricilla's feet. She searched for the source of the commotion. Pricilla wanted to hide, but it was too late. Mr. Muscle tipped over, leaving her—and Max—exposed.

And looking completely guilty.

Another drink teetered on the shelf before plunging to the floor. It burst open against the tile floor and splattered as it rolled across the aisle, spraying chocolate across the bottom of Pricilla's skirt.

Great.

"Mrs. Crumb?"

"Michelle. You. . .you startled me."

"I startled *you*?" Michelle glanced up at her companion and then back to Pricilla as if she wasn't sure what to make of the situation.

"Cleanup in aisle three," boomed over the loudspeaker. Pricilla spotted a back door that presumably led outside and wondered if anyone would notice if she sneaked out of the store. Probably. She glanced behind her. Where was Max?

She might as well take advantage of the situation. "I haven't met your friend."

"My friend. . ." Michelle glanced at the man. "No. . .he's not. . .we both just happened to be buying. . .cold medicine. I asked him which brand he recommended."

"Yes. Cold medicine." The man sneezed before grabbing a box of cold medicine and striding away toward the cashier.

"Cold medicine?" Pricilla repeated.

Michelle coughed. "Some brands will actually prevent a cold if you catch it early enough. I can't get sick right now, you know."

Pricilla frowned. The woman was lying.

"You're not sick, are you?" Michelle asked.

Changing the subject?

"Sick. . .no. Of course not. I'm here with Max. He needed some antacids." Pricilla forced a smile as she stepped out of the way of the young clerk who'd been assigned to clean up the aisle and mumbled her apologies. "You know how it is with all the rich foods we've been sampling."

"I wouldn't know, actually. I've been having the kitchen prepare my own low-fat meals."

Pricilla nodded, not surprised at all with the confession.

"We start again in just over an hour," Michelle reminded her.

"And I'll be ready."

"Good. I don't think I can handle any more surprises."

Pricilla didn't want to handle any more surprises either, but neither was she quite ready to end the conversation. "I can't imagine how difficult the past two days have been for you, as the director of the competition, in losing both a judge and one of the contestants."

A hint of fatigue showed beneath Michelle's eyes. "Out of all the things I imagined going wrong, murder never once popped into the picture."

"I don't suppose it would." Pricilla swallowed. It was time to push for answers. "I understand, though, that you had a fight with Norton the night of the murder."

Michelle's face paled. "That sounds like another accusation, Mrs. Crumb."

"Not at all." Pricilla prayed she hadn't just pushed the woman too far. "I just thought it interesting that you had a fight with the victim the night he was killed and never told the sheriff."

"Not that it's any of your business, but Norton and I were fighting over the show's credits. He believed his name should be highlighted on the rolling credits at the end."

"What did you do after the fight?"

"That's none of your business, Mrs. Crumb. But Norton and I fighting isn't exactly headline news. Anyone who knows me also knows that Norton and I never got along."

"Never?"

Michelle's knuckles whitened as she grasped her shopping basket tighter. "What are you implying now?"

"I understood that at one time you and Norton were. . .how shall I put it . . .more than friends."

Michelle took a step back. "I've done what I had to do to get where I am. Hiring him for this job was no different. I knew he'd boost the ratings."

"Which might have worked if he hadn't been murdered."

"It did work." Michelle smiled for the first time. "In an odd sort of way, hiring him became the one bright side of all this mess."

Max appeared beside Pricilla with a box of antacids. "The bright side of what?"

"With the murder of Norton Richards, the show's received more publicity than I ever imagined." Michelle's smile spread into a wide smirk. "It's a bit of poetic justice in a way, if you ask me."

"Meaning?" Pricilla asked.

"That something good actually came from Norton's death."

Pricilla frowned. "Well, I for one have a hard time imagining murder ever having a bright side."

"Ratings are up by 25 percent."

"Well. . .that's good." Or so she thought. It was a bit difficult to care about ratings with a man dead and Clarissa sitting in jail.

"One hour, Mrs. Crumb. And don't be late."

Pricilla glanced at Michelle's basket as she walked away—without a box of cold medicine. "That was strange. She was actually happy, in a weird sort of way."

"So what do you think?" Max asked. "That Michelle killed Norton in order to boost ratings?"

"Weirder things have happened."

*Still. . .*Pricilla frowned. *Surely Michelle wouldn't have sabotaged the show by getting rid of Norton no matter how mad the man made her. Or would she?* Despite Michelle's innocent stance, the murder had brought the competition into the spotlight. Perhaps that had been her plan all the time. Killing two birds with one stone.

Pricilla fastened her seat belt before leaning back against the seat and closing her eyes. The sun filtering through the window felt warm against her face but did little to ease the chill of reality that swept over her from the constant reminders of Norton's untimely death. Her lip twitched. For a moment, she was there again. Clarissa stood over Norton's body. Red blood. A scream. . .

She popped open her eyes. Closing them only brought back the scene. Something she didn't want to experience again. Instead, she stared out the window at the passing aspen trees, dwarfed by the majestic mountains behind them, and forced her mind to think in another direction. But no matter how hard she tried, the normally vibrant spring mountainside blurred into muted colors and took her in directions she didn't want to go. She glanced over at Max, who clenched the steering wheel hard enough to make his knuckles turn white. Chin set, jaw taut, gaze pointed straight ahead. She knew the situation had him on edge. He wasn't the only one. What if she'd gotten everything wrong? What if Clarissa had actually killed Norton?

No. No matter what the DA thought, she refused to believe Clarissa was guilty. Call it gut instinct, or simple intuition, but she hadn't lived sixty-five years without picking up a thing or two about human nature. She knew she was right. The police might have a monopoly on forensics and lab reports, and she'd be the first to admit that their scientific tactics made sense, but there were times when a routine investigation missed the subtle interactions, background, and volatile relationships of a suspect. And that was where she came into the picture.

Certain she was headed in the right direction, Pricilla shifted her thoughts to Michelle. "You know that woman was lying."

The car's tires grated against the gravel as Max turned onto the road leading toward the lodge. "Who's lying? Michelle?"

Pricilla nodded.

Max shrugged. "Maybe the guy was a boyfriend, and for whatever reason, she didn't want anyone to know. It makes sense. The press has taken an interest in her and the show, and while she seems to enjoy the publicity, I can understand her wanting to keep her personal life out of the limelight."

"So they arrange a secret rendezvous in the cold-remedy section of the local pharmacy?" She definitely wasn't buying that line of thinking. From what she knew about Michelle, the woman would take publicity in any shape or form. "Doesn't seem likely. Besides, apparently Michelle is engaged to some guy named Charlie. Sarah said that he called this morning to tell her that he wasn't going to be able to make it. He's playing some gig down south."

Max's brows rose. "A gig?"

"Apparently he's a musician."

"I know what a gig is. I just can't see Michelle, of all people, married to a drummer, or some electric guitar player. But either way, isn't there a possibility that Charlie changed his mind and decided to come?"

"I suppose." While Pricilla wasn't ready to entirely dismiss the boyfriend angle, that didn't seem likely.

"There's also another alternative."

"What's that?"

"Maybe the man was really who she said he was. Someone she ran into and asked advice on which was the better cold medicine."

Pricilla sighed. Of course he was probably right. All she'd managed to do was turn a typical encounter with a stranger into some top-secret meeting between two murder suspects.

"And you know that makes more sense than your clandestine meeting. If you start looking for trouble in every direction, then all you'll be doing is throwing another log onto an already out-of-control bonfire. Who that man was really isn't any of our business."

"You would be right except for the fact that we are in the middle of a murder investigation, and Michelle has already lied about her past relationship with Norton. I still think she has something to hide."

The gate to the lodge came into view, and Max slowed down. "I have to admit that I agree with you on that account, but your responsibility is simply to tell the sheriff what you saw and let him take it from there. That was the deal, remember?"

"Max—"

"No. All you are to do is pass on information. Sheriff Lewis is perfectly capable of doing the rest."

"I suppose." How many times was she going to have to back down and admit that he was right? Hadn't she gotten herself into enough trouble the past few days? Still, there was one thing she wouldn't forget. Clarissa was innocent, which meant there was still a murderer on the loose.

Five minutes later, Pricilla left Max in the lobby of the lodge and took the elevator to the second floor, wishing she didn't have yet another contest to emcee tonight. While she'd looked forward to the opportunity for months, Norton's death had managed to strip all the excitement from the event. And seeing Clarissa in jail had put an additional negative spin on things as well. She was now more determined than ever to ensure the young woman was found innocent, but with a growing pool of suspects, the truth seemed more and more evasive.

Pricilla stepped out of the elevator and stopped. Sarah stood in front of her, her arms loaded with books, files, and an expensive-looking silver cashmere sweater.

For the first time since she'd met the young girl Friday, Sarah's perky smile appeared forced. "So we meet again, Mrs. Crumb."

Pricilla shot her a sympathetic gaze. The young woman's work, it seemed, never ended. "I am sensing a bit of déjà vu."

Sarah's laugh rang as flat as her smile. "Michelle just called. We still have just under an hour until the next competition, but she's already got me rushing around."

"Maybe she's running behind. I saw her a few minutes ago in town." Pricilla decided to test the waters. "I thought you told me that Michelle's fiancé wasn't coming."

Sarah's eyes widened. "He's not."

"So he didn't change his mind and decide to show up?"

Sarah managed to reposition her glasses on the bridge of her nose with a swipe of her hand. "Far as I know, he's still in Texas. Trust me, if Charlie was coming I'd know. That six-foot-four cowboy doesn't make an entrance without a certain amount of fanfare, even if most of it is a figment of his own imagination."

"Six-foot-four cowboy?" That answered that question. Whoever Michelle had been with definitely wasn't Charlie.

Sarah shifted the load in her arms and eyed the elevator that had just closed. "Is there a problem?"

"No, of course not."

Pricilla pushed the button to open the door for Sarah, wondering how much information she should disclose. Considering the young woman was in the midst of negotiating an unauthorized biography about Norton, Sarah might be a great source of information, but Pricilla refused to be another conduit for gossip.

"It's nothing, really." Pricilla decided to drop the subject for now. "I'm sure she just must be disappointed."

The doors slid open and Sarah stepped into the doorway. "Trust me. Michelle can handle disappointment. Her skin's as tough as an alligator's."

Or so she wanted everyone to think.

Pricilla gnawed on her lip as the doors shut again, wondering what her next move should be. A glance down at her skirt gave her the answer she was looking for. She hadn't planned to change, but after her encounter with the milkshake mix on aisle three, it was necessary. Not that it really mattered. She was in the mood for something more subdued than the colorful silk blouse and deep purple skirt and jacket. Pulling the key card from her bag, she drew in a deep breath. She needed to put Michelle out of her mind for now, change her clothes, freshen up, and finish the day's last contest. Surely she could do that, though she had no idea how she was going to focus on her role as emcee when there was a murder to solve.

Pricilla shoved open the door. Trisha stood in the middle of the room dressed in her wedding dress with its ripples of glossy fabric around the floor while Riley made adjustments on a sleeve.

"Mrs. Crumb. It's good to see you again." Riley pulled a straight pin from her mouth and smiled.

"It's nice to see you, Riley, as well. It looks as if you're almost done with the gown."

"It's beautiful, isn't it?" Trisha's smile widened.

"One more fitting and I think we'll be finished. Trisha and I decided to change the drape a bit, and I wanted to make sure everything still fit correctly. We don't want any last-minute surprises, you know."

"You're right about that." Pricilla chuckled and set her bag down on the desk.

She crossed the room toward her closet, unable to keep her eyes off the gown. She stopped midway on the thick carpet. "It really is stunning, Riley. Absolutely stunning."

Trisha's dreamy smile spoke volumes. "I told Riley I was going to feel like a genuine princess on my wedding day because of her."

"Which is exactly how you should feel. Young, beautiful, and glamorous."

Pricilla laughed. "I'm glad someone in the room feels both young and beautiful at the same time. Enjoy it."

Riley took a step back and hit the bedside table, knocking her pair of shears to the floor.

Pricilla reached to pick them up and then ran her hand across the material. It was time she found something to wear at her own wedding. Up until now, she'd focused all her energy on her job at the lodge and helping Trisha with the unending details of her and Nathan's wedding. Maybe she could find time for a day trip into Denver during the next couple of weeks. While Trisha's gown was far too elaborate for what Pricilla wanted, there was no reason she couldn't find something simple, yet at the same time, beautiful.

Riley took a step back from Trisha's slender form. "Do you like it, Mrs. Crumb?"

"Do I like it? It's exquisite. I was just thinking about my own wedding and how I need to start looking for my own dress in the next few weeks."

"There's no reason why you can't have something just as beautiful." Riley made another small tuck before slipping a straight pin into the top of the sleeve. "If you ask me, beauty is timeless."

"Maybe Riley could design something for you, Mom."

Pricilla smiled at the term of endearment Trisha had begun calling her. "At sixty-five, I don't think I need something quite this. . .fancy, but it is time I found a dress."

In fact, there were still dozens of details left to be worked out—and just a month before the wedding! She felt a rush of adrenaline. She might be sixty-five, but that was no reason for her not to look forward to her own upcoming nuptials.

Riley set down her pin cushion. "I'd offer to make you a dress, but starting next week I have an entire wedding party to outfit. I'm going to have my hands full for the next few weeks."

Thoughts of eloping flittered through Pricilla's mind once again. Maybe it wasn't such a bad idea. A trip to the notary public might sound a bit unromantic, but the bottom line was that a marriage was far more important than the actual wedding ceremony. What she was looking forward to was the companionship that came with marriage. Marty had been that for so many years, and it was something she missed. Max had managed to not only fill that need, but the emptiness in her heart, as well.

Pricilla pulled a cinnamon brown pantsuit from the closet and headed for the bathroom. "If the two of you will excuse me, I need to change for my last spot as emcee for the night."

"Is it going all right?" Riley turned from the dress and caught Pricilla's gaze. "What I mean is, with a murder taking place right here. . .well. . .it has to change the dynamics of the event, even if the murderer is behind bars."

"That's the problem, he's not!"

"He's not?"

"The murderer. He. . .she. . .I don't know who it is at this point, but it's not Clarissa."

Riley's eyes widened. "You sound certain."

"I am."

"That's exactly what we've been discussing." Trisha ran her painted fingernails along the bodice of her dress. "I told Riley about our excursion in the lake and the knife."

"Any other new developments?" Riley asked.

"No. Not really." Pricilla sat down on the edge of the bed, her plans to change clothes momentarily postponed. She wasn't ready to mention her suspicions about Michelle, at least not to anyone other than the sheriff. More than likely, Max was right, and she was following a dead end. "I'm just worried about Clarissa. I visited her in jail today and the poor girl is at her wit's end."

"I can't imagine what she's going through," Trisha said. "Especially if she's innocent. Can you imagine being accused of something you didn't do, then end up having to go to jail because of it?"

Pricilla shuddered. No, she couldn't. The closest she'd ever come to the inside of a prison cell was when she'd borrowed—or rather, stolen—an ATV from the rental shop in Rendezvous. At the moment, the impulsive act had seemed necessary. Looking back, she knew there had to have been a better way to deal with the situation, which was a viewpoint that both Detective Carter and Max had made very clear to her.

Pricilla got up and hurried down to the lobby in better spirits. With Trisha's wedding taken care of, it was time to concentrate on herself and Max. Something she planned to do just as soon as this contest was over.

The sheriff caught her on her way down the hall. "Mrs. Crumb. I was just on my way out. Do you have a minute?"

Pricilla glanced at her watch. "I'm not due in front of the camera for another twenty minutes, but I can't be late this time. I'm hoping that our finding the knife in the lake will help Clarissa's case, but Michelle wasn't impressed with my appearance after I fell into the lake."

"I'm sorry about that." The lawman fiddled with the brim of his hat between his hands. "But I still owe you a tremendous thanks for what you did."

"Do you think the knife will help Clarissa's case?"

"I hope so."

"You hope so?" Pricilla fought back the frustration. While she understood that there could be no guarantees at this point, she'd thought the evidence would tip things more in Clarissa's favor. "You don't sound very positive."

"We're certain now that the knife you found came from Clarissa's kitchen."

"Which doesn't prove she killed Norton."

"No. And you're right in that it should help her case. If the knife had been found closer to the crime scene, things would probably be more cut-and-dried. As it is, the DA realizes that there was no way for Clarissa to kill Norton and dispose of the knife so far away."

As much as she didn't want to, Pricilla had to ask another question. "What about the possibility that she killed him, disposed of the knife, and then returned to make it look like she didn't do it?"

"The coroner believes there wouldn't have been time for her to kill him, throw the knife in the lake, and return to the point where you saw her standing over him."

"Then that should be our proof. Right?"

"Or, according to the DA, it implies that someone else was involved. Her lawyer is doing everything he can to get her released because of lack of evidence, but in the end we may be looking at a trial." The sheriff's expression tightened. "Any news for me?"

"There are a couple of things I'm worried about." A small group Pricilla had noticed from the contest's audience entered the lobby, making a lot of noise. Pricilla followed the sheriff down the empty, long hallway toward the Great Room to ensure they were out of earshot from anyone. "There have been more instances where I believe Michelle has been lying."

"You've got my attention."

Pricilla shared with the sheriff her concerns about Michelle.

The sheriff paused halfway down the hallway and shoved his hands into his front pockets. "It's not a crime to lie about who you're talking to, but in the case of her not disclosing her relationship to Norton, I am concerned. Maybe it's nothing more than her being embarrassed, but in a murder investigation, that's no excuse for lying."

"I definitely agree."

Withholding evidence and lying to the authorities were things Michelle would know were serious offenses. Had her lies sprouted from a guilty conscience? Or had they surfaced because of fear that her relationship with Norton would be seen as a motive to kill him?

"How did you find Clarissa?"

Pricilla noted the genuine concern in the man's voice as they started walking again. At least he seemed to believe in Clarissa's innocence. "Understandably, this has not been easy for her. She's a small-town girl way out of her league. I'm worried about her."

"So am I."

This time Pricilla heard a catch in the sheriff's voice. Something wasn't right. This wasn't simply another case for the sheriff.

"What is it? Is this case personal for you?"

The sheriff glanced behind him and then stopped again. "I'm not sure. . . ."

"What is it?"

"You're right that this case has become too personal. I've asked a colleague of mine to take it over for me."

"Why? Clarissa needs someone who believes in her."

"I know. The fact is, though, there's a problem with my working the case. Clarissa. . . I should have volunteered to step aside immediately, but I couldn't have Clarissa found guilty for something I know she didn't do." The sheriff combed his fingers through his hair. "Clarissa is my daughter from my first marriage."

The sheriff's confession caught Pricilla completely off guard. On the other hand, the man had seemed overly anxious to ensure that Clarissa wasn't convicted for Norton's murder. Now she knew why.

The sheriff's gaze darted to the floor in what she interpreted as a moment of regret over the admission. Or perhaps his guilty expression had more to do with regrets over the past. She pressed her lips together, determined to give him a moment to compose his thoughts while at the same time wishing she could remember what Clarissa's mother had told her about her first husband. Back then, she'd never expected to meet the man, let alone work with him, even if it was only in an unofficial capacity. Which was probably exactly why he'd been willing for her to help in the first place.

The sheriff cleared his throat and slowly raised his head until he caught her gaze. Pain, guilt, and remorse mingled in his eyes. "Clarissa was five months old when her mother and I divorced. It was. . .and still is. . .a moment I've spent my entire life regretting."

Pricilla glanced down the hallway to make certain no one was in earshot of their conversation. The staff was already preparing for the next competition in the Great Room, but their attention wasn't focused on the decades-old confessions of Sheriff Lewis. "Do you want to tell me what happened?"

He leaned against the wall, drew in a deep breath, and then let it out slowly. "Judy and I had been married three months when she found out we were expecting. We'd wanted kids, but not for several years. At the time, I didn't know if I should be angry, or happy. . .or what."

"It must have been a very stressful time for both of you."

"Yeah. You could say that."

His tanned brow furrowed as he motioned toward a set of glass doors and beyond, to a bench surrounded by rows of lush plants. Pricilla glanced at her watch. Clarissa was certainly a priority over the current food competition, but that didn't erase her concern of not fulfilling her commitment to Michelle. Thankfully, she still had a few minutes before the next contest.

He opened the door, and they stepped out into the breezy afternoon air. The sun sparkled against the water that lay below the majestic Rocky Mountains, but for now, she was more interested in what Sheriff Lewis had to say than the stunning view. A counseling session with law enforcement was the last thing she'd expected today.

He rotated his hat in his hand and sat down beside her on the bench. "I was trying to get into the police academy; she was working as a secretary. At first, even with the unexpected pregnancy, it didn't seem to matter that we were poor and living on macaroni and cheese. What's the old saying? Love covers a multitude of *sins*?"

Pricilla frowned at the emphasized word. "Sins?"

He glanced up at her. "Unfortunately, it's not always true."

"What do you mean?"

The sheriff stared at a group of lean aspen trees. "I've always said that the discipline of four years in the military and a career in law enforcement have been my salvation, but before that, I grew up with a bit of a temper and didn't have it under control when I married Judy. Losing her wasn't the first time my impulsiveness got me into trouble."

Pricilla winced. The confession struck too close to home. She'd fought her own battles with impulsiveness and almost lost Max in the process. What was it about human nature that made one tend to choose the wayward path?

His blue eyes seemed to pierce right through her. "Have you ever accused someone of doing something they didn't do?"

She hesitated at the question. "I don't know. I'm sure I have."

"I started drinking from stress, until one afternoon I lost my temper and accused Judy of seeing someone else. That the baby wasn't mine." The following pause was full of emotion. "I'd been jealous of her boss's attention, and while it had bordered on inappropriate, I never asked for her side of the story. Things got out of hand during that discussion and accusations flared. The bottom line was that I hadn't trusted her. She never forgave me for that."

"I'm so sorry."

"So am I. My impulsiveness lost me my wife and my daughter. In the end, we divorced, and I moved here."

"Did you ever see Clarissa again?"

The sheriff shook his head. "Judy remarried a year later. I decided that it would be better for all of us if I just walked out of their lives for good. I didn't want to compete with a stepfather. Now I wish I'd stayed around and been a part of her life."

"What about you? Did you ever remarry?"

"I finally got my act together through a local AA program and a preacher who wouldn't leave me alone. I met Paula at a singles' meeting at church shortly after I became a Christian. We have two boys, Seth and Michael, who are fourteen and sixteen."

Pricilla smiled. "That's wonderful, though I can't imagine how tough it must have been for you."

"At least Clarissa was too young to understand what was going on when I walked out. The bottom line is that Bruce is her father. She doesn't know about me."

"Doesn't seem fair somehow."

"In my years of law enforcement, I learned not only to curb my temper, but that life is rarely fair." Sheriff Lewis cleared his throat before standing. "Mrs. Crumb, look. I'm sorry for all of this."

"Sorry?"

"I shouldn't be dumping my problems on you. It's just that seeing Clarissa was such a shock. Especially when I was the one forced to arrest her. And seeing her again, well, it managed to drag me back to a past I thought I'd put behind me." He shook his head. "I have no right to drag you into my personal life."

"Please." Pricilla waved her hand in dismissal as she stood to join him. "What's important right now is that we do everything we can to help Clarissa, which I know is exactly what you want. Can I ask you a question?"

"Of course."

"How did you know she was your daughter?"

"I've been in touch with Judy off and on throughout the years. She sent me a photo of her two years ago. Clarissa had just graduated and had a job as a souschef. Judy thought I'd like to see how well Clarissa turned out despite the mistakes I made."

"Mistakes you both made," Pricilla underscored. "Are you going to let her know?"

"That I'm her father?" His eyes widened.

"Yes."

"I don't know—"

"I think you should."

"She's already gone through so much. . . ."

"Maybe. But what I do know is she needs people who believe in her." The five-minute warning bell rang. "I have to leave. Michelle will never forgive me for missing another session."

"Of course."

"I want Clarissa freed as much as you. She didn't do it."

"I don't know her the way you do, but I know you're right." He pressed his hat down onto his head. "And we have to find out the truth. Quickly."

Max strained his neck to see over the stocky man sitting in front of him who no doubt was enjoying the weekend with its large choice of gourmet samples. At the moment, though, Max's mind was far from appetizers and succulent entrees. Pricilla was—once again—missing. The past two days had proved to him that she'd still failed to put a curb on her impulsive tendencies. That had been emphasized by the fire alarm escapade and finding the murder weapon in the lake. Did he really want to live with that? He glanced past the man again. The five-minute warning bell had gone off at least four minutes ago, and she was still not in her place at the microphone.

He was rising to leave when he saw someone hurry across the left of the stage. The following flood of relief that swept over him managed to extinguish any anger that had briefly made him wonder if his heart would be able to handle life with Pricilla.

Her smile reached him and he melted. The past few days had wound his nerves into knots. Between murder victims, butcher knives, and her exploits, the weekend was far from what he'd envisioned when he agreed to a relaxing mini-vacation in the mountains. At least he wouldn't have to call on the cavalry this time to search for her. But in spite of the fact she was there in front of him, he was still worried. More than likely he was the only one who could tell that her warm expression was slightly forced. He returned her smile, hoping it would give her the boost of energy she needed. The bottom line was that Pricilla would always be Pricilla, and he wouldn't want it any other way.

She looked every bit the professional she'd been when he first met her almost forty years ago. Back then she'd organized yearly baking competitions for her girls at the academy but probably never expected that she'd one day be standing in front of a television audience. No one would guess this was her first time to do so.

Pricilla addressed the audience with the same poise and grace Max had admired all those years ago. "Ladies and gentlemen, welcome again to the Fifteenth Annual Rocky Mountain Chef Competition. This next competition is one of my favorites, and as I've observed in years past, I'm sure it is many of yours as well. It's the contestants who are sweating under their white coats."

The audience laughed on cue.

"Now we all know they can cook." Pricilla moved to the side of the podium, seeming to enjoy the interaction from the audience. "The question is, can they handle the pressure of cooking both an appetizer and a main course with only the ingredients found in these black boxes." A couple of audible gasps erupted from the audience as she continued. "So welcome to this afternoon's Black-box Competition, where it's all about improvising, nerves of steel, and of course, creating a winning dish.

"Every contestant must utilize all the ingredients in the box and will have exactly two hours to prepare a feast that will be served to both our judges and those holding tickets to tonight's gala. Points will then be awarded by the judges for taste, skill, creativity, and finally, artistic merit. And now for the list of ingredients. . .Michelle, the envelope please."

The audience hushed as Michelle handed a black envelope to Pricilla. The contestants stood before their boxes, the tension obvious on their faces. With a quarter of a million dollars at stake, it was no wonder. Pricilla slit open the envelope, pausing briefly to raise the anticipation before reading. "Here are the long-awaited ingredients of this year's Black-box Competition. Pork loin, smoked salmon, fresh prawns, calamari, asparagus, shallots, baby beets, onions, red potatoes, mushrooms, pear, mango, yellow—"

A loud *pop* exploded throughout the room. Max jumped from his chair. Someone screamed. It only took him a few seconds to realize the source of the commotion. Christopher Jeffries's stove was engulfed in flames.

Twenty minutes later, Max was sitting in on a meeting between the sheriff, Michelle, the hotel manager, and Pricilla. He reached for his fourth cup of coffee of the day. At this rate, he was going to be jittery from all the caffeine, but for the moment he needed something to do with his hands. The whole experience had him completely unnerved.

"How could this have happened?" Michelle paced the narrow meeting room.

Pricilla pulled out the cushioned chair beside her and motioned to Michelle. "Why don't you sit down? All you're going to do at this point is end up with a bill for the hole in the carpet."

Michelle grasped the back of the chair. "You all don't understand."

Max cleared his throat before injecting his opinion. "From what I've seen, the publicity of the show is anything but suffering."

"That might be true, but this has turned into a circus, which was not what I had in mind, publicity or not."

The sheriff held up his hand. "There's no use arguing. What we do need to do is to find out the truth about what is going on here."

"The situation is perfectly clear to me." Michelle finally plopped down on the offered chair.

"What are you talking about?" the sheriff asked.

"Someone's trying to sabotage my show."

"That has yet to be proven, but why would someone do that?"

She leaned forward and shot the lawman a heated glare. "If we knew why, none of us would be sitting here right now, would we?"

The sheriff frowned, grabbing his notebook. "Even I will admit that you might be on track about sabotage, a scheme that just might be working. I know I'm tempted to close down the competition."

Michelle shot up from her chair. "There is no way I will allow you to put a stop to my competition. I've worked too hard for this to be thrown down the tubes because of a few problems."

"A few problems?" The sheriff's brow furrowed. "Might I remind you, Miss Vanderbilt, that not only was one of your judges murdered, we just had an explosion that could have sent a man to the hospital. It's a miracle he wasn't hurt more than a few singed hairs."

"Believe me, I know. I almost lost another contestant."

Max frowned at the woman's coldness. A man could have been killed, and all she cared about was his worth as a contestant.

Pricilla leaned back in her chair. "Is it possible that Norton's death isn't related to the mishaps in the kitchen?"

The sheriff flipped through his notebook as if searching for an elusive answer to the problem. "I've considered the possibility. But there is also the possibility that these two latest incidents were nothing but accidents."

Michelle stood over him. "Do you really believe that, Sheriff? Because I for one am convinced that someone is out to sabotage my show, and I want to know what you are going to do to ensure I can finish my contest without any more incidents. Because if you can't—"

"Miss Vanderbilt, sit down." The sheriff combed his fingers through his hair. "Please."

Michelle hesitated and then complied without another word.

"Thank you. I'm already ahead of you. I'm posting a guard outside the kitchen for starters. No one will be allowed to enter the competition area without their official badge."

"That's a good first step."

"And there's one other thing. The other reason I called you all in here was to let you know that Michael Tanner, a good friend and colleague of mine who works for the local police, will be taking over the case as soon as I can brief him."

Max glanced at Pricilla, who didn't look surprised at all. Michelle, on the other hand, looked livid. "Don't tell me you're quitting the investigation."

"For personal reasons I won't go into. . .yes, I am. We'll leave it at that for now. I'll make sure Tanner knows everything that's gone on here, and in return, I expect full cooperation—and truthfulness—to be given to him."

Michelle squirmed in her seat and then turned away, avoiding the sheriff's telling gaze and leaving Max to wonder what else the woman was hiding.

Sleepless nights had become all too common. Pricilla glanced at the red glow of the clock beside the bed and groaned. Despite her concern over the turmoil of the day, she'd finally managed to fall asleep, but now, two hours later, she was wide awake again.

Pulling on her tennis shoes and a comfy track suit, she took the elevator down to the lobby to see if it was possible to get some hot milk to help her sleep. She passed the lodge's gym on the way, noticed the light was on, and wondered how anyone could be working out at this hour. She looked through the window and saw Maggie Underwood running on the treadmill.

Pricilla poked her head inside the room that contained a couple of treadmills, a stationary bike, and a few weight machines. "I see I'm not the only one who can't sleep."

Maggie's smile was bright despite the late hour. "Exercise has always been relaxing to me. Seemed like the best thing to do to combat my nerves."

"I don't blame you. It's been a tough couple of days." Pricilla leaned back against the treadmill next to Maggie. "You ended up doing well early today. I loved your prawn and calamari soup."

"Thanks, but even that dish probably won't be enough to win the competition. I'm afraid I'm too far behind at this point." Maggie punched a button and her speed increased to a jog. "It's hard to believe I could lose $250,000 over a pan of burned raspberry sauce." Maggie glanced at the other treadmill. "Why don't you jump on for a few minutes? Then I won't feel as if I'm the only crazy person working out when it's past midnight."

"Exercise. . .I. . ." Pricilla glanced at the updated version of a treadmill she once had. Hers had turned out to be the perfect coatrack in the winter. "This machine is awfully. . .high tech. I'm used to walking outside."

Maggie leaned over and punched a button on the machine. The screen lit up. Pricilla took a step backward.

"They might seem a bit complicated at first, but don't let that scare you off," Maggie said. "My grandmother still walks five miles a day on hers while watching soap operas."

"Really. . . ?"

"Here you go. All you have to do is step on and push this button." Maggie nodded as she reached for her water bottle.

"I don't know—"

"Start off slow. You'll get the hang of it before you know it."

Pricilla hesitated before stepping onto the machine. She'd given up going to the gym ages ago, settling instead for frequent walks along the wooded paths near Nathan's lodge. Maybe this wouldn't be any different. There were several more things she wanted to ask the young woman, and at the moment, a midnight jaunt on the treadmill was looking like her only option. Even if her muscles still ached from the fall into the lake.

"You're sure it will start off slow?"

"Positive."

Pricilla stepped onto the machine, hesitated another two seconds, and then pushed the START button. This was great. It was twelve thirty at night, and she had to walk—or land in a heap at the other end of the machine. But it did start off slowly like Maggie had said. Maybe this wouldn't be so bad after all.

Pricilla worked to catch her breath and forced in a lungful of air. Maggie hadn't missed a step. Oh, to be thirty-something again with no cellulite, clog-free arteries, and a pulse like an athlete. For now she'd have to settle for a few extra pounds around the waist, crow's-feet, and blood pressure that tended to rise in stressful situations. Like a weekend filled with murder and mayhem.

"Did you know Norton?" Pricilla finally managed to ask.

"I met him once, though I know he'd never remember me."

"Why's that?"

"He held a public signing for the book he published a couple years ago. I'd always liked his reviews. Brutal, yes, but honest. And definitely interesting. I always wanted to be a chef and figured I could learn from the man. Besides that, I suppose it's always been every chef's secret fantasy to get a rave review from Norton."

"I'm beginning to see that." Her breathing was becoming shallower. So much for her power walks through the mountains. "Any takes on his murderer?"

Maggie upped the speed on her treadmill. She must be kin to Wonder Woman. "You really don't think Clarissa did it?"

"No, I don't."

"I don't have a take on the murderer, but I do have another, shall we say, *ethical situation* I'm facing."

Pricilla fought to focus on the conversation and not the moving belt beneath her. "What do you mean?"

"I. . .I haven't told anyone this yet, because it just happened. That's why I'm here, trying to decide if I'm overreacting or if Freddie is really up to something."

Pricilla looked down and tried to stop the ensuing panic. Her shoe was untied. She fumbled for the STOP button. Her speed increased. "Maggie! Get me off this thing. . . ."

"Mrs. Crumb—"

"Now. . .please. . ."

Maggie pushed STOP on her own machine and leaped off in one easy bound. A few seconds later, Pricilla's came to a stop. She glanced down at her shoe. At least she was still upright and in one piece. She had panicked, maybe, but at the moment, she didn't feel as if she could be too careful.

Maggie held on to her forearm. "Are you all right?"

"I'm fine. Computers, treadmills, and well, anything electronic—except for a good oven—let's just say that I've never really gotten along with any of them." She sat down on the weight bench and tried to catch her breath. "What were you saying about Freddie?"

Maggie grabbed her towel to wipe away the perspiration on her forehead. "I overheard him arguing with Lyle Simpson, one of the judges, about an hour ago."

Pricilla frowned. Everyone knew the strict rules forbidding any interaction between contestants and judges. "What were they arguing about?"

Maggie shrugged at the question. "I'm not sure exactly. Freddie said something about Lyle keeping his side of the bargain. There were a few more harsh words exchanged, but that was the gist of what I heard. What bothers me, of course, is that Freddie knows he'll be kicked out of the competition if Michelle finds out they were talking. We all even had to sign forms that we would have no contact with the judges under any circumstances."

"Including blackmail," Pricilla mumbled under her breath.

"Blackmail?"

"I'm sorry. I was just thinking out loud." Pricilla took the hand towel Maggie gave her and wiped off the back of her neck. "Don't worry about what you saw, Maggie. I'll take care of it."

"That would be great. I'd prefer not to be known as the snitch in the competition. Not that Freddie doesn't deserve to be put in his place. The man's insufferable."

Pricilla said good night before heading out of the gym and down the hall toward her room. Had Freddie been so intent on winning that he found a way to make an unscrupulous bargain that would guarantee it? If so, Norton might have become the one thing standing in the way of winning.

A crash sounded on the other side of the lodge where the competition was held. Pricilla hesitated in front of the elevators. If Max were here he'd forbid her from investigating. But Max wasn't here.

A police officer rounded the corner, almost colliding with her. "Excuse me."

Pricilla pursed her lips. "Are you the officer on duty tonight?"

"Yes, I. . ." The man glanced back toward his post. "I just left to get a cup of coffee. . . ."

Pricilla rushed in front of the officer. "One cup of coffee might have just bought our murderer enough time to strike again."

The dimmed lights in the cathedral ceiling cast just enough of a yellow glow for Pricilla to make her way down the wide, carpeted hallway toward the kitchens. Max might disapprove of any late-night investigating, but at least this time she had reinforcements. The officer charged past her, his keys jingling at his side while he spat something into his radio, making more noise than a herd of elephants. So much for sneaking up on the suspect.

Something rattled, and this time it wasn't the set of keys. Someone was in the kitchens. A crash sounded again, like pots falling onto the tiled floor. Whoever it was must have bided his or her time until the officer left and then hurried to make a move. Ten more yards and they'd be there. But if they missed whoever had broken in. . .

Pricilla entered the room behind the officer and switched on the overhead flood lights, hoping to at least catch a glimpse of the perpetrator. She blinked, waiting for her eyes to adjust to the brightness.

The officer rushed into the kitchens that had been set up for the competition and shouted for the perpetrator to freeze. A door slammed shut. Whoever it was had just left the building.

Pricilla called for the officer to hurry.

"Don't worry, ma'am. I'll get 'em."

Pricilla started to follow but then stopped midstride. Her time on the treadmill had drained her of any energy she'd had left. She'd never be a match for a sprint across the lodge's grounds in the dark.

The officer returned a minute later shaking his head. "Whoever it was is gone. I wasn't even able to catch a glimpse of them."

Pricilla let out a sharp puff of air and then jumped as the sheriff's voice boomed behind her, "What's going on?"

She whirled around. "Sheriff Lewis. Don't you ever sleep?"

"Not lately." The shadows beneath his eyes were more pronounced than usual. Of course, hers probably were as well. "I suppose I could say the same for you. I was driving home and heard the message come in over Stew's radio."

Stew's gaze searched the ground. "They got away, Sheriff. I'm sorry."

"Man. . .woman. . .tall. . .short?"

Stew shook his head. "Nothing. I only caught a glimpse of a shadow."

"Well, that narrows it down." Displeasure shone in the sheriff's eyes as he turned to Pricilla. "And what about you, Mrs. Crumb? I told you I'd have one of my men working. What are you doing here?"

"I was on my way up to bed when I heard a crash." She glanced at the officer, not wanting to squeal on him, yet wondering if the sheriff needed to know that the man hadn't been at his post.

"And I was off getting a cup of coffee." The officer's confession saved her from saying anything.

"Coffee? We'll talk about that later." From the look the sheriff shot the officer, Pricilla was certain heads were going to roll before the night was over. "Did you see anything at all, Mrs. Crumb?"

"Just noises. Whoever it was must have heard us coming and taken off." Pricilla cocked her head. "I thought you'd been taken off this case."

"I am. . .or shall I say I *was*. Sheriff Tanner was involved in a hit-and-run this afternoon. Broke both legs and will be off duty for the next few weeks."

"I'm sorry."

"So am I. Tanner's a good man. Until someone else is assigned, I'll be continuing with the case."

Which might give him time to prove Clarissa's innocence.

"You need to take a look at this, Sheriff." Stew had moved into the kitchen area.

"What is it?"

The three of them stepped over a pile of pans that had fallen to the floor. Whoever had broken in had left behind a blow torch.

Sheriff Lewis let out a low whistle. "It definitely looks as if someone was trying to sabotage one of the kitchens."

"You're right." Pricilla nodded. "Maggie's burned sauce. . .the explosion in Christopher's oven. . ."

"We can sweep the room for evidence, but I'm not sure we'll find anything that will help us. Dusting for prints won't tell us much either, as too many people have had access to this area."

"At least it gives us a direction to take the case."

"That's assuming that these incidents are even related to Richards's murder. But why would someone want to sabotage the contest? In order to shut things down?"

Pricilla yawned, but her mind was now wide awake. "Maybe there's another angle."

The sheriff quirked his left brow, obviously not interested in having his night complicated any further.

"I found out an interesting tidbit tonight, though how it ties into this mess, I'm still not entirely certain."

The sheriff rubbed his eyes. The man was definitely overworked. The fact that his estranged daughter was in his jail had to exacerbate the fatigue. At least he was still on the case. Clarissa needed someone who would go the extra mile for her, and from everything Pricilla had seen so far, Sheriff Lewis was that person. "What is it?"

"Maggie overheard one of the judges, Lyle Simpson," Pricilla said. "He was talking to Freddie Longfellow about keeping his side of the bargain."

"What do you make of that?" the sheriff asked.

"Well for one, judges and contestants are strictly forbidden to interact at any point during the contest. Such behavior means immediate expulsion."

"Then why would they be talking?"

"That's what I want to know. The only thing I can think of is that they had some sort of unscrupulous deal going. Maybe a cut in the prize money."

"A huge presumption, but you might be on to something." The sheriff rubbed his chin. "If Lyle could somehow guarantee Freddie wins, then he'd take a cut of the prize money. But while it's not too hard to imagine $250,000 as motivation for breaking a few rules, how could one judge guarantee a win?"

Pricilla mulled over the question. "I don't know how they'd do it, but I suppose it might be possible. What I do know is for the whole competition, Freddie has had this cocky, I'm-going-to-win attitude."

"Which doesn't make him guilty but also doesn't dismiss the question, is he willing to do anything for the prize money?"

"Sabotaging the other contestants' workstations would give him the upper hand."

"So might murder. Especially if he believed, for whatever reason, that Norton might tip the votes the wrong way." He sighed. They both needed a good night's sleep, but after tonight, Pricilla feared that any rest would be hard to come by. "Whatever happened to good, old-fashioned bake-offs where the only prize was a blue ribbon for the best cherry pie in the county?"

"That's a good question," Pricilla said.

"For now, we all need to get to bed. Stew, don't leave your post. For anything. And call me if anything happens. I'll have your replacement here at five."

"Yes, sir."

"Tomorrow I'll bring Freddie and Lyle in separately for questioning to see if we can get somewhere with that angle. Does anything else look like it's been tampered with?"

Pricilla shook her head. "I don't think so, but it's hard to tell."

"I'm convinced whoever it was will be back."

"Then this time we better be ready."

Pricilla rounded the corner of the lobby the next morning and felt her breath catch. He stood at the edge of the room waiting for her. Coffee-colored Dockers, neatly pressed, buttoned-down shirt. . .and a wide smile just for her.

Her day suddenly brightened. "Morning, Max."

He handed her a cup of steaming coffee. "Morning to you, bright eyes."

Bright eyes? She wished. She felt more like she'd just emerged from a dark tunnel and was ready to crawl back in.

Max's lingering kiss managed to give her an extra shot of energy, but not enough, she was afraid, to propel her through the rest of the day without a long afternoon nap. One she'd probably never get to take because of today's schedule. Max, on the other hand, looked ready to run a marathon.

She squeezed his hand. "You look chipper. Too chipper, in fact."

"Didn't you sleep well?" He took a sip of his coffee.

Pricilla stifled a yawn, hoping the caffeine helped. Where should she begin? With her late-night exercise jaunt at the gym with Maggie, the mishap in the kitchen when the perpetrator got away, or the hour and a half of trying to fall sleep while suspects and motives scurried through her mind, refusing to leave her alone?

She tried to fill him in briefly on all that had happened during the past eight hours.

A flicker of concern registered in Max's eyes. "Let's leave right now. We could head back to Nathan's lodge and spend the rest of the weekend doing nothing but fishing, hiking, and napping on the front porch. Michelle can take over for you here. She loves the spotlight and probably wouldn't mind at all. In fact, I'd go as far as to say that she'd jump at the chance."

For a moment, Pricilla let her mind linger on the idea. All she'd wanted was a quiet weekend with Max, walks around the lake, late-night talks, and conversation over some five-star food. . .definitely not murder. A wave of guilt replaced her wistful thinking. Her relaxing weekend might have been replaced with interviewing suspects and late-night excursions to hunt down suspects, but Clarissa sat in jail right now with the possibility of a decade or two of prison hanging over her.

Max would understand. He'd have to. She'd made a promise she was determined to keep.

"I wish I could leave with you, but you know I can't."

His smile forgave her. "I know. It seems to be my job to worry about you."

She chuckled. "What happened to the verse in the Bible that talks about not worrying about your life, or what you will eat—"

"I'm not worried about my life." He tipped her chin up with his thumb.

"I'm worried about yours. Something I think God understands."

Blue eyes met hers. Her breath caught. "Then He also has to understand that I have to fulfill my commitment."

"I'm just concerned about you. Your proposed time to get away and relax has turned into chaos." He reached down and squeezed her hand. "And somehow I hadn't planned my retirement to be filled with sleuthing and undercover detective work."

"I know, Dr. Watson." She flashed him her best smile. "At least this is the last day of the competition."

The last day.

Reality hit hard. The four of them had made plans to attend church in Denver tomorrow where Nathan was friends with the pastor and then head back to Rendezvous after lunch. She could stay here and continue her investigation, but she had a commitment to Nathan as well. A large group was arriving at the lodge on Wednesday from back East, which didn't leave her much time to prepare. Misty, her assistant, would be there to help her, but she still had to shop for groceries, stop by the Baker's Dozen for bread and pastries, and start cooking for the dozen hungry appetites that were coming.

Which gave her today to find answers.

The five-minute warning bell rang.

"When's your next break?" Max asked.

She checked the schedule she'd carried downstairs. "The morning session lasts until ten thirty. Fondants, candies, and confections. Then all that's left is the afternoon's session and the award ceremony tonight."

"And tomorrow we can drive away from all of this."

Which brought her back again to the realization that she had far too little time to get to the bottom of who killed Norton Richards.

She gripped the schedule between her fingers. "What about Clarissa?"

"Her parents get in tonight. She'll be all right."

"But I promised her I'd help, Max—"

"You've risked your life helping her. You've done all you can. It's time to let the police do the rest."

Pricilla let out a soft "humph." She knew he was right, but that didn't erase the urgency she felt to find answers. She glanced up. Michelle scurried around in a peach suit, barking orders. At least she still had today.

Max watched the flutter of activity from the back row of the audience, thankful he had nothing to do with running the show. Michelle looked frazzled with only two minutes left before the cameras rolled. At least Pricilla was here.

Despite her lack of sleep the night before, she still looked beautiful to him in her black checkered suit. The contestants, outfitted in their matching chef coats, black pants, and tall chef hats, were busy setting up their kitchens.

All except Freddie.

Max frowned as he leaned forward and scanned the kitchens again for a sign of the cocky chef. No. He'd been right. All the chefs were accounted for except for Freddie, who apparently was late. . .or missing. Max squeezed his eyes shut for a moment to erase the thought. Freddie wasn't missing. That assumption was coming from an imagination sparked by a weekend that had been anything but normal.

Michelle swore, catching his attention. Apparently she'd just noticed Freddie's absence as well. Forget that the entire audience could hear her every word or that they were about to go live in another—he checked his watch—one and a half minutes.

"He knows the rules," she snapped at the cameraman. "We'll start without him. Pricilla, you're on in one minute."

The sheriff slid into the seat beside Max. "What's wrong now?"

"Freddie is late."

"Late?"

Or missing. Max knew he couldn't dismiss the thought. With a murderer on the loose as well as a possible saboteur, he wasn't the only one wondering what was going to happen next. He held his breath as Pricilla stepped up to the mike. She'd done an outstanding job the past couple of days, but the stress of the contest was beginning to wear on all of them. With less than six hours of sleep, it was no wonder her voice didn't hold its normal spark of energy.

The sheriff leaned in toward him. "Has anyone checked his room?"

Max shrugged a shoulder as Pricilla addressed the audience, announcing the next segment of the competition. "I don't know. Apparently they called his cell phone, but he didn't answer. I don't know if anyone checked his room."

Sheriff Lewis crossed his ankles in front of him and frowned. "If I'd have known how much trouble this contest was going to cause, I'd have talked to the mayor himself about refusing to host it."

"I can hardly blame you."

The timer was set and the contestants jumped into action. With or without Freddie, it was apparent that the show would go on.

Even the contestants seemed to have taken on the sullen mood of the day. Their expressions were serious, and their normal interactions with the audience were gone. The audience responded with its own subdued silence.

Max watched as Michelle reached into her pocket for her cell phone. Moving back from the stage, she answered it and then stopped short before dropping her phone and collapsing in a heap onto the floor.

14

"Freddie Longfellow is dead!" Sarah stood at the entrance of the Great Room with a look of bewilderment across her face.

Gasps from the audience followed her unexpected announcement. Pans clattered in the kitchens. Something crashed to the floor. For a full five seconds, no one moved, including Pricilla. She'd expected further incidents of sabotage but not another murder. Reality sank in, digging deeper than a rooted tree. If Sarah was right and Freddie was dead, the acts of sabotage had escalated—once again—into murder.

Sending up a quick prayer for strength, Pricilla forced herself to move across the stage to where Michelle lay. Judging by her startled reaction, Pricilla could probably delete the woman from her suspect list. Now if only she could erase the fact that their murderer had just struck again.

Surely there had been some kind of mistake.

A chair toppled over. Pricilla looked up. Apparently she wasn't the only one who had jumped into action. Sheriff Lewis barked into his radio for backup.

With Pricilla perched beside her, Michelle finally started coming to.

Max bent over the two of them, casting a long shadow from the stage lights. "Is she all right?"

"It must have been the shock of Freddie's death."

Or the probable end of the contest? Pricilla glanced up at the camera that had stopped rolling. Another murder might very well mean the canceling of the show. How many acts of sabotage was it going to take before the sheriff, or perhaps even the producers, nixed the show?

Which was, she was afraid, exactly what the murderer wanted.

Michelle groaned as she struggled to sit up. She pressed her hand against her forehead. "What happened?"

"You fainted."

"Fainted?" Her attempts to get up didn't work. "I've never fainted in my entire life."

The production manager joined the huddle. "I'm sorry to interrupt, but we're scheduled to be on the air and—"

"You're still on a commercial, right?" Pricilla asked.

"Yeah, but that only means that we're fine for another minute and a half or so. After that. . ."

Pricilla felt her joints protest as she rocked back on her heels. She'd been hired to introduce segments and interact with the audience, not make production decisions. She signaled to a burly cameraman for help. Michelle couldn't weigh over a hundred and twenty pounds, but there was no way she'd be able to lift the woman off the ground by herself.

"Did Sarah's announcement make it across the airways?"

The production manager shook his head. "I checked. She wasn't close enough to a mike for it to come through."

"Then get Sarah for me," she barked. She sounded like Michelle, but she didn't care. "Be ready to roll the cameras again as soon as the commercial break is over."

The manager jumped up to comply, while the cameraman hoisted Michelle over his shoulder, despite her unladylike protests, and deposited her on a nearby chair.

Sarah came up, panting, out of breath. "He's dead, Mrs. Crumb. I saw him myself. It was the most horrible thing I've ever seen. He was just lying there beside his bed with blood across his face."

Fear—mingling with excitement—showed in Sarah's eyes. Did she see the incident as fodder for the book she'd written? Either way, now was not the time to stop and examine Sarah's motivation. If the show was to be saved, they needed to get Michelle back in commission. And she was going to have to focus enough that the television audience wouldn't find out that another murder had just taken place.

Pricilla closed her eyes and took a deep breath. "Sarah, get Michelle something to drink. Maybe some juice would be best."

"Of course."

Pricilla opened her eyes again and turned back to Michelle, who was now at least sitting up and looking halfway coherent.

"You didn't eat this morning, did you?" Pricilla questioned.

"A cup of black coffee. I. . .I didn't have time."

"Which would explain why you just passed out."

"I passed out because Sarah told me Freddie's dead. Can you even begin to realize what another murder is going to do to my show?" Michelle shook her head. "They're going to cancel the show, Mrs. Crumb."

The woman was actually more interested in going on with the show than in Freddie's death. Not a good reflection of character by any means. But Pricilla couldn't worry about those implications. Not now, anyway.

"Forty-five seconds."

Pricilla groaned. Multitasking had never been her forte. How was she supposed to calm a distraught woman while at the same time run a live television show?

"I suppose that sounded heartless. I didn't mean it that way. . .not really." Michelle must have picked up on how she sounded. "It's just that I've been waiting for an opportunity like this for years."

Even Pricilla couldn't help but sympathize with her a little. "The sheriff's on his way upstairs now to see what's happened. In the meantime, there's been no mention of shutting things down."

"But we're down another contestant."

"You were planning to start without Freddie anyway—"

Michelle ran her fingers through her hair, which had lost its polished look. "They're going to fire me. Or at the very least, never let me produce another show again."

"No one's going to fire you. It's not your fault there's a murderer on the loose. And as you said before, any publicity is good publicity." Pricilla let out an audible sigh. Had she actually just said that?

The production manager hunched down beside them, addressing Pricilla. "We've got twenty more seconds until the commercials are over. Can you go on?"

Pricilla nodded. All she had to do was get through the scripted dialogue, and then the cameras would switch to the contestants in the kitchens. At least she wasn't on the hot spot that way. The poor remaining contestants were forced to think about cooking when another one of their colleagues had been picked off.

Pricilla took her place in front of the camera, waited for the red light, and forced a broad smile. "Good morning and welcome back to the third and final day of the Fifteenth Annual Rocky Mountain Chef Competition. . . ."

The room had been blocked off by the same yellow police tape Pricilla had seen in dozens of television shows. But seeing it in real life tended to put an eerie spin on reality. What was inside a person that could cause him or her to play God and take the life of another human being? The Bible said that money was the root of all kinds of evil, and if she was right, $250,000 had just sprouted into murder.

The sheriff stepped under the tape and joined her on the other side of the hallway. "Thanks for coming up here."

Max had agreed to let her go while he waited downstairs, but only because it was daytime and the hotel was crawling with officers of the law. "I've only got a few minutes until the next segment."

"That's all I need." He motioned inside the room. "I'd planned to bring Freddie in for questioning this morning. Don't have to do that now."

"No, you don't." Pricilla shuddered. The room was identical to hers, except for the lifeless body of Freddie Longfellow who lay motionless in the middle of the floor.

The sheriff tapped his hat against his thigh. "I'm considering canceling the contest."

"I can't say I blame you." Which was true, but the other side of her gave in to the urge to convince him to save the show. "Except today's the last day. It would be a shame for all the contestants' hard work to be thrown away. And it's not as if the crime scene is downstairs in the kitchens."

"True, but the body count is already too high for my taste."

She stepped a bit farther down the hall, thankful her role in the case was only as an informal consultant and not anything that had to do with forensics. The small group in the room right now was brushing for fingerprints and searching for evidence.

All she had to search for was answers. Like what did Norton Richards and Freddie Longfellow have in common, besides the fact that they were now both dead? The prize money seemed to be the obvious common denominator. . . .

Pricilla cleared her throat and tried to stop her mind from wandering. "So what do you think? Is there a connection between the two murders, or are we looking at two completely different cases?"

The sheriff shook his head. "I wish I knew."

"How was Freddie killed?"

"The coroner will have to verify, but it looks like a blunt object to the head."

"Both could have been acts of passion."

"That's what I'm thinking. Maybe a confrontation. Someone trying to cover the tracks of the first murder."

"That would make the two crimes related."

"I'm going to need to talk to Maggie, and then to Lyle."

"Can you wait until the morning contest is over? They've all worked so hard to get to this point."

The sheriff let out a deep sigh. "I suppose it will take me that long to finish processing the crime scene."

Pricilla nodded her thanks. "What about Clarissa? Is she holding up?"

"Her parents will be here soon. I know that will be a boost to her spirits."

"You should tell her who you are. It's bound to come out once Judy shows up."

"The thought has crossed my mind more than once, but I don't know." The sheriff clasped his hands together. "I haven't seen her in twenty-odd years, and I thought I'd buried any feelings from the past."

"But you haven't, have you?"

He shook his head. "And now knowing that Judy will be here. . .I don't know. I guess it just dredges up things I'd just as soon forget. Clarissa has turned into a fine young woman without me. Maybe it's best to leave it like that."

"I don't agree."

"But Judy—"

"Judy will understand. And besides, Clarissa is a grown woman. She deserves to know the truth."

"I'll think about it. Right now I have another dead body to deal with, and I'm not sure we're any closer to finding the murderer."

Pricilla glanced at her watch. She'd be gone in another twenty-four hours. For Clarissa's sake, she had to find out who was behind this before then.

The sheriff called Pricilla's cell phone at half-past twelve to tell her that Judy and her husband, Bruce, had arrived and might need to see a familiar face if she was up to coming by the sheriff's office. While their distress over the situation was to be expected, they weren't, he informed her, taking the arrest of their daughter well.

With an hour and a half until the final session began, Pricilla kissed away any thoughts of an afternoon nap and headed with Max to the sheriff's office. Anything she could do for Clarissa would be worth a few more hours of lost sleep.

Clarissa's parents were sitting in the lobby of the sheriff's office when Pricilla and Max arrived. They were still dressed in shorts and a sundress more suitable for a Caribbean cruise than a holiday in the mountains. While Judy now wore her hair longer and had gained a few pounds, she'd changed little since Pricilla had seen her last.

Pricilla stepped up and gave her a welcoming hug. "It's good to see you, though I'm sorry the circumstances aren't better."

"I know. My little girl. . ." Tears poured down Judy's cheeks. "I can't. . .I can't. . ."

"Has she seen Clarissa yet?" While she was glad Clarissa's parents had finally made it here, seeing her mother hysterical wasn't going to help the already-tense situation.

Pricilla looked to the sheriff and Judy's husband. Both men shook their heads no.

Judy reached for a tissue from her handbag. "Martin—Sheriff Lewis—said I had to get ahold of myself first. That it won't do Clarissa any good to see me this way."

Pricilla squeezed Judy's hand and prayed that God would give her the words to say. "He's right, you know. I know how hard it is, but you've got to be strong for Clarissa right now. Everything possible is being done to get her released, but until then. . ."

"I know you're right." Judy sniffled and then blew her nose again. "I just can't understand how this happened. Clarissa's never been in trouble before. Straight As in school, a hard worker—"

"None of that has changed. We're going to get her out." Pricilla glanced up at the two men. One who'd given life to Clarissa; the other who'd raised her as his own. Life wasn't always fair or easy. The past few days had more than proved that. "What Clarissa needs right now is for you to be strong. At least while you are in there with her. She needs to know that you can help her right now, especially when the system seems to be against her. Can you do that?"

Judy blew her nose and nodded.

"Good. Wipe your eyes, then go in there and just let her know you love her and that you'll stand by her through all of this no matter what happens."

Twenty minutes later Clarissa's parents emerged from the visitors' room. Judy's eyes were still red, but she'd stopped crying.

Pricilla stepped forward. "How is she?"

"Holding up. Somehow."

"And you?" Pricilla probed.

"Just praying that this nightmare will be over soon."

Judy stopped in front of the sheriff. "I want you to tell her who you are, Martin. She needs to know that you're on her side. I've never spoken ill of you, because what happened between us all those years ago was both our faults. Please, Martin. Do this for Clarissa."

Sheriff Lewis glanced at the door and shook his head. "I don't know. . . ."

Judy reached up and grasped his arm. "Please, Martin. She's a strong girl, but she needs all of us rallying around her. Do this for me. . .for her."

"I've just never been much for words. Put me in front of a group of officers or even a courtroom, and I know my place, but the daughter I haven't seen for over twenty years. . .I just don't know if I can do this."

"You can."

The sheriff turned to Pricilla. "You know her, Mrs. Crumb. Would you come with me to help her understand the situation?"

"Of course. If that's what you want."

Pricilla followed the lawman into the visitors' room. Clarissa sat in the same seat she had taken when Pricilla and Max had come two days earlier. Her face was still pale, but—perhaps because her parents were finally here—there was a spark of hope behind her eyes.

"Clarissa. . ." The sheriff stopped halfway across the room before moving to take a seat across from his daughter.

"Sheriff Lewis. Pricilla." Clarissa reached out and grasped Pricilla's hands. "Thank you for getting my parents here, Sheriff. You can't imagine what a relief it is just knowing they're in town now instead of somewhere outside the country."

Pricilla squeezed her hands. "I'm glad they're here as well. I know it's important."

Clarissa looked to the sheriff. "Please tell me you have good news about my case. It's been a nightmare for me, but now seeing what it's done to my parents. . .and I didn't even have anything to tell them."

"I wish I had something new to tell you."

Pricilla looked at Sheriff Lewis. "The sheriff does have news for you, but it's something. . .personal."

"Personal? I don't understand."

"You will. Just give him a moment to say what he needs to say."

The sheriff steepled his hands in front of him and took in a deep breath. Seeing them together, Pricilla noticed for the first time the striking resemblance in their reddish brown hair, blue eyes, and facial features. There was no doubt in her mind that Clarissa was his daughter.

"I'm not sure where to begin." He squeezed his eyes closed for a moment before continuing. "I used to know your mother."

Clarissa's eyes widened. "Wow. It's a small world."

"Clarissa, I don't know how else to say this than to simply say it. I'm Martin Lewis. Your mother's first husband and your. . .your biological father."

"My. . .my father?" Clarissa blinked, looking confused. "I know my mother divorced when I was a baby, but my father went back East. She never told me much."

"I worked in Philadelphia for a few years, then moved here to work with the sheriff's department."

"You're my father?"

Sheriff Lewis nodded.

Pricilla held her breath, wondering if another bombshell was going to be too much for the young woman to cope with. Another time, another place, maybe, but with a murder hanging over her head, maybe they'd all been wrong in thinking she needed to know about the sheriff now.

Clarissa's expression softened, relieving some of Pricilla's fears. "I always wanted to know who my biological father was. Not that Bruce hasn't always treated me like his own daughter."

"I'm glad to hear that."

"You're my father," she repeated.

The sheriff nodded. "Your mother's kept me up-to-date from time to time on how you were doing. I'm so proud of you. You've become such a remarkable young woman."

"Why didn't you ever tell me? Ever try and contact me?"

"I. . .we thought it best. Bruce is your father."

"I wish I'd known. Just a photo. . ." Clarissa's gaze dropped. "I need to know something. Do you believe I'm innocent because you're my father or because you're a lawman?"

"Clarissa. . ."

"I need to know."

Sheriff Lewis's Adam's apple bobbed. "As your father, I know the kind of woman you are. Not one who would ever take the life of someone else. And as a lawman, I honestly believe that the evidence is going to prove your innocence in the end."

"And if it doesn't?"

His jaw tensed. "We'll all deal with that if we have to. In the meantime, I just want you to know I'm on your side, and I'll do everything I can to get to the bottom of who murdered Norton."

"Tell me what the DA is saying."

"Honestly?"

Clarissa nodded.

The sheriff swallowed hard again. "He's convinced that we've arrested the right person. And unless new evidence turns up, there's a chance you will spend the next decade or two of your life in prison."

They were back to square one. Or so it seemed. Pricilla stood inside the lobby of the sheriff's office between Max and the lawman, wanting to make sure Sheriff Lewis was okay before she left. He grabbed a paper cup from beside the water cooler, filled it up, and then took a long drink.

"Are you going to be all right?" she asked.

Sheriff Lewis drew in a deep breath and nodded. "Believe it or not, I'm actually relieved. While it wasn't the meeting I've dreamed about for the past twenty-five years, at least my daughter knows who I am. And that I really do care about her."

"She's a grown woman now, and from the way things went, I'd say she's keen on the idea of further contact." Pricilla hoped her words were encouraging. "And the fact that you care about her enough to do whatever it takes to find out the truth will be worth something to her as well."

"But what if I can't?"

"There has to be a way." Pricilla fiddled with her purse strap. It was the lingering question none of them really wanted to face. "What about Freddie's death? Doesn't it prove Clarissa's innocent? If the two murders are related, then she couldn't have done it sitting in jail."

He crumpled the cup and tossed it into the trash. "The problem is that we still can't be certain that they are related. Or that she didn't have an accomplice who's still out there."

Max leaned against the wall and folded his arms across his chest. "Two murders occurring over the course of one weekend is a bit too much of a coincidence, don't you think? At least for them not to be related in any way?"

"I have to agree, but establishing exactly how they're related is what's proving to be the difficult part. Other than the fact that Clarissa was found over Norton's dead body, covered in his blood, I simply don't have any hard evidence. We still need something strong enough that will exonerate Clarissa completely. So far, with Freddie's death, we've found no real evidence leading to the perpetrator."

"What about the murder weapon?"

"Turned out to be the iron the hotel room provides, but it was wiped clean," the sheriff told her. "Apparently Freddie was pressing his chef's coat when the murder occurred. And because nothing appears to be stolen from the room, I believe it had to be an argument that escalated into murder."

"Did anyone see or hear anything?" Pricilla asked.

"No one that we've found so far."

Pricilla looked to Max. "Someone had to have heard something—"

"Pricilla?" Max asked. She knew exactly what he was thinking. One look at his frown told her that he'd had enough of her involvement in the case, especially after a second murder. And for once, she tended to agree. If only it weren't for Clarissa. . .

The brief reminder of Clarissa strengthened her resolve. "All I want to do is look around and ask a few questions."

"I think this time the sheriff should ask the questions. There's been another murder, Pricilla. It's not safe."

The sheriff nodded. "We'll continue to see if we can find a witness, but I believe that Max is right this time. The information you've managed to dig up has become an essential part of the investigation, but I don't want anything to happen to you."

Max reached out and squeezed her hand. "Me neither."

Max's smile made her forget what she was fighting for. Almost. The bottom line was that another man was dead, and Clarissa's future was still at stake—two things that she simply couldn't just ignore.

"I'll just keep my eyes and ears open," she conceded.

"No late-night treks though the hotel," Max told her.

"Or responding to any ruckus from outside," the sheriff added.

"Or—"

Pricilla held up her hand and laughed. "All right. I get the picture. I'll be careful. I promise."

Pricilla took another bite of her double-chocolate cheesecake and swallowed a measure of guilt along with it. While Max had ordered a chef salad for lunch, she'd opted for a scrambled egg, bacon. . .and cheesecake. She couldn't help it. A bit of comfort food had suddenly become essential. And thankfully Max had been wise enough not to say anything.

"I feel as if we've hit a brick wall," she confessed.

Max dabbed another spoonful of dressing onto the rest of his salad. "The truth is going to come out eventually."

"But when? We're leaving in the morning."

"And Sheriff Lewis is perfectly capable of solving the case. Give him time." They were both silent for a moment while the waitress refilled their waters before moving on to another customer. "You still have a few minutes left to lie down before the last session if you'd like."

"Maybe I will." But when Pricilla glanced out the window, a glimmer of purple caught her eye near the shore, giving her second thoughts about a nap. "I think I'll take a short walk before the next session."

"A walk? Now?" Max glanced out the window, following her gaze.

"I won't go far. Just need to clear my head, and it's such a perfect day."

She quickly finished the last bite of her cake, hoping he wouldn't notice—

"Violet Peterson?" Max adjusted his bifocals and frowned. "Is that Violet Peterson?"

"Violet?"

"Pricilla, tell me something. Why is it you didn't invite me along on this walk?"

She cleared her throat. "There's nothing wrong with my taking a short walk. And if I happen to run into one of the contestants, or a member of the audience—"

"Or one of the judges." Max squeezed a lemon slice into his water and frowned. "What did we just finish discussing with the sheriff?"

"All I'm going to do is keep my eyes and ears open. Just like I promised."

"And what if Violet's the murderer?"

Pricilla matched his frown. "There are plenty of people around. If she was the murderer, she's not liable to try something in broad daylight when the lunch crowd is eating on the balcony above."

"I'm coming with you."

"I don't need a guardian angel, Max. I'll be fine. Really."

While she loved playing Sherlock Holmes alongside his Dr. Watson, something told her that Violet would open up better to her if she went alone. They didn't need to take any chances of intimidating the woman.

"You'd better get used to my role of guardian angel. Your habit of taking off without a thought about what could happen, well, take it from me, you need all the help you can get."

She decided to plead her case. "Max. I just think she'll respond better if it's just me. Woman-to-woman."

He hesitated before answering, clearly not agreeing with her reasoning. "Fine, I'll wait here, but don't be late. Michelle's going to hang you out to dry if you miss another session."

Pricilla glanced at her watch. "I'm not going to be late. I've still got another thirty minutes before I have to be back in the Great Room."

He leaned over and kissed her cheek. "The bottom line is that I love you, Mrs. Pricilla Crumb. Despite your stubborn ways—"

She kissed him on the lips to keep him quiet. "You know I love you, too, Max."

She made her way down the incline, hoping it would look as if she were out for a short walk along the shoreline and not looking for a chance to further a murder investigation. Violet stood at the shoreline in a purple-colored tailored pantsuit that looked more suitable for a boardroom than the mountains, even with the loaf of bread she carried to feed the ducks. A half dozen ducks had gathered around the middle-aged woman, thrilled with the free meal. But while she assumed that the city woman probably didn't know the difference between a trout and a bass, she definitely knew the intricacies of cuisine and how to run a business.

Pricilla approached Violet from the side, the lake spread out before them, shimmering beneath the early afternoon sun like hundreds of tiny crystals. The colorful array of columbines, poppies, Indian paintbrush, and a dozen other wildflowers only managed to add to the beauty she'd grown to love.

"It's stunning, isn't it?"

Violet tossed another piece of bread before turning to Pricilla. "Absolutely. I've been trying to figure out how I can arrange a month or two off so I can just sit out here watching the view. Maybe that would erase some of the stress of city life."

"I'd say your ducks look pretty carefree." One came up to Violet and nipped a morsel of bread from her fingertips.

"The only thing they have to worry about is where to get their next meal." Violet's laugh was light and contagious. "My father always gave me a loaf of bread to throw to the ducks back home. I loved to watch them gobble up the food I gave them. Life seems so simple when you're six."

Pricilla sensed the layer of sadness underneath her professional persona. "And today?"

Violet's smile withered. "After two murders and a contest that probably should be canceled? The world has turned into a complicated mess that's absolutely frightening to me. And that's not even taking into account the stress of normal everyday life."

Pricilla tried to gauge the woman's expression. She looked too genuinely upset, even scared, to be guilty. "At least it's almost over."

Violet sat down on the stone bench overlooking the lake. "As much as I really would love to hide out here for the next couple of months, I can't wait to jump on my plane tomorrow morning."

"I can hardly blame you. Do you mind if I join you for a moment?" Pricilla took a step closer. "I know we don't have much time, but I was hoping a bit of fresh air would help clear my mind."

"Not at all. I could use the company. I haven't wanted to be alone lately."

"I understand completely." Pricilla sat down beside her. There was nothing like a couple of murders to get you wanting to leave the light on at night.

"It's absolutely frightening, if you ask me." Violet threw out her last piece of bread and then wadded up the plastic bag. "I've seen you talking to the sheriff a number of times. You're not on his suspect list, are you?"

"His suspect list. . ." Pricilla shifted in the seat, taken aback by the question. Her relationship with the sheriff wasn't something she wanted to explain. "I'm working with him as a. . .a consultant."

The woman's eyes widened. "You mean a spy?"

"Well, that's not exactly the term I'd use."

Violet leaned against the back of the bench as if considering the idea. "That's not bad, actually. You're pretty much the one inside person, besides Michelle and maybe Sarah, I suppose, who can talk to both the contestants and the judges."

"And I've had some experience in working with the police." Pricilla paused before expanding on her exploits. Maybe she shouldn't have mentioned her past experience working with the authorities at all. It had never been on a professional level, and she had tended—to a degree anyway—to frustrate Deputy Carter more than help him, even though in the end her madcap escapades had eventually helped solve the cases.

"You've actually worked with the police? I'm quite impressed."

"It really isn't anything I like to brag about."

"Well, I have no idea how one might get involved in a murder investigation, so I say the more help, the better," Violet continued. "It frightens me knowing there's a murderer on the loose. I've judged contests before, but the worst thing that ever happened was missing ingredients, or maybe a refrigerator that wasn't keeping the correct temperature. There was no mention of murder in the contract I signed."

"I certainly agree with that." Pricilla decided to press further. "So you don't think Clarissa is guilty?"

"I don't know the girl, but she definitely didn't look like the murdering type."

"What does a murderer look like?"

"No one ever knows, I suppose, which is why I'd be willing to bet that Michelle's involved somehow. That woman will do anything for publicity."

"But murder?" Pricilla leaned in slightly. "That's an awfully strong accusation."

"Truth be told, Michelle's not the only one who once held a vendetta against Norton Richards. Besides, I'm not accusing, just observing."

"Anything specific?"

Violet shook her head. "I already told the sheriff I hadn't seen anything."

Maybe it was time for another angle. "I understand you knew Norton?"

"Knew him?" Violet fiddled with the plastic bag she still held between her fingers. "Hardly. I wouldn't have shaken hands with that man if my life depended on it. I've never understood where his popularity came from, and when I found out he was the substitute judge. . .well, you can understand my annoyance. Made me wish I could simply drop out."

"And your feelings toward him stem from a review he gave your restaurant?"

Violet looked surprised. "You heard about that?"

"I believe it was a review on your Coquille St. Jacques and stuffed mushrooms—"

"The man had some crazy agenda. He had to, to lie the way he did about my food. My restaurant has a solid reputation, which is something I've worked my entire professional life to uphold. Then he comes along and compares my cuisine to an overcooked microwave dinner." Violet's voice began to rise in volume. "You can imagine what that one negative review did for my reputation, after Norton Richards had the gall to waltz into my place like he was some sort of. . .of a god pronouncing judgment."

"I wouldn't go so far as to compare him to God."

"You get the point."

Pricilla forged ahead. "And you're sure that your staff wasn't just having an off night?"

It was obvious from Violet's wide-eyed expression that the question was insulting. "I have quality checks every step of the way to ensure my cuisine is top-drawer in every respect."

"Do you have any idea why he would give your restaurant such a negative review?"

"Of course I do."

Bingo. Pricilla hadn't expected such candidness, but maybe she was finally on to something.

"Which is. . ." she urged.

"Well, it's never been proven—and probably never will be now that Norton's dead—but it was never beneath him to use his power. And while I admit he found fame as a reviewer, he had always wanted to be a world-renowned chef—something he never achieved. So his fame became a poison dart he could throw at will to show he was still the one in control."

Pricilla crossed her legs. Clarissa had said nearly the same thing. Her boss, Jake, had been admitted into one of Europe's most prestigious cooking schools, but Norton hadn't been accepted. Grudges might run deep, as Clarissa had said, but there were still things that didn't add up.

Pricilla proceeded carefully. "What I don't understand is that a false review would, in the end, only serve to discredit Norton. Was it really worth the risk of his reputation?"

"Norton became more than just a reviewer. To the public, he was an icon who could do no wrong. If he said my Coquille St. Jacques tasted like a microwave dinner, then it tasted like a microwave dinner. That was simply the kind of power he held. Even so, I was in the process of suing him."

While she wasn't sure she would ever understand the hold Norton had once had on his readers, there was still one more question Pricilla wanted answered that could lead to a possible motive for Violet. "Was there ever any kind of settlement for you in the end?"

Violet shook her head. "I was hoping to have the whole thing over with this fall, but now that he's dead, there's no case."

Which meant that Norton's death would potentially cost Violet the settlement. Still. . .

"While it's sad the man is dead, most people I've talked to seem to believe that his death will work to their advantage."

Violet shook her head. "Not for me. I'll never be able to hear him apologize."

There were now four contestants left for the final session of the contest. Pricilla watched as Maggie Underwood, Christopher Jeffries, Brad Philips, and Gayle Wright worked feverishly in their kitchens to finish the final round of the contest. A task that for the moment, anyway, seemed to be anything but easy.

They had started five minutes late, and unfortunately, things had gone downhill from there. Pricilla studied the serious expressions of the contestants. Gone was the friendly interplay that had existed between the contestants and the audience. The spirited mood that had once filled the Great Room had now been replaced with a heavy sense of tension that was affecting the chefs' concentration.

Pricilla could feel the jumbled nerves. She'd bumbled over two lines in her script, and the audience had failed to laugh at her joke. Even Trisha's good news that her wedding dress was almost finished and their honeymoon reservations had been found had done little to lift Pricilla's spirits. All she could do for the moment was to paste on a smile when the camera rolled and pray she could keep it up until the red light went off.

For now Pricilla watched from the sidelines as the contestants worked to complete their last session, the Wild-card Dish. Ranging from elaborate desserts to sophisticated main courses, the chefs' goal during this segment was to blow away the judges—and the audience—with their unique creativity and style.

One of the cameras zoomed in on Christopher Jeffries, whose eyebrows were still noticeably singed from yesterday's explosion in his kitchen. His hands trembled as he set the top layer of his four-tiered cake. Pricilla gasped. Somehow he managed to save the triangular piece before it toppled off the side and onto the floor. But that lucky save couldn't be found for Brad Philips. The camera caught the chef pulling the hot water bath from his oven and then flipping it onto the floor. So much for his savory butternut flan appetizer. At this point Brad was more than likely out of the running. Hardly the grand finale they'd all hoped for.

The final bell rang, announcing the end of the wild-card segment. Pricilla let out a sigh of relief. All she needed to get through now was the formal award session that would be held later this evening.

Max joined her at the edge of the Great Room where she'd found a pot of hot coffee. "You made it through this afternoon."

"Barely." She took a sip of coffee that tasted more like her father's bitter campfire sludge. As long as it helped keep her awake... "Just remind me never to accept another honorary position as emcee."

He squeezed her free hand. "You've done terrific. Really."

"Maybe, but I can't tell you how relieved I'll be when all this is over. The tension in those kitchens this afternoon was thicker than this coffee."

The sheriff joined them, and Pricilla offered him a cup of the coffee. "I probably need it, but no thanks. I've been drinking so much coffee the past few days it's amazing I've gotten any sleep at all."

"Which is exactly what you need."

"You're probably right." The sheriff glanced across the room. Most of the audience had left, leaving only the crew to set up for the award ceremony. "I just received some news from the coroner I thought you might want to know."

"Good news, I hope?"

"At this point, I'm not sure how to interpret it."

"What do you mean?"

"The knife you pulled out of the lake. . .it wasn't the weapon that killed Norton Richards."

16

It took a moment for the sheriff's news about the knife to sink in. Pricilla had wanted the knife she found to be the murder weapon, because it proved—at least in her mind—that Clarissa was indeed innocent. Even the DA would have to agree that the girl couldn't have been in two places at once, a fact that was more than enough evidence for her.

"You're absolutely sure the knife wasn't what killed Norton?" Pricilla asked.

The sheriff took off his hat and nodded. "According to the coroner, that knife couldn't have made the wounds inflicted on Norton. They were a quarter inch too narrow and a half an inch too short."

Pricilla shrugged off her jacket and folded it over her arm. Even with all the overhead lights turned off, the room was still unpleasantly warm.

Max gripped her elbow. "Are you all right?"

"Honestly? No. I want this to be over."

She'd been so sure that the knife would be the evidence that threw out Clarissa's case and set her free. Hadn't the knife come from Clarissa's kitchen, meaning someone had recently thrown it into the lake? But why? She tossed the rest of her coffee into the lined bin and pondered the question. If it wasn't the murder weapon, what reason did anyone have to throw it into the lake in the first place? If it hadn't been for her jaunt with the metal detector to find Trisha's ring, the probability of anyone discovering the knife would have been next to nothing. It just didn't make sense. None of it.

A wave of fatigue swept over her. She slumped down into one of the extra chairs someone had lined up and leaned her head against the wall. If she could just close her eyes for five minutes. . .

"Pricilla?"

She caught the concern in Max's voice and opened her eyes again. "I'm fine. Really. Just tired after all that's happened here the past few days and frustrated that we're no closer to an answer."

Max didn't look convinced. "Why don't you go to your room and rest for an hour or two? You have plenty of time before the final session. Or we could go get something to eat first. Maybe that's what you need."

What she needed was for this to be over, for the real murderer to be behind bars instead of Clarissa. She sank deeper into the fabric-covered chair, surprised at how comfortable it was. Or maybe she was simply so tired anything would feel comfortable. "How about I meet you in the restaurant in a few minutes. All I need is a few minutes of quiet and I'll be fine."

"Alone?"

She grinned. The room was empty now, except for a couple of crewmen and one uniformed officer. "Max, I'll be fine." She looked at the sheriff. "Your guard isn't going anywhere, is he?"

"Stew will be here until this is over, and he knows I'll have his job if he leaves for any reason."

"See, Max. There's nothing to worry about."

Max still hovered in front of her. "All right, but don't be long. I'll be in the restaurant trying to avoid the coconut pie."

He spoke as if that fact would get her there faster. It probably would, but for the moment, Pricilla closed her eyes and took in a deep breath as the men walked away. The room still smelled like chocolate, something that normally would have been a temptation. But while the audience was enjoying samples of the chefs' creations in one of the other rooms, all she wanted to do was find a few minutes of escape without actually moving.

She pressed her fingers against her temples, hoping to ease the dull ache of her head. A second murder had underscored just how serious the situation really was and left her wondering if the murderer was finished.

I just don't understand any of this, God. It all seems so. . .wrong. Two men are dead, Clarissa's in jail. Why?

It all seemed to keep coming back to motive. Why kill Norton? Why frame Clarissa? Why kill Freddie in a fit of rage, if that's what it had been? Why were the answers to her questions continuing to be so elusive? She did know at least one answer. Sin had come into this world and, with it, pain and consequences. It had begun shortly after creation when Adam and Eve had to deal with the consequences of leaving the lush Garden of Eden and again when Eve must have asked God why He'd allowed Cain to kill her son.

Pricilla had asked God the same question when Marty died. The truth was that life was full of both pain and joy, and as the years had passed, she'd also learned the amazing truth that hard times stretched, polished, and strengthened. And joy could actually be found after tragedy. It was a reality that didn't always make sense. But one she knew to be true. Especially when God was in control.

Footsteps echoed beside her. Pricilla opened her eyes and then blinked.

Michelle had slid into the empty chair beside her. Flawless makeup, every hair in place, and not one wrinkle in her chic New York suit. How did the woman do it?

Michelle pulled her ever-present clipboard to her chest and grinned.

"Well, Mrs. Crumb, we did it."

The fatigue had yet to lift. She should have gone upstairs like Max had suggested and slept for the next two hours. "We did what?"

"Finished the last session of the contest with a bang."

"A bang? I hardly see an almost-falling cake and splattered butternut flan as a triumph in the kitchen. I'd say every one of the contestants made at least one major mistake this afternoon, some of which were downright disastrous to their standings in the contest."

"That is true." The smile hadn't left Michelle's face.

"The pressure they face during a normal session with no problems is great enough," Pricilla continued. "Add a couple murders, sabotage, and a police investigation into the mix, and well, you saw them. They were all nervous wrecks."

Michelle's grin somehow managed to widen without drawing any lines across her face. Definitely Botox. "Don't you see? That's what made today's show so exciting. It's good television. Watching the chefs as they sweat over who will be taken in for questioning by the police next, all the while trying to create a masterpiece that will awe the judges. You just wait. Everyone will be tuned in tonight to see who will win the quarter of a million dollars—and to see who's left in the competition."

"That's horrible."

"Not at all. It's like Agatha Christie's famous book *And Then There Were None*. If she can make a story about people dropping like flies on some deserted island into a best seller, then I can make this contest, with its own reality-show mix of disappearing players, number one in the Nielson ratings."

Pricilla gasped at the woman's exuberance. If she had been in charge, the contest would have been canceled before it had even begun without a second thought as to whether or not they were wowing the audience or what the sponsors might think. It seemed to her that common decency and propriety should always come before reviews and good television.

Michelle leaned in slightly. "And by the way, the audience loves you as well. You add that homespun, grandmotherly charm to the show."

Pricilla coughed. Homespun and grandmotherly? She wasn't sure if thanks were due after that compliment—or whether or not it was even a compliment. "If you ask me, it's a pity that it took two tragedies to thrust the show into the limelight."

Michelle caught Pricilla's gaze. "Believe me, I agree that what has happened is horrid, but what's wrong with finding a bit of success in the midst of all this tragedy?"

Pricilla's eyes widened. "What's wrong with it? Two men are dead, Clarissa's in jail, and there is still both a saboteur and, even worse, a murderer on the loose."

Michelle clicked her tongue. "Like I said, good television."

Pricilla clenched the armrests of the chair before standing up, praying that she'd be able to keep herself from giving Michelle a tongue lashing—or worse. The younger woman didn't have a sympathetic bone in her entire body, and there was no doubt in her mind about one thing. If she had to choose from her list of suspects today, Michelle Vanderbilt would be number one on that list simply because, apparently, she had the most to gain from this string of disasters.

Pricilla stood to face Michelle. "I think it's sad, Miss Vanderbilt, when profit and prestige come before the respect and needs of people. God never intended us to treat each other this way, and your treating this as a spectacle, well, I believe it really breaks His heart."

"I'm not exactly into religion, Mrs. Crumb."

Pricilla shook her head. "I'm not talking about religion. I'm talking about treating people with respect and dignity, the way God intended. The problem with this world is that sin has taken over and trickled into every crack and crevice, and the only hope is realizing that Jesus' death on the cross is what can redeem each and every one of us. And if you ask me, this world could use a bit of redemption."

Michelle pushed her bangs back with a graceful swoop of her hands. "Do you really believe all that?"

Pricilla took in another long, slow breath. She hadn't intended on a sermon, but a deep frustration had taken over. God's laws weren't meant to be a bunch of mumbo-jumbo regulations to make life complicated and confining for mankind. They were made to bring life to His people. "Yes, I really do believe all that."

Michelle folded her arms across her chest. "How do you see me, Mrs. Crumb?"

"How do I see you?" Pricilla wasn't following.

The younger woman held up her hand. "Wait a minute, let me try. Driven, cold, and uncaring. Does that about sum it up for you?"

"Well, I wouldn't exactly. . ."

"Say those things out loud? That's okay, because I know you're thinking them. The thing is, sometimes that's what it takes to get ahead. And I'll do anything to get where I want to be."

Pricilla grabbed her jacket from the chair, poised to leave. "Even murder, Miss Vanderbilt?"

Pricilla rushed out of the Great Room and down the hall, wondering what had just happened. She'd once again practically accused Michelle to her face of murdering Norton Richards in order to up television ratings. A shiver ran down her spine. Surely even Michelle wasn't that coldhearted.

Or was she?

She pushed the button on the elevator and tapped her foot. If it wasn't for the awards ceremony, she'd be heading back to Rendezvous right now to the peace and quiet of Nathan's lodge. The bottom line was that Max was right. The sheriff could handle Clarissa's case better than she could, and the truth would eventually come out.

The elevator doors opened and Trisha stepped out in front of her. "Great news!"

She could use some good news at the moment. "What is it?"

"Riley just called. My dress is ready, and she wants me to come pick it up."

"That is wonderful news."

Trisha slung her purse onto her shoulder. "You'll come with me, won't you? It won't take long."

Pricilla hesitated. There was still time for her to lock herself in her room and take that nap, which would ensure not only that she felt more rested tonight, but that the bags under her eyes wouldn't be quite so obvious. Trisha's hopeful smile changed her mind. How could she even think about bailing on her soon-to-be daughter-in-law at this point?

"Of course, I'll come with you. I'll just need to let Max know that I'll be late for dinner." She glanced at her reflection in the mirror hanging on the wall before the doors closed, wondering if Botox wasn't such a bad idea after all. Her face looked pale, but at least her makeup still looked decent and her hair had a bit of bounce left. It would have to do. The last thing she intended to do was dampen Trisha's spirits. "Let's go."

Fifteen minutes later, Riley opened the front porch door of her log cabin-styled house before either of them had the chance to ring the bell. Wearing jeans and a purple T-shirt, she welcomed them in and led them through the veranda to the entrance of the older home.

"You'll have to excuse the mess. I just haven't had time to keep up with everything."

Trisha laughed. "I suppose that's my fault, keeping you so busy with my dress."

"Oh, I love every minute of the sewing, but these past few months have been extra busy."

Pricilla stepped around a table piled with unopened fall magazines, junk mail, a small FedEx box from Sally's Scissors Emporium, and two empty boxes of Froot Loops. She followed Riley into the house, which wasn't any cleaner. While the woman had a way with design and sewing, her housekeeping skills were on a completely different level altogether. The two couches in the living room were covered with laundry, newspapers, and magazines. And it appeared as if no one had eaten at the dining room table for months. It was covered with books and an assortment of dishes and knickknacks.

"I would have dropped the dress off at the lodge myself, but I'm running behind. I'm supposed to leave tonight for Denver."

Pricilla tried to ignore the mess without tripping over any of it as she crossed the gold shag carpet and continued down the long hallway. "Your next job?"

"Six bridesmaid dresses plus an antique wedding gown complete with ten yards of lace, an eight-foot train, and two hundred pearl buttons."

Pricilla let out a low whistle. "You really do have your work cut out for you."

"According to the bride, they found the patterns in her grandmother's cedar chest. She decided to recreate the vintage look and go for a truly old-fashioned wedding."

"So you're not going to make it to the awards ceremony tonight?"

"For the contest?" Riley stopped in front of one of the closed bedroom doors and shook her head. "I've got something to do before I leave town, but even if I was going to be around, I have no desire to watch someone win $250,000. It's a bit ridiculous, don't you think? I've always wondered why school teachers make minimal salaries while sports stars and movie stars—and apparently chefs—are paid a fortune to look good in front of the camera."

Funny. Pricilla had been paid to look good in front of the camera and promote the contest, but somehow she'd missed out on the fortune part.

Trisha peeked inside the room. "Can I see the dress before we leave, or do you have it wrapped up?"

"I thought you might want to see it, so I left it out in the back room." Riley motioned them toward the other end of the hallway.

Pricilla walked past another closed door and then an open one that must have been Riley's bedroom. A large red suitcase halfway packed with clothes was open on top of the queen-sized bed, and the floor was covered with more clothes, making it as bad as the living room. On the walls of the hallway were a half dozen photo collages.

Pricilla stopped for a moment to study them.

One of Riley's parents' restaurant, The Krab Kettle, caught her eye. Riley, who had changed little in the past few years, stood smiling between a woman who looked enough like her to be a sister, and a rotund young man with glasses. There was something familiar about his eyes, but she couldn't place him. Perhaps someone she'd met at the lodge. . .

"Family photos?" she asked.

"Yeah. My mother never could get rid of any of them. The dress is this way." Riley herded them down the hall toward the back of the house. "Sorry, I'm in such a hurry."

Pricilla brushed past the rest of the photos, wishing she had a few more minutes to study them.

While the entire house required a visit by Britain's own *How Clean Is Your House?* duo, Riley's sewing room was crowded but neat. How was it that some people could be organized in one area and a complete disaster in another? She'd never understand.

The sewing room, though, would be any seamstress's dream. From the sewing table and machine, to the shelves full of fabrics, threads, and other sewing notions all arranged by color and function, the contrast to the rest of the house was enormous.

"What a wonderful work space."

"It is great, isn't it—though what I wouldn't do for a proper store where I could hire a couple assistants and work full-time. The problem is that this town can't support me. There will simply never be enough business."

"What about Denver or some other large city? You've got the talent to make yourself known in a place like that." Pricilla studied the penciled dress designs on the large table, impressed with the uniqueness in Riley's style. "I've done my own fair share of sewing and tailoring, and my talents don't run near your level."

Riley laughed, her impatience apparently forgotten. "Who knows? Maybe one day I'll give the big city a try. For now, though, I can't complain too much. I have plenty of work, and the location isn't too bad, either."

Trisha's wedding dress hung on the far side of the room. Pricilla crossed the wood floor and ran her finger down the smooth fabric, impressed at the intricate details Riley had added. The beaded handwork Trisha had asked for was now complete and ran across the bodice in simple lines trailing down the front.

Riley pulled an extra-large garment bag from the closet and began unfolding it on the worktable. "So the two of you are leaving in the morning?"

"Bright and early," Trisha responded. "And I have to say, I've never been so ready to leave a place as I am this one."

Riley looked up from the table. "Because of Norton's death?"

"I guess you haven't heard the latest news from the lodge." Pricilla helped the younger woman lay out the bag they'd used to cover the dress.

"No, I've been here all morning and haven't heard anything. Didn't even turn on the television."

Pricilla dropped the edge she'd been holding. "There's been another murder."

"Another murder. . ." Riley's face paled. "You can't be serious."

"Unfortunately, she is," Trisha said.

Riley shook out the bag and began to unzip it. "So what do the police think? That there's some crazed serial killer on the loose?"

Trisha shrugged. "I suppose that could be one explanation."

"I doubt it's a serial killer," Pricilla began, "though the police still have no idea who's behind things."

"So they think it's the same killer?"

"There's obviously a bit of discrepancy on that one," Pricilla said. "Clarissa's still in jail, even though there is no way she could have murdered both men."

The room was silent for a moment. "Who was killed?"

"One of the contestants," Trisha told her. "Freddie Longfellow."

"Longfellow. And the police don't have any leads?"

"Not yet."

"Maybe it's a good time to leave town then." Riley lifted Trisha's dress down off the hook. "Living alone, I certainly don't like the idea of staying around with some crazed murderer on the loose."

Trisha nodded. "I agree completely."

"So who do you think the killer is, Mrs. Crumb?"

"Honestly? I'm not sure at this point. Norton had a bone to pick with everyone. But Freddie, his death adds a twist to the entire situation that I just don't know how to decipher. The man was a bit too cocky in my opinion, but that's certainly not a reason to kill someone."

Riley shivered. "Somebody obviously had a reason."

Ten minutes later, Pricilla and Trisha left with the dress lying neatly in the backseat of the car.

Trisha glanced at it. "I admit that the dress was a bit of an extravagance, even when I first bought it, but Riley transformed it into a masterpiece."

"I'm so glad you're happy with it. It is beautiful."

"How much time do we have until the next session?" Trisha asked from the passenger seat.

Pricilla glanced at her watch. "We're fine. I've got forty-five minutes until I have to be there."

"Good."

Pricilla took the sharp turn toward the lodge and felt the car shudder beneath her. She pressed the brake, fighting not to run into the ditch that ran along the side of the road.

Trisha grasped the armrest as Pricilla finally came to a complete stop. "What's wrong?"

Pricilla glanced in the side mirror and smacked her hands against the steering wheel. "Look's as if we've got a flat tire."

Pricilla stepped out of the car to examine the back tire and groaned at the shredded tread. She'd been right. The tire was flatter than her aunt Bell's infamous creamed corn soufflé. The woman never had been able to cook. And Pricilla had never changed a tire. Three miles from the nearest town on a narrow gravel road made that reality even more serious. At least they had a cell phone.

"A flat tire?" Trisha came around the back of the car, stopped abruptly, and then let out a low whistle. "You weren't kidding, were you?"

"I wish I were." Pricilla struggled to formulate a plan while trying not to worry about what Michelle would say about this latest excursion—especially if Pricilla was late for the contest's last session. "You know Michelle's going to kill me if I'm late."

Trisha rested her hands on her hips and frowned. "Not a very appropriate cliché to use considering all that's happened the past few days."

"True, but that doesn't change the fact that if I don't show up on time for the final awards ceremony, Michelle will be furious."

Pricilla started to lean against the side of the car, stopping when she noticed the layer of dust that would end up on her pale yellow skirt. She needed to show up on time and as smudge-free as possible.

"Let's not worry yet." Trisha started digging in her purse and pulled out her cell phone. "Nathan can be here in less than ten minutes, which means we'll be back in plenty of time for you to change."

Pricilla glanced at her watch. "I've got thirty-five minutes and counting."

Granted, thirty-five minutes of worrying wasn't going to do anything but add to the stress of the weekend, which definitely wasn't worth it. All they needed to do was call Max and Nathan who could in turn worry about getting the tire changed—after they rushed her back to the lodge.

"Pricilla. . ." Trisha held the phone up above her head and frowned.

"What is it?"

"A problem. There's no signal."

Pricilla felt her blood pressure rise. "There's got to be a signal."

"We are out in the middle of nowhere." Trisha dropped the phone back into her purse and eyed the tire. "You do know how to change a flat, don't you?"

Pricilla cocked her head and stared at the black mess of rubber. "Sort of."

"Sort of? It was a simple yes or no question!"

"I learned how to. Once. My father made me take an auto mechanics course in college."

"Which was. . ."

"Forty-five years ago, give or take."

Trisha folded her arms across her chest. "You're joking, right?"

"No." Pricilla eyed the tire again, wishing she was joking.

"And you don't remember how?"

"You take off the screws, then jack up the tire. . ." Pricilla caught her lower lip between her teeth. "Or is it the other way around. . . ?" She glanced up and caught Trisha's gaze. "Nope. Not a clue. What about you?"

"Somehow I missed that lesson in driver's ed."

"You missed that lesson?" This couldn't be happening. "Where's my ever-reliable, independent, soon-to-be daughter-in-law?"

"It rained the day we were supposed to take How to Change a Tire 101. Besides, up until now, I've never needed to change a tire. Back in New Mexico, I'd simply call a tow truck."

"Something we can't do considering we don't have any phone service."

"True."

"Then it looks as if we have two options at this point," Pricilla began. "One, we can attempt to change the tire, or two, we can start walking. We're about halfway between town and the lodge, so you can even take your pick which direction, though I'd prefer at least walking in the direction of the lodge so I can feel as if I'm making progress."

"I would normally agree, but. . ." Trisha looked down at her two-inch heels, which looked great with her dark jeans and her short-sleeved green sweater, but weren't made for an impromptu walk down a gravel road. "You don't have a third option? One that doesn't include a hike down a deserted road in heels?"

Pricilla looked down at her own shoes, thankful she'd opted for the tan flats and not the brown heels. "You do have a point, but so far I haven't come up with a door number three."

Trisha's gaze dropped to the ground. "There is another problem to consider as well. The fact that there have been two. . ."

Trisha stopped before finishing her sentence, but she didn't have to for Pricilla to know exactly what she was thinking about.

Murders.

She shuddered. "Two murders? I know. I've been thinking the same thing."

Pricilla glanced at the tire again. Not that she thought her car had been sabotaged, or even that there was any chance that the murderer could be out here, but there was something unnerving about being out on a lonely road after having to deal with not one, but two unsolved murders.

Pricilla worked to shake off the eerie feeling. "If you can think of another option, I'm up for trying."

Trisha eyed the tire again. "We could try to change it. How hard can it be?"

"Forget it." They spouted the words in unison and then laughed, easing the tension slightly.

"Okay then." Trisha slung her purse over her shoulder. "You know we're being silly, really. It's not as if we're hitchhiking after dark. We merely need to make it back to the lodge, which is only a couple miles from here. It'll be a snap."

Pricilla did a quick calculation in her head. If they walked an average of four miles an hour, she might make it in time, though she could forget about freshening up and changing clothes. This was definitely going to be her last time in front of a camera.

Pricilla locked the car and tried to find a bright side of the scenario as they started walking toward the lodge. "Look at it this way. We now have time to brainstorm the murders."

"Brainstorm the murders?" Trisha shook her head. "That's not exactly the topic I was wanting to dwell on."

Pricilla swerved to the right to avoid a large rock, wondering just how long her semicomfortable flats would make it on this terrain, let alone Trisha's heels. "We could discuss the appetizers and floral arrangements for your wedding."

Trisha hobbled alongside her. "But you'd much rather discuss a whodunit."

"Only because I've got just over twelve hours before I leave, and I intend to make some headway in finding the truth before then."

"I know you believe Clarissa's innocent, but didn't the sheriff say you needed to stay out of the investigation? Another murder is serious business, and I, for one, have no desire to get involved in it."

"You sound just like Max," Pricilla countered. "I promised to stay out of trouble, which I intend to do—to the best of my ability. But I also promised Clarissa I'd do everything I can to help get her free, which means that until I have to leave, I intend to do exactly that."

Along the road, golden leaves from the trees danced in the light breeze beneath the shadow of the Rockies. Clean mountain air, the warm sun on her face, and a mountain jutting up above them. . .she should be enjoying it, not worrying if there was a murderer on the loose.

Trisha shoved her hands into her back pockets. "So who's at the top of your list?"

"Twelve hours ago, Freddie Longfellow was right at the top."

"Who just took himself out of the running this morning."

"I'd much rather be a suspect than a dead victim."

"True," Trisha admitted. "And I'm sure Freddie would wish that as well if he were still alive."

Pricilla glanced down at Trisha's shoes. They had to be uncomfortable. Barely half a mile down the road and her own feet were already starting to ache.

"What about now?" Trisha asked. "Anyone surfaced to the top of your list?"

"Michelle's the first person that pops into my mind."

But while it was true that Michelle had both motive and opportunity, Pricilla had learned that things weren't always as they seemed. She wished there were a convenient way to study the printouts Max had given her. Seeing the suspects and their motivations laid out side by side helped tremendously in organizing her jumbled thoughts.

Instead, Pricilla shook her head and let out a long sigh as they turned right at the fork in the road and started uphill. She was beginning to sound like a genuine sleuth, instead of the formerly retired chef and soon-to-be-grandmother—she hoped—that she was. No. She should be reading whodunits instead of trying her hand at solving murders like some escapade from Agatha Christie's Miss Marple books. Murder was police business, as Max was always quick to remind her, and the bottom line was, he was right.

The only problem was that not getting involved in a situation where she was needed had never been her strong suit. And Clarissa definitely needed her.

"Michelle had motive and opportunity," Pricilla finally continued, feeling breathless. With the uphill incline increasing, her lungs gasped for air. "And she doesn't have an alibi, according to Sarah. Add to that that she's lied—or at least withheld information—about several key situations."

Trisha was starting to limp slightly. "From outside appearances, Michelle seems to have enough motivation and drive to bend the rules and to get exactly what she wants."

Including murder? The same question continued to surface. Pricilla hoped not, but someone who was obviously driven by something had killed both Norton and Freddie.

"I'm afraid you're right about Michelle."

"Mom?" Trisha's voice came out like a squeak a few steps behind her.

Pricilla spun around. Trisha was standing on the side of the road, bent over. "What's wrong?"

Trisha slipped off her shoe. "The heel just snapped off."

"You're kidding."

She held up the broken piece. "I wish I was."

"Well, you can't go barefoot. This road is full of gravel."

Trisha pulled off the other shoe.

"What are you doing?"

"If I can break off the other heel, at least I won't end up throwing my back out of whack by walking unevenly on this surface."

Trisha fought to break off the heel. Nothing. She bent down and whacked it against a large rock.

"It's not working." She struck it against the rock again and then quickly drew back her hand. "Ouch!"

"Trisha—"

"I'm fine." Trisha groaned. "I just managed to bash my finger along with my shoe. So much for my Elizabeth Long originals."

"Expensive?"

Trisha laughed. "Twenty-five bucks on sale."

"It looks as if we're back to option *A*."

"Limping back to the lodge."

Trisha started off at a brisk, lopsided shuffle. "This is nuts, you know. Hiking back to the lodge in a pair of mismatched heels with a murderer on the loose. I should write a book about all that's happened this weekend."

"Let's just hope this story has a happy ending," Pricilla added.

At the moment, a happy ending included getting back to the lodge in time to change and freshen up before she was due in front of the camera. She glanced at her watch and quickened her pace. They were down to twenty-five minutes before Michelle expected her and at least another two miles. She was never going to make it.

Trisha, still struggling to keep up, pulled out her cell phone again.

Please, Lord. . .

"Anything?" Pricilla asked after a moment.

"Nothing." Trisha shook her head, dumping the phone back into her purse. "There is a bright side to all of this."

"A bright side?" Pricilla wasn't convinced.

"We're walking off some of the calories from the weekend."

Pricilla chuckled. "You do have a point, but right now I'd prefer the extra pound or two to this."

Gravel crunched behind them. Pricilla turned around. Maybe they would get a ride to the lodge after all. She shielded her eyes from the setting sun with her hand and caught a glimpse of Michelle's red sports car, top down. She pulled up alongside them and crawled to a stop.

Great. Pricilla bit the edge of her lip. How was it that their one ticket back to the lodge was also her number-one suspect?

Trisha was the first to speak. "Oh, Michelle, I can't tell you how glad we are to see you."

Pricilla wasn't quite as convinced. Obviously the opportunity to avoid walking back to the lodge with a broken shoe far outweighed any fears Trisha might have that they might be catching a ride from a murderer.

Michelle smiled. "Well, well. It seems as if my favorite emcee and her sidekick have once again managed to find themselves in yet another predicament. How do you do it, Mrs. Crumb?"

Pricilla shook her head. The woman didn't have a sympathetic bone in her entire body. "We had a flat tire."

"Yes, I passed your car just now. So there were no metal detectors or sabotage involved?"

"Sabotage?" Trisha threw Pricilla a concerned glance.

"Of course not," Pricilla said, dismissing the idea. She wasn't going to let the woman scare her. Her imagination had done enough running for the day. Which meant it was time to change the subject. "You wouldn't by chance happen to know how to change a tire, would you, Michelle?"

"Change a tire?" Michelle shifted her car into PARK. "This suit cost five hundred dollars, which means even if I did know how to change a tire, I wouldn't. I'm sure the lodge will be able to send someone to change it for you."

Trisha dangled her broken heels behind her. "Then would you mind giving us a ride?"

"Of course not. Jump in, and I'll drive you both back to the lodge."

Pricilla hesitated as an eerie sensation brushed over her. If Michelle were the killer, that meant. . . No, she was definitely overreacting. Just because she had motive, opportunity, and means didn't automatically mean she was guilty. She was simply being helpful. They had nothing to worry about.

Pricilla must have hesitated too long, because Michelle leaned over to pop open the front passenger side door. "Come now, Mrs. Crumb. You look as if you've seen a ghost. Surely you don't really think that I killed Norton, or Freddie, for that matter. Is that the problem?"

"Of course she's not worried." Trisha had already climbed into the backseat of the immaculate convertible and had a smile on her face. Apparently she had forgotten that they were about to get into the car with their number-one suspect.

Pricilla winced as a wave of guilt washed over. She was being unreasonable, but she couldn't help it. This probably wasn't the time for a bit of sleuthing, but. . . "To be honest, Michelle, you do have motive for at least Norton's death."

"Something you've made quite clear. And so do half the contestants and judges," Michelle quipped.

"She has a point." Any traces of fear had left Trisha's voice. The chance for a ride back to the lodge had obviously pushed her over to the other side.

"Come on and get in, Mom. After all your worries about being late, we're actually going to make it."

"I'll even make a deal with you, Mrs. Crumb," Michelle said as Pricilla gave in and climbed into the car. "Ask me anything you want, and I'll give you an answer."

"An honest answer?"

"I didn't say that, but, yes, an honest answer. Then maybe, just maybe, you'll finally agree with your future daughter-in-law that I'm not the horrid monster you think I am."

"I never said—"

"One question, Mrs. Crumb." Michelle pulled back onto the narrow road and continued on to the lodge. "Any question."

"Okay. Where have you been? The final award segment of the contest starts in less than an hour, and we're supposed to be there thirty minutes before that. I expected you to be rushing around making sure everything was in place by this time."

"I had a business appointment. Sarah can handle things without me for the moment."

"Who was the meeting with?"

"The deal was one question, Mrs. Crumb."

"True, but. . ."

Michelle clicked her cherry red nails against the matching steering wheel. "But I'm feeling generous. I had a meeting with the man you saw me with at the pharmacy."

"So you did know him."

"I presumed you figured that one out, so call it a freebie. I suppose it was a strange place for a meeting."

At the local pharmacy? You could say that.

"Then you don't mind explaining," Pricilla probed.

"Yes, actually. I do mind. It was a personal matter that has no bearing at all on the sheriff's murder investigation. Which is, I assure you again, the truth."

"Okay. I suppose it is your business."

"Yes, it is."

The only sound for the next few moments was the wind rustling through the open convertible. Michelle's short hair flew in every direction, but she didn't seem to mind. No doubt, like her perfectly made-up face and elegant, unwrinkled suit, once they returned to the lodge, her hair would automatically fall perfectly back into place. Pricilla's own short curls, on the other hand, would take a miracle to tame before she stood in front of the camera again.

"Can I ask you a question now, Mrs. Crumb?" Michelle's question broke the silence.

"I suppose." Pricilla squirmed in her seat and pressed her fingertips against the cherry red leather interior that had to have cost a pretty penny. Michelle might be fighting for a prime-time spot in front of the cameras, but she was still obviously doing well financially.

"You've been pretty chummy with the sheriff these past few days," Michelle began.

"I've been. . ." Like with Violet, Pricilla paused, once again wondering just how much information she should offer. Clearly, though, her interaction with the sheriff these past few days hadn't gone unnoticed. "I've been helping him as a sort of consultant. In an unofficial capacity, of course."

"She solved two murders back in Rendezvous this past year," Trisha piped up from the backseat.

"You're kidding."

"Unofficially, of course," Pricilla clarified again. "I just happened to be in the right place, or shall we say the wrong place, at the right time, and was able to help."

"I thought amateur detectives were only found in mystery novels and maybe a rerun of *Murder, She Wrote*," Michelle said.

"Like I said, it's all been informal and completely unofficial."

"So here's my question. Where am I on Sheriff Lewis's list of suspects? You must know."

Pricilla noted the woman's stern profile. Her normal confidence had rapidly melted into something that sounded like pure fear.

"To be honest, I don't know," Pricilla confessed. "The sheriff doesn't let me know everything regarding the case. He just has looked to me for insight on things I might pick up by being part of the competition."

Michelle took her foot off the accelerator as they went over a couple of large bumps in the road. Pricilla drew out a sigh of relief. In another couple of minutes, they'd be back at the lodge.

"Then maybe you can tell him this," Michelle said. "I've worked hard, made some mistakes, and taken advantage of opportunities, and in the process stepped on a few toes, but I never killed anyone. And I didn't kill Norton."

"Is that what you're afraid of? That the sheriff is going to arrest you for murdering Norton?"

"Wouldn't you be afraid if you were me? I know what it looks like. Not only do I have motivation and opportunity, I panicked and didn't tell the sheriff about my relationship with Norton." Michelle gripped the steering wheel until her knuckles turned white. "We. . .we had an affair a few years ago."

"I know."

"You know? Then I can assume that the sheriff knows as well."

"He knows that you've been covering up some things, including the affair.

But whether or not he's planning to arrest you, I don't know."

"People are so predictable, it's scary."

"What do you mean?"

"Have you heard of Brandt Watson?" Michelle sped past a grove of aspen trees whose yellow leaves dripped like gold from the white limbs.

"Brandt Watson?" Pricilla shook her head. "I don't think so."

"He was a famous outlaw back in the late eighteen hundreds from this part of the country, though there are a few people who believe he was actually a hero. He was worth over a million dollars when he died."

"And what does that have to do with us today?"

"It's interesting how things are," Michelle continued, not answering Pricilla's question directly. "You get ahead and people assume you did it in some unscrupulous fashion. Newspapers print the sensational, filling in what they want between the lines, and sometimes, out-and-out lying. It was that way with Brandt Watson. People saw him with his money and power and found it easier to believe that he'd gained wealth by some sort of evil deeds instead of hard work. And do you know what? People are exactly the same today as they were back then."

"So he wasn't an outlaw?"

"Oh no. He earned his money the old-fashioned way. A lot of hard work and a bit of luck."

"How do you know?" Trisha asked.

"Brandt Watson was my great-grandfather on my mother's side."

Pricilla began to see where Michelle was going. "And the same thing has happened to you?"

"Did you know that last year I was arrested for assaulting one of my colleagues? Marcy Lee knew I was up for a promotion and wanted it. She deliberately picked a fight with me, knowing my temper would get the better of me. Then she brought a lawsuit against me, claiming I had 'harassed' her. She almost won her lawsuit and the promotion, but they finally had to drop it because it was her word against mine."

"Why'd she do it?" Trisha asked.

Michelle continued down the bumpy road that was flanked by purple wildflowers on either side. The sun had already dropped behind the mountains, leaving the horizon a hazy band of orangish yellow.

"Isn't that obvious? Marcy wanted the promotion and figured that the easiest way to get it was to get rid of me."

"But none of her accusations were true?"

"Oh, we had a fight, but I never struck her. In the end, though, it didn't matter because I was still made out to be the bad guy in some people's eyes. Innocent or not. I managed to get the promotion but learned in the process that you can't get ahead by being Mr.—or Miss—Nice Guy."

"So why are you telling us this?" Pricilla asked.

"Because I'm tired of the lies and rumors and gossip. I'm tired of working hard, only to be snubbed because people perceive me as some kind of hatchet woman. I've gotten promoted by hard work and sweat. I'm always the first one at the office, and by the time the rest of them show up, I've already put in a half-day's work."

While Pricilla was certain Michelle would never admit it, Pricilla could hear the deep hurt in the younger woman's voice. "It's called being driven, Michelle, something that can be a positive quality. But sometimes that drive can be the very same force that ends up running over people. And in the end, you're the one who ends up feeling isolated and alone."

Michelle's chin jutted out. "So then I'm the one who suffers, because I'm driven and disciplined?"

"Sometimes."

"Maybe they're right."

"Who's right?" Pricilla asked.

"I've heard the names they call me. Ice Woman. Heartless. Cold-blooded." Michelle shrugged, looking more deflated than Pricilla's back tire. "But it doesn't mean I don't have any feelings. And now everyone has taken those old rumors and twisted them once again. The truth is, Marcy Lee didn't have the drive it takes to become what she wanted, so she decided to take me down any way she could. Nobody wants to hear the truth. They would rather hear that I socked a woman in order to get ahead.

"And you know what else I'm tired of?" she continued without hardly taking a breath. "People assume things about me before they even know me. Men don't want to date me because they're threatened by me, and women don't want to befriend me because they're jealous. Yet I've worked my way up from living on a shoestring to. . ." She held her hand up. "To this."

Pricilla looked around at the car, the expensive suit, and the manicured nails and knew that one thing was true. "But you still want more, don't you?"

Michelle's laugh rang hollow. "Who doesn't?"

"In the end, it's all meaningless, Michelle. Nothing more than a chasing after the wind."

"So you're back to your religion again?"

"Are you happy with all this, Michelle?"

There was no response as they passed the carved sign announcing the Silvermist Lodge in half a mile, which made Michelle's answer clear. Pricilla hadn't missed the sadness in the young woman's gaze or the loneliness.

Michelle turned and caught Pricilla's eye. "Do you still want to know whether or not I killed Norton?"

"Did you kill him?" Pricilla asked. She didn't like the way the conversation had abruptly switched, but she needed to know.

Michelle swung the car around and headed back toward town.

"What are you doing, Michelle?"

"Pricilla?" Trisha spoke up from the backseat.

"Michelle, I'm not sure that now is the time to show me whatever it is you want to show me. We need to get back to the lodge."

Michelle stepped on the gas. "Don't worry, Mrs. Crumb. What I have in mind won't take long at all."

Max sat at the table waiting for Pricilla—something he'd been doing a lot of lately, it seemed. Not that he minded waiting for her, but he was hungry, and the water the waitress had brought him had done little to curb his appetite. He glanced at the menu, wondering if they'd have time to even order. The restaurant was busy and the awards ceremony was supposed to start in less than an hour. He could always order an appetizer to hold him over until she arrived, but if she wasn't here in the next few minutes, there wasn't going to be time for her to eat.

As if she could read his mind, the waitress reappeared at his table. "Can I get you something else until your party arrives?"

Max eyed the list of options, debating between a side salad and hot wings.

Charlotte, as her name tag read, flipped open her order pad. "The appetizer special for tonight is crab stuffed mushrooms in a rich butter sauce."

Butter sauce. Even better. Max tapped his fingers against the table. Pricilla would tell him that it was off limits, but in his defense this was their last night here. It couldn't hurt. Not really.

"I'll take one order of the stuffed mushrooms and a refill on my water."

"Coming right up."

She skirted away from the table and barely missed knocking into Nathan who'd come up behind her.

"Excuse me." Nathan spoke to the waitress as he slid into the seat across from Max. "Sorry I'm late. Where are the women?"

"I was about to ask you that." Max glanced toward the entrance of the restaurant. "They're not with you?"

"I thought Trisha said she'd meet me in the lobby between five and five thirty. Maybe I misunderstood her." Nathan shook his head. "Or we've both forgotten that they've gone to pick up my bride-to-be's wedding gown."

Max laughed. "Which explains a lot. Three women and a wedding dress. . ."

Nathan pulled his cell phone from his shirt pocket. "I'm sure there's nothing to worry about, but I'll still give Trisha a call. Too many strange things have happened this weekend."

A sliver of guilt sliced through Max as Nathan made the call. He should have gone with them to pick up the dress. The only reason he hadn't offered was because Pricilla already thought he was being too protective. But when had things like chivalry and gallantry become passé?

Nathan flipped his phone shut. "There's no answer. They must be out of range."

"I'm sure there's nothing to worry about."

"No. Nothing to worry about at all."

The waitress set Max's appetizer on the table and took Nathan's drink order before leaving. Max glanced at the plump mushrooms piled on the plate. His appetite had disappeared.

He forced himself to pick up one of the mushrooms and dipped it into the sauce. No use letting good seafood go to waste. "Help yourself."

"Thanks." Nathan glanced at the door. "But I'm not very hungry."

"Let's wait a couple more minutes and call again. You know how these mountains can interfere with reception."

Three minutes later and there was still no sign of the women. Nathan picked up his cell phone. "I'll try again."

Max watched as Nathan's jaw tensed.

"No answer?" Max asked after he'd flipped the phone shut.

"Trisha always carries her phone with her."

Max ran his fork through the butter sauce. "Think we should worry?"

"I don't know how not to. Logic tells me they're drinking tea with Riley and talking about bridesmaid gowns and wedding appetizers. Then on the other hand, there's the fact that there's two people dead and a murderer on the loose."

"Well, when you put it that way. . ."

Max bit his lower lip. He'd been determined not to let the weekend's events turn him into a worrywart. Of course, the last time Pricilla and his daughter had gone missing, they'd shown up soaking wet with a knife in their hands. And that didn't even begin to include things that had happened in the past with Pricilla. The woman was a magnet for trouble.

Nathan nodded. "I think we should find the sheriff."

Max pushed out his chair and stood. At the same moment, Sarah approached their table. "Mr. Summers? I'm sorry to interrupt your dinner."

Max looked down at the young woman. "No, that's fine. How are you?"

"I'm okay. . .well, no. I'm really not okay."

"Do you want to sit down?"

"I thought you were both leaving."

"We were, but if there's a problem. . ." Max sat back down.

She pressed her hand against her chest and sat down beside him. "Have you seen Michelle? I can't find her anywhere, and all the contestants and judges are supposed to be ready in the Great Room by six thirty. Michelle's never late. For anything."

Max glanced at his watch. "Did she leave the hotel?"

"She told me she needed to rush into town for something and would be right back. I offered to go, but she said it was something personal." Sarah gripped the wooden handle of her wicker bag. "I suppose I'm overreacting, but with all that's happened this weekend. . .let's just say that while Michelle can be a tyrant to work for, I still don't want anything to happen to her."

"Is the sheriff around?" Max asked.

Sarah covered her mouth with her hand. "You don't think something's happened—"

"No, Sarah. I'm sure Michelle's fine," Max scrambled to reassure her. "She probably just got held up or had a flat tire or something."

"Like Pricilla and Trisha?" Nathan threw out.

Sarah's eyes widened. "What's happened to them?"

"They're missing as well," Nathan said.

Max pushed out his chair. "Listen, I'm sure we're all overreacting. I say we go to the Great Room. They're probably all there right now."

At least he hoped so. The only thing Max did know at the moment was that Trisha and Pricilla were missing, along with the person he considered to be the top suspect in a murder investigation.

Max tried not to panic as he quickly paid the bill and hurried behind Nathan toward the Great Room. Already the staff was busy preparing for the final ceremony that would be the culmination of the weekend. And with a quarter of a million dollars at stake, Max was certain that the evening would be spectacular. But at the moment, none of it interested him. What he needed now was to find either Pricilla and Trisha. . .or the sheriff.

Sheriff Lewis stood in the back of the room, leaning against the wall, a serious expression written on his face.

"Sheriff Lewis. I. . ." Max stopped in front of the lawman, then hesitated. Was he panicking for nothing?

"Anything wrong, Mr. Summers?"

"Pricilla's missing. . .again."

"And Trisha," piped in Nathan.

"And Michelle," Sarah added.

The lines on the sheriff's forehead seemed to multiply. The man looked tired. "Well, this is exactly what I need. Along with a string of murders, I now have an epidemic of missing people."

All doubts vanished from Max's mind. No. Something was definitely wrong. Three grown people couldn't just disappear.

The sheriff threw up his hands. "Start at the beginning. Where did Pricilla and Trisha go?"

"They left for town about four thirty to pick up Trisha's wedding dress," Nathan explained. "We were supposed to meet them for dinner about forty-five minutes ago."

"Where was Trisha's wedding dress?"

"At the house of a local seamstress. I think her name is. . .Riley?" Nathan looked to Max.

"Riley Michaels," Max finished.

"And what about Michelle?" the sheriff asked Sarah. "Where is she? With barely an hour left until the show begins, I would think the woman would be here pacing a hole in the carpet."

"So would I. And that's why I'm worried. All she told me was that she was going into town and that she'd be back in plenty of time." Sarah's forehead creased. "And as I told Nathan and Max, Michelle's never late."

Max felt his blood pressure rise. Never late until they were facing two murders, a murderer or murderers on the loose, and three missing people. He glanced at his watch and tried to convince himself that Pricilla had lost track of time, that the cell phone towers were down, and that she was, right now, having tea with Riley.

Except Pricilla would never skip a professional obligation for a cup of tea. Something was wrong.

The sheriff pulled out his cell phone. "There's still forty-five minutes until the show starts. I'm not sure this is the time to panic."

"All participants are required to be here early, which means Michelle would—"

"Okay." The sheriff held up his hand for Sarah to stop. "I see your point, but I can't exactly send out a search party without at least narrowing down the parameters. It will be dark before long, so anything you can tell me will help."

"I'd start between here and town," Max suggested. "It seems the most obvious."

"What about Miss Michaels?" the sheriff asked Sarah. "Have you talked to her?"

"I'll call information and try to get ahold of her now." Nathan stepped back from the group while the sheriff put in a call to the station.

A moment later, Nathan snapped his phone shut. "Riley said they left at least thirty minutes ago."

"Thirty minutes ago?" Max questioned. "Town's not even ten minutes away."

"Where were they headed?" the sheriff asked.

"Back here, she said. Pricilla said something about not being late for the awards ceremony."

The sheriff shoved his hat on. "Then they should be somewhere between here and town. It's probably nothing more than a flat tire or dead battery."

Sarah didn't look convinced, and Max had to agree. "Both cars? It doesn't seem likely, sir."

She was right. What were the odds that both cars had broken down on the way back from town? It simply didn't make sense. If anyone wanted to put a stop to tonight's show, taking out both Michelle and Pricilla was a sure way. And if. . . Max shook his head and tried to rein in his wandering thoughts. Worrying only made things worse.

"So what are we waiting for?" Nathan fished his keys from his pocket. "Let's go."

A minute later, Max slid into the passenger seat of Nathan's car, praying that they would find the women. Quickly. The chance to spend the remaining years of his life with Pricilla had been a gift from God. He wasn't ready to lose her.

"This whole weekend has been a disaster." Nathan peeled out of the gravel driveway of the lodge, the worry evident on his face.

Max tried to think of something positive to momentarily offset his apprehension. "It hasn't been a complete disaster. Your mother and I managed to set a wedding date. Or at least narrow it down to a month. Which for us is progress."

"If I'd have known that a wedding was so complicated, I'd have convinced Trisha to elope."

"The thought has crossed my mind a time or two."

"Why is it that women have turned weddings into something rivaling the Academy Awards, with all the fancy clothes and food to serve an army? The money for flowers and decorations alone would be better off invested in a college fund for future children."

Max chuckled but kept his gaze on the road for a sign of Pricilla's car. In another thirty minutes or so, the sun would set, making it harder to find them. "I don't know. When I married my first wife, which seems like forever ago now, things were different. All you needed was your friends and family, a homemade cake, and the local preacher."

Nathan flipped down the visor to block the setting sun. "Think Trisha might go for that?"

"I'd say it's far too late for homemade cake and a guest list under twenty-five."

For a moment, they were both quiet, lost in their own thoughts. *If something had happened to them. . . No.* Max reined in his thoughts. "They're going to be fine, Nathan."

"You can't know that."

"No, I can't."

Max gripped the armrest and started praying out loud. For Trisha and Pricilla. For Michelle. For the upcoming weddings. Clarissa. . .and the murderer. A chill that ran up his spine as he said "amen" was followed by a strange measure of peace.

"Thanks," Nathan said. "I guess I should have prayed before I started panicking."

"You and me both. I don't know why we think we can rely on our own know-how until things are completely out of our control, but that seems to be the time that we normally send out the SOS."

Please, Lord. We're trusting You to help us find them.

Max searched the road ahead for any signs of a breakdown or a car that had gone off into the ditch. So far, nothing seemed out of place. They came to the T-junction and took a left toward town. If they hurried, there should still be enough light for them to search the other direction if they couldn't find them before getting into town.

"You know how much I love your daughter."

Max glanced at his future son-in-law. "Yes, I do."

"If anything were to happen to her. . .or to my mother. . ."

"Remember what I said earlier. It's far too early to give up."

Nathan tossed him his phone. "We're halfway to town. Why don't you try and call Trisha again. The reception's got to be better soon."

Max adjusted his bifocals and peered straight ahead. "Wait a minute."

"What is it?"

Max leaned forward, his heart stuck in his throat. "It's Pricilla's car."

They'd been kidnapped. Or so Pricilla was convinced. Why else would Michelle drive off with them, away from the lodge, while rambling on and on about who murdered Norton Richards? She glanced again at her watch for the umpteenth time, unable to brush aside the question. Even if Michelle wasn't the murderer, planning to add another two victims to her rampage, something was still wrong. With the awards ceremony starting in just over thirty minutes, there was a good chance they weren't going to make it back in time. Which meant that Michelle, who seemed to personify professionalism, had found something more pressing than the fulfillment of her contract and was now risking her career for it.

Pricilla studied the unfamiliar territory with its thick rows of pine trees. "We're going to be late."

"Don't worry about that right now." Michelle slowed down as she turned off onto another narrow dirt road. "We're almost there."

Trisha leaned forward and rested her chin on the red leather between the seats. "Almost where?"

"You told me you wanted to know if I killed Norton or not?" Michelle turned on the headlights.

"Well, yes, but—"

"Then that's exactly what you're going to know."

Pricilla worked to regulate her breathing. "Michelle, I think it's time you told us exactly what is going on."

"Like are you planning to murder us?" Trisha squeaked.

"Murder you?" Michelle's high-pitched laugh was far from reassuring. "Of course not. I'm planning to clear my name from your suspect list."

"Oh." Pricilla studied the open field nestled at the base of the mountain and frowned. "Then to be honest with you, Michelle, if your intention is to clear your name, at the moment you're not doing a very good job."

"Then I'm going to have to ask you to trust me."

Trust her? Right. Pricilla tightened her grip on the armrest, still unsure where they were going as Michelle accelerated down the dirt road. As far as she was concerned, Michelle was either the murderer as she'd feared, or. . .or completely nuts.

"Max is going to think something has happened—"

"Mrs. Crumb, all I want is for you to believe that I'm more than a career woman on the fast track who would do anything to get what I want. Like murder."

They were all silent for a moment while Pricilla silently prayed that Michelle was telling the truth.

A small cabin sat fifty feet ahead. Michelle parked the car in front of it and shut off the engine but made no move to get out of the car. "When I was five, I remember watching the evening news with my father. I was mesmerized by how the newscaster was dressed, the way he talked, and the stories he recounted for the audience. They were full of drama and sadness and sometimes laughter. From that moment on, I wanted to do that. Find stories that made a difference in the lives of people. Except. . .except somewhere along the way, with the competition and rush of getting ahead, I realized that I'd lost that drive to discover the truth."

"I think we've all done that before," Pricilla said. "Forgotten why we're doing what we're doing."

"Like I forgot about the girl who had a dream to make it big in newscasting."

The truth hit Pricilla hard. *The Lord doesn't see things the way you see them. People judge by outward appearances, but the Lord looks at the heart.* For the first time, Pricilla began to see the woman sitting beside her in a different light.

Young, vulnerable, full of ambition and hope. . .

The sun teetered on the edge of the mountain and then fell behind it, leaving the valley in a hazy golden dusk.

"So what do you want to show us?"

"Have you ever heard the story about Naomi Tucker, the librarian who was found dead eleven years ago on the bank of Lake Paytah wearing a purple scuba diving suit?" Michelle asked.

Pricilla's brow furrowed. "Yes. That was right in our neck of the woods. Far as I know the case was never solved."

"That's right. Well, Naomi Tucker had this fascination of history, perfect for a librarian. But she also had this strong sense of moral obligation. Unfortunately, it was this very passion that got her killed in the end."

"I don't understand."

"I've finally found my chance to prove I can do more than just host a cooking show or write an article about a bunch of food recipes."

"There's nothing wrong with that," Pricilla stated.

"Maybe not, but I still want more."

"What does Naomi Tucker have to do with any of this?" Trisha asked.

"I know who killed her."

Pricilla swallowed hard. "You know who killed her?"

"Fifteen or so years ago, a man by the name of Caleb Fountain bought ten thousand acres of land that included Lake Paytah."

"And he is somehow responsible for Naomi's death?"

"Yes. The man I met with at the pharmacy is Naomi's son. He's been trying to find out who killed her for the past eleven years, but he's never been able to prove anything. Nor have the police."

"So how does this all connect with your big story?"

"What would happen if I told you that I've stumbled onto something that could actually make headline news on CNN?"

"Sounds like something huge."

"It is. You see, ten years ago Naomi accidently stumbled onto something big that ended up costing her her life."

"What was it?" Pricilla asked.

"It has to do with Caleb Fountain and his land." Michelle opened her car door. "But first, I want you both to meet someone."

Pricilla moved to follow suit but then stopped. Someone had stepped out from the cabin. It was the man from the pharmacy.

He stood on the front porch, his arms folded across his chest, and frowned. "Michelle, what are you doing here?"

"I need you to meet someone, Greg."

"Michelle—"

"Mrs. Crumb, Trisha," Michelle began, interrupting the man. The three of them made their way toward the cabin. "I'd like you to meet Greg Tucker."

Pricilla held out her hand, still not certain as to what was going on. "It's nice to meet you, Mr. Tucker."

"You can call me Greg." The man's expression softened slightly, but he still wasn't smiling.

"All right, Greg."

Michelle swung her purse across her shoulder. "I need you to answer some questions for Mrs. Crumb."

"This isn't how we planned—"

"Please. You know I didn't want to involve you in any of this, but I'm a suspect in that murder case I told you about, and I'm not going to prison for something I didn't do." Michelle dipped her head toward Pricilla. "You can trust them."

Greg rubbed his goatee. "I don't know."

"Please, Greg."

He shrugged a shoulder. "I suppose it doesn't really matter at this point, does it? By tomorrow the whole country's going to know."

"Know what?" Pricilla pressed.

"You didn't tell her?"

"Of course not. But now. . ."

Trisha shivered beside Pricilla. "What's going on, Michelle?"

"He's my alibi, Mrs. Crumb. The one person who can prove I didn't kill Norton."

"If you have an alibi, then why all the secrets?"

"It's. . .complicated."

"Okay." Pricilla decided to leave it at that for now and forge ahead, even though she was still at a loss as to what was going on. "Were you with Michelle Wednesday night?"

The man nodded. "We met in town at Gardner's Bar about. . .ten o'clock I'd say."

"Why so late?"

He cocked his head toward Michelle. "She had a lot of work to do with the contest and couldn't get out until then."

"How long were you there?"

"They close at midnight. The owner locked the doors behind us."

"You're certain it was midnight?"

"Positive. Frank Gardner's a stickler for closing on time. You can ask anyone. He's too cheap to pay his workers any overtime."

"Then I drove directly to the lodge," Michelle continued. "I had just walked into the hotel when the sprinklers went off."

Pricilla quickly calculated the times. She'd glanced at the clock in her room right before she saw the two figures struggling in the darkness. It had been five minutes after midnight. If Michelle had left when the bar had closed, she would have indeed arrived just in time for the sprinklers to have gone off.

Pricilla cleared her throat, wishing the sheriff were here. "And you'll vouch for her whereabouts to the authorities?"

"Of course I will, though you're not exactly the authorities."

"No, but I'm certain that the sheriff will want to talk to you at some point."

"Are you satisfied now, Mrs. Crumb, that I'm innocent?" Michelle asked.

"I'm not the one you need to convince, but, yes, I am. What I don't understand is why you didn't tell this to the sheriff in the first place."

Michelle glanced at Greg. "We couldn't take a chance. As soon as things are over tonight, I'm going to break the story to the media."

"What story?" Pricilla asked.

"You'll have to watch tomorrow's news for the answer to that."

"So this is your big break as a reporter?"

Michelle actually smiled. "Yeah. You could say that."

"But why bring us here?" Trisha asked.

"Because I'm tired of the rumors and accusations. And, I suppose, of always being the bad guy."

"I guess we've all been guilty of judging you. I'm sorry," Pricilla admitted. "I do have one more question. You still haven't told us the reason for the clandestine meetings between the two of you."

Greg shook his head. "I said I'd vouch for you. I didn't promise anything else."

Michelle hesitated. "It's okay, Greg. They won't tell anyone. Will you?"

"Tell anyone what?" Trisha asked.

"I told you about the man who owns most of this land around here. Greg has been working undercover in his jelly lab where they make temazepam."

"Temazepam?" Trisha asked. "What's that?"

"It's an illegal drug that's in high demand internationally." She nodded at Greg. "He can explain better than I can."

Greg sighed. "Temazepam is a hypnotic drug that ranks as one of the top-abused drugs in the world. In the past, most of the labs have been located throughout eastern Europe, but Mr. Fountain decided he wanted to try his hand at bringing in a little extra cash and set up his own indoor lab where he manufactures the drug."

"A little cash?"

"So that's a bit of an understatement. It's a billion-dollar industry for those who choose to get involved."

"I want this man shut down, Mrs. Crumb." Michelle's gaze dropped. "Three years ago, my brother died from a drug overdose."

"So this story is personal."

"It will make a difference to hundreds if this man is stopped. And I'm hoping for a CNN headline as well."

"And that's not all," Greg said. "Fountain killed my mother."

"I thought she drowned."

"No one scuba dives in Lake Paytah. They killed her because she was going to go to the authorities with information about his labs. The purple diving suit was either someone's idea of a sick joke or some crazy stunt to try and throw off the police."

"And you can prove all this?"

He nodded toward the house. "I managed to get the rest of what I needed today."

"So you're planning to break this story tomorrow."

"I came to Michelle because we're old friends, and I wanted a reporter I could trust with the news."

Michelle glanced at her watch. "For now, we'd better hurry back to the lodge. Sarah's probably in a tizzy, but we'll make it."

Pricilla started for the car, still trying to digest what Michelle had just told her.

"Thanks, Greg." Michelle followed them to the car. "Do you believe me, Mrs. Crumb?"

"Yes. Yes, I do."

Michelle pulled a U-turn and headed back toward the main road. She'd been telling the truth when she told Michelle she believed her, but now there was another problem. If Michelle hadn't had anything to do with Norton's death, then who had? Maybe she'd narrowed the field too much, as there still were all the ticket-holding audience members, and any of them could have had a vendetta against Norton. But if—

The blaring of sirens interrupted Pricilla's train of thought. She turned around to look as Trisha spoke.

"Mom. . ." Trisha started from the backseat.

Four police cars with flashing lights and sirens were blaring down the road behind them.

"I think you'd better pull over, Michelle."

They stepped from the car. Half a dozen officers had come out of their vehicles, their guns aimed directly at the three of them.

There she is!" Max jumped from the car and started running toward Pricilla.

"Wait." The sheriff grasped him by the forearm. "Until we know what's going on, I want the three of you standing right here behind the car. We don't need what could be a hostage situation going bad."

"A hostage situation. You can't be serious." Max felt his heart about to explode. How in the world had their relaxing weekend turned from sampling fresh prawns and asparagus to murder and kidnapping?

"After two murders and a few rounds of sabotage, I'm deadly serious."

Pricilla stepped out from the front of the red convertible and approached them slowly. Max adjusted his bifocals. Her face was pale, but otherwise she looked fine.

"Mrs. Crumb, are you all right?"

"Yes, I'm fine."

The sheriff moved in front of his vehicle. "Miss Vanderbilt, I want you to put your hands in the air where I can see them."

"Michelle's not the murderer, Sheriff," Pricilla called out.

Ignoring the lawman's order, Max took a step forward. Pricilla's life was at stake here, and he wasn't willing to stand back and do nothing. A bit like Pricilla, he supposed. "Are you really all right?"

Pricilla nodded. "I'm fine. This has all been a huge. . .a huge misunderstanding."

"What about the fact that you went missing with the number-one suspect of a murder investigation?" Max asked.

Pricilla looked to Michelle. "She decided she needed to prove to me that she's innocent."

"Innocent? And you actually believe her?" Max countered.

"Yes, I do. This whole. . .stunt. . .was because she wanted to show me the truth. She has an alibi for the night Norton was killed."

"And what is your alibi, Miss Vanderbilt?"

"A very long story," Pricilla jumped in. "And one all of us will know very soon."

The sheriff shook his head. "I don't understand."

"I'll make a deal with you, Sheriff Lewis." Pricilla glanced at her watch.

"We've got exactly fifteen minutes to get back to the lodge for the awards ceremony. After it's over, I'll explain everything."

Red veins bulged in the sheriff's neck. "And you actually think I'm going to let the show continue after all of this."

"I think you should."

"Give me one good reason. There's a murderer on the loose, and I'm still not convinced that there isn't something strange going on here—"

"Those contestants have worked hard to prepare for this day. Michelle's worked hard. They deserve this opportunity."

"But—"

"Think of it as a chance to have all the suspects together one last time. At least you'll know where they all are."

"I don't know."

Michelle stepped forward. "Please, Sheriff Lewis. I realize that I haven't always been completely forthright with you, but I really can explain. There have been. . .extenuating circumstances."

"Is this a confession?"

"Only that I was wrong in not telling you the complete truth. But that aside, Mrs. Crumb is right. The winner deserves a moment in the spotlight and the television audience deserves to see who wins."

"What about you?" The sheriff obviously wasn't finished yet. "I'm sure you could use the limelight as well."

Michelle lowered her hands. "I didn't kill Norton or Freddie, but I can promise you that after the show is over, I'll tell you everything."

"You're certain about this, Mrs. Crumb?"

Pricilla nodded.

"Okay. Then I expect to see all of you back at the lodge in five minutes. Looks like somebody's got a show to put on."

Pricilla slid into the backseat of Nathan's car and slouched against the leather interior. "I can't believe I have to cross my number-one suspect from my list. Number two is dead, and there isn't enough evidence against anyone else to make a solid case."

Nathan started the engine and headed toward the lodge behind the sheriff. "You should be glad your field is narrowing."

"Narrowing? That's the problem. It isn't. Not really. But for the moment, I have more pressing things to deal with."

"For instance?"

"Those cameras are about to roll, and I look—"

"Beautiful." Max reached out to squeeze her hand. "As far as I'm concerned, you always do."

"You know I don't deserve you." Pricilla fished in her purse for a tube of lipstick. She pulled out a pair of sunglasses, her powder compact, and the stack of papers Max had printed out for her.

"You never told me if any of that information helped."

"It became my late-night reading." Pricilla glanced at the stapled pile. "Honestly, though, I think it only made more questions by adding to the motives of most of the suspects."

Trisha sat snuggled up with Nathan in the front seat. "What are they?"

"Pages Max downloaded from the Internet the other day."

"I figured the sooner the investigation was closed, the sooner Pricilla would be back to. . .back to being Pricilla," Max admitted.

"You wouldn't want me any other way now, would you?"

Max chuckled as the truth hit home. "Holmes and Watson always did make a good team."

"And they always managed to solve the case. Something we haven't been able to do."

"At least you were able to cross one suspect from your list," Max said. "And speaking of Michelle, did you notice her photo?"

"Several of them gave me a good laugh, to be honest. Look at this picture of Michelle." Pricilla handed the page to Trisha.

"She's obviously lost all her small-town image," Trisha said.

Pricilla passed a second page. "And Freddie. I'd never recognize him. The man must have had some plastic surgery to have those ears pinned back."

"Wow. You're right. You'd never recognize him, would you? Seventy-five pounds lighter at least, short hair, no glasses."

Pricilla froze at the description. "Trisha?"

"What is it?"

"Can I have that page of Freddie again, please?"

Trisha handed the page back to Pricilla. "What is it?"

Pricilla sucked in her breath. Everything clicked.

"I can't believe I didn't see this. I knew I'd seen him somewhere before. It all makes sense now."

"I don't understand," Max said. "What are you talking about?"

"The killer. We've been on the wrong trail this entire time." Pricilla leaned forward and tapped Nathan on the shoulder. "Flash your lights at the sheriff. I've got to speak with him immediately."

"What?"

"Please, Nathan. Flash your lights. I need him to stop."

Nathan flashed his lights and started to slow down. "Would you please tell us what's going on?"

"I know who killed Norton. . .and Freddie."

Pricilla had obviously been wrong. She scanned the audience and tried to calm the butterflies knotting up in her stomach. To the left, the judges sat at their private table. Max, Nathan, and Trisha sat near the front, looking as anxious as she felt. They were already twenty minutes into the evening's ceremony, and so far, everything had gone without a hitch. The sheriff's deputies were in the process of searching the grounds, but from her perch in the front of the Great Room, her plan hadn't worked. There had been little time to explain her suspicions to the sheriff. Even Max had been left in the dark as she'd flagged down the sheriff and driven with him back to the lodge. But the bottom line was that the murderer hadn't shown up for the grand finale as she'd anticipated.

The red light came on and Pricilla forced a smile. "Ladies and gentlemen, it's been a privilege to be a part of this weekend's Fifteenth Annual Rocky Mountain Chef Competition. This evening is the culmination of three days of activities, and *Food Style* magazine is now prepared to award the quarter of a million dollars to the winner of this year's competition. So now for the moment we've all been waiting for. The winner of this year's competition is. . ." Pricilla took the black envelope from Michelle and started to open it.

A streak of yellow crackled along the edge of the room and caught her eye. Someone screamed. The curtains lining the large windows burst into flames. Someone shouted. The fire alarm went off, followed by the sprinkler system.

A shower of water sprayed on Pricilla. She felt her knees go weak as the soggy envelope slipped from her fingers.

The sheriff quickly took charge, shouting above the noise. "I want everyone to leave the building through the south exit in an orderly fashion. No running. No panicking. Everything's under control."

Trying to catch a glimpse of her suspect, Pricilla watched as the audience scurried from the room. She was still standing in front of the camera when Max appeared beside her. "We've got to go!"

"I can't leave. Not yet." A drip of water splashed off the end of her nose. Between the sprinklers and a fire extinguisher, the fire seemed to be out, but if they didn't catch the murderer in the act. . .

"Come on, Pricilla."

She nodded and followed him out the door. There was nothing else she could do here.

The sheriff met her outside the building, soaked like the rest of them. "We did it!"

Her eyes widened. "We did?"

The sheriff wiped his chin with the back of his hand. "Not only is the sprinkler system working, but it seems as if you were right, Mrs. Crumb."

The sheriff was smiling for the first time all weekend as one of the deputies walked toward them, gripping Riley Michaels's arm.

Pricilla caught the young woman's fiery gaze and felt a ping of guilt. "I didn't want to be right."

"One of my deputies caught her with a box of gasoline-soaked rags. She managed to set the curtains on fire by using a fuse, but that's as far as she got." The sheriff turned to Pricilla. "If you hadn't told us who to look for, we might have had a real disaster on our hands right now."

"Riley?" Trish slid in between Pricilla and Max. "I don't understand. . . . I thought. . ."

Riley tried to jerk away from the officer's grip. "I didn't do anything. This is nothing more than a big mistake, like the arrest of. . .of Clarissa. I was just. . ."

"Just what, Miss Michaels?" the sheriff asked.

Pricilla shivered in the cool breeze and pulled her sweater tighter around her shoulders. Part of her still wished she'd been wrong, but the smell of gasoline on the girl was all the additional proof Pricilla needed. "I never would have believed it, if I hadn't seen the pieces laid out before me like some crazy jigsaw puzzle."

The sheriff took a garbled call on his radio and then turned to Riley. "We lucked out and caught the judge at home, and thankfully, he was willing to grant us a search warrant."

"And. . ." Pricilla prodded.

"And one of my deputies just found the murder weapon in Riley's house. A pair of eight-inch sewing shears."

"You have no right to search my house—"

"No right? You should have thought of that before you decided to kill a man. Two men, actually. And then tried to burn down the lodge."

"I didn't plan to kill Norton." Her voice was lathered with anger. "He. . .my parents lost their business because of him. He deserved anything he got."

The sheriff shook his head. "I found out this evening that The Krab Kettle went out of business because your father was dipping into the till to feed his gambling habit, and your parents went bankrupt."

"None of it would have happened without that review he posted of the restaurant." Riley's expression was one of a trapped animal. "That restaurant meant everything to my parents. They worked for years to build up their clientele until Norton ruined it all with one stroke of his deadly pen and gave them a two-star rating. When I found out he was coming. . ." She dipped her head. "All I planned to do was talk to him. . .and to tell him how he ruined my life."

"But you had your scissors with you. Sounds pretty premeditated to me," the sheriff told her. "And then there was Freddie."

"I never meant to hurt Freddie, but he. . .he wanted out."

"Out of blackmailing Lyle and sabotaging the kitchens in order to win the contest? I hardly blame him."

"The sabotaging was Freddie's idea." Riley's jaw tensed. "I'm not saying anything else until I have a lawyer."

"That's just fine, Miss Michaels. You've already said everything I needed to hear. Take her away, deputy."

Riley started crying. "You don't understand. I needed the money. Freddie promised me he could win. And if I wasn't going to get the money. . ."

Max shook his head as they led Riley toward the squad car. "Now that this is all over, do you think you might explain, Sheriff? I have to admit I'm still a bit confused as to exactly what tipped you off."

"Would you like to do the honors, Mrs. Crumb?"

Pricilla smiled at her captive audience. She'd liked Riley and hated that she'd been the one they were looking for, but her arrest also meant that all charges against Clarissa would be dropped.

"There were several clues that on their own didn't mean anything," Pricilla began. "But I started to wonder if we hadn't been looking in the wrong place. First of all, I knew Norton had reviewed Riley's parents' restaurant, which was my first connection with Norton. Then there was the overnight express package I'd seen from Sally's Scissors Emporium on Riley's veranda table. Why would Riley suddenly need a new pair of scissors?"

"Because she'd used hers to kill Norton?" Max said.

"Exactly. She had them overnighted to replace the ones she stabbed him with. And then there was Freddie," Pricilla continued.

"Freddie?" Trisha asked.

"You remember the family photographs hanging up in Riley's hall. When I saw those printouts from Max the second time, I recognized that the rotund figure standing outside the restaurant beside Riley was Freddie—a hundred or so pounds heavier. Riley convinced Freddie they could rig the contest and win the quarter of a million dollars."

The sheriff nodded. "That's not all. Lyle Simpson admitted to us that Freddie had a photo of him and a woman who wasn't his wife. When they added a few acts of sabotage to blackmail, Freddie and Riley convinced themselves they were on the fast track to winning the prize money. Clarissa's arrest worked right into their plan. The young woman made the perfect fall guy. Riley even stole the knife from Clarissa's kitchen in hopes of further incriminating her."

"I'm sure she didn't plan for anyone to find the knife so quickly and prove it wasn't the murder weapon," Pricilla added. "But Trisha's lost ring messed up those plans. I'm sure Freddie's death was unplanned, but Riley couldn't have Freddie panicking and confessing what they'd done."

Pricilla turned to Trisha. "Even you and I played right into her hands. Riley knew I was helping out the sheriff, so every dress fitting ended up giving her an inside look into what was happening with the case. And we never suspected a thing. Plus, it gave her access to the lodge without anyone questioning her presence.

"When Riley said she had something left to do tonight, I wondered if she had something else planned. As she just implied, if she couldn't get the money, then she didn't want anyone else to get it."

Another call came through for the sheriff.

"That was one of my deputies I sent over to Riley's house after we got a search warrant," he said. "They just found what we believe to be the murder weapon—a pair of shears."

"Wait a minute," Trisha began. "You just told Riley you'd already found them."

The sheriff smiled. "I decided to gamble. When Mrs. Crumb told me she suspected that Miss Michaels's shears were the murder weapon, and the coroner confirmed that they could be, I decided to try to get a confession out of her."

"It worked, but I have a question," said Pricilla. "Where were they? I saw her house today, and I can't imagine anyone finding them quickly."

"I've got a couple of smart deputies. They were hidden in the tank of her bathroom toilet."

"A bit of a cliché, don't you think?" Max said.

"It only goes to prove who's the amateur and. . ." The sheriff glanced at Pricilla. "Who's the professional."

Pricilla felt her cheeks blush in spite of the chilly breeze and her wet attire.

"I'd be privileged to work with you again anytime, Mrs. Crumb," he added.

"Thanks for the vote of confidence, Sheriff." She turned to Max. "But now that Clarissa's about to be released, I'd say we have a wedding to plan."

20

Pricilla entered the elegant dining room that was situated on the fourth floor, set up for Nathan and Trisha's rehearsal dinner. She took Max's proffered arm and glanced out the row of large picture windows. The twinkling lights of Denver began to emerge as the sun sank behind the lofty Rocky Mountains, making the perfect backdrop. The stylish table, set for twenty, was adorned with a white tablecloth and crystal candlesticks with gold candles. Already more than a dozen of Nathan and Trisha's friends were gathered around the table, ready for the appetizers to be served.

"Marriage isn't as easy today as it was when we were young, is it?" Max said.

"Nor, it seems, is the actual wedding. After all that's managed to go wrong with this one, I'm glad we're almost through with it."

"I have a feeling they'll make it."

Pricilla nodded, amazed at how God had brought them all together. Her son and his daughter, Max and her. . .

"You're late, Mom." Trisha and Nathan approached them from the other side of the room. Trisha's deep purple dress fell in soft folds around her waist and swirled to her ankles.

"Everything looks beautiful, Trisha."

Her son kissed her on the cheek. "And so do you. But I was getting worried."

Pricilla winked at him. "Worried I'd managed to get myself caught up in another murder mystery?"

"I admit I'm not quite as worried as I have been now that Riley's behind bars."

"You don't have to worry about me." She looked at Max and laughed. "I've decided to just read my mysteries and leave the investigations to capable people like Sheriff Lewis."

Nathan cleared his throat. "Now why do I have a hard time believing that? With your knack for finding trouble, there always seems to be plenty of it."

"Plenty of trouble? I'd say quite the opposite. Clarissa's record has been wiped clean, Michelle was offered a position as an anchor with a major network after her story broke, Christopher Jeffries is now studying in Paris, and Sarah landed a book contract that will allow her to hire her own girl Friday if she wants." Pricilla glanced at Max and smiled. "Besides, I've already found everything I need right here."

She felt her breath catch. There had always been something mesmerizing about his eyes that left her breathless. She might not have expected a second chance at love, but she'd be forever grateful to God for giving it to her.

"Mom?"

Pricilla turned back to their kids, forcing herself to focus. For tonight she was going to leave any daydreaming behind. Tonight was for Nathan and Trisha. "Sorry, I—"

"What is it with you two?" Trisha cocked her head. "You look positively... positively blissful."

Pricilla shook her head. This wasn't the way she wanted things to go. "This weekend is for the two of you, remember, and nothing's going to get in the way of that. Tonight's the rehearsal dinner, then tomorrow's the wedding ceremony at the church." She shot Max a dreamy look. "You haven't seen the church yet, but the eighteenth-century building has the most stunning stained-glass windows in the front. Then it's off to the Bahamas for your honeymoon—"

Nathan folded his arms across his chest and shot her that familiar look of his. She knew that look. She rambled when she got excited, and he clearly had no intention of letting her off the hook. "Mom, something's up. What is it?"

She attempted to dodge the subject. "Why do you assume that because I have a smile on my face something's up? And besides, you were right when you said we were late, which means it must be time we all sat down to eat. Right, Max? There's nothing more disparaging to your guests than to serve the appetizer lukewarm—"

"We've got to have the most exasperating parents alive." Trisha nudged Nathan. "I've just never seen the two of you look so...so glowing."

"And young," Nathan added.

"Yes." Trish nodded. "And young."

Glowing. Blissful. Young. Pricilla couldn't help but giggle. She could get used to descriptions like that. And while she knew the cream-colored suit and moisturizer she wore couldn't really erase the years, she did feel about twenty-five again tonight.

"Mom?"

"Dad?"

Max clasped her hand. "We might as well tell them."

Pricilla shrugged and then nodded. "I suppose it's the only way they'll let us sit down and eat. I don't know about you, but I'm starving."

"Me, too. I hear the food is great, but the servings leave a bit to be desired—"

"Dad. What do you have to tell us?" Trisha threw out.

"Your father and I. . ." Pricilla began. "We eloped."

"You eloped? You didn't."

"We did."

"You eloped?" Nathan repeated.

"Yes, we did."

Trisha's shocked expression melted into a broad smile. "This is wonderful, but. . ."

"But what?"

"What about the church and the wedding gown and—I was looking forward to another wedding."

"But I, for one, didn't want the hassle of misspelled invitations, oversized wedding dresses, and—"

"And a seamstress who turns out to be a murderer," Trisha said.

"Exactly, and—"

"Hold on." Nathan laughed and pulled Trisha toward him. "I'd say we get the point."

Pricilla smiled. She'd meant it when she said she didn't need a fancy dress, dozens of guests, and piles of rich food as an essential backdrop to her proclaiming her love to Max. A wedding ring on her finger and a marriage certificate from the courts really was enough for her.

"All I've wanted all along was to be Mrs. Pricilla Summers. I don't need the hassles of a wedding ceremony for that."

Trisha scurried to the table and grabbed four of the crystal fluted water glasses. Ice chinked against the sides as she handed them out and then turned to the rest of the guests sitting at the long table. "If I could get your attention, everyone, I'd like to propose a toast to Max and Pricilla, who somehow managed to make it to the altar before we did." She held up her glass. "May you both enjoy years of love and laughter ahead of you. . .together."

"Hear, hear!"

"Bravo!"

"Congratulations!"

"Thank you." Pricilla felt the heat of a blush rush to her cheeks as she turned her face to Max.

He leaned down and brushed his lips across hers. "Whoever said that eloping was scandalous had no idea what they were talking about. Isn't that right, Mrs. Summers?"

Pricilla held up her glass and smiled. "That's exactly right, Mr. Summers."

Lisa Harris is a wife, mother, and author who has been writing both fiction and nonfiction for the Christian market since 2000. She and her husband, along with their three children, live in Mozambique where they are missionaries. Life is busy between ministry and homeschooling, but she cherishes the time she has to escape into another world and write. She sees this work as an extension of her ministry. For a glimpse into Lisa's life in Africa, visit myblogintheheartofafrica.blogspot.com or visit her Web site at www.lisaharriswrites.com.

You may correspond with this author by writing:
Lisa Harris
Author Relations
PO Box 721
Uhrichsville, OH 44683
or e-mail her at contact.harris@gmail.com

A Letter to Our Readers

Dear Readers:

In order that we might better contribute to your reading enjoyment, we would appreciate you taking a few minutes to respond to the following questions. When completed, please return to the following: Fiction Editor, Barbour Publishing, Inc., P.O. Box 719, Uhrichsville, OH 44683.

1. Did you enjoy reading *Colorado Crimes* by Lisa Harris?
   - ❑ Very much. I would like to see more books like this.
   - ❑ Moderately—I would have enjoyed it more if ______________

____

____

2. What influenced your decision to purchase this book? (Check those that apply.)
   - ❑ Cover ❑ Back cover copy ❑ Title ❑ Price
   - ❑ Friends ❑ Publicity ❑ Other

3. Which story was your favorite?
   - ❑ *Recipe for Murder* ❑ *Chef's Deadly Dish*
   - ❑ *Baker's Fatal Dozen*

4. Please check your age range:
   - ❑ Under 18 ❑ 18–24 ❑ 25–34
   - ❑ 35–45 ❑ 46–55 ❑ Over 55

5. How many hours per week do you read? ______________

Name ______________________________________

Occupation ______________________________________

Address ______________________________________

City______________ State__________ Zip__________

E-mail ______________________________________